The Magic of Prophecy

Book 1 of the Annals of Prophecy

Mark Kingshott

Published by MDA

ISBN: 978-0-9576067-9-1

DEDICATION

To my wife Dawn and my two beautiful children, Ashlynne and Ethan.

CONTENTS

	Acknowledgments	i
Prologue:	Fear and Fire	1
Chapter One:	Executions and Exile	5
Chapter Two:	Flight and Fatalities	30
Chapter Three:	Revelations and Revenge	59
Chapter Four:	Rings and Retribution	90
Chapter Five:	Magic and Meetings	122
Chapter Six:	Tricks and Traps	154
Chapter Seven:	Torture and Treason	178
Chapter Eight:	Prophecies and Power	213
Chapter Nine:	Plots and Pirates	242
Chapter Ten:	Preparations and Prisons	269
Chapter Eleven:	Violence and Violets	300
Chapter Twelve:	Rest and Rescue	327
Chapter Thirteen:	Swords and Shields	360
Chapter Fourteen:	Schemes and Studies	393
Chapter Fifteen:	Augury and Ambush	430
Chapter Sixteen:	Monsters and Mayhem	458
Chapter Seventeen:	Siege and Sacrifice	481
Chapter Eighteen:	Duty and Destiny	506
Chapter Nineteen:	Death and Destruction	534
Epilogue:	Demons and Devils	564

ACKNOWLEDGMENTS

Thank you my wife and children for putting up with my inattention as I reedited the manuscript countless times. Thanks also go to Bruce and Stuart for helping me cut the teeth of my story telling abilities all those years ago. Finally thank you to the many friends who proof read the manuscript and to Laura who ensured I did not have to rewrite an entire chapter when it was lost to a bad choice of backup media.

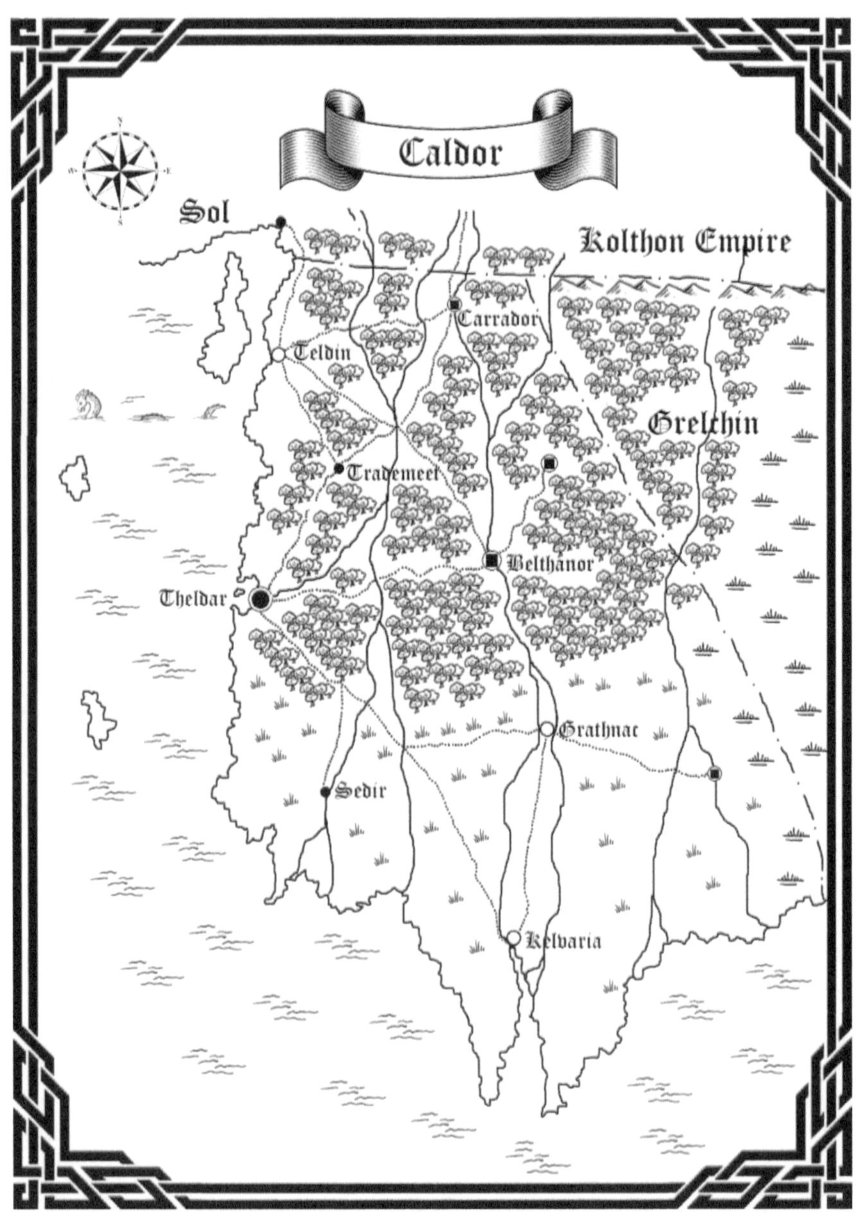
Caldor
Sol
Kolthon Empire
Carrador
Teldin
Grelchin
Trademeet
Belthanor
Theldar
Grathnac
Sedir
Kelvaria

THE PROLOGUE: Fear and Fire

A thin mist crept out of the dark woodlands and slowly into the open valley they surrounded, its white vapour devouring and diluting the light of the morning sun. With it came a cold, damp breeze that made the already oppressive atmosphere of the village almost unbearable to its inhabitants. It was a small, ramshackle affair, consisting of some twenty crudely built huts of mud and straw with a centre square and a single meandering mud track that served as a road. Normally it would be filled with the inhabitants and their animals yet today the village was empty and almost deathly quiet. All activity was occurring in two areas just outside the settlement, each on almost opposite sides. At one end, women and children could be seen moving rapidly into the trees, carrying whatever meagre belongings they could carry, hoping that they could escape ***them***. On the other side the men were making their own preparations for ***their*** arrival.

The villagers had known for months that ***they*** were moving closer, yet the community had believed that it would be overlooked. They were a small settlement and were no threat to anything, or anybody, yet they had been wrong. The smaller village of Grelc had been cleansed only yesterday and only one of the scouts they had sent out to investigate had returned. The news he had brought had not been good. The entire population had been destroyed and their village burnt to the ground. ***Their*** next stop was almost certainly here, and the villagers knew they had waited too long. This knowledge had not prevented them from trying to do something, for they all held out hope that this last desperate gamble would pay off. The men were to remain and hold ***them*** off, whilst the women and children fled to the woods. It was a near hopeless gamble. The hastily erected earthen barricades would prove no obstacle for the monstrous beasts ***they*** rode, even with the wooden stakes set in its damp soil. The crude clubs and farm implements would never penetrate ***their*** armoured shells and the villagers wore nothing that would shield them from ***their*** hideous weapons. Yet the defenders clung defiantly on to the one hope in their hearts, that they would buy their families the time they needed to escape. It was this one hope that prevented most from running when ***they*** suddenly emerged from the trees ahead.

They were truly an awesome sight; row upon row of towering warriors riding monstrous beasts from which smoke seemed to curl from their mouths. As ***they*** slowly moved closer, the weak sunlight glittered off their metallic shells making it seem as if ***they*** were surrounded by an aura of light and energy. The light flickered almost menacingly, as if alive and it seemed to reach out for the defenders as if to hold or grab them. More than one villager went pale and fled at the sight as the light seemed to strike at their very souls, and many more felt the blood drain from their faces as sickening fear grabbed them.

Suddenly ***they*** stopped. The defenders felt a momentary surge of hope, before realising that this was merely the calm before the storm. The horde parted and from their midst a single warrior rode to face them. As its beast came to a halt, the massive warrior slowly raised its weapon high into the morning light.

It was by far the most fearsome sight that the villagers had ever seen. It was encased in its glittering silver shell, and it towered above all others. Power radiated almost visibly around it and its fearsome silver visage almost seemed to snarl at them. The black beast it rode stared malevolently down at them and none of the villagers could stare back at it for more than a few seconds. Vapour poured from its mouth in slow waves, and for the villagers, it was as if time had slowed down. The silence of their foe was total and unnatural. The breeze died, as if the weather itself held its breath, and fear began to drain the villagers of the last vestige of their resolve. Yet one stood tall. He raised one of the few hunting bows in the village, aimed it, and loosed an arrow. It flew straight and true, yet it seemed to slow its flight to almost a crawl before vanishing as if it had never been.

That one act destroyed the last vestige of hope in many of the villagers. Some turned and fled, others broke down in choking sobs, knowing death herself was here. It was at this moment that the lead warrior moved. The weapon was lowered and the horde behind it moved as one towards the barricade, yet still not a single sound could be heard; even the beasts' thunderous gallop was mute. The wall of silence proved too much for many of the villagers, who turned and fled, their screams swallowed up by the approaching silence. Suddenly the wooden spears on the barricade exploded into tiny fragments, showering the few remaining defenders with thousands of needle sharp splinters, and as the warriors reached the barricade's remains, sound returned to the world once more. The warriors roared out a battle cry and the pounding of the beasts' shod hooves mingled in to create a terrible cacophony that caused the remaining doomed defenders to turn and flee. In no way could their two legs carry them faster than the four legs of the warriors' beasts and their screams were added to the horrifying sounds of the erupting conflict. Their cries lasted but a few minutes, for that was all the time needed for the massacre to be completed.

It did not end there however. The warriors swept onwards through the village towards the fleeing families. Even with their head start, they had no hope of fleeing the warriors' beasts. Yet more screams filled the air as the women and children were cut down from behind, or trampled beneath the stampeding beasts. In one part of the village a warrior came across two children, huddling together fearfully. With a barely repressed shudder the warrior cut them down before continuing the chase.

The battle was over in minutes and soon a new silence rose up. The commanding warrior rode slowly into the village centre. It reached for its head to remove its helm and survey the scene. The knight nodded his head in satisfaction. It had been a good clean fight. He had lost no troops and met with little resistance, yet, like all battles, the weariness of battle magic would soon be upon him and he still had much to do. At that moment a junior officer rode up to him.

"We believe that some may have escaped into the woods. Shall we organise a search for them, my lord?" she asked calmly.

"Yes," he replied, "but be quick about it as there are many villages in need of purification today."

She bowed in obedience and turned her horse back to the reserve contingent, always on hand for such occasions. As he watched her go he noted the ambitious look in her eyes. He knew she would become a great knight one day.

He shook his head in weariness. He was too long in the saddle for this, but he did not have much longer to go. A few more battles and he could retire home to his family for a while, though that could not be his concern today. Villages were waiting to be cleansed, though nothing could be done until this village had been dealt with completely.

Knowing the chase would not take very long he took a brief glance around. He noticed a severed head of a villager lying in the filthy mud of the centre square. He decided to take one last look at his most hated of enemies. He carefully lifted the head up slowly with the tip of his sword and examined it slowly. It had probably been male, but was so caked in mud and filth that identification was difficult. It had dark matted hair that seemed almost alive with lice. Its skin was heavily tanned and weathered, making it seem even dirtier. It had small grey eyes, a large flat nose, and swollen lips. The smell was nauseating. He shuddered with revulsion and felt like an old fool. He flicked his sword out violently and sent the goblin's head spinning through the air. It struck a nearby hut with a sickening crack and fell to the ground. He looked away from the crushed head in disgust. He had purified some fifty villages in this war, and he still found them completely hideous to look at.

He turned his thoughts to other things. Tomorrow his tour of duty in Grelchin would be over and in a month he would be back home, if only briefly, and spending time with his wife and daughter again.

A moment later the junior officer returned, breaking off that pleasant train of thought.

"It is done, my lord. They have all perished under the fist of Toric!" said the young woman with an almost exultant look on her face.

"Very well then," he replied, returning his thoughts to the task at hand. "Let flame purify this village."

"By the will of Toric," she said, bowing her head swiftly.

"By the will of Toric," he replied wearily.

Fortunately she had been too flushed with success to notice his apparent lack of enthusiasm. As he watched her ride away, he sighed in resignation. He had spoken the ritual command many times and still he could not see why it had to be used. It seemed just a little unnecessary to him. He quickly moved his thoughts to other matters. Thoughts like that could earn him another visit to the Chambers. He shook his head again, angry with himself for losing control like that. If the Covenant caught it…

He did not allow the thought to continue, resolving to spend this night in prayer to Toric. He replaced his helm and rode out of the village. He never once looked back, entrusting the remainder of the purification to be handled by the junior officer.

The command to burn the village broke the relative silence of the settlement. Knights with flaming brands rode through the village setting fire to everything they passed by. The straw and wood, though damp, quickly caught fire with a little magical aid, and soon the whole village was in flames. Screams rose from a nearby haystack where a goblin woman had hidden herself and her baby, hoping to escape the knights' wrath. The knights rode past, ignoring the screams completely, and formed ranks behind their commander. They rode out of the village and on towards the next in their path.

The screams soon died out, as did the flames. When the mist finally lifted, all that remained was the black and charred pieces of what had once been a bustling village. The air remained still and all was quiet; the lively chatter of the villagers silenced forever.

Chapter One: Executions and Exile

I

Dawn.
A time of beginnings; a time of endings.
The birth of a new day; the death of a dark night.
With the sun comes hope for a fresh start; fear of a bitter demise…

It was thus when the sun rose in the western skies over the dazzling white city of Theldar. As the light slowly filled the marble clad streets movement could be seen; people were wandering slowly through the softly glowing streets and alleyways. For some it was the beginning of a day's work; for others it was the end of a hard night of toil. In the marketplace, stalls had already been uncovered and items placed upon them. The owners of the stalls called out to the people passing by. All were hoping to sell their goods; most feared that they would sell nothing.

Elsewhere in the city guards patrolled the outer walls and stood watch at the three main gates. On the docks men hauled crates on and off the ships that were moored to Theldar's many piers and jetties whilst fishermen carried ashore the night's catch. Smoke rose from the many bakeries and the smell of freshly baked bread drifted across the city on a soft breeze. Darker smoke rose from other buildings as smithies stoked their fires in preparation for the new day. Several carts, filled with piles of scrap metal and assorted jumble, were pulled through the streets by large, lumbering horses. Upon the carts sat tired men and women who punctuated the quiet morning air with cries for iron and scrap. Occasionally a door would open and a man or a woman would leave with arms filled with a bundle of items. These were placed onto the cart and money exchanged hands. One such cart ambled slowly along the walls of the palace, unaware that within one of its inner courtyards knights on horseback were forming ranks with stately grace. Inside the glistening palace itself, servants went about their daily tasks; some cleaning its vast halls and many chambers; others preparing breakfast for the many noblemen and courtiers that resided there, most of whom would not be up until mid-morning.

Unlike the most noble, King Naithan II, of the House Tara'non; Lord of the County of Daranshire, Protector of the People, Ruler of Caldor, and Bearer of the Truth of Toric was already awake before the first rays of the sun had risen over the Western Ocean. He now stood at his window looking out over Theldar. It was the First City of Caldor and also the largest. From his window he could see most of the city as it radiated around the hill upon which his palace was built. He could even see some of the movement in the streets as the city began to awaken. He clenched his fist angrily as he watched the apparently peaceful scene. It was all a facade. The dazzling white beauty of Theldar was false. The buildings had not been made of marble, merely covered with it; the outer shell built merely to disguise the ugliness of the old, decaying buildings beneath.

This could also be said of his people. Many appeared to be good-natured people who walked in the Light of Toric. However the old saying often quoted by his mother entered unbidden into his mind. Beneath the skin of beauty often lies great ugliness and sin.

This had been true when she had been queen and was still true today. He was surrounded by problems. Crime was rife, public discontent was high and heresy widespread. He smiled sourly at the bitter irony of it. He was supposed to bring the truth of God to the heretics of Kolth and Sol, yet could not do so in one city in his own land. The smile turned to a scowl and he slammed his fist angrily onto the windowsill. All of the power at his command and still he could not bring order into his own city, Theldar, First City of both the king's country and the king's land!

In fact, the troubles seemed to be growing worse. Almost two months ago a knight had been found with his throat slit. This was not completely unusual for people *were* murdered in Caldor; although very rarely. What made it unusual was that the knight had been asleep in his room with the door closed and locked from the inside. The window had also been locked inside and there was no other entrance to the room. Naithan's personal friend and sorcerer, Matthew, had been there personally and had only been able to discern that magic had been involved; as if that was not plainly obvious to everyone already that this was so.

To make matters worse, this had not been the only killing that night. There had been four other murders, all of them knights, and all with their throats slit. The following nights several more knights had been killed and the same happened every night since. The problem was that only one person had ever seen the killer, and she was a drunkard and a woman of the streets, another problem he had yet to stamp out. She had seen one of the murders and claimed to have seen a man leap silently from the shadows and swiftly kill a knight. She then claimed that he had then disappeared back into the shadows; that he had literally vanished into thin air. Naithan would not have believed the report of such an unreliable witness if Matthew had not confirmed it. Apparently he had sensed faint traces of magic at the scene of death which meant that the man could have indeed vanished. They had returned to every other site and each time the result had been confirmed. They had all involved similar magic, but once again that told them very little, as Matthew had said that the patterns had been unusual, whatever that meant. Even armed with that knowledge, his Seekers from the Covenant Knights, commonly called Grey Knights, had thus far been unsuccessful at finding this evil practitioner of the dark arts.

An involuntary shudder went through Naithan. He shared his people's distrust of sorcerer's magic, even though his best friend used such magic, many of his commanding knights used magic, including the Seekers, and even he himself had been schooled in it. The only magic he felt comfortable with was that granted by Toric and the rest he tolerated so long as he had some control over the users, even Matthew.

A distant shout in the streets broke his concentration and he looked out at the city once more. Somewhere in the streets a loud argument had begun but Naithan could not find the source of the commotion. It had to be somewhere just past the palace walls for it was close enough to hear snatches of the argument. Intrigued, despite himself, he had leaned out of the window in an attempt to hear more. Suddenly a gentle cough behind him caused him to jump and set his heart racing in fear.

"Excuse me, Sire, " said an infinitely formal voice behind him, "but may I be of service?"

A relieved Naithan groaned slightly and turned to face his ageing valet.

"For Toric's sake, Luca, how many times will I have to say I'm sorry?" he asked almost desperately.

"I beg your pardon, your Majesty?" asked Luca with a stiff questioning bow.

"I'm really sorry about the way I snapped at you Luca," said Naithan, almost pleading. With Luca, kingly dignity or commands rarely worked as expected. "Now, please could you stop playing the part of my formal servant and let bygones be bygones? Please!"

"I'm sorry, your majesty," replied Luca, his voice betraying no emotion, remaining strictly formal, "but I distinctly remember you telling me to keep to my station of life and not to meddle in yours, if you'll pardon my bluntness, your Majesty."

Naithan gave up. Luca Horne had been his valet for as long as he could remember and the old man was like a father to him. He was also one of the few people who had not treated him differently upon his coronation, until now. It had started two days ago when Naithan received news that both the Kolthon Empire and the country of Sol were sending ambassadors to discuss his intentions over the invasion of Grelchin. Naithan had been expecting those from Sol, as he had been planning a formal visit to their ruler, Sulan XXV, but the fact that Kolth had sent an ambassador too had disrupted his plans. Luca had made some helpful comment and in a flare of unexplainable rage, Naithan had shouted at his manservant. A pained look had then crossed the weathered face and he had been unbearably polite and formal ever since.

"I see that your Majesty had dressed himself," said Luca, eyeing him critically. You could hear the capital M in every *Majesty*. "Does your Majesty require my services at this precise moment?"

"As you have correctly assessed I am dressed and I have no further need for your services, Master Horne," replied Naithan in resignation.

Luca stood there regarding him for a few minutes. Then he spoke.

"You no longer require my services?" he asked in mock amazement. "Have yer seen yerself in the mirror? Yer look a right state. Yer couldn't dress well if yer life depended on it. Let me see to it."

The old man came closer to Naithan and began to fiddle with his clothing. Naithan stood trying to hide his pleasure that his old friend had returned to him. To do this he waited there patiently and gazed at his reflection in the mirror. He could not see what was wrong, but knew that Luca would not leave until he was satisfied that Naithan was dressed properly. He shook his head and smiled slightly. A slight glance from Luca and he promptly fixed his face back at the mirror, the smile almost disappearing.

"Have yer heard the news from Gareth yet?" asked Luca without bothering to look up from his work.

"No, the last I heard was that the main forces were nearing Grelchi."

Gareth, his brother, was leading his army into the heart of Grelchin. Naithan had not intended to go to war quite so soon for his troops were still small in number; however the increasing number of goblin raids in the eastern counties had forced him to retaliate until the conflict had escalated into full-scale war. Thankfully his brother was a skilled general and had consistently led his forces to victory. He was also aided by the fact that the goblins had put up very little in the way of organised resistance. According to the weekly reports it was more of a massacre than a war. At the rate his forces were advancing Grelchin would be taken within the next couple of months.

It was this that had likely caused both the northern lands to send ambassadors to him. Sol was evidently worried that he would move his campaign northwards and the Kolthon Senate almost definitely wanted to see if Caldor was weak enough to invade. Now he would have to try and convince the heathen ambassadors that his intentions were essentially peaceful. That meant lying and treating them with a respect that they did not deserve.

Surely Sir Caldor the Pure had not had such problems! he thought as he sighed softly.

"I'd bet that Sir Caldor didn' have such problems," said Luca, fumbling with Naithan's shirt. Naithan had become used to the way that the wizened old man seemed to be able to read his thoughts. "What with that man they call the Shadow killin' knights right, left and centre, as well as the war and the problems with the Empire and Sol. But I'm sure yer'll see 'em through admirably. 'Course if he'd finished what he'd started we wouldn' be in such a pickle."

Naithan nodded in agreement. Many years ago his people had been enslaved by the vile goblins and forced to do all manner of tortuous work. Then Caldor, with his magical sword Caliburn, united the humans and led them into a revolt against their goblin oppressors. Not only that but he had carved the kingdom of Caldor from the western lands of Grelchin before leading them to victory against the legions of Kolth. The treaty he forced them to sign on his victory had lasted to the present day. The emperor Tynarsis would love to get revenge for that ancient defeat. If Sir Caldor had finished what he had started Naithan wouldn't be in trouble today. However, that was all in the past and could not be altered. One day he would finish the work and the entire human race would stand in the Light of Toric.

"Finished," said Luca, stepping back to admire his work, "Now yer look like a real king should."

"Thank you Luca," replied Naithan daring to give a smile.

He looked at himself in the full-length mirror that stood in the corner of his room. He was not surprised to see that he did look much better. Somehow the clothes seemed to hang on him in a much more regal manner. Luca seemed to have a magic touch when it came to clothes. It was a shame that this touch did not extend as far as his face. He could see that it was drawn from lack of sleep and his thin blond hair lay haphazardly upon his scalp. His short beard did not hide the paleness of his face and nothing could be done about his bloodshot eyes, which all but drowned out the blue irises. He knew that he might be considered fairly handsome, if he could get a good night's sleep but he doubted if such a thing existed. He wiped away the tears of tiredness from his eyes, ignoring Luca's concerned look.

"You may go and get some breakfast," he said, returning his gaze to the window.

"Will you be eatin' t'day?"

"Yes, after I have attended to a few matters of State," replied Naithan.

"Good," replied Luca with a nod. "Yer know that breakfast is the most important meal of the day."

He walked to the door then turned back around.

"But be warned," said the old man, waving his forefinger at Naithan, "if I find out that yer skipped it then I'll personally see to it that yer do it from now on. Even if I 'ave t' spoon feed yer!"

With that Luca walked out of the room. Naithan shuddered as he thought of the warning that he had been given. Luca was quite likely to carry out his threat. He had done so once before when Naithan was twelve and even now he flushed with embarrassment at the memory. Luca could be worse than a mother hen sometimes. However Luca's friendship was worth every bit of his mothering. He was Naithan's link to the general population. Through him he found out how the peasants were reacting to his new laws and taxes. How the old man found out he never knew and did not really care. He was just glad for his advice and the fact that it meant Naithan was not completely tied to the information of his Spymaster, a shadowy figure whose identity was unknown to even him. Knowledge of the man's existence had only been passed on to him on the day of his coronation. He had found it very difficult to put faith in such a man, especially one that seemed to know so much. Luca's information helped relieve his unease, and gave him a slight edge during their encounters. At least, he hoped it did.

"I almost forgot t' tell yer," said Luca, startling Naithan as he reappeared at the door. "Malcolm is lookin' for yer. It's somethin' 'bout the next Royal Council."

Naithan groaned as Luca left. That was all he needed. There would be no avoiding the small man and he could be forced to make a decision on the next council meeting.

Why today? He asked silently.

A loud clatter of metal drew his attention back to the window. Down in the courtyard a young knight had just fallen off a horse. Naithan smiled with pride as he watched the commanding knight swing off his horse to help.

"A young man to be proud of," said a voice by his ear.

Naithan swung round in surprise, reaching for the sword at his side. It was half-drawn when he saw that is was his friend and advisor Matthew that stood before him.

II

Matthew Kelreon, Lord High Priest, personal advisor and friend to the king, smiled at his friend's startled reaction. It was one of his favourite tricks. Many people often thought that he used magic to maintain his silence. Very few people knew that he had in fact begun his apprenticeship as a king's ranger, not the court magician. Then again nobody really cared.

"How could you do that to me?" asked Naithan angrily. "You saw what I almost did to that...that...that creature the other day! My nerves are on edge as it is!"

"I'm sorry, " replied Matthew, cursing himself silently. *How could I forget that?* "It won't happen again."

Naithan looked at him a moment then began to laugh. Matthew stared at his friend feeling a little puzzled. Usually he could read Naithan's thoughts as he would a book. Evidently the incident had really unsettled him.

"Are you all right?" he asked anxiously.

"Of course," said Naithan when he stopped laughing. "It was just the look on your face when you realised what I meant. I've never seen anyone go so pale so quickly."

Matthew's face creased in confusion. It was then that he realised he could feel the blood rushing to his cheeks. In the heat of the moment he had ignored the feeling of fear and panic that had gripped him when Naithan had mentioned the incident. He now realised how close he had been to losing his head. His throat suddenly felt very dry and very tight. His arm also seemed to tingle somehow, as if in recognition of the fact. He wondered if Naithan had thought that far enough ahead to consider what would have happened had he killed him. Matthew felt it wise not to bring it up at this juncture. His friend rarely smiled these days, let alone laughed.

"I'm not surprised that I went pale. You almost cut the wretched creature's head off!" replied Matthew, his voice shaking.

"Well it *was* trying to assassinate me," replied Naithan in a dry voice, "and you weren't much help."

"I had everything under control," replied Matthew, regaining his composure.

"Eventually. Anyway your flashing blue lights only postponed the inevitable. It's going to die under the executioner's axe today; chopping its head off then would have achieved the same thing," replied Naithan. "It would also have been less trouble."

"You know what purpose it will serve today. It will let those knights in the courtyard see the creature's true colours," replied Matthew wearily. He was growing tired of this old argument. "They will have physical evidence of the evil that scourges our land and will also be able to see what we intend to do about it."

"I'm still unsure about this. The last time an execution was made public the king was removed from his throne by a mob of angry peasants. You know how they feel about them."

"This isn't public, and besides, the creature isn't human," replied Matthew with forced patience. The peasants were not alone in their beliefs. Naithan's beliefs were often as strong as, and frequently stronger than, those of his subjects. "What you're really saying is that you're scared that Tristan isn't far enough through his training to witness this."

"The thought did cross my mind," replied Naithan. "He has only been the King's Knight for three months. He still has regular doses of treatment and he hasn't even begun to learn the ways of magic. For Toric's sake they haven't even finished adjusting the ceremonial armour for him."

"You know that the armour's all but finished," replied Matthew in irritation, "and he'll begin his training in the arts of magic soon enough." *Once the treatments finally force those stupid superstitions out of his mind*, he added silently.

"You mean you have the results of the test?" asked Naithan hopefully.

"Yes, he will be an adept student of sorcery."

Matthew thought he saw a slight frown appear on Naithan's face. He knew how his friend felt about sorcerers' magic. However, the two types were very different and a person was usually only able to use one form or another. Only one person in recorded history had ever been able to wield both and he was that person. Why that was so he did not know, but he could somehow use priestly magic as well as sorcery, though he was less adept at it.

No, the young man would have to study with him. Almost all the commanding knights were trained in magic and that was what made their armies so strong. In Caldor sorcery was hated and reviled by almost everyone. It had also been made illegal. This meant that there was nowhere for wizards to study. In Kolth there was a wizards' university where all those with the spark of sorcery in them were trained. In Caldor those people were rounded up and placed into the army. When they had been sufficiently trained and treated they would then be raised into the commanding ranks. Here they would be tested and taught how to use magic. This had many advantages. All armies employed the so-called war wizards. However they were few in number and often weak in physical combat.

In Caldor, though, all those capable of magic were enlisted and taught how to cast minor offensive and defensive spells. Many of these were also taught some of the more powerful spells. They would easily neutralise and overwhelm enemy sorcerers because of their superior numbers. Their magic was also useful in demoralising and frightening enemy troops. It was a brave army who could fight with the knowledge that the majority of their opponents could wield magic as well as they could a sword. Of course, this was all theoretical strategy at present, as it had been kept a secret practice since the idea was introduced, in order to prevent the other nations following their example and filling their own ranks with spell wielding warriors.

Of course not all of those enlisted were capable of sorcery. When a priest did the initial testing on the naming day, it only indicated whether the infant was capable of magic. Only the extensive testing of the knighthood could determine that and many were found to be strong in clerical magic. Most of these joined the clerical orders of the church, although many chose to stay in the knighthood.

"Are you still with me?" asked Naithan.

Matthew cursed silently, bringing his attention back to his friend. His mind had a tendency to wander when he was tired and he could often lose himself in his thoughts. He had lost whole days that way and often he had only been thinking about trivial matters. A dangerous habit, especially if casting spells…

Blood and Hellfire I'm doing it again! He thought angrily digging his nails into the palm of his hands.

Thankfully they were tucked inside the sleeves of his white robes so Naithan could not see. However the tiredness reminded him of something that had been worrying him.

"Luca said that you were awake and dressed when he arrived. Is that true?" he asked with concern.

"Yes," replied Naithan wearily. "That old man is too fussy for his own good."

"He was concerned about you," replied Matthew. "As am I. You know how your safety concerns me." He thought he saw Naithan rub his arm but did not take offence. Now was not the time. "You need sleep."

"How can I sleep with the evil that plagues me?" asked Naithan plaintively. Matthew just stood gazing silently at him with his arms folded. Naithan sighed. "If you must know the potions are becoming less effective at keeping me asleep."

"I will brew up a stronger batch this afternoon," replied Matthew, ignoring his friend's shudder. The matter had been decided a few years ago. "But I think we had best attend to the morning's agenda."

He started to yawn, but caught himself. Unfortunately Naithan saw it.

"Late night was it?" he asked dryly. "Let me guess; you spent the night theorising with that student."

"Yes I spent part of the night discussing the mechanics of magic with Jalim," he replied with a sigh. "It was very interesting."

It certainly had been that. As the young man was a Free Wielder he had some very interesting ideas. It also meant that his progress was considerably faster than most other students. He was a joy to teach, unlike the young King's Knight. Teaching Tristan magic would be like teaching a cat to bark.

"So that's why you keep going distant on me," said Naithan, breaking the flow of his thoughts. "You know you really ought to get some sleep, or am I to order servants to ensure you drink one of your own potions each night?"

Naithan's voice dripped with sarcasm as he said this. Matthew sighed in resignation. He had left himself open to attack. He decided to make his life a little simpler and give in.

"All right I'll cut down on my late night discussions with Jalim. Satisfied?"

"Certainly," replied Naithan a little too smugly. Matthew was too tired for this. "Shall we go to the execution?"

"As you wish, Sire," he replied with a mock bow.

They moved together, Matthew standing a little behind his king, and walked towards the door. Matthew pulled the hood of his robe over his head, allowing his face to disappear into the shadows. He liked to maintain an air of mystery around himself and the hood was only one of the many devices at his disposal. Naithan stopped by the door and looked back at him.

"Oh by the way," he said with a smile, "Malcolm's looking for me, something about the time of the next council meeting. Let's see if we can get down to the courtyard without Malcolm finding us."

"If you can do that, Sire," replied Matthew with a smile, "then I can move a mountain with one hand whilst pigs fly around the other."

It was an old saying, but then it was an old game. They had never once succeeded in avoiding the weasel faced little man when he was looking for them. Matthew suspected that the man would find them even if they were invisible. It was a theory worth testing one day, if it were possible to become invisible. It was one of the many things people incorrectly thought wizards could do…

"Well are you coming of not?" asked Naithan impatiently.

Matthew nodded briefly. He vowed silently that he would never again spend the whole night talking with Jalim. It seriously affected his concentration. He hoped fervently that he would not be called upon to use his magic today. There was no telling what might happen if his concentration slipped. Suddenly noticing Naithan's irritated look he dug his nails deeper into his hands and followed the king into the hallway…

III

The King's Knight, Sir Tristan Pathfinder, Knight of the White Plume and Commander of the Armies of Caldor, rode his white stallion back down the line of stationary knights. They were all sat upon horses, though none of their steeds were as magnificent as his. He had chosen it when it was still a foal and had named it Galahad, after the first King's Knight. It had grown to be as powerful as his namesake and was the envy of many other knights.

He stopped briefly by one of the knights. The young man was shifting uncomfortably in his saddle.

"Are you all right Michael?" he asked quietly. The inexperienced knight had fallen off his horse earlier and was obviously in pain.

"I'm fine, sir," replied Michael, suddenly sitting rigidly in his saddle.

"You will make a fine knight," said Tristan with a smile.

"Thank you, sir," replied Michael as his eyes lit up with pride.

Tristan stopped smiling and continued down the row of knights. He stopped by another young knight who was slumped slightly in her saddle.

"Sit straight, Karene," he commanded a little harshly, and just a little too loudly.

The young woman immediately complied, although the look she gave him could have melted firestones. He was not surprised. She had openly opposed him when he had been granted the position of King's Knight and his insult did not help matters. She was a junior officer and should not have been reprimanded in that way, even though she had deserved it.

He hastily took his gaze away from her and moved his thoughts to other things. He had not been the King's Knight for very long and he still found himself a little bewildered by all his training, as well as the extent of his power. To be King's Knight was to be in a very important position. It was highest honour that could be given to a knight and it meant that he was superior to all knights in active service. It also meant that he was keeper of the legacy of Caldor, the holy sword Caliburn. That mighty blade now rested proudly at his side, though the ceremonial armour that also came with his position was still being altered.

He was one of the youngest men ever to be awarded the honour. This had caused several problems. Many other knights who had also been candidates for the position became very angry and probably a little jealous, especially some of the older ones. They had felt that he did not deserve the position, even though most had seen him succeed in drawing Caliburn in the Ceremony of Choosing. When he had first begun his new duties they had made life very difficult for him. They had subverted his orders and openly disobeyed direct commands in an attempt to undermine his authority. He had been forced to challenge them to a test of arms. They had demanded that he faced them all in a one-day tournament and he had been bound by the rules of chivalry to comply. So he met every challenger on the field of combat in front of a very large crowd of people, both knights and civilians. By the day's end he had fought every one, and won. It had delighted the crowd and the ease with which he had won had humiliated the knights. He was not once unhorsed and his lance splintered only once. By the end of the hot summer day he had barely broken into a sweat, despite his bulky plate armour. Tristan had taken this to mean that he had been chosen by Toric and the majority of those he had defeated seemed to agree with him. This had produced a new depth of respect for him and most of them had ceased their subversive activities. Only a few of them still plotted to embarrass and humiliate him. Karene was one such knight.

This did not excessively concern him, for he had the situation well in hand. Karene was the only such opponent present this morning and she would be next to him. The problem was that he enjoyed using his power to humiliate them. He knew that it was unseemly and discourteous. He also knew that it was not the expected behaviour of the King's Knight. However he just could not seem to rid himself of these unsavoury emotions. Even his regular Treatment seemed to have no effect.

A soft whinny from Galahad brought him out of his reverie. He briefly glanced down at the two rows of knights facing each other in the courtyard. They formed an aisle that led from the palace doors down to the execution block. Seeing that everything was in order, took his place at the head of the knights by the foot of the stairs that led from the doors. His troublesome knight sat next to him with a badly concealed scowl on her face.

The minutes passed by slowly. Time seemed to slow down and drag forever. Tristan could not understand why the king was taking so long. But then he could not hope to understand the mind of one as powerful, wise, and intelligent as his king. This execution had been scheduled for dawn, yet the sun had risen quite high into the sky. He could also hear more sounds coming from the city as its streets became more crowded.

Tristan just wanted the whole procedure to be completed. He hated the idea of an execution. To his knowledge there had been only one such execution in Caldor, and for Tristan that was one too many. Even other such would-be assassins had never been punished in this manner, although none of them had been goblins. Even so it still did not feel right. Matthew, the High Priest, had spent many hours trying to explain why it was necessary and once or twice Tristan had almost understood.

Then again Tristan was beginning to have grave doubts about that man's integrity. Several times when they had spoken the thin man had spoken highly of sorcery, almost as if it were from first-hand experience. If Tristan had not seen the man heal a small cut on his hand then he would almost suspect that he actually used sorcery. But then that did not shock Tristan as it once would have. In fact on several occasions, usually just after a dose of treatment in a Redirecting Chamber, he had found himself actually thinking about the merits of sorcery! However such feelings wore off rapidly. They were obviously a side-effect of the Chambers.

His concentration was broken once again when the palace doors suddenly swung open.

IV

"…and as you can see Malcus…"

"Malcolm, Sire."

"…there are several matters that need attending to," continued Naithan, seeming to ignore the small man's interruption.

"That is exactly my point…your majesty," replied Malcolm. "If you would just set a date for the next Royal Council then you can go about your…other duties unhindered. I still believe that next Whitsunday is the ideal time."

"Oh I just couldn't do that," replied Naithan, rolling his eyes in apparent shock.

Matthew smiled at his friend's play-acting.

"Why not?" asked Malcolm with a dark expression.

"Because you know that Whitsunday is my hunting day! You *can't* have forgotten that?" asked Naithan innocently. "You're my head beater, blazing a trail through the undergrowth for everybody else."

Matthew's smile grew as Malcolm's face turned sour. The greasy haired man hated to leave the city and he detested hunting. He always seemed out of place without a pen behind one ear and a pile of paper under one arm.

"Of course not, Sire," replied Malcolm with a forced, slightly twisted smile.

"And besides," continued Naithan, "that wouldn't give either the Count of Harkshire or the Countess of Northshire enough time to reach Theldar."

Malcolm's face darkened and his smile turned sour again. That had obviously been his intention.

"You did say that it would be an important meeting, didn't you. What was it you said again…"

Naithan appeared to be deep in thought, Matthew knew that his friend's memory was almost as sharp as his own.

"That's right," said Naithan, his eyes suddenly lighting up. "Something about the *division of the territorial acquisitions from the annexed state of Grelchin*, or something like that. That definitely sounds too important to discuss in a minority council."

The look on Malcolm's face could have melted firestones. It was all Matthew could do to prevent himself from laughing out loud. Naithan always pretended to hate the Game of the Council and, having come to the throne at an early age, was often thought by others to be a poor Player with a lot of luck. However, the king revelled in the chance to play it, as well as play it up. Malcolm thought himself to be a strong player, yet was constantly blocked by Naithan, who did so with ease. The king made the man feel superior by playing the part of a fool. This made the man arrogant and meant that he was easily manipulated. It was easy for Naithan to accidentally let slip some vital piece of information that would be reported to his former lord. The Duke of Kempshire had given the man to the king as a coronation present. The man was obviously sent to work for the duke's benefit. If he had not been as good as he was at administrating affairs he would have been removed from office years ago. He was also useful in keeping the duke confused about the king's true intentions. It made him cautious and easy to control.

"Bring out the vile creature that would see me dead!" said Naithan loudly making Matthew jump.

The king now stood at the top of the stairs, looking at the knights in the courtyard. Malcolm was nowhere to be seen. He bit his lower lip until it began to bleed. He would never stay up all night again.

V

As the king spoke Tristan moved his eyes so that he could see down the aisle created by the knights. He expected to see the goblin being dragged kicking and screaming to the executioner's block, like the snivelling cowards its race were reputed to be. Instead he saw a creature leading the way to the block with its head held high and a look of defiance on its face. It had obviously suffered in the king's dungeon for, although torture had been technically banned in Caldor for centuries, it was well known that those rules did not apply to those considered evil, such as goblins.

As Tristan watched the creature he found it hard to believe the stories of the atrocities its race were supposed to have committed. He also found that it did not look like the savage, wild eyed, animal-like creatures they were rumoured to be. Even at this distance he could see the glint of intelligence that it obviously possessed through its eyes. It had somehow been able to penetrate the king's elaborate defences to the point where it had actually attacked the king. It was only the intervention of the High Priest that had prevented its immediate execution at the king's hands.

He watched as the creature laid its head upon the block waiting with resignation for its death to come.

This is wrong, he thought angrily, *we should not treat intelligent creatures this way.*

He cursed under his breath. He could not believe that he had allowed that thought to escape. If Matthew had caught it then it would mean another trip to a Redirecting Chamber. All knights were treated in the

Chambers, for it allowed them to see the true glory of their king and protect them from evil thoughts. It also helped clear their minds of cluttered, sinful thoughts. However, despite the feeling of calm that always followed Treatment, and the realization that he had needed it, he always felt discomfort at the possibility of another trip. He could never remember exactly what happened but he knew that it involved quite a bit of personal discomfort.

He nervously glanced over to the king and sighed with relief when he saw that his thought had gone unnoticed.

"When I have gone," commanded the king, "kill it and have its remains used for pig swill."

That is truly barbaric, though Tristan in disgust. *How could they treat a living creature in such a cruel manner; even if it is only a goblin?*

He cursed once more. He could not understand why his thoughts had slipped again. It seemed to happen too often for his liking. It was strange, but it seemed that the more times he was treated, the more often his mind slipped like that.

He glanced back at the stairs and thought he could hear the sorcerer whispering in the king's ear. It was clear to Tristan that the sorcerer had caught that thought. He knew that he was in deep trouble.

"If you're going to escape more Treatment I'd start running now; if I were you," said a soft voice in his mind.

VI

Matthew was getting a little bit worried. He had connected with Tristan's mind, just in case he had not been trained enough, and had found it to be a maddening swirl of confusion. The young man's thoughts seemed to be pulling in many different directions at once. He had almost lost himself to it. Something was terribly wrong. He couldn't understand what Tristan was thinking. He could only get vague impressions of emotion and they all seemed to be contradicting each other.

Suddenly the link was broken and a sharp pain struck his mind. Tears filled his eyes as the pain numbed his mind. His spell had been broken. He did not know how but he had been forced out of the knight's mind.

"I'm a little concerned about Tristan," he whispered to Naithan, trying to conceal his pain.

"Don't worry," said Naithan without moving his lips. "He's a strong man. And you did say that his training was enou…"

He was cut off by the sudden clatter of hooves. Tristan was spurring his horse toward the goblin.

"Now look what you've done," said Naithan with a smile. "You've scared him."

A feeling of foreboding crept throughout Matthew and he began to prepare a spell. His head still throbbed in pain but he began to empty all thought from his mind. Now he really wished that he had got some sleep last night. He knew that it was going to be one of those days…

VII

Groltch the goblin was having a really bad day. He had just spent several nights in a disgusting cell, suffering all sorts of physical abuse. He was about to be executed and now he had a knight charging towards him on his thundering giant white horse! He had been ready to die under the blade of an axe and now it seemed that the humans had prepared another way for him to die.

To be fair, it had been a pretty bad month. He had returned home from a hunting expedition in the forest around his village to find nothing but charred remains. The home of his new wife had been destroyed and he later found her body out in the trees. It had been among many other corpses of friends and relatives from the village. He had found one still clinging to life, his *tenget*. The old one had told him what had happened and he'd given him the amulet he now wore. He had made Groltch swear to avenge their deaths and then passed into the long night himself.

He had burned them all, releasing their shadows to the light of Toric and spent several days mourning his life-mate's death whilst he plotted his revenge. He had heard of the knights' rampage through his homeland but believed, as all his friends had, that it would never affect him or his village. He had been wrong and he had to make amends. It was then that he decided the only way to get revenge would be to kill the human leader who had ordered this destruction. Then perhaps the bloodshed would cease and the spirits of his friends would rest.

His preparations had begun almost at once. He had acquired a robe from a human village, so that he could disguise his appearance in the human towns and cities. He had practised stomping around in a human-like walk and had even gone as far as taking a bath, to make him smell more human. That had been the worst part of his plan. He hadn't had a bath since his mother had thrown him in the river as a youngling, ten cycles ago. That had been after he had accidentally set fire to his mother's house and she had been forced to suffer the humiliation of living in his father's house until she had built a new home. His people were very independent. They preferred to live in their own buildings, even after joining with a life-mate. The only mixed households that had several residents were females with younglings. To live in another person's house was to impose upon their personal space and also a sign that one needed to rely on another person's help, such as younglings relying on their parents. It had taken his mother years to forgive him.

Having prepared himself and buried his memories, he had then set out to travel into Caldor, one of the many human lands. Once there he discovered that the king, a title given to human rulers, lived in a large city called Theldar. He had set out upon one of the many roads and walked towards the city. As he drew near he saw more and more humans, and the more he saw of them, the more they disgusted him. Their many weaknesses were apparent. They usually lived in mixed groups of several generations, usually in one building and often in one room! They constantly punished their younglings by forcing them to immerse in water, and kept them constantly under control and supervision, allowing them almost no freedom. He had come to the conclusion that for a supposedly civilised race, they were extremely barbaric and uncouth.

He had eventually arrived at the city they called Theldar and the most difficult stage of his plan; getting close enough to the king to kill it. He was very surprised when he managed to sneak into the castle without encountering any real obstacles. He had only needed to kill six or seven guards before he found the opportunity to sneak up on the king. Unfortunately, after he managed to finish the blood feud rites a weasel faced human with greasy black hair had spotted him and alerted the king. The king had then spun round, drawing its sword and screaming curses at him. Groltch had known that to succeed he had to strike fast, but its skinny wizard intervened on the conflict, using its magic on him. Blue light had flared from its fingers and wrapped itself around him, paralysing him completely. The king had seemed ready to send him into the Long Night there and then, but the wizard had spoken in its ear and he had been thrown into a dungeon. There his jailers had put him through the most unbelievable torture. They had even tried to remove his amulet, though it could only ever be given, never taken. This had only made them angry and they had intensified his torture.

By the time they had finished with him he had resigned himself to the fact that he was going to die. When the guard had arrived to his cell this morning, he already knew that this was the day, and had decided to die with dignity and would not struggle. Death came to all things and evidently Toric had deemed that today was his turn. This new development was just too much, however. His lack of sleep combined with the stress, pressure and fear of imprisonment and his mind gave up. He fainted.

VIII

Tristan had no idea what impulse had driven him to spur his horse down towards the goblin, but he knew there was no turning back now. He had heard the king commanding the guards to stop him, so he knew he was now committed to this course of action. He did not know why he was doing this. It had been rash and foolish and he was already regretting it. He reached the goblin and brought Galahad to a halt. He looked round swiftly, wondering what to do. Unfortunately his mind was mired in confusion and thoughts were pulling in all directions. Part of him wanted to give in and lay down his weapons, leaving himself to the king's mercy. However, another part of his mind contemplated the fact that this would mean another dose of treatment and desperately wanted to flee. With these came dozens of other options, but in his panic, Tristan could not decide what to do. He longed for the peace of mind that followed Treatment, yet shuddered in revulsion at the same time.

"Grab the goblin and get out of here!" said the voice in his mind, *"or else you'll never escape!"*

Confusion mounted in Tristan's mind. He looked to the king and down to the goblin. If the executioner had not chosen that moment to act, Tristan's indecision would have led to his capture. As it was, the big man moved towards him with his large axe. The threat triggered Tristan's training and he became devoid of all thought, losing himself to the action and needs of the moment. All he knew was his opponent. He drew Caliburn and swiftly cut the man across his unprotected stomach who then dropped his axe in pain. Tristan barely noticed him fall to the floor clutching his stomach as if to hold it together, nor the blood spilling across the floor. He merely grabbed the goblin with his left hand and hoisted it across the horse in front of him. He then surveyed the situation. There were still some fifty knights between him and the gate leading from the palace. At present they seemed stunned with shock at his actions, but even he was not quite fast enough to incapacitate that many in the short period of time he had before they recovered their senses.

"Knights and their crazy way of thinking with only the sword!" said the voice in his head, sounding exasperated. *"Raise the sword above your head then close your eyes for a second. It will do the rest."*

He did as ordered without question. In this situation, he needed all the help he could get, no matter how strange it seemed. As he closed his eyes he saw the sword begin to glow softly and he felt a strange tingling sensation grow inside of him. Suddenly his stomach knotted in pain and he heard startled screams from the direction of the knights. He opened his eyes to see them all cradling their eyes in pain.

"Now run!" screamed the voice.

IX

Naithan stared in horror as Jon, one of his best torturers and executioners, collapsed to the ground in a pool of his own blood. He looked at the man who had committed the vile sin of murder and rage rapidly burned away the shock.

"Knights, stop him at all costs!" he screamed, his rage taking over completely.

The knights were slow to react and only one, a young woman, was moving when Tristan slung the goblin over his saddle.

"What in Cal's name is he doing?" he asked Matthew.

There was no reply. He turned and saw that Matthew was lost in the trance he took on before casting a spell. He presumed it would be one similar to that used on the goblin. Knowing better than to disturb him he looked back to the evil young man and saw him raising the holy sword high into the air. The insulting gesture was not lost on Naithan and his rage was beginning to boil over.

How dare he! He thought angrily. *He will suffer for this.*

Suddenly the sword began to glow in light and he looked to Matthew to see if it was of his doing. Seeing that he was still in the midst of his casting he looked back in confusion, just in time to catch sight of a blinding flash of light. It took his stinging, watering eyes over a minute to recover sufficiently to see again and when he could, he saw that Tristan had gone, along with the horse and goblin. Tendrils of blue smoke appeared suddenly, wrapping round the spot where Tristan had been. He turned to his sorcerer with a scornful smile on his face.

"Oh well done!" he said, his voice dripping with sneering sarcasm. "You've managed to capture a whole six feet of air!"

"Your Majesty," said a female knight with a swift bow, "I can hear the sound of his horse. It's heading towards the palace gate."

"Well get after him then before I get angry and do something we both won't like!" he screamed, his rage seeming to leap like fire from him as he spoke.

The young woman's face turned pale.

"Yes sir."

She quickly commanded some knights to follow her and rode towards the disappearing sound of the galloping horse.

Naithan watched them ride off before turning to Matthew.

"Well what are you still doing here?" he asked, eyes blazing. "Get to your laboratory now and contact the guards at the city gates! Those idiots don't stand a chance of catching him. Tell the guards to apprehend him, but not to kill him. They can do what they wish to the vile creature with him."

"Yes, my lord, I'll go right away," replied Matthew looking a little hurt.

"I knew something like this would happen," continued Naithan, more to himself than his friend.

He barely noticed Matthew dash off into the palace and it took him a few minutes to notice that many of the knights were still in the courtyard.

"Well don't just stand there!" he snapped. "Get off to whatever duties you've got today!"

The knights left hurriedly and soon the courtyard was empty. Naithan stood silently on the steps, allowing his rage to slowly disperse.

What in hellfire went wrong? he asked silently, putting his head in his hands.

He knew as soon as this was all over he'd have to make a few drastic changes to the knights' Treatment.

X

Groltch was not the only one who was having a bad day today. Captain Bertram Brünholt of the East Gate Guards was feeling just a little fragile. He and the watch boys had spent most of the previous evening in the Broken Axe Tavern, celebrating Martin's twentieth birthday. They had had even more reason to celebrate, as it also had been the birthday of a rather rich gent too, who had been rather free with his cash, especially to the friends of his fellow drinkers. The drinks had flowed gloriously all night, and had meant that he had arrived home rather later than planned, and just ever so slightly drunk. Unfortunately his wife had heard him creep in, helped by the fact that he'd knocked over half the kitchenware stumbling round in the dark, and been forced to suffer yet another scolding.

Of course, it was just before dawn when his wife had woken him up, reminding him he was now on mornings. At this point he realised he might have drunk just a little too much. His head had felt as though three giants were pounding on it with stone clubs and his thick, dry and furry tongue had not been dulled enough to ignore the taste of foul bile in the back of his mouth. He also had that sick feeling in his stomach from a night of having his bed spinning round and round. Of course, he had conceded, the drink may have been partly responsible for the feeling.

He had staggered down the stairs to find his wife just as unsympathetic, if not more so, than the night before. She had not helped him do anything, and his hands had been shaking so much that he had cut himself shaving four times. He had then left the house with his ears still ringing from his wife's maltreatment of various pots and pans and his stomach churning from the smell of the fried breakfast she had eaten in front of him. For some reason he had not felt like eating much this morning.

He had left the house and stepped into the painfully blinding light of the summer sun and was so sick that he had emptied the little breakfast he had eaten all over someone's cart. Of course the owner had been upset, and loud with it, and he had been forced to part with what little money he had left just to get some peace and quiet.

That noisy incident had set the tone for the rest of the day. All the men under his command were just as rough as him and twice as clumsy. Young Martin had dropped the breastplate he'd been polishing five times and Don had knocked over the entire weapon rack. The gate had been unusually busy and noisy, with screaming children and braying mules. Five violent arguments had erupted that he had been forced to sort out personally. Now, just when the noise had died down and he had just prepared himself for a quick, quiet cup of tea, that blasted mirror had flared to life.

Bertram jumped to his feet and saluted the High Priest, spilling his hot tea over his legs as he did so. He managed not to scream out loud, knowing it would do nothing for his raging headache and looked respectfully at the mirror. The image seemed a little hazy, as if the High Priest had been in a rush when contacting him. He also looked a little pale and gaunt, a fact Bertram put done to the bad connection, as his voice seemed a little muffled as well.

"Greetings, Captain," the image said, just a little too loudly. "I bring you some urgent news. A traitor may be approaching your gate with the intention of escape. If so, you are to apprehend him. He will be easy to recognise, even to one in your present condition, as he is in armour, riding the horse of the King's Knight with a goblin over his saddle. Do not believe any claims to power he may make, and don't injure him too much, else you'll answer to the king. The goblin may be dealt with as you please..."

Captain Brünholt did not like the implication of that last statement.

"Now don't just stand there!" said the High Priest, cruelly raising his voice. "Go and get your men ready."

"Yes sir," he replied with a salute, trying not to wince in pain.

The image faded as he turned to leave and was almost knocked over by Martin, who had been on sentry duty.

"Sir, there's some fella riding like a madman towards our gate on a monster of a white horse!" he said breathlessly, and a little too loudly.

Great! He just had t'choose my gate! he thought with a sigh.

"Go tell the men to load their crossbows and drop the 'cullis!" Bertram commanded shivering inwardly at the thought of the noise shutting the gate would make. "I'll be there in a second or two."

The young man saluted and left, with surprising speed considering he had drunk the most out of all of them last night. Bertram paused for a moment to gather himself together. The sudden excitement had sent his stomach into somersaults and his vision wavered and blurred for a second. With some effort he shook it off and then climbed the stairs to oversee preparations from the parapet.

XI

Galahad and his passengers had charged into the streets of Theldar and through the palace gates unchallenged. The men on guard had just gazed at them with open mouths as they had ridden past. Tristan barely noticed them. The clarity of purpose he had gained from need of survival was draining away and confusion was replacing it once more. So disturbed was he that he all but left control of their speed and direction to his horse. Galahad was an intelligent and well-trained horse and seemed to realise Tristan's urgency. It ran at a fast trot through the streets that were now full with people going to the markets. The area became even more cluttered the closer they came to the central square. In the beginning people were able to get out of the way quite easily, but as the streets became more crowded, some began having difficulties. Galahad was forced to slow a little so that it was possible to dodge and weave round the stragglers. This created a little panic in the people and they began to move more and more frantically. This then grew and grew until people began to desperately push past everyone in their way. Some were even pushed to the ground, forcing the horse to jump them, making more than one scream out in fear. This grew fear rapidly, like a flame across paper and soon the whole crowd was screaming.

By the time they reached the Royal Market, it was easy to see that word had spread, as there was what seemed almost like a riot as people tried to get away. People swayed this way and that, and Tristan wondered how one horse could cause such panic. It was then that he heard the sound of the other horses, those of his pursuers. It seemed that they were being less careful of pedestrians than he. He steered his horse towards the East Gate, which was closest to their position. Yet it seemed his hunters would reach him before he made it to the gate. Panic began to fill him, and he lashed out with the sword still in his hand. The air filled with the sound of splintering wood, smashing glass and metal clattering as market stalls fell beneath the holy blade. This was intermingled with the screams and curses of the stall owners. Tristan looked back and found the desperate ploy had worked as the knights behind him were being forced to negotiate their way through the market with a little caution. They began shouting out to the people to stop him, and as he returned his gaze ahead he saw that someone had moved to obey. An astute merchant seemed to have realised the financial possibilities and had pushed his stall across the street leading to the east gate. Tristan froze in fear. Galahad was going too fast to turn or stop in time.

"Jump it!" the soft voice commanded.

Without pausing to think on the fact that the stall was too high to jump, he spurred Galahad onwards. Just as Galahad began the leap, blue and white lightening leaped from the sword's blade to the stall. It exploded in flames and crashed to the ground and the merchant followed, sobbing at the loss of his livelihood.

The horse barely even flinched at the event, leaping calmly through the flames, which Tristan was surprised to discover, emitted no heat. The goblin twitched violently, and he noted its presence with surprise. It was all he could do to force down the urge to throw it from the horse in disgust.

Suddenly he felt very light-headed and also a little ill. He took his attention from the creature and concentrated on controlling Galahad. He steered the horse towards the gate, knowing that this brief ride was almost over.

XII

Captain Brünholt was reaching a state of absolute panic. There had been a sudden explosion and something had burst into flames at the top of Eastern Avenue. From these flames had emerged an armoured man on horseback, holding aloft a sword, though this description was inadequate for the exact image he saw. The sword glowed brightly and the knight seemed surrounded by a blue aura of energy. The horse was a magnificent beast that seemed to possess its own glow, and the thundering of hooves that should have accompanied it were merely the soft clattering of a horse half its size. The scene was like something born of legend and he momentarily forgot his headache. Yet a cold realisation struck him. This warrior had used magic of some sort…

How can we fight magic? He thought frantically. He knew that some knights were trained in the arts but not so the city guards.

"Get that accursed portcullis down!" he roared. "And where are those men below to apprehend him?"

"I can't work it sir!" replied the gate operator on the verge of complete panic. "The winch is stuck!"

"'E must be usin' 'is magic on it!" muttered Martin fearfully.

"Don't be daft!" growled Bertram.

We're doomed! he thought in despair.

"Get that crossbow loaded!" was all he said though.

Martin complied. Unfortunately the rest of his men were still rushing around getting their weapons ready. Even he was still desperately focusing on his crossbow, winding its windlass frantically in order to load it. He paused for a moment, as the world seemed to spin before his eyes. It stopped and he found he was feeling extremely light-headed and more than a little sick. It soon passed.

What if this was part of his magic? He thought worriedly.

He swallowed his fears and completed loading his crossbow. He glanced back and saw that Don had gone over to help the guards at the winch. Normally six would be enough to operate the ship winch installed to make opening and closing the two ton gate, yet not today. Looking at it Bertram noticed that there seemed to be something stuck there. He ordered Martin over to help and prepared himself. Today could be a very short day…

XIII

Tristan could now see the gate before him and knew that he would not make it through. The gate would close and his escape would be blocked. He would then be surrounded by crossbow wielding guards and captured.

He drew closer and eyed the two protecting towers with apprehension. He could not understand why the portcullis had not yet dropped down. He bent low and spurred Galahad through with visions of the gate crashing down on him and was soon well beyond the other side. Within minutes he was well outside the city grounds.

XIV

Back at the tower nothing moved. The bodies of the guards littered the floor, their faces frozen in the agony each had felt on death. Captain Brünholt lay with his loaded crossbow upon his chest, tears of pain trickling down his cheeks. He saw something stir in the shadows and a man stepped out. It was the man who had been so generous last night…

XV

He moved towards a fallen guard and felt for the pulse. When none was found he smiled to himself. The poison had worked well. It had been expensive, imported from the desert regions of Karsisia. According to the merchant who had sold it, the poison came from a creature called a scorpion. Its sting was as dangerous as that of a wasp, unless the person stung began to panic, or get emotionally excited. This caused the heart to beat faster and concentrated the poison, making it deadly.

He looked at the strange knight now galloping from the city. He had no idea who or what he was, but he was evidently against the king, as he carried the king's failed assassin with him. The assassin had almost spoiled the Shadow's plans for the king. It had only just been stopped, with a little intervention on his part. Whoever the knight was, he was taking the annoyance out of harm's way, and who was also saving him from having to organise an event to excite the guards and trigger the poison. Its effects only lasted a day but were incredibly painful to the victim, and that was all that mattered. They would suffer as she had. They all would…

The sound of more horses broke his train of thought and he realised that these must be the knights sent to pursue the first. He quickly moved over to the portcullis mechanism. There was a thick hemp rope that connected the gate to the wooden mechanism used to open it. He removed the bolt that he had wedged in to make the mechanism stick and released the gate. After he heard the clash as it struck the ground, he covered the winch with oil from nearby lamps and set fire to the mechanism.

"That is in thanks for your help," he said softly to the almost vanished form of the knight in the distance.

A groan from the floor made him spin round. One of the guards was still alive. The crest on his brooch marked him as the captain. He slowly pulled out a dagger and a piece of paper. He then kneeled down by the captain's side. The man was trying to aim his crossbow at him. He smiled contemptuously and slowly slid the dagger into the man's chest. He then watched the life fade from the captain's eyes before placing the piece of paper behind the crossbow wire. He stood, gave a mocking bow, then span on his heel and disappeared into the shadows.

When the guards finally arrived they found the tower devoid of life and a small note addressed to the king. All it said was *Watch your back* and it was signed *The Shadow.*

CHAPTER TWO: Flight and Fatalities

I

"…and here's some money for yerself," whispered Luca as he handed the cloaked figure a money pouch.

They were stood in the dark corridor leading to one of the servants' entrances.

"Now yer remember what t'do?" he asked worriedly.

"Yes," she replied softly. "I *have* done this before. I'll have yer messages delivered on time."

"Remember you've only got a couple of days t'get there and back. After that I'll not be able t'cover for yer no more."

"Yes, yes, I know," she replied in a bored voice. "Can I go now?"

Luca nodded and she turned towards the door.

"One more thing," he called softly and she stopped and turned round. "Take care of yerself."

She put her hands on her hips and he could feel her glare, even though he could not see it.

"I'm not a little girl," she replied just a little too loudly. "I've filled in for my mother before and I'm just as capable as her!"

Luca had no doubts about that. She had inherited all of her mother's qualities and talents, including her rash temper. He just did not like sending either of them on such potentially dangerous errands. The countryside was not as safe as it used to be especially for a girl…woman carrying so much money.

"I'll be fine," she said soothingly. "And in two days I'll be back, so don't worry!"

Although her face was hidden he was positive she had just flashed that mischievous crooked grin that usually preceded trouble. Sometimes she was a little too like her mother.

Suddenly he heard hurried footsteps echoing from an adjoining corridor, coming towards them. He gestured frantically for her to leave, and for once she obeyed him. She gave a quick, farewell wave and moved quietly out of the door. He hurried up behind her and ensured she had locked the door before turning back and walking towards the sound of the footsteps. As he turned the corner he saw it was one of the young corridor cleaning girls. She seemed to be in tears and was in full flight. Luca sighed in relief before swiftly diving to catch her as she stumbled to the floor. She did not try to stand and just continued sobbing. He looked down at her. Her red hair was tied back and tears were streaming down her face.

"Yer Sal, aren't yer?" he asked gently and she nodded her head. "What's wrong?"

She did not answer immediately, but Luca was a patient man. He waited for her to calm down a little before repeating his question.

"It's the king, sir" she replied, looking up at him. "He's took away my job. I was jus' cleanin' the floor an' he storms pas', trips over my bucket and paupers me. That job was all I had."

With this she started crying again. He put his arm around her and helped her to her feet.

"Don't worry," he said softly. "I'll sort this out. Yer not paupered. Come with me and I'll sort it with Lynn so that yer work some other corridors till I can speak t'the king."

What has happened now? He asked silently.

Naithan's reign seemed destined to be fraught with troubles.

II

Naithan marched angrily towards Matthew's room, swearing and cursing under his under his breath as he went. He had just received a report from one the knights who had pursued Tristan through Theldar and he was not pleased with it. Apparently the guards at the east gate had failed to stop him and now the young traitor was heading out into the countryside. Matthew had failed in his duty and Naithan had lost control in a fit of rage. He had almost knocked the unfortunate messenger from his horse and sent him scurrying for safety. He had then turned and entered the palace. Servants scattered before him and his glare had reduced more than one of them to tears. Even Malcolm had turned and gone the other way. However nothing would cool his anger and he remained resolutely on course.

As soon as he arrived at Matthew's bedroom door he burst in screaming, "Of all the incompetence I have ever seen…"

His voice broke off as he realised the room was empty. This puzzled him a little and a tingling sensation in his arm turned confusion to concern. He went to the door on the other side of the room and waited long enough for his anger to completely slip away. The door led to Matthew's laboratory and Naithan had seen first-hand the damage that could be done if he disturbed him even in the simplest of spells. He cautiously opened the large marble door and peered into the quiet, dark room.

There was a soft glowing light at one end of the room that gave enough light o allow him to see into the room. He looked round, and found that the room appeared to be empty, though it was still dark enough that he could not be absolutely certain. His view was also partly obscured by the large granite table that occupied the centre of the windowless chamber. It was then that he realised where the light was coming from. The mirror on the opposite wall was glowing softly and had no reflection upon it. Instead it showed the inside of what looked like the captain's office of the southern gate house. This meant that Matthew was most likely somewhere in this room. Naithan's concern grew and his arm seemed to go numb, as if to confirm his fears.

He moved slowly round the desk, frightened that he might knock over one of the many coloured potions or break some of the fragile glass apparatus. It seemed to take hours to finally make it round and when he did he almost cried out in shock. Matthew was lying in a heap on the floor. Naithan dropped to his knees and checked for a pulse. He gasped with relief when he felt the soft throb of blood surging through the man's neck. He tenderly picked the young sorcerer up and carried him through to the bedroom. As he walked through the door Matthew suddenly screamed out in pain. Naithan cursed himself angrily. He had forgotten that it was painful, and sometimes dangerous, for a wizard to have a spell broken by an outside force. He looked down to Matthew and was relieved to see he was still breathing, though visibly pale.

He placed Matthew gently onto the large four-poster bed. He had seen Matthew in such a state before. It usually occurred after he had used too much magic too quickly. Even so it was unusual for him to collapse as quickly as this. Naithan knew enough about magic to know that the feats performed today were very minor. Evidently his friend's lack of sleep the previous night had diminished his power.

Naithan looked over to the door leading to the laboratory and saw that it had vanished. He shuddered at such visible evidence of magic, but knew it was now safe to summon Matthew's valet. He leaned across the bed and pulled the bell chord that hung there. He then checked Matthew's breathing. It was ragged and a little irregular but that was to be expected. He sighed with relief. Hopefully Matthew would be up and about in a few hours.

The door leading in from the servants' corridor opened and Matthew's valet, upon seeing the king, stepped nervously into the room. He was a young man called Eward who had only recently entered Matthew's service.

"How may I be of service to you, your Majesty?" he asked, nervously rubbing his hands together.

"Close the curtains and stoke the fire," replied Naithan in a hushed voice. "Then see to it that he is not disturbed by anyone but me."

"Yes, your Majesty," replied the valet with a small bow.

The man then went and began to hurriedly fiddle with the curtains. Naithan would have been amused if he had not been so worried for his friend's health.

"As soon as he wakes up he'll need some food and water. Make sure that it is brought to him as soon as you are called."

"Yes, your Majesty," he replied with another bow and Naithan could not help wondering if all that bobbing up and down made him sick.

The valet then picked up the poker and began coaxing more heat from the fire. It did not take long for the heat to diffuse through the relatively cold room. Matthew's east facing window only ever caught the sun during the afternoon and evening and even then it had little effect on the room, yet the fire's warmth seemed able to spread through the room with almost unnatural speed.

He looked up and noticed the valet waiting to be dismissed. Naithan groaned inwardly. He had gotten so used to Luca's informality that he often forgot to dismiss other servants. Luca always left when the job was finished, with or without his command.

"You may go, Eward," he said with a smile.

The young man looked a little startled then bowed and left swiftly, leaving Naithan alone with his friend. He took a quick look around to make sure everything was as it should be. The glow from the fire bathed everything in a soft orange light giving the room a somewhat more cheerful atmosphere than usual. It was quite a plain room, consisting of only a bed, small table, wardrobe and bookcase.

As his eyes rested upon Matthew's bookcase, a smile appeared on his face. Matthew had liked books for as long as Naithan had known him. He loved to collect books and his personal collection was beginning to rival that of the palace. He even owned what they believed to be the only piece of goblin literature, if it could be called that, known to exist. It was from that piece of scrawling script that they had found the key to the means to fulfil their holy quest.

A heavenly messenger who had taken on the form of a gardener had given the quest to them. They had both been children at the time and had known little of the world and its sins. Then they had met him and he had revealed to them in vivid detail the sins and evils of other folk. The images had been so strong that they still burned with extreme detail in his mind.

He had not told them what to do, he had not needed to, they had known instinctively.

They had never seen him again, and on checking palace records they had found no trace of the man, though they had found the goblin parchment whilst looking. This confirmed their belief that he was a heavenly messenger and the goblin scroll would lead the way. Matthew had set to translating the script and it quickly revealed how they could carry out the divine plan. Soon peace and light would reign in the world and the likes of this so-called *Shadow* would no longer exist to blot the lives of the pure. Anger welled up inside of him again and he looked at the note from the Shadow the messenger had given him.

"You'll pay for this," he muttered angrily. "You, that treacherous knight and all those who dare try and prevent me from cleansing the world!"

He placed the note on the small table and quietly left the room. As the door closed a figure stepped out of the flickering shadows created by the fire's dancing flames.

"So I'll pay, will I?" he asked, softly. "Well not before I've made you suffer as much as I have."

With that the figure returned to the shadows and vanished, leaving only the flames to bear witness to his passage.

III

It took Tristan almost half an hour to reach the forest that surrounded Theldar's eastern border. When he reached the first of the trees he finally allowed Galahad to slow and stop. The horse was foaming slightly at the mouth and was showing signs of extreme fatigue. Tristan dismounted feeling a little ashamed of himself. He had never treated Galahad in this manner before. He moved Galahad into the trees and tethered him to a small sapling. He looked at the horse and saw that the goblin was still lying across the horse's back. He shook his head with disgust and returned to the main highway.

When he reached it he raised the visor on his helm and looked back towards the city in search of anyone who might be following him. The road was relatively empty except for those few travellers he had passed by. A confusion of thoughts swirled round in his head as he tried to sort out the day's strange events. He should have been caught before he had even left the city and now there should be at least one or two people riding from the city in pursuit. It all made no sense, and worse still, part of his mind was crying out to be caught. He was also at a loss as to what to do next.

"I suppose I should get to somewhere relatively safe," he said quietly to himself.

"Now that would seem like a pretty good idea, wouldn't it?" said the voice in his head dryly.

Startled, he looked round for the source of the strange voice.

"Who are you?" he asked nervously.

His question was met with silence and Tristan shivered fearfully. The voice was obviously caused by magic of some sort or another, but what kind? If it was priestly magic, why had it advised him to go against the head of the church? And what if it was sorcery? That would mean, despite all the High Priest's attempts to show the good nature of such magic, that some evil person or creature sought to gain control of him. If so then why now when he was no longer in a position of power?

Finding no answers he walked back to Galahad. The goblin was still on the horse's back and Tristan avoided his initial instincts to drop it to the ground and leave it, deciding it might help in answering some of his questions. Galahad seemed unusually calm, not at all like a horse that had been forced to gallop for almost fifty minutes. Tristan forced his suspicions to the back of his mind and remounted, spurring the horse back on to the road. At a lack as to what to do now, he decided to go the village of his birth which was situated nearby.

As he emerged from the trees he saw a contingent of knights ride over the crest of the hill. His heart almost stopped before he realised they were going towards the city, not coming away from it. One of the knights broke away from the main group. He rode towards Tristan and stopped just before him.

"Sir Balin, Blue Knight and Claw Leader of Belthanor," said the knight by way of an introduction. "I'm travelling for Theldar with this squad of initiates. Are you our escort?"

Panic suddenly set in as Tristan realised he was still in his armour. He could not say he was their escort for he would then have to return to Theldar. On the other hand, knights rarely rode out on their own, especially without their squires. His mind locked into a fierce battle as it pulled in all directions. Tristan's head seemed to explode in pain. He was obviously going mad.

The knight regarded him suspiciously, looking up to where Tristan's plume of rank should have been. Tristan could recall it having fallen off some time during his flight. On not seeing any symbol of rank, the Blue Knight's eyes moved down towards the goblin.

"Is that a captured raider?" he asked.

Tristan just sat there frozen with fear and indecision.

"Ride into the woods…now!" screamed the other voice.

That was just too much for Tristan and he screamed in an attempt to drown out the soft voice. Captain Balin's eyes widened in surprise and he began to edge his horse backwards.

Tristan's horse cocked his head as if listening to some unheard command. Suddenly Galahad sprang for the woods, surprising the other knight, who just sat there, gaping in amazement. That gave them time to reach the trees and soon Galahad was racing between the massive oaks, avoiding the fallen branches as skilfully as he had avoided the people in Theldar.

The decision taken for him, Tristan's mind cleared a little, leaving just a dull ache. He began to take control of the situation by looking around him, searching the trees for a familiar landmark. He almost whooped for joy when he saw a familiar, large gnarled oak tree. He had grown up in these woods and his father, a King's Ranger, had shown him everything that had lived in the woods that surrounded his village. The oak had been one of his favourite childhood haunts. He could vaguely recall spending many hours climbing through its twisted branches. He should know this area better than almost anyone in the region, though his memories of that time seemed strangely dulled.

He spurred his horse on, trying to slow the pursuing knights by jumping low shrubs and riding down a small brook for several yards before leaving on the opposite bank. He knew this would not hide his trail well, but it would give time to think.

He began to move in a wide circle back towards the old oak, trying to remain in the territory he knew. He made sure he avoided crossing the stream. This was fairly easy, as it emerged from the ground some fifty yards from where he had originally crossed, caused by something like chalky hills and low tables of water, or something to that effect. He had forgotten many of his father's lessons. He did remember one thing, though. The result of this disappearing stream was that trails could often be confusing to those who did not really know the land, and that could work to his favour. Already the vague outlines of a desperate plan were forming in his mind. He had to act soon though, because although Galahad showed no signs of tiring at the moment, a worrying observation considering the length of time they had been running, it surely could not last.

He had a slim advantage, with the knights travelling at the slower pace, trying to keep on his trail, but it would not last. He had to mislead them somehow, and he had an idea of what to do. He aimed to reach his own trail some ten feet after the oak, such a visible landmark being too recognisable for the plan to work. When he reached it, he was pleased to note his own trail was obscured by the trails of the other knights. He joined it and rode along it until he reached a specific clearing he had marked on his way round. In an attempt to lose the knights he had made Galahad leap a bush to the left, leaving little evidence in the tracks as to the direction he had taken.

He looked down and as expected, he found deeper marks of the knights' horses, where they had been forced to stop and wait whilst one dismounted and searched for the trail. He was amazed at how easily his knowledge of reading tracks had come back to him. It had been one of his worst fields of study as a squire, despite his father's teaching.

He stopped Galahad and quickly dismounted. He then proceeded to walk around the area, forcing his tracks into the ground in places, as if he had been standing there a while. He even dragged the goblin off to create different sized footprints, despite the difficulties of carrying its limp form around. He returned the still unconscious goblin to Galahad's back and then prepared for the difficult bit. Unfortunately, the ground here was quite soft, and he just hoped desperately that they would not make to deep a set of tracks as they left, in a direction different to that in which he had left the first time. He led them off and after several hundred yards they found a game trail frequently used by the king. He made his way down to a nearby clearing that was surrounded by dense undergrowth. He tethered Galahad quickly and glanced briefly at the goblin before leaving to cover their trail as best they could. He made his way back the way he had come and found the trail very faint. As he went back further and further he also discovered that it faded until it eventually disappeared some ten feet from the clearing. He looked at it in amazement and wondered how on Loden it had happened.

Suddenly the world spun before his eyes and he dropped to his knees clutching his stomach, as it seemed to twist and churn about in painfully long spasms. For many minutes he could barely breathe, and it felt as if he would collapse, but it gradually cleared up until he was almost ready to stand once more. Unfortunately at that moment he heard the sound of horses entering the clearing, so had to keep low and quiet, observing them through a gap in the foliage. He prayed fervently that his armour would not glint in the sunlight.

There were some thirty men in the clearing dressed in armour similar to his own, all with blank white shields and no feathered plumes on their helms. This confirmed that they were indeed uninitiated, which meant that they were all a little inexperienced. This could help his desperate plan somewhat, though not by much.

"Squire Gilder, you are the best tracker of the company. See if you can determine the direction in which our quarry left in," commanded the captain, who had obviously already made up his own mind on the answer.

He's treating the whole thing like an exercise! He thought incredulously. *Of course! The final quest!*

All squires were required to take a final surprise quest before knighthood, and the Blue Knight must believe this was it.

One of the knights dismounted and began to slowly pace round the clearing, examining the ground cautiously. As he did so, Tristan noticed that other knights were looking round the clearing, as if it was sparking off some memory. Tristan prayed to Toric that none would recognise the area, though part of him doubted any would as he barely recognised it himself.

Time slowed down to a crawl and a shiver of fear went down his spine. He went through the plan in his mind. He realised just how desperate and foolish it was. It was a child's trick that any experienced tracker would see through, even with the almost magical lack of a trail in his direction. How could he have been so stupid? He was not truly wise in the ways of the woods. What little skill he had was what was left of his childhood memories, all of which seemed so few and distant now.

The young squire carefully looked round and for one horrifying moment seemed to look directly at the spot where Tristan was hiding. He held his breath as the young man stood and contemplated everything. Just as Tristan was beginning to feel faint, the squire spoke.

"It appears he was not alone. The tracks indicated that there were numerous forces here and at least two or three men were stood a while, as if awaiting someone and one of whom was heavily laden. It appears the quarry met with them here and then they rode off together in that direction."

As he said this he pointed in the direction of their own older trail, as Tristan had hoped they would.

"Very good," said the captain. "That matches my conclusions almost exactly. You may remount and we will ride on. We shall apprehend these goblin friends and enhance the honour you will receive upon your knighting ceremony.

"We ride!"

With this the captain raised his sword in the air and galloped off. The others followed at a slower rate, some still looking round cautiously at the clearing as they left.

As the last one left, Tristan felt a sudden desire to call out. He had wanted them to find him. He wanted the peace of mind that followed Treatment. He stood up and it was only with the greatest of efforts that he remained silent.

He turned sadly away, knowing his last chance to surrender quickly was now over. He made his way slowly back to the other clearing. As he did he thought back to the captain. The man's arrogance had prevented him from finding Tristan. It was he who had truly allowed Tristan's plan to work. He had obviously decided on what he thought was the truth then fitted the facts to fit his theory. Tristan had never noticed this trait before, yet on thinking back, most knights he had ever known were like it. What made it worse was that he had obviously been the same, for his piece of trickery had probably been based on what he would have done in the man's position. Admittedly the captain had expected a quest of some sort, which would have influenced his thinking but still…

That's one group of knights who've failed their test! said the voice dryly. *My my, the knighthood really has gotten worse over the years.*

Tristan ignored the voice, and soon forgot all about the odd comment, for on reaching the clearing he found that the goblin was no longer there.

IV

When Groltch returned to consciousness the horse had stopped moving and there was no sign of the knight, the courtyard, or the executioner. In fact he seemed surrounded by trees. This confused him. It had to be some kind of cruel human trap, or form of torture.

He waited for what seemed like hours yet nothing happened. Birds were singing in the trees as the leaves rustled in the wind, and occasionally the horse shifted slightly. Even more confused, he looked around him. He seemed to be in the middle of a forest. After waiting for a little while longer, he decided to risk it and rolled off the horse's back. He landed with a jarring jolt on the exposed roots of the tree to which the horse was tethered. He grunted loudly, but tried to ignore the pain. He then closed his eyes and prepared to be skewered on the end of the sword. Nothing happened.

He opened one eye, then the next. The clearing was still empty. He dared to hope that he had somehow escaped. He tried to get up but found he was still bound with rope. He began to roll about in a desperate attempt to break free. He was fortunate that a sharp piece of fire rock was settled amongst the roots. His frantic movements allowed the stone to weaken the rope, but it also led to numerous cuts and bruises. Luckily his hands were still numb due to the tightness of the bonds and so he felt little pain. He steadied his violent rocking and forced his thoughts into calmness. He then began to work carefully at sawing the rope apart. When he finally achieved this, he swiftly leapt to his feet, immediately regretting doing so. His head suddenly felt dizzy and his vision blurred as the world before him began to spin round and round. His mind became cloudy and unfocused and he was forced to lean on the tree for support.

Just then he noticed movement in the bushes to his left. He staggered off hurriedly in the opposite direction, gripping his stomach as it began to churn violently. He tottered into the bushes and managed to cover about two hundred metres before the ground seemed to suddenly swing round and strike him in the head. He slipped thankfully into unconsciousness.

V

Naithan sat in his private audience chamber listening to his chief engineer explain the reasons why the east gate could not be opened until sometime in the evening. The poor man was so scared of Naithan's reaction that he stammered and stuttered and his report was almost entirely incoherent. However the king had other things on his mind. As soon as the engineer had left this chamber, Naithan would have to speak to Jon's mother. Ostensibly it was to inform her of her son's death, but in reality it was to ensure that no rumours of executions would leak out. This had potentially lethal consequences for both him and his family. Only once had the kingdom of Caldor seen a public execution, about two hundred years ago. It had resulted in first riots and then revolution, which had included the killing of the king, one Henry III, or Henry the Black as he was popularly known. It had also seen the destruction of nearly his entire House, ending the reign of House Faithe permanently.

More importantly, it had led to the coronation of the first Tara'non, William I. Of course, executions had been publicly renounced, whilst continuing in secret as it had for generations. Only in the time of Sir Caldor the Pure had it been possible to rule without execution, the people gliding on the wings and euphoria of freedom. There were always those for whom Treatment could provide no cure and as many as ten or twelve executions a year were held. If even a hint of such knowledge leaked out to the public, riots and bloodshed would soon follow. It was all a throwback to the time when they had been enslaved under goblin rule. The vile creatures had used executions as the principle form of punishment, and the king in no way intended to be associated with those monsters.

It was also part of the paradoxical nature of his people. They were generally very peaceful in their beliefs and the way they lived. They hated violence and anything man did outside the Laws of Toric. However they were renowned for forming the most violent and merciless mobs in the southern lands, especially when it involved the likes of kings, witches and wizards.

Ordinary people who sinned were considered to be misdirected and in need of treatment. However kings who did so were considered evil incarnate and magic users by their very nature were evil. It was one reason why all those with even a spark of magic were brought into the knighthood. It was also the reason why Matthew's official title was Lord High Priest, and not as Lord High Sorcerer. Even though he was the first ever to hold that office who truly possessed priestly powers along with their wizardly ones, something Naithan had been taught was impossible, they would still detest his use of evil magic. Even Naithan found discussing the subject difficult, and it often left a foul taste in his mouth.

Deciding that he had no wish to face a rioting city, he had decided to deal with the matter personally as it was too important to leave to an underling. Malcolm had tried to persuade him otherwise, and of course that had made him even more determined to do so. Now he was bitterly regretting the decision. He kept running through his mind for suitable stories he could tell her, yet none had sounded correct. He had even once contemplated telling her the truth, even though he knew it was not an option. To tell her that her son was a cruel, mean, brutal, sadistic, vile, and violent man who enjoyed torture and slicing men's heads off with an axe was not really a good idea.

He also knew that Jon's mother did not have many friends and it was likely that she still lived for her son. Her husband had apparently died shortly after Jon's birth and she had lived alone ever since. He wanted to give her a story that would one day ease the pain a little, as she could then speak with pride of her son's courage and he could steer clear of any mention of the word execution.

He was so engrossed in thought that he did not immediately notice that the chief engineer had managed to stutter out his report. The poor man had probably then spent several minutes in agonising silence for the king's reply. When Naithan finally noticed the silence he waved his hand negligently towards the door.

"Very well you may go," he said automatically.

The engineer bowed swiftly and hurriedly left the hall. He was sweating profusely and Naithan knew this day would probably be the stuff of nightmares for years to come. He was barely out the door when Malcolm entered.

"I have some good news, Sire," he said, bowing stiffly to conceal his sneer. "The Lord High Priest has recovered from his collapse and is asking to see you. Unfortunately you have Mrs Harper to see you."

Naithan pretended not to notice the almost smug look on the oily man's face. One day he would find some suitable position for the little man somewhere far away.

"Show her in," Naithan said, a little wearily.

VI

Tristan removed the last piece of his elaborate armour that came off suddenly and crashed to the ground. It had taken him several hours to remove the whole suit. This was because it was ceremonial armour with more parts than absolutely necessary. He was also unused to removing his armour without the aid of a page or a squire. This made him glad, for the first time, that they had never finished altering the Armour of Caldor, the armour he should have worn today as King's Knight. It was probably the most complicated and spectacular suit of armour to have ever been made in Caldor, if not the whole of Loden. Now he would never be allowed to wear the sacred suit. He had no illusions. He knew that when he was finally caught he would never again be allowed to hold the position of King's Knight. He sighed and focused his mind on his present situation.

It had been many hours since his escape from the knights. He had immediately ridden towards Havelock, his home village, intent on staying there the night. As he neared his old home though, he came to the realisation that it would be a mistake. His presence would only complicate village life and get those caught harbouring him into trouble. It was an offence that required Redirection and he did not wish to be the reason for anyone suffering that. He had decided to set up camp some five miles or so east from the village. When he had finally reached a suitable clearing he had immediately set about removing his armour.

Now that he had finished that task he realised that he was very hungry. It was so bad that his stomach began to make its protests heard in a very loud voice. He stood and immediately went in search of some food. Once again he thanked his father for his training. He knew which roots were edible and where to search for them. He also knew where the nearest stream was as well as a nearby clearing often frequented by numerous rabbits.

When he reached the clearing he attempted to set several snares with whatever came to hand. Unfortunately time and large doses of treatment seemed to make it difficult to recall the fine details of his father's lessons. The snares he made were both clumsy and inefficient. He eventually gave up, content to eat whatever roots and plants he had already found. He returned to the site where Galahad was tethered. When he got there he set about unsaddling him, cursing himself for not doing so sooner and when he had finished, he let the horse graze. Unfortunately Tristan knew that Galahad could not survive solely on grass. He needed some proper feed if he was to remain fit and healthy.

Tristan slumped to the ground. He had no hope of surviving for any length of time. He was just too ill-equipped. He closed his eyes and tears began to trickle from the closed lids. Everything was hopeless. He would have to go and surrender in the morning. There was nothing left to do. He would have to go and face the Treatment.

This made the tears flow faster for he knew that treatment would lead to great pain. He could even remember a little of what had happened on his last visit. He had cried then too, as he recalled. Grief overwhelmed him and he finally gave himself up to tears.

VII

Naithan walked quickly to Matthew's bedchamber. The audience with Mrs Harper had gone well. He had spun some tale about an evil knight and several goblin followers attempting to assassinate him and how Jon had stood against them, fighting bravely to the end. He had defeated all but the knight who killed him in a cowardly attack from behind. He smiled bitterly at the irony of the tale. He had reversed the personalities of the two antagonists. He had made Jon, a vile man of intrinsic evil, but a necessary tool for now, into a hero of epic proportions, and had placed Tristan, a good man merely in need of redirection, in the role of villain.

The story had served its purpose, however, for he had seen a glimmer of pride shine in her eyes behind the inevitable tears. He had then handed her a pouch full of money, enough to last her to the end of her days, and then personally escorted her to the state carriage that had brought her here. He had helped her climb aboard and waved farewell, before turning hurriedly to get to Matthew's room.

As he arrived he knocked softly three times before opening the door. He looked in and saw Matthew propped up with cushions, reading a book. His friend looked up and ushered him inside. As Naithan came in he took a closer look at Matthew. He still looked extremely tired and haggard. Obviously the magic had worn him out more than Naithan had originally thought.

"How are you feeling?" he asked as he sat on the edge of the bed, concern showing in his voice.

"I'm not feeling too bad, just a little lightheaded," Matthew replied, his soft voice almost hoarse. "I heard about the problem at the gate so I thought would try and locate him, to speed up the search. It was fairly easy because he's not gone too far. He's about five miles east of his old home village. He seems very confused at the moment. You should be able to get some men out to him before dawn."

"You shouldn't have done that!" said Naithan in exasperation, "not so soon after a collapse. No wonder you feel lightheaded! The best thing to do is to have complete rest until tomorrow. I'll send some knights out as soon as the gate is repaired."

"I also read the note left by that monster." Matthew's voice was now edged with concern. "That means I don't have time to rest because I've got to set up some stronger protective wards around you, just in case."

Matthew struggled with his blankets as he tried to stand up, but Naithan pushed him back down gently.

"No you won't," he said sharply. "You will get some rest and leave the worrying to me for the moment."

Matthew smiled and shrugged his shoulders in resignation. He sank back down into the feather filled cushions. Within minutes he was asleep and the worn look faded slightly. Naithan smiled softly and quietly rose from the bed.

"I had better see to those knights," he said softly to himself. "I'll make him pay for what Matthew's suffering."

He did not know whether he meant Tristan or the Shadow. At the moment it didn't matter; they would both suffer a little after they'd been captured.

He took one last look at the sleeping sorcerer then left the room, closing the door quietly behind him. He walked off down the corridor.

In the silence of Matthew's room the fire still burned in the hearth, casting strange shadows on the walls and furniture. If Matthew had been awake to see, he would have noticed that one of the shadows seemed somehow darker than the rest. If he had continued to watch, he would have seen it break away suddenly and slip out of the room, almost as if it were following the king…

VIII

It was nearing dusk when Tristan woke up on the hard ground. He realised that he must have fallen asleep, but could not remember when he had slipped from consciousness. He got to his feet and felt a sudden chill as a cold breeze cut through the rust stained clothing he wore under his armour. Tristan groaned. Summer nights could be exceptionally cold when the skies were clear.

He shook off a little of the euphoria of sleep and cleaned himself in the nearby brook. The cold water washed the last vestiges of sleep from his mind and he returned to the campsite. When he arrived he was surprised to see that near where he had slept was a pile of clothes, food and basic tools for survival. He looked round, but could see nothing so cautiously approached the small pile. When nothing happened he prodded it with one foot. The items certainly felt solid and not like an illusion. He looked around but could not see anyone. He carefully removed his dirty clothing and dressed himself in the white shirt and brown trousers. He was surprised to find that they fitted him almost perfectly.

He sat down and began to think. There was only one place where they could have come from, yet he could not see why. He decided to go to Havelock to have a look, a decision partly influenced by a sudden feeling of homesickness.

He searched through the clothes and found a pair of brown leather boots. He put them on and found them to be a little tight. He forced his feet into them with a slight grunt and stood up. It felt quite strange wearing the light boots after the heavy sabatons and greaves he had grown accustomed to, but it provided relief for his tired legs which, like all of his body, seemed strangely drained of strength. He was not unaccustomed to heavy exercise and today he had actually done less than on a usual training day, but felt much more exhausted. He shook off the thoughts, finding them too unsettling and confusing to bear. There were many questions that needed answering. Maybe he could get some in Havelock.

He bent down and picked out a brown leather jacket, put it on and set out towards the village. It took him over an hour to get there and as he arrived he saw that it was still full of life despite the darkness. Suddenly shy, he pulled himself up into an old oak tree from where he could get a good view of the village. There was a big bonfire in the centre square and all down the street and in every house candles burned. People were dancing, drinking and singing and revelling in merriment.

Of course! He thought as memories sparked. *It is the Festival of Light!*

It was a week-long celebration of the light of the summer sun. It was held in the seven days before the longest day of the year, and culminated in the Lighting. The village would stand in darkness and in silence, all waiting with unlit torches. The local Headman or Lorewoman would then come out and start the fire. If priests were around, they would draw upon the power of Toric and set fire to it with their power. Then each villager would light their torch then move through the street, lighting all the candles along the way. The festivities he was now witnessing then followed it. They usually lasted until dawn, followed by a long day of recovery. Strangely, Theldar had celebrated this last week, as Tristan had been required to attend as torchbearer for the king. Then again, he could see the brightly coloured clothes of a taleweaver worn by one of the revellers, which meant the festival had probably been put off a week to await his arrival.

He lost his train of thought as the scene before him brought back memories of his childhood. He had always loved the summer festival, especially if a taleweaver had been present. He could have sat listening to their tales of knights and dragons for hours on end. He would have had to be dragged physically from his front row seat by his father before he would leave a good taleweaving. For some reason his passion seemed to die after he had joined the knighthood. He knew it must have been due to the Treatment, and he was beginning to feel more than a little resentful of the fact. He felt a surge of sorrow for his lost dreams rush through him, and he was forced to think of other matters before he broke down in tears.

He scanned the crowd looking for familiar faces. Havelock was a small village and he had known almost everyone, so it was not hard. They all seemed to be a little older than he remembered, and he found it difficult to recall their names. In fact, trying to do so was almost painful, sending echoes of pain through his mind. He had just given up trying when a hand clamped over his mouth and he felt himself being pulled back into the foliage.

IX

When the area for Theldar had been chosen almost a thousand years ago, there had been two features that had made it a prime site for development. These had been the vast natural resources nearby and the large bay that formed a perfect natural harbour. Though but a small port town initially, it soon began to grow until it was one of the largest ports in the southern lands. The wealth brought in by the trade allowed the small Ruling House, Tara'non, to gain in power in the Royal Council until it had finally made use of the Revolution some two hundred years ago to put one of its own on the throne. It was a position they had retained until this day.

However, the city's position did create a few problems as well. In late spring and through most of the summer, warm currents of air from the north-east would flow out across the sea. This would create a dense fog that would then roll across the city as it was caught up by the prevailing offshore winds. The result was that on many summer nights, such as this night, the streets of Theldar were filled with dense fog that severely limited visibility and people often preferred to remain inside. This was because with the fog often came an ominous silence and many unseen dangers. Thieves of all sorts were abound and crimes were so rife that the fog had earned the name Thenril's Breath, after the evil, dark nemesis of Toric, who reputedly breathed smoke to hide his minions as they moved.

There were, of course, those without such intentions who would venture out into the misty streets; those who were returning from work, ship workers and others unable make it to the safety of their homes before the fog appeared; and tonight was certainly no different. In the most easterly side of the city, engineers had just finished repairing the gate that, as rumour had it, had been almost destroyed by magical fire, and were rushing home to their families. Other people scurried around lighting the city's many lanterns, though they actually made the streets yet more frightening, as the light caused strange, evil looking shadows to flicker out of the corner of your eye, as if waiting to pounce on the unwary.

The sound of marching guards broke through the silence, hoping to deter the many would-be thieves, not realising that they only succeeded in warning them of their approach. In the harbour, men manned the two large beacons that had been lit to warn ships they were nearing the Jaws of Death, the two rocky headlands that had been the cause of so many shipwrecks in the past. More guards patrolled the palace to prevent people seeking unauthorised entry and in the main courtyard itself, knights of the Talon were mounting up, preparing to leave on some quest. One seemed to be having difficulties with his horse, and seemed to feeling the effects of the cool, damp, suffocating air that always accompanied the fog.

Above the fog rose the central spiralling tower of the palace, its marble walls glimmering in the half-light of the two half-moons. In one of the windows near its summit a light shone and a dark silhouette could be seen moving slowly about, as if trying to put off getting into bed. Higher still upon the tower's roof, a dark figure could just be seen, looking down upon the city, as if it could see through the white wall of fog, and to any who saw it, it would appear as if it were waiting for something…

X

Sir Michael, Green Knight of the Talon, took a deep breath, which did little to dispel the feeling of suffocation that seemed to surround him in the fog. He tried to take his mind off it by concentrating upon the task at hand, yet he still found it difficult to finish saddling his horse. It looked as though it was going to be the perfect end to a miserable day. He had started by falling from his horse whilst lining up for the execution of the foul goblin, then had proceeded to witness the betrayal of the King's Knight, a figure he had always idolised. Then he had been shouted at by the furious king when he had brought word of the Knight's escape and now he was to hunt down and capture the man he had once been prepared to protect with his life. It all left a bitter taste in his mouth, and things were made worse by the fact that this was to be his first quest since being knighted some two weeks earlier.

His stomached churned and his hands would not stop shaking in nervousness. He fumbled with the harness once more in a desperate attempt to fix the mess he had already made, and found that he only succeeded in making it worse. The only good thing about the day was that the fog was hiding his efforts to do what should have been the simplest of tasks.

"Are you all right?" asked Captain Feltworth, as he emerged from the fog.

"Yes, sir," replied Michael, trying to conceal his nervousness.

"Feeling the butterflies a bit?" he asked quietly, obviously so that the others of the patrol didn't overhear.

Michael remained silent, wishing he were better at concealing fear.

"Don't worry about it," continued the Blue Knight. "We all feel it now and again, especially on the first mission. You'd be a fool not to. Even I was a little scared on my first real quest."

"Really sir?" asked Michael incredulously.

"Yes," replied the captain with a wink and a quick smile. He then lowered his voice conspiratorially. "But you breathe a word and I'll deny this conversation ever took place. You understand?"

"Yes, sir," replied Michael quietly.

"Now let's get this horse of yours ready."

Captain Feltworth spent a minute or so fiddling with the harness, then patted the horse and indicated to Michael to mount up. He saluted in obedience, and with a returning salute, his commander turned and faded back into the mist. He mounted up, ensured his sword was in its saddle scabbard and gently spurred his horse forward as the command to ride was given. He moved close enough to the knight in front so that she was visible and they rode out of the large courtyard. As they passed through the main gates and into the street a quick shiver of excitement subdued the slight sensation of nausea in his stomach.

This is it! He thought. *My first adventure.*

XI

"Yer slippin', yer know!" said Tristan's father with a smile. "Even when yer were a nipper I could never spook yer that well."

Tristan felt the blood returning to his cheeks and his heart begin to slow as the shock faded.

"Why in all Loden did you do that father?" asked Tristan, his voice still shaking a little.

"T'remind yer that yer need t'be alert."

"Many thanks to you. I will remember that in the future," he replied dryly, momentarily forgetting who he was talking to.

"Be sure yer do!" began his father, before pausing to look at him thoughtfully. "I thought the knighthood had rid yer of yer humour…"

Tristan flushed red and looked away. He recalled his father's complaints the last time he had visited about how the knighthood seemed to be ruining him. Yet he could not keep his gaze from his father's deep blue, penetrating eyes for long. As he looked back he noticed that he had visibly aged from their last meeting. Streaks of grey could be seen in his dark brown hair and there were more creases round those glittering eyes.

"I'm growin' old," said his father, noticing his son's stare. "It's been almost three years since yer last saw me and a lot has happened."

"It cannot have been so long!" replied Tristan, shocked.

He was sure he had visited recently, but then…he had not thought of home in quite some time. It seemed that as he had progressed through his training he had lost the urge to see the man who had first raised him. He wondered if this too was in some way related to the treatments.

"Well it has," replied his father, breaking off Tristan's thoughts. "And I'm glad t'see yer've finally seen sense!"

"What?" asked Tristan, more than a little confused.

"Yer've broken away from the knights. It's about time as well, yer were never meant fer it."

"How did you know I had broken away from the knights?"

"It was just a *little* obvious!" his father replied with more than an edge of sarcasm. "Firstly, yer come chargin' through my forest on that thunderin' great war-horse o'yours, chased by thirty knights or so. Then yer camps down with no supplies just outside Havelock, when if yer were comin' t'visit yer'd have just come straight in. It was just a little plain yer were running from 'em, but don't worry, I set down some false trails, so they'll be out most the night without findin' yer. I see yer got the food and clothes I left yer and tomorrow I'll give yer some saddle bags and oats, and a sack an' polish fer yer armour..."

Tristan found his head was spinning. Why was his father knowingly and willingly aiding and abetting a criminal?

"...which of course yer'll have to sell when yer come to a town."

"Why?"

"So yer can buy passage on a ship at Kelvaria of course!" replied his father rolling his eyes.

"Why would I want to go on a ship?"

"So yer can get out o'Caldor of course!" replied his father in amazement. "Yer can't stay here, the king's sure to find yer."

Tristan could see the sense of the idea and he knew it had to be his best option. What he would do afterwards or where he would go were decisions he would make later. For now he had a lot of questions that needed answering.

"Why are you doing this?" he asked.

"'Cause yer my son and yer need me!"

"Why are you not angry with me?"

"Fer what? Fer seeing sense? Don't be so daft! I've always said yer should have been free t'choose yer own way, and now yer can. Yer free t'do what yer want."

This seemed to strike a chord with a distant memory in Tristan's mind. It was of his father and a priest, both of whom seemed to be arguing about him. It was all very vague, but it was something about his being chosen for the knighthood. They had argued often, and it seemed that his father had been against the idea, even though Tristan had felt blessed about the fact he had been chosen by Toric. Or had he? He recalled his ambitions in taleweaving, and could recall faint urgings to be a ranger like his father. In fact his father had taken to training him from an early age and he recalled that at one point all he had wanted to do was be like his father. When had it changed? What had...?

"Are yer still with me?" asked his father, snapping his fingers before Tristan's eyes.

"Yes father," he replied. "What were you saying?"

"I said yer'd best be leavin' now before yer seen. I'll deliver yer stuff jus' pas' dawn. Now go!"

Tristan had dropped down from the tree and was about to leave before he realised what he was doing. He turned back to see his father starting to leave.

"Father, wait!" he called. "I have so many questions to ask you."

"They'll have t'wait!" replied the dark haired man, turning back. "And besides, there are some things yer better off not knowing."

As their eyes locked, Tristan noticed a deep heaviness behind them he had not seen before. The man also seemed to be struggling with some inner torment. Suddenly he came closer and pressed an object into his hands. Tristan looked down and saw that it was a ring of polished blue quartz with a thin band of silver and gold entwined around it. He looked back to his father in confusion.

"If yer ever need help, put it on yer right index finger and go to a tavern. Hopefully yer'll get what yer need, or at least someone who can point yer in the right direction. Keep it hidden at all other times."

With that he gave Tristan a fierce hug then slipped away into the nearby bushes towards the village. Tristan desperately wanted to follow him, but was suddenly frightened of what he might find. He turned and ran back to the clearing, almost blindly, tearing his way through shrubs and bushes, heedless of the many thorns that scratched at him. Upon reaching the clearing, he threw himself to the ground. He reached over and took the sword from the bush he had hidden it in and fell into an exhausted and troubled sleep. He had been so preoccupied that he had not seen the small fire that burned in the next clearing, nor the squat form peering out of the bushes at him.

XII

Michael rode through the silent, misty streets with only the occasional hazy light and the back of his comrade to guide him. As they went, shadowy half formed figures seemed to appear in the mist and Michael gazed intently at each one. In his mind's eye he saw each one as an evil denizen of Thenril, preparing to attack them, and each time he was the only one who could save the squadron. He hoped that one day such a thing really would happen so that legends would then speak of his brave and heroic deeds. His greatest desire was to have taleweavers speaking his name in hushed awe to the large crowds that would flock round to hear the tales of the great Sir Michael of Ashby. He smiled, knowing that they were, in truth, only fantasies, but it was always fun to dream. It had been something he had always been good at and if he had not been selected by Toric for service in the Knighthood then he fancied he would have become a taleweaver. Though maybe not, for his imagination seemed to be less active of late and it was only as his next Treatment loomed that he found himself regularly gripped in the vivid world of his dreams, such as now.

In fact, he had been so busy dreaming he had not noticed that he had dropped behind the others a little. As he did, he realised he could no longer see them due to the fog. He spurred his horse on after the still audible clatter of the horseshoes of his comrades. As he did so he almost rode over the still form of a person on the ground.

He stopped quickly and dismounted, bending down to take a closer look. It was the crumpled body of a city knight. He was lying in a pool of his own blood that seemed to be seeping out from his back. The knight turned his face towards Michael and beckoned him closer. He did as instructed and moved closer. As he did so the knight whispered to him in a hoarse and strained voice.

"Shadow…that way."

He moved an arm to indicate a direction and Michael peered into the fog. He could see nothing so looked back to the knight only to find that all that returned his gaze were two dull, lifeless orbs that had once been used to see the world. Michael felt sick. He had never been this close to brutal death before. All his training had not prepared him for this sight. He looked away in horror. As he did so his mind swirled wildly, trying to work out what the knight's last statement had meant. The word "Shadow" echoed through the halls of his mind. He recognised the term, yet in every direction his mind searched, all he found was the image of the dead knight's face. He closed his eyes and forced the image from his mind, trying to sort through the maze of horror, fear and confusion.

Anger suddenly surged through him and he almost hit the ground in frustration. The anger cut through the barriers in his mind and suddenly he remembered.

The Shadow.

The word continued to echo through his mind. Now was his chance for glory. He would become famous for catching the notorious knight killer. He was about to stand when he remembered the dead man beside him. He gently closed the man's eyes and whispered a prayer to Toric to watch the man's soul, then stood up, eyes blazing. He thought briefly about calling the other knights for assistance, but then decided that he needed no help. He had been trained in the art of swordplay and this Shadow was but one person.

He walked in the direction indicated as the knight had died and found it was an alleyway between two buildings. He drew his sword and boldly stepped into the shadowy corridor.

XIII

He stood before the main doors to the palace. Inside he could hear the king's voice, raised in anger. It was cursing a vile man who had betrayed him. A man he had trusted, befriended, and heaped honours upon that had been given to no man so young.

He knew the king talked of him, and he felt shame flow through him. The man had aided him, seen personally to his training, and even allowed him to choose one of the best foals from the king's stables. Now he had betrayed him, and he had hurt him, reneging on all he had promised. He dropped to his knees, tears in his eyes, and placed his head in his hands.

"I can help you, you know," said a voice, softly.

Hope entered his heart and he looked up. Before him was a man with a face almost like that of a weasel, with slicked back hair, wearing ceremonial robes of office.

"You can?"

"Of course!" replied the man. "If you wish, I can help you restore your name with the king and more. I can arrange it so that you ride at his side once again, sharing in the power and glory as before. I see you and the king sweeping through the world, bringing peace, prosperity and the light of Toric to all. The light of history will shine upon you and all will marvel at your courage, wisdom and skill. All this can happen…with my help."

"What must I do?"

"It is simple," replied the man, running his fingers through his hair. "All you have to do is swear fealty and obedience to me, then prove it by one simple act of obedience. After this, together we will work through all your problems and you will be whole once more."

He looked at the strange man and his gaze was caught up in his strange eyes. They seemed like those of a cat, with vertical pupils. Images of him riding at the head of the army, victorious over all those who opposed him, flashed through his mind. In his hand was the mighty sword, shining in glory and at his side rode the king, praise shining in his eyes.

Tears filled his eyes and his body trembled at the thought of the glorious visions.

"What act of obedience do you require?" he asked, not really caring.

"It is but a simple one. Cut the head from this goblin traitor," replied the man.

It was then that he noticed a goblin tied and bound with its head on the executioner's block. The man handed him an axe and indicated towards the goblin. It would be a simple thing, to kill this creature of evil. The price was so small for a prize so great. He lifted the axe high into the air, knowing that with this simple act, he would restore all.

Suddenly more visions filled his mind. He saw a man dressed as executioner, before him a long line of condemned prisoners. The executioner sliced and hacked off the heads with seeming glee, until one prisoner broke free, killing the executioner. As the executioner's masked head rolled down the floor, the mask snagged and came off. The head of Tristan Pathfinder was revealed.

Tristan looked down at the goblin and he realised that to kill only one creature in cold blood, even if it were only a goblin, would diminish his respect for life. That path only led to utter destruction, as he became more and more like the man he had killed today.

"Go on! Kill him!" commanded the man behind him.

Tristan turned and discarded the axe.

"Never," he replied firmly.

"Fool!" hissed the man as he sprang at Tristan.

His teeth elongated to fangs and his face began to stretch and distort. His body seemed to shift and slide, as if becoming something else. Tristan felt a moment of panic, before realising Caliburn still rested at his side. He drew the sword from its scabbard and sliced out across the creature. The sword flashed in light and suddenly there was darkness.

Tristan faded from the dream and drifted back to the safety of deep sleep…

XIV

The alley that Michael crept down was cold, dark and damp. The initial anger he had felt had slowly seeped away, as if drained out by the fog, and fear began to replace it. He thought it might actually be better to return to the others and get assistance, just in case.

In the swirling mist, thousands of shadowy forms swirled around him, silently taunting him, reaching for him, clutching at his very soul. They seemed to be slowly sucking the life from him, enveloping him, destroying him. Panic surged through him and he found himself gasping for air. He turned to stumble away, but could only see walls and shadows around him. He seemed trapped like some caged animal and his breathing became shallow and erratic.

Then a voice sounded in his head. It was a strong voice, like that of his father, telling him sternly to have courage, and reach for his dreams. Images of his glorious past flashed through his head. He saw the lines of his ancestors all lined up dressed in dazzling silver armour, and courage filled him. His imagination flared to life and it was not long before he was lost in this magical world, as the real world seemed to merge with the dream, and time became obsolete.

In the dream both he and the Shadow fought with all their skill and might. Sparks flew from their shining swords as they struck together with mighty clashes. Blood dripped from the many wounds they had dealt each other and yet still they fought. On and on the battle raged until they were both ready to collapse with exhaustion. Finally the Shadow collapsed to his knees as his sword shattered, and begged for mercy. Michael raised his sword high into the air then placed the flat of the blade onto the man's right shoulder, the mark of mercy. So touched was the evil man by

Michael's compassion that he repented and agreed to go with the knight to the king and suffer what punishment may come. Michael brings the man before the king to exalted praise by both king and courtier, and is offered a reward. Michael refuses the king modestly, impressing him to the extent that he raises his rank and begins to consider him as a future candidate for King's Knight…

Michael was so enraptured in his dream that he did not notice the cloaked form slip out from the shadows behind him and he never knew about the blade that slipped behind his breastplate and into his heart.

XV

Captain Feltworth ordered his men to halt when they reached the newly repaired East Gate. He paused wearily before speaking. He had not been prepared for a night ride after one of the best knights in Caldor. The king had insisted that it be done as soon as possible and his sickly looking magician…High Priest…had told him the exact location of Tristan's camp. Despite his treatment, the Captain still distrusted sorcery. His magic was priestly and he was proud to carry the power of Toric. However, he had to follow the man's orders, so was about to spend a dreary night riding through the countryside. It would be a long haul, especially with Tristan's knowledge of the land. The captain had been chosen especially because he knew the land reasonably well, but that would only make things marginally easier. If Tristan did not wish to be found, he could hide out for quite some time.

He glanced over at his men but could see little of them due to the fog. He rode down the line of knights making a quick head count whilst checking each was prepared. When he had finished he frowned. The squadron was one person short. He had a good idea who that might be and a quick name check revealed that it was indeed Michael. He sighed heavily, hoping the young man had not lost his nerve.

"We will wait ten minutes for his return then leave, whether Michael is with us or not," he said quietly to himself.

They all waited as time dragged slowly by and the Blue Knight counted through the minutes in his head. They stood in silence with only the occasional snort of a horse or the slight jingle of armour to break it up. It was as if they were in another world, a world of silence and shadowy, misty forms. Captain Feltworth shuddered and tried to think of something else.

Ten minutes were almost up when they heard the sound of a horse riding towards them. The captain sighed with relief as Michael's horse emerged from the mist. He went up to greet the man, who had wrapped himself up in his long cloak.

"Where have you be…" He stopped in mid-sentence when he saw the face in the hood. "Who are you?"

The face staring out from the hood at him was twisted with hatred and rage and the eyes positively glowed with anger. It was the last thing he ever saw before the Shadow's blade ended his life.

XVI

He was stood in the middle of the village he had once lived in, and all around he could see the people playing, laughing, singing and dancing. Yet it all seemed distant, as if he were not really a part of it. He felt alone and separate, knowing he could never again be a part of this peaceful, simple world.

"But you can," said a soft voice behind him.

He turned to see a woman stood before him, dressed simply, hair tied back as was the custom with young woman. Her green eyes sparkled joyfully, yet had a strange intensity about them.

"What do you mean?" he asked, confused.

"With my help, you can return to this life," she replied. "If you wish, you could stay here, become a ranger, marry, and live peacefully forever. All you have to do is ask, promise obedience and renounce all interest in the greater world. All the confusion will cease, and your cares will become once more the simple things of daily life."

As her eyes seemed to draw him in he found images of life flashing before his eyes. He saw himself working out in the bright green forests. He saw himself marry a beautiful woman, and himself holding their firstborn child in his arms. Years passed by and he saw his children grow up and have children of their own. He saw himself as an old man, surrounded by his family for Juletide celebrations. Tears of happiness filled his eyes at the scene. The promise of a peaceful life filled him, a life free of cares and worries. All he had to do was promise to remain out of the affairs of the world.

His mouth opened to speak the words and suddenly other scenes flashed through his head. He saw the world blackened and charred. He saw a towering dark form laugh loudly. He saw villages destroyed, burnt; villagers killed and tortured. In the midst of it all he wandered, unable to help them, bound by his promise, knowing that he lived in joy whilst thousands lived in terror.

He shook the images from his mind and he saw that the eyes were cat-like, with vertical pupils shaped like the blade of a dagger. Remembrance flooded through Tristan and he reached for his sword. The woman's eyes widened and she screamed angrily.

"Say it! Promise me!"

Tristan ignored her, even as her body began to shift and he sliced out with Caliburn. The sword glowed in purifying white life and the dream dissolved before his eyes, returning Tristan to peaceful sleep.

XVII

It took a few moments for the other knights of the squadron to realise what had happened. By the time they had reached him it was too late. Their captain was dead and his killer was escaping. They immediately took up the chase. They were going to catch him and make him pay. Vengeance was the only thought on their minds. Anger surged through their bodies firing them up with energy and they strained to hear the sound of their quarry's horse.

It took the knight in front several minutes to catch the horse and when she did she found it was rider-less. Confused she looked around, only to find that she was alone. Fear replaced her confusion and she began to move away slowly. Suddenly her horse reared in fright and she was thrown from its back. Her last memory was of a sudden explosion of pain in her head.

XVIII

The Shadow stood over the body of the last knight to fall and stared at her contemptuously. He put his hand inside one of the many pouches on his belt and removed another note addressed to the king. He then unsheathed one of the knight's daggers and used it to pin the note to her chest. It would be a shame to waste one of his own for such a trivial purpose.

"I'll make you suffer for what you and your knights allowed to happen to my mother!" he muttered, barely containing his bitterness, sorrow, anger, and hatred.

Dawn broke, washing away the last remnants of the fog and the emotions he was feeling. Suddenly he was very tired, so he turned to the morning shadows, slipped in and disappeared.

XIX

He stood before an open door. It was made of black marble and housed within a granite wall. It opened into a large room. In the centre was a large table made of obsidian and at each end was a chair made of ebony. On the walls hung black velvet drapes and blackened torches with black flames that somehow seemed to glow with a dark light. At the furthest end of the table was sat a man dressed all in black.

"Please, be seated," hissed the dark figure, indicating the chair nearest the door. "I wish to talk."

Tristan moved cautiously into the room and sat down. The chair was comfortable with cushions of black velvet. He noticed that despite the slightly overdone blackness of the whole room he could still see quite clearly. He quickly glanced back at the door and was relieved to see it was still open. He then looked back to the stranger. He appeared to be observing Tristan with interest and his golden, cat-like eyes glittered with dark light. In his hand was a pendent made of onyx and he was swaying it back and forth in a hypnotic motion. Tristan's eyes followed it and he could feel tiredness sweeping over him. The urge to close his eyes and sleep was almost overwhelming. He knew that the sleep would bring relief to the confusion and pain in his mind. All he had to do was close his eyes and it would be all over…

He shook himself violently and looked into the stranger's eyes.

"What do you want?" he asked coldly.

"Why you, of course!" replied the man with his almost reptilian voice. "You are a very unique individual. Few have ever reached this dream and none have ever denied the stone's hypnotic power. As for what I want, the answer is quite simple. I want you to obey me."

"Why should I do that?"

"Because I could bring you wealth and power beyond your wildest dreams," he replied. "I need someone with your willpower. I have been searching for someone like you for many years."

"Wealth and power do not interest me. You do not interest me," replied Tristan in a cold, dispassionate voice.

"Think carefully what you say, human, and also what you are refusing. Together we could bring order to the chaos of this world. I can achieve this without you, though your help would be invaluable. Of course, if you refuse, I'll be forced to destroy you."

"Then kill me," replied Tristan angrily. "As you say, this is only a dream."

He tried to force himself to wake up but failed. Suddenly worried he leaped up and ran to the door. Unfortunately it was no longer there. He heard soft laughter behind him. He spun round to find the room had shrunk and that all its furnishings had vanished. Before him was the stranger, stood with a dagger in his hand. Tristan fumbled for Caliburn but found that it was missing. The stranger placed the dagger at his throat.

"Do you know that even dreams can kill you?" the man asked, in his soft, taunting manner.

Suddenly Tristan felt something sharp press against his neck and suddenly the dream began to fade rapidly. The man's face twisted in horror and he screamed in rage.

"I will not be cheated of your death!" were the last words Tristan heard as he woke, with relief, into the light of dawn.

Relief turned to fear when he realised that he could still feel the blade pushed against his throat. As the blurred haze of sleep faded from his eyes he saw a humanoid figure stood over him with a dagger at his throat.

"Good morning!" said a deep grating voice, bringing with it the foul smell of an unclean mouth. "Remember me? Not that it matters if yer do as yer gonna die anyways."

Chapter Three: Revelations and Revenge

I

The dream began as it always did, with fire. Intense, burning flames flickered around him, their red heat searing through to his very soul. The pain was so great that his mind sought the safety of insanity to escape. As usual an unseen shield blocked the way and his mind was forced to comprehend the sheer enormity of the pain. He could feel parts of his body bursting into flame and he could do nothing to prevent it. He was unable to move the slightest of an inch. All he could do was sob and watch his tears fizzle to steam.

Then the flames began to fade and the silhouette appeared before him. All that could be seen of this shadowy figure was the eyes. They seemed to burn with an inner light that drove all thought of pain from his mind. This brought little relief though, for with the intense stare came a different kind of pain; one that did not affect his nerves but burned straight through his mind like a white-hot poker. He screamed in pain and tried to shut his eyes, but once again nothing moved.

"What do you want?" he asked, tears now streaming from his eyes.

He already knew what the answer would be. It was always the same.

"To help you revenge yourself," it replied with its soft, silky, yet penetrating voice.

With this statement the tall, the cloaked form placed a large ring made of white gold and inlaid with runes of onyx into his hand. As the ring touched his flesh its cold metal seemed to soothe the pain in his mind and with this came freedom of movement. Once he had tried to run, but he had learned that greater pain lay in that action. He stood his ground and listened to the stranger say what he always said.

"As long as you wear this ring you will have access to another world that will provide you with all the protection and transport you need," it said its voice almost hypnotic.

He placed the ring on his finger with the eyes of the stranger intently watching him. It seemed to shrink to fit his finger perfectly. When it was firmly in place, the flames vanished and with them went the pain. He sighed with relief and stuttered out his thanks.

"Wear it always and never forget the pain; her pain," said the stranger, his voice and body fading to nothing.

Then his vision blurred and shifted, before seeming to melt away and he found himself crouched down in his old village behind several barrels of Grathnacian ale. He peered round them and saw two knights approaching. He ducked back behind the barrels, straining to hear the knights yet already knowing what they would say.

"The old hag has been spreading more rumours about the Redirecting Chambers. She's been saying that the people taken there are often tortured and sometimes executed," said the first knight, trying to keep his deep voice down to a whisper.

"That's no worry!" said the second knight, her light voice contrasting strongly with that of the first knight. "She's just a harmless old woman."

"I'm afraid it's gone a little further than that," he warned before gulping down what was probably stolen ale.

"What do you mean?" she asked.

"I overheard some of the villagers talking," he replied. "They're beginning to wonder if she speaks the truth."

"That doesn't sound good. Do you think it's the common view?"

"At the moment it's just idle chatter and nonsense," he replied. "We still have time to act before it goes any further. Do you think we ought to bring her in for more Treatment?"

"No," she replied, "that would just make them think there's fire with the smoke. I think the best way is to let her be dealt with as in Selene."

He had later discovered what this phrase meant. It referred to an incident that had occurred during the time of the Great Revolution some two hundred years ago in a small village called Selene. During the hysteria that broke out, many villagers were certain that the forty members of their small community had supported the king and were therefore possessed by Thenril. This led to the obvious truth that they had also been involved in his art, witchcraft. All had been taken and burned at the stake. Whenever knights used the phrase in Caldor today it usually meant that they would organise a witch burning. It was an effective way of executing a possible threat to Caldor without doing much themselves. In burnings there were rarely trials and few escaped the mobs that formed against them. Yet this knowledge only confirmed what was to happen and what had happened before.

"Do they have a Returner in this village?" asked the first knight.

He had yet to discover what the term Returner meant, though he had his suspicions.

"Of course. Those Grey Knights have probably been placed in every village in Caldor, for all the use they are."

She said this statement with a definite tone of disgust. Whatever they were, the knights obviously disliked them.

"You have to admit, though, no one can stir up a witching as well as a Returner."

"Yes but that's about as far as their use goes."

The image suddenly melted away like hot candle wax to reveal another scene. He was now stood in front of his mother's house. In the square behind him stood Adam the blacksmith. He was talking to a large crowd of villagers.

"I tell ya I saw it wiv' me own two eyes," he cried loudly. "She jus' said a word an' the fire sprung up like it was from Deeprealm itself! It jus' had to be magic I tell yer!"

"Yeah my cow died las' week without any warnin'. She jus' keeled over all dead like, an' tha' was the day after she'd gone past it muttering them evil things to herself like she does!" cried a voice from the crowd.

This was followed by more claims of mysterious events. One man had accidentally tripped her and was now going blind. Another had started to go bald after speaking with her. As each claim was made more and more people began to blame their misfortunes on her. He desperately tried to disclaim the rumours about his mother, but he couldn't be heard over the cries of the villagers.

Suddenly some people rushed off to prepare the fire whilst others, led by Adam, began marching towards his mother's house. He stood in the doorway to try and prevent them from entering but was swiftly overpowered by six men and dragged out of the square. When they reached the edge of the village one of them hit him on the head with a stone and he collapsed to the ground. They returned to the village, collecting firewood as they went.

Once they were far ahead, he staggered up to his feet, his head throbbing and his vision blurry. He staggered on towards the village square and arrived in time to see the villagers binding his mother to the centre post. Though she had now ceased to struggle, it was plain that she had not gone quietly to the post. She was covered in cuts and bruises and more than one villager was nursing injuries.

He looked round to try and get some help. He saw the two knights drinking ale at *The Winespring Tavern*. He rushed up to them, swaying violently as he did, and begged them to help.

"I'm afraid we can't," replied the male knight, shrugging his shoulders.

"It's a local matter and we're not allowed to interfere."

With that they returned to their drinks, leaving him to just stand and stare in shock.

"Do you mind?" asked the woman. "We are trying to have a quiet drink and we don't want you gaping at us."

He stumbled away from them. They were knights. They were sworn to protect the citizens of Caldor and they were just sitting there whilst a woman, his mother, was being falsely accused of witchcraft. They had left him to face the mob alone.

He rushed at the crowd surrounding the stake and desperately tried to force his way through. He was constantly hit and shoved back by jeering villagers. The violence of the mob left bruises on his body and made his head, still pounding from its initial knock, hurt even more. Despite all this and his blurred vision he could now see they had completed the bonds tying her to the stake. Panic surged through him and he began to lose control to an overwhelming wave of emotions that threatened to engulf him.

His control suddenly snapped and he screamed in fear and rage, forcing his way fitfully through the crowd. Unfortunately he was too late. He arrived just in time to see the flaming brands being tossed onto the oil covered kindling. The flames immediately sprang to life. He attempted to put them out but was held back by Adam who was still much stronger than him, despite his frenzied strength from surging emotions.

He clawed at Adam's arms as the flames swiftly surrounded his mother. She stood there, weeping, begging to be released. All she received in return were cold looks and clenched fists from the villagers. Then the flames enveloped her and her sobs of fear turned to shrieks of pain. He could see the agony in her face as the heat and the pain began to distort it. Anger, guilt, bitterness and nausea swirled round inside of him. He could see the flames eating away at her living flesh and the smell of her burning flesh filled his nostrils. He wanted to be sick, but found his stomach unwilling to comply.

He tried to look away, but his eyes seemed drawn constantly back to hers. They stared accusingly back at him, burning more fiercely than the flames surrounding her. She then looked past him and the accusation became a look of hatred. He strained his neck to follow her gaze and found she was looking at the two knights. They were still outside the tavern, drinking and laughing as if nothing was going on. The rage and hatred grew within him and the image of his mother's burning face became burned in vivid detail on to his mind's eye.

Suddenly he felt pain. It was a burning sensation that grew rapidly across his body. He looked down and saw that it was now he who had been tied to the stake. Flames were now devouring his flesh, causing intense pain as each nerve screamed in agony. The fire grew around him until it was all that he could see and feel. Then an image formed in front of him. The eyes of the familiar figure gazed into his mind.

"Remember her suffering always; her pain and misery. Revenge her death. Destroy those who allowed her to suffer so...Remember always...Revenge."

The voice and the image faded away to reveal his mother's face twisted in agony. Then darkness fell and the dream ended.

II

The man known only as the Shadow woke up on the cold stone floor of the cavern drenched in sweat, the image of his mother still hanging vividly in his mind. The ring on his finger glowed with a soft red light and seemed to burn the skin around it. The dream always left him this way.

"I will avenge you, mother, I will," he said angrily, clenching his fists together. Tears were trickling down his face. "They will all suffer."

III

Matthew looked out at the soft light of the morning sun as it gently illuminated the glistening marble city. Though its golden rays did not strike his room till evening, the view of its passage over the dazzling city was one of the most beautiful, calming sights he could imagine. He had woken up with the dawn after a refreshing night's sleep and wondered how the king had fared the night without one of his sleeping potions. He had decided that he would stop by the king's bedchambers after he had watched the sun's majestic rise and eaten his breakfast, which Eward had already gone to fetch up.

He yawned and stretched before returning his gaze out of his bedroom window. It was a beautiful day, and he had personally seen the mist vanish as the sun had risen. The whole city seemed to glow in warm light, yet despite that a shiver of cold ran down his spine. Thinking it was merely the lack of light within this room he moved closer to the crackling fire. Despite the fact it was already blazing with heat, he actually found himself feeling even colder. He narrowed his eyes in confusion and suspicion and he began looking closely around the room. All around were the distortions of the magic wards and remnants of previous spells he had used, just as expected. These were due to the fact that magic, when wielded, created small ripples in the fabric of reality that were often very difficult to hide. The ripples usually lasted for a few days, though incredibly powerful spells could leave such ripples for thousands of years. This echo of magic was often known as the Kilsbur Effect after the man who had first noticed the phenomenon. He was the first to notice the tiny distortions in the air, and had discovered what caused them with minimal investigations. He was also the first to realise that different spell-wielders left different imprints in reality, making it possible for skilled observers to discover just who had cast the spell. The imprint was different, according to Alex Kilsbur, due to the fact that all wielders of magic drew and expended the energy in their own way. It meant that magic wielders who delved in crime or banned magicks could often be caught by recognition of their spellprint, a name derived from the ancient method that guards used to detect criminals by matching their fingerprints with those on the crime scene. It also meant that other users of magic, who were always taught how to recognise the effect, could tell when others had used magic nearby.

It was this that was worrying Matthew. The pattern here was different from either his priestly or his sorcerous spells. In fact, it was almost unique, even for spellprints, though he had seen it many times before today, and had in fact seen one similar only the previous day. It seemed to have a double ripple, as if draining energy from two sources, and Matthew was rapidly reaching a conclusion as to the reason. The print the day before had been from Tristan when he had used the sword to create light, but more worrying, the other, which matched this one before him almost perfectly, had come from the murder sites of the Shadow. Obviously the two had interdependent magical…

His thoughts were broken by a sudden burst of panic. The Shadow's magic had occurred in this room without setting off his wards, where his magic was strongest. This meant that he could have gone anywhere in the palace. Matthew's arm went numb at the thought, though it could have been in warning…

Matthew pushed the terrifying thought from his mind and dashed for the door. Unfortunately Eward, who had just returned with Matthew's breakfast, halted his desperate dive through the door. They both crashed to the ground in a flurry of arms and legs spilling the tray of food across the floor and out into the corridor. Even before the last piece of toasted bread had hit the ground Matthew was back on his feet and running down the corridor. His panic was so great that he did not even think to prepare a spell as he reached Naithan's door and flung it wide open. He ignored the guards' disapproving frowns and looked fearfully into the room. Naithan lay on the bed, motionless. Panic was now replaced by abject terror. He rushed to his friend's side.

Tears of relief poured from his eyes when he saw that Naithan's breathing was strong and regular. He even thought he could hear a soft snoring. The feeling returned to his numbed arm and he smiled at his own over reaction. But he knew his fears could have quite easily been recognised. He quickly examined the room and found almost no spellprints, for he had not renewed the wards here in some time. He muttered a quick spell and was pleased to see his complex maze of wards arching round the room. He resolved to strengthen them later, but knew that for the moment he would have to rely on old-fashioned methods. He turned to the two Silver Knights who were peering in suspiciously.

"You men are to quietly stand guard inside the king's chambers," he commanded, his voice still shaking a little.

One of the knights looked ready to object but a quick glare from Matthew kept him silent. They both entered the room without a word.

"You will stay here until commanded otherwise, and keep a careful eye out for anything unusual."

As one they turned and nodded their heads in salute as Matthew left the room. He ignored the insult. Now was not the time to force the higher, spiritual rank he held in the knighthood. Most knights chose to ignore it when they could, and Matthew was too relieved to care. At least these men had a modicum of power. If the Shadow was to come, he would be in for quite a nasty surprise. He stepped out into the corridor and as did so, found himself being approached by Luca who was looking at him suspiciously, though concern was also visible in his eyes.

"What's up?" the old man asked.

"Nothing yet," he replied. "He's sleeping soundly for the moment."

"Where are the guards then?"

"They're inside," Matthew replied. Upon seeing Luca's suspicious frown he elaborated. "I've discovered that I had a visit from our friend the Shadow sometime yesterday."

"What?" asked Luca, his eyes widening in shock.

"It appears that he can enter without tripping any of my alarms or wards, so I thought it best to ensure Naithan's safety," replied Matthew, still feeling a little shaken. "Could you go downstairs and order two more guards to stand outside, and organise a new watch rotation order as soon as possible. Some of the more *talented* knights if possible."

Even though they were in the heart of the king's territory, there was still the possibility that foreign spies were around, so the cover name for knightly spell users was still used.

"Of course," replied Luca, still looking a little dazed.

Luca turned to walk away, then suddenly span back.

"Did yer say that he was sleeping?"

"Yes, why?" asked Matthew, a little confused.

"I jus' thought that he'd run out of yer potions."

"He has," replied Matthew with surprise. "Evidently the dreams have stopped. At least there's some good news today."

Luca nodded in agreement then hurried off down the corridor. As the old man disappeared from sight he felt a tap on his shoulder. He turned round and barely prevented himself from groaning when he saw Malcolm.

"What's wrong?" asked the weasel faced man with that irritating, nasal whine he had when he spoke.

"Nothing," replied Matthew. "The king has need of rest and has empowered me under the nineteenth decree of the coronation treaty of William I with temporary regency powers for the period of one day."

He watched in satisfaction as the greasy haired little man scribbled this all down on a piece of parchment that he always seemed to have under his arm. Matthew hoped this would have satisfied the clerk, or at least sent him scurrying to check the nineteenth clause. His hopes were quickly dashed.

"I'm afraid I'll have to confirm this with…Where are the guards."

"Naithan requested they remain inside to prevent anyone from disturbing him. Their positions are now being filled as we speak," replied Matthew quickly.

Malcolm eyed him suspiciously before his expression suddenly brightened.

"Well as you are now acting regent, perhaps you could set a date for the next meeting of the Royal Council. I have a few suggestions…"

Matthew groaned as the little man began to chatter away incessantly. Unlike Naithan, he positively hated playing the Game of the Council. He began his journey back to his room with Malcolm in tow. He was already regretting his kindness in letting Naithan enjoy his first natural sleep in years.

IV

The man stared deeply into Tristan's eyes with a vicious sneer on his face.

"I'm goin' t'enjoy killin' yer," he said as the sneer spread to an evil grin. "I knew it was yer last night up that tree with yer dad. I knew you had come to gloat and to take her away from me. Now yer'll die slowly and me and Davine will be safe ferever."

Tristan felt the pressure on the blade grow as the man pushed it harder to his throat. He knew he was completely helpless and that any move would be fatal. He did not even wince when he felt it break the surface of his skin. In fact he welcomed the pain. For some reason the prospect of dying was more appealing than that of living. At last he would find relief from the pressures that seemed to be ripping apart his mind. He slowly closed his eyes and began to pray to Toric. He would finally go to meet his creator.

Suddenly the pressure disappeared, leaving just the initial cut trickling blood from his throat. He opened his eyes in confusion and almost jumped with surprise. Stood before him was the goblin he had rescued. In its grubby hands was that holiest of swords, Caliburn, dripping with Caldorian blood.

"Just what I need," mumbled Tristan bitterly. "To leap from the hot pan into the fire."

The goblin began cleaning the sword. He looked at it in confusion. What was it doing? Was this part of one of its vile sacrifice rituals? He raised himself from the ground a little to get a better view. As he did so the creature span round and presented Caliburn to him, hilt first. Tristan just stared at the creature in amazement.

"This yours, Groltch think," said the creature, its guttural voice grating through the human tongue awkwardly, revealing its low intelligence.

"Yes," he replied uncertainly, slowly reaching out to take the sword. "Err…Thank you."

The creature merely shrugged.

"Match-nah…debt repaid."

It then turned round and began to walk off. Tristan staggered to his feet and the world span briefly before his eyes.

"Wait," he called out, hoping it would understand. "What debt are you talking about?"

"You save Groltch," it replied, turning to face him. "Groltch save you. Groltch now not owe debt. Groltch go now?"

"No wait…please. I would like to talk to you."

"You want talk to me?" it asked suspiciously.

"Yes, there are a few questions I would like to ask you, if you would not mind," he replied. "I have food to share if you wait."

He held out the food as he would to a dumb creature. It seemed to ignore him and studied the sky. He was just wondering what to do next when it looked back at him.

"Have time. Will talk. Food good too, but first body to…deal with?" It seemed to study the corpse for a while. "Who was it? Knew you, did it not?"

The strange way that the creature spoke made it difficult for him to understand exactly what the creature was saying. When he finally understood he looked at the corpse for a minute. It seemed familiar yet his mind seemed clogged up. He could recall a few details though.

"Yes I know…knew him," replied Tristan, more to himself than the goblin. "We used to live in the same village. I remember he loved to bully me around, and we quarrelled a lot. It is strange, but I thought he had been put in for Redirection…"

He broke off when he saw the creature looking blankly at him.

"You speak too fast. Groltch not know all of what you say. Speak less fast please."

Tristan looked disapprovingly at the creature. He had forgotten he had been speaking to a lesser race. He had known they were stupid but had not realised to what extent this went. He repeated himself very slowly, taking five minutes to ensure the creature understood fully. It looked at him in what seemed to be a scornful manner.

"Just for Groltch not know all of how you speak not mean Groltch stupid. No need for you speaks so slowly," said the creature slowly, imitating Tristan.

"As you wish," he replied, trying to measure the speed of his speech.

"Why it want kill you?"

"Possibly because we had a disagreement over…" he paused in mid-sentence. "Just one minute. I wanted to ask you the questions, not the other way around."

"Okay," replied the goblin with a shrug of its shoulders. "You say we to deal with body first."

Tristan searched through the equipment from his father and found a trowel. It was small but would have to do. He then started to dig a shallow grave.

"What you does?" it asked, sounding confused.

"I am digging his grave."

"You mean you stick it in ground?" it asked as its eyes opened wide in horror. "That dis…gusting. We even not treat animals in this way."

"What do you suggest?" he asked sourly.

"Stick in fire, so shadow is free from prison of body," it replied and Tristan's eyes opened wide in surprise. "It also not so slow and not attract those."

Tristan looked at the body and saw that it was already attracting flies. He found himself left speechless by the creature's logic and reasoning, even if it was based on some primitive type of Thenril worship.

"Face it, the idea's a good one!" said that strange voice, and Tristan was forced to agree.

He turned and left the clearing to collect firewood for the pyre. It was not too difficult and he soon returned with his arms full. As he arrived he caught the goblin searching through the dead man's clothes. Tristan dropped the wood to the ground.

"What are you doing?"

"Groltch search body," replied the goblin, stating the obvious.

"I know that! But why?"

"Groltch need coin."

Tristan found himself speechless once more, this time in horror. How could it be so mercenary? He now knew why the goblin had thought to burn the body. It had nothing to do with shadow worship. It had obviously killed people for money before and burned the body to destroy the evidence. Rage consumed him.

"That is sacrilege," he replied angrily. "You are defiling a dead body."

The creature just looked at him.

"What you mean?"

"It is unholy to steal from the body of a dead man."

The light of understanding flickered in its hideous green eyes. To Tristan's further horror it merely shrugged its shoulders.

"You got coin?" it asked, cocking its head quizzically.

This confused Tristan and succeeded in diffusing his rage. His father may have left some but it would not be all that much and he certainly would not tell the creature that.

"Well no but…"

"You got no coin," interrupted the goblin, showing it lacked even in the decencies of politeness. "Groltch got no coin. We got no coin. It got coin. Not need it where it go."

It looked up at him and seeing that Tristan was not completely convinced, concluded by saying, "Anyhow, Groltch get money from clothes, not body."

It gasped for breath, the lengthy sentences obviously straining its inferior lungs, but Tristan did not really pay much attention. He was trying to puzzle through the logic of the creature's argument, even though it had ended on an obviously lame note. There was no way round it though. The creature was correct in asserting that they needed finances, from whatever source they could get it at the moment. He set to building the pyre, muttering angrily to himself until it was complete. Then, with the creature's help they placed the body atop the pyre and he kneeled down it a brief, silent prayer to Toric. Having completed the last passage rites, he lit a torch then set light to the pyre. He stood and watched until the pyre had completed its task and died down, then ensured the last remnants were completely out. Though the bones were largely untouched, he left them buried in the ash, for time was moving rapidly and soon knights, who should have been here already, would make their long awaited arrival.

"Why take so long over killer," asked the goblin when Tristan had finished.

It had remained, thankfully, silent throughout out the whole funeral.

"Because life is sacred to my people and the soul should be adequately prepared for the afterlife," replied Tristan coldly.

The creature looked at him, and for a moment he could see that look of nobility and intelligence that he had thought he glimpsed yesterday before the execution. It closed its eyes and muttered something in its own guttural tongue then turned to Tristan.

"You not quite like man things Groltch meet before. Maybe not all bad," it said softly, almost to itself. "We go now?"

"We?" asked Tristan, a little confused by the last the creature's last statement.

"You still want ask of Groltch questions?"

"Yes…" he replied slowly.

"Then Groltch go with you for short time. Not want to stay here you would, Groltch bet!"

Tristan struggled through its convoluted Caldorian and gave a resigned nod. Thrice he had been bested by the logic of a mere *goblin* and a pretty filthy one at that. He prepared to leave by saddling Galahad, much to the goblin's obvious discomfort. He looked at his armour and remembered his father's promise of a delivery of more equipment. He vaguely recalled seeing it nearby whilst collecting wood, so began to return to the spot.

"Where you goes?" the goblin asked.

"To collect some more equipment I saw when getting firewood," he replied. "Wait here."

The creature raised one of its bushy black eyebrows in an almost sarcastic, questioning manner, but seemed to obey the instruction. He ignored it and made his way back to the pile of equipment. As promised, there were several saddlebags, packs of oats, and a sack for his armour. There was also a letter addressed to him, written in his father's thick, sprawling handwriting. He unfolded and read it quickly.

To my son Tristan,

I hope that this equipment and the small sum of money I left will aid you in your flight. I would also ask that you keep the goblin close to you…

Tristan's eyes widened in surprise and he re-read the sentence several times before proceeding to the end, more than a little confused.

…flight. I would also ask that you keep the goblin close to you and that you deliver him safely to an inn called the Hog's Head in Kelvaria. When you go there wear the ring as instructed and the goblin will be safely removed from your hands. I know this will be hard for you as you view him as an enemy, but I would ask you to honour this request as the last that I will make of you. I know we will never meet again, but I would wish you luck on this journey and on your new life, and pray to Toric that you will one day forgive my weakness in allowing them to take you away. Toric's will grant you speed and fortune, Tyrone, the man who could once claim to be your father.

Tristan gazed at the note in absolute horror. His father was asking him to protect this vile, barbaric creature. He could not see what possible motive his father had for demanding this terrible price. Yet the note was correct, this would be the last time the man would be in a position to ask such a favour, so he would honour this last request. He knew though, that from this moment on he was an orphan. The man who had been his father had died with this letter.

He returned to the clearing determined to be in a brisk, focused attitude.

"Well we had better start moving before the knights find us," he said to the goblin loading up the equipment and sacks on to Galahad. "Help me with this."

The creature came nearer and helped him pack up his armour, then load it onto the horse's back. He hated the thought of Galahad as a packhorse, but he had no choice, and to ride him, laden as he already was, would have been an act of cruelty. Despite the load, though, the horse stood the strain with seeming ease.

"Let us be going then," said Tristan coldly.

He began to lead the horse from the clearing.

"You saids you had food," said the creature, catching up. "Groltch hungry."

Tristan's stomach turned at the thought of eating so close to the funeral, but took out some provisions and tossed them in the goblin's direction.

"Is…Groltch…your name?" he asked, thinking it best to find out if they were to travel together.

"Yes," replied the goblin, barely pausing its eating enough to speak and definitely without swallowing first.

"I am Si…Tristan Pathfinder, formerly King's Knight," he replied formerly.

The goblin looked at him.

"Groltch just Groltch, and Groltch call you Trista…Trist…Tris," it replied, struggling over his name.

Tristan's gaze turned to ice. He hated being called Tris.

V

Tyrone Pathfinder watched as his son left the clearing. He wished that it did not have to end this way, but he wanted his son as far away from Caldor as possible. He had wanted to tell him what was going on, but knew that Tristan would be unable to cope with the truth. He did not know what they had done to him in the knighthood, though there were strong suspicions amongst the others, but the man was nothing like the boy he had been. At the time Tyrone had been cajoled, tricked and practically forced into sending his son away where they had perverted his true nature. Hopefully this unexpected bonus of a breakaway, he had truly believed his son would be killed in the planned events, might restore a little of the old Tristan. If it did then perhaps he would gain his son's forgiveness. But for now, there was work to do. Knights would surely be on their way, and he had to disappear. It was obvious that they would take him for questioning under which he might give away their plans. It was too late in the proceedings for that. He took one last look at the young ex-knight and then disappeared into the bushes.

VI

Tyrone was not the only one who was following Tristan's movements. In the city of Theldar, deep within the palace laboratory, the Lord High Priest, Matthew, had linked his mind to that of the errant King's Knight. It had been hard to restore the connection over the long distance. Interestingly enough, he was still largely shielded from magical intrusion, and when he had finally slipped through, had discovered Tristan's mind to be spinning in a whirlwind of confusion. It had taken more time than he had planned to extract the relevant information. He now knew of the knight's plan, plus the disturbing news that there was an underground group of goblin friends in Caldor. By the looks of the way it operated, it seemed Queen Anne II might have been less successful than had first been thought. He slowly slipped out from the consciousness and broke the link with Jalim. His young apprentice had an amazing gift, aside from free-wielding. He was able to transfer energy to others, enabling them to cast more spells of greater power than they normally could. It was an exceedingly interesting subject of study, as was the source of Tristan's magical shielding.

"Take this down," he instructed his student, whom also served as personal scribe. "Under the heading, further theories on dual power magical items. Due to the symbiotic nature of the magical item, it may confer upon its owner a limited form of mental protection similar to that of those who have been trained in the arts of sealing the mind. This is possibly the reason for the Shadow's seeming immunity to generalised mind sweeps of the city I have performed in searching for him. It may also be responsible for the disruption in Tristan's mental training in Treatment that led to his sudden breach of loyalties yesterday. Possible reasons for Tristan only being affected may be due to the fact he is the first King's Knight to have been gifted in the arts of sorcery since pre-Treatment days."

Matthew quickly checked over his student's notes before thanking him and dismissing him. He then quickly made his way down to the private audience chamber where he hoped the next knight to be sent out to catch Tristan would be waiting. He opened the door and was dismayed to see Malcolm stood there. Matthew tried to hide his disgust.

"I don't recall requesting for your presence, Malcolm."

"But you assured me a date for the Council Meeting would be set today," replied the small man.

"All I said was that it was the king's decision to make. As for a rough date, I can't see a full meeting being convened until after the ambassadors have arrived. They are the prime concern of the king at the moment," replied Matthew testily.

Upon seeing a barely stifled grin Matthew realised he had probably said something that he should not of, but it made no difference. The ambassadors would be here shortly and soon all would know. He curtly dismissed the man, who complied just a little too quickly for Matthew's comfort. As the little man left, the knight he had requested entered, brushing him aside curtly. Matthew waited long enough to allow Malcolm to be well out of ear shot before turning to speak to Captain Skellan.

"Greetings, Sar Karene," he said formally.

She merely nodded her head in what passed, barely, for a small bow. Matthew hated the way the knights seemed to treat him with such little respect.

"You are no doubt aware of the situation of the renegade King's Knight," he began, knowing she had been one of the knights who had been at the ceremony, "and of the fate of the squadron sent to retrieve him last night."

She nodded curtly in reply. He was really beginning to dislike her.

"I need you to lead the next squadron of Talons in pursuit," he began. "He is presently on his way to Kelvaria…"

"We shall lead immediately…Sir," interrupted the knight.

"I hadn't finished, Karene," he replied, ignoring the glare for his informality. "You are to first proceed to Havelock and bring in his father, Tyrone Pathfinder, for questioning."

"What?" she asked angrily. "Why…Lord."

"I believe the man is a member of an underground group of goblin friends. If true, then he may be a danger to the country. If we are lucky he may lead us to them."

"But…"

"No!" replied Matthew, his voice turning icy cold. "Your personal vendetta can wait. You are one of the best knights left in Theldar and I need your expertise to bring in Tyrone. Then you may proceed to your quest."

"That will give Tristan almost two days head start!" she complained. "By then he could have reached Kelvaria and left by sea."

"You have the advantage," he replied. "He's travelling across country, and you'll be on the main highway, and there are contingency plans should you be too slow in catching up. Now go."

The thinly veiled insult did the job and she bowed formally then turned to leave.

"One more thing," he said, hoping to get her whilst she was being at least slightly obedient. "Due to the killings all knights and guards are commanded to travel in pairs, even when not on duty. Inform them before you leave, and be on guard at all times when departing."

"I'm always on guard, my Lord," she replied, with a glare that could melt firestones.

"Then you'll have no problems then," replied Matthew with just a hint of sarcasm. "You may leave now, Sar Karene."

She stormed out of the room after a quick bow of obedience. Matthew sighed. He was glad he was not the king.

VII

Malcolm pulled back the small viewing shutter and rubbed his hands together. With all the information he had collected today he might even be able to afford that marvellous mahogany writing desk he had seen last week. He dashed off to meet his contact.

VIII

Tristan and Groltch sat eating some freshly cooked rabbit in front of a small fire. These were the only pieces of meat he had found in the provisions from his father, though fortunately there were also several lengths of snaring wire which meant he had a better chance of catching something this night.

He looked up at the goblin. It was still eating. They had stopped briefly to satisfy their hunger, which had become ravenous due to almost a day without food. The creature looked up at him.

"You cook not too bad for human," it said, its mouth still full with food. "Next Groltch cook and show human good cooking."

"Not if I have anything to say about the matter," muttered Tristan under his breath.

"What you say?"

"Nothing," replied Tristan tersely.

The rest of the meal passed in relative silence, if the noise of the creature eating was discounted. Tristan took the opportunity to examine his new *companion*, as he had never actually seen one of these creatures before the execution, save for the goblin head moulded onto the hilt of Caliburn. The goblin was similar in shape and size to himself. Its build was slightly smaller than Tristan's, and it was several inches shorter, but from a distance it was possible for someone of poor sight to mistake it as human. At close quarters such a mistake would be impossible to all but the blind. Its head was like a flattened human head though the forehead was more sloped and it had prominent ridges across its brow. It had a relatively weak chin that disappeared into a large lower jaw. This made its large lips even more prominent and this in turn made its flat nose seem smaller by comparison. Its skin was heavily tanned and its thick, tangled hair was almost jet black. These dark features made its light green eyes stand out, despite their relatively small size. He also noticed that the creature often squinted in the bright sunlight.

Its body was also different from that of the average human. The arms were slightly longer and the legs shorter than proportion required, making it seem as though distorted as in the Carnevale mirror hall in Theldar. From what he could see from beneath its grimy clothing, its body was slightly more muscular than a human its equivalent size and its large hands seemed clumsy and a little ungainly. The most noticeable thing about it, though, was the dirt that covered it. It was even visible beneath the clothes and it did nothing but add to the foul odour that it emitted.

He found that he had to look away, for it was obviously so inhuman, and he was disgusted that he was going to help it escape. He prayed to Toric that it would be a swift journey.

It was not long before they had to stand and continue their journey. This began in an uncomfortable silence as he tried to force all thought of the hideous creature from his mind. The creature seemed unnerved by the lack of noise and soon broke it by speaking.

"So you want ask me questions," it stated cautiously.

"Yes," he replied uncertainly, trying his best to avoid looking at the sight of the creature. "I…I would like to know how you knew I was in danger and why you took my sword."

"Groltch was going…returning…yak, returning to kill shadowless one, human king, when Groltch heard…"

"My king is not shadowless!" replied Tristan angrily.

To be shadowless was to be in league with Thenril himself, for the legends told that those who made deals with Thenril sacrificed their shadows to show their allegiance. How the creature had known this ultimate of insults he did not know but was not going to hear a single slight to his king.

"King is!" retorted the goblin. "Only shadowless one would kill Groltch's people, children too!"

"You are correct, but it was your kind that started the war by raiding and destroying our villages. They too killed children."

"Humani…humans were ones who started. Humans not help in time of…of…great chaos. When floods came Groltch's people ask for help like treaty said, and humans not."

"There has never been a treaty between Caldor and Grelchin," replied Tristan in outrage.

How could this foul creature even say such a thing!

"Was," replied the creature petulantly. "When we give humans

Caldor…"

Tristan was almost speechless by now.

"…and while Groltch try speak human tongue, you not even say name right!"

Tristan was so outraged by this distortion of Caldor's history that he almost struck down this ugly little, foul smelling creature.

"Sir Caldor the Pure fought long and hard for our land," he cried angrily.

He glared angrily at the creature that returned the glare with vigour. Suddenly Tristan recalled the creature's last statement and his anger faded to confusion. The realisation that he had briefly lost his emotional control helped erase it completely. Nothing was achieved by irrational emotion.

"What do you mean I say the name wrong?" he asked.

"You call home of Groltch Grelchin. That wrong. It called Grel-Chin."

"What is the difference?" he asked, having heard it say the name in what seemed to be exactly the same way.

"Grelchin mean nothing. Grel-Chin mean Hope Land, or land of hope. It two words, not one! It like First City of Grel-Chin called Grel-Chi, Hope City."

Tristan suddenly realised that this conversation was not going where he wanted it to go. Angry with himself for letting his confusion of mind show, he gave a brief, dismissive nod.

"Grel-Chin. Now could you please finish what you were saying about last night," he said, forcing himself to remain calm.

The creature seemed to pause a minute as its slow-witted mind worked its way back to where it had left off.

"Was going back to kill…king, when Groltch heard voice in head. It say Groltch have chance to repay debt, if Groltch do what it said."

"A voice in your head? From where?"

"Groltch get to that soon, not you worries. Where got Groltch?" it muttered to itself, pausing for a minute to think. "Ah, yak. Told Tris was in danger by voice." It looked at him, directing the next words at him. "Voice tell Groltch where go, and Groltch follow. Groltch found you and voice say 'pick me up.' Groltch ask who voice are. Voice say it sword."

"Wait a minute, you said the voice claimed to be the sword?"

"Yak, let Groltch finish," it replied, sounding annoyed. "Groltch take sword and it say leave. Groltch leaves and then hears ano…ther human. Groltch hide in bush and watch. Human creeps near you and put something to neck of you. Sword say 'Now' and Groltch creep behind it. Rest you knows."

"How can you be sure it was definitely the sword that spoke to you?"

"It…it…" the creature seemed to be searching for the correct word.

"It…it shakes when voice spoke. Made hand…tingles when it says things. Groltch as sure sword spokes as Groltch name Groltch."

"Why would the holy sword Caliburn speak to you?" replied Tristan in contempt. "It is reputed to have only ever spoken to the most pure of knights. It has not spoken for centuries."

The irony of this struck him at once. If it had not spoken in such a long time then obviously its previous owners must have been less than pure.

"*Well spotted!*" said chuckled the soft voice in his head.

Tristan cautiously touched the hilt of Caliburn. It was vibrating softly and seemed to crackle like gentle lightening.

"*Yes I am the sword. I had hoped you would figure it out on your own. I guess that was just a little* too *much to hope for.*"

Tristan found himself speechless. The great and holy sword was speaking to him, a man not even a knight, and had spoken to a *goblin* of all things. The whole thing was too confusing for words.

"*Oh and whilst you seem in a state to listen, you might want to know that the humans did indeed break the treaty, making the way for war.*"

IX

Naithan woke up shortly after midday feeling extremely refreshed and relaxed. It had been one of the best night's sleep he had had in years. It had been deep, uninterrupted and, best of all, dreamless. He had enjoyed this the most because he had been plagued with nightmares for years. They had begun shortly after his mother's death when he had ascended to the throne. At first they had only been short terrors and occurred once or twice a week. At the time he had believed them to be due to his mother's death. However they continued for months after, gradually getting longer and longer and more and more frequent. Some two years ago it had reached the point where he could not sleep because of them, and his health had begun to deteriorate. It had been then when Matthew had struck on the idea of sleeping potions. They forced him to sleep no matter how hard he tried to remain awake and, although not stopping the nightmares, they took away a little of the terror. This meant he was able to endure them without waking. It had worked, and his health had been largely restored and he had been able to resume his functions as king of Caldor.

Last night had been different though. Despite the fact he had not consumed a potion, he had slept better that night than any other he could remember. Suspicion flashed briefly through his mind. Could it be possible that Matthew's potions had prolonged the nightmares?

He immediately dismissed the idea and buried it deep into the back of his mind. He was not going to let anything spoil his day. It was then that he noticed the two guards either side of his bedroom door.

"What is the meaning of this?" he asked angrily.

"We were told to stay here until you woke up, your Majesty," replied one as they both bowed deeply.

"And who gave you this command?" he asked, already suspicious of who it might be.

"The High Priest, Sire," replied the guard, bowing again.

"Get out of my room!" he commanded angrily, his suspicions having been confirmed.

The guards bowed and left the room. As they did so Naithan pulled the bell chord by his bed. Within minutes Luca had entered the room carrying a tray of food.

"Why were there guards in my room?" demanded Naithan.

"Matthew thought yer were in danger from that creature the Shadow," replied Luca, quietly placing the tray before him as he spoke. "And before yer ask, I don't know why. He tried to explain it t'me and I was confused before he'd barely begun."

Naithan looked suspiciously at his manservant. Luca could be tighter with information than a miser with a golden goose when he wanted to be. He ate the food quickly, still remembering the threat from yesterday, and then allowed Luca to dress him. As soon as he was finished Naithan asked him to fetch in Matthew. The old man left taking the empty tray with him and within minutes Matthew had arrived.

"What has happened?" asked Naithan. "Why were there guards in my room?"

Matthew sat down and relayed the morning's events concerning matters of the Shadow.

"Why didn't you wake me?" asked Naithan accusingly.

"Because you needed the sleep and I knew with my magic I could do more about it than you at present. I contacted the Council members and told them of Tristan's flight. I believe he's too long gone for it to remain a secret any longer. They've agreed to inform their barons to be on the lookout. After this I located Tristan's position and sent out Captain Skellan to intercept him, though she has a more important task to see to first, a matter I will speak to you about later.

"I also informed the families of the knights killed last night and have summoned another two squadrons of Talons to replace those we've lost. Two squadrons of Lion's Claws reached us from Seafordshire and will stand for them until their arrival."

Though curious as to what this other task Captain Skellan had been given, he had sat patiently till the end, agreeing with each one of Matthew's actions. He forced all suspicion to the back of his mind. Matthew was his friend.

"How did my brother take to you ordering his knights around?" he asked with a smile.

"As begrudgingly as ever," replied Matthew. "He seems to think that we are slowly reducing his armies. Do you know that the Shadow has killed more knights than have died in the entire Goblin War so far?"

"That doesn't surprise me," replied Naithan wearily. "Hopefully he will not be a problem for too much longer."

"If I can discover what device he's using then I might be able to trace him."

"At least there's some good news today."

"I have some more," continued Matthew, "because Gareth seems to think that the war will be over within two to three months. He's even able to return from the front to see you before the proposed visit to Sol."

Naithan smiled. He had not seen his brother in many months now. It would be good to share some time with him before the State visit to Sol. His brother's loyalty, friendship and courage always left him feeling refreshed and prepared to continue the fight.

"What of this important mission given to Sar Karene?" he asked, bringing his thoughts back to matters at hand.

"She's to pick up Tristan's father and bring him here for questioning."

"What?" asked Naithan incredulously. "That's absurd! Why in all Loden should we want to question him?"

"Well he helped Tristan to escape…"

"I would have expected nothing less from a father to his son," interrupted Naithan.

"…and the methods he was employing lead me to believe that the *Circle of Light* may still be operation."

"What?" asked Naithan in horror. "That's impossible."

The Circle of Light was a revolutionary group probably formed sometime during his grandfather's reign. They were a group dedicated to overthrowing the monarchy. They had been convinced that the present monarchy had been corrupt since the time of Henry III. Their solution had been an attempt to overthrow the reigning monarch and his entire family, then place an *untainted* line on the throne. Fortunately they had been crushed at the height of their power during his mother's reign.

"Are you sure?" he asked.

"No I'm not," replied Matthew. "Tristan received a troubling note from his father. Apparently there are people aiding goblins in their flight from Grelchin. The methods described are similar to those used by the Circle during Queen Anne's time, when they smuggled out possible spell casters to Kolth."

"Very well, the decision was wise. The moment he is brought in I would speak to him directly."

"Certainly," replied Matthew. "'I'll see to it personally."

"Very good, you may go," he replied. "You may return to your studies as well, for I will finish the day's duties."

Matthew smiled in apparent relief. His friend had always hated using Regency powers.

"Will you be needing a potion for tonight?"

"You can bring me a potion, though I will try to last the night without one," he replied, watching for any reaction on the wizard's face.

There was none. He merely bowed and replied:

"As you wish."

With another bow his friend turned and left the room. Naithan allowed himself a little time for thought before following suit.

X

"What do you mean the goblin is correct?" asked Tris loudly.

The sudden noise startled Groltch from his thoughts. The strange human, if there was such a thing as a normal human, had fallen silent for several minutes. Its blue eyes had gone glassy and Groltch thought he might have entered some form of meditation.

"Why would we have a treaty with someone who enslaved us?"

Groltch looked around to see who or what the human was talking to. He knew that humans were quite mad, but he hadn't realised that it extended to talking to themselves.

"What was that you said?" asked Tris, sounding completely horrified.

Groltch started to answer but realised that the question had not been direct at him.

I wish that stupid human would stop talking like that, he thought irritably. *It keeps breaking up my concentration.*

He was in the process of planning another assassination on the life of the *miklahna*, the shadowless, and every time the human spoke it disturbed him, forcing him to start again. Not that he was getting anywhere with the plans. He took the human's distraction as an opportunity to look at it. It was taller than its kind, and without its metal shell looked rather thin and ungainly, though its muscles were apparent. He studied it hard, trying to determine its sex, but it was difficult. One human looked pretty much the same as another. This on had a little more fur on its face and head than many, and its fur was lighter in colour than that of his own people, but that could mean anything. He could see it was different to the *miklahna*, but that was only because he had etched the king's image into his mind's eye. He had discovered that the *miklahna* had pompously ordered the image of its head etched onto one side of the round metal disks of metal they used for currency. He had found that the image was not exact, but close enough to allow him to recognise the king when he had found him.

He returned his thoughts to the present dilemma trying to ignore the human that had started talking to itself again. Deciding it was too difficult, and seeing that the human had finished its enquires with him, he stood and turned to leave. Just as he started to slip away Tris called out, obviously this time in his direction.

"What are you doing?"

Groltch thought he could hear worry in the human's voice, which was rather deep and effeminate.

"You no more questions. Groltch go now," he replied, trying to pronounce the almost unintelligible words of the human tongue.

He knew when they spoke of themselves they used the word *I*, but trying to pronounce such a short word with no solid sound at the start was practically impossible and hurt his vocal chords.

"Where are you going now?"

"Back to kill king," he stated.

Evidently humans knew nothing of blood debts.

"Are you insane?" asked the creature that moment's ago had been speaking to itself. "It would take an army to get to him now."

That was quite logical reasoning for a human. His first failure would make the *miklahna* very wary, and to merely cut the head of the wyrm off was not necessarily to kill the beast. Another far worse ruler could take its place. The best way to end the threat completely was to destroy the human capability of war. To do that an army would be needed. His people were too scattered and defeated to provide this, so he would have to travel to other human lands to raise his army. He dredged his memory in search of what little he knew of them. As far as he could remember the only nation strong enough to defeat Caldor was probably Kolth, so that would have to be his destination.

"Where you goes?" he asked.

"I intended to leave Caldor by sea and go somewhere like Kolth or Sol."

"Good," he replied, knowing a human guide in this strange territory would be useful. "Groltch come with you."

XI

Tristan would never have noticed the goblin leaving if Caliburn had not alerted him. He had been so busy arguing with the sword that a platoon of knights could have thundered past him without disturbing him. Now that he had seen the goblin, he could not believe it still wished to kill the king. However, this was not his main concern of the moment. He had been asked to escort the creature to Kelvaria. His conscience would not allow him to break his father's trust, yet at the same time he could not force the creature to accompany him. His mind quickly ran through all the possible ways he could persuade it and was dismayed to discover that there were not very many, and the few ways available were not all that effective.

He was on the brink of despair and seriously thinking of battering it unconscious when it suddenly changed its mind. He looked at it suspiciously. What had caused its sudden change of heart? He rose and walked in the direction the creature had been headed. Even as close as he dared go he could not read the expression on its ugly face. He pointed in the opposite direction to which the goblin had been moving.

"Very well, you may stay with me, but Kelvaria is this direction," he said, not bothering to hide his contempt from the creature.

"Thank you great master," replied the creature with a mocking bow.

Great! Thought Tristan as they began their journey anew. *That is just what I need. A sarcastic goblin following me around.*

"Where's your sense of humour?" asked Caliburn. *"You would probably be much nicer to talk to if you weren't so serious all the time."*

"Oh please be quiet," snapped Tristan irritably.

"Wha…oh," said the goblin, irritating Tristan further.

The creature probably thought he was insane or something.

"Well I'm sorry," replied Caliburn. *"I'll leave you alone then."*

With that the strange presence of the sword left his mind and the journey continued in silence. They travelled in this way until dusk, when Tristan suddenly broke the silence.

"Oh no, I think we are lost."

XII

The dream began as it always did. He was sat on a cold stone chair in the middle of a large dark hall. The deathly silence made him shiver almost as much as the cold air that shrouded him. Upon his head he could feel a heavy object which bore down on his skull with such force that he felt his neck would soon end and snap. He placed his hands on the object and almost screamed in agony as their bare flesh touched icy cold, frozen metal. He removed the object from his head, already knowing what he would find. In his hands was a black and twisted crown set with onyx. He tried to throw the perverted object to the floor but his hands had been stuck fast by the ice.

He tried to keep his gaze from the hideous object but his eyes were drawn to the largest piece of onyx set in the crown. It was almost completely smooth and reflective, yet as he watched the surface seemed to ripple like water. The jet black stone began to fade in colour to a murky grey, thin black lines being all that remained of its former darkness, and all began to swirl round in a dizzying motion that hurt the eyes to look at. From the centre of this black and grey whirlpool emerged the image of a face, surrounded in white light. It was a face well known to him, one he had seen almost every night for several years. It spoke to him in the soft, calming voice and its eyes burned through his in righteous fury.

"Remember your mission," it almost whispered. "There is evil all around you, in every shadow and behind every door. It knows you and your mission and it seeks to destroy you. It fears you and its fear makes it dangerous. Watch and remember."

With that the face faded away. He knew now what would happen. He knew he was dreaming, and that he would not wake until it was finished. He tore desperately at the crown still fused to his hands and with a scream, kicked it off across the hall. His hands throbbed in pain, the skin torn off revealing only the bloody flesh beneath. He leapt from the throne and saw that the large onyx centrepiece of the crown had shattered, and the grey misty haze it had contained was released. In the half-light created by this fog, images swirled around him, each seeming to be figures, holding daggers ready to strike. He moved round, trying to see each swirling form, knowing that one would indeed be his attacker.

A sudden glint of light and flurry of movement behind him alerted him to the danger and he flung himself to the floor. His bloodied palms screamed in pain as they struck the floor, spraying blood around and striking his face. He ignored the pain, rolling forward and springing up to his feet. He knew he had to escape. He looked from left to right. The hall was filled with arches, each leading to a different time and place. Knowing he had little time left he leapt for the nearest. This was the best known to him and while it was not the most painful of the arches, it was certainly not the least painful. As he dived through he heard the howl of the attacker and he smiled, knowing he would not suffer its cruel torture this night. The mist swirled round him, caught him up as if in the arms of the wind or currents of the sea and led him to the second, more painful stage of the dream.

He suddenly found himself behind a cask of wine in the cellar that had become so familiar to him. Peering round he could see a room filled with men and women, all stood in a circle holding a candle in their hands. For the first time the significance of this struck him. It was the Circle of Light. All were talking of him, and he knew they planned the revolution. More striking to him was the fact that despite the light provided by the candles, none had shadows. They were servants of the Dark One himself, and he knew that their shadows were now used against him in the form of that evil creature that now stalked him in the streets of his very own city.

He stayed quiet, trying to hear; yet knowing their plans would be barely audible, and that the creature of his undoing in this dream was already scuttling towards him. He tried not to look at the rat-like creature and ignore its light feathery touch. He instinctively moved to brush it away, despite himself. It leapt at him, sinking its teeth deep into the unprotected flesh of his hands, tearing away another strip of his torn palm. He screamed in agony. The people turned towards him and on seeing him began to move swiftly in his direction.

He reacted immediately, spinning round and fleeing. The creature took another bite, this time of his foot, and he stamped down hard, knowing this would only serve to release its poison. He limped away, pain flowing through him as the poison surged through his arteries.

He leapt through a steel door and began to run frantically up the stairs that lay behind them. The cries of pursuit began to draw nearer and he doubled his efforts to escape. Arrows flew past him as his pursuers reached the base of the stairs, yet by now he had almost reached the top. But as he reached the penultimate step he found yet another step behind the last, and another behind that. No matter how fast he ran it seemed that he could not reach that elusive step and safety. By this point the poison was spreading through his abdomen and panic grip him to the point of hysteria.

A sharp pain in his back reminded him of his pursuers and looking down he saw the point of the arrow that had hit him sticking out of his chest. Twice he slipped, his head smacking hard onto the granite steps, causing cuts and wounds that seeped blood into his eyes, blinding him.

Suddenly the blades of weapons slashed and stabbed into his back, announcing the arrival of his pursuers. The poison surged through his neck and into his head, causing an explosion of pain and agony. It was at this moment that he reached the last step and burst out into the dark landscape that marked the final stage of the dream. In his panic he barely noticed the cliff in time to stop. He stood, panting for breath, dizzy with exhaustion and poison, which now filled him. He cleared the blood from his eyes and discovered it had turned black from poison. As he looked at it he could see and feel the black ooze eating through his flesh. He was being dissolved from the inside out. He raised his head and howled in pain. He could feel the venom burning away his eyes and hands. He rubbed at his eyes with his arms and looked down. He could see before him a drop of many thousands of feet and it seemed to be swirling around and around before him. He wished to step over the edge and end it all but knew that would only lead to more pain. He stepped back, yet it seemed to move with him. He tried again but it followed, seeming to move faster than he. He turned and ran, feeling the cliff edge crumbling away beneath his dissolving feet.

A man suddenly emerged from the shadow of a boulder before him. He was stood still, yet seemed to move no closer, despite the fact his own movement was in the man's direction.

"I will not let you purify the world," said the shadowy man. "I will destroy you, and if I fail, another and another shall rise in my place until we succeed. Now you die!"

With that the man stepped closer and pushed him off the cliff. He plummeted downward with a sickening speed and he screamed as parts of his body dissolved and disintegrated. As his eyes finally dissolved, the last image they saw was the familiar face with the burning eyes.

"Remember who wishes to do this to you. You must prevent them before they halt your sacred mission. You must wipe out evil and teach those humans who have lost the way exactly what the truth is."

As those last words were spoken he struck the ground and the world exploded.

XIII

Naithan awoke in a cold sweat and fumbled for his gas lantern. He lit it quickly, but its little yellow flame brought no comfort. He reached across for the sleeping potion, knowing that he would need it to sleep after this dream. He had hoped that he no longer needed them, but the dream had proved him wrong. He drank it down swiftly and rolled over to return to sleep. It was at this moment that he felt the pain and saw the blood covering the sheet, his own blood. He tried to scream for help but the potion's effects had taken hold and he was dragged remorselessly into sleep. As his consciousness slipped away he cursed himself for not retaining the guards in his room…

XIV

The dream began as it always had. He was returning from the nearby forests of his village. His people had been luckier than most, for they had lived in the northern reaches of Grel-Chin, in the province of Nar'atch, which had suffered the least in the upheavals of the great catastrophe. Their lands were actually pushed higher, and not lower, meaning that the land remained good. The forests retained plenty of game, including the flightless Garou Garou bird, of which he had caught three. All was bright and glorious day. Nothing could disturb him, not even the unusual amount of smoke rising from the direction of his village. Feast days were often marked with great fires, to create light for their shadows to play in.

He walked over the rise and suddenly he realised all was not well. Where his village once stood was a blackened, smoking ruin. He dropped his prizes from the hunt and ran down the hill. His sharp eyes picked up the faint images of burnt corpses several hundred metres before he reached the first hut. Tears now streamed down his eyes as the smoke filled his lungs and the smell of burnt flesh filled his nose. He moved through the village, house by house, searching for anyone still living. Yet all were dead. He reached the home of his mother and dropped to his knees in despair as he saw a corpse with his mother's favourite neck wear. He wept long and hard, moving next to the house of his father, and then his beloved engar. Despair filled him and the agony tore and twisted at his heart. It was all so real, so vivid, yet the horrors around him were in the past. Buried deep within…

XV

Groltch awoke with tears in his eyes. He had not had such a dream in several months now. He had thought himself hardened by it, strengthened. He had expected to die in killing the king, and to be reunited in Toric's realm with his loved ones. That comfort removed from the immediate future, the sadness filled him once more. He saw Tris looking at him and, determined not to let the human see his weakness, stood and muttered that he needed a drink. He went to the nearby pool the human had found and took a drink. He then sat quietly for a while, gathering his strength together before returning to the fire. He thought of the past and lost himself to the now bittersweet reverie of earlier days.

XVI

Tristan, like many others that night, was having difficulties with sleep. The events of the past two days along with the strange dreams of the previous night had left him more than a little unsettled. He had offered to take first watch, a precaution he had once thought unnecessary. He had watched the creature sleep, and noticed it tossing and turning restlessly, obviously having difficulties sleeping with its past crimes on its mind. When it had woken he had seen something he had never expected, tears. He had been brought up to believe goblins could not shed tears, yet this creature was. As it got up and went for a drink Tristan found himself wondering, not for the first time, just how much the things he had heard about goblins were true. Even more confusing was Caliburn's acceptance of the creature, and its lessons of history as it knew it, all of which left him feeling confused as to what was the truth. Added to that was the very real threat of the dreams he had last night meant that he knew he would not sleep this night.

"What is the problem?" asked the sword, its presence filling his mind and breaking his thoughts. *"Why don't you sleep?"*

"I had some strange dreams last night and I am afraid that they might come again."

Tristan could face any enemy with little fear but the bizarre world of dreams and magic petrified him.

"I wouldn't worry. They won't come again."

"How do you know? Do you know what they were?"

"Yes, they were an ancient form of magic that I supposed long vanished," replied Caliburn.

"Magic," said Tristan in disgust, as if the word had a sour taste to it. "What was it for?"

Caliburn took on the cadence of speech similar to that of the knightly instructors in Belthanor making Tristan smile slightly in remembrance.

"Dreams can be used in many ways. It is the point when everyone's mind is most open to attack. If a powerful magician can penetrate the dreams of a person, then he can often gain much control over them. Before he does, however, he must try to break or trick the person's spirit into obedience. They have three attempts to do so before the conscious intervenes, closing the mind off to the sorcerer forever. Usually they try to lure people with promises of power, glory, comfort and security. The first is usually the probe to discover the desires of the person, the second the attack. If resisted the third is usually a last desperate attempt to either trap or ask you to give up. The sorcerer who met you was powerful indeed for he was not only able to cast this spell, but he was also able to genuinely hurt you, even kill you. I tried to aid you, but his last attack was too strong. You were lucky to be woken when you were."

Tristan shuddered with the mere thought of dying that way.

"Can he try it again?" he asked worriedly.

"No," replied Caliburn softly. *"Your mind was closed off forever from his control. The greatest dreamweaver, Elflord Kaneril could not do such a thing, even when at the height of his power."*

"Why would anyone want to do that to me? And why now, after I have lost my position?"

"The High Priest's magic no doubt protected you whilst you were in the king's service."

"That still does not explain why he chose to enchant me now, when I have lost all power."

"You never really had such power," replied Caliburn softly. *"The kingdom would probably be in a better state if you did. If anything, you're more powerful now than you ever were before."*

"What do you mean by that?" asked Tristan.

"The power of the King's Knight has never been anything more than symbolic," replied the sword. *"As such, those chosen are trained specially from the very outset on idealist sentiment. Idealism is easy to induce in those whose personalities contain a spark of it already. You are shielded from much, so as to retain your sincere belief in the king and his work."*

"What do you mean by that? What possible reason could they have for doing that?"

"Simple," replied Caliburn. *"You are supposed to represent the descendent of Caldor. He never became king, yet on the strength of his word the first Council Leader*

was elected. Subsequent leaders used his image to gain themselves the title of King. Your presence is seen as Caldor's blessing on the present king. Through you will be seen the fulfilment of Caldor's promise to return again in his nation's hour of greatest need. As a free man, with me at your side, you will become a potent figure for other would-be kings. They could use you to lead the country in uprising against the present king. That is what I believe this particular sorcerer was after."

"Why was I given you then, if I was only necessary as a symbol? Why not a replica, so that a more worthy knight could wield you?"

Caliburn made a strange buzzing sound that Tristan took to be laughter.

"Until yesterday people thought I was just a symbol. I've concealed my powers and abilities until I found one such as you who I believed were truly worthy of wielding them without abuse. I was considered just to be a wonderful addition and continuation in the myth of Sir Caldor. You're lucky, the earliest knights had to change their names to Caldor! This is also the reason why women are never allowed the position, because that would destroy the continuity."

"I do not believe you. It cannot possibly be as bad as you say it is."

"That's exactly what you are trained to believe, though something seems to have gone in your training. The magician tripped up on that one."

"What do you mean *magician*?" he asked.

"I mean that the High Priest is a magician," replied Caliburn.

"Then I was correct!" replied Tristan in joy. "I can return and expose him. Then my punishment will be a little more lenient."

"I'm afraid the king already knows," replied Caliburn.

Part of Tristan believed Caliburn but he stubbornly held to his disintegrating beliefs. However, he knew that it was a futile battle, and that such beliefs would not survive long.

"I refuse to believe you, even if you are a holy sword," he replied petulantly, before slowly becoming suspicious. "Anyway, how is it you seem to know so much about it all?"

"Just as I can speak in your mind, it can talk to me, which you might want to start doing if you don't want everyone to think you're crazy. If someone is near enough I can pick up their stray thoughts and as I'm usually surrounded by people in power, I can usually learn quite a lot of secrets."

"Can you pick up the goblin's thoughts?" he asked slowly.

"Especially the goblin's."

"Why is that?"

His original intention had been to discover the creature's motives, but that was now superseded by curiosity and surprise.

"Because my creator was a goblin, his face even adorns my hilt" replied the sword. *"Now I think it's time for you to get some sleep. I've answered all the questions I want to tonight."*

Despite the fact that the statement shocked him and he was supposed to be on watch, he swiftly drifted to the land of dreams. Obviously he had just misheard the sword.

As he drifted to sleep he heard the sword say softly.

"Don't worry, I'll wake you if something comes."

XVII

Groltch returned to find the human asleep. Evidently it had not learned from the previous night's experience. He settled down to take over where the irresponsible human had left off. Yet barely before he had sat down he found himself drifting to sleep.

Soon the gentle snores of the two companions where the only sign of life in the clearing. A gentle blue light encased the sword.

"Thou art cruel, my friend," said a voice, apparently from nowhere. *"In the morn both shalt be at each other's throats once more."*

"But it means they'll speak to each other, and they shall never know each other any other way," came a second voice, seemingly from the sword. *"Besides they need the sleep and both are too stubborn to admit it."*

"Thou art truthful with these words, though I cannot but think that thou also enjoyeth thyself in the baiting."

"Well, a sword's gotta have some pleasure in life."

Anyone who had been conscious in the clearing would swear blind that they could hear a gentle laughter from nowhere that spoke of many years of warmth.

CHAPTER FOUR: Rings and Retribution

I

As the dawn sun rose into the sky above Theldar a shadowy figure flitted through the half-lit streets. Sometimes it would suddenly slip into a shadowy corner and just as suddenly emerge from another across the street. If anyone saw it, they would immediately suspect the figure's dark identity.

The Shadow of Death.

It was often said that people saw shadows of their own deaths. If a person saw this Shadow then their death was almost a certainty.

The man who bore this dark title was returning to his temporary home. This was the dark series of caverns that lay beneath the palace. They were used to store and *treat* political prisoners. He found it highly amusing that he spent so much of his time in the very place where the king most wished him to be. Even after all this time the thought brought a smile to his face.

Of course, it was the perfect place to hide. It was the one place where they would not even dream of looking for him. It was so well hidden a secret that almost no one ever went there. The jailer was as much a prisoner as the rest, never being released, lest it become public knowledge. The fact that the only entrance he had been able to find was built beneath the royal jetty in the harbour, unguarded, concealed and only accessible during very low tide which meant that its designers had not intended it to be easily found. He suspected another entrance might connect the caverns to the palace, though he had not yet found it. He could not imagine the king getting his feet muddy just to see mere prisoners.

The noise of guards patrolling the street disrupted his concentration and he slipped silently into the dark recess of an alley.

Of course, he *had* discovered the entrance, although somewhat by accident, and had discovered the secret that lay behind it. The tide had initially caused him some difficulties, before he had discovered that his ring allowed him to enter even when the tide was at its height. It allowed him to kill at will and disappear from sight, as he was about to do now. This time he had not killed anyone though, just left the king a personal message.

It had been an easy thing to do. He had used the ring to enter the king's bedroom unobserved avoiding all of the clumsy wards set by his pet sorcerer with ease. He had then placed a poultice on the king's arm that numbed the skin to pain, before slicing the flesh open and inserting a poodberry into the wound. He had closed the wound, causing the berry to split open and release its poison. It was not deadly. It would merely debilitate him and cause him much pain. It could never equal his own pain but the important thing was that the king would suffer. The effects would last about a week, even with the ministrations of priests and their spells, and that would give the king a lot of time to think. He would realise that he was not safe from justice, even in his own palace. To add a little more emphasis to his message he had used his dagger to open a larger gash in the other arm. The king would have to live with the fear and certain knowledge that his death would come at any moment. The Shadow's reign of personal terror had begun.

Suddenly he heard movement in the adjoining street. He moved deeper into the shadows and peered out from the alley. He smiled when he saw the source of the movement. It was a tall knight and she was alone…

II

Matthew suddenly woke up in a cold sweat. He could feel a tingling sensation in his left arm accompanied by a slight numbness. There was no mistaking this feeling and he knew that this time he was not imagining it either. Naithan was in danger. He tumbled from his bed and sprang to his feet. His vision blurred suddenly and his mind began to spin but he ignored them. Naithan was far more important than any temporary discomfort. He ran to the door and prayed desperately to Toric that he would get there before it was too late.

III

The knight looked a little tired and dirty. It was obvious to him that she had just completed a long journey. She had no doubt just returned from the war front, or some such thing, for these past few days all knights had been travelling in pairs on new orders and she was alone.

The woman looked happy enough too, obviously unaware of her dangerous situation. He could even hear her whistling a popular folk song called "The Lion and the Thorn".

He sneered to himself. It was obvious that it was all a facade. Beneath the exterior lay a rotten core. She had probably whistled just as joyfully whilst untold numbers of innocent people had been burned to death. He shuddered with rage and slowly drew his razor sharp Kolthon dagger. The ring on his finger began to glow deep red. It knew that blood would soon be shed.

IV

Matthew burst into Naithan's room and saw that his friend was convulsing with pain on the bed. He also saw the white sheets stained with his friend's blood.

He rushed to Naithan's side and began praying. He had always found it difficult and often painful to use his priestly magic but Naithan was in dire need. Thankfully the meditative state brought on by the praying came swiftly today. He stretched out his feelings from his body and began tapping into the energy that began coalescing around him. It was an agonisingly slow process but if he were to retain full control of it he could not rush. The bittersweet energy filled him and his muscles gave an involuntary spasm of pain. This was the sign he needed.

Using a little of the energy he had gathered he slowly began probing his friend's body and psyche, in an attempt to discover the problem. His senses reached out and he could feel Naithan's chest rise and fall as he breathed. He could feel the weakened heart pumping, the surge of blood through the arteries, and more importantly, the pain. An alien body, probably poison of some sort, was reacting badly to the sleeping potion, mixing into a lethal combination. The pain was excruciating. The numb sensation in his arm helped him clear his head by reminding him of his duty. He had to go on and separate the two, by drawing one onto himself. It was the only way for either of them to survive.

He pushed his senses deeper into his friend's body till they touched the living core, the soul. From here could be felt the rhythms of Naithan's life, which were rapidly slowing down. He then allowed his own soul to link with his friend's. He allowed it to be guided and instructed, and soon his bodily functions, the rhythm of his own life, slowed down to match that of Naithan's. Within moments they were living in total unison. Their hearts beat as one. Their feelings and thoughts merged together and suddenly they were one person and they felt the pain. Their nerves screamed as one and both screamed out in agony. They were dying.

V

The Shadow waited until the knight had walked past the alley's entrance then stepped out silently behind her. It took but a few gratifying seconds to slit her throat and almost as much for her to die. At that precise moment the door to his right opened and a small girl came rushing out.

"Mummy's back!" she called out joyfully.

Upon seeing her mother's dead body her joy turned to confusion. She knelt down beside her and began shaking the now lifeless corpse.

"What's wrong mummy?" she asked with concern. "Are you all right? Mummy…Mummy!"

She saw the blood at her throat and gasped. She stared at the body and grasped the cooling hand in shock. The fingers opened and a little golden bracelet fell to the ground. Tears filled her eyes and she looked up. It was then that she saw the cloaked figure of the Shadow, still holding the bloodied dagger in his left hand. He was transfixed by the scene before him.

"Can you help my mummy?" she asked hopefully.

She did not seem to realise his crime but the look of hope in her eyes was far worse than any of the most accusing looks she could have given him. He had once healed people, yet knew he could do nothing here. He had destroyed part of someone's life, just as the knights had once destroyed part of his. Whilst they remained faceless, anonymous, it had been easy. Now, he was not sure what to do. He had killed; taken the lives of people where once he had tried to preserve. The thought made him sick. He wanted to flee. He needed to think. In seeking revenge, what had he become?

A man appeared in the doorway, hastily dressing himself. It took him but a few seconds to appraise the situation. The girl turned round.

"Daddy, can you help mummy?"

The Shadow, what was his real name again…he could not recall…cringed in horror. Her hope was still there.

"Come to me, Calandra," said the man nervously. "Come to daddy."

The Shadow could bear it no longer. He threw the dagger, that which had been his most prized possession moments ago, to the ground and ran almost blindly to the nearest shadows. He leapt at them and the ring flared in white light. The last sounds he heard before leaving his native world were the sounds of a girl's sobbing.

It was the dreams, he thought in misery. *It wasn't me. It was the dreams. It wasn't my fault…*

VI

I am Matthew.

The thought came from nowhere, yet it was heeded. They were not one. They were two separate individuals. This awareness allowed Matthew to begin withdrawing from the union he had created. He slowly dragged himself from his friend's consciousness and with him came the poison. It was the only way, and the poison was not deadly. He could not force the long sickness the poison would bring on his king, so had left him under the effects of the potion.

Suddenly he was alone. He had pulled himself free of Naithan's control, and with this freedom came exhaustion and pain. All of his energy had been drained, so much so that he could barely move. He moved his head towards Naithan, sobbing as a spasm of pain struck. Naithan was breathing deeply and regularly. Satisfied that he had succeeded he allowed himself to slip painfully back into unconsciousness.

VII

"The probes proved the villagers to be telling the truth, Sar," said the young Green Knight. "None have seen Tyrone Pathfinder since last evening. Having searched his home it seems he has left on a permanent basis. All his personal effects are gone, Sar."

"Very well. Contact a friendly agent here and inform them to be on guard in case it is just a ruse then return at once, for we have no time to spare," replied Sar Karene.

She waited upon Saracen fuming at the delay. Now she would have to return to Theldar to inform the king of the man's escape. His very absence indicated that there may have been something to the High Priest's fear and just the mere possibility of that odious little man being in the right was enough to make her angry.

The Green knight returned and she ordered the knights to form up and ride out.

If that wizard has cost me Tristan, I will not be amused, she thought angrily as they rode out of the peasant village.

This was her chance to win the king's favour and become the first female King's Knight. She knew that Tristan would never hold that position again after she brought him to justice. She had to be the next logical choice.

VIII

"Yes. I agree. You can cook better than me but that still does not mean I should not take my turn at cooking tonight," argued Tristan loudly.

They had been travelling for almost a week now and the goblin was beginning to really annoy Tristan. It had insisted on cooking the meal on their first evening together, despite all his attempts to prevent it. It was only with a great deal of persuasion, largely at Caliburn's insistence that he keep party harmony, that he had even dared taste any of it and, to his dismay, he found it had been cooked with some skill. Tristan's later culinary attempts had culminated in disaster. The last meal that Tristan had burned had caused so much smoke that they had been forced to move to another campsite.

"Groltch…Yi cook well. You not. Yi like to cook. You not like…" Groltch finished in mid-sentence.

"What is wrong no…"

"Shush! Grol…Yi ham listening!" replied the goblin in a hushed voice.

Tristan had been trying to teach the goblin…Groltch to speak better Caldorian, once again at the sword's insistence. He was amazed at how quickly the creature was progressing, though he had to work out how to make it easier to pronounce words beginning with vowel sounds, as it seemed utterly incapable of doing so without sounding like a strangled cat. Evidently, the creature was more intelligent than he had originally thought, though how much was debatable as most of the time it still seemed like a backward, spirit-worshipping barbarian. However, one thing not in question was the sensitivity of its hearing. He stopped talking and let the creature listen. They stood in deathly hush for a moment before Groltch finally broke the silence.

"Groltch think we nearing ha village. Can hear laughing," it said in a hushed voice.

"How far?" he asked quietly.

"Very faint. Maybe one hof your miles, hor so."

"A mile!" said Tristan incredulously.

The creature was probably not that accurate and probably measuring distance in terms of its own kilmetras, or whatever it said the word was. These were certainly shorter than the Caldorian mile by a long way.

"I think Groltch is right. I can sense a vague presence at about that distance," said the sword quietly.

Oh, for Caldor's sake keep out of it, thought Tristan angrily.

The sword had an annoying habit of starting arguments and causing more interaction between himself and the goblin than he thought exactly necessary. He was also pretty certain it was done deliberately as well.

"Okay, but I wish you'd stop calling him Caldor. He hated it when he lived, so I don't see why it should be any different. And a few abbreviated words wouldn't go amiss. Have you any idea how stilted and unnatural you sound when you speak?" replied

Caliburn testily.

I am sorry ***Caliburn*** *but I did not ask you for your opinion on the matter now, did I?* Thought Tristan, trying to refrain from being too sarcastic.

He had finally mastered the art of communicating with the sword without speaking. This seemed to have eased the goblin's fears about his seemingly senseless ramblings, though he still forgot himself on occasions.

"That's a little better, but you'll never match Jim the Fifth King's knight, or was he the sixth? He had a real flair for sarcasm."

"If you mean James, he was the fifth King's Knight," replied Tristan, forgetting to speak silently in his anger. "And do you ever call people by their full names?"

Tristan heard the goblin start in surprise then mutter something about crazy humans.

"No I don't ***Tris****,"* replied the sword.

Oh just go away! thought Tristan sullenly.

"As you wish, but I thought I would point out that you might be able to use your father's ring in the village to try and hire a guide. As much as I ***love*** *travelling with you, I don't wish to spend the rest of your life wandering lost through these trees following every false trail we come across."*

Tristan grated his teeth at the reminder. A few days earlier he had been positive that he had found a familiar trail and had immediately convinced the goblin that they should follow it. Along the whole way Caliburn had insisted that they were going the wrong way but Tristan had been adamant. This had meant that they ended up going deeper into the forest and had left them even more lost than before. It was one of the reasons why they had been wandering aimlessly through the forest for almost a week. His temper had not been improved by the fact that the wandering had done nothing for his feet. The boots from his father were a size too small, and they had yet to find a place where he could trade or buy a pair that fitted better.

I thought I told you to go away, snapped Tristan.

"Sorry. I just thought it was an idea. I'll go then," replied the sword, sounding genuinely contrite.

Many thanks!

Tristan felt Caliburn's presence fade from his mind and he sat glaring into the fire that the goblin had just lit. He barely noticed the creature as it began to prepare dinner. He had lost his appetite. The great sword Caliburn was a disappointment. It was nothing like the sword of legend. It was not wise and did not have a sober personality. It was incapable of speaking seriously and he was beginning to wish it had never spoken to him at all. It was on its instigation that he had got into the whole mess in the first place. However, speak it did, though only to poke fun at him, or throw in some devastatingly unfunny witticism. He wished he could just get away, even if it was only for an hour or so.

"I was thinking that we might be able to hire a guide at the village to help us get to Kelvaria," said Tristan sourly, startling the goblin again.

"Good idea. Glad you thought of it."

"But Yi just started to cook. Food will go bad if left!" whined the snivelling little sub-race.

He truly needed to get away as his companions truly were grinding away on his nerves.

"I was planning to go alone," replied Tristan coldly.

"That good yidea," it replied, looking back to the one pot they owned. "Yi have food cooked when you get back. Yi even look after Gal…Galha…horse."

"Galahad," said Tristan absently.

He had been trying to teach the goblin the horse's name but like all words of more than two syllables, the creature seemed incapable of pronouncing them. He did not like the thought of the creature's filthy paws touching his horse, but he wanted to get away quickly and Galahad did need grooming. The goblin had also proved itself adept at other menial, household chores it performed.

"Very well. I should be back some time later this evening," he said as he removed the scabbard from his belt.

"What are you doing?" asked Caliburn.

I said I wanted to go to the village alone. Besides it would cause a stir if I walked into a village wearing a sword. I will be much less apparent if I go without and dress simply, he replied quickly.

"Good thinking," replied the sword sullenly.

It had obviously guessed his true intention.

He put the sword down and walked off towards the village. As he left he heard the goblin begin to hum. It always hummed whilst cooking, another of its infuriating habits. He prayed, not for the first time, that this journey would be a short one.

He soon found a well-used trail that evidently went in the direction of the village, so he joined it and began to walk down it, feeling in better spirits already. Even the pain in his feet from the boots seemed lessened.

The village Tristan entered just after dusk was quite small. It consisted of several buildings made of stone and pine wood connected by several well-worn gravel pathways. It was probable that barely a hundred or so people lived here. However the streets seemed deserted and the laughter Groltch had claimed to hear had stopped. He went into what seemed to be the central square where he could see several lit windows in a large building. He crossed the square, carefully avoiding the various livestock that wandered freely about and listened at the door. He could hear several voices behind it so went to knock on the door. Just then a particularly vicious, evil looking goat bleated at him. He forgot all propriety and entered without knocking. He had hated goats since one had butted him as a child. He had been convinced from that day on that they were servants of Thenril and this was a conviction he had never shaken off, despite the tireless efforts of the Instructors during his Treatments.

So shaken was he that he did not immediately notice that the voices had stopped, or that some two hundred heads or more had turned in his direction.

"Do you mind?" asked a voice irritably behind him. "I'm trying to begin a tale!"

Tristan turned round and looked at the room he had just entered. It appeared to be the common room of a tavern and was crowded full of people, all of whom were looking at him.

So much for not being noticed! He thought dryly.

"Please, do sit down. I would very much like to begin my tale, if that is all right with you, my friend."

The speaker was a man stood on a table in the centre of the room. He was dressed in colourful clothes that seemed to contain every shade of red, green, blue and yellow imaginable. His clothes marked his profession. He was a taleweaver. One of a number of travelling minstrels who travelled from village to village spinning the villagers tales of high adventure, comedy and tragedy. The best of such people Tristan had seen were able to draw the audience in so completely that at the end many would swear themselves blind that they had actually been there.

"Are you deaf, drunk, or just plain stupid?" asked the taleweaver, breaking Tristan's train of thought.

"I beg your pardon?"

"You may beg all you like," replied the gaudily dressed man, "but all I wish is for you to be seated."

This brought a smile to the faces of many of the people and some even began laughing. Tristan felt the blood surge to his face as he searched for a place to sit. The weaver made several more sarcastic comments about his state of sobriety, and Tristan was not aided by the fact that the boots were so painful to walk in by now that he had to almost hobble to make it easier.

"Now that we're all settled," said the bard with his eyes on Tristan, "I may continue with the true tale of Sir Caldor the Pure as seen and told by one of my very own ancestors."

Tristan's eyes lit up at this. He had arrived in time for the best tale. Most Taleweavers followed the same order when weaving. They would begin in the afternoon with a humorous, often bawdy tale, then a tragedy and then begin the evening with a rousing tale of Sir Caldor the Pure. An evening of dancing, singing and drinking would then follow this. Then, if the weaver were skilled and well-paid, or just plain drunk, the night would end on a solo ballad.

Tristan's favourite part of the tradition had always been the story of Sir Caldor. He settled down to listen. The taleweaver had just started his version of Sir Caldor's search for Caliburn. Tristan had heard the story before but had never grown tired of it. Of all the stories about Sir Caldor this had remained one of his favourites, and even his knowledge of the true nature of the sword was not going to spoil his enjoyment.

"…and the whips flayed across his back as his cruel goblin masters tried once more to force Caldor to work," said the taleweaver, his voice soft and melodious, "but no matter how hard he worked his tired limbs to move, nothing now could induce them. His energy was now spent.

"Seeing that he was now of no more use to them they threw him out of the mine shaft and on to the snow covered mountainside. A blizzard raged on around him and, unable to move, he began to feel the numbness of cold flow through his body. He was dying, yet he felt no fear. He was the greatest of Toric's sons and knew not the meaning of fear, or despair. He called out to the Great Father to give him the power to free his people, and his cry was answered. From the howling winds came His voice. From the flames of Caldor's soul came His spirit. From the mountain stone rose up His body. From the ice and snow spread His flowing white robes. Toric stood before him blazing fire and light in all His glory. All became still and there, in that isolated spot, did He first speak to Caldor.

"'THOU ART THE GREATEST OF ALL MY SONS AND FOR THY LIFE COMES THE GREATEST OF QUESTS.

"'THOU MUST GO UNTO THE HEART OF ALL MOUNTAINS WHERE THOU MUST COMPLETE TEN TASKS. IF THOU DOEST SUCCEED THEN THOU MUST FLY WITH THE BIRD WITHOUT WINGS TO THE VERY CENTRE OF THE MOUNTAIN OF FLAME. UPON THY ARRIVAL SHALL I BEQUEATH UNTO THOU THE GREATEST OF ALL GIFTS. WITH IT THOU SHALT LEAD THY PEOPLE OUT OF THE TYRANNY OF THY CAPTORS AND FOUND THE GREATEST OF ALL NATIONS.'

"Upon saying this the Great Lord returned from whence he came and left Caldor to make his long trek to the heart of the mountains."

"I'd love to tell them what really happened. For Cal's sake don't they know there weren't even any snow covered mountains in Grel-Chin at that time."

"Shhh! I'm trying to listen," hissed Tristan angrily.

Several people sat near him turned and looked at him in confusion.

What are you doing here? I thought I left you at the campsite.

"Just because I'm not near you doesn't mean I can't speak to you. I can speak to people up to fifty miles from me," replied Caliburn.

Fine, thought Tristan. *Go speak to one of them then. I left you at the campsite so that I could have a moment's peace.*

"Sorry!"

With that the presence of Caliburn left his mind and he was once again caught up in the weave and flow of the story.

IX

Groltch sat huddled by the small fire as the cold night began to descend.

"Hope Tris not be too much longer," he said in Caldorian, his teeth beginning to chatter violently. "Grol…Yi will go mad hotherwise. Halready talking with myself."

"Don't worry, I'll keep you company," said a familiar voice in his mind.

"Yi thought that you honly talk to Tris now," said Groltch.

After several days of Tris talking to himself he had noticed that it was not solely incoherent ramblings, but that he was probably talking to the sword.

"Why you want speak with me?"

"I thought I'd talk to someone who wasn't so boring and uptight as Tris. And besides, it looked like you could do with the company."

"Thanks. That would be nice."

Suddenly something strange dawned on him.

"You're speaking my language!" he said, reverting to his own tongue.

"Of course!" replied Caliburn.

"How?"

"I was created by your people as part of the treaty between your people and those of Tris. The human forged sword still lies in your lands somewhere, so I've been led to believe," replied the sword.

"So the great sword Caliburn was created by Tu'ran-tha," said Groltch with a malicious smile. "I bet Tris hates that!"

"He'll get over it."

"He? So Tris is male?" asked Groltch, relieved to find out at last.

The sword seemed to buzz in his head and Groltch decided it must be laughing.

"What's so funny?" he asked suspiciously.

"Sorry, it's just that Tristan's been having exactly the same problem as you!"

"Oh!" replied Groltch, not really seeing the humour of the whole thing. Then again it was a sword, so it wasn't necessarily going to have the same view of life as him.

"What shall we do now?"

"I think I'll teach you the proper way to speak Caldorian," replied Caliburn.

"But Tris has started that already," he replied, feeling more than a little confused.

"He's been teaching you what he calls High Caldorian, but what I call total and

utter gibberish," replied Caliburn in Caldorian.

"What gib…ber…rish mean Caliburn?" asked Groltch, also returning to the human tongue.

"That shall be our first lesson," replied Caliburn, *"and please, call me Cal."*

X

Tristan sat mesmerised by the tale as it had unfolded. He had been with Caldor when he had completed the ten tasks. He had felt despair when Caldor almost died of an infected wound and joy when a man healed him he had once saved. Now he felt exhilaration as he flew with Caldor, who was being carried to the heart of the Fire Mountain by a woman who could grow wings and fly.

"…Caldor felt the wind whipping through his golden hair as he sped through the air in the arms of the woman he loved. Over vast mountains they soared, and through the deep valleys, past waterfalls, forests and seas. Far and wide they flew, never stopping or slowing in speed.

"Finally they reached the great island that was the fiery mountain. They alighted at its base for they knew it was here that they must part. Yet for ten more days they remained in the arms of each other before the day of their parting arrived. Both ached with sorrow yet knew they must follow the needs of destiny.

"'I leave you now,' she said as tears trickled down her soft face, 'but you shall never be parted from me. We are tied together with strong bonds and you will remain in my heart forever.'

"He placed in her hand the Ring of Fealthe with which she could return to her people, honour intact and with that his fair love grew her wings and leapt high into the sky. Caldor watched until he could see her no more then began the long climb up the mountain, sorrow weighing him down.

"Long and hard was his climb, yet never once did he forsake his goal. When the rocks tumbled down from on high, thrown by the Demons of Thenril, he held tight to the rock, using the Shield of Harn to protect him. When a demon lord leapt at him, screeching in fury he held up the Spear of Lokus and let fly. It struck strong and true, and none leapt down on him again.

"Suddenly Thenril himself caused the mountain to spew fire yet with the Boots of Fury he outran it. At last he had reached the cave within the mountain and the last obstacle in his quest. The great daemon sat there and demanded a fee. From his pack he removed the great Crown of Thrawn, which the daemon then grabbed and vanished. The mountain trembled in fury and rage and Caldor smiled in joy at his trick. For many years now would Thenril be unable to plot for now he had a usurper challenging his reign.

"Caldor walked through the cavern and emerged in the crater of bubbling magma. As he reached the edge he looked for his gift, yet saw nothing but fire and rock. He knelt down before Toric and prayed for His guidance. When he opened his eyes he saw God's reply. In the centre of the bubbling pool of molten rock rose a magnificent sword that glowed in magical light held aloft by a pale hand robed in white satin.

"'THIS SWORD SHALL BE NAMED CALIBURN AND AS LONG AS A MAN OF PURE HEART DOTH WIELD IT, HE SHALL NEVER KNOW DEFEAT. HE SHALL ALWAYS BE STRONG AND MY HAND SHALL ALWAYS GUIDE HIM. COME AND TAKE THY REWARD.'

Caldor stepped onto the burning liquid not fearing that he would sink or burn. He found it to be solid and cool underfoot and so walked further onto the lake of flames. He strode to the pool's centre and grasped the sword in both hands. The pale hand sank back down as he raised his mighty gift above his head. It began to glow with a dazzling white light that flowed out and enveloped him. He shone as brilliantly as the sun and could be seen by all for miles around. Exultation filled him, though part would never feel joy again. He spoke out and his words rang out across the world.

"'I do swear by this holy sword that I shall carve my people a kingdom so that they might never be slaves again.'

"Suddenly lightening flashed from the heavens and struck the mighty blade, infusing his oath with the power of Toric. The resulting light was so bright that it lit up the world for all to see. Then he began his return to Grelchin, ready to forge the land of his dreams, a tale not to be spun on this day."

The taleweaver ended his telling with a flourish then bowed deeply to the breathless audience. For several minutes the audience sat in rapt amazement before first one, then another, began to applaud. Suddenly the room was filled with the sounds of cheers and clapping hands. The taleweaver wiped the sweat from his brow, bowing as he did, then went to the bar for a drink.

After the applause had died down and the people had realised that the show had ended many left to continue the celebrations outside. They were soon followed by the taleweaver who carried a stringed instrument out with him. Within moments music, singing and dancing could be heard.

Those that remained sat talking in awe about the tale they had just heard and the quality of its telling. Tristan was glad the taleweaver's skill was being appreciated, even if it was only for a few minutes. In his own opinion it was one of the best taleweavings he had ever heard. Even though he now knew something of the *true* tale of the sword's origin he had still found himself enthralled by the almost hypnotic voice of the taleweaver. It also reminded him of his childhood and had brought back vivid memories that he had thought forever dulled by Treatment. He was suddenly consumed with homesickness and the urge to return to those happier days.

He swallowed back the emotions and walked to the small bar. When the barman finally came to serve him he ordered a flagon of local ale and sat on a bar stool. As he drank he quietly observed the people in the room. They were all just sat, casually drinking, talking and laughing with their neighbours. A barmaid bustled past him holding a large tray to her hip and he found himself staring at her. It was not the girl that caught his attention though, but the ring on her finger. It was only a plain wooden one but it reminded him of the ring his father had given him. He slipped his hand into the small pouch hanging from his belt and scooped it up into the palm of his hand. He then casually placed it onto his right index finger. Fortunately, unlike his father's boots, it was quite large and slipped on easily. He took the opportunity to look at it once again. He could not see what was so special about it. It was just a plain band of gold with a thread of silver wrapped around it.

He waited a couple of minutes before drinking the rest of his drink down in one and attracting the attention of the barman. He was a thick set, well-muscled man who looked more suited to working a field than to working a bar.

"How can I help yer?" he asked, his voice deep and gravely.

"I would like the same again, please," he replied, trying to hide his accent as much as he could.

As the large man poured the drink Tristan tried to casually reveal the ring. He had no idea how this was supposed to work so he just left his hand in plain sight.

"You wouldn't happen t'know where I could hire the services of a guide to lead me t'Kelvaria, would you?" he asked, praying to Toric that this would work.

"Kelvaria is it?" replied the barman raising one eyebrow as he spoke. If he had seen the ring he made no show of it. "I reckon that's a long way from 'ere it is. I don' be reckoning you'd find any in this village as would like to leave, but we've folks from all over t'day so yer might be in luck. Go sit at that table at the back there and I'll go take a look-see for yer."

He sat down at the small table indicated by the barman. It was set in the corner of the room, hidden from sight from most people in the room. He sipped his drink and waited. Time seemed to drag on and he ordered a third drink. Just as he was gulping down the last few mouthfuls it, an action he was regretting as he had not drunk in a while and this was a very strong brew, he saw the barman talk to another large man and point in his direction. As the man approached he took the time to study him.

He seemed to be a thick set man, though his general build was difficult to discern due to the thick, dark brown clothing he wore. This was unusual for it was still mid-summer and the day had been warm. His long, tangled and almost black hair and large shaggy beard that grew down to his chest made it difficult as well. What he could see of the face was that it was ragged and ruddy brown in colour. Even the eyes were difficult to see due to the vast overhang of hair.

In his right hand he held a long staff of dark wood that seemed to be partially wrapped up in his long brown hooded cloak. As he sat down Tristan could see that the clothing was largely of some kind of treated leather, yet what immediately took his attention was the ring on the man's right index finger. It was similar in design to the worn his father had given him, yet appeared to be made of some sort of inferior metals to his. The big man placed his hand on the table and waited. Unsure exactly what to do he followed suit. The man's hand briefly touched over the ring and Tristan saw the man jerk his head a little, as if startled, then draw his hand away and remove his ring. Tristan once more copied the man's actions.

"I hear yer lookin' for a guide," said the man, though Tristan could definitely hear the tone of respect within it.

When he spoke his deep voice almost seemed to growl and his smile revealed his gleaming white teeth that seemed to be a little longer and sharper than usual.

"Yes…" replied Tristan uneasily.

"I'm probably the best you'll find in these parts."

This statement was met by a burst of laughter from a drunken young man on the next table. His friends suddenly went exceptionally quiet and all seemed to put some distance between themselves and their friend. He carried on laughing, oblivious to their actions. A shroud of silence fell over the entire room, broken only by the man's laughter.

"How can yer guide someone when yer as blind as a bat?" gasped the man, trying to breathe through the laughter.

Tristan looked back at the large man and peered through the tangled mass of hair that hung from his forehead. He discovered, to his shock, that the man was correct. Though each iris was deep brown in colour, the pupils were both milky white, the most common sign of blindness. The young man on the other table continued laughing until he was almost choking.

There was a flash of movement from the blind man and a dagger flew from his grasp. It whistled past the young man.

"Yer missed!" said the other, doubling over in laughter.

"Check yer right ear," replied the large man, "then bring me back my dagger."

The young man's hand went to his ear and came back covered in blood. He went deathly pale and scurried off to collect the dagger. He found it buried hilt deep in the wall. He pulled it out and then threw it as hard and quickly as he could. The large man merely moved away slightly and caught it with his left hand. He then roared in deep-throated laughter.

"Yer'll need t'be quicker than that t'catch me out." He turned back at Tristan and winked. "I may be blinder than a bat, but like a bat, my other senses make up for it, as yer've no doubt jus' seen."

He extended his hand.

"The name's Belthar and, as I believe I already said, I'm probably the best guide yer'll find in these parts."

XI

The words on the page began to spin before Matthew's eyes as tiredness gradually crept up on him. He was still very weak due to the poison he had drawn from Naithan, but he was determined to find what he was searching for. He had been reading through every book he owned that had references to devices that allowed its wielder to travel on other planes and worlds. Unfortunately nearly every single book he owned that was not a spell book contained at least one reference to such a device. There were also a large number of books in the libraries of Theldar that could also include the information he sought. This meant that it was going to be a long and tedious process.

Ordinarily studying books would not have been a problem for him as it was one of his favourite pastimes. However he had been doing it solidly now for several days and had barely made an impression on the books in his personal library. He was growing very weary of staring at pages and pages of hand printed words of all different sizes. It was also infuriating, because the time spent here could be better spent researching the sceptre. He was sure that Naithan had not realised the full potential of the device, having deemed it of secondary importance. For Cal's sake, the last report of the Shadow had been almost a week ago, and the impression left was that the killings had finished. They even had his accursed dagger, and no knights had been killed in all this time.

However Naithan, seeing knives everywhere, insisted that finding the man was of paramount importance to discovering the plot against him. Matthew was just getting weary of the whole thing. This, coupled with the residual traces of the poison that had proved so resilient to healing spells, meant he was very tired. Even after only five hours of intense study, it was all he could do to keep his eyes open. It was not long before he finally gave up and allowed himself to sleep…

XII

…He was stood in a room looking at a familiar man whose eyes burned with a strange light. It was a man he had not seen in many years.

He gasped in fear as he thought back to the parting words of their last meeting. He started to back away and felt his hands tremble with fear.

"You need not worry," said the man softly. "You have served your king well, as I instructed. I only came to help. I agree with you, the evil man is of secondary importance to the sceptre, therefore I will speed your search."

He felt relief flood through him. He realised that he would not be shown the pain that would follow any betrayal, this time.

"Turn around and ye shall find all that you seek," said the man quietly.

He obeyed and turned round to see the shelves that held his prized books. He just stared in amazement as it floated from the shelf and began moving towards him. He had felt no magic being cast.

When it was close enough to him he studied it intently. It was a dark blue book called *Realms of Shadow and Darkness.* He had no recollection of ever owning a book with that title. It dropped into his hands and the dream ended.

XIII

Matthew suddenly woke up at the desk in the laboratory. How he could have fallen asleep whilst studying he did not know. He looked back to the book he had been reading before he had fallen asleep. Its title had given him hope that providence was smiling on him. It was one of the smaller books he had kept in his collection for years. It was called *Realms of Shadow and Darkness…*

XIV

Groltch was sat trying to make the fire a little larger in an attempt to warm himself up and prevent him from shivering. It was nearing midnight and Tris had yet to return. Cal's presence had left him about half an hour ago. He looked out again to where he had last seen Tris but the light of the fire was making the red-light he used to see at night almost invisible. At that moment he heard the heavy clomping of human footsteps. Judging by the uneven sound it had to be the human knight. He wondered why the human persisted in wearing boots that were just too tight for him. Some five or ten minutes later Tristan emerged from the trees.

"Well?" he asked grumpily. "Find a guide?"

"Yes I did," replied the human.

He could smell alcohol on its…his breath. I…he had been in the warm drinking ale whilst he'd been sat out here in the cold.

"He is called Belthar. He will meet us here in the morning. He is very nice. He is going to bring some boots with him too."

Groltch wondered just how much of their limited money he had spent drinking.

"Suppose Groltch…I have to wear disguise now," he stated, knowing the answer.

The sword had taught him an interesting way of pronouncing the vowel sounds that it had developed with a goblin colleague years ago. It was still difficult, but at least it didn't feel or sound as stupid when he spoke.

"No, that is the best part of it," said Tristan with a triumphant smile. "He is blind and will not even know your race!"

"Blind?" he asked incredulously.

Only a human would hire a blind guide.

"Yes, but it is all right. He can move around just as well as you or me," replied Tris with another smile.

This was unnerving Groltch. In their entire time together he had never seen Tris smile, and now he had done so twice in a row. He had visions of spending half the night looking after a drunk human and the thought wasn't a pleasant one.

"He is also very good with a dagger. You should have seen what he did with it. His aim was deadly accurate. He says that his other senses make up for the loss of his sight."

"Blind?" he asked again.

Tris must be in a worse state than he feared. He was seeing blind men throw daggers with deadly accuracy. Evidently the alcohol must have been playing tricks on his vision. He'd heard that humans were prone to strange false visions, but not usually through the influence of alcohol. Then again, he was human after all…

"Yes, he is blind."

"And how much is this *blind* guide asking for?"

"This is where it gets even better," replied Tristan with his third grin of the day. "He will do it for free!"

"Free?" asked Groltch. "Why?"

Evidently alcohol affected humans' ability to hear as well.

"Err…" it…he replied, as if unsure what to tell him. "The man is a druid and…and…he does not need money…and…he knew my father."

The human seemed to hesitate and Groltch waited for the rest. When it was not forthcoming he let the subject drop. The human was not a very good liar, yet Groltch could see that most of what he had said was true. Groltch had the feeling he had merely omitted parts of the truth, which made him suspicious as to why. But he knew it was pointless trying to find out at the moment, and the part about the druid was interesting. He had known a couple living near his old home, and knew that many, often those gifted with the Sight, were blind. He hadn't realised that humans could become druids too. If it was true then somehow Tristan had managed to get them what was most probably the best guide for miles around.

"I see if he work out when he get here tomorrow," Groltch said with a yawn.

At least he knew this human's sex in advance, so he wouldn't make mistakes. He heard in the back of his mind that strange laughter of the sword again. Cal was almost as strange as a human, though not quite.

"You cook own food and take watch first," he said and then rolled over, closing his eyes.

He heard the human's nightly mutterings as usual, though the alcohol had made him loud. Groltch had forgotten that the human had drunk tonight. He realised that if he slept, he would awaken to find the human asleep again, as he had on their first night together. Sighing he got up to find the human already well on his way to sleep. Just as Tris began to snore Groltch swore he heard the human mutter something about new boots.

Humans. Would anyone ever figure them out?

XV

It was well into the morning after hours of study that Matthew had finally found what he had been looking for. It was in a section entitled "*Methods of Transportation into the Realms of Shadow*". It had been a treatise some four hundred pages long, much of it pseudo-magical nonsense. It had listed some thirteen magical devices and after researching and confirming the whereabouts of eleven of them, had decided, more on instinct than anything else, on the one it had to be. The passages about it read:

> *The most powerful and effective device that I have studied in this field was called the Ring of Shadow. It be a large golden ring inlaid with onyx. Its origins I was unable to ascertain in the short space of time it was in my care. What is known of its history after my care is as follows. It was stolen from my laboratory and ended up in the hands of the evil Elflord Kaneril where it was used in his failed attempt to escape the victorious Southern armies as they marched into Veltharia at the close of the Second Elf-War.*

Matthew's eyes had widened in interest upon reading this. He had read about both Kaneril and the second Elf-War in his search for information on the sceptre and its whereabouts. It had to be more than a coincidence that the same creature had used both objects last. It had been this that had finally decided him on it being the object used by the Shadow, along with the belief that the Shadow Crown, which he would have to wear, would have been mentioned in the few eyewitness accounts. The passage continued thus:

> *Due to it being removed from my care and its subsequent disappearance, the list of abilities here is merely a combination of rumour, legend and my extensive knowledge of magical items. This means that the list is largely conjecture and probably incomplete.*
>
> *I believe that the ring's primary function was to allow one or more person to have access to the plane of shadow. It does so by creating portals out of existing shadows (unlike the shadow creating properties of the crown) through which the bearer and one or more other person may enter. All passengers would have to remain in contact with the bearer for the ring also acts as protection for the wielder from the dangers of the Shadow plane. (See above for the complete description of the Shadow Plane and its dangers.) If the ring is lost whilst on the Shadow Plane then the bearer is trapped and doomed to death in this horrifying land. Fortunately, for the bearer that is, the ring has protection for such a case and will only leave a person's finger if removed by that person himself, and may only pass ownership if given from one to another. If the bearer dies with the ring, it is possible that it will remain with them forever. (I believe this has something to do with its creation prophecy.)*
>
> *The ring has several unusual side effects for the bearer. As long as he or she is in contact with the ring then part of their mind remains in the Plane of Shadow. This makes it impossible to read the bearer's thoughts, even through direct contact. It also allows the bearer to become a shadow and in that form can go anywhere where the light is enough to make shadows. In a room with no shadows the bearer is forced to resume their original form.*

It went on further to detail possible dangerous side effects, but this did not really bother Matthew. He was annoyed that there was no discourse on the symbiotic properties of the ring, and had decided that most of this man's writings to be a meaningless, shallow collection of myth and superstition. However, the information would be enough to direct his search to more useful texts and he was already forming a plan of capture in his head. He returned the book to its correct place on the shelf then entered his bedroom, sitting on the bed to put on his boots. Or so had been his intention. He was still feeling fatigued and on deciding to lay down for just a minute or two he found himself fast asleep, and he did not awaken till the afternoon.

XVI

Tristan was woken up very early by the goblin, who was shaking him violently around like some rag doll. He groaned, as the morning light seemed to pierce straight through his eyes into his brain.

"Big ugly human coming," it whispered fearfully. "It look fierce. Have sword ready in case it attacks!"

Tristan looked up and, on managing to focus his bleary eyes, saw Belthar approaching.

"Calm down, it is only Belthar," he replied with a yawn, shuddering as what felt like a thousand titans beat upon his skull with heavy clubs.

The creature's eyes opened wide in amazement.

"It…he no walk like he blind," it said, sounding astounded.

"He says he uses all of his druidic senses and that staff to move around safely," replied Tristan who, with a start, suddenly remembered the creature's so called *sense of humour.* "By the way, do not make jokes about his condition, for the sake of Caldor. The last person to try that very nearly lost his ear."

"You not worry, I not dare say nothing," whispered the creature as the big man emerged into their campsite.

Tristan, hoping that the creature did not intend the literal meaning of the double negative statement it had employed, stood up sleepily and greeted Belthar with a shaking handshake. The world seemed to spin around before him. He knew he would come to regret those drinks he had drunk the night before.

"Good mornin', my friend. I didn't arrive too early did I?" asked the big man, his booming voice doing nothing for Tristan's headache.

"No, it is fine. We were hoping for an early start," replied Tristan. "May I introduce to you my companion, Greltch…"

"Groltch."

"I beg your pardon?"

"You says Greltch. My name Groltch."

"Did I say that?" he asked, genuinely surprised. "I am sorry. I had not forgotten. It is just I am still a little sleepy from my abrupt awakening."

"Liar!" said the sword.

Please, do not start again, he thought, but only said, "As I was saying, this is my… companion…Grultch."

"Groltch."

"Groltch," repeated Tristan.

"Pleased t'meet yer Gr…friend," replied Belthar and shook the creature's hand, making it wince at his strong grip. "Now yer'd be a goblin then, wouldn't yer?"

Both Tristan and the goblin looked at the big man in fear.

"How do you know that?" he asked, trying to sound as calm as he could.

"I may be blind, but my nose is as good, if not better, than yours and I'd know a goblin from a mile off," replied Belthar who, seeming to sense their fear, added quickly, "Don't yer worry now. I'd figured as much last night. That's the usual reason a person with that typ'a ring comes lookin' fer help. I've taken more than one t'Kelvaria before."

Tristan felt relieved. The goblin seemed to be more offended than anything, probably due to the insulting, but truthful, comment on its smell. With the mention of the ring it looked at him suspiciously.

"Of course, this'll be the first renegade knight I've taken though," continued the big man with a smile.

Tristan went cold in fear and he looked again at Belthar. He was sure the druid was enjoying revealing the strength of his observational powers.

"What makes you say that I am knight?" he asked, trying harder still to sound calm and composed. "And what makes you think that if I am one, that I am an errant knight?"

"Well firstly, yer armour's almost as easy to smell as yer friend here," he replied, smiling viciously at the goblin. "And as t'yer status, only a renegade, sorry, errant knight would be travelling in disguise with a goblin."

"Why are you willing to help me then, if you are so certain that I am a deserter?" he asked, confused.

"Because any who's bein' hunted by the king, fer whatever reason, is a friend t'me, that's why," replied Belthar.

"Why do you dislike the king then?"

Everywhere he went it seemed there were people who disliked the king.

"'Cause it's him who's destroying acres of natural wilderness in his attempts to increase the size of his armies. He's huntin' down bears an' wolves as creatures of Thenril, and at the rate he's going, he could well hunt them from these woods completely."

Tristan just could not believe this. His father would never allow such a thing. At that moment he was reminded of the weariness in his father's face, the streaks of grey, and most of all, the ring that was in his possession. He wondered just exactly what his father had involved himself with, and just how deeply.

"I suppose the King's Rangers have little to say in this matter?" he asked, knowing the answer already.

"What do you think?" asked Belthar. "They're the ones who round up game to ensure the king's own hunting grounds aren't depleted when he rides out."

"Why is it I get the feeling that I am the only person who does not know what truly happens in Caldor?" he asked softly.

"Quite possibly because you're the only person who doesn't," replied Caliburn.

Unusually for the sword, it sounded quite saddened and did not throw in an ironic comment.

"We're gonna have t'do something about yer friend here," said Belthar.

Tristan ignored the insult. He was no goblin friend.

"Luckily I happen to know someone who can sort it out for us, and he doesn't live to far from here either," continued the blind man.

"Certainly," replied Tristan. "I just have to get on some fresher clothing."

He was turning to leave when a pair of boots landed heavily on the ground before him.

"There are the boots, as promised," said Belthar, chuckling. "It'll save yer from hobbling round like a lame duck from now on."

He picked up the boots and removed himself to the bushes. He still disliked the idea of undressing in front of a goblin, though the creature had shown no such compunction with him. It did not take long and he quickly returned to the others. The dangerous glances he had seen sent from the goblin to the druid made him feel that a fight could be imminent. Upon arriving he found nothing was further from the truth. They were both roaring in laughter.

"What is so amusing?" he asked suspiciously, believing himself to be part of whatever joke they had shared.

"Yer wouldn't understand," replied Belthar, gasping for breath. "It's a private joke."

"I see," said Tristan coldly, his suspicions having been confirmed.

He turned to Galahad and groomed him as best he could. He fed him then loaded up the saddle, armour and packs onto its back. He hated to see this magnificent animal reduced to the status of a packhorse. Having finished, he turned back to the others. They were still chuckling at their *private* joke.

"Shall we go and meet this friend of yours then Belthar?"

"Yes. I think we'd best be leaving 'cause I think you were spotted by a Returner last night in the inn."

"A what?" asked Tristan.

"Yer a knight and yer don't know what a Returner is?" asked Belthar, sounding amazed. "Does it help if I use the term Knight Errant?"

That helped a great deal. A Knight-Errant was a knight sent upon special quests for the king and country. They would often be gone years, and some never returned. The term errant was also used for knights like himself who had deserted, though placed before knight, as a derogatory adjective.

"Almost correct," said the sword.

Why only almost? he asked silently.

'Because Knight Errant is the disguised term for those who are returned to their village to watch for traitors, and keep the king, or their immediate superior, of the local situation," explained the sword.

"You mean they are spies?" asked Tristan, so shocked he spoke out loud.

"That's one word for 'em, yes" replied Belthar. He obviously believed the question had been aimed for him. "By now the king 'imself could be aware of yer whereabouts."

"Then we had best be on our way then," said Tristan, his confused mind barely noticing the impact of another belief shattering revelation. "Well? What are we waiting for? Caldor's return? Let us be on our way."

Without a word Belthar turned and moved silently out into the woods. Though leaning fairly heavily on the staff, he still moved sure footedly and, if Tristan had not known better, he would have never thought him to be blind.

Groltch followed immediately, moving equally as silently and steady footed. Tristan noticed, however, that the previous laughter had left its face, and was now regarding Belthar with a suspicious eye. The initiative having been taken, Tristan shrugged his shoulders and followed, leading Galahad at the rear.

A shroud of silence fell upon the party as they moved, and Tristan began to feel very heavy footed and clumsy compared with his two companions and was aware of every noisy step he took. He turned his thoughts away from his own ineptitude to the other more important problems facing him. All his beliefs, the foundations of who he thought he was were being demolished one by one, leaving nothing but a hollow emptiness in their wake. For the first time in his life, he felt genuine uncertainty about almost everything. His future was empty, and he no longer knew his function in life. He felt displaced and out of time. He had no goal, no purpose, and had never felt so alone and afraid. He tried to turn over possible solutions in his mind. As far as he could see life as he knew it was over.

A deep-throated whisper from Belthar forced him from his inner turmoil.

"We'll have t'stop here for a while, 'cause I can hear knights approaching from up the road."

A nod from Groltch in agreement convinced Tristan, though he as yet could hear nothing. It was then that he noticed they were near a highway. He guessed that this was probably the Souward Highway that connected Theldar to Kelvaria. It was then that he noticed the other to whispering furiously to each other.

"If fight comes Groltch need weapon and Tris not give Groltch one."

The big man sighed and reluctantly passed the creature a dagger.

"Be sure yer use it against the right humans though," whispered Belthar with a growl.

"Oh, I will, not you worry," replied the goblin with a malicious glint in his eyes.

"Shut up, both of you," hissed Tristan angrily. "There will be no fighting. I will not allow it."

"If they attack us, we'll need t'defend ourselves, even the little one here," replied Belthar, fixing his sightless gaze unerringly at Tristan.

Groltch seemed angered by the patronising term used by the big man, but seemed to pass it over to present a united front against Tristan. He was not about to be stared down by a blind peasant and stupid goblin.

"I will not fight or kill any knights and I do not want anyone else to either," he said defiantly. "I will not fight someone who once trusted in me."

"Start talking any louder and yer might have t'fight 'em 'cause with the racket yer're making is sure to attract 'em," hissed Belthar, his sharp teeth seeming to gleam menacingly.

"Groltch need weapon," put in the creature stubbornly. "But if fight comes, I swear by Toric that I not kill unless not have other choice."

Fortunately Tristan was still too angered to register the blasphemous use of his God's name by the worshiper of Thenril.

"I do not care. Have a weapon if you so desire, but if a fight breaks out, I will not aid you in anyway whatsoever."

"Fine, then yer'll die," retorted the big man, "'Cause they don't give tupence fer yer outdated honour."

The big man turned to Groltch.

"Here, catch," he said, tossing the creature another sheathed dagger that seemed to appear from nowhere.

The creature caught it deftly and in one motion, unsheathed it and its companion before crouching in a defensive stance, holding the now naked blades in readiness.

"If I die then that is how Toric wills it to be so," said Tristan, more to himself than anyone else.

The creature's sharp ears must have picked it up for it looked at him in shock and anger. Tristan barely noticed, for he was too preoccupied with the thought of fighting knights.

"Shhh, they're here," whispered Belthar.

Tristan crouched down and peered out through the bushes at the approaching knights. He inhaled sharply at the sight of the commanding knight's shield. It was Sar Karene and she had to have been sent in search of him…

XVII

"May we halt for a moment, Sar?" asked Red Knight Jax. "A horse in back has picked up a stone. It'll go lame if left."

Karene Skellan, Blue Knight, and Captain of this troop agreed to the request almost with resignation. This journey seemed fraught with difficulties. Upon returning to Theldar she had found the palace in uproar and had been unable to make her report for two days. Upon finally gaining admittance to the king, she had been personally instructed to oversee the arrangements and duty rosters for the newly arrived knights from Belthanor. This had taken yet another day, yet the king's personal request, for that was what it had been, was not to be refused. Having finally gotten everything in order, she was able to leave and began at full speed towards Kelvaria. However, several sections of the road were un-tithed, and therefore in ill repair, and twice already they had been forced to stop to remove stones from a horse's hoof.

She sighed. Tristan had probably left for Sol by sea now.

To take her thoughts from the possibility, she took the brief stop as an opportunity to survey the surrounding landscape. She had no fear of an ambush, and highwaymen had not been a major problem since the time of James I when the notorious Dark Knight had been captured and redirected. Yet, as she informed the High Priest, she was always on guard, for in times of war, strange things often happened, such as the flight of the King's Knight. She still could not fathom his reasons for rescuing so foul a creature as that.

Her thoughts were distracted by what she thought was a flash of metal in the trees to the left. She quickly channelled in Toric's power and used it to enhance her sight. The sudden nearness of everything that had just moments ago been so distant still disorientated her and it took her a few moments to adjust. She scanned the area closely, but only found bushes. Adding to the magic, she forced herself to see heat patterns, in search of the red to white glow of warmth emitted from animal bodies. Whilst she saw many creatures, nothing was large enough to be of threat to them. She reluctantly released the exhilarating energy and allowed her vision to return to normal.

"We have finished and are ready to proceed, Sar" said the Red Knight, forcing her gaze from the trees.

"Very well, we ride on," she replied.

"Yes Sar," replied the other, with a swift bow.

She returned the bow and allowed him to return to his position as they moved off. As they went she looked back at that spot again, certain she had somehow missed something. Yet she could not waste time. If Tristan was indeed travelling cross-country, then she might still have a chance to capture him. Turning her thoughts towards this goal she set the horse to a light gallop. The position of King's Knight still lay in her grasp…

XVIII

Tristan watched the knights ride away with confusion. Sar Karene had looked straight in their direction and had stared at them for almost four or five minutes. How could she have failed to see them? The cover here, whilst good, certainly could not have held up to such close scrutiny. Even the goblin had looked surprised when they had left. Belthar had been the only one unaware of the danger, not having been able to see her gaze. So why…

He grabbed hold of a nearby bush, feeling sick. His head spun and throbbed in pain. The feeling died out, but not completely, leaving him feeling even more hung-over. He really should not have drunk as much as he had last night.

"You all right?" asked the goblin, actually sounding concerned.

"Yes, fine," he replied. "They've gone now, so we can cross."

The goblin looked at him in amazement and he heard a strange buzzing in his ears. What had he said?

"Yer right, let's go," said Belthar, moving out to cross the road with the goblin following immediately.

Confused by everything that had happened he followed behind, trying to ignore his throbbing head and vowing never to drink ever again.

XIX

The man known only as the Shadow woke up screaming. The dreams had plagued him, hounding him, time and time again. For almost a week he had resisted, despite all the pain, all the suffering. They had gradually changed, bit by bit, as if probing him for some weakness, yet the image of that young girl's face had made him strong, until now. Her image had been in the last dream, the face full of hope. He had seen behind her the mother. The female knight had laughed as his own mother had burned to death. He had not deprived the young girl of a mother, but opened her eyes to the truth of the world, that knights were corrupt and evil. By liberating the girl from her evil parent, she would grow wise to the world and be a start in the renewal, the rebirth of Caldor from the decadent depths its monarchy and their knights had dragged them. The corruption they spread to those such as the girl was yet another reason he had to destroy them. And they would suffer…

XX

They entered a small clearing in the forest about mid-afternoon. In the centre was a small grey, half-timbered cottage with a thatch roof. All the doors and windows were open, though from this distance he could see nothing of what lay beyond them. Alongside the cottage ran a small, sparkling stream of water, and surrounding it were thousands of pieces of wood and stone, much of it blackened almost beyond recognition. The rest of the clearing was filled with lush green grass and an abundance of summer flowers, including what looked like a bush of wild roses. Near where they entered the clearing lay a small black kitten basking in the afternoon sunlight. Upon their entrance it merely rolled over and observed them with a half opened eye.

Suddenly a large explosion sounded from within the cottage, shattering the relative peace of the clearing. The house seemed to shake slightly and bits of the wooden panelling and thatch began to fall off. At the same time a small human like figure surrounded in blue light could be seen flying backwards out of the front door. It landed in a crumpled heap by the stream, the blue glow fading to nothing. Belthar rushed towards the figure with unerring accuracy. Tristan and the goblin were too stunned to move.

Belthar rapidly reached the crumpled figure and was helping it to the stream. By this time Tristan had recovered from his shock and began moving to the two by the stream. It was obvious that it had to be a sorcerer of some kind and, whilst not wanting anything to do with it, did not want to incur his or her wrath.

When he reached them he saw that the figure seemed to be a young man, though his individual features were too blackened from the explosion for him to get a clear look. Belthar was presently helping the wizard to drink some water and the goblin was nowhere nearby. He took a look round whilst the druid washed some of the soot from the wizard's face and saw that the goblin was still stood wide-eyed with shock at the edge of the clearing.

Tristan returned his gaze to the *wizard*. He was surprised to see that the person before him was more of a boy than a man. He had untidy, sandy blond hair that tumbled haphazardly above his shoulders. He was tall and thin and his clothes seemed to hang limply about his small frame. He wore a large shirt and trousers with a pair of tight fitted boots. They were all grey, except for the boots that were dark brown. It was obvious that the clothes had once been white and that the explosions were probably quite frequent. He wondered how the boy had escaped being Redirected.

The most striking thing about him, however, was his face and in particular, his eyes. His face was small and appeared quite delicate in structure. He had high, prominent cheekbones and a small nose and mouth. As for the eyes, they were slightly almond shaped and deep violet in colour, and it seemed as though the large black pupils would swallow them up. This was definitely not a normal human being. He took his gaze away with a shudder.

The young man seemed uncomfortable under the scrutiny of his visitors and nervously invited him into the house. His voice soft and melodious, making it hard for Tristan to hear everything he said. Tristan agreed to follow them in then returned to the edge of the clearing and unsaddled his horse. He then left Galahad to graze and dragged the still stunned goblin into the house.

They entered into a small, sparse living room and sat on the floor, the only chair having been taken by Belthar. It was here that the druid introduced them to his friend.

"May I introduce to you, Matthius the Magnificent," he said with a large flourish.

Matthius seemed more than a little embarrassed.

"Just call me Matt."

"Just what we need," muttered Tristan to himself, his suspicions now confirmed. "A wizard."

'Be quiet, he could come in useful,' said Caliburn. *'Now get on with it and introduce yourself.'*

"My name is Tristan Pathfinder, formerly King's Knight and th…"

'NO!' screamed the sword in shock.

"The King's Knight?" asked the two humans in unison.

"Yes…"

"You've brought a knight into my house," said Matthius, angrily turning to Belthar. "And not just any knight. Blood and Hellfire! You've brought the bloody King's Knight here, of all people! I thought we were friends!"

"It's all right," replied Belthar, sounding a little shaken. "He'll not take yer in, he's hiding from 'em himself…I think."

"You think?" replied the boy angrily. "You never think."

"Belthar is correct," replied Tristan quickly. "I would not turn you in. Please believe me."

I am crawling to a wizard, he thought in disgust.

'Because you need him,' replied the sword.

"Well I guess it's too late now," replied the boy in resignation. "Who's the goblin?"

"Grultch," answered Tristan.

"Groltch!"

"Groltch."

Matthius looked hard at the goblin, as if only really seeing it for the first time. Tristan could see the creature physically flinch at the strange eyes.

"So I gather you need my help."

"Yes," replied Belthar.

"In what way?"

"We need t'disguise the little 'un here, 'specially the smell, and I thought yer magic would do jus' the job."

The goblin shot the big man such a dark angry look that Tristan feared that the creature would attack him. Fortunately the creature just got up and paced angrily round the room.

"I'm afraid I can't do that," replied Matthius.

"Why not?" asked Belthar. "Yer've done it before."

"I'm sorry," replied Matthius. "I'm not going to leave my home to help a man who would slam me into a Chamber at the first available opportunity, and as for the goblin; you'll have to rid him of his smell the old fashioned way. I've an old bath tub he can use."

"Groltch not take no bath!" snapped the goblin angrily, storming out of the house and slamming the door.

"Then I believe it's time for you to follow the goblin's actions and leave," replied Matthius haughtily to Belthar.

"I don't suppose we could stay here the night. There's a few *Light* problems I've to discuss with you," said Belthar gently. "And that way we might be able t'persuade our goblin friend to have a bath."

"All right," replied Matthius slowly. "But only for one night and if I'm captured then by Toric I swear to you that you'll bloody pay."

Tristan looked at the boy in horror. Not only did he use magic, but he was irreverent to the High Lord himself. At that moment they heard the goblin shout outside.

"Groltch not take one more bath! I happy as am!"

"Well I tried but he wouldn't listen to me," said Caliburn, entering Tristan's mind.

Belthar looked at Tristan.

"We're gonna have t'find a way t'make him wash regular, like us."

"Oh that won't be necessary," said Caliburn.

Why? Asked Tristan.

"Because all goblins have fluids in their skin that keeps them clean. It's only when they are so dirty that their skin gets clogged up that they need a bath. In fact frequent washing often destroys the fluids, causing many skin irritations."

"We will not need to wash it regularly," replied Tristan, trying not to think of why the sword would know such things. "All we need do is wash it once, then its own body will take over and keep him clean."

Belthar looked at him questioningly, his milky white pupils fixing themselves unerringly to his own. Tristan merely shrugged. The eyes left him and the big man looked thoughtfully into space.

"Very well then," he said after a moment's pause. "What we need is a plan to get him soaking wet, and I think I have jus' the one."

Belthar's last statement was accompanied by a wink that did not put Tristan at ease in the slightest.

XXI

Matthew finished relating to Naithan everything that he had learned from the *Realms of Shadow and Darkness*. He also mentioned some of the possible traps they could use, if the information was verified. Much to Matthew's annoyance his friend dismissed them all with a wave of his hand.

"The problem is we don't know how to lure him out of his hole. His attacks are at random, with no visible pattern and, as you pointed out, he hasn't killed in a week. We now need more information on the man himself," Naithan said, frowning in concentration. "We'll have to increase the reward for the information anyone can supply on him, as long as it leads to his capture."

"That's a good idea. Shall I go and organise it?" asked Matthew, not really feeling the enthusiasm he was displaying. "I think two hundred mareks should be enough."

"No, you need to conserve your strength until the arrival of the ambassadors. I believe they are due to arrive *unexpectedly* some two days early, meaning the conference is only three days away. I'll get Malcolm to see to it," replied Naithan. "You ensure you have a good night's sleep. I don't want you going back over that book again. You almost wasted away when you found that goblin manuscript mentioning the sceptre."

"Yes, my great and wise king," replied Matthew with a bow and a smile.

Naithan often complained about the mothering attitude of Luca, but could be just as bad, if not worse, than him on occasions. This time it was welcomed, however. The reward would do nothing but attract vultures, and he had no intention of going over that badly written book again. He was not even sure why he kept it in his collection.

Naithan smiled and gave a resigned shake of his head.

"What am I to do with you?" he asked.

"Make me the Merlin?" asked Matthew with a sly smile.

"When we have the sceptre that will be my first act," replied Naithan. "Now go to bed, by order of the king."

Matthew bowed and walked silently towards his room. Naithan was right. One day he would be Merlin, but for now there was still plenty of research to be done.

XXII

The two moons rose into the sky above Theldar. One was full and the other half, the time of full conjunction merely weeks away. Their combined light filled the streets with shadows. This made them the ideal hunting ground for the man whose name was spoken in whispers.

The Shadow had returned and on this night the streets would run red with blood.

CHAPTER FIVE: Magic and Meetings

I

As the red morning sun sent its light creeping slowly out across the marble city, a horrific scream broke through the almost silent shroud of fear that had smothered Theldar that night. As the light crept silently through the streets, it slowly revealed the horrors that the darkness had concealed. Near the docks, not far from the inner wall, the first such scene was revealed. A knight sat cradling the dying form of a companion whose stomach wound was taking a painfully long time to kill her. He had been luckier, the tendons of his legs merely having been severed, though he knew it was likely he would never walk again. In a darkened alley the body of a knight lay still, the hands clutching the gashed throat that had been her demise, the face frozen in twisted agony. On the opposite side of the city yet another body could be seen, hanging by rope from a ladder that had been wedged across an alley. In the Square of Caldor, knights were gathering together the bodies of an entire patrol that lay scattered about the marble statue, its white stone flecked with the red of blood. One of the patrol members had the misfortune to be a survivor, his mind torn apart in madness at the horrors he had witnessed.

A morning mist began to wind its way through the streets, its tendril like fingers reaching out and clasping at all that dared walk on this day. The dawn's red light diffused through the vapour, turning it a shade of blood red, as if the city itself were bleeding. High upon the tall temple dome a dark figure could be seen, its presence mocking the beautiful and sacred symbol of Toric. In its hands could be seen a newly crafted knife, its shine dulled by the drying blood on its blade. Any seeing this figure would feel dread in their heart, for it would tell them that this man, this "shadow" had returned, and that it had barely begun its day's work.

II

...The village lay about him in ruins, the charred and blackened bodies scattered everywhere. He ran to the house of his *engar*, half blinded by the tears he had shed for his family. He collapsed to his knees and clasped the body of his beloved close to his breast, his betrothal gift still hanging round her neck. It was all too much to bear and he broke down completely, overwhelmed by grief and tears. How long he wept he did not know, yet when he had calmed enough to see and think even remotely clearly, he noticed that not all his people had been killed...

III

The wariness induced by his training caused Groltch to break off the dream, and the pain it brought. His training had been so intense that he had developed *Mistah*, the almost instinctive sixth sense that warned him of danger, even when sleeping. Unfortunately this time it came too late. By the time he had woken, a matter of less than a second, hands had already grabbed him. He was hauled up and felt himself being carried. He struggled violently, managing to strike one of his assailants and upon hearing a roaring curse, realised who one of them was.

So that's Belthar's game! He thought fearfully. *I knew I shouldn't have dropped my guard!*

The big man obviously had some plan with him, probably to do with some human druidic traditional sacrifice or something. He bit at the hand and a loud curse followed it. At last he could see and some of the panic left him. He felt he could master this situation if he remained calm. Looking around he saw that the humans had turned on him. All of them! He struggled violently, but realised they had learned from his first attempt, and were holding him with great strength. Suddenly the hands were gone and he felt himself flying through the air. Panic gripped him as he struck the ground only to find it parted around him. Water! They planned to drown him. Panic the like of which he had never felt flooded through him as the water closed around his head. He knew he was doomed. He couldn't swim and had always feared deep pools of water. Water clogged his nose and mouth and he found himself choking as the water began filling his lungs. His brain started to go numb and dizzy as it became starved of that life giving air. He heard cruel laughter from the shore and knew his death was near. His eyes closed and he felt his consciousness drift away. A strange sense of calm filled him and he felt distant and cold.

At that moment hands grabbed him and he was hauled to his feet. He heard a familiar voice raised in anger, though he barely comprehended the meaning. Then the human looked at him.

"Are you all right?" asked the man in that strange language.

The voice broke through the dreamy haziness and he felt his mind begin to slowly clear.

"Yes," he croaked, coughing out water. "What happened?"

"Belthar felt you needed a bath and that this was the best way. I tried to stop him."

Groltch looked round and saw the big man walking towards him.

"I'm very sorry, my friend, but 'twas only two feet o'water. I didn't think yer'd react the way yer did," said the druid, looking genuinely sorrowful.

Groltch glared at the human angrily before looking down. Two feet of water, it barely reached his waist. Suddenly feeling rather foolish he began laughing, largely in hysteria, but partly in embarrassment. He felt very giddy as the adrenaline slowly drained away and he knew that he would have collapsed if the human hadn't held him up.

IV

Tristan held tightly to the hysterical goblin, worried that fear had finally deprived it of what little sense it already had. He glared angrily at Belthar, who merely shrugged apologetically, and Tristan fumed inwardly. He had spent the whole night trying to discover the big man's surprise, even consulting the sword, who refused point blank, for the first time, to meddle in the affairs of humans. He had awoken this morning to hear the goblin struggling and curses vile enough to draw the Eye of Thenril himself! Despite his protests, and attempt to remove the creature from their grasp, they had succeeded in throwing Groltch in the stream, the results of which he now had to deal with.

"Pass soap, Belthar," said the creature defiantly.

Surprised, Tristan looked at Groltch and saw that same look of pride and courage in his eyes that Tristan had seen when Groltch had been marched to his execution. The goblin turned and, seeming to notice for the first time that he was still being supported, broke free of Tristan's grip.

"We are again in *Match'nah*," said Groltch solemnly. "I stay with you till debt repaid."

Tristan did not like the sound of that. He wanted to be rid of the creature as soon as possible, but, in the hopes of creating some form of unity between them, accepted the creature's hand and bowed his head formally. Seemingly satisfied, the creature then turned to its task of washing, humming to itself softly. Not wanting to let that particularly irritable habit get on his nerves, he moved out of the water and returned to the house.

V

Sar Gemma, newly promoted to the rank of Green Knight, looked out across the Norward highway that led towards Teldin from the north gate. Unlike many of her fellow knights, she actually quite enjoyed guard duty, especially First Watch atop the so-called *Seeing Tower.* She loved the silence and the grand panoramic view it offered. She also loved the long seeing device, marvelling at how close it made distant objects seem. It was a new device, invented by someone or other in Kolth, and worked completely without magic. It truly was a marvel. She scanned up the road, extending the device as far as it would go and caught a flash of metal. Waiting a few minutes she saw the beginnings of what looked like a column of Kolthon infantry moving down the road. The captain's instructions had been correct. The foreign ambassadors were arriving, and two days early at that. She replaced the device and turned to inform her captain of the news.

VI

The Shadow cursed his luck. The guard had moved unexpectedly, and he had missed his chance. That move had saved her life, though next time she would not be so lucky. His reflexes had truly slowed down quite considerably, evidently due to tiredness. But the hunger for vengeance had not yet been satiated, so he vanished into the shadows in search of his next victim…

VII

Tristan finished drying himself off as he entered the small house. As he passed through the door he felt something rub up against his leg. He looked down and saw Matthius' little kitten circling round his legs. It looked up at him with large green eyes and opened its mouth in a small squeal that Tristan took to be its attempt at a meow. He stooped down and ruffled its soft fur. The creature rolled onto its side and began purring.

"I don't care!" cried a voice from another room, startling Tristan. "Didn't you hear him? He's the King's Knight, for Cal's sake! I'm a wizard! You know what that means don't you? I'll be Redirected! It's bad enough that I live this close to Selene as it is, but they're too scared to accuse anyone of magic-use anymore, not with Cleric Anya's leadership!"

Loathed to eavesdrop, he started to turn and leave, but curiosity made him stay, for he still wished to know exactly why they wished to help him escape.

"I don't know!" said the sword in his head, sounding its usual droll self. *"First you ask me to spy on their minds and then you crouch down eavesdropping like*

some young child. I thought you were supposed to be…"

Shut up and be quiet! snapped Tristan angrily. *If you had told me what was on his mind then Groltch could have been saved the humiliating display he was forced into today!*

The sword left his mind quietly, which worried him. Caliburn never left his mind quietly, especially when it had such a golden opportunity as this to tease him. He pushed it to the back of his mind and turned his attention to the voices.

"Calm down," replied the gruff voice of Belthar. "I'm sure it'll be fine. Anyone with that ring's in it far too deep to risk it turnin' yer in!"

"How do you know it was the correct ring?" asked Matthius sounding angry. "You're blind!"

"You know exactly how I found out!" replied Belthar, actually sounding a little hurt.

"I'm sorry, I shouldn't have said that, but there's still no way I'm going with you."

Tristan lost track of the conversation for a few minutes. What had they meant about the ring? He moved his hand from the kitten and reached for the ring to take another look. The kitten looked up at him in disgust for having stopped petting it. He ignored it and looked closely at the ring, yet could find nothing truly distinguishing about it. Having been left alone, the kitten began circling round Tristan's legs and rubbing its head against his knees. He began petting it again absently. What had his father gotten himself into?

"No Belthar, no!" shouted Matthius, breaking his concentration. "I don't care if the milk's spilt! I'm not going anywhere! It's all right for you. You're used to stomping round in woods and such. You've been doing it all your life! You are a…"

Matthius stopped as Tristan sneezed loudly. He looked at the kitten accusingly, yet it just stared up at him with its big, green, innocent eyes. He rose up, putting the ring into his pouch as if he had just found it, trying to cover his impoliteness. He waited for Caliburn to say something, as it would usually, but oddly, nothing was forthcoming. This was puzzling to say the least. He wondered if there was something wrong with the sword.

"Is everything all right?" he called out, tying to sound a little concerned. "It is just that I heard shouting and thought…"

"Everything's fine," broke in Belthar as he entered the room.

"Good. I believe Groltch has almost finished bathing, so it might be a good idea to finish the preparations to leave."

"Sure fine," said Belthar testily. "Whatever you say."

Matthius had entered the room by now and was pointedly ignoring the big man. The sorcerer looked at Tristan, as if searching for some clue as to how much he had heard. Tristan began to feel very uncomfortable caught as he was in the gaze of those eyes. They seemed very penetrating, as if they were slicing through the layers of his mind, making him feel suddenly very naked. He was suddenly filled with the feeling that the young boy was in fact much older than he looked. He shuddered and looked away.

"Blood and Hellfire!" swore Matthius, causing Tristan to look back at the young man in disgust. Someone should really have taught him some manners.

He noticed the young man seemed to be very worried and was fumbling in the many pouches that hung from his belt. He pulled out something that looked like coloured sand and threw it at Tristan, mumbling something that just had to be an incantation. He flinched and reached for Caliburn, but found the sword seemed somehow stuck in its scabbard.

"Leave him be," snapped the sword testily. *"I've been waiting for him to do this for some time now."*

Do what? he asked, fear swelling up inside him. He feared magic more than anything in the whole of Loden, including goats.

"Wait and see," continued the sword, still sounding irritated. Suddenly its tone softened. *"Don't worry, it'll not harm you, in fact, it will do you a lot of good, and I wouldn't let him harm you, whatever you think."*

The sand sped towards him, glittering in the light of the morning sun that shone in through the west-facing window. Its sparkling light seemed to merge together to create a glowing blue line that coalesced to form a halo around his head. Almost petrified by the sight Tristan stood, watching in amazement as the blue glowing sand suddenly shot from his head and formed a line leading from his head to the roof. He heard Matthius curse again, someone was definitely going to have to teach him some manners and soon, and reach for his pouches again. The sorcerer pulled out something he could not quite see and began the muttering of yet another spell. Tristan hoped he could keep from fainting in fear as yet another spell was hurled at him. It took all his training to remain calm as he felt the magic swirl round him. He could even see the air around Matthius distorting and shimming as it would on a hot day. He felt anger welling up within him and noticed that Matthius' eyes widened in shock.

"Calm down!" said the sword in his head. *"The magic can be blocked if you try and resist!"* Tristan tried to calm down and thought he heard the sword mutter something like *"Of all the times to start independently!"* as it faded from his mind.

He forced himself into the calming meditative stance he had been taught in training, allowing all thoughts, all feelings to drain from his body. As he did so he felt a sudden surge of energy rush through his body, seeming to suck energy from him as it did. He opened his eyes in fear then saw that a large sphere of crackling blue energy had formed around his head. As he stared in horror, it surged up the line of glowing sand and exploded through the roof of the cottage, causing a shower of straw and thatch to shower down around them. Matthius looked as shocked as he felt. What had the boy done?

"Matthew had better be prepared for that one, or the boy may have just saved Groltch the effect of killing the king!" said the sword, sounding genuinely shocked.

What do you mean? Asked Tristan, confused. Yet, as usual, the sword remained silent, leaving Tristan alone to try and puzzle out what it meant.

"What did he do?" asked Tristan, so worried he forgot to speak with his thoughts.

"The High Priest had established a mind link with you," replied the boy, sounding more than a little scared. "I think I just broke it."

"Broke it?" asked the sword incredulously. *"He just shattered one of the most powerful thought link spells as if it were thin glass, and sent back a sting capable of disintegrating the High Priest himself. And I think he tapped in…"*The sword trailed off without finishing the thought. That did not worry Tristan though. Matthius could kill the High Priest like that. Fear flowed through him in an icy river. He was glad the young man was staying behind.

It was then that he noticed that the young man was packing rather hurriedly. His body felt like it had been enclosed in a block of ice as the fear began to change to terror.

"You have decided to come with us?" he asked, unable to keep the tremor of fear from his voice.

"Well I have no choice now, do I?" snapped Matthius angrily. "Whatever happens at the palace, they're sure to come hunting for me soon, and I'd rather not find myself thrown in a Chamber, thank you." The young man glared at Belthar accusingly, though the big man seemed not to notice. "Come on then, let's be going."

He snatched up the hastily packed bags and gently scooped the kitten into his arms, which began purring as he did so. At that moment, Groltch entered the building, drying his hair with a towel. Despite its initial objections, the goblin had certainly done a good job of cleaning itself up. It…he looked almost civilised.

"You coming too then?" asked the goblin suspiciously.

"Yes, so get ready and let's go!" snapped the young wizard.

Tristan tried not to appear hurried as he packed his bags. He had no intention of letting anyone see how scared he felt. A cold pit seemed to have opened in his stomach, and he felt weak and dizzy. Whatever the boy had done to him he would show no weakness. He finished packing his clothes and moved into the bright morning sun, yet even that could not dispel the cold sense of fear that now grasped him firmly in its hand.

VIII

Energy came spiralling down his thought link with incredible force and speed. Panic gripped Matthew as he hurriedly raced to complete the wards of protection around himself. The magic came with difficulty, another problem of the poison that could now be a fatal one. He knew that if he failed, all would be lost. Energy swirled round him, pushing at him, striking at the wards as he put them up. Three shattered immediately and he was force to hastily erect three more. He hoped these would hold. They just had to hold, for he had exhausted what little energy he had…

IX

"It is like a war zone, your Majesty," said the reporting knight. "We've discovered some thirty knights dead or dying, and reports are still coming in." Thirty knights. Blood and Hellfire, thirty knights in one day. They could not afford to keep losing such numbers. At this rate, the war would have to be called off within days. The ambassadors' visit would certainly have been wasted. "We've cleared the bodies from the parade route as best we can, and many are washing down the streets to clear the blood." The blood of his knights stained the streets of his own city. This "shadow" would pay when caught, and for a long, long time. "We have still enough knights to make the parade, though some have had to be drafted in from the northern barracks, and they are not entirely ready. They may make mistakes."

The Blue Knight actually looked nervous when she said this. He raised his hand in a command of silence, and she stopped and bowed.

"Very good," replied the king, concealing his anger. It was not worth cursing the messenger, despite what he might feel. Yet the Shadow's attacks had one beneficial side effect. The ambassadors had arrived early, in an attempt to surprise him and put him on lower ground in the negotiations. He had been prepared for this, but commanding knights who were proud of their abilities to ride and manoeuvre in perfect formation to make deliberate mistakes would have been difficult. At least, with knights genuinely unprepared, mistakes would seem natural, as if they truly had been caught off guard. He noticed the knight still bowed before him. "Are the preparations ready for their arrival?"

"Yes, Sire," she replied. "We will guard them every step of the way."

"Very good. Return to your post, Sar Shoran."

The knight seemed surprised that he knew her name, and pleased as well. It was a simple trick, but one that paid back in three fold. He ensured he knew the name of every knight who might be sent to speak to him. To know their name was to encourage them, to make them feel he was aware of them and their problems, as well as their achievements. It was a simple trick that boosted his image among his troops. If only other problems could be solved simply. He sighed wistfully he watched as the knight bowed, then span on her heel and marched from the palace.

"They've arrived then, your Majesty," said a voice behind him.

Naithan knew it was not really a question. His Spymaster never asked questions. More often than not the man knew the answers before him. He did not even turn to see him, knowing that he would be cloaked in the shadows nearby. Not that Naithan was worried. He knew that his Spymaster was tied to him almost as tightly as Matthew.

"Yes. Your scouts were correct about their advanced positions, though how your men knew when mine did not I'll never know." He knew better than to expect an answer. His Spymaster was effective because even the king did not know his methods, or his identity. Yet the man was tied to him, a bond that could one day be broken, but not yet. "I don't suppose you would care to tell me how my preparations are coming along?"

The man always seemed to be prepared for every question he asked in advance, with papers and reports when requested. He suspected magic was involved somehow, for the man could not be omniscient. It was true that he had somehow managed to have a report on the cactus rose flower already prepared when Naithan had asked him, just to throw the man off balance. Such a thing had seemed impossible, yet the man had had a report on it, waiting on the top of the pile, no least. Only in the search for the Shadow had he come up short, and Naithan had not entirely discounted the possibility that one day soon he would walk in with the Shadow in chains.

"Certainly, your Majesty," replied the Spymaster. Naithan was certain he had made a mocking bow behind his back. Naithan bit down his temper. There were some forms of behaviour unacceptable between a king and a servant, no matter how they were linked. Yet he needed the man, for now. "Everything is as planned. The ceremony will be enough to ensure you do not lose any honour, but will still look frayed at the edges. They will no doubt think they have you at a disadvantage, and will probably press for the meeting to be moved forward tomorrow. My advice would be to accept, and let them make the mistake of over-confidence."

"Thank you, I believe that was the plan. You may go now."

There was no doubt the man had already gone. One day, when the war was won, and Toric victorious, people such as him would not be needed. His thoughts were interrupted by a loud scream from Matthew's quarters. His arm went numb and cold fear ran through him. He ran as fast as his legs would carry him, not caring about the indignity of it all. Sometimes that blasted link with Matthew was more of a threat than security. He flung open the door and raced into the room. He found his friend cradling his head with blood seeping from his ears. As he looked up he saw that his friend was incredibly pale.

"Are you all right?" he asked worriedly.

"Fine!" replied Matthew sourly. "But it seems our knight has enlisted the aid of a wizard, and quite a powerful one at that. Karene will be no match for him. I will have to go to Kelvaria personally to deal with it. If I hadn't moved quickly enough he could have…"

Naithan did not let him finish that disturbing thought.

"You may go to Kelvaria in two days. It is likely the meeting will be held on the morrow, so I hope you will be ready."

"Of course I will," snapped Matthew. "He may have been powerful, but that's all it was. There had been no skill to the spell. Just speed and strength."

Naithan glowered at him. Why today of all days did all his servants and courtiers seem so disrespectful?

"Very well. Put on your best robes of office and meet me in the courtyard of the fountain in five minutes. No. On second thoughts, go to the audience chamber and ensure the room is in order. Make it seem like we are rushing to get everything ready."

"As you wish," said Matthew with a small bow.

Suddenly Naithan regretted being so cold and commanding. Matthew was his friend after all, one of the few he could truly trust, and he had just suffered a shock. It was too late to go back now though, the ambassadors' entourage would be reaching the north gate even now. As he turned to leave he heard Matthew berating himself for lack of preparation. At least he had survived to learn from it, as the saying went. He turned and marched off towards the central courtyard to meet the ambassadors.

X

The Shadow held back in the darkness, cautiously observing the knight before him. The pain in his arm was enough to make him wary. The last knight he had attacked had been alert enough to spin and attack him. One knight alone would not have been enough, but his companion had leapt out, seemingly from nowhere, and attacked. It was not the first such trap he had encountered, yet with his reactions slowed down due to tiredness, he had found it difficult to kill them, taking a slash in the arm for his troubles. This knight definitely seemed alone, yet he seemed to be waiting for someone. The Shadow moved himself to a better position to see. This would have to be the last one today.

XI

Marie Romano walked along in open-mouthed wonder at the beautiful streets of Theldar. Though told about the glorious city from a young age, seeing it was the only way to believe it, and now she had, she believed she would never see a more beautiful place next to the Celestial Palace, the realm of the afterlife. She knew she would never leave here, not that she had anywhere to go to. She had lived her entire life in a village that had been called Ashby, before *he* had destroyed it. The worst of it had been that he had once been her betrothed, and she had once thought him the perfect man. Evidently she had been wrong, even though she had been partly responsible for his change in character. However, no crime on her part called for what he had done to the village, but at least he had died for his crimes. Before it had all began she would never have believed someone deserved death, but he had definitely changed that view. She choked back the tears as memories of her family and what he had done to them flooded back.

No, she would be strong. She had almost died of grief when she had returned to the village that day, yet that would have made his crime complete. Her dreams had led her to this wondrous city, where a new life awaited. True, the streets were not paved with gold, and she had certainly seen poverty near *The Dolphins' Wake,* the small inn in which she had rented a room, yet she was sure it was possible to make good here. The carnival atmosphere of the day had also stirred her spirits. According to Madame Croates, the landlady of the inn, the rumour was that folk from foreign parts were coming to see the king and a parade was expected. Everywhere people were hurrying about, trying to put up banners and decorations. Apparently they had arrived earlier than expected.

As she made her way through the crowd she saw a knight stood alone, something they had not done in days, yet that was not what made her stare. Behind him she was certain she had glimpsed a dark figure crouched close by him. The image filled her with a sense of nameless dread, and she felt it would be best to inform the knight, as he seemed unaware of the danger she felt sure he was in. A black shadow seemed to swallow the knight for a split second and she knew she would be too late…

XII

He had to act now. The woman had seen him and soon his chance would be gone. He stepped up behind the knight and drove his blood stained dagger deep into his back, tearing a kidney apart. The knight dropped to the floor with a strangled cry of pain and the Shadow's attention turned to the witness who had forced his hand. His eyes locked with hers and he felt a stab of ice cold recognition slice straight into his heart. The smiling blue eyes; the golden hair cascading round the shoulders; brief moments of joy before his holy mission had begun. He froze, locked in his place as questions bombarded his mind. Why here, and why now? What did it all mean? What should he do?

A shout broke through his paralysis as another knight came charging towards him, sword drawn. The Shadow turned to the alley to dive into the shadows but to his dismay found it was suddenly filled with light. Magic. Magic had robbed him of his escape route. Panic gripped him and he frantically looked round, desperate for help. The shadow of the knight loomed towards him and the Shadow smiled in relief. The fool had forgotten his own shadow. He threw himself to the ground at the shadow, willing the ring to life. It flared up in a rainbow coloured spray of light that surrounded him and the doorway to the dark realm opened up before him. He felt a sudden jerk backward as a hand grabbed at him, but the realm's hold on him was too strong, and he was pulled through.

XIII

Marie stood in stunned amazement at the spot where the two men had disappeared. Yet what had stunned her was not the magic, but the man, the killer. It just had to have been the man they called the Shadow, yet she knew him. She had thought him dead, but she had been wrong. Fear, confusion and sadness flooded through her, leaving her in a state of near panic. She turned and fled down the street.

XIV

Colours seemed to leech out of everything around him, swirling and spinning, mingling and meshing into a nauseating pattern. His eyes throbbed and his stomach clenched tightly together, though he had become used to these feelings by now. The sounds emanating from the knight behind him showed that he was obviously not faring as well, a pleasing thought to the Shadow. A sickened knight was a weakened knight and therefore less of a threat in straight fight. A fight that he had merely postponed by this trip. He looked at the ring on his finger, watching what little colour it had leech away, following the strange inversion, as the onyx runes became a dazzling white and the pale gold a dark black. He had not known it could bring others to the realm to which he now travelled. It was not a surprise, he knew little of it save the dream, but it would be interesting to discover if it possessed other powers.

A flash of black disrupted his thoughts and the hand on his shirt released its grip. He spun round to face his unwanted companion and was startled. The man looked strange in this world of black and white, for he still retained his colour. Admittedly they were pale and faded, yet this hint of colour in a world without made him seem as if wearing the gaudiest of clothes. The Shadow watched the man in amusement, as he looked this way and that at this realm, for he must have looked the same on his first visit. For the ignorant, this was a perilous realm, and this knight was certainly in danger. Yet the Shadow allowed him time to look around, knowing it would take more than a few minutes for a mind to grow accustomed to this land. In most physical respects it was identical to the realm they had just left. This was an exact copy of the street in Theldar they had just left, even to the newly laid piles of rubbish in the alley, and it was situated in exactly the same area as it was in the true Theldar. Yet other than the physical look, it was completely different than from home. For one thing, there were no colours, only blacks and whites with shades of grey. Even stranger was that the extremes of white and black played reverse roles here. In Caldor, the sun was almost completely white, yet here, almost completely black and set in a grey sky. Nights however, brought white skies with black stars. This even extended to the shadows, the lighter areas around marking where they lay. Temperatures too were strange. The coldest place on a sunny day was in the black light of the sun, the shadows providing gentle warmth that often took the edge off the mid-summer chill, were there anybody here to take advantage.

This was the other difference; people. In Theldar, on a day like this, the streets would be filled with people all rushing to see the parade, yet here, nothing. There were things that lived here, of many sorts. Strange, shapeless forms, grey and almost transparent could often be seen, and were always drawn to him on arrival. On his first visit they had surrounded him, reaching out to touch him, with strange, wailing like noises that were terrifyingly human. The ring had flared up in light and protected him, yet he could never cease wondering if there was a limit to this protection. It was this fear that had always made him avoid the other, often gigantic creatures he had occasionally glimpsed in the distance or, as on one occasion, almost ran straight into one as he had entered.

"Where am I?" asked the knight, his shaking voice breaking the Shadow's thoughts.

"The Land of the Dead," he replied, noting with satisfaction the sudden look of fear on the knight's face. Even knights, it seemed, believed in old superstitions. "But don't worry, you'll soon be joining them."

The knight drew his sword and dropped into a stance, showing a sense of courage the Shadow would not have credited him with. It was said that one slight wound was enough to bring Thenril's evil gaze upon trespassers in his own lands, and even the Shadow had been almost insensible with fear on his first visit. The Shadow drew his rarely used sword from its scabbard and barely managed to defend against the knight's opening strike. A twinge of fear struck him, for in an open fight he stood little chance against a well-trained opponent. A flurry of attacks flew out at him and the Shadow realised that the knight knew his superiority and aimed to kill quickly. He looked round, desperately seeking advantage or shade, but realised in horror he had been manoeuvred away from any such escape route. He felt panic rising inside, and his head swam, tiredness catching him up. His attention wavered and he felt an icy stab of pain strike his left shoulder as the knight took advantage. The pain merged with the confusion in his mind and he rocked unsteadily on his feet as all thoughts merged and swirled. He was open to the killing strike. Fortunately the knight's superstition saved him, as the young man suddenly withdrew the attack, looking around as if expecting Thenril to suddenly appear. This gave the Shadow enough time to recover, though barely in time to ward away the next strike.

The knight attacked and attacked with increasing vigour, his training evidently overriding his fear of this land. The Shadow was cut again and again, the blood beginning to pour from the wounds. Suddenly the world span as the lack of blood and sleep combined to make him almost insensible, and he felt the icy cold cobbled street strike his face. His vision swam and as he watched the knight approach him he saw his own blood pooling out before him. To his dazed mind it seemed as if the strikingly rich red colour drained away as it sank between the cobbles, and he knew that death was upon him. Yet no deathblow came and it was then that he realised the knight needed him alive to get home. He felt the man's hands upon him and healing energies flowed through his body. He felt the wounds closing, and whilst not completely, it was enough to ensure his survival. The knight had raised him up and was asking him something, yet consciousness was fast fading and all he could see were grey mists that seemed to be enclosing his vision.

Fear brought him back to sensibility. The grey mist had not been an imagined sight, it was them. The knight had not seen them and was still staring angrily at him.

"How do we get…"

His words were cut off as the grey, shapeless forms took hold of him. Several reached for the Shadow, but his ring flared in warning and they moved back slowly. The Shadow's relief was short lived, however. As he watched, more shapeless forms grabbed at the knight's body. They seemed to take on human-like forms with legs and arms, yet instead of fingers they had claws. The creatures raked at the now screaming knight. Pieces of flesh and spurts of blood flew from the mass of grey and the screams seemed to last an eternity in this silent place. One of the forms suddenly began to devour the still living human form, tearing up the flesh and gulping it down. The Shadow felt bile rising up in his stomach, yet could not turn away. His mind screamed at his muscles to obey but nothing reacted. Blood ran down his face and into his mouth, the world seemed to spin in madness, then nothing.

All movement ceased and silence followed. He watched the motionless creatures, still paralysed with fear and horror. Then the largest creature turned and made its way towards him. It seemed larger now, and more solid. The Shadow even felt he could see flecks of colour within its grey form. Yet its face was still the shifting, horrifying swirl of diverse, part bestial, part human features. The eyes however, had become fixed, steady. As it moved its head close the Shadow smelled the blood and flesh on its fetid breath, yet it was the eyes, those eyes that held him. The ring on his finger flared and the creature looked down at it. When its eyes returned to his they held anger, yet at the same time pity. Something else struck him at that moment. He had seen these eyes before, on the knight the creatures had just killed. He screamed and crawled backwards, clawing himself into the shadows. He willed the ring to life and sunk into the shadowy doorway, the contents of his stomach emptying as he did. His mind span in horror, unable to cope with sights just witnessed, and as he emerged into the safety of his native realm, his consciousness finally slipped into darkness.

XV

"We're almost there," said the human magician in that hissing voice that was starting to annoy Groltch. "If trouble does break out then we'd best split up and meet back later back along that old eastern trail I showed you. I'll create some sort of diversion if I can then catch you up later."

Groltch glared at the human, disliking being told what to do, then looked at the coin the magician had given him. He trusted that violet-eyed human about as much as the large gruff one, which wasn't saying much. At least the knight had some sense of honour, the other two…

He tried not to get too suspicious, yet the fact was that for some unknown reason the thin human had changed its…his mind and decided to accompany them. They seemed friendly enough on the surface, but there were dark undertones in their conversations with each other and he felt each one was concealing something. At least Tris was honest enough in his open dislike of him.

"Selene? If I recall my history correctly there were a number of witch burnings here during the Revolution, were there not?" asked Tris.

"Yes, it was a terrible thing," replied Matt. "Why do you ask?"

"I was just wondering why they tolerated a wizard on their doorstep. I thought old hatreds were hard to bury," replied Tris, his tone revealing that the villagers were not alone in their dislike of wizards.

"I'm sort of considered a ward against other magicks and such. I sell the villagers charms and such to protect them from incantations and such. It was the same with my master before his death."

Groltch looked at Matt and saw how young and alone he looked. The death of his tenget had affected him deeply.

"When was that?" asked Tris.

"Last year. I've been muddling along as best I can since then."

That statement cleared up some of the questions that had been gnawing at him, such as the human's relative youth and seeming inexperience.

"I suppose that's a good thing about my leaving. I'll be able to join the Great Academy in Kolth and get a new teacher," said the young man under the shadow of breath, Groltch's sensitive ears barely picking the words up.

"Are we going to do something about the goblin before we enter?" asked Tris.

Groltch glared at the human but let the insult pass. He wished that they would stop using that derogatory term for his people

"Oh! I'd forgotten!" said Matt looking genuinely distressed. "This should do it."

The boy began muttering to himself in a strange language that seemed similar to High Shar'antua and started waving his arms and fingers about in an ungainly fashion. Groltch closed his eyes nervously and waited. When nothing happened he opened his eyes to see Tris looking at him in amazement.

"What?" asked Groltch.

"It is incredible! I would never believe he was a goblin!"

Groltch almost strained his neck trying to look at himself but couldn't see anything different and he certainly felt the same as before.

"Let's get a move on, time's awasting," said Belthar sourly, muttering " He certainly don't smell no different!"

Groltch resisted the urge to reach for the dagger at his belt and settled for glaring at the big man. One day these humans would push him too far.

XVI

Fanfares blared out across the city of Theldar and the sounds of music, laughter and shouting filled the afternoon air. Banners hung across many streets and people were lined all the way down the Kingsway, the main road of the city. Stalls had opened up wherever there were people, all selling sweets, decorations and sparkle crackers. In many areas tables had been set out and all the local inhabitants had turned up with food and drink to celebrate this impromptu holiday. Most were dressed in their Torsday best and others in brighter, more colourful clothes often frowned upon in temples. The people lined along the Kingsway all jostled for the best position, children often sat on the shoulders of obliging parents, all in the hope of getting a glimpse of the foreign princes. There were even marketplace rumours that the Solmen had brought some of their great elfants, creatures that were said to be as large as houses. The fanfares blared a second time and an expectant hush fell over the awaiting crowd.

The sound of marching feet soon broke the silence and all eyes turned to the North Gate. Marching at the head of the procession were the famed foot soldiers of the Kolthon Empire, all walking in step and in perfect formation, their ceremonial armour almost glowing in the midday sun. Behind the formidable warriors came the emissary of Kolth, bedecked in the finest tailored uniform, sat within a gilded carriage. To the trained eye it would seem that the man was more than a little uncomfortable with the grandeur of it all and just a bit irritated. That confirmed the suspicion that the Emperor had sent none other than the great Mortan Kractus, famed straight talking Senator of the Begral Province. He also seemed perturbed by the lumbering beast thundering down the road behind his carriage.

Even the most detailed description by the most accomplished taleweaver could not have done the gargantuan creatures justice. Standing at somewhere between twenty and thirty Imperial feet high they dwarfed the entire parade and even some of the buildings alongside. Their large ears flapped their sides lazily and their long trunks hung loosely towards the ground. The large tusks were almost invisible beneath all the jewellery covering them and the earth seemed to tremble as they walked. Most spectacular of all were the fabulous jewelled carriages that were strapped to their backs. In the centre carriage of the three beasts lounged a woman wrapped up in colourful silks, the face veiled so that only the eyes could be seen. To the casual eye she seemed to be relaxing upon the silken cushions around her, enjoying the festivities around her with just enough aloofness as to add an air of mystery. The trained eye, however, caught the occasional glance here and there that, though seeming to be casual, revealed a cautious alertness, as well as a deep probing intelligence behind them. This confirmed reports that Genia Mahjats, First Ambassador of Sol, concubine to the First Prophet of Sol and important member of the Royal Clan, had come to meet with the king. Naithan II of Tara'non was truly honoured today.

Behind the elfants marched the black clad Shar-meer, Royal Guard of Sol, in perfect silence. The only colour in their uniform were the coloured sashes that denoted their life's station and held their long curved swords for which they were famed. Either side of the procession rode the Caldorian Elite knights, their armour shining gloriously, pendants flying from the upright lances, horses in perfect condition. The Knights were of the Royal Regiment, the Falcon's Talons. To the casual eye the knights seemed to be shining perfection that almost put the other companies to shame. The trained eye, however, noted that some occasionally fiddled with their armour that had been obviously donned with haste. There were others who wore armour not completely polished, as if it had not been expected to be used for several days and yet others were forced to calm horses that were in obvious discomfort, as if saddled in haste. Even members of the crowd looked a little confused, as if unaware of what passed before them.

Yes, it was all working splendidly, for the trained eye saw that both ambassadors had noticed these flaws. Not enough to offend, but enough to show surprise. The king's Spymaster smiled whilst moving away from the rooftop vantage point. It was time to write out reports for the king on how best to approach each ambassador. Trumpets flared and the Spymaster knew the king would be almost ready to greet them at the Palace Square. Time was short and there was much to do.

XVII

Cleric Anya stood at the large bay window that looked down on the small village of Selene that she had now governed for some forty years. It still gave her pleasure to watch the life go by, a life which she had been a fully integrated part of as a child. That had been before Lord Arendale's wife had been taken sick and she had been summoned, as the best healer closest to hand, to tend to her. The woman had recovered and in gratitude for her services the Lord had given her this governership. She could still remember her first reactions to what had been a young and handsome lord. She had fancied herself in love and had even cursed his wife's survival in some of her more emotional moments. Feelings she had come to regret upon coming to know her, for she had become a close friend until her death five years ago.

"Sorry to disturb you," said the voice of her maid and lifelong friend May, "but Lord Arendale has arrived to see you."

The tall man walked in moments later, taking Anya's hands and bowing his head to kiss them.

"How are you today, my lord?" she asked.

"The same as ever," he replied. "The back aches, the hearing is going, and matters of state seem more confused and complicated than ever."

"I'm sure you're enjoying every minute of it, and as for that back, it's not as if I've not offered to fix it up for you!" she retorted with a smile. "Is that why you're here?"

"No, I'm afraid not! I've been instructed by the baron himself to search this stretch of land for some renegade knight and a goblin accomplice. Apparently they were last seen near this village so it's my responsibility to track him down. I guess I was just born lucky." The sarcasm in his voice was heightened by the feigned look of resignation on his face. "I don't suppose you could offer some assistance in this matter and save me looking behind every blade of grass before I learn that he left days ago?"

"Well that depends really. If he happens to also own a magnificent white charger and is travelling with a big man and…Matt?"

"You've seen them?"

Anya looked down at Matthius Faldare, who seemed to be giving some sort of farewell hug to his mother. The goblin had been magically disguised, but her magically enhanced eyesight saw straight through the flimsy disguise. What had the young man gotten himself into this time?

"Where?" asked Lord Arendale as he joined her at the window.

"Down in the village square," she replied, her eyes not leaving the boy that she had been forced to magically deliver.

She had also lied for him after discovering his latent magical power on his naming ceremony. Her gift of foresight had shown her that he would be physically weak as an adult and the life of the knighthood would have been too harsh for him. He would have died, as she almost had before it had been discovered her magic came from Toric. She had somehow known Matt would have had no such choice.

"When?" asked the lord, his tone of voice betraying that he had already asked more than once.

"Sorry, my lord," she replied quickly. "It's just that they are down there now."

"What? You can see all the way down there? I have difficulty seeing past the front gate without my glasses on, and I'm sure I'm not that much older than you."

"Well why don't you wear the glasses then, my Lord?" she asked, hoping to stir up another of their old arguments in order to give Matt some time to leave the village.

His look spoke strongly of his views of glasses. He had never been one to give in to weaknesses.

"We'll continue this wonderful conversation later, Blessed Sister, after I've seen to my task."

"As you wish," she replied with a soft sigh. He was a man rarely distracted when there was a task to do.

They bowed their heads in respect and friendship, the forms always had to be obeyed, and he left, shouting orders to his men outside before he had even left the room. She looked back to the village, and her face creased in a frown as she considered a difficult dilemma. It took only one glance at young Matt to make up her mind. She reached out with her will, touching the spiritual energy in the objects around her in which the power of Toric flowed. She gathered a little to her, feeling the light touch of her Lord's power flowing through her, filling her with a sense of joy and peace. She allowed the energy to pass through the amulet she wore, upon which Toric's symbol of a lion's head surrounded by a flaring sun was etched, and sent it spinning down towards Matt. She saw him look round and see the knights. He seemed to shout a warning to his companions and they all turned and fled.

"You're on your own now Matt," she said softly. "Good luck and may Toric guide you."

She knew she would never see the young man again, the curse of foresight striking once more. She turned and went to her favourite seat by the fire. She sat and picked up the novel she had been reading, a new innovation sparked by the intellectual flowering of Kolth a few generations ago aided by their invention of something called a printing press. Though it was an interesting read, age and tiredness caught up with her and she drifted slowly off to sleep.

XVIII

"A little to the left. That's it. Perfect," commented Matthew as he guided the servants in placing the large gilded mirror in the conference room.

Another fanfare blared out, signalling the official meeting between the king and the two ambassadors, distracting him momentarily. The grandness of the whole charade was beginning to grate on Matthew's nerves, though to have treated them any other way would have been to imply insult on the part of the king and the political implications could have been grave. As he looked back he saw the servants almost drop the mirror.

"Be careful!" he snapped, "unless you desire Thenril's Eye to turn on you."

The servants went pale and doubled their efforts to handle the mirror delicately. It was magical and could not be broken by ordinary means, yet the servants' reaction gave him some form of grim satisfaction. Being the High Priest, Mouth of Toric had some advantages, even if he had little real power over the church itself. He gazed at his reflection and felt the desire to test its enchantments again, yet knew the Ambassadors or their aides would probably detect any magic he cast. He just hoped the spells weaved around it would be as undetectable as he hoped. Even Jalim had found detecting them difficult, and his was one of the strongest magicks in the kingdom, next to his own and that strange wizard who had sent back that feedback spike.

"Excuse me, Lord High Priest," said a voice hesitantly behind him.

"Yes?" he asked tersely.

"Sorry to have troubled you, sir," the old man replied, "but the advisors to the ambassadors are here to inspect the meeting room."

They were moving fast. They had to suspect something and it was long believed that his true position and power was well known to the spies of the nophiles, the Caldorian name for the people of the northern lands.

Well he certainly could not risk leaving a spellprint now. He checked himself in the mirror quickly. His unusually dark brown hair was a little unruly, but no more so than usual, and his face seemed fresh, if a little pale and drawn from lack of sleep. He quickly smoothed down his robes and returned his gaze to the servant.

"Very well, let them in."

"Yes sir."

Matthew greeted each one formally, gazing at them deep in the eyes as he did so. Four advisors, two wizards, two priests, to judge by the robes and symbols they wore. He guided them around the room, pointing out the various precautions set up against spying and assassination attempts. Yet as he went his skin prickled at the flow of magic around him, the true reason for their visit. He could even recognize some of the mumbled spells used as they scanned for magical auras. It was very difficult to prevent beads of sweat forming as the energy, visible as slight distortions in the air, swirled around the mirror.

"Is this mirror really necessary?" asked one of the wizards, her accent revealing his Kolthon origins. Wizards of the academy liked to claim independence from individual nations, though they often meddled in the affairs of their former lands and in times of war.

"Yes, I'm afraid this room, by necessity, is rather deep within the palace. It loses a lot of heat and the small windows do little to light the room," Matthew replied, hoping his voice remained level and calm. Both he and Naithan were still very new to their roles, having been in power for only a few years and Matthew had never had to face a test such as this before. "I believe the last ambassador to visit Queen Anne from Kolth had disliked the cold and had sent it to her as a gift. As I gather part of this new learning about light reflection and refraction or something. Apparently the sunlight bounces off this mirror and is sent around the room by the smaller mirrors you see around the ceiling and walls, at least that's what I'm told, it's all rather complicated and I don't really understand it myself."

The lie seemed to be swallowed whole, though probably because the mirror also contained a small Kolthon enchantment. It allowed someone in the Imperial City to watch all that passed in front of it, though the previous High Priest had discovered it and had altered the enchantment so that they had control of what was seen. The wizard looked closely at the mirror and Matthew felt a powerful spell build up and disperse, her eyes widening in surprise. She turned and conferred briefly with her fellow advisors.

"Very well," said a dark skinned Sun Priestess of Sol. "The preparations are adequate, though Ambassador Mahjats will require more comfortable seating as she has been…unwell of late and requires some comfort for the pains with which she still suffers."

Matthew wished that Mishlanese, the Old Tongue still used in diplomatic exchanges, was not so difficult to understand, especially when thickly accented, as the priestess' was.

"It is nothing serious I hope?" he asked, trying to sound genuinely concerned. "For I humbly offer any assistance you require within my powers so that she is in the best of health for the meeting tomorrow."

"Thank you, that would be most kind," replied the man with a slight bow of his head. "Any aid would be most welcome. If you could meet her before supper, I am sure she would be most grateful."

"Anything I can do to be of service," he replied, mimicking the Solman's bow.

So they did not know for certain what his powers were. His predecessor had warned him before her death that this could happen. They would watch him closely and test if his were truly 'god-given' powers. Well, they would be in for a surprise, though he would have to prepare himself, for spiritual magic always came more difficultly to him. He wondered how the High Priests before him had ever managed without such magic to cover their tracks.

The advisors bowed in unison, breaking his thoughts by their movement, and after replying in kind, he was left alone in the room.

"You did well."

The voice behind him made him jump and he span round to see who it was.

"I see your reactions haven't dulled since we last met," said what could only be the king's Spymaster. Matthew could just see a vague outline of someone in the only part of this room that was in shadow.

"What do you want?" he asked, his voice still shaking.

"The portfolios you requested are ready," replied the Spymaster, throwing two neatly bound bundles of paper at him. "As you know the meeting is tomorrow and you had better be prepared by dawn."

Matthew had already ceased to listen though, as his eyes were already probing through the notes in his hands. Somehow the man had obtained exactly the information he needed and had even placed the most important first. He was obviously intelligent and why Naithan allowed him such freedom and to keep his anonymity was a mystery to Matthew. Yet he was good at his work, and had saved him a lot of time, though there was still at least twelve hours work ahead of him. He was not surprised when he found himself sat in his laboratory having walked from the chamber with his nose in his book. He rang the bell chord and ordered Eward to bring him up a mug of the strong black coffee that the Kolthon's liked to drink. It was going to be a long night and he could not afford to sleep.

XIX

Tristan rode through the trees and bushes, half-cursing, half-praising their luck. If Matthius had not seen those guards when he had, they would have most certainly been captured, taking away one of the two confusing options before him, to run or return. So now he was still forced to continue the struggle, with only a goblin, wizard and blind-man as companions.

"Stop moaning and watch where you are going!" said Caliburn in his mind.

Oh yes, he had forgotten the sarcastic *holy* sword that seemed to delight in his troubles and stir them up whenever possible. He could still feel the sword's presence in his mind, its resentful feelings manifesting themselves as a dull, throbbing headache.

"There!" called the goblin in his ear, pointing to a clump of bushes.

Tristan slowed the horse and directed him towards it. As they neared it he realized that the bushes surrounded an old campsite clearing that had probably fallen into disuse about the same time as the old game trail they were following.

"Well, it is as good place as any," he muttered quietly to himself.

"Best place Groltch seen so far," said the creature behind him, revealing once more its incredible hearing.

Tristan made a note to be more cautious about saying things aloud, and dismounted to lead Galahad to the clearing. Once the creature had hopped off the horse Tristan began grooming him, largely for something to do. Looking back at the goblin he saw it had sat down with a stick and had begun whittling away at it with Belthar's dagger. Time passed by slowly and Tristan soon began to find the noise of the metal on wood very irritating. By the time the sun had passed its midday peak and begun its descent towards the eastern lands Tristan felt ready to throttle the hideous creature.

"Groltch not like this," it said, finishing yet another stick, both ends sharpened to points.

"That is: I do not like this," corrected Tristan with a snap of the voice. "What do you dislike?"

"Groltch not trust the others. Something not right. Grol…" It corrected itself swiftly after a glare from Tristan. "I think we should go not with them now and leave now."

Tristan agreed silently and, as the chase had split them up, it was certainly their right. Unfortunately he knew that he needed the other two. He had no idea where they were, and Groltch's magical disguise had disappeared when they had parted ways. Suddenly the bushes beside him exploded outwards, showering him with twigs and leaves. Before the first leaf had settled both he and the goblin had spun to face it, weapons drawn in readiness.

"It's all right," said a familiar voice, and Matthius emerged from the bush. "You could have chosen a spot that was a little more open, I almost ended up inside a tree!"

Both Tristan and the goblin sheathed their weapons slowly, the dislike of the open display of magic apparent on their faces.

"Where's Belthar?" asked Tristan.

"I don't know. I thought he was with you!" replied Matthius.

"No. We have not seen them since we left the village."

"Great. Wonderful," muttered the young wizard. "I got the spell right once, now I've got to try again. Great! I guess I'd better try and fetch him though, but not here. Come on, we're moving to a more open space. I wouldn't want to get Belthar angry by putting *him* inside a tree. Well, what are you standing there for?"

Matthius was out of the clearing and already on the trail before Tristan began to move. Would his soul be tainted by the closeness of this dabbler in the dark arts? He hoped not, for it was tainted enough already.

XX

Lord Arendale was more than a little annoyed. They had lost the knight, but he took a little consolation in having captured his large companion, who was now chained to the ground outside with several thick chains. The man had managed to injure four men before he had been captured, though fortunately none had been killed. Hopefully this man would be able to lead them to the knight, though in his heart he knew it was unlikely. The man had too great a lead now to be caught, the big man had seen to that.

"Sir," called out one of his knights outside in alarm. "Come quickly!"

He emerged from his tent to see all his men stood, pale faced, looking in the direction of the prisoner. He followed their gaze and felt the blood drain from his face. The big man was gone, the chains lying on the ground, yet still staked deeply into the earth. He swallowed back a gulp of fear. Though trained in Belthanor, he had never possessed the talent for magic, and had never found himself at ease in its presence. His men had all been specifically chosen for their lack in such skills and the empty chains seemed to positively glow with magic. He turned back to his tent, deciding that the whole event had not happened, a sentiment that his men would quite happily agree with. He nodded his head in satisfaction. He was best off out of the whole affair.

XXI

Malcolm was fuming. With the arrival of the ambassadors, a date for the next Council meeting would be impossible to get. He cursed the fact that he had nothing to give by way of information to his employer, and he had had his heart set on buying the beautifully carved writing desk he had seen at the market. He decided that he would have to return and see if he could not work up the funds from the Royal Exchequer, though recent changes in the system made such things difficult to do nowadays. It was as he was turning that he heard a girl's voice raised in anger nearby.

"But I tell you it's true! The other knight vanished with him so he can't say I was there, but I tell you, I know who the Shadow is!"

"Yes, I'm sure," replied a bored male voice. "You and every other Tom, Mick and Sally who's seen the reward posters all over the city. Report it to your local garrison or, if you really wish, queue up with the others on the next Torsday Audience and tell the king himself!"

Malcolm could understand the man's irritation. This woman had probably been the hundredth person to come here since the offering of the reward. Yet the incident she mentioned caused alarm bells to ring in his mind. He quickly scanned through the notes in his hands and found that in the list of Shadow related deaths, there was indeed a disappearance. However, it could still be a coincidence, so he would have to make certain. If correct, he could make himself a handsome sum of money, and would not have to risk another visit to the vaults. He tucked the papers back under his arm and went over to introduce himself to her.

XXII

A dark form slipped out behind Malcolm and followed him. It was possible the weasel-faced little man was about to involve himself in something he would be ill prepared to handle, such as his bungling attempts to embezzle the Treasury money. The Spymaster felt that it was definitely time to take a closer eye on the activities of this underestimated viper. It would not take long to get a detailed report in to the king.

XXIII

Naithan slammed down the report he had found on his desk this morning. It seemed that Malcolm had been slightly more intelligent than he had given him credit for, a mistake that needed rectifying, though not now. At this moment he needed a clear, calm head, for the dawn meeting was almost upon him. Malcolm could wait, and the results of his meddling had been minor, though some explained why Tristan had still so far evaded capture. It had been believed by his mother that the Circle of Light had been led behind the scenes by one of the Council Lords, though had never proved the belief. With the circle's involvement in Tristan's continued freedom, it may have been that the Duke of Kempshire, Malcolm's previous Lord, was somehow involved. He made a mental note to speak to the Spymaster to intensify operations in that area. Tristan could be a powerful symbol to a would-be king. Things would be much safer if the meeting was already over and Matthew already in Kelvaria preparing the trap there.

A light tapping on his door disturbed his thoughts and Luca entered. The man looked a little weary, as though he had not slept much. In his arms was the official meeting robe, the white dove on the front being the traditional symbol of truce under which foreign dignitaries met.

"Tis almost time," said the old man, barely concealing a yawn.

He's getting a little too old for this, thought Naithan with sadness, knowing the old man would never retire. *Well hopefully the upcoming voyage will allow him some rest. If I can arrange it with Ambassador Mahjats of course.*

He gazed out of the window as Luca placed the robe over his head and prepared himself for the mental battle of wits ahead of him. He hoped desperately that Matthew would be ready.

XXIV

Matthew looked over the final preparations for the meeting in his laboratory. The various components were ready and assembled close to hand. The door to the room had been sealed so as to prevent any interruption during his work and he felt fresh of mind, even if a little tired of body. He took a seat and finished the cup of Malton tea, its special blend of herbs being one of the reasons his mind was so clear, and ate the rest of the small breakfast Eward had brought to him early this morning. Having finished he took one final look over the notes then cleared his mind of all clutter. As he did so, the one and only lesson he received at the hands of the former High Priest came to his mind.

For magic to work, one must first clear the mind of all clutter, to lessen the chance of being distracted. Then one must draw upon the inner energy that burns within so that the spell can become empowered, gathering it together until every part of the body tingles with the joy that comes from holding the power in control.

For those of the priestly order, such magic would be drawn from without, though Matthew had been forced to learn this the tiresome way with the most boring priest that had ever lived, such magic usually being an anathema to all wizards. For him to draw upon it, as he would have to today, would be hard and tiring, as it seemed in constant conflict with his other magic. He was also careful to measure just how much energy he drew, made especially difficult as he was drawing upon both forms of energy, inner and outer, something magically impossible before him, ensuring that he did not draw too much. To draw too much could lead to madness and even death; sorcery burning the wielder up from within, leaving nothing but a hollow husk; divine energy attacking from without, causing them to explode in flame.

Matthew pushed these thoughts aside as unnecessary distractions, trying to control the fear they brought. Yet fear was not the only emotion brought on by magic, for to hold the energy around you was intoxicating, exhilarating and the most pleasurable, exciting feeling he knew of. Of course, this too had its dangers, for whilst not distracting, the desire to draw more energy was incredible and was a pathway that many wizards had destroyed themselves upon. Using a combined effort of will and practise, he prepared himself for the second stage.

The second stage of magic is the image. For the energy to function, a caster must retain a clear image of the effect he desires in his mind, for this is where the caster begins to shape and mould the energy, to give it form and direction. Without the image, the energy would have no focus, breaking apart before even half-forming, bringing with it often devastating effects.

With this stage, Matthew had never had problems, for he had always had a very vivid imagination. In fact the problems he had faced initially had been to limit his imagination so as to have enough energy to power the grand images that he could create in his mind. As this was a simple spell the image came fast and he was soon ready for the third stage.

The third stage of magic is the setting of form. All spells need size, dimension and direction, which are provided by word. The words are ancient in origin and bind the energy to the form imagined in the mind. Without the words, there is no control; without control, there is only chaos; where chaos rules, anything can and will happen, often with lethal results.

Once again this part was simple for Matthew, though he never allowed himself to become complacent. He had performed this spell countless times and in that could often arise the feeling that it was a simple task, but no task of magic was simple. As he spoke the words seemed to fly from his mouth and take form, binding the raw energy within him, refining it shaping it, constricting and metamorphosing it into a copy of the image in his mind. For speed and direction, Matthew preferred to use his hands and fingers, their movements melding in perfect unison with the words, the energy an almost visible thing in their grasp. Failure in this part could often mean insanity, as the energy would suddenly implode drawing itself back into the body in a random direction and often bringing the caster's mind with it, or worse still, explode outwards, destroying everything around him.

The fourth and penultimate stage is a stage that can be missed, if the caster is in a hurry, or lacking the objects required, though this is the most dangerous and most tiring part. For in this part there is involved a physical component through which the energy can be amplified and leave the caster with more of his own energy for other spells. Those who proceed without, often find themselves very drained, or worse still, that the energy is not constant, fluctuating into wild, random forms of which the caster has little or no control, if they are still alive or sane after the event.

For this part of the spell Matthew had been prepared, his frequent use of this spell meaning the component was of almost always at hand. He placed his hands in the bowl of milky fluid, infusing it with the energy as he did, ready for the final part of the magic, the magic of prophecy.

The Magic of Prophecy is so called because it is, indeed, a separate kind of magic, capable of being cast independently of the other two, though the other two forms both require prophecy. When used alone, it can bring on curses, geas and quests, bestow blessings and blights and perform things seemingly impossible to occur. In the Art, it has a much more significant purpose. Magical energy, once released, cannot survive more than a second unaided, its effect disappearing within the blink of an eye or less. The magic of Prophecy allows spells to sustain themselves until a set of conditions is met. For spells of war, such conditions are met almost instantaneously, yet others can be sustained for minutes, hours, days, years and even generations. It is thus that magical items retain their energies that often exist with obscure prophecies, designed specifically to make it difficult to destroy the item. Some prophecies are so powerful that they eventually warp the events around them to fulfil the conditions, and others have even sought to discover the prophecies to rob powerful men and creatures of their weapons. Such was the case with the mighty Karcalus, who completed twelve tasks, each a part of the prophecy contained in the wand of the last god-king, Makatrutus. This was also believed true of another legendary figure, Tratus, whose mother cast powerful enchantments of invulnerability on him, saying that no weapon could kill him lest it be made of seven year willow and struck him in the left heel at dawn. Of all magic, Prophecy is the most powerful, useful, and volatile of magicks. Always keep this in mind when casting and when empowering it, remember, the more cryptic the prophecy, the more powerful the spell and the more energy it drains. There is many a wizard who became so wrapped up in Prophecy that they drained themselves of all life without knowing, for the energy required is taken painlessly, effortlessly, and no wizard ever truly knows how much it has drained them until the spell is completed.

The most useful of all the advice, Matthew had spent many hours building up stock prophecies for certain spells, so as to know roughly how much energy was drained, though it often varied from spell to spell. The prophecy of this spell was simple enough however. *Till blue eyes look away, all things shall be clear.*

The milky fluid, charged with energy, flew from his hands, washing over the mirror. As it ran down its silvered surface, it began to clear and images could be seen within it. By the time it had covered the mirror, the image had become clearly focused, almost as if he were looking at it through a window. It was of a large room and in the centre were a large table and three chairs. Upon the chairs were sat three people, looking as if in deep conversation. One, a blond haired man with piercing blue eyes had the manner of royalty about him and was smiling as if the conversation was a pleasurable one. The second man in the room was slightly shorter than the other with the dark brown hair and eyes so common to nophiles. His nose was large and slightly hooked, resembling the beak of a hawk, and his face was lean, drawn and clean shaven. By the sour expression on his face, he was plainly irritated, and his twitching fingers indicated an air of impatience about him. The third figure in the room seemed at odds with the whole room. She was lounged comfortably, as if relaxing before an open fire, and her brightly coloured clothes were in direct contrast with the dark, refined clothes of the hawk nosed man, and the simple black and white robe of the king. She seemed to be enjoying the conversation and her eyes seemed to sparkle as she laughed. Her dusky skin added to her exotic beauty, and whilst she was veiled, the thin silk did little to hide the fine boned, delicate features of the face.

Slowly, gradually increasing in volume, sound could be heard emanating from the figures which soon became clearly audible to Matthew and by the time the spell was firmly in place, it was as if they were all seated in the same room, Matthew, Naithan, Ambassador Kractus and Ambassador Mahjats.

"Your Majesty, Lady Ambassador, if we may please now get to the business at hand…" said Kractus, sounding more than just a little irritated.

Good, thought Matthew, *Naithan's playing it just as discussed.*

Mortan Kractus, according to all reports, was an excellent debater, keen minded and intelligent. He was of very strong views and had a way of debating that often ended with his opponents agreeing with his opinions with such vigour that they could barely recall their original opinions. His flaw, however, was his irritation with political niceties. He was a man who liked to get straight to the point, throwing in his idea, listening to criticism and other ideas. He would then go about destroying each and every one of them so that only his idea remained. He hated the Great Game, believing it a waste of time and the worst side of it all was that which could now be seen passing in the form of niceties being bandied between the king and the Ambassador of Sol. As his irritation grew, so did the cracks in his mental armour; cracks through which Matthew intended to enter.

Genia Mahjats was a different matter altogether. The love of her life was the Game, played with often lethal vigour by the Rajas of Sol. It was believed she had been behind the sudden rise of the recent Light of the Heavens, spiritual and material head of the Council of Princes, leaders of the various principalities of Sol. In fact, it was believed that his position was still weak and that this visit was more about gaining a political ally, than a complaint about the goblin war. Yet they could not take the chance that they were wrong, and he would have to subject her mind to the same treatment, a very risky proposition indeed, for her mind would be a maze. She was famed for the talent to talk to a dozen people in the same room, each with differing opinions on the same subject and, by the time she had left, each person present would swear to Thenril himself that she had agreed wholeheartedly with them. Her ability to think in may such ways would give a confusing series of paths to follow that, if wrongly chosen, would leave him lost and trapped; a body without a mind. The only weaknesses he could see was her total belief in the fact none knew of her complete abilities and that none could best her. This arrogance of mind would hopefully be the string to lead him through the maze, as Herassius had used to exit the pyramid maze of Zartheus. This would undoubtedly be the most difficult mind to deal with, but first there was the mind of Ambassador Kractus to play with…

XXV

Ambassador Kractus sat at his desk, feeling very confused. He had achieved exactly what he had expected. The king had signed the Treaty of Renewed Trade and had also, inadvertently, given away the strength of his forces. He had discovered that the assassination of Queen Anne had achieved its aims by removing the strongest wizard in the country (due to the strange funerary rites of this country) and leaving the new king with only a priest in the highest advisory position. The spies in this realm had reported back that whilst magical ability was evident in some of the army officers, it was always of a weak nature, no match for even one weak war wizard. He had also learned the true skills and weaknesses of the new king and could probably have an accurate guess as to how he would react in certain situations. He had battled a tough opponent and won. Yet why was the thrill of victory missing? Why was it the he felt somehow out-manoeuvred; out-debated; that somehow he had lost?

XXVI

Sweat had broken out all over Matthew's body and a very real fear was welling up within him. Ambassador Kractus had been simple, the spell working smoothly, just as planned. The man had even left the meeting early, confident in his victory. Yet from the moment he had started the spell with Genia he had encountered problems. Firstly, he had not expected the sheer number of magical charms, protections, and spells that encased her in an almost impenetrable shield. He could have simply broken through many of them, but to do so would have destroyed many of them and that would have left too many suspicions in the minds of her advisors. He had therefore been required to prod at each layer gently in order to discern weaknesses he could wiggle and squirm through unnoticed. Yet even that had been planned for and on at least three occasions he had almost been caught in spiral charms; enchantments that looked like spell flaws, but were in fact traps that spiralled downward into infinity, dragging his mind with it. It had only been the combined might of both his magicks that he had been able to escape, and even then just barely, for the timing of the two spells to escape had had to be exact. He had finally penetrated the final layer, but after too much time. Matthew was aware that Naithan seemed to be gradually moving out of his depth, the ambassador's agile mind slowly out-manoeuvring the king's. Though he was good at the Great Game, she was much better, and the time when she had him where she wished was fast approaching. Worse still was the fact that she was obviously suspicious, as she had been gradually piecing together information from his unspoken words and gestures.

Unfortunately the problems had not ended with his successful entrance to her mind. To affect the mind as intended, he had to practically merge his mind with hers so that they ran together in tandem and he could offer gentle, persuasive thoughts that would gradually alter her point of view so subtly that she would not know they were not her own. In this way his meddling would be invisible to all but the most detailed and thorough probing spells. The problem was that her complex mind was moving in ways that Matthew could not comprehend. Her purpose and motive seemed in a perpetual state of flux and as her thoughts darted around they would often shoot off in tangents or oblique directions, making it practically impossible for Matthew to attune himself. In fact, whenever he tried to redirect a thought, he would often find it overpowering and that his own thoughts would change to those of hers. Panic clutched at him, its icy claws seeming to constrict his lungs, breaking up the steady, rhythmic breathing needed to maintain perfect focus. His mind, strong and keen as it was, had been outmatched by a mind so alien to his own that he was unable to comprehend it, to match it, and therefore defeat it. In truth, he was finding his own mind and thoughts lessening, becoming merely a tiny oblique part in this swirling mass of thought. Slowly and surely he was losing the battle and with it, his own awareness.

Eyes, burning eyes, glared at him in his mind's eye, cutting through his panic, his fear. With them came a stab of icy pain and in the moment of clarity it seemed to provide, he had an idea; a last desperate gamble. His consciousness floated through the myriad of thoughts until he found one, tiny thought he felt he could use. It was a small thought that most closed minds would have rejected by now, yet here, in this maze, was the small consideration that Naithan was being truthful. Matthew desperately fired what little energy he had left at it, striking it as hard as he could in a vain attempt to enlarge it. The energy merely deflected off of it, knocking the thought a little of course. But this was enough. It struck another thought, becoming stronger and gathering momentum, as thoughts and ideas often do. The new thought grew again as it struck one thought and deflected another and Matthew watched in amazement as a chain reaction began; thought striking thought, each growing, changing in direction as it did. A swirling pattern of chaos and order swirled through the mind and suddenly

Matthew realized he could see a pattern forming. In this whirling, spinning mass there was structure, an answer to a question Matthew could not recall. He felt himself on the verge of a revelation, an unquestionable truth; the ultimate answer. The view began to slip. The prophecy had been fulfilled. He had completed the task. He desperately tried to gather his little remain strength to remain, to see it all through to the end, yet the magic of prophecy was too powerful.

With a sudden flash of pain it was all gone, his consciousness back within his own body, the thoughts and memories of what he saw rapidly fading away. He placed his head in his arms and wept, breaking the mirror's enchantment as he did. By the time the mirror's reflection had returned to normal, all Matthew could remember was a sense of loss and sorrow; an empty yearning for something he could not recall.

CHAPTER SIX: Tricks and Traps

I

Naithan watched with concern as Matthew walked slowly up to the platform set in the centre of his private courtyard leaning heavily on his apprentice Jalim. He seemed to have aged since yesterday. Several grey hairs had appeared where they should not be on one so young. Naithan wondered just how much their victory with the ambassadors had cost his friend. The fact that he had worked a miracle was not in any doubt. Not only had the royal visit to Sol been confirmed, but the implications had been that the Light of Heaven had plans to wed his daughter to Naithan in a marriage of alliance against the possible threat of Kolthon aggression, which would also help Naithan consolidate his own plans. The Kolthon Ambassador, meanwhile, knew only what they had planted. The Spymaster had confirmed this by providing several copies of the reports that the ambassador had sent. Yet looking at Matthew he knew that the magic had somehow aged him, and realised that this may have shortened his own time on Loden. Fear gripped him at the thought and a tingling sensation ran down his arm.

"Are you certain you're fit to go now?" he asked his friend.

"Yes," replied Matthew. "I have to get there soon. You said yourself that you wouldn't leave Tristan's capture to Lewis Hanton. Even your trusted *friend* said he was a risk."

"I know, but is it necessary to go right this minute? If your condition weakens and you are unable to return, you know what the consequences will be."

The king's arm went numb at the thought of it. A blood-link had its merits and certainly ensured the High Priest's loyalty, but in situations like this it could be a real drawback. If other nations discovered that they still used the banned practise, the problems that would ensue would be immense and Matthew could even become an assassin's target. He turned his thoughts away from the terrifying consequences of such actions, lest the Eye of Thenril see them and decide to use them against him…

"Don't worry," replied Matthew, rubbing his arm as if his thoughts echoed those of Naithan. "We'll be fine. I'll be back well within a week."

A week apart was generally harmless enough, but Naithan was worried nonetheless. He watched carefully as Matthew began chanting the spell. The platform he stood on had counterparts in each of the other eight original county capitals, the one in Feranshire was still under construction, and upon them were mosaics of a twelve pointed star within a ten pointed star. In each city, a different point of the ten-pointed star was coloured gold and he had been told that the familiar pattern allowed sorcerers to travel from one city to the next in an instant with almost no danger. He was not sure of the technicalities, and never had been. The realm of magic was left to Matthew to worry about and Naithan was more than happy for this to be the case. The tenth point, however, had always been a mystery and Naithan had taken it to be a sign of his success, along with the empty twelve-pointed star in the centre. He had already created the tenth county, though the Earl of Coombshire had complained bitterly at his loss of territory. Upon the conquest and conversion of the northern races, he would divide them out into another twelve counties, or provinces; he had yet to decide on the structure of the enlightened empire that he planned to build.

A flash of light brought him from his reverie and he saw that Matthew had vanished, leaving him with his unnerving apprentice, Jalim. Though vital to their plans, he could not bring himself to feel comfortable in this young man's presence and those strange, piercing eyes of his.

"Thank you for your assistance," he said, trying to hide his hesitancy. "You may return to your…er…studies."

The boy bowed silently and walked away. In all the infrequent times he had seen him, the boy had never once spoken, though Matthew swore that he did. A cold shudder ran down his spine and he turned his thoughts away. A slight cough caused him to turn round and he saw Luca stood there with the official robes of office. Today was the second Torsday of the month, the day of his monthly audience with the people when he tried to settle their petty excuses. Yet today could be the day that saw the end of the Shadow's run of dark luck. The Spymaster's report on a young female witness had indicated a high probability that she knew of the man's identity and that they would be able to use her information to snare him. Thinking of the girl his thoughts returned to the weasel Malcolm. He decided that he would send him to some undeserving lord as punishment. The thought made him smile and he walked in to the palace, ready to meet his people.

II

Tristan stifled yet another irritated sigh as the druid and goblin started up yet another argument, this one being as pointless as the rest, concerning snoring of all things. This was the latest in what had been a series of disputes that had occurred throughout the past two days since their flight from Selene. From the moment they first argued onwards he had wished that the journey had finished already and that he had rid himself of the whole bothersome company. It would have even been worth the risk of travelling the main highway to have arrived there early, but Belthar had insisted that they take the 'scenic' route to avoid any more chance encounters with knights. For that reason alone had Tristan agreed to the plan, for he had no desire to see any knight harmed by the likes of these people.

"Wha…what that?" asked the goblin, its voice quaking with fear.

"It's the sea yer idiot!" replied Belthar with a glare.

Tristan looked about in surprise. He had been so preoccupied with his own thoughts that he had not noticed that they had emerged from the trees and onto a thin strip of headland. All around it the glistening blue of the Southern Ocean swayed gently in the light of the summer sun. In the distance two ships could be seen gliding smoothly past each other, foam spraying off their bows as they went. Before it all stood the goblin, its mouth gaping open and its small eyes almost bulging out of their deep sockets.

"Groltch…I not know so much water could be in one place!" it said with awe. "How we cross it?"

"In one of those things over there," replied Matthius, who also seemed to be a little in awe of the blue expanse before them. "They are called ships."

"Gro…I not think I like ships," it said with a nervous glance at the young wizard.

"Yer'll be fine," replied Belthar softly, "and who knows, with all that water, even you might be able t'keep yerself clean!"

The goblin turned back to the big man and yet another argument erupted, leading Tristan to feel once more that one day blood would be shed between the two. Yet in a few more days that would be none of his concern. It was just a shame there was no way of speeding up the journey.

III

Karene Skellan sat in the guard room scowling. Guard duty indeed. She had ridden into the town of Teldin only a few days ago to find that the High Priest was already there. His first orders had been to oversee the city gate guards to ensure the precautions were adequate and then to join them at the west gate. She was a blue knight and going to be a future King's Knight and she had been reduced to the level of a city guard. She scowled as one of her knights roared in victory, having just won his fourth hand in a row in cards.

I long for the day we meet, Tristan Pathfinder, she thought darkly, *and you'll pay for the suffering you are causing me!*

IV

King Naithan sat on the throne trying to seem interested in the problems brought before him, whilst attempting to hide the discomfort he felt wearing the heavy crown and thick, hot ceremonial robes. He waited restlessly for the girl his Spymaster had informed him would be here today, the one with information possibly vital to the capture of the Shadow. He had already been offered a lot of information from the many greedy citizens seeking the reward. The information had been politely written down along with their names and addresses in the event that it proved useful in his capture. Yet his Spymaster had been emphatic that this woman was a definite possibility, though her exact whereabouts had somehow proved beyond the Spymaster's talents. He scanned the mass of people before him, hoping to catch a glimpse of her, yet could see nothing. It was with a start that he realized that the plaintiffs before him had ceased talking. He tried to look as if he had spent time in serious contemplation of their plight whilst frantically trying to remember what the case they had brought before him was. It had been something about one having slandered the other or something to that effect.

"You have committed the sin of false judgement on your neighbour. You are required to pay four silver geldons in compensation to your neighbour, and are banned from speaking to him for one week," said Naithan in a commanding voice.

The offender turned visibly pale at the steep sum, yet bowed in silent agreement. As he did so, Naithan saw the woman he had been waiting for. She seemed paler, dirtier and thinner than the description, and Naithan guessed that she had probably been sleeping rough since her last visit to the palace. She was stood some way to the back of the crowd and would probably never reach him before the day had finished, but that mattered little for he had no intention of letting her information become public knowledge. He made a slight nod of the head to the Red Knight at his side then looked out in the direction of the woman. A look of concentration passed over the knight's face and suddenly the woman collapsed to the floor. Within moments several knights had removed her from the chamber and the commotion had died down, for people collapsing in the stifling heat of this chamber were common occurrences. He congratulated the knight with another slight nod of his head and prepared himself for a long day of impatient waiting.

V

When Marie awoke she found herself in a strange room, far from the crowd, whose cloying presence had made her faint. It was a fairly small room, though richly furnished and decorated. Small golden candle holders were set in the walls, providing her with enough light to set by and found herself lying upon a couch made of dark wood and sumptuous red velvet cushions. Before her was a small table with a tray set with food and drink left on top. She began tearing ravenously at the food, the hunger of several days without food gripping her violently. Theldar had not been the glorious city she had expected. The people here were often cold and aloof, the majority having walked straight past her despite her obvious need for food and shelter. Her landlady had thrown her out the moment she had failed to provide coin and finding work had proved nigh on impossible. The atmosphere in the city itself was as cold as its marble streets on a long winter's night and for days she had longed for the warmth and friendliness she had known in her village. Yet it was gone, its people dead, its buildings destroyed by fire, and all that remained of her memories of her childhood home was sadness. With this thought came the tears and despair that even now threatened to overwhelm her and she blinked away the few that escaped her eyes. She realized that someone must have known what she had come to see the king about, for the small weasel faced man had said her information would be of vital interest to the king, and felt that she was probably here to await a meeting with one of his advisors.

The door to her right opened up and a man dressed in very formal, expensive looking clothing entered. This had to be the man who had come to speak with her.

"Have you finished the meal, ma'am?" asked the man politely.

Marie stared at him in confusion, not sure how to respond. She had not expected such a question from a so obviously important man.

"Yes, sir," she replied, not knowing exactly how to respond to a gentleman of the court but hastily adding thanks to prevent the possibility of insulting the man.

The man quietly walked over to the table and picked up the tray, seeming surprised that the knife and fork remained clean.

"There is water in the basin, should you feel the need to refresh yourself," said the man quietly, before bowing his head slightly and leaving the room.

Suddenly feeling very dirty she walked over to the basin and washed her face and hands, wishing she had enough water to do more. She shuddered upon seeing the murkiness of the water and tried to tidy herself up a bit, all the while worrying about the man's reaction. Had she slighted him in some way, or made some error in courtly ways? She had not thought to use the knife and fork in her haste to eat, and had not even stopped to clean before eating. Was that why he had acted so strangely, almost coldly? Had she disgusted him in some way?

The entrance of yet another man interrupted her thoughts. He seemed a little younger than the first and had blond hair and piercing yet kindly blue eyes. He was dressed in a more casual manner, wearing plain, soft grey clothes that hung loosely around his frame and obviously designed to allow easy movement. From this she gathered the man was dressed for work, probably a servant to an advisor. It explained many things. The first man had obviously seen her and decided that her station was too low for him to speak with her in person, and that he had sent another in his place better suited for the meeting. She certainly felt more comfortable at the sight of this man than the first.

"Did I do something wrong with the Lord?" she asked worriedly.

"What?" asked the man sounding somewhat confused.

"He was here just now and I think I insulted him or something, for he just took my tray away and left. If I did I didn't mean to or anything…"

She saw understanding dawn in his eyes and he smiled reassuringly at her.

"Don't worry. You've offended no one here," he replied, his voice soft and kind. "I'm just here to ask you about the man they call the Shadow, for I have been led to believe you have some information on him that may aid our enquiries."

"What do you wish to know?" she asked, relief washing over her and removing much of the tension she had felt.

"Start at wherever you feel appropriate and tell me everything you know in your own time," he replied, taking a seat and indicated her to follow.

She sat down and related briefly their childhood days together, and their subsequent engagement, before moving on to what she felt was the cause of their split, the burning of Galen's mother four or five months ago, though she omitted her part in the proceedings. The woman had been accused and found guilty of witchcraft and for weeks after her death he had seemed preoccupied, distraught and bitter. Marie spoke of the problems that had arisen between them, the coldness, his attempts to isolate himself and the fits of rage that would suddenly consume him, causing him to lash out at the nearest piece of furniture. Then there was the change, the sudden brightening in his demeanour and often-happy days of joy that marked the last two weeks of their relationship together, along with the occasional glimpse of the icy anger and rage she had caught when he thought she had not been watching. Then, of course, the final, fateful day that had changed her life forever. This had been the warm day when he had suggested a picnic in the woods near Grelchin before springing upon her, knife at her throat, eyes burning with hatred, as they had the last time she had seen him, in the alley with the knight. She spoke of her struggle to freedom and flight through the woods, before making her way back to the village, only to find it destroyed by fire. She broke down into tears as she recounted the horrific scenes that had assaulted her senses, the smell of death, the cruelly dissected remains of several villagers and the charred bodies.

The man held her closely as the tears streamed down her face with the memories and patiently waited for her to continue until she had finished her account. Even when describing her attempts at burying the bodies and subsequent journey to Theldar that had led to the meeting of the man whose body she swore she had found in the village. During the whole meeting the man sat quietly listening, asking only one question, the name of her village upon which he had frowned slightly when she had answered. It was at this moment when they were disturbed by a knock upon the door.

"Enter," said the man, whose name she had not even thought to ask.

"Sorry for the disruption, your Majesty," said the young woman that bowed and entered, "but an urgent message from the Lord Warrior has arrived."

The woman bowed once more and left.

Marie looked at the man in confusion. Had the woman really said *Your Majesty?* Could this man really be the...

"Yes, you are correct," said the man, as if reading her thoughts. "I am your king, and I, Toric and all the people of Caldor thank you for your help, and if you are ready, we may require your help again. However, I must take my leave of you for the moment to see to some urgent matters. My servants shall see to your needs until my return."

With that the man stood up, bowed his head slightly and left the room, leaving Marie sat on the chair in amazement.

VI

The bodies lay all around him, charred, blackened and dead from the fires, some of which still flickered around him. He stumbled on through the street, dazed, stunned and appalled. His head had taken in many sights, yet his heart was not quite ready to believe, and in his thoughts ran one thought, *tenget*, "beloved". He picked up his pace, half-staggering, and half-running to the area of the village where her home was placed. As it came into view all sights and sounds left him. All he could see was the remains of her hut and the huddled form in the centre, both charred and blackened. Fear closed icily around his heart as he ran towards the small form, the hope that it was not she being barely enough to keep him from panic. He dropped to his knees besides the still body and searched for some clue of its identity. Then he found it, the small and delicate gold and silver ring he had made for her. He clutched it to his heart and screamed as fear and abject desolation ripped him apart.

Hands sprung to his throat and the eye-less sockets gazed blankly into his eyes.

"You failed me," its lip-less mouth rasped. "You failed me…"

VII

Groltch woke up, drenched in cold sweat, the feel of those icy fingers remaining round his throat. He sat up and reached for the ring that no longer hung round his neck. The humans had that now, in that cold white palace. He closed his eyes and began running through his thought calming exercises. As his breathing began to slow and regulate he stretched out his sensations, feeling the soft breeze on his face, hearing the sounds of the birds' morning chorus and smelling the dew on the grass around him. As his emotions settled down he allowed himself to open his eyes and found the human knight looking at him in what appeared to be concern.

"Are you all right?" he asked worriedly.

"Bad dreams," replied Groltch, not wanting to discuss them further.

"Do goblins dream then?" asked Tris.

Anger flared up within him, threatening the inner peace he had achieved and he glared at the human.

"Why you always call me that?" he asked, trying to reign in his anger. "I know word not a nice one in human speak."

"What else can I call you and your people? I know of no other term!"

"You could call us *ran-the*, what we call us-selves!"

"Well you never told me that before!" snapped Tris.

"Well you never ask!" snarled Groltch, the anger almost overtaking him.

"I…I'm sorry," replied the human, sounding genuinely remorseful.

"I too," replied Groltch, all anger slipping away at the apology.

They then sat for several minutes in an awkward silence before Tris ventured to break the silence.

"What does it mean?"

"Well, ours full name are…is Tu'ran-tha. In human speak it means…" Groltch paused as he searched for the correct translation. "…The Chosen Ones."

Tris arched one eyebrow in what seemed to be the rather overstated human version of a sarcastic expression.

"I know," said Groltch shrugging his shoulders. "We once thought much like humans. Name not mean that much anymore."

As he finished speaking he gazed into the fire, his thoughts returning once more to his people. He barely noticed the remarkable tact, for a human, of Tristan moving away to leave him to himself.

VIII

The Shadow woke with the dawn, his whole body shaking violently from the horrifying dreams that had plagued him since the knight's death in the Shadow Realm. He was covered with the morning dew and the filth and grime of almost a week without washing. His stomach had drawn tight from lack of food and his throat dry and hoarse from lack of water. His arms and legs ached from lack of use and his head swam with every movement. He knew his shattered form would not support life for much longer, and he welcomed his death with his arms open wide. The pain and misery would at last end and he would know dreamless sleep at last, even if it was the sleep of the Damned. He had no illusions. He had become a creature of Thenril, a being far worse than any knight or king in this land. For his crimes he felt that death was a just penalty and hoped that the city would sleep safer in their beds once he had passed away.

Yet he could not go without one last look at the city whose beauty he had only truly seen in the last few days. He crawled to the edge of the alley to watch life return to the city, as people would make their way down the Kingsway to the market. As he gazed out he realized something was wrong. The streets were already crowded and shouts could be heard in the distance. As the cries became more comprehensible he heard one word that sent his cooling blood boiling once more. The word was witch. He staggered to his feet in an attempt to see the victim, yet could not see over the top of the crowd, so he began dragging himself up a drainage pipe to the roof of a small porch, his muscles shuddering violently from the sudden exertion. Once above the crowd he looked across to where the cries were coming from and saw that a woman had been bound hand and foot and was being dragged through the market square towards a pile of wood that was being thrown together. Visions of his mother's burning flashed before his eyes and as they did, he realized that he knew the woman.

A memory flashed up of a picnic; the last moments of joy he had savoured before his descent into darkness, a final compassionate act before his total consumption to revenge. He had forced her to flee to prevent her from dying at his hands, and now she was going to die the same way as his mother. Once more he was powerless to help.

No. Not helpless; not this time. His eyes went to the ring still on his finger. He could save her, but it would mean entering the Shadow Realm once more and risk a meeting with old ghosts. He looked back to the square and saw them tying her forcefully to the centre stake. He could almost see the look of fear in her eyes and watched, his body shaking, as the burning brands were brought forward.

He looked to the ring once more, its dark light laughing at him, knowing his dilemma and revelling in his pain. His eyes narrowed in anger. Very well, his last act would be one of redemption. It could never cleanse the evil that had now cloaked and obscured him, but he could give himself some comfort in his dying moments. He dropped to the shadowy side of the porch, its shadow opening up before him, and he was drawn through one last time.

IX

The Spymaster watched the square with interest from a nearby roof. It would be interesting to see if the trap would work. By all the calculations the Spymaster had made, it would seem that this trap would most likely cause the Shadow to break his cover. The king had been dubious but it all fitted with the profile that had been created from all the evidence that had been collected about him. Of course, the brilliance of the plan was that if it should fail the only loser would be the girl, and she was of little consequence. They had all the information they needed from her and so all the use she had left was as bait. All the Spymaster hoped was that the Shadow would bite.

X

Marie watched the approaching flames with mounting fear. The king had promised her that she would be protected and that no harm would come to her, but it was proving more and more difficult to believe it as the heat began to intensify. She could feel panic flickering to life within her and frightening thoughts began to flash through her mind. The crowd had seemed a little too violent and enthusiastic, and she had very real bruises from where she had been dragged and pulled to this spot. She had been told that they would try and make it realistic and believable, but even so, this seemed a little too real.

The flames reared up before her and seemed to be growing out of control. She wondered how they would put it out if Galen did not show up to rescue her. Or were they just planning to leave her to burn?

She pushed the thoughts out of her mind. The king had given her his personal assurance that she would be safe. Yet as the grey smoke began to fill her lungs and sting her eyes her faith began to desert her. She tried to scream but a fit of smoke induced coughing prevented her and her chest was wracked with spasms of pain. She struggled futilely against the strong bonds and suddenly the realization struck that she was going to die. He was not coming and they were leaving…

Her thoughts were interrupted by the appearance of a demonic apparition. It seemed human, in a dark, sickly way, its face white and stretched out, the eyes burning and deep-set. Thenril's servant had come for her, for whatever sins she had committed. She smiled giddily at the odd form, hysteria and smoke confusing her mind. Suddenly her hands were free and she fell towards the figure, which caught her, almost tenderly. A familiar voice spoke into her hazy thoughts.

"It's all right mother, I'm here to save you."

Somewhere in the back of her mind a small moment of recognition flickered and with it came the apparition's name; Galen Faithe. Somewhere in the distance screams could be heard, though it mattered little to Marie now. Consciousness was rapidly slipping away and as it did she was filled with the sensation of rising up into the air, as if floating on water…

XI

The Spymaster was impressed and amused. The Shadow's sudden appearance had certainly been spectacular, as had the crowd's reaction. Faced, possibly for the first time, with a person who truly had some control over magic, the people of Theldar had turned pale and fled. Admittedly, the almost demonic demeanour of the man would have been enough to scare away the bravest of men, but the Spymaster doubted whether the reaction would have been any different if the form had been more human.

The truth was that deep down Caldorians only burned those who they knew to be untalented in magic, for fear of bringing down upon their heads the wrath of a true magician. That was of no consequence, however, for the Shadow had taken the bait and rescued the girl. Now all they had to do was wait for him to return to the Shadow Realm, closely followed by the Spymaster, who owned a similar travelling device. Yet the man did the unexpected once more, by leaping through the flames and staggering into the streets. This contingency had been planned for, however, and an elite unit of Talons was on guard ready. The moment the Shadow leaped, they began to move in to capture the man. Hopefully the girl had removed the ring, as they had asked her to, and the Shadow would be captured. Two such devices would certainly aid the Spymaster's work. The knights circled the man and, satisfied that the job was done, the Spymaster returned to more important work…

XII

The Shadow, the man once known as Galen, began to stagger as fatigue, hunger and the weight of the unconscious woman combined to almost completely debilitate him. He had barely made it out of the square and he could already hear pursuit. Evidently the woman, whom at one point he had actually seen as his mother, had been used as bait to trap him and it was clear that they had been prepared to let her die in order to maintain the charade.

A leg gave way beneath him and pain shot through his knee as it crashed to the ground. He knew he could carry her no further but felt that he had to get her to safety somehow. He looked at her unconscious form and dredged through his memories to the time when he had once healed and not harmed men. He realized that she was merely overcome and exhausted, and even if he revived her she would not be in a fit state to run. He looked once more at the ring on his finger. With that she could escape, yet would she be safe? Would he just be condemning her to the hell of the Shadow Realm?

The voices of the guards drawing near forced him to make a decision, for good or for ill. He swiftly searched through his pouches, looking for something he could use to wake her. After all but emptying their squashed and mouldy contents onto the floor he found what he was looking for, a pinch of mireweed that still had a white berry on it. He removed the berry and placed it to her nose, squeezing it tightly to release its foul smelling liquid as he did so. The effects were immediate and the woman came round with a jolt, coughing furiously as she did so. Galen wished he had time to mix a drink to ease her pain but time was fast running out. He took one last look at the ring and with a great force of will, slipped it from his finger. He placed it in the hands of the woman, who looked up at him, almost petrified with terror.

"Don't worry," he rasped weakly. "This will help you to escape."

She glanced dumbly down at the ring in her hands.

"Put it on!" he commanded sharply. "Then think of a door in your…head…"

He paused briefly, waiting for the fit of dizziness to subside. As his vision returned to normal he caught a glimpse of a cloaked figure in the corner of his eye. Death herself was waiting for him.

"Step into a shadow and you'll be in a strange place, like this…but…not. Go where you will be safe then think again…of a door…" Death was now looming above him, cold and pale. "…then step into the…light."

A cold numbing sensation was flowing through him as Death's icy claws reached down for him. He saw the girl place the ring upon her finger and watched as it shrank to fit her tiny fingers. He made one final, silent command to the ring and hoped it would obey his last wish. Apparently it did for the woman vanished suddenly into the shadows and he was left alone with Death. He made one final breath and closed his eyes for the last time…

XIII

Naithan stood in the prison corridor looking into the cell of the now captured Shadow. He smiled in joy. He had finally caught him. How pathetic the man looked now that his power to instil fear and commit sin had been stripped away by righteousness. When Naithan had first seen him he had feared that the man was dead, and according to Sir Harken, his commanding Phoenix warrior, it had taken all of their magic to save him from Thenril's clutches. Had he died Naithan would have been upset, for this man needed earthly punishment before his eternal damnation, and he had been assured by his priests that as long as he was tended to that could be a long way away. Naithan intended the man should know the pain his knights had suffered before he died, yet before that could be arranged questions had to be answered. Who had he worked for? What were their plans? Who was he, in truth? The girl, who had not been seen since her disappearance in the trap, had raised more questions. The man went by the name Galen Faithe, but that was impossible for that Royal House had been totally wiped out, every man, woman and child, during the Great Revolution; the revolution that had brought his family, House Tara'non to power.

Naithan sighed and turned to leave. Such questions would have to wait until Matthew's return, when they would have two people to question. He walked away and prayed his friend's trap would prove as successful as his own.

XIV

Matthew stormed angrily through the bustling streets of Kelvaria, fuming to himself about all the worthless, stupid guards of this dark-cursed city. He had informed them to install mirrors at each guardhouse so that any illusion covering the goblin could be found and had issued a description of Tristan with instructions on how to proceed upon sighting them. The guards had merely shrugged and done nothing, not even reacting to the financial incentive he offered. The so-called lord of this small farming and seafaring county, Lewis Hanton had only been a little more helpful, proving to be often *indisposed* and unable to meet with him. And as for that obstinate, arrogant, pig-headed Blue Knight, Sar Karene Skellan…well he would certainly recommend a particularly large dose of Treatment for her upon their return.

The upshot of all these problems was that each day he had to check on each of the main gates each hour to ensure that the guards were not lounging about playing Chase the Elven maiden, or some other ridiculous card game. Matthew and his two armed "escorts" (placed on him on the specific command of Lord Hanton) pushed their way towards the western gate. He almost screamed with rage when he reached it, for it seemed unmanned and a score of people were moving through it. His eyes blazed with fury and magically flung the door wide open, storming in for yet another pointless confrontation. If Naithan had been here not one single person would have even dared to question his authority.

XV

They had first seen the port town of Kelvaria just before dusk the previous night and had unanimously decided to enter in the morning, when there was more traffic to hide amidst. They had then spent what would hopefully be their last night together camped out just a few miles away from their long sought after destination. The night had seen the usual squabbles and the morning the ritual preparations, including Groltch's magical transformation into a human. They had left an hour after dawn and at long last were approaching the town.

The first thing that struck Tristan about Kelvaria was that it had none of the planned look about it that the cities of Theldar and Belthanor had about them. As they neared it he could see that it seemed to sprawl across the land and even over its own defensive walls, so that some of the buildings were nearly a mile outside them. Many were so far away from a gate that in the event of an attack many would probably never reach the safety of the outer walls, let alone the inner defences. Of course such an attack was unlikely, but still there were as many possibilities under the sun as there were stars in the sky, as his father used to say. He was suddenly filled with the vision of a town in flames and shivered in cold, foreboding fear and was forced to turn his thoughts to other matters.

Such a task was not difficult for as they entered the *outer* city his senses were assaulted by the abject poverty about him. The houses, if they could be called that, were largely shelters of wood and mud, loosely bound together by rotting hemp ropes. They had been constructed with no sense of order springing up here and there, making it difficult to navigate through the streets, if they could be called such. They were muddy tracks that rambled in any direction, often stopping at a building or particularly large pile of refuse, most of which was scattered across the floor anyway. Mangy rats and other vermin swarmed around scavenging through what edible remains were left. The people, for the most part, were covered in filthy rags and grime, the dirtiest of which were sat along the roadside begging for alms. Others had the look of honest folk, walking about in relatively clean clothes and looking as if engaged in some type of work or another, though their faces seemed haggard and worn. The only real sign of joy he could see came from a group of young boys he saw running through the streets chasing after a half-starved, frightened dog. Yet worse than all these visual signs was the smell. Tristan had smelled nicer sewage wells than this.

"We needn't have washed the goblin," muttered Belthar softly to himself, Tristan's ears barely catching the words. Belthar had not been looking all that well of late, and it was beginning to worry Tristan. "The smell o'this place is enough t'put off stink rats!"

Tristan agreed silently with the big man's sentiments. He wondered how such a place as this was allowed to exist. It seemed more like a go…ran-the's village than a human town. The cities of Theldar and Belthanor contained no such places.

"Of course they do!" muttered Caliburn. *"You were just never allowed to see them!"*

Tristan glared at the sword wondering, not for the first time, if he should just throw it away and be done with it all.

"Oh you wouldn't do that now, would you?" pleaded the sword, sounding almost sincere.

Tristan sighed heavily and shook his head in resignation. He could no more rid himself of the sword than he could the magnificent horse he now led, which at present resembled an old packhorse, thanks to Matthius's magic. Galahad was almost as well-known as he was himself and too fine a horse to be legally in a company of traders as they were now posing. Tristan patted the horse's neck, glaring at a ragged, filthy youth that had gotten too close.

"Be careful o'them urchins," muttered Belthar, "They'll rob yer blind if yer let 'em."

Tristan looked at the druid in surprise as he left himself unusually open to one of the gob…Groltch's barbed comments, then turned to the goblin in greater surprise when no insult was forthcoming. He was amazed to find Groltch looking around in what seemed like pity and understanding. The creature before him was nothing like the vile, child eating creatures he had been led to believe. In fact, he had found himself moving closer to Groltch since the night of its nightmare, if only in defence. Matthius and Belthar had each other and mutual distrust had been gradually shifting the group into two sections and Tristan was beginning to feel that he might actually have the better of the three companions. He shook his head angrily. Groltch was his enemy, a creature he was only helping as a last favour to his father, nothing more.

"Remember, let Matt do the talkin…" Belthar's words were cut off by a by a sudden hacking cough. It was part of the growing symptoms of illness Tristan had seen these past few days, a condition the big man had put down to his extended absence from the northern forests. "Because yer accent stands out a mile, Tris."

Tristan glared angrily at the druid. The other two had adopted Groltch's nasty habit of calling him by his *shortened* name, a habit that was really beginning to grate upon his nerves.

"Halt, who goes there?" Said an obviously bored and disinterested voice, breaking his thoughts. "State ya name an' business, please."

The guard was appalling. His appearance was unkempt and dishevelled and his uniform was in a severe need of cleaning and polishing. He also seemed to be concentrating on another matter completely for he kept glancing back at the guardhouse as if expecting someone or something to emerge.

Matthius began to reel hastily and rather awkwardly off the false names and business they had prepared last night. Tristan groaned inwardly. Even a goblin would know he was lying. As Tristan looked back to the guard another one appeared at the door. Fear welled up inside Tristan. He knew they had been caught.

"Torslud, Jim, hurry up and get back in 'ere! It's your hand," said the newcomer, sounding more than a little irritated. "That priest fella's been gone some five or ten minutes now!"

A look of relief spread across the first guard's face and he waved them through as he turned to enter the guardhouse.

"Excuse me," said Tristan quickly.

"What?" asked the guard sourly.

"Could you please give us directions to the *Hog's Head*, please?

"Sure! Follow the road to the market main market square and it's on yer left!"

"Thank you," replied Tristan who need not have bothered for the man had already left, muttering something about bloody foreigners.

"Come on!" growled Belthar, whose temper had grown as his health had dwindled. He also seemed to be glaring at something just off Tristan's left shoulder, a look he presumed was meant for him. For the first time since Tristan had met the druid, he found it possible to believe that Belthar was indeed blind.

They made their way slowly up the bustling main street, which Tristan was relieved to see was cobbled and reasonably clean. Even the houses, though not as magnificent as those in Theldar, were relatively well built and looked more like places to live than crude shelters. They were all largely of the same half-timber design, with grey stone forming the ground floor and dark black timber and white plaster forming the first and subsequent floors above. All had the slanting roofs that seemed common to these parts, covered with thatch or, in some cases, red clay tiles. Most even had windows, using the diagonal square cross lattice design of metal strips to break them up, as had become the fashion recent years. It was even becoming popular in Theldar, so he had heard, and apparently they were less likely to break or shatter than windows of plain sheet glass. Though Tristan liked the idea, he still preferred the older, original style.

"No accounting for taste, obviously," said the sword sarcastically.

Tristan was about to retort when he noticed that Matthius was stood before him and apparently saying something.

"…and then we…are you listening?" the young sorcerer asked suspiciously.

"I am really sorry, something distracted me," said Tristan quickly, gripping hold of Caliburn's hilt tightly. "Could you please repeat what you said?"

"I said: We'll stay and order the rooms at the inn whilst you go and sell your armour. Then…Oh wow!"

This time it was Matthius's turn to be distracted. Tristan turned to see what had caught the young man's attention. At the far end of the main square was a large colourful tent. Surrounding it were several covered cages from which strange and bestial sounds were emanating. Immediately outside what was presumably the tent's entrance flap was a large, misspelled sign painted in gaudy shades of green and orange. It read: ***THE GREATIST SPETACOLAR IN ALL LODEN. THE GREAT AND WONDERFULL SEARKUS OF THE MANUCCI BROTHERS.*** Beneath it was a list of events and times of each show. Tristan could recall only ever seeing one such show, though it had been a long time ago, and nowhere near the size of this one. It was probably much better than the disaster he had seen, but he had no desire to go and find out.

"Sorry," said Matthius, who had begun an attempt to close his kitten inside his bag. Tristan looked at him in disgust. "It's only until we have a room. They might not accept pets."

"You were saying," prompted Tristan, hoping to get Matthius back to the relevant subject.

"Oh yes…urm…After you get back we'll get some rest, look into passage dates and times then decide what to do in the morning…If that's all right with you?"

"Certainly," replied Tristan, more than happy to get a little time to himself. He knew he had to approach the barman or something with his father's ring, but he had plenty of time to do that.

"No. I'm gonna have t'pop off t'that park we saw back there. It's got some trees, so it might help restore some o'me spirits. Don't worry. I'll be back by dusk," said Belthar, turning to leave before anyone could argue.

No one did. Even Matthius had been getting irritated with Belthar's sudden fits of anger and occasional bouts of melancholy. They all hoped he came back at least a little refreshed.

The group separated in three directions. Matthius and Groltch took the horse to the inn to be stabled whilst Belthar moved slowly in the direction of the park that Matthius had pointed out, using his stick as a guide and occasional resting post. Tristan hefted a huge sack towards the part of town where black smoke could be seen, the usual sign of the smiths' quarter. If any of them had bothered to look back, they might have seen a robed figure lurking in the shadows watch them go before smiling and disappearing, as if by magic.

XVI

"Karene, I really need your help in this."

Karene smiled as those words slipped from the High Priest's mouth. She had been waiting for this moment since she had arrived. She had seen his difficulty in motivating the guards, and had even offered her assistance, which the stubborn man had turned down flatly.

"The guards don't seem willing to do their utmost and I…we need more dedication, if I…we were to catch the King's Knight," continued Matthew, squirming in discomfort.

She allowed herself a few moments to savour the moment before, with an elaborate sigh, agreeing to help.

"But only if you are absolutely positive that you can't manage it alone," she added quickly.

"You know I can't," he replied tersely. "But enough gloating. We need to get things in motion immediately."

At last, sentiments that she agreed with completely. She stood up quickly, marched out of her room with sparks seeming to fly from her eyes. Within minutes the entire garrison was scrambling to obey her orders.

XVII

Groltch was sulking. He was being treated like a prisoner. Matt had shown him to his room and all but commanded him to "stay put" before leaving and locking the door after him. Yet it was those two that truly needed locking up, of that he was sure. The two of them were hiding something and Groltch was determined to find out what. He was positive that it had something to do with the mysterious illness that had struck Belthar. All druids he had met were fine away from forests. Yet here he was, locked up in this poky little room, whilst the answers to his suspicions were wandering about out there, free to do whatever they pleased.

But then again, locked doors had never stopped him before…

XVIII

Carlos One-Eye watched the blind man as he stumbled into his hunting grounds in the park. He was a big man, who made Carlos very wary, but his keen ears had heard the sweet jingle of coins. He observed the man for a while, a man did not do well in thieving if he was not cautious, and after half an hour or so, he decided that the potential gain outweighed the risk. Besides, how dangerous could a blind man be?

He sneaked up quietly on the mark, unsheathing his dagger as he did so. He waited until he was behind and in range, then struck what would quite possibly be his last victim…

XIX

Tristan worked his way back through the crowd towards the inn, his pouch heavy with mareks. He could not believe how much his plain suit of armour had earned him, even though he still felt guilty at selling something that technically was not his to sell. At first he had had no luck, until, following an instinctive guess, he had slipped the ring onto his finger whereupon he had found himself inundated with offers. Not for the first time he wondered what this ring meant and what his father's role in it was. He had even been offered a handsome sum for Caliburn, though he had declined it, after some considerable prompting from the sword. Of course he could always go back later…

"Hey now, less of that!" said Caliburn quickly.

Just checking if you were listening, thought Tristan smugly.

He turned round the corner that led to the front of the inn and almost walked straight into Matthius, who was hurriedly rushing out of the door.

"What is wrong?" asked Tristan.

"He's gone!" replied a frantic looking Matthius. "I locked him in his room and when I went back to check on him he had vanished!"

"Calm down," said Tristan, trying to remain calm himself. "We will go to the park and speak to Belthar. Then we can discuss how best to search for him."

Secretly Tristan wanted to do nothing of the sort and was glad to be rid of the rotten creature whose very presence was such a source of confusion. But he had yet to fulfil his final obligation to his father and could never go back on his word. Upon seeing Matthius calm down he turned and walked in the direction of the park. Matthius began to follow and they had barely gone a dozen yards when they saw two familiar figures walking towards them and, as usual, they were arguing. As they drew closer the actual words of this particular dispute could be heard.

"…ind you, there was a bear!" said Groltch angrily.

"Of course there was! It heard my cry for help and came to my aid. We *can* communicate with animals yer know!" replied Belthar, equally as heatedly.

"But where it come from?" snapped back the gob…ranthe.

"The Chearkus of course!" snarled Belthar, "Or didn't yer see them beautiful animals, caged up in such cramped, filthy cages?"

"Well, yes," replied Groltch grudgingly. "But I saw it stab you and you not hurt!"

"I am a druid!" roared Belthar, "Or have yer never heard that we can't be harmed by some weapons?"

Tristan vaguely remembered hearing that old saying about druids when he was younger, but there was also something else to it. Unfortunately his memory was too vague and hazy to recall what it was. He muttered another curse to add to the many he had already placed on his Treatment.

Groltch seemed satisfied with the answer, however, and yet another argument ended. Yet, as always, suspicion lay lurking in the creature's eyes.

"What are you two doin' here as well?" asked Belthar angrily.

He seemed to look better, though his tone of voice revealed his anger had not been tempered.

"We thought we had lost Groltch and were on our way to the park to inform you," replied Tristan quietly. "Shall we return to the inn?"

"Okay by me," replied Belthar. "The sanctity of that place has been spoiled now anyway."

They turned round to return to the inn, another argument, this one about sleeping arrangements, erupting between druid and ran-the as they did. Tristan ignored it and looked to the inn, his eyes widening in fear as they rested upon the sight before them.

"Be quiet!" he hissed to the still squabbling pair. "Look!"

He pointed to the inn where a whole squadron of knights was slowly converging upon the building.

"What?" asked Belthar.

"Knights!" replied Tristan quietly.

"Let's go then," said Groltch, but even as he spoke it seemed too late. The man and woman at the back turned in unison, as if touched by premonition, and looked directly towards the group. Tristan gasped in horror as his eyes rested upon the High Priest himself.

"Here we go again!" said Caliburn with what sounded to Tristan like a deep sigh.

XX

Thom yawned as he removed the last food bag from the last horse in the stables. Today had been a very long and busy day, as they usually were in summer. Well…they had been last summer when he had first been apprenticed here. He liked the job, but on warm days like this he often wished to be outside more with his friends, rather than stuck in here shovelling out horse manure in this stuffy building. He was certain the horses did not like the atmosphere of the place but his master, Mister Wilkinson, the owner of the inn next door, had no plans for any modifications.

At least I'm finished now, he thought, cheering up as he did.

A growl from his stomach warned him that he was close to missing his tea if he tarried too much longer. He took one more, quick look at the horses then turned to go out. He paused for a moment and spun back to the horses. No he was not imagining it. The horse in stall four was shimmering.

It must be the heat an' all he thought.

Within seconds he was proved wrong and he was ill prepared for the truth. The shimmering stopped suddenly, leaving behind the most magnificent white stallion he had ever seen. Its coat positively gleamed and as it turned to look at him, he swore blind he could see a deep intelligence that lay within their brown depths. It was an awesome creature, coming close in beauty to the legendary unicorns he had once dreamed of seeing, and he felt tears of pure joy well up within him.

Suddenly it leapt its stall, a feat he would have deemed impossible, and galloped towards him. Without realizing what he was doing he opened the main gate and as it passed it slowed a little, glancing at him as if in thanks, before galloping out into the courtyard and onwards to freedom. In the days that followed Thom would swear blind to all who asked and many that did not, that as it emerged into the sun, light had sparkled off the top of its head, revealing what could have only have been a gleaming pearl horn…

XXI

The four watched in fear tinged with stupefied amazement as the men came moving slowly towards them, drawing their swords as they did. Looking first left then right, they could see that more guards were approaching from all sides, their scruffy uniforms marking them as the city guard. Tristan realized that they were surrounded, outnumbered and seemingly out of options.

"If you give in peacefully now, then none of you will be harmed," said the High Priest. "If you choose not to come peacefully then I cannot assure your safety.

"Damn," Tristan heard Belthar mutter. "If only we could distract them then I might be able to do something!"

"I can provide one," replied Tristan without thinking. The part of him that wished to be captured screamed in frustration. "It might not work though!"

"It'll have t'do!" replied Belthar before turning to the goblin.

Tristan tried to hear what was said but failed, though the gobl…ranthe seemed to agree with the druid, though it still looked suspicious. At that moment Tristan heard a familiar rumbling in the distance and he began to feel like someone or something was manipulating the events for everything seemed a little too convenient; a little too perfect. Yet Belthar rapidly destroyed his line of thought.

"Give us yer distraction then!" whispered the druid harshly.

"Very well then, but close your eye…" Tristan thought about who he was talking to. "…Tell the others to close their eyes."

"Ready!" came the terse reply.

Tristan looked out, the guards were almost upon them so he raised his sword high and heard the High Priest and Karene shouting out warnings.

"As bright as you can go!" he told Caliburn, shutting his eyes tightly.

"As you wish, master," came the almost mocking reply.

The flash was bright. Tristan knew this because it stung his eyes even though they were closed, and he heard the screams of the guards not quick enough to follow orders. He opened his eyes, which were now watery with pain, and saw the guards around him stagger about in confusion, most clutching their heads as if in pain. He also saw that Belthar and Matthius had vanished, leaving him with the ran-the again. Just as his thoughts turned to what course of action to take he saw Galahad leaping over several guards who had dropped to their knees, blood pouring out of their eyes. As the horse came by it slowed just enough to allow him to vault onto his back. He was surprised to find a pair of hands gripping his waist and he looked round to see Groltch mounted behind him.

"Go near cages, then leave north," the ran-the screamed in his ear.

Tristan merely nodded in reply, unable, at present, to think independently. His head hurt badly and a severe pain in his stomach was making him feel nauseous. His head suddenly went very light and he almost fell off in the resulting dizziness.

"Snap out of it!" said the sword in his head, clearing his mind just enough to steer the horse to the cages.

As they approached, Tristan felt the hands leave his waist and he looked back, worried that Groltch may have slipped. He was able to catch sight of him moving towards the cages. Tristan had no idea what the others had planned but he knew he could do nothing else to help them, so he spurred Galahad on to the north gate. As he raced through the panic stricken streets he got the distinct impression that he had done this all before.

XXII

Groltch quickly examined the lock. It was a simple thing and with the quick twist of the wire the lock came undone and he opened the cage door. The black and white stripped horses seemed puzzled at first, but suddenly their ears twitched as if hearing a distant sound and as one they fled their cell. Evidently Belthar really could communicate with the animals.

Without giving it a second thought he went to the next cage and, upon finding it empty, knew that Matt had been at work as well. Glancing back he could already see animals everywhere, either pursuing or being pursued by humans. Groltch smiled at the bizarre sight around him, his first true smile since her death. His heart seemed to lighten a little and the mischievous scamp of his youth came out. He ran on to the next container, laughing as he opened it and after several minutes' work he found that all the cages were soon empty. As the chaos swirled on around him a moment of seriousness struck him in one thought. What were they to do now, as it seemed they were stuck in this land?

XXIII

Tristan saw the north gate flying rapidly towards him. He was just beginning to wonder just how he would get passed them when he saw a guard come running past screaming, covered in what looked to be…monkeys? As he rode passed the gatehouse he looked inside and found it looked like a scene from a taleweaver's tale about the famous monkey houses of Sol. He smiled grimly at the bizarre sight then found himself once more in the slums that surrounded the town.

Free again he slowed his pace to that of a more gentle canter, as riding bareback was something he had not done in years. As he rode he tried to decide what to do next, for he had not yet helped Groltch to freedom, but found nothing but tiredness and this brought confusion. He had done practically nothing all day yet he felt as if he had fought a thousand battles. His head sagged and he soon found himself sliding from the horse's back as the tiredness overtook him.

XXIV

"No, absolutely not!" ordered Matthew angrily. "You can see the chaos that is reigning here! You're needed to help me tidy up this mess we're in!"

"But he'll escape," retorted Karene angrily.

"Don't worry about that," fumed Matthew. "He's gone north, which means he's between the rivers Life and Blood. There is no way across either until Grathnac unless they use magic and I should be able to prevent that, or at least set up wards to alert us as to where they crossed. We'll have them, don't worry."

He saw Karene glaring angrily at his logic, trying to see a way through. For the first time he noticed her deep green eyes as they seemed to stare through him whilst she thought. He could almost see her thoughts working. If it became known that she had left a town in turmoil solely to pursue a private vendetta, then she would lose honour and much standing within the knighthood, something she could not afford to do.

She nodded her agreement and replaced her helm covering up her thick brown hair. Orders suddenly echoed across the streets and Matthew prepared the spell for transport. The blood-link was beginning to call and he dare not stay much longer. In fact, he was not entirely sure why he had momentarily wanted to stay longer. He pushed the thoughts aside and prepared to give Naithan the bad news. As the spell activated he found himself wondering exactly why he desired the position of Merlin with all its added responsibilities. Perhaps he was just quite simply mad…

CHAPTER SEVEN: Torture and treason

I

Tristan was awake before the first rays of the morning sun touched the River of Tears. He had slept the entire night through and had not been woken by the others for his turn at watch. He had no idea why he had fallen asleep like that. He had done barely anything at all and yet he had collapsed as if he had just finished a week-long jousting tourney.

He had vague recollections of the sensation of falling, and of many dirty faces around him. Instinctively he checked his pouch to ensure he still had the money gained from the armour and was surprised to find it still there. An image surfaced in his mind of a goblin face looking down and forcing the other faces away, but beyond that he had no memory of the previous evening's events.

Upon waking up he had found that both Matthius and Belthar were still with him and concluded that they had elected to stay with him for some reason. He had also found the goblin, and its…his presence had extended the duration of the vow he had made to his father. He sighed softly. It seemed that he was doomed to travel with the foul creature for a while longer. He looked down and sighed again. His chances of return had faded almost completely now and it appeared as if he would need to begin a new life. He looked up at the western sky, watching as the red light of the morning sun painted the clouds in a breath-taking array of rich colours. He was a man to whom symbols held great importance and he decided that with this dawn he would change his life. It would be simple at first, allowing himself to grow a beard, leaving Caldor and finding employment in some village somewhere, once he had rid himself of the goblin of course. He closed his eyes and breathed in deep, drinking in the cool morning air then returned his eyes to the sunrise.

"They say a red sky in the morning is a Solman's warning," said a voice behind him. "But it sure makes for a beautiful start to the day, don't it?"

Tristan did not need to turn to recognize that it was Belthar who spoke. He decided the question needed no answer and this morning he chose not to leave himself open to the big man's rough sense of humour.

"'Well, 'tis good t'find yer at peace for a change," continued Belthar softly.

Surprised by the druid's sober attitude Tristan turned to face him.

"Why are you still here?" he asked. "I thought our agreement ended at Kelvaria."

"Well it did, but we're just as trapped as you are. There's no crossin' the two rivers till Grathnac, so me and Matt thought we'd stick with yer that far at least. There's no hope of going back t'Kelvaria and with that Priest so close there's no risking leaving magically. Besides we're all just startin' t'get along!"

Tristan ignored the last statement and chose to sit in silence. Unfortunately the big man seemed to have other ideas.

"Yer do need us too."

"Why would I need you?" asked Tristan, getting more irritated at the interruption to his need for contemplation.

"'Cos yer almost as recognizable as that fella there!" said the druid, pointing at the goblin. "We're all gonna need magical disguises to get into Grathnac, whether yer like it or not."

"Magic?" asked Tristan in horror. "You wish to use magic on me? I most certainly will not agree to any such absurd idea!"

"Oh yer will, 'cos there's no other way, my friend," said Belthar, seeming to revel in the creation of yet another argument.

This time Tristan was ready to take the bait.

"I am certainly no friend of yours and I stand by my beliefs. I will not resort to magic under any circumstances!" he replied.

"Yer don't seem t'mind using the sword's magic when it suits yer though!" growled Belthar, raising the level of the argument.

Within moments it had erupted into a full blown argument. In fact, so intense did the fight become that Tristan completely forgot to question just how the blind man had known it was a red dawn…

II

They were all around him, hundreds and thousands of them and all too familiar. Each face was frozen in the agony they had felt upon his killing stroke. They moved closer to him, their now rotting and decaying limbs brushing against his bare flesh. They pressed closer and closer, pushing their bodies against him. The air was filled with the fetid stench of long dead flesh. He could feel the movement of the many maggots writhing beneath the cold, clammy skin and the echoes of their wailing, haunting screams lingered inside his ears. His was pushed to the ground and felt their bodies collapse on top of him. His breathing became ragged and shallow as his face was smothered and his chest crushed. He knew he was suffocating yet worse was to come. The skin split open and the maggots wriggled and squirmed out, forcing themselves into his mouth, nose and ears. He could taste them on his tongue and feel them squirm down his throat. His stomach churned and wrenched violently and he tried to scream as the realization that his fears had been met. He was in the Dark Realm, the land of One Eye, the land of Thenril, Lord of the Damned. He shuddered violently as the creatures within him slowly began to eat their way out of him. Madness consumed him and he flailed about desperately. He wanted it all to stop. He would do anything to make it stop.

Suddenly all the images and sensations stopped and he found he was lying on a cold stone floor. He looked around to find himself in a small dark cell, mired in his own bodily excretions. His eyes vaguely focused upon a shadow by the door and found it to be food and water. Almost without thought he began to eat, even though his stomach still churned from the nightmarish visions that occasionally flashed before his eyes. As the last mouthful went down his throat he noticed a familiar figure stood before him; his most hated and despised king. He leapt up with his remaining strength, determined to throttle the king as his last act of violence. He crashed into the wall on the other side of the man and lay in a heap, looking at the king in confusion.

"Did you really think I would be that stupid?" asked the king in a mocking voice. "That I would risk my life to stand before you physically?"

"Then you still fear me," muttered the Shadow, his voice hoarse and sore, getting a little pleasure from the slight start the king had given at his actions.

"That is of no consequence." Images of fire flashed before him. He felt his flesh first prickle then sear, before melting from his bones. The Shadow screamed in agony, tears streaming down his face. "Ask me any more questions and such pain will be visited upon you again. Move in my direction and the same will happen. Fail to answer my questions and the pain will be of a like to which you have never felt before."

As if in confirmation of the king's statement, prickling ripples of pain ran throughout his body and he shuddered involuntarily.

"Who are you working for?" asked the king.

"No one," he replied.

Pain flashed across his body and a scream leapt from his throat.

"You lie. Who hired you? Who do you work for?"

"I can help you," whispered a voice in his head. *"If you answer as I say then*

I can ease your pain."

"No one!"

Pain flashed again and again and the voice whispered perpetually in his mind. Before long what little strength he had had been diminished to nothing and at that point the pain was so great that he would have sold his soul to the Demon Lord for a moment's peace. Instead, he settled for the voice's offer and almost immediately the pain eased. When he spoke as instructed he found that the pain almost disappeared completely and upon completing the voice's words he collapsed gratefully into a fitful, feverish sleep. As his consciousness broke away the voice spoke one last time:

"You did very well for me. Soon your task will be finished and I will allow you eternal rest. Very soon…"

III

Naithan looked at the shattered wreck of a sinner that was shown in the viewing chamber, a look of consternation crossing his face. He was not entirely sure whether to believe this man or not, for he was obviously a follower of Thenril, Prince of Lies. Yet so much had fitted in with his own ideas of a plot against him, to which his nightly dreams had pointed. For the first time he regretted the need for the trip to Sol, yet it was vital to him if his plans were to succeed. The heretics of Sol had to be converted and, unlike the more cynical nophiles of Kolth, their strong superstitious beliefs could aid in such a conversion.

The people of Kolth would require open warfare and subjugation, until they had been dragged into the light of Toric. He shook his head and tried to clear his thoughts. He would require more than one or two more interviews with this man before he would believe him, though there was such little time left before the visit. But for now the punishment would continue. He nodded to Sir Robert, a Black Knight who's sick, but rather essential for the present, pleasures with magic and pain who then began the dreams anew. The man grinned and Naithan shuddered a little. One day men such as Sir Robert would no longer exist. A scream broke his thoughts and he returned his gaze to the illusionary image of Galen before him. A feeling of righteous pleasure surged through him at the sight of the sinner being punished and he decided to watch for a while, as a lesson to himself to never become like the man before him.

"Naithan, I hate to disturb you but your brother has just arrived from Grelchin to see you," said Matthew's voice in his head.

Naithan felt the shiver of fear run down him that always happened when Matthew communicated like this. If the man could place thoughts into the head, what would stop him from taking things out?

Very well, he replied. *I shall be there anon.*

"How did he get here so fast?" he wondered aloud, before he noticed Sir Robert glance at him in confusion.

He nodded for the man to continue then left quickly as his smile widened at the sounds of the screams. Naithan prayed that Matthew could finish the device soon so that the vile man could be executed. There was no treating those like this Black Knight. He turned away and headed up the stairs towards the cleansing warmth of sunlight and his brother Gareth.

IV

Marie huddled into a ball looking down on the gruesome sight before her. How she had got here she could not recall, as it had all been an almost dream-like journey. She had woken in the night having been plagued with eerie, strange nightmares and had decided to go for a walk. She had still been hungry and had been moving towards the palace to go and claim the reward that she had not the courage to collect. Though the rational part of her mind had tried to dismiss her fears, her instincts had overruled it. Some part of her knew that had Galen not come to save her, she would have been left to burn. The thought that the king had been prepared to use her in that way still left her shaking violently inside.

She had moved away and wandered through the streets, everything seeming dull and dim, as if not quite there, even in the light of the sun as it slowly began its ascent in the western skies. No one had seemed to see her and after a short walk through the streets had found herself within the walls of the palace once more, almost as if drawn. She had walked past the palace guards in amazement that they did not stop her. Their eyes seemed to slip over her as if she were not there.

She had found the king and had followed him to this place; a place of darkness where she saw the true colour of her king's soul. She had been sick several times throughout the 'interview' and felt light-headed. The king had then walked straight past her and off back up to the main palace.

She sat there quietly clutching her aching stomach, wondering at what to do. Galen had done evil things, but surely he did not deserve this. Confusion, revulsion and fear filled her suddenly and she ran up the stairs. As she ran through the palace corridors she barely saw anything as tears filled her eyes. The world around her seem to fade in and out of focus as she ran, but paid it no heed. She barely noticed the servants she ran past, or the surprised and startled looks some had given her. She was even vaguely aware of one screaming, and dropping a pile of porcelain plates on the floor. All she wanted to do was escape.

Within a few minutes she was out onto the streets, tears flooding down her face. What they were doing was horrific but he was the king and she but a poor girl. She had no way to help Galen in his suffering, a suffering that she had been responsible for in more than one way. Tears flooding down her face she ran as far from the palace as she could get.

V

Naithan rushed up the stairs to the fresh morning air and saw his brother dismounting from his magnificent rowan horse. He was of a larger build than Naithan, having been trained from an early age to serve as House Warrior, and his darker, almost brown hair set off a pair of sparkling green eyes that he had inherited from their mother. When clean he was quite a handsome man and court gossip had it that he had already fathered several bastard children, though Naithan knew how such gossip could be exaggerated a little at times. Though reasonably different in personality, they had nearly always found themselves getting along with each other and Gareth, though older than Naithan, was fiercely loyal to the crown and he had served admirably in the first Great War. Naithan smiled. Gareth had been away several months and it was good to see him back again.

"Naithan!" cried his brother, breaking into the largest grin possible. He ran up and gave Naithan a fierce hug. "It's good to see you again."

"It's good to see you again," he replied, feeling a little embarrassed Gareth's open display of emotion. "How goes the war?"

"Well, very well, though you look none too healthy I must say."

"Why thank you, you really know how to cheer someone up, don't you," he replied, relaxing as he entered the private wing of the palace. "But you, on the other hand, look absolutely filthy and you stink of horse and sweat."

"Well you try riding like the Godswind through two countries with barely a break and we'll see how you look and smell. I'd be willing to bet you that it wouldn't be much better than this," replied his brother with a grin. "What's it all about then? We're approaching Grelchi and my place really should be with the troops."

"So soon? That is good news," commented Naithan, half to himself. "You're here because I will be leaving in a matter of weeks to Sol and I need to discuss the leadership of Caldor in my absence. Helena will be arriving tomorrow and we shall have to organize things so that they continue to run smoothly."

"Is that wise?" asked Gareth, sounding a little worried. "You're leaving in a time of war, and with the problems you have here with that Shadow person, things could go quite badly wrong you realise."

"Don't worry about that," replied Naithan with a secret smile. "That's one problem that has been dealt with."

"You caught him?" asked Gareth incredulously. "Excellent. So I won't have to send you any more replacements from Belthanor. You realize he has killed more knights than the whole goblin nation has in twice as much time, though I hear that goblin assassin managed to triple our losses when he came here. Is he caught yet?"

Naithan looked at his brother in surprise.

"I didn't realise you knew he'd escaped!"

"Your mystery man told me about it a couple of weeks ago when he came with your instructions to come here."

Naithan stopped suddenly.

"You mean you came here normally and didn't…?" asked Naithan warily. He was always a little uneasy about his brothers 'talents'.

"No," replied his brother. "Peggy is afraid of heights, though she'll never admit it. I ought to really think about changing her name, as she certainly doesn't seem to fit it."

Naithan shuddered at the reminder of Gareth's power to communicate with animals. He swiftly turned his attention to the reason for the question.

"So you left a few weeks ago?" asked Naithan a little confused. He had only sent word for his brother to return after the ambassadors had left a few days ago. He had assumed that his brother would have used less than ordinary measures to get to Theldar.

"Of course I did," replied Gareth just a little indignantly. "You don't think I'd disobey a direct command do you?"

"Certainly not!" replied Naithan, hoping he sounded more confident than he felt.

His Spymaster had to have known of his plans in advance to have issued such orders and Naithan now wondered just who was leaking such information to him. For a moment twinges of pain rippled down his arm and he thought of Matthew, but quickly dismissed such suspicions from his mind. The sorcerer just had to be loyal; they both knew the consequences for any harmful treachery. He decided he would take the matter up with the Spymaster when they met next time. It had saved them some time, though, for none were as gifted at travel spells as Matthew and his apprentice and a journey from Grelchi, even with his brother's magic, would not have brought him here on this day. It meant that they would be able to spend some more of the little time they had together, a luxury they had not had since they had been children.

"…and the buildings and walls there are still pretty much intact so we could face some difficulties there as well…" His brother went silent momentarily. "You're not listening to me, are you?"

Naithan shook himself out of his reverie.

"Of course I am, I'm just a little tired, that's all!"

"Still with the same dreams then?" asked Gareth worriedly.

Naithan felt that the whole kingdom seemed to know of his dreams and troubled sleep. Worst of all, all turned into doddering old nursemaids when the subject came up. He had to change the subject fast or his brother would soon be suggesting he have an early night.

"Occasionally, yes, but don't go thinking you can use it as an excuse to avoid my drinking you under the table tonight!"

"You'll never let me live that one down will you?" replied his brother in mock irritation. "I had spent a hard day hunting and had been tired, that's all!"

"The cook didn't think much to you wearing that food instead of eating it. He'd spent all day preparing it and you barely touched it, apart from those morsels you breathed in when you were snoring," replied Naithan with a grin.

"Well this time it'll be you and Matthew with yer heads in the stew!" replied Gareth with a roar of laughter. "If we can drag him away from his books that is!"

"Well, he sends that odd student of his away today so you might stand some chance of that" replied Naithan repressing a shudder. Something about that boy truly did unnerve him. "You've got an hour to freshen up then all night to revel until the prude turns up."

The prude was the name they both used for their dourer and quieter older sister, Helena.

"You've got a deal!"

They reached a split in the corridor and separated to go to their respective chambers to prepare for the drunken night ahead of them.

VI

Matthew watched as Jalim finished packing. The young man had taken the news of the sea voyage and their separation as stoically as ever and Matthew found himself wondering if anything would ever surprise or unnerve the boy. Though he refused to admit it to Naithan, Jalim made him feel uncomfortable on occasions, usually when he seemed to look at him with those strange eyes that would seem years older than even the most elderly of men. The boy had even seemed to have guessed Matthew's intentions for his continued studies by asking to go to Belthanor to study among the knights there before Matthew had asked him. He looked closely at the young man, wondering if he truly did have the gift of foresight.

"I'm ready," said the boy laconically. Only when they talked about magic did the boy really ever become animated in his conversations.

"I'm afraid you'll have to travel by ordinary means for I'm going to have to save my strength for Sol."

The boy said nothing but opened up his hands towards Matthew, gentle ripples of prismatic light radiating from his fingertips. Energy suddenly rushed through his body and Matthew almost fell to his knees as the fierce, intoxicating joy of power surged through every part of his body. It was all over too soon, yet left him trembling with emotion. The boy had never passed him so much energy before and Matthew had never felt so alive. If he could unlock Jalim's mind as he had the ambassador's, Toric only knew the power he could possess. He looked up and saw the boy sagging against the bed support, his face pale and grey. An icy stab of fear struck at Matthew, almost wiping away the thrill of magic.

"Are you all right?" he asked, moving to help the boy to stand.

"Fine," said the boy softly, "but use it wisely, you'll find you'll need it in the next few weeks."

Matthew's started in surprise. He knew better than to ask what he meant for Jalim inevitably denied all knowledge of such prophetic statements after they were spoken.

"If you need to rest before you leave…"

"No, send me now and all will be well."

With the extra power he now had, it would be simple to magically teleport Jalim to Belthanor so he sighed and began to work through the various parts of the spell, bringing to mind the image of the transport chamber in Belthanor. The boy disappeared and Matthew sighed again, this time with regret. There was always so much to learn with him around and he had been sure he was getting closer to the truth of Jalim's magical heritage. Free-wielders were rare and he was the first to have existed for centuries, at least according to all records he had ever read. Yet that would have to wait for the moment, for there were still some preparations to make for his own journey.

He returned to his room to find that Eward had completed the bulk of the packing for him, yet there were a few less than ordinary objects he needed. He entered his laboratory and collected the various components he felt he would need then moved to the communications mirror. Muttering a few words of activation its surface rippled like mercury and slowly the image changed. Instead of his own reflection he could see an alcove that had shelves containing his more valuable artefacts. He reached through and took out the ornately carved ivory and gold box that sat behind the enchanted helm he had discovered as a boy. He moved back to the bench and placed it in the place it had rested last night during his experiments. He put his head upon the table and looked deep within the mirrored metal plates that resembled eyes in their oval shape. He stared deep into the reflection of his own eyes and watched as the pupils seemed to dilate. He muttered a few more words and suddenly the pupils expanded enough to cover the whole plate. Pain stabbed at his eyes and it seemed as though the world around him was spinning and that his eyes were being dragged from their sockets. Colours from objects around him seemed to drain away and soon all had gone, leaving only black and white in its place.

The only colour left in the world could be seen in the two metal plates, that now seemed to hold the reflection of two brown eyes staring out, his own eyes. Matthew moved away with a shudder. He caught sight of them blinking briefly, their action confirmed by the momentary darkness that flashed before him. He hated using the box but it was the only totally secure way of protecting the item within.

He reached in and the eyes on the box closed, leaving him in darkness to feel the cool metal of the short rod within. It positively tingled with energy and life, sending shivers down his spine. He clasped it and held it close before closing the box. With a rush and swirl of nauseating colours his eyes returned to him and everything seemed as normal once more. He swiftly drank the potion beside him and the nausea stopped. He then dropped some into his eyes and the blood that had begun to flow from them ceased as they healed over.

When he had first performed this magic it had taken weeks for his eyes to recover fully, yet he had now perfected the potion that reduced this to minutes, though they would still often ache for days after. It was worth it however, for the prize he would eventually gain. He looked at the seemingly plain rod. It was just a five-inch piece of brass that was jagged at one end, revealing it had once been part of a much larger object. However, even without its counterparts it was still a very powerful artefact, capable of enhancing prophecies in ways impossible when unaided.

He had spent years researching this, or so it seemed for in the memories of earlier High Priests he possessed due to the blood link, it was something they had been studying for almost two centuries. It had been only two years ago, however, due to his own research, that he had discovered the "*forbidden*" information. All his predecessors had known that the rod had existed as part of the ceremonial sceptre since the time of the Second Elf Wars, but information as to why this was so had been impossible to find, until he had found an ancient tome of forbidden lore. Even this had been sparse on details, claiming only that the Elflord Kaneril had used a rod known as the Sceptre of Prophecy, a powerful item which had been magically broken into five parts on his defeat. The sections had then been given to each of the five kingdoms involved in the war to guard in order to prevent its misuse. It was partly in an attempt to collect the goblins' section that the war against Grelchin had been initiated; at least they were part of the reasons for Matthew's approval of the conflict. Naithan was, as yet, unconvinced as to the power of the sceptre, yet he would be once they had collected all the parts together and had it at their disposal.

For the moment, however, he had to make do with just this small fragment for the task ahead. Naithan wished to dispose of his torturer's services, feeling that the Shadow should remain completely isolated from any form of human contact. He feared that the fiend may somehow be helped to escape by whoever employed him if his presence was discovered. It would mean the death of the Black Knights who had been involved in other executions, but they were perverted abominations anyway so that mattered little to him. The death of the guards who fed the prisoner would be more of a waste but nothing compared to the cost of keeping the Shadow's incarceration a secret. That was if he could perfect the device in time. It would have been simpler could he have brought Jalim into his confidence about the sceptre, but Matthew trusted only the king with the knowledge. No one was going to become Merlin before him.

He shook his head angrily as he picked up the device he had been working on the previous evening. It was still difficult getting the balance of energy correct when using the rod. He had already caused three of the eye shaped disks to explode by magnifying the energy too much with the sceptre. He had almost decided after the third failure to resort to the more traditional method but he knew that if he could not even master a fragment of the sceptre, he would be overwhelmed with the power of the fully completed device.

He forced the thoughts away and concentrated on the task at hand. The process to prepare the metal disk would take most the night and one mistake would force him to begin again. Unfortunately that would mean another day's delay for him to regain the energy required to cast the spell, even with the extra energy given to him by Jalim that morning, and with their visit to Sol now only days away it was time he could not afford to lose. Once more he found himself wishing for his apprentice and his special talents.

"Blood and hellfire," he muttered angrily, "what's getting into me of late? If I'm not careful I'll burn myself out!"

He closed his eyes and reached out with his mind, clearing away all thought. As his emotions quelled to nothing and his concentration focused, he heard the footsteps entering his room. Needing no distraction he issued a brief spell and his door sealed. As it closed all thought but that of his task faded to nothing and soon the night was spent away in magic and energy.

VII

Naithan tottered through the corridors, draped between Luca and Gareth, humming merrily away to himself. The world around him seemed a little blurred and the ground beneath him seemed to pitch and roll, almost as if he were on a boat. He had been singing but his good friend and brother had reminded him that he was king and therefore should not run through the corridors whooping and singing for all the servants to see. That had not stopped him, however, and it had taken his overzealous manservant's threat to tie and gag him to actually stop him. Despite his age, Luca was quite capable of carrying out the threat, especially if his brother had helped. They could not stop him humming though and that thought made him chuckle. Even if they bound him they could not stop him doing that. He looked up at the old man holding his left arm.

"Have I told you how much I appreshiate your work for me, Luca?" he asked with a smile.

"Yes, sir," he replied sounding strangely resigned for some reason. "Just five minutes ago."

Naithan creased his forehead in confusion. He could not recall telling Luca that at all, let alone just five minutes ago. He tried to think back over the night's events. He could vaguely recall drinking a few flagons of ale, some rather swiftly, and also a few glasses of Grathnacian wine, some of the more potent ones if he recalled correctly, and he could recall several glasses of that fortified wine as well. After that however, happenings and events seemed to blur together a little. There was definitely some singing and dancing in the main hall with other nobles. He could also recall being sick, though fortunately that had been whilst he was alone with his brother.

"Right, 'ere we are," said Luca, helping to throw Naithan on the bed.

"Should we undress him?" Naithan heard his brother ask.

"No," came the reply. "Let them add to his discomfort in the morning."

Naithan's eyes began to close as sleep began to sweep through him.

"Besides, we'd be 'ere all night undoin' the tangle he's gotten himself into!" were the final words he heard as darkness swept over him…

VIII

…The dream began almost as soon as the darkness overtook him. It was the same but different, as they always were. This one was the dream of Caldor. The truth of Caldor. People of Caldor believed the great knight their first king in all but name and in that they were partly correct. Yet they also believed that he gave up his throne to become advisor and protector to his successor, a role that he fulfilled for some two hundred years. In this they were not correct. The truth was closer, in fact, to his dream. He was Caldor, in his final moments before his first, true death. The dream washed over him, consuming him and he lost himself completely to the events.

He was sat at his desk, looking over his plans for the continued conquest of Grelchin now that he had secured himself a firm base of operations at Belthanor from which to strike at the evil goblins. It had been years in construction but would ensure that no goblin horde would ever again be able to set foot in Caldor. As he made a few more amendments he noticed the shadows behind him shift. Knowing that the treachery of the foul creatures could strike even here he reached down to the magical sword by his side. Caliburn glowed with life and it spoke one word.

"Danger!"

Caldor span round and drew the sword, its blade lighting up and expelling some of the shadows. Stood before him was a man in armour, his armour. Anger filled him at the sight of his own armour being worn by another. With an oath to Toric he sprang at the armoured form and Caliburn sprang to life in his hand. He brought the sword round to strike at the figure's exposed side and the knight before him barely managed to block him. Yet Caldor was not finished for he twisted the blade in an over arm loop in an attempt to slice into the less protected area of the shoulder. The figure twisted and barely avoided a serious injury, bringing its own sword to bear on Caldor, almost slicing through his unarmoured side. Caldor knew that he was at a disadvantage, being clothed for his monthly open audience with the people. He also knew that calling for his guards would be fruitless for the figure before him would have had to have killed them before entering this room. Caldor's only hope was that the man's skill with the blade was not equal to his own.

A few minutes of battle soon proved that this hope was a spurious one. With this realisation came the inescapable certainty of death that had never touched him before, even when he had been forced into the cold and left to die in the goblin prison mines. His thoughts briefly contained the possibility of a parley but dismissed them equally as quickly. A man that attacked you without a word was not a man who would talk to make a deal.

He looked around to see if escape was possible, at all times fighting off an attack that was becoming quicker, faster and more deadly with every second. Once again he saw that his opponent had been too good, having chosen his ground well. There was little space in this room, barely enough to swing these swords to their full extent and the figure before him had most of it available to him. There was not even anything close enough at hand to throw at the knight to distract him.

He closed his eyes and fought off the panic. There was so much that still needed doing and he would not have the time to complete them. Anger surged through him and one thought dominated his mind. This man would not live long enough to enjoy his death. He thought back to his training, recalling the one move that Kree-thar, his winged companion and sword instructor, had shown him that would help him in this situation. The words that had accompanied the lesson came back to him as he moved into the best position to begin the final deadly dance.

"This move is known as Kissing the Blade and should be done only if you know that you are doomed to die. It is inescapable once initiated and fatal to both combatants,

at least when humans fight…"

Not for the first time Caldor regretted not possessing wings like those of his friend. He closed his eyes and with a cry began a swirling, spinning attack that began to force their blades higher and higher. It was the opening to a similar series of strikes that had once been deemed unbeatable and against unskilled opponents it often was. However, it had been discovered that if the defender was skilled enough to suddenly reverse the spin of their blade they could bring its blade under their opponent's guard and simply skewer them in their now exposed stomach. Caldor counted on his opponent being skilled enough to carry out the manoeuvre and was not disappointed. He gasped as the sword blade slid into his stomach, the pain being almost beyond belief. This was now the crucial stage of the manoeuvre and he prayed for the strength to retain the focus required for the next move. Rather than pull away from the knight, as was expected, he pushed himself towards the knight. The pain was excruciating and he was unable to stop a scream from erupting from his throat as the blade's tip emerged from his back. Yet still his focus remained and he reversed his grip on Caliburn whilst placing his left hand round the blunted part of the sword blade close to its hilt. He lifted it above his head and brought it down with all his strength onto the damaged shoulder plate of the knight. As he did so he channelled all the energy available to him through the blade. There was a flash of light and he felt the blade slice first through metal, then flesh, and then bone. The two figures crashed to the ground and lay upon the floor. As they did so, the knight's helm rolled away to reveal his attacker's face and Caldor's heart ran cold. The face of the knight was his own.

The knight before him looked as confused as Caldor himself, probably mirroring exactly his own expression.

"She said I would not die…" said the knight as his eyes began to glaze over.

"Who?" asked Caldor with a struggle. His limbs were going cold.

There was no reply and the room lay in silence. Caldor closed his eyes and died, at least that was what usually happened. This time, however, it was different. A figure moved from the shadows, a feminine form and Caldor widened his eyes in recognition. His strongest rival on the royal council stood before him, Countess Angeline of Northshire. She bent down towards the dead knight and removed what appeared to be an almost transparent scarf. The face, his face, shimmered a moment and then changed, revealing it to be the face of Matthan Faithe, his closest friend and advisor. Confused he looked to Angeline. She looked at him and sneered.

"He was a pathetic fool who would do anything for love," she said coldly. "I guess I'll have to find another to take his, and your place at my side as champion to the Queen."

"Queen?" asked Caldor softly. "We were not to have inherited power, only divinely appointed leaders."

"I am divinely appointed," she replied quickly, "and with *your* support I will have no problem convincing the Council of this. Goodnight, sweet prince!"

Caldor shuddered at the name she had once used when they had both been young and in love. As life faded away from his body the world shimmered and suddenly he was Naithan once more, lying in pain on his study floor. The body of the knight had gone and in its place was the figure of that most hated of men, the Shadow. Stood above, in place of Angeline was the form of someone more familiar, Countess Michelle, also of Northshire. Anger filled him as he drifted into death once more. The pitiful wretch had been honest about his employer…

IX

…Naithan woke up in a cold sweat, the alcohol already gone from his body. His first thought had been of the Countess and her betrayal, but a stab of suspicion swiftly followed it. Why had the dream changed? They had never changed so much before, so why now? It all seemed too neat and tidy. Was it possible that he had somehow changed his own dream to suit the prisoner's story? Was it the Shadow himself altering his dream, setting suspicion where none should exist?

For the first time he questioned a dream and its contents. He would have to find some way of observing the Countess from afar. A smile came to his face. He had wondered what to do with Malcolm and his meddling, for whilst a little amateurish, it could cause complications whilst he was away in Sol. Now he could remove him and hopefully surprise his seemingly unshakeable Spymaster who already had agents watching the weasel faced little man. By sending the man there with instructions to watch her, it would have several beneficial effects. The first would be that the man was away from anywhere his petty machinations could cause trouble. The second would be that it would send the man into a fit of curiosity as to what was going on and send him snooping around and distract the Countess from the presence of his Spymaster's better agents. It would also confuse Malcolm's employer by sending confusing signals about his actions. The final and most satisfying of these would be Malcolm's reaction to being sent into what was essentially an uncivilised border Shire that had little need for the comforts of the palace. Chuckling at the idea of Malcolm "slumming it" to use a peasant phrase, he rolled over and returned to sleep with the dreams that followed it…

X

"I do not care in the slightest. I will not agree to this and that is the end of it!" shouted Tris angrily.

Groltch sighed and returned to basking in the warmth of the summer sun. It had been getting steadily warmer throughout their journey and the countryside had been slowly undergoing an amazing transformation. The usual lands he had seen in Caldor had consisted of trees interspersed with farms and villages, with the occasional towns. Here however, there was much more open space and there were many fields, most growing hops, grapes and malt. Apparently this land was ideal territory for growing such plants and had become the centre for the drinks trade in Caldor. It had been an alien concept to Groltch as his village had been almost completely self-sufficient and the idea of relying on one area to provide something such as wine to the rest of the areas seemed rather unusual. But then, this was a human kingdom and could therefore be excused such strange customs.

Another shout from Tristan disturbed his thoughts so he closed his eyes and tried to clear his thoughts. It was too difficult though, for it was an argument that had been going on since their escape from the port town. Belthar and Matt had decided that Tristan would also need a magical disguise, as it was obviously his face that'd given them away in Kelvaria. He would not be alone, for all of them would probably be known by now and so all would need disguises when they entered Grathnac, the city where the two rivers met and the only place they could cross one or the other inconspicuously. Tristan had other ideas though. Unfortunately that had meant arguments had occurred throughout the long trek north. They had now reached the gates of Grathnac and it looked like the argument would soon erupt into physical violence. Groltch decided it was time to stop this. He flipped up onto his feet and walked over to Matt, who was sat despondently playing with his small black kitten. Groltch looked at the other two and seeing them still in heavy debate he sat down next to the human boy.

"What do you want?" it…he asked.

"I have idea, if you want, to stop this silly thing," replied Groltch cautiously.

"What's that then?" asked Matt.

"This magic you want use. It like one you use on me?"

"Yes, almost identical in fact," asked the boy, his violet eyes turning on Groltch with curiosity.

"Then when you…" Groltch searched around for the words.

"Cast it?" offered Matt.

"Yes, think so…cast like use?" he asked. Seeing Matt nod in reply he then continued. "Then he not see that he magicked. It not feel anything and he not able to see, true?"

"Yes!" said Matt with understanding in his eyes. "I have never used it on myself and I never thought of that! How could I have missed that?"

"You want tell or me?" asked Groltch.

"You'd better *solve* the argument, say something like we'll have to just disguise him better or something."

"Why me?" asked Groltch suspiciously.

"Well he seems to trust you more than Belthar or me," replied the boy.

Groltch saw that there was more behind the boy's meaning and for a second he saw an age of knowledge seem to appear in the boy's eyes. He suddenly had the impression that the boy had already thought of the idea and that he had merely been waiting for someone else to arrive at the same conclusion. Once again Groltch found himself agreeing with Tristan's sentiments. The two were hiding too much to be trusted.

"And besides, I'll be able to explain what's happening to Belthar whilst you help Tristan *disguise* himself."

"True again," replied Groltch.

Suddenly Cal appeared in his mind.

"You'd best get over here quickly," said the sword, sounding genuinely alarmed, *"Tris is about ready to draw me against Belthar!"*

I'll come anon! Thought Groltch springing to his feet.

He ran towards the two humans and saw that Tris's face was almost scarlet with anger. He put himself between the two and pushed them apart. His sudden appearance seemed to startle them and they stopped and looked at him.

"Matt want you Belthar, needs to magick you. He says it not worth the fight and Groltch agree. Think best if we try make Tristan look disguised normal way, okay?" he said, firmly, imitating his *tenget* when she was breaking up two squabbling *hytani.* He must have got the tone exactly right, for Belthar had moved down to Matt before realising he was doing so and Tris just looked at him in amazement.

"Don't stand there with mouth open," he said briskly. "Sooner we get through and over water we can leave them and that be better for all, true?"

Tris still seemed a little stunned by the whole turn of events and was easily led to the nearby river. Groltch reached into his pouch and took out some black root in order to create a paste to darken Tris's complexion. For his plan to work Tris had to be convinced that he looked different by natural means. It was a task made more difficult by the sudden transformation of Tris into a dark skinned human reminiscent of the legendary human sailors of *Tear-thowl-ri* folklore. Tristan seemed satisfied by the final result, though Groltch had no idea what Tris now looked like without the illusion, and they were soon ready to enter the gates of

Grathnac.

XI

Justace Strongman, court scribe to the Earl of Seronshire Lord Anton of the House Gethrel and uncle to the king himself, sat rubbing his hands together silently bemoaning his fate. Until a month ago he had sat in the relative luxury of the palace hall to pursue his work. Now he was sat in a dark, draft filled guard tower on the lookout for several fugitives. It was, ostensibly, an important role, for one of the men he sought was viewed as highly important to his Lord. So important that he had sent his chief scribe to oversee the security checks at the gate. Justace had protested profusely, and not only on the grounds of the personal discomfort he would suffer in the process. He had pointed out to his Lord that there were three land gates at least to check and there was no guarantee that they would pass through this one. However, Lord Anton had merely looked at him in that infuriating yet knowing way, tapped his nose as if implying an instinctive knowledge and said *"He'll go through that gate all right, mark my words he will!"*

With that he had been forced to move his possessions, especially his sloped, mahogany writing desk to this miserable tower that never seemed to see the light and was perpetually damp and dank. Semi-literate, Neolithic and moronic guards surrounded him, all of who found his every complaint a source of amusement and who had seemed to take evil delight in his discomfort. They had even gone as far as having played *practical jokes* upon him and every complaint he had sent to Lord Anton had been returned with the statement *one more week and they'll be here.*

Four weeks in a row he had heard that same phrase and was beginning to doubt he would ever leave this miserable Thenril spawned hole of iniquity and depravity. He was starved of any intellectual conversation and the only form of diversion from the boredom available was the constant card playing of the guards. He had given up trying to play himself after he discovered that they had been "stacking the deck" in order to keep him from victory.

He reached down into the small drawer beside him and pulled out a small bottle of apple brandy he kept there to help the days go by just that little bit quicker. It was watered down of course, he had never been much of a drinker and he needed to retain a clear head to maintain the official records that he was working upon. That was a little bit difficult at present for the market season was well underway and there were many people moving through the gate, all of whom he had to question and note down their names and business. At least that was what the travellers were told. In reality he was there to check the mirror fixed above the door to see if there were any magical illusions covering them.

Justace could not see why he had to perform this task, for even these dim-witted fools around him could manage to look into the mirror. However, Lord Anton had insisted that it was a task of utmost secrecy and that he was to tell no one of his true reason for being here. That he could understand for the buffoons around him were rather slack-jawed and could never be trusted with any matter of a more delicate nature. Unfortunately that meant that he was doomed to stay here until they arrived or Lord Anton realised that they were not coming through at all.

He was distracted by the loud cry of halt uttered from outside from one of the more intelligent gorillas known as Sergeant Wilberforce. He quickly un-stoppered the bottle in his hand and swallowed down several mouthfuls. He spluttered violently as the liquid seared the back of his throat and made his eyes water. He looked at the bottle in amazement. Even watered down it seemed strong, and certainly did not taste as bad as watered down brandy usually tasted. The warm sensation inside him and the pleasant tangy after bite distracted him and persuaded him to have just one more drop before the next line of peasant refuse was ushered past him. Suddenly the smelly cell he was sat in did not seem quite so unpleasant, the alcohol removing the chill that seemed to have settled into his bones of late. He stopped a warm smile from encroaching upon his face, for his task was serious and he needed to project a sober, composed and efficient image to those about him. Even if it was largely wasted upon the black hearted guards who were posted here.

"If yer'lls go through there the gate keeper will takes yer details," said Sergeant Wilberforce in what had to be the longest sentence of his limited vocabulary.

Justace looked up and almost laughed openly. There was never a bunch of peasants more unlike the people of the description before him. Two were women for a start, and never a more ugly, filthy pair of wretches had he ever seen before, though he had to admit there was something akin to attractiveness about the tall one with blond hair. It had to be the gappy teeth she had, though there were rather more than would be expected on a peasant woman of her age. The two scrawny men that accompanied them were probably their menfolk, especially by the rather worn and resigned expressions on their faces. The short dumpy woman certainly appeared to be the unruly and domineering type.

With a sigh and repressed giggle, for he was glad he had no woman to wear him down, he asked for their names. By the relieved looks upon their faces he assumed that they were obviously as stupid as they looked and that they had feared to be asked questions they could not answer. As it was, one of the women stumbled over her name, and another could not spell hers. He looked to the sky, or at least where the sky should be, and silently asked Toric what he had done to deserve such punishment as this.

The reply was rather quicker than he expected for as his eyes moved down they caught a glimpse of the mirror above the door.

What they saw made his blood run cold and he felt the flush drain away from his face. The people stood before him did not belong to their reflections. In fact, they matched exactly those of the descriptions he had of the fugitives.

The man with the *dusky* skin had to be the knight, for his bearing had everything of nobility about it and the short, squat creature that stood in place of the second man just had to be the goblin. The tall woman with the gappy teeth turned out to be a large man with shaggy beard and white eyes, most likely the druid, and the other, short dumpy woman had to be the wizard, though he looked barely old enough to bear the title. From the books he had read most wizards had not the power to be called such until well into their thirties and forties, and this boy could not be out of his teens. He took a deep breath to try and steady his nerves. The fugitives were here, stood before him. He could barely stop his hand from shaking as he wrote down the last of his details and his voice seemed to fail him.

Justace looked around knowing that he was rapidly approaching a fit of blind panic and his eyes dropped down to the bottle of brandy that he had not been fast enough to conceal upon their entrance. He picked it up and drained it of its contents. The burning sensation tore through him and for a moment he felt that he was going to be sick. His vision blurred momentarily and he felt himself stagger. Evidently with his heart pumping in panic the drink was coursing through him rapidly and enhancing its effects. He felt a hand grab him and he saw the woman that was a boy look at him with concern.

"Are you all right?" the he-she asked.

Justace chuckled to himself at his own wit. The he-she indeed! Unfortunately that seemed to make the he-she more concerned.

"Come, let's get away from here," said the large he-she, pulling the littler one away.

"Oh no you don't!" said Justace, finding his voice at last.

"What?" asked the big he-she with a dangerous glint in its eyes.

Justace looked round for a weapon and, seeing only his quill, grabbed it and brandished it before him like a weapon. By now the brandy inside him had dissolved any trace of fear he had previously felt.

"You thought you wash clever, didn't you?" he asked, feeling truly superior over these intellectual gnats. "You thought thoshe magic dishguishesh would fool me, didn't you?"

Their eyes widened in alarm and a feeling of smug satisfaction washed over him, in much the same way it did when he beat someone at chess whilst playing the black pieces. They started to back away from him. Justace thought it was time for the guards to earn their pay.

"Guardsh!" he cried out, moving himself round towards the door, still brandishing his quill before him. "One move and you'll regret it!"

He waved the quill threateningly at them. The people before him seemed to stare at him in stunned amusement.

"I'm sherioush you know," he replied, bracing himself as the world span briefly before him. The alcohol really seemed to have had a rapid effect upon him. "You know the ancshient proverb, don't you? The shword is mightier than the…no wait…"

He creased his forehead in confusion. Fortunately the guards were not as slow physically as they were mentally and were already surrounding the fugitives.

"Take them to the royal dungeonsh," he said absently, trying to recall the proverb that he gotten wrong.

The guards soon had the men under guard…he chuckled at his own wit once again…and began to lead them away. Justace noted that with little interest, the puzzle of the proverb taking full priority. It did not last long though for he soon found the world go dark around him and the last thing he remembered as unconsciousness claimed him was his head hitting that precious mahogany writing desk…

XII

Tristan sat on the floor of his cell with his head on his knees. The events surrounding his capture were still a blur to him yet he could not escape the reality of his present situation. He was an Errant Knight captured and awaiting his fate. If he was lucky he would be offered the chance of the Challenge which could help decide his fate, though regardless of its outcome, he was guaranteed another trip to the Chambers and he would lose his position of King's Knight. Bitter tears welled up inside him. All this had been his own fault, yet he had given up everything he had believed in to save the wretched life of a goblin, or ran-the, or whatever the hell it was. Anger began to mingle with the bitterness and he got to his feet. He paced rapidly around his cell, thoughts swirling through his mind. Plans emerged and were soon discarded. He could see no way out of his predicament, even though his companions were only a few yards away from him. Belthar had seemed a little despondent, Groltch had been knocked out with a club and Matthius injected with some sort of drug to keep him unconscious and prevent him using magic. The situation was quite simply hopeless.

"You there!" said a guard who seemed to appear suddenly at the viewing grill in his cell door.

"Yes?" asked Tristan, fear beginning to gnaw at the pit of his stomach.

"Lord Anton requests your presence at dinner."

Tristan looked at the guard to see if some cruel joke was being played upon him. The guard, however, looked deadly serious and was obviously of a better quality than those who had captured him. Tristan wondered at the request. The Earl had no need to summon him as if he were a courtier. There had to be some mistake here. The guard opened the door and removed the shackles that had bound him. Two others stood behind him, swords at the ready, obviously to ensure his co-operation. Tristan knew that even unarmed he could probably take all three and win, yet knew that would not help his position, stuck deep within the heart of the central tower of Grathnac. Though not as formidable a fortress as Belthanor, it had withstood at least three sieges, including the two during the Elfwars when even Belthanor had fallen.

"Come on then," said the guard, belatedly adding, "sir."

Tristan's eyes widened in surprise. The man before him was using his rank, something not usually granted until after the Challenge, and only if the defender was successful. He followed the guards out through the corridor. As he went the knights and guards around him all knelt and bowed with their right arms on their chest, the traditional and formal bow that knights had to give the King's Knight on ceremonial occasions. This completely confused Tristan and he barely noticed the courtyard as they moved from the prison tower to the central tower. He did notice that it was in the process of several alterations that seemed to turning the place into an ornamental palace. Looking around he could see that if any army made it into the courtyard, the central tower would not be as well equipped to defend itself as before. Tristan wondered at this, especially in a time of war such as they were in.

He had little time to ponder too deeply upon it for he was soon within the tower itself and being led up what appeared to be a newly constructed central stairway. At the top of the staircase was a set of double doors at which two guards stood, pikes at attention. The door opened and what appeared to be a gentleman in waiting appeared and bowed before him.

"If you would accompany me, milord, I will take you to where you can freshen up and prepare for dinner."

Dumbfounded by the whole experience Tristan followed mutely, leaving the guards behind. He was led up a spiralling staircase onto the uppermost floor; the area generally reserved for high ranking courtiers and the Earl's family. He was taken to the steam room in which he was finally able to scrape off the travel dirt he had acquired and left feeling fresher than he had in months. Servants then flocked round him, much as they had in Caldor, and attended him. Some cut and trimmed his hair and beard in what was said was the latest court fashion and others saw to perfuming him and dressing him. By the time they were finished he found that he looked something like the old Tristan in Theldar, though the beard made him seem older. As he looked at himself in the mirror he found that he was wearing a deep red silk shirt with golden lions brocaded onto the sleeves and the jewelled sword, his symbol of office, attached as pins to his collar. Yet that was not all. Even as he stood looking at his reflection in a full length mirror a squire approach him holding Caliburn in a highly decorated scabbard.

"How's that for an entrance?" asked the sword in its usual mocking manner.

Fantastic replied Tristan dryly. *Any idea what's going on here?*

"No, but a rather attractive maid polished my blade up rather skilfully. It quite stirred me up!"

Tristan looked at the sword in shock and disgust.

"I knew that would bring the old prude back out in you!" said the sword with that soft buzzing that acted as a chuckle. *"Shall we go?"*

Tristan looked round to see that another servant had arrived. She informed him that the Earl awaited his company with his knights in the dining hall. This was an even greater shock to Tristan than the treatment thus far, for even as King's Knight it was custom for him to be seated before all nobility. The position of King's Knight was as high in society as a commoner could ever expect to climb to in Caldor. He followed the servant back down the grand central stairway and was ushered into the main dining chamber. Tristan was stunned to see it half full with all the occupants' eyes upon him. They all stood as he entered and as the servant led him to the high table the knights and courtiers around him knelt in the ceremonial bow as he passed. Feeling suddenly very awkward he made his way through the hall keeping his eyes fixed upon the servants back. It was a breach of dining etiquette but he did not care. This was the last thing he had been prepared for and he wanted to avoid possibility of insulting some minor noble by looking at them in the wrong way.

"I wouldn't worry too much about that!" said Caliburn softly, *"there aren't many people of note here anyway, only those unlikely to question your presence. Evidently the Earl wants to make a show to you without playing his hand to the other Houses. I would be very careful what you say and do here. He is a very clever, very dangerous player in the Royal Game."*

I thought he was just an idle noble concerned with nothing but gambling, drinking and wenching on his mind! Replied Tristan, recalling his history lessons.

It had been for that reason that Queen Anne, Lord Anton's younger sister, had been elected to the throne by the Royal Council over him.

"It's an image he has recently taken care to reinforce, so I'd be very wary if I were you!" replied Caliburn, fading slowly from his mind.

"Welcome, Knight Errant!" said Lord Anton, rising to meet him.

Tristan took a moment to look at the man who ruled this shire. He bore little resemblance to his nephew, being unhealthily obese, with very little hair and quite a swarthy complexion. His clothes were elegant and rich, yet exceptionally gaudy. In his hand he held a golden goblet and before him was a sumptuous feast.

"Please, *Knight Errant*, take the seat at my side," said the man with a gravelly voice and a wide grin.

It was a grin, however that did not reach his eyes and it was there he could see the resemblance to the king. There was a cold, calculating intelligence behind them and suddenly Tristan felt the urge to follow Caliburn's advice to be cautious. The Lord's emphasis on the title Knight Errant also showed Tristan why he was being treated as he was. Either Anton thought, or wanted those around him to think, that Tristan was on a sanctioned quest. He sat down beside Lord Anton.

"I would like you to meet my daughter Miranda," said the Lord, indicating the woman to his left. "Is she not one of Loden's great beauties."

"You speak truly for she is a wondrous sight to behold," replied Tristan politely, recalling his lectures on court protocol and speech.

As he looked though, he realised that the earl had not exaggerated. She was indeed quite beautiful, with elegant features, long brown hair and sparkling, intelligent green eyes.

"Beware Mannamen bearing gifts!" quoted Caliburn softly, referring to a lost civilisation said to have once waged war over a woman of surpassing beauty.

She's not a gift for me, replied Tristan sharply.

"A fine prize for any that would take her hand in marriage, I'd wager!" said the Lord rather too loudly with none too subtle a wink at Tristan.

He blushed furiously and thought of Caliburn's words once more.

"Told you so!" came the smug comment at the thought.

Oh shut up! Replied Tristan in irritation.

He wished that just once the sword would be wrong. He turned back to the meal and ate his fill, feeling only a little guilt at the incarcerated state of his companions. Almost as if reading his thoughts Lord Anton turned to Tristan.

"Your companions have been released and are presently eating in the servants' quarters. I have to apologise for the behaviour of my guards, they did not realise your status and position."

Stunned once more Tristan was barely able to mutter his thanks and soon was feasting and drinking as if he had not done so in years.

XIII

Groltch moaned and spat the blood from his mouth. The guard had been less than gentle when he had delivered the evening meal. It had happened, as before, when the human had seen the gold chain round his neck, his *methram*, given to him by his dying *tenget* on the day his village had been destroyed. Magical in nature it could never be forcefully removed by anyone other than the wearer. It could be given and generally was passed on from *tenget* to *hytan* at the correct time, for those still worn on the death of the bearer were lost forever, the prophecy of their creation fulfilled. It had not saved his *engaral* ring, for the guard in the human king's prison had twisted and cut at the ring until it had yielded. No blade could slice or damage his *methram* however, though this guard had tried for almost half an hour before giving in. Unfortunately, for Groltch, the man had then vented his frustration on him by beating him to unconsciousness. He was unsure how long he had been unconscious but the pain in his chest and face told him it had not been long enough. He moved over to the food that had been brought to him. Stale bread and water was all he had and one sniff of the liquid was enough to know that it had been polluted with urine. He staggered to his feet and moved to the cell door.

"Anyone about?" he called, hoping that the guards stayed in the guardroom he had seen whilst being dragged to this filthy, rat ridden cell.

"Yeah," came the grizzled reply of Belthar. "Got a head that won't quit playing the drums, but other than that, fine."

"I know feeling," replied Groltch, leaning against the door as his head suddenly seemed to spin round violently. "What of others?"

"Mat's down and poisoned," replied Belthar almost growling as he said it, "and Tristan's gone turncoat with them guards."

"Turncoat?" asked Groltch unsure what the expression meant.

"Yer know, turned traitor."

"You not know that!" replied Groltch, not knowing why he was defending the odd human.

"Well they took 'im away an' removed his chains," muttered Belthar clanking his own chains as he spoke.

Groltch looked at his own chains and inspected the locks on them. They were simple affairs, especially compared to the chains of the king's prison which were welded shut. He still had these scars on his wrists from that procedure.

"That not prove anything!" replied Groltch angrily.

The one thing he knew about Tristan, and even admired, was the fact that when he gave his word it was locked in the strongest steal. He suspected that Tristan was one of the few humans who he would trust to enter a *matchlahna*, a shadow pact, with.

"Well that counts fer toffee in this pickle," replied Belthar, once again using the human slang that he rarely understood, and this time there was no Cal to translate it for him.

"What you mean?" he asked.

"I mean, so long as we're down here and he's up there it counts fer nothing!" the big human replied.

"Well chains here are no problem but door lock on other side so Groltch no better for not having chains!"

"They're not stupid here either, they've put me in iron and that tends t'cancel out mi powers."

"Then we stuck then!"

"Not tonight, my little friend!"

Groltch would have killed the human for that comment, were it not for the two doors between them. Little friend indeed!

"It's a lesser conjunction tonight," replied Belthar, not making himself any clearer. "The two moons are full tonight and so I might just be able t'manage yer door. If yer quick enough, I'll have mi chains off in time to give yer a hand with any guards, for the door'll not be a quiet affair."

Groltch removed one of the wires he always kept entwined in his gold chain, straightened it out and attached it to one of the pins kept in the small chamber magically concealed within the medallion that the chain held. Within seconds he was free of his chains.

"That quick enough for you?" he asked.

"It'll do, but yer'll have t'wait a while. For me to break through the iron I'll have to wait until both reach high ascension, about an hour from now."

"How you know the time?" asked Groltch quickly.

"If yer power depended upon the cycles of the moons yer'd soon learn their movements! Now clap yer trap and wait fer mi signal.!"

Groltch assumed that the human wished his silence so he sat down took out the medallion and began to meditate in order to retain his composure, a skill he was rapidly developing to a fine art among these infuriating humans…

XIV

Tristan sat in the private audience chamber of Lord Gethrel in a luxurious armchair with a glass of fortified wine in his hand. The meal had gone by quite quickly, though quite embarrassingly for Tristan, with Lord Anton, Anton as he claimed he preferred to be called, constantly referring to the various assets of his daughter, both financial and physical. This had been backed up by Cal's even cruder running commentary on the true meaning of Anton's insinuations. He had been more than a little relieved when the meal was finished and the woman was returned to her quarters.

Better still had been the fact that the rest of the dining hall had also now retired to their own pleasures and he had been left alone in the company of Lor…Anton. Throughout the meal Tristan had the impression that the Earl had been guarding his words and he was curious to discover why he, an errant knight, was being treated almost as a minor noble. He had not been satisfied thus far, as the old Lord had seemed content to prattle upon meaningless niceties since they had reached this room.

"If you're clever you might be wondering exactly what's going on here," said the earl, startling Tristan by his sudden change in conversation.

Evidently the sly old fox, as Caliburn liked to refer to the Lord, wanted to keep him off balance.

"Well I had wondered, especially due to the sensitive nature of my departure from the King's service," he replied cautiously.

"Smart, I like that!" replied the earl with a smile. "Just what I would expect from my future son-in-law." Tristan started at the comment but the Earl did not give him a chance to reply. "Actually, you're departure surprised me as well and kept many of my agents guessing for quite some time. It was rather sooner than expected."

"You expected me to leave?" asked Tristan, who felt like he was being battered around by this conversation, constantly being pushed this way and that.

"Of course!" replied the earl slapping his thigh with a laugh. "I've had agents doctoring yer training since yer started."

"What do you mean?" asked Tristan, now completely confused.

"Let me ask you," said Anton slowly, "did you start to experience doubts recently about the exact nature of your training and role within the kingdom?"

"Well, some yes, why?"

"Well that was due to me," replied the earl with a satisfied grin.

Tristan could not help liking this jovial man, despite his mistrust.

"How was that so?" he asked, still a little confused.

"A major part of your training consists of visits to the Redirecting Chambers. Do you know what the purpose of this is?"

"To help purify our minds so that we can live up to the ideals of Caldor," replied Tristan, even though he suspected otherwise.

Sometimes it was prudent to maintain the illusions that others held about you.

"I'm impressed," said Caliburn softly. *"You can be sneaky when you wish!"*

Tristan just ignored the sword.

"That's just poppycock!" said Anton with a snort. "It's to ensure loyalty, in fact obedience, to the crown. It's a kind of brainwashing that clears the soldier of their own personality and turns them into walking killing machines. Only those who need to think get altered treatment, such as those who need to use magic, which you are able to do I hear. Then Treatment is used more as a threat or punishment to ensure obedience."

"Nonsense!" retorted Tristan heatedly.

He had suspected something similar, but nothing so insidious. Unfortunately, it all had the ring of truth about it.

"It's true, trust me," replied Anton with sadness in his eyes. "I underwent similar treatment to help me mend the error of my ways, but fortunately for me I had won this necklace in a game of cards and it protected me. Unfortunately it wasn't enough to allow me to free myself in time to claim the kingship."

"But what has all this to do with me?" asked Tristan, feeling confused.

"You can help me. Naithan has fallen, Tristan. He is the worst king this kingdom has seen. He is slowly destroying our life. More people enter the Chambers under this reign than under any other. It is killing our originality. What makes us who we are, and he wishes to force this upon the other nations." Tristan listened with disbelief. "I was passed over for my sister to succeed after our father's death, and then again to allow a boy barely grown to take power. He had even promised to pass the crown to me, the rightful heir, but the power got to him; corrupted him and changed him. Together we can help lead an uprising to cleanse our nation. We can even cease the war with the goblins. They are weak and certainly no threat to us. All the killing is senseless, can't you see that? They even worship our god, for Cal's sake, so why try to *cleanse the heathens*, as he is so fond of claiming?"

Tristan heard the words, almost transfixed by their power. He could see the restoration and rebirth in his mind. But questions from a familiar voice, somewhere distant in his mind, kept the image from becoming whole. Anton's eyes almost shone as he spoke and once again he was reminded of the king. Yet still the questions came.

"Why do you need me for that? My role is just that of a figurehead, trained to die heroically for Caldor. How can I help you?" he asked, trying to keep the bitterness from his voice.

"Shortly after Caldor was formed, a member of the Royal Council made a bid to become Caldor's first queen, Queen Angeline. Before she did it, she secured the support of Sir Caldor, who was growing weary of struggling with the squabbles of the council. She would have failed had she not done this. You are his successor and a symbol of the continuity of Caldor. You are he incarnate, at least to the peasants. If you lead them, then they will follow. I need this, for my reputation, through no one's fault but my own, has become tarnished among many. Your reputation would help cleanse mine and strengthen my appeal to the people, especially if you were to marry my daughter and sire the next heir!"

Tristan could see it all before him in his mind's eye. He found his head swimming with the prospect. Yet still the questions came, though fainter than before.

"What of my friends?" He asked. *Are they my friends?*

At that moment there was a knock on the door. Anton called for them to enter and the tall scribe that had greeted them at the gate appeared.

"My lord, sorry for disturbing you, but the guests of the King's Knight have just left and bid me to say farewell to their companion and send their regrets at not being able to speak to you personally."

"Thank you Justace," replied Anton quickly. "I have spoken to the guards about the brandy. Apparently they used fey wine, so for that they are on double guard duty until further notice. You may go."

"Thank you, milord," replied Justace with a bow.

After the scribe had left Tristan looked at Anton with suspicion, the questions in his head now much louder than before.

"Take a look through the window. You may just catch them as they leave. I have given them provision and protection enough to get your goblin friend to safety," he replied to Tristan's unasked question.

He got to his feet and went to the window. Sure enough there were three forms, remarkably similar to his friends, leaving through the east gate towards the bridge of blood, just as they had planned. The large one paused and turned to look back. Tristan was sure that the figure waved at him before turning back and leaving through the gate. Tristan returned to his seat, his head throbbing as it warred between acceptance of the kind old man's ideas and the questions that the sly old fox had left open.

Why had Belthar, of all people, waved at him?

His hand touched the hilt of Caliburn and for a moment he felt exceptionally clear-headed, and suddenly very tired. On seeing this, the old man's face creased in concern.

"I've been a terrible host. I'm sorry," he said softly. "You've had a long day and this has been a lot for you to take in. Retire to your chamber and give me your answer in the morning. You have a choice here young man. It is more than Naithan ever gave you."

Pondering Anton's final words he followed the servant across to the chamber set aside for his personal use and went to bed.

XV

Anton smiled and rubbed his hands together. Yes, the knight had surprised him by leaving so suddenly, but the other instructions his agents had been introducing to Tristan's treatment seemed to have taken root. He finished the coded messages meant for his allies on the Council. With his nephew's rash plan to visit Sol, his brother out of the kingdom on this foolish campaign and the King's Knight under his control, the conditions for a coup in Theldar would be almost set. If he could then manipulate his agents in the so-called Circle of Light then everything would be complete. He sat down and drank his wine with a smile. Not only would he be taking his rightful position as king of Caldor, but he would also have vast tracts of land ceded from Grelchin with which to bribe the dissenters into submission. Yes, Tristan had been early, but maybe it had merely been a sign from Toric that now was the time for him to strike…

XVI

Jeremy had almost dropped the drink he had been serving Lord Anton at dinner when the errant knight had entered the chamber like a lord. His Master would need to know about this. It seemed that whatever plans the Earl of Seronshire was hatching involved Tristan in some way. Yet he was not sure the errant knight was in complete agreement. He would first watch and wait, as all in his profession often had to do. He would have to ensure that all the facts were correct. Rashness was a fault of beginners and amateurs, and he was neither. He helped the knight undress, his hands lingering just a little on the fabled sword, before blowing out the lanterns and returning to his post outside Anton's room.

XVII

"You ready there little one?" asked Belthar in that patronising tone of voice that Groltch was beginning to hate.

"Of course!" he replied tersely.

"Then stand back, I don't know which way it'll fall."

Groltch moved back towards the opposite end of the cell from the door. He closed his eyes, unsure exactly what the druid's powers would do, never actually having seen them. There was the sound of wood cracking and splintering, followed by a loud crash. He opened his eyes and saw that the door had collapsed, the wood around the hinges having warped and split beyond recognition. Without paying it a second thought he leapt through the gap and over to the cell door with the large, manacled hands protruding from the viewing grill. It took but a few moments to unlock them, yet guards were already entering the corridor.

"Stand back Groltch, I'm coming through!" roared Belthar loudly.

Groltch backed down the corridor away from the approaching guards. Just as they reached Belthar's cell, swords drawn there was an almost bestial roar that rumbled out from within and the door suddenly exploded into a thousand deadly sharp splinters, ripping through the approaching guards. Groltch ran up to the first guard and saw, with revulsion, that its body had been ripped apart in the explosion.

"You kill them!" he cried angrily. "We agree not to!"

"You may have, but I certainly didn't. I intend to get outta here. We druids don't do well all cooped up like that!"

Groltch glared at the big man then picked up the keys attached to one of the unfortunate guard's belt. He ran down the corridor, searching until he found Matt. When he did, a stab of ice sliced his heart, the boy was in a lifeless heap upon the floor. He twisted the keys in the lock and flung the door open, rushing immediately to Matt's side. He reached round the boy's neck to feel for the Life Rush. His heart went limp. Though the body was still quite warm, there was no Life Rush. He held his head in his hands.

"What is it?" asked Belthar as he entered the cell.

"Matt dead," replied Groltch simply.

"What?" roared Belthar, leaping instinctively to the boy's side.

For some reason, unfathomable to Groltch, he placed his hand to the boy's throat.

"Yer idiot," said Belthar with tears in his eyes. "He's just unconscious!"

Groltch looked at the boy in confusion, then realised he could see his chest rise and fall. Relief welled up inside him, for although he mistrusted the boy, he had never wished him dead. Evidently humans did not have the life rush of blood surging down the back of their necks.

"Let's get movin'" said Belthar, lifting Matt up tenderly in his arms.

"Okay, I find Tris and you get horse!" replied Groltch.

"Tris? Are yer crazy? He's deserted us!"

"Groltch not think so. I go look!"

Belthar looked at him a moment with that unnerving blind gaze of his.

"Okay, I'll get the horse, we could do with it to help Matt till he recovers. You've got half an hour, yer hear me? Thirty minutes!"

"I be back in half that!" replied Groltch.

"Good, meet us at the East Gate!" called Belthar after him, for he was already flying up the steps at the end of the corridor two at a time.

When he reached the top he found himself in the guardroom. On one side was a weapons rack and he instinctively reached for a sword. As his hand touched the hilt he recalled his pledge. He was skilled with a sword, but not enough to ensure that he would not kill his opponent. He reached instead for a wooden staff that looked like it might once have had a blade atop it, possibly a pike of some sort. He tested its weight and balance, spinning it round a couple of times. It was a little long, and a bit too heavy, but it would do for now. He slipped silently up the next set of stairs, knocking two guards to sleep before reaching the courtyard. Looking around he decided that Tris had to be in the central tower. He slipped across the open ground as a cloud passed over the full moons, and began his assault upon the castle.

XVIII

Tristan tossed and turned in bed, his thoughts spinning round and round on themselves. Anton's words rang of truth, but always there were questions, none of which he could resolve. What was more was that Caliburn's voice, always so strong in his mind, seemed somehow distant and remote, leaving Tristan feeling more alone than he had ever felt. If only the others had stayed around long enough to talk to, which was another question. Why had they left so quickly? And why had Belthar waved? They were not exactly on the friendliest of terms…

He sat up in the luxury four poster bed, lit a lamp and stared at the wall. Before him was a picture of Anton's daughter, an image that he now recalled had haunted him for years. But why? He had never seen her before tonight, yet now his thoughts seemed to return constantly back to her.

The door to his chamber swung open silently, disturbing his thoughts. In one fluid motion he was off the bed, Caliburn in his left hand, bedpost guarding his right flank. He stared in amazement when he saw Groltch enter.

"I thought you had gone already!" he said loudly.

"Shhhh!" replied Groltch, putting a finger to his lips.

Tristan noticed that Groltch seemed a little bruised, and his clothes were torn and covered in blood.

"Have you been killing the guards?" he asked angrily.

"No, just, making sleep with this," replied Groltch pointing to the three-foot staff in his hands. "It broke on one with hat on."

"What of the blood?"

"It mine. Guard wanted this but Groltch not give," replied the gob…ran-the pointing to the necklace it always wore.

"When?"

"After you go. Not know exactly."

"But they set you free!"

"No, we escape jus' now, only we must go. Belthar and Matt ready to leave with Gala…horse. Groltch swear all true."

Groltch placed his hand on the floor to his shadow then pressed it to his heart. Caliburn had said that the gob…ran-tha believed that their shadows contained their souls and any oath made in the method he had just witnessed were like the sacred oath to the knights.

He looked into Groltch's eyes and saw complete honesty. The answer to one of the questions he had been pondering suddenly came to him. What was to prevent Anton's meddling with his treatment from going beyond just revealing the truth, but to manipulating him as well. The answer was, of course, nothing and, given Anton's treatment of Groltch, it was obvious he was not a man of his word. Tristan then did something he had never dreamed he would ever do. He placed his trust in a goblin, a creature he had once hated.

"Let's go," he said throwing some clothes on quickly.

Groltch's relief was evident. Tristan grabbed some items of clothing and threw them towards Groltch.

"To replace those you're wearing," he said quickly.

"Too big," said Groltch and for the first time Tristan saw Groltch smile. "Groltch not exactly tall, even for ran-tha. My *engar* Sherlatch always tease me on it when we together."

Tristan nodded then moved to the door. He looked back to Groltch.

"The guards?" he asked quietly.

"Asleep," replied Groltch with a shrug.

Tristan led the way towards the entrance. Everywhere they turned there were guards lying unconscious upon the floor. Tristan looked at Groltch with renewed respect. If his race possessed skill like this then why were they unable to fight better against the king's troops? He wondered silently. It certainly revealed how Groltch had gotten so close to the king in his own palace. He counted some thirty men in the corridors they passed through and that would not account for those he encountered in other corridors whilst searching for him. He looked back at Groltch and noticed with concern that the ran-the was limping. He looked back to see two guards approaching.

"Stay back," said Tristan quickly, "I can deal with them."

XIX

Jeremy followed the two as they made their way down the stairs to the main exit, desperate to avoid that goblin's staff. He had seen it work on two guards already and they had fallen almost before they could blink. He had also seen their two companions waiting by the East Gate. He could wait no longer. He had to send word to agents in Belthanor and also send a report to his Master. They could not head into Grelchin because of the number of troops in that area, so they would have to pass near Belthanor and hopefully that fortress would be more secure than this rat's nest here.

He saw two guards running towards them and the errant knight ran to meet them. He needed to see no more. He had once seen Tristan in a sword tournament and had never seen his equal. They would soon be out of the city, especially as Anton would not wake for a few more hours due to the herbs Jeremy had slipped into the fat man's drink. By then they would be well on their way north. Jeremy smiled. He loved this part of his profession most of all, the knowing that he had help damage the plans of those who opposed the king. He turned and moved in the direction of his pigeons. As he disappeared down the corridor he heard the sound of swords clashing…

XX

Groltch was one of the best swordsmen he knew, which was not saying much, but compared to Tris he knew he would seem like a youngling playing with sticks. The speed and fluidity with which the human moved were incredible. The first guard had foolishly rushed in an attack that Tristan had parried then swiftly twisted the flat of his own blade down on top of the guard's head, flooring him with one stroke. The second had been more cautious, coming in with a measured series of attacks designed to test Tris's defence. It was flawless and with an amazing cross hand changeover that saw the sword Cal leap between Tris's hands and exposed the guard's unshielded left side. Tris had sliced open the tunic to the mail beneath, making the guard shy away. This was his fatal mistake. Tris brought Cal down hard on the sword arm of the guard, forcing it low, before slamming the hilt into the guard's face. Groltch thought he heard the man's nose break but was amazed to see that there was not a scratch there. He had merely slammed the helmet hard enough to knock the guard senseless.

Suddenly the first guard Tris had fought, hooked his leg round the knight's, bringing the knight toppling towards the dagger the man had waiting. Tristan twisted mid-fall and placed his free hand round the blunted section of blade at Cal's hilt. With one swift jerk he brought the hilt down into the guard's stomach, winding the man and causing his dagger to fall to the floor. Tris then rolled to his feet, brought his foot down heavily on the guard's head and sheathed his sword.

"Let's go," he said and Groltch noticed that the human had not even broken into a sweat.

He found himself looking forward to the next time they fought, just to see if the human really was as good as he seemed. He jogged up behind him and they ran swiftly towards the East Gate. No guards approached them as they ran yet about halfway across the yard Groltch's sensitive ears picked up the sound of whispered voices. It was Matt and Belthar who had to be waiting in the shadows of the gate.

"I don't care. I've always known about it! It's just that I've never seen it happen before!" whispered Matt's voice, sounding annoyed and more than a little scared.

"It was the fact that both were full," replied Belthar quickly. "It's always difficult to control when both are full!"

"I know! You've said that before, but look what you did!"

"He damn near hit me with his sword, for the love of Gathra!" replied

Belthar angrily. "Shh! They're coming. Please, don't say a word!"

"I promised you secrecy and you'll get it! All right?"

"Of course, of course! Though I never realised how difficult it would be to resist the temptation though…"

As Belthar's voice trailed off he sounded extremely worried.

"Ho there!" called Tristan softly.

"Ho there! Thought you'd left us for a while there!" came Belthar's reply.

"Never, I have my oath to fulfil, remember?" replied Tris a little too quickly. "Did you get Galahad?"

"Yes," replied Matt, his voice sounding a little shaky. "He's outside. A horse is a little difficult to hide in shadows, especially white ones!"

"The guards?"

"Distracted," came Belthar's quick reply.

They were now close enough for Groltch to see what he thought was a warning glance at Matt from Belthar. Groltch eyed them suspiciously, curious to know what secret lay between them.

"Let's go," said Matt, nervously eyeing the guard tower. "The plan is to head out as if to enter the swamps of Grel-Chin then cross back at the ford some miles north."

Groltch scowled angrily. In his haste to cover their secret he had spoken the plan for all to hear. They joined up and headed through the gate, Groltch taking rear guard. As they passed the tower he could not but help looking in the dark recess of the door. His sharp eyes managed to pick out the shape of what appeared to be a severed human arm in a pool of blood. Most startling of all was that the damaged stump seemed to have large teeth marks in it, like that of an animal…

XXI

The woman who called herself Hannah watched them go with interest. She knew of their plan and also that the spy Jeremy would be sending word of their approach to Belthanor by pigeon. Yet Anton required the knight for his plans. The Circle of Light had not been very active in this area recently and she had been getting a little bored. It was time to do a little more free-lancing for Anton.

She did not mind juggling the two around so long as Anton's business did not adversely affect that of the circle. She could not see how giving him a rogue knight would do that, though they would probably wish to aid the ran-the, so technically it would be aiding both causes. It would also have the added advantage of helping her out of this pit of boredom she seemed to have dug for herself. Infiltrating Belthanor would certainly pose a challenge. She watched them disappear round the corner and then moved to beat them to the city gate. She had some guards to distract, for she could not have them capturing the hapless four as they left and thereby spoil her fun…

CHAPTER EIGHT: Prophecies and Power

I

Meredith moved back the picture silently from the wall of what appeared to be this family's study. Sure enough, as if lifted straight from one of those cheap prose adventure tales so popular in Kolth, there was the safe. Even better was the fact that it was one of those magical dial safes that had a numerical code that had to be entered in sequence before the door would open. The merchant, a Caldorian, would, of course, not know that it was in fact a magical device, but believe it to be one of the new amazing mechanisms currently being designed and built in the Empire. For nophobs, they certainly seemed to put a lot of faith in this supposed technology.

Meredith had once lived there, some ten years ago, and it was nothing like these southlanders seemed to think it was. For some of them it seemed to have taken on an image of mythical proportions where there were no poor and the streets were lined with gold. She knew the truth. Kolth had just as many, if not more, poor districts than this marbled city of Theldar. She shook her head angrily. There was a time and place for old memories and that was not in the midst of a heist. If she were not careful her spotter and apprentice Jack would pick up some career threatening bad habits.

She reached into her belt pouch and removed a metal ear cone. When put over her ear it would amplify the sound made by the crackle of magical energy that where emitted when the central dial was moved. She knew from past experience that when the crackle became an almost inaudible pop that it was time to move in the opposite direction until the pop occurred again. It was a delicate procedure that only the best of her trade could master and it required near complete silence. Unfortunately, Jack was not helping, stood as he was just outside. He appeared to be getting bored and was leaning against the wall drumming his fingers against the wall.

"Jack! Silence, or its dredging for you!" she whispered quickly.

Dredging was the wonderful task performed by "sewer rats" that involved standing in the refuse sewers with a net and pan, dredging for any valuables lost by the topworlders, as they like to call those people who spent most their lives above ground. It was not the most pleasant, or wealthy, division of the guild and was often performed by those being punished, or those who were too hot to remain above ground. She had done a stint there herself and had vowed never to do it again.

The threat had the desired effect upon Jack, who had been sent there himself on several occasions. He was not the most suitable of candidates, particularly for this area of work, having little patience with it, but he was now too old for any of the street rat gangs and they were searching for a suitable role in the older sections of the guild. He would never make a good panther, as the night cats like to call themselves. The day cats had taken to calling themselves the lions, though it was more a source of amusement than sign to respect. To housebreak in the day was one of the least risky sections of the guild.

Meredith cursed again. She was getting too old for this. She placed her ear against the safe door and began to twist the dial to the left. The first number was always found by dialling left, the Kolthon safe makers never really being known for showing much imagination in such things. It was a slow, tedious process as she could not afford to move one number past the one required at any point for to do so would trigger the re-lock and she would have to start again. The dial reached seventy-six before the distinctive pop could be heard. She almost screamed when the drumming of fingers began again.

"Once more boy and I'll cut them all off, one by one then feed them to you for your naming day," she whispered harshly.

It was an idle threat but Jack was not to know. She had once cut off a man's member when he became too friendly with her and ever since the mere mention of amputation from her lips sent the men who heard her into a cold sweat. She was not, in truth a harsh woman, but in this profession it had to be believed you were or others would walk all over you. The drumming had stopped so she slowly twisted the dial round to the right. She almost missed it when the click came for it was only three numbers around. Anyone of lesser patience would have been fooled by it.

She began turning it back to the left and after ten digits she heard a pop, yet it was not quite the same as before. A bead of sweat rolled down her face and she continued to twist it to the left. The pop had been the initial trigger of a booby trap being switched. Anyone of lesser skill would have taken it for the lock popping and turned back to the right, triggering the incapacitating trap. This family evidently had more wealth than it seemed. This was often the case with merchants, for to look too rich was to attract the wrong sort of eyes, but Meredith always enjoyed a challenge. Her efforts were rewarded by a pop followed by a click and the door swung silently open, though only because she had already oiled the hinges. The merchant had probably employed a cat to design these alarms and defenses, for they were all tricks that panthers, or any cat of lesser experience, would have triggered.

She peered inside, using the light of the two full moons to see by, something the designer of this room had not counted upon. She scooped away the money and gems inside, placing them upon the shelf beside her. Though quite valuable in total, it was merely a lure designed to fool cats and divert them from the true stash. Ordinarily that would mean the safe itself was a false lead and that the stash would be elsewhere in an obvious place that would be over-looked as too obvious. The man who owned this however, was too security conscious to risk such a ploy and would use double bluff. She reached into the safe and pushed the back wall at the top. It gave way and revealed a veritable treasure trove of gems. She took a handful of the smaller, less valuable, but less recognisable gems and put back the false wall.

Greedy thieves were often caught thieves and the prospect of a visit to this kingdom's *Redirection Chambers* was not something she ever planned to allow. The man, though a city official as well as a merchant, was also honest and had a family. This loss would be enough to allow her to live comfortably for a while, after the guild had taken its cut of course, but not enough to seriously inconvenience this family. It was a moral stance she could now afford, and helped her sleep better at night. She would only ever steal from those who could afford it and never enough to cause them to hunt her down remorselessly, as had happened to one panther recently. The Night Owl, as he had liked to style himself, had stolen everything from a Solman living here several months before. The victim, less squeamish about violence than these Caldorians were, had hunted down the Night Owl and taken him prisoner. He had been found only yesterday by a dredger, well, his head at least. Apparently they were still fishing out body parts when she had left this evening to do this job.

The drumming of Jack's fingers reminded her that she had become lost in thought again. Cursing silently once more she replaced the show money into the safe and closed it up, returning the dial to the exact position she had found it. She lifted her leg up and tapped the heel of her boot three times. It swivelled round revealing a hidden compartment and she pushed the gems inside until it was full. She then repeated the exercise with the other foot. Jack's fingers stopped drumming against the wall and she thanked Sivran, god of thieves for his mercy. She replaced the painting and looked round her eyes widening at what she saw. A middle-aged man with red hair and light eyes had a dagger to Jack's throat.

"Burgle me, will you?" asked the man, his voice harsh and loud.

Meredith did not know what to say or do. She had not been this close to capture since her early days. Her mind raced with escape plans, yet none would help Jack. Unfortunately she would probably have to cut and run. The guards had taken their quota this week so Jack would likely be free in a few days anyway.

"Hah, I got you, didn't I?" continued the man with a sneer.

Judging by his size, the middle-age spread was in full flow on this man. She was probably swifter than he was; yet he filled the door. That left only the window, which was of the recent, stronger, cross-lattice design. It was also sealed. Her eyes scanned the room. It had been designed specifically for a moment such as this and she cursed herself for not seeing it sooner. The false wall had probably been attached to an alarm in his bedchamber.

"What are you going to do, little mouse? How does it feel to be the victim?" asked the man.

She looked at him whilst sliding the painting that hid the safe away to expose the dial. She dialled seventy-six left.

"What are you doing, little mouse?"

She dialled three right.

"Putting them back won't save you from the Chambers."

She dialled ten left then held her breath. A hissing sound erupted from the various holes she had noticed dotted around the walls. She thanked Sivran for the moonlight that had allowed her to see them clearly. The man's eyes widened suddenly and he backed quickly out of the room. A white mist began to fill the room and her lungs began to burn. She ignored it, however, and dived for the now empty doorway. Blood was pounding in her ears and her lungs felt about ready to explode. She kicked hard at the man as she sprang past him, hoping to force him to release Jack, but his grip was to strong and his eyes shone with an obsessive fervour.

Cutting her losses she ran down the corridor, taking out her weighted silken scarf. She leapt through the open window, tossing the heavy end of the scarf above her. It arced over the rope she had attached there and she swiftly grabbed the weight with her free hand. She slid rapidly down the greased rope that had been attached to a clothes' pole in the garden. She released the scarf near the bottom and crashed heavily into the ground, painfully jarring her legs. Nevertheless she staggered to her feet and swiftly removed her tinder striker from her pouch; a clever device that used a spring mechanism to strike flint onto steel and created sparks. The grease on the rope caught light first time and made its way rapidly up the rope. She threw herself at the back wall and hauled herself over to the other side. By now the entire wooden framed window was alight and the occupant had worries other than her on his mind. She thanked Sivran for her escape and slipped into the maze of sewers beneath the marbled streets of Theldar.

II

Councilman Oliver Talbot looked at his burnt out window and anger welled up inside him. A thief had managed to enter his house again, and escape, though with ingenuity and audacity that he would not had credited a thief as having. It was a problem he was determined to stamp out, starting with that thief. He had only seen the eyes and the rest of his face had been heavily covered but Oliver was certain he would be found. If only the City Council would listen to him. Well they would. The light of Toric would shine in every nook and cranny of this city of sin if he and the king had anything to do with it. Oliver admired King Naithan for his strong religious stance, but knew that he had not had the chance to look over his crime preventing proposals. His weasel-like scribe just took them and filed them away somewhere, but they would be seen eventually, and then no amount of arguing on the council would top them being enforced. He looked at his window once more and then turned to the guard beside him.

"I want to be there when they question that wretch of a boy, you hear?"

"Yes, councillor," replied the guard with a slight bow.

Guards never showed Councilmen the respect they deserved, but that too would change. He turned away from his house in disgust and went to oversee his shipping company finances before the afternoon council was convened.

III

Malcolm sat at his desk, staring at the writ issued to him that morning by the king. There had to be some mistake. The bumbling fool of a man was sending him away from Theldar at a crucial time. The idea that he would have to keep an eye on the Countess of Northshire was sheer absurdity. She was no more a traitor than himself. It was true that he looked after the interests of his former master, yet never to the detriment of the kingdom.

It dawned on him that the king could suspect his extracurricular activities. He shook his head. That could not be possible as the idiot did not have the wit to see through Malcolm's carefully hidden schemes. Still, he had seemed to have known of that girl Marie and her connections to the Shadow. Suddenly a little nervous, he began to think through the myriad of explanations he could give about the incident. Then rational thinking took over. If the king had known of his activities more would have happened to him than this brief exile to the border county, for Malcolm was sure that it would indeed be brief, after the chaos that would reign here in Theldar.

He shook his head angrily. That should not matter, for what mattered was that he was being sent to the wilderness of the borders and all the hardships that such a life would entail. He did not wish to spend any amount of time in that land forsaken by Toric himself. He had to find some way to ingratiate his way back into the king's good graces, for he was sure that this was merely a case of the fickle king being annoyed by some action or another on Malcolm's part that had inadvertently upset him.

He smiled in satisfaction. That had to be what had happened. Yet how could he do this, for time was short and he was due to leave after the proxy Council's decisions had been made and sent out to the various council members this afternoon. He sat there, spinning his most prized possession, a Kolthon device designed to replace the quill known as a *Penna Acquias* in their tongue, literally translated as a fountain pen, through his fingers. He only used it on special occasions, and he deemed this moment as one.

His thoughts were distracted as Princess Helena's entourage swept past his office on their way to the royal quarters of the palace. Evidently she would be here to confer with the king before the Council meeting this afternoon. Suddenly the pen stopped spinning as an idea slipped into his mind. She would obviously be here to find out her role during her brother's absence, which would probably be the running of the kingdom as regent, especially as Gareth was away fighting the goblins. This first, private meeting would contain all the pertinent information on the whole situation, the council meeting being merely a forum to allow the various Lords to learn of the details. If he could get to eavesdrop on this then he could find out something useful to get him out of the trip to Northshire.

He quickly tidied his desk and made his way out into the corridor. If he was lucky he would be able to get into one of his vantage points and see all the proceedings. He made his way into the servants' corridors, and found his way to that certain section of wall he had fortuitously discovered shortly after his arrival here. He had been drunk and lost at the time, one of the few times he had allowed himself to get in such a position, after he had been forced out on the king's hunt as a beater for the first time.

He pushed the second stone to the right of the small table and with a grating noise the stone door swung open, allowing him into the secret corridors that seemed to crisscross the palace. He had not had the time to explore them all and was sure he did not know all of them, or even half. Yet this one was possibly the most ingenious of them. He soon found the large sheet of glass in one side of this particular corridor. He had been given the most almighty of frights the first time he had found it, for the king had been looking straight through him from his private chamber. He had since realised that somehow this window was only clear on this side.

Though he had never seen the chamber from the other side, he had assumed from the way people would often preen themselves before it that it was a mirror of some sort on the other side.

As he stood there, the king and his brother and sister all entered together and sat down. Behind the king was that manipulative, irritating Lord Priest of his, a man who often seemed to be the bane of Malcolm's life. The king opened his mouth as if to speak and Malcolm realised the reason for Matthew's presence. He smiled in satisfaction, however, for this was a common occurrence in these chambers, magic being used to hide the voices. Malcolm, however, had been trained for this eventuality, so set about observing the movements of their lips so as to ascertain the words they were producing. It was not foolproof, yet would hopefully provide him with enough information to aid him in his plight.

IV

"...travelling these roads is the same as it always has been, brother. You really should do something about them, they really are starting to become a bit of a mess," continued Helena in her usual, nasal whine that she had perfected as a child.

Naithan nodded and assured her that he would get on to the local barons to start reconstruction of their local sections of the highway before he was forced to introduce further taxes. She nodded in assent then continued moaning, as she often did. Naithan was glad that he was about to bestow upon her the Regency of his kingdom. Perhaps a little first-hand experience of the problems of ruling a kingdom would help stop her almost constant complaining whenever they met, though he doubted it. His brother was sat behind their sister with a grin on his face and making his hand flap up and down in mock imitation of their sister. Momentarily distracted, Naithan could not help but return the grin.

"You're not listening to me, are you?" asked Helena with a snap. "And what's *he* doing that's so amusing?"

"Nothing!" both answered simultaneously, trying to conceal their grins.

Their sister had always been the most serious of the three and they had often joined to tease her on it. However, this time it gave Naithan a chance to think back to what she had been saying, a gift he had gained from constant daydreaming as a child. It had always been useful to pay enough attention to the schoolmistress that he was able to recall the last few sentences she had spoken. He used that gift now.

"I have already tripled guard patrols on the main trade highways," he said, enjoying the startled look of his sister as he answered her question. "There's not much more we can do about these so-called *dark knights*. I believe some of the peasantry must be hiding them, or may be members of the Circle of Light."

"What?" asked Helena with a start. "I thought mother had well and truly crushed that?"

"Evidently not," replied Naithan sourly.

He wished his sister would read the reports of his Spymaster, though she rarely did as she did not approve of the man's profession. It had been one of the initial reasons he had continued the man in royal service in the earlier days of his reign. Anything that would cause discomfort with his sister had once been enough of a motive to do it. That had been in the more juvenile days of his reign, and now was not much time to relive such moments. He gave a nod to his brother and instantly the smile disappeared. This was the time for serious discussion.

"That is one of many things you will have to take care of when I am gone," continued Naithan quickly.

"I'll do my best," replied Helena, looking only mildly surprised. "Anything else?"

"We have…a special guest in the lower suites," said Naithan slowly, knowing his sister's aversion to torture and imprisonment.

"Who?"

"The one who styled himself *the Shadow*," he replied. "It seems his name is Galen Faithe and it may be that he has somehow restored the ancient alliance with the an'Tharons."

"I thought the Faithes had been wiped out in the Rebellion?"

"Evidently not, but your question leads me to another subject."

"What's that?" she asked suspiciously.

"All these questions would have been answered by my agent's reports, all of which he has assured me reached your desk."

"They did," she replied curtly. "I just didn't read them. You know my feelings on the subject."

"Yes, I do," replied Naithan, equally as curtly. He ignored the quick flash of a grin Gareth gave him. "Yet if you are to take the Regency whilst I'm gone, you will have to use him."

Helena scowled at him.

"Now don't give me that look. I'm no longer twelve you know. You cannot bully me around anymore. He is a vital link in maintaining power here. You know that there are many here that would use my absence to further their rank if they could, and I need you to be as prepared as possible for any eventuality. There are plots within plots swirling round this kingdom and the an'Tharon-Faithe alliance is just a small part of it. Without the help of him and his predecessors, all this could have ripped the kingdom apart generations ago. You know that someone is involved in some plot involving Tristan. We recently discovered that he also has some agents meddling with knights' training, including Tristan's."

That information, received only this morning, had been a bitter pill to swallow. The possibility of disloyalty being programmed into his knights had never occurred to him. In his rage in hearing this news he had wanted to have them all subjected to Treatment there and then. His Spymaster had borne out his anger before pointing out that they were not exactly sure who they were working for and that it would be useful to keep them under observation. It was possible, with time that they would be able to trace them back to their ultimate master and cut off the threat from the source. The man had been correct, of course, but Naithan found himself wishing this mission to Sol were not so pressing. He would not be happy to return to a broken kingdom. He looked back to his sister and realised the news had taken hold.

"Very well, I shall use him," she replied sourly. "But he shall have to start reporting to me at Teldin though."

"Why?" asked Naithan quickly, as he had assumed that she would remain here to oversee the administration.

"I've problems of my own," she replied tersely. "Someone is undercutting our trade and the merchants are getting restless. I've a dozen city-wide problems, including nearly three outbreaks of fire that threatened to destroy the town. It really is a rat's nest you know, and we suspect arson. We believe that some Solmen traders are at the heart of it, trying to destroy their opposition, something I would like you to discuss with the Light of Heaven when you meet him."

"What of the administration, and the ruling of Theldar and Daranshire?" he asked angrily, not wanting his own shire to be left unguided.

"Those responsible for the kingdom administration will accompany me to Teldin, we have quarters they can use. It has been done before. As for Theldar, you'll have to assign a Lord Protector whilst you're gone."

"Yes," put in Gareth quickly. "It's worked well enough in Belthanor. I checked in with Lady Julia Bellsi on my way through and she has done wonders with the city under her Protectorate. They tend to have more time for the little things, something you should have thought about years ago. Ruling a kingdom, city and shire at once is spreading yourself way too thin. It might do you a favour in the end."

Naithan sighed. It was not often that his elder siblings joined against him on anything and this happened to be one of those times. Unfortunately, with his sister's ready compliance to co-operate with the Spymaster, Naithan would be left as the intractable one and they would have achieved the moral high ground. He was stuck between the two of him and on seeing the rare, impish smile of his sister, realised that he had actually been outmanoeuvred by the two, something they had not done for some time now. He narrowed his eyes petulantly.

"All right, all right, I'll appoint a Shire Protector, though I'll need your help in choosing, as you both seem to be so good at that."

Helena smiled and placed the papers she had been carrying on the floor before him.

"Where..." he began in confusion.

"You said to start co-operating with your Spymaster, so I got him to provide me with records on the local councillors. We've short listed these ten for you."

Naithan almost growled in anger. He had not just been outmanoeuvred, but out classed as well. He would have to have words with his agent about this, for the man had not uttered a word on it this morning. He looked at Matthew who was sat there silently, looking the picture of innocence. Due to the spell used, even his sorcerer could not hear what was passing between them, yet his involvement in their scheme would have been a necessity.

Feeling extremely annoyed he turned to the papers looking through the short-list. Admittedly, they were all competent men and women, many of whom he would have picked himself. They eventually decided upon a councillor called Oliver Talbot, a man not noted for his vast intellect or imagination, yet he was a capable leader, an able administrator and, more importantly, completely devoted and loyal to the king. This had been a stipulation that he had insisted upon, not wanting any chance of a rebellion whilst he was away. Oliver had only once ever been sent to the Chambers and the effect had been a determined, deep-rooted loyalty that Naithan trusted. With that decided, they returned to the business of Helena's period of Regency and the various problems they could face. It took most of the morning to sort out and the rest was filled with details of the war and eventual division of Grelchin. In what seemed to be no time at all it was time to face the council, or at least their permanent representatives in Theldar, and tell of some of the details that had been discussed.

V

Malcolm could not believe it. They had picked someone to lead the city, a job he was best suited to, and they had picked Oliver Talbot, of all people. The imbecilic king had gone for loyalty over intelligence, and that was a big mistake. Oliver's loyalty was renowned, but it bordered on fanaticism, a fanaticism that tainted everything he did. He was vehemently anti-thief and the ages old treaty between the ruling families and the Guild of Hawks would not be honoured by this man. He would cause strife and turmoil in Theldar not seen since the time of Henry the Black, and could even precipitate a similar revolt if left unchecked.

Malcolm had to see the king and inform him of his error. This just had to get him out of going to Northshire. Even King Naithan could not be so stupid as to ignore his reasoning. Smiling at the grace of Toric for granting this reprieve he returned to his office to collect the various covert reports he had collected on the man. He collected information on all the notable figures of Theldar, knowing that there was often a lot of hidden information about people that they would pay a lot to keep secret. Even if Naithan did not listen to him, he could stall his exit long enough to use the information to keep himself here as *advisor* to the new Protector. Either way he could not lose.

VI

Oliver Talbot was annoyed. In fact he was more than annoyed, he was angry. He had managed to secure some time to observe his personal Redirecters work on the boy thief Jack when a summons had come from the council chambers in the lower palace, former residence of kings of old. He had arrived there only to be told they had already proceeded to the new palace to where a joint Council was to be held. That they had left without him had only riled him more.

To make things worse, that odious little man Malcolm, the person who possessed too much information on some of his own, more distasteful habits, had tried to speak to him. For once he had merely swept him away in a rush to get his fellow councilmen and give them a piece of his mind. The man had looked shocked and that would probably mean an increase on the price of the little man's silence, which added yet more fuel to the fire of his anger. As he approached the Royal Council Chamber, a place he would usually feel honoured at entering, the two guards on either side crossed their halberds over the door.

"Halt," said one formally. "State your name and business."

"Councillor Talbot and I'm here for the Joint Council meeting," he replied, further irritated by the delay.

"Talbot?" asked one quickly.

"Yes, Talbot. Do you wish me to spell it?"

"Councillor Talbot. The king requests your presence in the Green Chamber."

"The king?" he asked, worries suddenly filling him.

He was a loyal servant and all his indiscretions were on sinners who deserved it, yet could the king have found out and be disapproving somehow? Was that what Malcolm had tried to talk about? He suddenly found himself regretting his haste.

The guard before him motioned to the door on the left. Oliver walked cautiously through the door, panic swirling through his stomach. He stepped through the door and saw the king stood at the window. Oliver bowed a full one-knee bow and bent as low as he could when the guard announced his entrance. His mind began desperately seeking ideas and possible solutions to his predicament. He made a quick prayer.

Toric, of great and wondrous Lord of the Heavens above, he prayed silently.

Please grant me peace this day so that I may repent for all my sins, even against thieving sinners like Jack. Save me from discovery and I shall be the best of your followers, humblest and most devout…

The king interrupted his prayer.

"Please, rise Councilman. It really is not necessary."

Oliver rose up quickly, trying not to show his panic. It was always possible that he was wrong and that the king had some other reason for inviting him here.

"Councilman," began the king, "you may have heard that I leave for Sol in several days' time, and I shall be leaving my sister here as Regent."

Oliver nodded mutely, wondering where on Loden this could possibly be leading.

"Well, 'tis true and, unfortunately, she will be unable to protect and rule my interests here in Theldar. Therefore, I am in need of a truly devote and loyal man to guard and protect this city and shire in my absence. You are that man."

Oliver's jaw dropped as the words reached him. Him a Protector? Toric be praised at such an offer.

"You will have the power to act as you see fit, so long as not act be treasonous or to fulfill your own ambitions, both of which shall be observed by my sister, Princess Helena. Yet so long as you work for the furtherance of my cause then you shall enjoy complete powers, even to overrule the council, though only in times of need. The full details of your appointment shall be explained in full time, yet for now we need to inform the Joint Council of this development, unless, of course, you wish to refuse the position?"

"N…n…no, your M…m…majesty," he replied, falling over his own words. "I have many ideas that w…will further our c…c…cause, your Majesty."

"I thought that would be the case," replied the king with a knowing smile.

With a start Oliver realised that the king must have read his proposals on the ways to reduce crime in Theldar. He was not given time to wonder upon this, however, for the king whisked him through into the Great Chamber and into a whirlwind of politics that lasted well into the night.

VII

Tristan sat and watched the sun go down in the eastern sky, watching the last of his hopes and ideals disappear with it. Everything he had believed in had been torn down, ripped to shreds by events and people. His training had been doctored to the point when he no longer knew the truth or who to believe. Even the usually comforting voice of Caliburn, though he would never tell the sword that, only seemed to add to his misery. Everything he knew was turned upside down and inside out.

It had only truly dawned on him this evening, for the day had been spent leaving various false trails for any that would possibly seek to find them. The poison that had been injected into Matthius had left him weakened and he had been unfit to travel. That had meant they had had to risk of spending a whole day leading the many patrols of knights seeking to follow them astray. What was more disconcerting for Tristan was the ease with which this had been achieved. Tristan had always thought that knights were the best soldiers on the entire planet, yet most seemed to be unthinking zombies like those found on the Isle of Night by Zaccharius on his epic journey as told in the Melathar Cycle.

Now that they had stopped for the night he had time to think and what he thought was not pleasant. The king was not the godly image he had portrayed and he openly flaunted his wizard Matthew at his side. Goblins were not goblins but Tu'ran-tha, an intelligent, skilled and seemingly noble race, at least if Groltch was anything to go by. Not only that, but they also worshipped Toric, meaning that the so-called Holy War was nothing more than a war of extermination and conquest of a lesser, well not lesser but different, race.

Tristan's head hurt with the thoughts and his vision seemed to spin, probably after effects of the Treatment he had received. Music suddenly filled the air and Tristan looked up to see its source. It was the camp of colourful horse caravans and carts that they had seen setting up earlier. The people wore bright, almost garish clothing and were now singing and dancing round a large, communal campfire. Tinkers, travellers, or whatever they liked to call themselves. A kingdom-less people doomed to wander the twelve lands of Loden since the time of beginnings. As he remembered it, all men had once been wanderers, moving from place to place in search of the perfect kingdom. As time had gone by they had gradually settled down into their respective kingdoms, or been captured as had the people of Caldor, until only a few tribes remained, still wandering in search of the perfect land, or so the legend went. Most people tended to think of them as unprincipled, heathen thieves who had no desire to bring order to their lives. They were infertile baby snatchers, yet they were also traders, fixers of tools and bringers of information and so generally tolerated by villages and towns for a week or two before forcing them on.

As Tristan looked at them now, however, they looked nothing like the image he had been brought up to believe in. He half expected Caliburn to pipe up with some comment on the truth about tinkers but the sword seemed to be valuing his privacy for a change, one of the small mercies Toric seemed prepared to grant at present.

He sat and watched them dance and laugh, envying their freedom and the peace that seemed to surround them. An overwhelming desire to join them swept through him and he stood to his feet swiftly. He looked at his sword sorrowfully, for tinkers did not believe in weapons, the remnants of such belief still evident in his own people's lack of desire to commit acts of violence. If he left with them, he would have to leave everything behind. He would be free from all that now hurt him. Anger filled him and he drew Caliburn, thrusting it deep into a rock, so that no other could use it in violence, his rage clouding the fact that swords should not pierce rock, even magical ones. He did not even hear the sword's cry of pain as its metal grated the stone.

He went to the river and made to dive in ready to swim to the tinkers' camp, yet a hand gripped his arm, stalling him. He spun around and saw Groltch stood there before him.

"I thought you were sleeping?" Asked Tristan angrily.

He had offered to take first watch so as to think and the others had all retired, each shattered from the day's events. Matthius had been recovering from the poison with Belthar's druidical aid and Groltch had been out helping lay false trails all day. Evidently the ran-the had more stamina than he credited it with.

"You make enough noise to wake a Rathalmak with Cal," replied Groltch, "and if not that the sword's scream certainly noise enough!"

"Well, go back to sleep, none of this concerns you."

"You leave not concern Groltch?" asked the creature incredulously. "You not leave me here with them. There something not right with them and I not like. Not one bit! You only one I can…trust."

Tristan felt genuinely touched by this comment. Groltch pointed over to the tinkers.

"In my tongue, they called Tu'Quar-tha. It mean *the free ones*, but also *the lost ones*. They lost, with no home. Yet they also lost in themselves. Many there run from things. Problems, crimes, pain. Though they free, they also lost for they not face what wrong and never will. You not such a human. You not run. Things never get better that way. Never. Groltch know this for I tried it. Can never hide, ever."

Tristan looked at Groltch with new eyes. The ran-the had startled and impressed him once more. As he looked he could see an age of pain behind his eyes and suddenly found he wished to talk to this odd being and find out something about it.

They returned to the camp and talked well into the night and Tristan learned with horror the devastation wrought upon Groltch's village in vivid detail. Tristan recounted his own fears and found that, though Groltch could offer no solutions, just talking about them made it a little easier. Yet both knew that it would soon be time for them to sleep and Belthar to take watch. They bade each other goodnight and prepared to sleep.

"You might want to pull Cal before sleep or wake Belthar," said Groltch quietly.

"You do it," said Tristan wearily. He had no time for the sword's pointless and annoying jokes. "As you seem to get on so well."

"I can't," replied Groltch. "I try, yet it stuck good and deep. Think you have to."

Suddenly worried he got to his feet and noted that the sword had been buried up to its jewelled hilt into the stone. He had no idea how he was going to get it out.

"Just pull me and I will slide out," said the sword softly, almost sadly.

Why could Groltch not do it then? He asked, confused.

"Because you put a prophecy on me that I would remain here so that no other could use me for violence!" replied Caliburn.

Me, use magic? He asked incredulously.

"It's a certain type of magic, perhaps the most powerful. It binds all others to make them last, yet can be used on its own by anyone in times of extreme emotion as a curse or blessing, as you did," answered the sword, though not as acerbically as it was usually inclined to do.

He drew out the sword with ease and noted that there was no mark left upon the stone.

I'm sorry if I damaged you or anything, thought Tristan, suddenly remembering the sword's scream.

"Don't worry about it, my friend," replied the sword softly. *"You all need sleep. Do so and I will guard. Belthar is more drained than you realise, he did more last night than he should and is paying the price for it now."*

Tris meant to ask Caliburn what it meant but found his eyelids closing, almost of their own accord. As they did he noted that Groltch was already asleep. If he had remained awake for a minute more, he would have noticed the sword begin to glow softly with blue light. Had he been awake just a few minutes more than that he would have heard a strange yet almost familiar voice in the night speak.

"Thou had the perfect chance to speak of his gifts, good friend," it said softly.

"He is not yet ready, though the time must be soon."

"I knoweth, for I heard thy scream. He hath fulfilled the first part of the prophecy of thy making. Our time on Caldor grows short, does it not?"

"Too short, my friend. I just hope it's time enough."

With that the glow died and the camp was left to the light of the fire and the songs of the Tu'Quar-tha.

VIII

Malcolm cursed as the stagecoach jostled once more on the bumpy road. Everything had gone wrong today. He had approached the king only to be brushed away like some insignificant gnat. He had then received the same treatment from that boy loving, pompous son of Thenril, Oliver Talbot. Even his attempts to stay for the king's departure had failed and he had practically been bundled into this draughty, rickety carriage by force of arms.

Well, hang them all, he thought sourly.

As far as he was concerned, the whole city could sink to the Dark Realm for all he cared. He had tried to warn them and only hoped he could survive until the time when he would be needed to help reconstruct it all. At least he would be far enough away to escape blame. Suddenly the carriage came to an unscheduled halt. He stuck his head out of the window to shout at the coachman and found himself facing the sharp end of a quarrel, fixed into the crossbow of a masked man on horseback.

"What do you want?" he asked, barely keeping a sudden fit of panic in check.

"Well I believes the traditional cry is *Stand and deliver, your money or your life!*"

Malcolm eyes rolled and he fainted dead away.

IX

Naithan watched with his brother as the long chain of his sister's entourage moved slowly out under the portcullis of the main palace gate. With her went practically all of the scribes, courtiers and administrators, along with their servants, vital to the maintenance of the kingdom's affairs, leaving the palace comparatively empty. Naithan felt glad that he was to depart in a few days too, for he disliked the seeming emptiness that their departure left. It was not empty, of course, merely down to around half strength, and would seem worse on his own departure, which would deplete it still further. Yet the fact that he would be able to walk through parts of the palace and find them empty of life was a little unnerving, reminding him of some of the more ordinary nightmares of his youth.

"Well, I guess this is it," said his brother softly.

Naithan turned back to Gareth with sadness in his eyes.

"You have the ring Matthew gave you?" he asked, pushing back his feelings of sorrow.

"Of course," Gareth replied, "and I'll contact him the moment we reach the outskirts of Grelchi."

"Good, it'll give him something to think about other than the ship's motion."

The both broke into a soft chuckle. Matthew had never been the best of seafarers, ever since a slight sailing mishap the three had been involved a few years back.

"Well, take care and bring me the *Jewel of the South*," said Naithan, using the ancient, and probably erroneous, name of the goblins' capital city.

"Of course," replied Gareth, mounting his horse as he did, "and you make sure you take those guards I brought with me to Sol. They are among the best and are not really required in the war at present."

"You're sure you'll not take any with you?"

"They can't exactly follow me and it would only slow me down to keep pace with them. Don't worry! Peggy may not like it, but she'll get me there fine! We can protect ourselves!"

Naithan shuddered at the thought of the methods his brother was alluding too. He truly wished his brother was more normal, but then no one he knew could ever be described as that. He prepared himself, determined to watch until his brother had gone, determined not to flinch as he did. Gareth wheeled his horse round at a trot to one side of the long courtyard before turning back swiftly. With a cry from his brother, the horse extended its stride reaching almost a full gallop before passing the centre point. There was a sudden flash and two white, feathery wings seemed to explode from the horse's shoulders and its tail flattened out and elongated, sprouting feathers as it did. With a single leap they were in the air and as they approach the top of the palace walls they seemed to shimmer in the air and vanish. Naithan was sure that such showmanship was not exactly necessary, but Gareth always seemed to love upsetting and teasing him in such ways, even now. He sighed and returned back to the palace, his court retainers surrounding him as he emerged from the door. Though the duty of ruling the kingdom was temporarily out of his hands, there were still a multitude of things to do before his departure, one of them being the overseeing of the new Protector's training. Yet a movement in the shadows made him pause.

"Leave me for a moment," he told those surrounding him. "I require a moment to freshen up."

The people swarmed away from him and for a moment he smiled at the irony of his situation. To think he had thought he stood a chance of being alone here. Privacy of that nature was denied to people such as he. He moved down the corridor where he had seen the movement, heading towards the nearest guarderobe.

"Well?" he asked softly, not looking around.

The stealth of his Spymaster amazed him sometimes.

"All seems well," came the whispered reply. "My agents follow the Redirecters, two of whom have led us a step closer to their leader, though it will take time. No sign of the girl, I think she may have fled the city, but with the sort of protection that ring gives her this is only conjecture. I have business elsewhere to attend to, so I'll be out of the city through most of your trip. I'm a bit concerned about that Protector of yours, as I recently found some interesting information on him from Malcolm's reports. An agent of mine…*relieved* him of some of his possessions last night. I'll have a couple of my best agents watch over him in case he proves to be unusually accurate for a change. What's more important is the fact that some of the information throws some doubt on the loyalty of the Hanton brothers. I intend to go in person, for it may even be related to the Faithe-an'Tharon threat, if it exists…"

Naithan ignored that comment knowing that the man was always sceptical about information gained outside of his usual channels.

"Good, anything else?" asked Naithan.

"Not much, but to wish you luck and remind you that my files on the Solman court are in your study."

Naithan turned to glance at his Spymaster suspiciously to see if the man genuinely knew that he had not yet looked at the reports. Unfortunately there was no trace of him, as usual, and Naithan was left to speculate alone.

X

Anton sat looking across at the girl Hannah before him. He had never in his entire life met a more disconcerting woman, next to his late wife of course. Nothing ever seemed to faze or startle her at all. She was a member of that group known as the Circle of Light, of that he was sure, yet he had never once been able to prove it, despite his close links with the group. She had also seen off a large number of Kolthon assassins sent after her when she broke into their *impregnable* Imperial Jewel House on his orders. He had been attempting to set her an impossible task that she would have to refuse; something to bring her supreme arrogant self-confidence crashing down to the ground. Not only had she succeeded but she had also taken the Imperial Crown and brought it to him and almost the entire might of the Empire with it. She had then returned it, for Anton had wanted nothing to do with it, despite the innovations and improvements the Kolthon safe makers had made.

She was cold, calculated, highly professional, and highly mercenary.

Yet somewhere inside her there had to be some passion involving Caldor, for the Circle of Light did not pay the prices someone of her skill demanded. A price his little Kolthon *test* had forced through the roof. He often wondered how she would react to the knowledge that he was, in fact, the true leader of her precious Circle, though it was a risk he was never willing to take. Not one member of that group knew of his involvement, a safety precaution vital to his survival. Though his involvement had only started during his meddling sister's repressive actions, it was a revolutionary group that had brought down kings, and would do so again, if he had his way. Tristan's flight had put a small spanner into the cogs of his plans, though the girl before him seemed to be hinting that she could somehow remove it.

"What are you saying, exactly?" he asked guardedly.

To say too much was to reveal too much with Hannah.

"Only that I know a certain...friend...of yours left unexpectedly last night and that you have some pressing need to see him again. I merely say that, for the correct price, I can get the message to him."

"And what would that be?"

"Only a thousand mareks, that's all."

"What's the catch?" asked Anton suspiciously.

Hannah usually demanded at least double that for her services.

"Let us only say that there is a little, private challenge involved in it for me and I'm at a bit of a loose end at the moment."

"So I would really be doing *you* a favour then," he replied with a smile.

"Well, in a way, hence the price. It's a bargain that one of your ambitions can't dare to miss..."

Anton studied the woman before him closely, knowing that it was useless as he did so. She was a person he would not like to play at cards, her poker face was unreadable. If she were not so valuable to him, he would have found some way of disposing of her, whatever the cost. It was quite possible she knew far too much about his plans, though she never mentioned them outright.

"May I ask exactly what you intend to do?"

"The grant first, then the plan," was all she said in reply.

He scowled angrily, and wrote out a quick banker's note for a thousand mareks and sealed it with a wax impression from his signet ring.

"Thank you," she said, taking the scroll from his hand. "He's on his way north, though he'll pass near Belthanor as he goes. Several of the king's agents spotted him and one is following, preparing an ambush. I intend to get him out of Belthanor and back to you, if you so wish."

Anton went cold. King's spies had spotted the knight here and seen him go. He would have to set to work finding them. Hopefully they would not have discovered his plans.

"Don't worry, they're uncertain as to your intentions at present, so no information has been sent yet." She threw a scroll of her own onto his desk. He looked at it suspiciously. "In case I'm unable to penetrate the castle, or bring him back, that list will earn me the money I need. It's a list of people you might need to Redirect, or whatever. You really should be more careful about who you employ."

With that she was gone. He unrolled the parchment and looked down the list, going deathly cold as he did. Many of the names were some of his closest advisors. Naithan was obviously more astute in matters of internal security than his mother, or possibly more paranoid. Anton had found it almost impossible to get agents close to the king, only getting one evenly remotely near, whilst the king had infiltrated his entire household. Fortunately, for Anton at least, he rarely shared his plans with anyone, yet his co-conspirators, the Hanton brothers, might not be so careful. He quickly penned two coded warnings to send to them and organised the removal to his interrogation chambers the various traitors of his household. None would survive it, for he could not risk any more leaks and he had proved the Redirection Chambers to be too unreliable a device.

As for Hannah, well, her help in this matter was worth the price already, and if she were to manage to infiltrate the dungeons of Belthanor it would be doubly useful. They were so strict on their personal servants that he doubted that even she could penetrate it, leaving herself open to capture. If she succeeded, though, he would have Tristan back and information on how to follow her example. He rubbed his hands together gleefully. What had started as a bad day could well be turn into the most vital of his plans.

He looked down at the reports on their escape and read over the details of the devastation the druid had wrought. He had been certain that the iron chains would hold the big man. Evidently it was not always enough. It could have had something to do with the night's double full moon for he had heard they held some sort of lunar link. Yet it also seemed to loosen his control, for the damage had been savage, like that of a fox in a hen house. He wondered if the knight realised exactly how dangerous the creature he travelled with truly was.

XI

Luca finished his packing quickly. The king had granted him leave and he intended to make the most of it. There was so much he needed to do whilst the king was away and hoped he had enough time to do it before the king began to suspect his secret. He knew that Naithan would react badly to the news, for he had always hated being kept in the dark, as the expression went, yet he could not afford to be dismissed from the service, not yet. He closed the case and went to the back wall of his small cell. He placed his hand on the familiar stone and the false wall slipped away. He moved into the tunnel beyond and with an hour he was on the streets of Theldar.

XII

Marie woke up screaming, as she had every night since that accursed day. The flames always leapt around her, searing her face, burning, melting. Demons pounced on her and tore her apart, all bearing the king's face. They had torn, shredded and ripped until she could bear it no more. Then the face came, offering relief, freedom. All she had to do was submit to its will and obey it. It offered her revenge, riches, love. It had taunted and cajoled her, and every time she rejected it, the pain had returned, more intense than before.

She lay on her bed, spirit almost broken. Why had this all happened to her. She had not wanted to see all she had seen. Before she had come here she had been content. Blissful in ignorance, she believed the term was, and she wanted ignorance. It was the one thing the face would not offer though, for it sought to control through knowledge and pain.

She staggered up from her bed, feeling tiredness she had not thought possible. The sleep she had was not restful and was slowly killing her, yet death would bring relief. She dropped to her knees and for the first time since the day her village had burned, she prayed to Toric. She begged to be released from it all, for him to take her into the next realm and free her for eternity. In the village she had forsaken him over her parents' grave, believing he had abandoned her. For that she prayed for forgiveness, and for all the sins she had committed. Tears streamed from her eyes as prayed, and her head span from tiredness and pain. She clung to the wooden pendent with the lion's head etched onto the image of the sun, Toric's holy symbol she wore round her neck and that she had never quite been able to throw onto the fire. It had been a gift to her from Galen before his change and a reminder of the good man he had once been.

How long she remained there, praying on her knees she did not know, yet the light in her room had begun to slowly fade when tiredness finally took control, sending her falling to the floor. As consciousness left her she felt an overwhelming sense of peace and calm fall over her. When the darkness finally overcame her completely, a smile played across her face, the first in a long time…

XIII

Naithan watched Galen squirming on the floor, screaming and weeping all at once. His eyes were open yet they were not seeing the cell he was in, only the images of retribution that were his punishment.

"See, it works just as well as Robert," said Matthew smugly.

"We don't know that, because we can't see what he's seeing!" retorted Naithan. "How can you be sure that he is truly suffering?"

"Isn't it obvious?" asked his friend.

Naithan had to admit that the magical device the Matthew had created certainly seemed to be doing an adequate job, though he mistrusted what he could not see. That was the advantage with men like Robert, they could tell you or show you what their victim was seeing, and the images would be limited only by the imaginations of the men. This device could not think in such away, could not improvise and change on a whim if the victim did not respond. But he had already mentioned such complaints to Matthew.

"It truly works," said Matthew, a little too pleased with his creation. Apparently the piece of that precious Sceptre of his had been the key in its creation. "It taps into their darkest fears, showing them over and over again, randomly changing the intensity to keep them off balance."

"Well, it will do for now, as an experiment," replied Naithan slowly. "Have Robert executed straight away as I do not want anyone knowing of this place's existence, other than the guard that feeds them."

The guard was a deaf mute and a simpleton to boot, so there was little chance of it being discovered. The man worked for scraps and any shiny baubles they could give him and had little time for the outside world that tended to treat him with cruelty.

"Certainly, Sire," replied Matthew, bowing to hide his triumphant smile. "This is but the first of the many things we shall be able to do, and when we have all the pieces…"

His friend left the thought hanging, yet Naithan was still not fully convinced. He would only truly believe it when he saw it. The tiny device that was Matthew's dream making machine did not seem to be anything that special, despite his friend's claims.

"If the device is still working when we return then I might consider your idea with more care," said Naithan, hoping to keep his friend from feeling he had won that major a victory.

The truth was that if it did work as planned, and when they returned they would hopefully have more of the pieces of the Sceptre then he was prepared to use it. It was largely due to his dreams, however, than any other form of persuasion, that had made the idea even worth thinking about. The dreams had promised that the sceptre was the key, though Naithan was sure that he would succeed by force of arms alone. However, if it was truly as powerful as Matthew said, then it was worth keeping, if only to prevent others from using it. He personally would probably not use it until the last possible moment.

"Let's go," he said, wearily. "The ship leaves tomorrow and we need to be fresh for the long, stormy journey..."

"Don't say things like that," replied his friend, going green at the mere thought of it.

"Can't your magic do something about your condition?" he asked.

"I've not really put much thought into it. There always seems so much more to do."

Naithan smiled. It was nice to know that his friend's magic could not solve everything. They returned to the main area of the palace and headed towards their respective quarters. When Naithan reached his he prepared himself for bed, already regretting his decision to give Luca leave to depart early. He would miss the old man over the coming months, but he was getting too old to make such long journeys. Not for the first time he thought about allowing his manservant to retire to old age. He climbed into bed and drifted off to the inevitable dreams...

XIV

She floated softly through the dreams, the events slashing down upon her and around her, but none touching. The face came again and again, beating at her, calling to her and pleading with her. Yet it could not touch her, the light that surrounded her seeming to deflect all that came at her, protecting her in a warm serene cocoon.

Suddenly the events ceased and she was stood alone in a room. Before her was a creature, humanoid in appearance, but not quite human. There was something about it that did not seem correct. As it looked up she could see it was a man, though not the healthiest of men she had ever seen. The face seemed very elongated and she could see his cheekbones clearly beneath his skin. The head was bald and the flesh was pale in colour, verging on white. Its texture seemed dry and tight, as if stretched as much as possible around his skull. The eyes were hollow, deep-set and dark. The iris was the colour of faded gold and the pupils were not round, but slits, like those of a cat. Its body was very thin, yet seemed quite lithe through its dark clothing. As she looked closer, she noticed that parts of his body were almost translucent and that in some areas she could even see the floor behind it.

"You hast bested me," it replied in a soft, almost croaky voice. "Never before hath one of your kind resisted so long, and all the power I possess is drained. My former Master now rages beyond yet is powerless to stop it. I am yours, great Mistress."

The man bowed his head low before her. She looked at him in confusion.

"Who are you?" she asked, fear edging her voice.

"I am the ring you bear, the Mythel'Vaneer," replied the man. "I appear thus so as not to alarm you and so that you mayest comprehend me easier."

"The ring?" asked Marie, confused.

"Yes, tis my way that I fight to control and dominate those who bear me. When I win, the power is then wrested from me by my Master, and the he may exert control of limited power. Through that of dreams, for dreams are the world of Shadow and I be a creature of Shadow."

"I don't want power over others," said Marie, horrified at the thought.

"Then, if you doth command it so, I shall obey the bearer till you doest wish control, or serve you solely. I canst do what you wish to aid you in whatever you choose, though I am limited to Shadow."

"Like what?"

"I can bring you into my realm and protect you and those who you wish protected. I can enter men's dreams and read their deepest thoughts. I can transform your body to the likeness of shadow and protect your thoughts from those who would intrude upon them."

Marie looked at the man, or creature, or whatever it was. It could do all that? Then it could help her. She could rescue Galen, and maybe even restore his goodness. He had rescued her from the flames when the king had not, despite his crimes, and she was not blameless herself.

"Ring, did you have anything to do with Galen's change?" she asked.

"I admit, great Mistress, I did. I fuelled the fire of his rage, kindled his desire for revenge then helped him unleash that energy."

"Why?" She demanded angrily.

"For it was my former Master's wish," replied the man.

"Why did he want that?" she asked.

"I know not, for I only obey."

"Could you help me free Galen from his prison?"

"If you command I could make you Shadow, or take you to that realm, where there are no such boundaries, and you couldst then bring him back, if you would command his protection."

As the man spoke she heard a slight emphasis on the word command. She looked at the creature closely and behind its eyes she could see, buried deep, a burning hatred.

"I wouldn't command you to do anything," she said in disgust. "I'd ask you, I'm no lord!"

Of that she was certain, and after her brush with the king she wanted no link whatsoever with such people. She recalled a sermon the priest Dernath Caldon had once made in her village church before his first visit to the Chambers.

"All creatures are free in the eyes of Toric and none are slaves to another," she said, repeating the words aloud for the creature before her.

"None hath asked me since my entrapment here," said the creature suspiciously, but also sounding a little awed.

"You were trapped here?" she asked, intrigued.

"In a manner of speaking, yes," replied the creature. "My former Master, my creator, tricked me into giving life to this ring, by way to aid our cause. Yet 'twas but a trap and now I am trapped, never to die, always to serve. I know little of my life before."

"Will you help me free Galen?" she asked the hatred in the man's voice scaring her into reverting to her previous idea.

"If you ask, then yes," replied the creature with a vicious gleam in its eye. "Methinks it would harm my creator's plan, and may lead to my freedom."

"What do you mean?"

"All magic is bound by prophecy, and that used to ensnare me is no exception," replied the creature. "When you asked me to aid you, my bonds loosened, and methinks part of my prophecy was fulfilled. For that alone I would aid you fight the gods on high!"

She looked at the creature trying to find any deceit in its eyes, yet she could see none.

"Thank you," she replied quickly.

"You must go now, for my power is weak. I need rest to replenish, yet we will move when I am recovered," said the creature as the world around her faded.

She woke up instantly and found herself lying upon the floor of the room she had rented. The ring had helped her steal the money needed to pay for it, though she had felt bad doing it at the time. She got to her feet and looked around. It was almost dawn outside and she felt truly refreshed. She looked at the ring, thinking of her peculiar dream. She noticed its black stones seemed to be glittering brightly. She looked closely at them and found that one, slightly larger than the rest, seemed to hold something within it. As she looked closer, she saw that it was the image of the man she had seen, curled up and still, as if in sleep.

She sat down heavily upon the bed, stunned. It had not been a dream, yet she was not sure she truly wished to release Galen from jail. He had killed, and killed many, yet the ring may have been responsible. Yet if that were so, how could she trust the ring? Worried and confused, she stayed on the bed thinking on the matter until well past midday.

XV

Matthew watched the white city of Theldar drift slowly away into the distance, the nausea striking his stomach already. He had spent the last few hours on land desperately seeking a cure to seasickness, but had failed. He had spent too much time working upon the small dream device, though he was immensely proud of it. He had even been able to create quite a specific prophecy to prevent it failing too soon. He could foresee it lasting quite some time, maybe even longer than a year, something that would be close to impossible without a prophecy enhancer. Admittedly he could have achieved a longer lasting result with some of the other components that could increase the length of prophecy, even those not already enchanted. Yet this was only one fifth of the total device and each segment did not merely add to the overall power but magnified it five-fold, if the writings he had read on it could be believed. Two segments alone would make it one of the most powerful prophecy magnifiers on Loden, so the full thing would be almost unstoppable. It was stoppable, of course, else it would still be in the hands of the previous owner, but he had not discovered what its weaknesses were. If he were able to enter the forbidden section of the Kolthon Imperial Library, he might find out more, yet he had been unable to get there as yet.

A sudden swell reminded Matthew where he was and he emptied the contents of his stomach into the sea once more. He ignored the chuckles of the sailors around him and staggered back towards his cabin. He passed Naithan as he did, ignoring the argument that was currently erupting between him and Captain Sirius. Though the Caldorian navy was not as large as those of its neighbours, the Solmen in particular, it still had strict rules and one of those was that when onboard and at sea, the captain was supreme ruler and all ship members obeyed his law. Unfortunately, Naithan had chosen to question that and it looked like his friend was close to being thrown overboard. As the captain's hands went towards Naithan, some twenty knights, unarmoured yet with swords in hand, rushed to defend him. Matthew groaned. This trip was going to be more miserable than he had ever thought possible. He pushed his way through the knights and placed himself between the two men. He looked angrily at both of them.

"Captain Sirius," said Matthew softly, hoping the nausea would not overcome him. "You speak with the king, therefore you will treat him with the respect accorded to him by right of birth. You will listen to his ideas and think on them seriously before replying."

The big man looked on the verge of an angry retort so Matthew raised his hand as he cast a spell and gave him a sudden stomach cramp that forced him to double over in pain.

"Your Majesty," he said turning on the king. "This man is captain of the ship with years of knowledge and experience that we do not possess. We would best help by not disrupting his job as he knows it well enough not to have sunk this ship before now. You may suggest ideas, but respect any answer he gives as you would that of your advisors and act accordingly. We only have ten ships in this fleet and do not wish to be thrown off all of them before we reach Sol!"

Naithan looked about ready to explode in anger but Matthew raised his hand threateningly and he backed down, though there was a dangerous glint in his eyes.

"Agreed?" he asked each in turn.

"Agreed," they said in unison, both looking angrily at each other.

Matthew sighed. At this rate the journey could become a very long one indeed. He glowered at the two men who had shaken hands and moved away before returning to his cabin. The king could be truly childish when he wanted to, especially after he had recently met up with Gareth. The king's brother had always been a corrupting influence. As his thoughts turned to the Knight Commander his ring began to grow warm. He sent his thoughts into the ring.

What? He asked sourly.

Still feeling ill? Came the jovial reply.

Do you want something or are you just contacting me to gloat? Do you realise since your visit Naithan has practically gotten himself into a fist fight with the Captain? Replied Matthew, trying to ignore another twist in his stomach.

No, really? Well good for him. I always told him he should have listened to me and taken up wrestling, replied the voice.

Gareth! Warned Matthew angrily.

All right, all right! Came Gareth's hasty reply. *I just thought I'd let you know that the attack upon Grelchi is commencing in an hour, that's all!*

Truly? Asked Matthew, momentarily forgetting his sickness. *Let me know as soon as it's taken and I'll inform Naithan.*

As you wish, enjoy the trip! Came the reply with a snicker.

The ring went cold and Gareth faded from his mind, yet that did not matter. Matthew's thoughts were already on the imminent conquest. The second part of the sceptre was almost in his grasp. Unfortunately his thoughts were disturbed by yet another stomach curdling lurch of the ship and Matthew was forced to leave his cabin very rapidly.

XVI

Oliver sat back in the chair of his new office, sighing contentedly. He had only been in office for a few hours and he was already beginning to enact a series of reforms to reduce the general crime level of the city. The first had been to remove those corrupt officials on the council who had blocked his proposals, then to instate those of a like mind instead. It was not exactly legal, yet he had many powers and, with the role of Protector being a new one, those around him were not entirely sure what the limits to his position were.

Having completed this he had passed the reforms in record time and already announced the city-wide night curfew. He had the knights and guards out in force to patrol the streets and ensure that the decree was obeyed. Though not all crime was committed at night, much was and the darkness could conceal many things. To that effect anyone found out after dark could therefore be committing a crime. To prevent this, all found out after dark without a special permit were to be sent to the Redirection Chambers where the law would be instilled permanently into the person's mind. It might get a few mostly innocent people, but, logically, if they were innocent, then the Redirection would only reinforce their lawful tendencies.

The curfew would also put an end to some prostitution and would prevent many fights, as men would have less time to drink in the pubs and taverns at night. He smiled softly as the sun began to lower in the horizon. Thieves would soon learn the error of their ways and the king would be eternally grateful for the ordered and lawful city he would return to him when his mission to Sol was finished. He might even decide to make the position of Protector a permanent one.

More importantly, however, was the fact that he now had as many knights as he needed to search out that wretched thief who had dared steal from him. His partner, Jack, had died too swiftly, one of the Redirecters getting a bit over zealous in his attempt to extract information. The boy's mind had been unable to take the strain and had simply given in before any relevant information had passed his lips. It had been a shame, but that did not matter now, for there was nowhere for the thief to hide. Eventually he would find him and he would pay.

XVII

Twilight descended over the great marble city of Theldar, lengthening shadows turning into vast patches of darkness divided only by the pools of light given off by the street lamps. As the darkness fell, so did the silence. Men, usually out to spend time in the taverns, rushed home to be in before the city bells rang. No one stopped to talk as they passed and all looked to their feet as the many guards on the streets passed. Market stall workers and shopkeepers hastily stored their wares and travellers made their way hastily to the various inns around. Fishermen rushed from the port in their hundreds, determined to be out at sea before the light failed. Here and there figures shifted hastily through the shadows, trying to complete their transactions before the curfew began. As the last ray of light disappeared from the heavens the bells of Theldar rang out through the night, slowly marking the start of the curfew. Soon the silence of the city was almost complete, broken only by the sound of marching feet,

Every so often, people late from work would scurry home through the darkness. Some made it to the safety of home and hearth. Others ended their night in prison cages, awaiting transportation to the Chambers. In other areas, people walked more boldly, either not knowing of the restrictions or, like many lords, feeling that the law did not apply to them. All such people were rudely awakened to the truth as all caught were taken to the cages, nobleman and commoner alike. As the night passed more were caught and just as dawn broke, many more, unaware that the restriction covered all hours of darkness, were also taken and led to the cages. Mid-morning soon came by and the cages were pulled through the streets by horses for all to see as a warning for the coming night's would-be curfew breakers, and so passed Theldar's first night with its new Protector...

CHAPTER NINE: Plots and Pirates

I

"We'll use Galahad to ferry us across," said Tristan quickly.

They had been travelling for almost a month since their flight from Grathnac and unfortunately it had rained for almost the entire time, turning what was ordinarily a calm ford into a deep, fast flowing river. Using Galahad was their only hope, as the others seemed incapable of going across the river alone. Matthius had protested that he knew no way to affect water and that he could not swim. Groltch was in almost the same boat. He could swim, but he was too afraid of the foaming water to risk it and Belthar's health seemed to be deteriorating, once more for reasons unknown.

Things had changed somewhat since they had escaped Seronshire. Groltch and Tristan had agreed to confront their companions as to what secret they were keeping and came up against a wall of silence. From then on they had moved firmly into two camps, each suspicious of the other. Nightly guard duties had been altered so that two were always awake at anyone point and always one from each *side*. They were also staggered to ensure that one was always a little more awake than the other, a stipulation of the other two, evidently hoping that on occasions either he or Groltch would be too tired to notice what the other on watch was up to. They were not experienced at this though and more often than not it was either he or Groltch that could have done something whilst the other on guard had drifted to sleep.

What confused Tristan most, however, was the fact that these two insisted on going on with them, despite the hostilities between the sides. He was verging on desperation in his efforts to discover why.

"I'll take Groltch first," said Tristan crisply.

"No, take Belthar, please," replied Matthius. "He's in little shape to do anything over there when you leave him."

Tristan had to admit that the big man certainly did not look in much shape to do anything. As the days had passed he had become less and less sure footed and had collapsed twice already on their journey. Yet still neither had ever said what this ailment was, though both seemed to know. All they had said was that he needed time alone and neither he nor Groltch would accept that. They had refused to leave accompanied and so were caught in a deadlock while Belthar's condition grew worse. Tristan had even resorted to asking Caliburn, but the sword had been reticent about telling him and a fight had erupted in which the sword declared that it would not speak to Tristan until he had grown more sensible. So far it had been as good as its word and not uttered a word since.

"Very well," replied Tristan, moving to help the man up onto the horse.

The man felt unusually light for one his size and Belthar was soon atop Galahad. Tristan led the horse out into water, carefully feeling his way as he did. The stones underfoot were slippery and the water's current strong, yet he had trained in many such exercises, occasionally even involving this ford, as it was reasonably close to Belthanor. The journey across seemed to take hours and the return trip longer still. As he pulled himself and Galahad out of the water, he noticed Matthius and his cat wink out of existence. Tristan span round and saw that the boy was now on the other side of the river, trying to help the big man to his feet.

"Damn," swore Tristan, possibly for the first time in years.

Since his meeting with Anton he had allowed some of the rigid forms of self-control he had employed as a knight to slip for he no longer had an image to maintain, though only a little. He was not a total barbarian after all.

He turned to Groltch, only to see the ran-the leaping up onto Galahad's back.

"Go," was all he said.

Tristan plunged into the frothing waters, ignoring the tiredness gained from the previous crossing and only hoped Galahad could make it. He patted the horse upon the neck to reassure him as they moved. Galahad's ears pricked up a little and his pace became a little quicker and a little surer.

It was not the same for Tristan, however. His head suddenly started spinning and he lost his footing, sliding beneath the foaming waters. As the world muted around him and the waters began to carry him off he felt his head strike something solid and all thoughts of swimming left his mind. He felt a cold moment of peace as the world bubbled round him and darkness began to take him, the pain in his head disappearing to a dull throb.

Suddenly the world exploded in light and pain as his head was pulled above water. His lungs ached and he coughed and spluttered as water tried to force its way down his lungs.

"You all right there," said a voice, not sounding all that calm despite its intentions. "I got you."

Tristan's mind barely registered the words or their source, and barely noticed when he finally felt himself free of water. As he lay on the bank, he rolled over and allowed his stomach to heave, something instinctively telling him that this was vital to his survival. When he had finished he looked up to see Groltch arguing with Matthius. Tristan also noted, with relief that Galahad had made it across safely.

"I no care for that," said Groltch coldly. "If you no say why, you no go away alone less you want leave."

Matthius almost seemed to consider it, but looked over at Tristan for some reason, then refused.

"Then you stay," replied Groltch angrily.

Matthius almost seemed about ready to speak, but the throbbing in Tristan's head became too much for him and unconsciousness swept him away.

II

Meredith gingerly walked about her room, carefully testing her well-rested legs. The incident with the almost failed heist had left her almost incapacitated after landing so heavily. It had only been mere fortune that she had had an escape prepared. Usually she would not have bothered, but had done so to get Jack into the habit of providing one. He was inept enough to have needed one.

She had not felt that she needed one in some time now and felt more the fool for the recklessness with which she had used it. The man she had robbed seemed to be the obsessive type so she had decided to lie low, giving her the added bonus of allowing her legs to heal up enough that she would be able to resume her activities. Of course, during this time this new *protector* had announced a curfew. She was sure that the inner circle or Dark Circle, as they liked to call themselves, of the Guild of Hawks would not like that. It went against the generations old agreement with the rulers of this city. Though only verbal, it had made certain guarantees that this curfew had curtailed. The thieves guild was allowed to work relatively unmolested, as long as enough thieves were given up to make those who cared in the city feel that something was being done about crime. In return, the guild strictly regulated its activities to ensure crime was not too rife in the city. Many of those handed over were, of course, freelance thieves not affiliated to the guild, and those members of other guilds that tried to form.

In effect, it had guaranteed the Guild of Hawks a monopoly on crime with a measurable protection from the law.

Meredith had already received the summons issued about a fortnight ago to the emergency meeting of the Circle, of which she was a minor member, to resolve the issue, though she had declined on grounds of ill health. She was not so important that her presence was vital and she had no wish to face the embarrassment she already felt at the amateurish mess she had gotten herself into at the Councillor's house. Yet she had to face them some time, and now was as good a time as any. She chose to leave in the day, just in case the Circle had been unable to solve the problem of the curfew. It was unlikely, for most officials were easy to get around if offered a little financial incentive, though she did not want to take any risks, not with the way her luck had been running recently.

She finished dressing herself and moved out into the streets. They were quieter than usual and those that were speaking seemed to be complaining. She heard several mentions of what the *Circle* would do and had done to people like him, though she knew that the circle they spoke of had been that revolutionary group of some years ago. She believed the last queen had crushed it, and the Dark Circle had adopted the term for their own amusement. Caldorians were funny people sometimes.

She made her way to the *Fig and Thistle* inn and sat at her usual table. It was strangely empty today. Even the usual spotters were not sat in their usual alcoves. She motioned to the barman with a quick twitch of her fingers. The man came straight over.

"What can I do for you ma'am?" asked the man politely.

His fingers said something quite different. The Guild had developed a series of special hand signals designed to be used in times when open talk was not advisable. Over the years it had become quite and expressive language.

Dangerous to talk, you're needed desperately, they flickered.

"I don't know, I feel a little adventurous today, what do you have?" she asked.

Why? she signed quickly.

"Well, we have..." began the barman before going into a long list of beers and beverages, allowing them to talk more freely.

The Circle gone. All taken by the ruler. Arrogant fools thought they had him in their pockets and went to take some of the royal treasury. They had been given permission *by the new Protector!* he said, his quick, sharp movements indicating his irritation. *It was a sting of course and the greedy fools all walked right into it. Guild fallen to pieces. You only Circle member left.*

Meredith sat there in stunned amazement. How could the idiots have fallen for so simple a ploy? Then the realisation struck her that she was the only Circle member left and her head swam.

The Headman gone too? She asked in amazement. The headman had not been in active duty for some ten years.

Yes, apparently the thought of the money went straight to his head, suspect Redirecters involved! Came the reply.

Well, that would explain some of it. Those head messers could often create havoc like that. She sighed. With them all gone it left her at the head of the Guild, if there was any of it left. She had to free them somehow, but how?

Where are they? She asked.

"What exactly is a Kolthon Square?"

"A cocktail ma'am, its ingredients include…"

Unknown, possibly palace cells though position unknown. Circle might know.

Circle imprisoned, remember? She snapped sarcastically.

"And that Elven Death Wish?"

"Well, ma'am, that is a wonderful mixture of…"

Not Circle, he emoted, drawing a small circle in the air with his index fingers from top to bottom. *Circle*, he continued, drawing the circle in reverse.

But they crushed years ago, she replied quickly.

"Fey wine sounds a little too strong for this time of day. How about the Knight's Lance?"

Not according to my brother. Has links, if you want look, came the reply.

"Well, we start with a wee dram of…"

Sounds good. I look into matters. Where your brother now? She asked.

Dockside, working the Mary Queen.

"That sounds perfect," she said, trying to sound bored as her mind began working on plans to free the Circle. She was never intended for leadership. "I'll have one of them."

"I think, ma'am, you might prefer the Jolly *Tom Jones*," he replied with only a slight emphasis on the name.

Hand talk was all well and good for most things but things such as personal names could often create problems, especially if the receiver or teller spelt it incorrectly. This way there was no doubt.

I go after this drink. Make sure no alcohol!

"Very well, ma'am," he replied bowing slightly.

Luck of Sivran to you, came his final, emoted reply.

She bought the drink and drank it down slowly, watching the few patrons around her. After seeing that no one appeared to have taken much notice of her conversation with the barman she rose from her place and returned to the busy, if a little quiet, city streets. The *Fig and Whistle* was centrally placed in the city, being set up ostensibly to provide for the merchants that lived in the area. A well-kept, lawful inn was always a better base than the more seedy, back street inns that Caldorians often established for such uses. That had been one of many improvements she had been quick to suggest on her arrival in the city. In many ways the Caldorians were rather primitive in their guild structures and group thinking.

It took nigh on an hour to reach the filthy stench of the harbour quarter and another to work her way through it. The tide was high so there were many ships presently arriving and departing, making for a very busy time. Meredith personally hated the area, the constant smell of fish always turning her stomach when she came here. She grimaced and bared it all, though, for her own personal dislikes were of less importance than her present quest.

It took close on half an hour to find the barman's brother after she had placed a few discrete enquiries among the various dockers. They looked very different from each other and quite possibly only shared the same mother. She approached the large, muscular man as he moved to take a break. As she went she rearranged her clothing and hair to make it sit a little more awkwardly and look more of a general mess.

"Tom Jones, you old cheat! How dare you treat me like this!" she cried in her best shriek.

The man jumped at her cry and looked round to see where it had come from.

"By Torslud," she shrieked, rolling her eyes. "Yer be lookin' to act as if yer don't know yer *friend* Bess…" We *need to talk. Your brother sent me.* "…Who yer slept with after makin' such pretty promises then never came back!"

"I don't know what yer talking about you old crone!" he replied indignantly. *Can't talk here, Redirector to your left. Meet at Roof Garden, noon.* "Be goin' about yer filthy business, yer whore. I paid yer fer yer services an' that were that. I didn't make no promises as yer claimin'!"

"Why you old, pea brained…" *Okay, noon.* "…jack-assed dirt grubber. If yer think that trinket were worth what I gave yer then yer've another thing comin'!"

"No, darlin', the first time weren't good enough fer me t' do yer again!" he replied crudely.

"Why yer…" she began, the rest of the words being obscured by the following shriek.

She picked up some crushed fish left on the floor and threw it at Tom, much to the amusement of his colleagues. She then threw up her hands in disgust and stormed away from the docks to prepare for their meeting. She hoped the information he had would be worth the effort required in gaining it.

III

Matthew felt like beating his head against the walls of his cabin in frustration. The journey had been much worse than he had expected, though not for the reasons he had expected. His seasickness was almost forgotten in the problems of a more personal nature that had continued from the king and the captain's initial confrontation. Both men were used to leading and commanding without outside interference, and neither was prepared to allow the other to command.

The worst incident that had broken out came on the first night when the king found some of the sailors performing an ancient pagan ritual still used by Solmen. They had been about to sacrifice a chicken to the ancient sea goddess Giarna, who was supposed to roam the oceans in the form of an ancient sea creature with jaws large enough to tear ships apart. It was believed that the small sacrifice helped appease her and would also please her consort the moon god Luranthio. Matthew had often wondered why the Solmen had never worshipped the second moon, though when he questioned a few Solmen on the subject they had all sworn that there was only one and that only unbelievers saw two.

It was an odd custom, yet one believed by the superstitious sailors. Of course, Naithan had been prepared to imprison the lot of them for heresy and devil worship. It had taken all of Matthew's powers of reasoning and persuasion to get through to his friend that without them they would have no one to sail the ship. He had succeeded, though barely, and convinced him to let the matter drop. Unfortunately he had insisted that the ritual not be performed and that any caught doing it would be taken on deck, flogged a hundred times then dropped into the sea water.

That, of course, infuriated the captain and a fight had erupted, almost resulting in armed conflict. It had taken a quick dunking in the sea, courtesy of one of his spells, to calm them both down, though Naithan had had a look of complete hatred in his eyes on his return. Matthew had then needed to stand up on deck and pray for the blessing of Toric on their journey before the crew, then use his power to becalm the sea around the ship to indicate Toric's blessing. That had partially calmed them, though he had had to repeat the same actions on each of the other nine ships. That had come very close to draining him completely and he had suffered for days with severe tiredness and sickness. However, he had been unable to rest up long enough before yet another argument erupted. Matthew felt glad that he had use of Jalim's parting gift of energy and had found himself wondering once again about the boy's apparent talent of foresight.

To make matters worse, the conquest of Grelchi, the completion of which would have given Matthew a perfect excuse for a week's absence, seemed to be taking forever. The reports he had been receiving from

Gareth had been of severe, bloody and vicious fighting, with the goblins using all forms of guerrilla tactics to slow down the knights. They had evidently expected the same resistance they had received in the villages and walked straight into one vast trap. Overnight the casualties of the war had increased a hundred fold and it seemed that the knights were having to take Grelchi street by bloody street.

A sudden rolling, pitching motion of the ship jarred his thoughts, another of the little problems this voyage was having. They had first been becalmed and forced to make the sailors down oars and row, then been struck by a ferocious storm that had severely damaged two of the other ships. One had been so badly damaged that it had been forced to limp to shore for repair with the instructions to catch up with the fleet once it was able. They were then left in stormy, volatile waters that had sought to give even hardened sailors a slight feeling of sickness in their stomachs. Of course, these events had caused the men to start grumbling about the wrath of Giarna and giving the king looks that would kill if they could. The whole ship was a war just waiting to be declared.

Matthew sighed miserably and wondered what he had done to deserve this cruel fate.

Matthew! Came Gareth's thought in his head.

What? He asked, hoping for some good news for a change.

We've done it, replied Naithan's brother.

At last! Thought Matthew, feeling a sudden surge of joy rush through him. *I'll tell the king at once, so stand in a clear area and I'll join you shortly. That is if Naithan and the captain can be kept from killing each other.*

They're still fighting then? I'm sure they can survive without you for a few days. Oh, you won't need to use me as a fixing point though, came the reply.

Why's that? he asked, suddenly interested.

To successfully teleport anywhere, there needed to be something to use as a point of reference, such as an item or person, hence the reason for the twelve pointed star within a ten-pointed star pattern in each of the major cities of Caldor.

They've got one of those star patterned fixing points in the central chamber of the main palace here, though it's now exposed to the open air, replied Gareth.

That meant that the hints in some of the older texts were correct. The links between Caldor and Grelchin had not always been hostile, for goblins were unable to cast sorcererous spells, so the pattern on the floor had to have been of human design.

Let me guess, the tenth point is filled in, he thought quickly, conjuring the image in his mind.

No, replied Gareth. *They are all gold.*

That made his jaw drop. That meant that it was the pattern of origin in ancient hierarchy. Local legend had said that the city of Toric had held the star with golden points. The ancient holy city thought lost centuries ago in the mountains north of Kolth was actually in the swampy marshland of Grelchi. Matthew smiled despite himself. It would certainly come as a shock to many priests to learn this. A series of precepts of the faith were based upon facts that were not true.

We can't tell anyone of this, he said quickly.

I know. I had the room sealed when it was discovered and have erased the knowledge from those others who saw it before, then concealed it beneath illusion, though it won't hold for long, replied Gareth.

Good, thought Matthew.

Privately he rejoiced at the news, for it meant his presence was a necessity there. The design had to be permanently covered lest the wrong eyes see it. Whilst Matthew took private delight at the possible discomfort of the priests, he knew that knowledge that Grelchi was the holy city had to be suppressed. If known it could destroy the system of Caldorian belief and bring anarchy reigning down on their heads.

Wait in that room, he said quickly. *I'll be there shortly.*

Gareth faded from his mind, indicating his compliance as he did so. Matthew packed together the essentials for this particular trip and ran out onto the deck. For perhaps the first time in days the king and the captain did not appear to be fighting. Thanking Toric for small mercies he went swiftly over to the king.

"They've taken the city," he said as the king looked towards him.

"A great day," replied the king, sounding a little sour.

"What?" asked Matthew.

"It means you leave us, as agreed, and that means the only person here remotely capable of any intelligent conversation will be that oaf of a captain," replied Naithan,

"Well it was you who insisted that the courtiers remain on the other ships," replied Matthew.

He remembered that conversation very well. The other ships had to arrive one by one before him so that they had all offloaded their cargo when he made his final appearance. It was designed to make a show of his power by having a procession prepared before him and show that he was above all other people in Caldor, requiring a ship of his own to carry his magnificence. Matthew had thought it all a little too much, but then he had never really played the Royal Game.

"When are you going?" asked Naithan with a sigh.

"At once. There are likely to be many traps round the device and I don't want those bumbling idiots stumbling into one and setting it off. There's no telling what damage that might do."

"You really think it's that powerful?"

"More so. Much more so in fact. That's why we need it."

"Very well, then take care and listen to my brother's instructions as you would my own."

"I'll be back well in the week," he replied.

"Well you'd best be, hadn't you?" said the king, making Matthew's arm go cold at the thought.

"Yes," he replied softly. "Take care yourself and try not to get yourself keel hauled."

"What's that?" asked the king.

"An interesting form of punishment they have here. Ask the captain if you truly wish to know."

The king smiled then faded away as Matthew cast the spell. The world blurred around him and he suddenly found himself in the midst of a ruined room. He looked down wonderingly at the golden stars at his feet, before concealing them more permanently with his magic. Gareth was powerful, but not that strong in this mode of magic. Knights had little use for illusion in battle, or so they claimed. He had tried to show them the error of their ways, but they had centuries of rules and tradition clouding their vision.

"That was quick," said Gareth as he entered the door.

"Well this needed concealing and quickly. Take me to those that have seen it and I shall check the alterations. Then I'll have to do so, even to you. The king ordered it be so."

"I understand," replied Gareth.

It was at that moment Matthew noticed that the man was covered in blood. Gareth saw him stare.

"There are still many goblins in the city creating ambushes and the like. I got struck just after I finished talking to you. You'll have to be careful here."

"I intend to," he replied. "Shall we visit the men?"

"Certainly. If you will follow me."

Matthew followed the armoured man out, desperate to get this minor task out of the way before beginning the search for the second piece of the sceptre. It was all turning out well at last.

IV

Meredith sat on the roof garden awaiting Tom. It was, basically, a flat roof on one of the taller buildings in Theldar from which the city could be observed and meetings such as this could be held in relative security. Tom arrived, a little late and sat before her.

"When do you want out of the city and where do you wish to go?" asked the big man.

Meredith covered her surprise. By his statement it seemed he was used to ferrying thieves out of the city. She had heard this Protector was tough on crime but this was verging on tyrannical.

"I'm not about to leave," she replied. "I'm preparing to help my Circle to freedom before it's too late and I need the help of *your* Circle to do it."

The man eyed her suspiciously.

"I'm the last of my Circle still free and I don't intend to leave them imprisoned. I was reliably informed that your Circle might know of their location and be able to give it to me. I'll take it from there. I can pay for any inconvenience."

She shook her money pouch and showed the Hawk and Circle tattoo on her shoulder to prove her claim. The man's eyes widened in surprise; evidently he was also a guild member and knew the tattoo's significance.

"I don't know about any such prison, but I'm only a runner. I'm barely even involved as I'm actually more a guild member than a Circle member. The Hawkmaster seems to have felt that it would be useful to keep connections open to this Circle."

The Hawkmaster, head of the Guild and one of those still imprisoned. It was quite possible that if he had still been free she would not have to be on this search. No matter though.

"Can you take me to someone who can lead me further?" she asked.

"I can try, but it'll be tough. They've been tight on security ever since Queen Anne. They don't want it happening again. They watched me for months before letting me get this far."

"Then I'll do it the hard way. When are you next due to meet them?"

"Tomorrow evening. I'm getting some more Hawks out in the curfew. We meet in Church Gate Crossing."

"I'll be there, but don't look for me because you won't see me. Now, act annoyed and then storm off. When they ask tell them I wasn't prepared to pay the price."

"What do you mean?" he asked, raising his voice as he did.

They still have men watching you. Don't look but two roofs away, she signed quickly.

"Fine, then stay here and rot," he said loudly.

Okay, I go now. Sivran's luck to you, he replied.

And you, she replied as he turned and left. She waited a while and noticed that the small figure she had noticed had not yet left. Cursing silently she slipped down to street level. Now she was going to spend the day playing ghost chase with her observer. Obviously she had not been as careful as she should. She was really getting too sloppy for this profession. She slipped into the crowds and did her best to disappear.

V

Hannah watched her prey silently. She had been observing this guard since she had arrived in Belthanor. Getting in had been simplicity itself, yet the trick had been getting into the central keep. She could have used the transport device that she had used to travel the distance between the cities, yet with so many magic-wielding knights in the city that would have been a potentially foolish error to make.

As it was, on her entry to the keep a young man with strange eyes and a white cat in his arms had looked straight at her as if he could see straight through her disguise. He could not of course, as it was created by the magical scarf she wore, yet even thinking of it now made her adjust it nervously and check it in the mirror. It was not like an illusion as it actually altered her form, though rather painfully, and was almost impossible to see through. It had fooled her father every time she had met him and he was paranoid about such things. She often wondered what he would do if he ever found out where she truly was when on one of her trips to the country manor. It was not a surprise that her father seemed to be preparing to marry her off on one of his schemes and she was not going to allow that.

No, there was no way that the boy could have seen through it, particularly one as young and probably untrained as he. Even so she had been doubly careful since that day, maintaining her role as cleaner whilst shadowing the guard she had picked. She had chosen a woman, as they were always easier to imitate, unsurprisingly, and observed her for nigh on a month. The King's Knight had not yet been captured, but guards had been posted throughout the county in preparation.

If she had guessed correctly, the druid with them would have to cross the western highway to reach the holy circle before the passing of both new moons. The first had almost gone and the other would be barely a week behind it. There was little time left so it was the moment to act. She would normally require more time to get the impersonation of the person down so well that his or her own family would not know the difference. She did not have that luxury though, and hopefully the regimented orderly style of the knightly life make would make most of the duties simple enough.

She moved through the corridors to the knight's room and entered quietly. The complacency of the inner sanctums of this place made her job so much easier. People inside never expected any threat to get this far and rarely locked their doors. She dropped to the floor and rolled under the bed, waiting for her return. It seemed to take forever, but Hannah had done this every night for the past four nights and the woman, a Cassandra Mistelle, had a strict routine that she followed every night. First, polish the plates then wash the face and hands. Take a drink to the bedside of her small cell then brush through the hair and then finally the removal of her clothes and the putting on of her night shift.

It took almost an hour of tossing and turning for the woman to finally enter deep sleep and that was Hannah's cue. She rolled out quietly from the bed and took the small wire and vial from her pouch. She allowed a small drop of the liquid onto the wire and gently lowered it into the woman's open mouth. Any field knight would have reacted to her close proximity, even in sleep, but Cassandra was now a permanent guard after making a major mistake some time ago. The woman had really let herself go in the years that followed, which made it all the easier for Hannah. It would make any mistakes in protocol she made seem more due to sloppiness than inexperience.

The poison dropped into the woman's mouth and Hannah smiled. It would not kill her straight away but do so slowly, keeping her unconscious as it did. It allowed her the freedom of not actually disposing of the body or having to live with the smell of a decaying body. She could just leave it beneath the bed during the day, safe there as guards cleaned their own rooms, then leave it on top whilst she slept under. Hannah trusted no bed other than her own and being here would give her some chance of surprising any unwanted guests. She practised changing her form to match that with the woman before her until she felt the match was as near perfect as it could get, then retired to sleep.

VI

Tristan sat there watching Belthar shift uneasily. He had always thought it odd that the druid took watch with the rest of them, even though the big man had proved on numerous occasions that his blindness was in no way a handicap. Tonight though, it was pointless. He was obviously ill, though why he could not fathom and Belthar had pointedly refused to say anything other than he needed to be alone, something neither Tristan nor Groltch were prepared to allow. So the stalemate continued leaving Belthar the loser, something that was plainly evident at that moment.

Despite these problems though, Tristan felt better than he had done in his entire life. Since his near encounter with death that morning he had never felt freer. Caliburn claimed that the knock to his head, combined with all the other events since his flight from Theldar had helped disrupt the majority of his redirection. It was true that many of his early memories were still unclear, but that was probably an irreversible effect of the years of training he had received, though he also still retained the skills he had gained in training. Yet he was finally free of many of the conflicting emotions and feelings that had seemed to strike from all sides then try and tear him apart. There were still many problems to come but the difference was he now felt he could face them all.

"Good," said Caliburn softly, *"because there is something we need to talk about."*

Tristan glared at the sword at his side, annoyed at the way it seemed to indiscriminately enter his head and hear his thoughts.

What do you want? He asked sourly.

"It's about what happened to you today, and about the various other strange events that seemed to occur from time to time," replied the sword.

What do you mean? He asked, his curiosity piqued.

"Remember the times when I've lit up to distract the guards? And that time when Karene looked directly at you from the road shortly after you met Belthar?"

Yes, vividly, he replied.

"Do you recall that you often felt ill shortly after, occasionally leading to dizziness, like that you felt today?" it asked.

Now you come to mention it that does strike a chord. Why do you ask?

"Well, it has to do with you and magic," began the sword hesitantly.

This now really caught Tristan's attention. The sword was rarely hesitant about anything.

In what way? He asked, getting the feeling he was not going to like the answer.

"Well, you see, I'm not exactly magical in the way that you seem to think I am," said the sword, still measuring its words. *"I cannot perform magic, as such, like make myself glow, at least not as brightly as I have done."*

How do you mean? Asked Tristan, hating himself for all the inane sounding questions he appeared to be asking. *How did you do it then?*

"That's just it," replied the sword. *"I didn't do it. Not alone, anyway. You did it with me."*

"Impossible! I'm no wizard! Thought Tristan angrily.

"That's true, you're not yet. But you will be, to some extent, regardless of what you want," replied Caliburn. *"When you are a child, at your first naming ceremony, the priest does a search, checking you for magical talent. Some are faint, meaning that they are trainable and are occasionally sent away to the north to let them see a seeming constant trickle of magic emerging from here. The rest are then picked for the knighthood.*

Others like you, showed a high level of energy at birth, meaning that they would eventually begin tapping into the magical energy and are immediately destined to go to the knighthood. Now at that age, it is impossible to tell what kind of magic they use, whether or not they are wizards or priests, to put it simply. That is discovered when people reach your age. Those who could be priests are allowed to leave for the orders if they choose. Those who could be wizards remain in the knighthood for life."

Then I could be a priest then? Asked Tristan hopefully.

"No," replied the sword sharply. *"The power I can tap is that of sorcery, not Toric, which is why I have been able to contact you and help you resist your Direction."*

Well, it matters little, replied Tristan. *I will never use it again.*

"It's not that simple, I'm afraid, for your power is latent. It is a part of you and when you need it you will use it. Without instruction you will surely kill yourself by trying to do something for which you don't have the power," explained the sword.

I was able to partially resist treatment. I can resist the temptation to use it, replied Tristan tersely.

He was surprised at how easily he had accepted the idea that his blood was tainted with sorcery.

"You can't. Remember at the ford when you feared for Galahad? Well your soothing pat was in essence a simple spell to restore his vigour and strength, much as you used on the horse when fleeing Theldar," continued the sword. *"The dizziness you experienced was the after effect of using the energy. Until your body adapts to those levels of power you will always suffer them, and every time you use more than you have become accustomed to."*

No! I won't listen to you. You lie! Shouted Tristan, if it could be called such.

"I speak the truth, Tristan. You need instruction, which I can give you, but only when you are ready. It's a lot to think about, I know, and I'll leave you to think about it, though not for too long. I've been able to prevent you using too much power but as time has gone on you've been drawing more and more. Eventually it will be more than I can contain and if you don't know how to do it, then it will kill you. Think on that…"

The sword faded from his mind and Tristan almost screamed. Just when he thought he had got it all under control and that he could manage, then the sword dropped this bolt from the sky on him. His head throbbed dully, and not just because of the earlier knock to it. A hand grabbed his shoulder and he almost jumped out of his skin.

"My turn to watch," said Groltch softly. He looked at Tristan with worried eyes. "What wrong?"

"Nothing," replied Tristan quickly. "My head just aches, that's all."

"Oh, then rest but no sleep straight away. Me watch you, might be after fall pain. Can be dangerous."

Suddenly the ran-the's eyes glazed over.

"Oh, Cal say you fine and can sleep, okay, night Tris," said the ran-the softly.

"Night Groltch," replied Tristan.

He closed his eyes knowing sleep would not come for hours yet but for some reasons his body seemed to overrule his mind and he was soon off in the land of dreams.

VII

"Tis time, Marie," said the ring in her mind. *"You knoweth what needs doing?*

"Yes," she replied softly.

She still was not sure if releasing Galen would be the correct thing to do, yet she had to do something and if he did try and harm her then she could use the ring to escape. It had told her that its former master had corrupted Galen through dreams with its help, though it still had not known why.

Well, there was nothing for it but to take the risk and see what happened. She formed the image in her mind of a door then stepped into the shadow. It had none of the nauseating effects that she had previously experienced, or any of the fear. When she emerged on the other side she could already see the other creatures moving around the streets. Even the ring had not known what they were, but this time they ignored her presence.

She moved quickly through the eerie streets, a feeling she still could not shake, and sighed with relief when she made it to the cell she had seen Galen in. She imagined the gate open then stepped through it. She looked back to see it closed as before. She took several deep breaths to calm herself then stepped back into the real world.

She was not prepared for the sight that greeted her. Galen was lying in a gibbering heap on the floor, his eyes wide open, though they were not seeing anything real. Around him was his urine and faeces that had just been left there to rot. His face was drawn and he had torn out almost all his hair leaving large tears and scabs across his head. His nose seemed broken and his fingernails withered and blackened. Most of his teeth were missing and his gums were bleeding profusely. It was all she could do to prevent herself from throwing up. In his hands was clasped a little bronze framed crystal lens in the shape of an eye from which his eyes never seemed to leave.

"The Master hath left him to die. He be'ath his own creature once more, though the device in his hand tormenteth his dreams still," said the ring, sounding almost sad. *"Best he is left. He is for this world not much more."*

"No!" she said firmly. "I will save him. Can you help me take him away?"

"If that be'ath thy request, then yes."

Marie became aware of other voices around her from the other cells. Cries of "*who's that?*" and "*Can you save me?*" filled the air. She ignored them all. The only one she had come for was the one she had helped put here. She put her arms around him and disappeared into the shadows, leaving the pitiful and heart wrenching cries behind her.

VIII

Meredith looked round carefully. She had to have lost her pursuer by now. It had taken her the full day and a half between her meeting with Tom and his meeting with the Circle of Light members. Her tracker had been of the highest calibre and even now she could not be sure that she had lost him. She looked over her shoulder again, but could see nothing. The feeling of being watched was still with her though, which probably meant he was still out there, somewhere. Yet she could not miss this meeting. Meredith only hoped her pursuer did not wish the Circle of Light harm, at least until she had gained what she needed from it.

She secured herself in a position that gave her a clear vantage point looking down on Church Gate Crossing, one of the central city cross-roads. She could already see Tom there with two others he was helping to escape. From here they looked to be a couple of recent recruits to the Guild, both foreigners. Both had used pseudonyms, as was quite usual with the older criminal recruits. The smaller one was a jumpy fellow, always drawing daggers at the slightest hint of danger, had called himself Sivran, god of thieves no less, and had the arrogance to match. His companion, the tall, muscular figure took his nickname from all the scars that criss-crossed his huge frame, evidently gained from too many fights with the two large swords on his back. He was a quiet yet loyal companion who seemed to follow the little character around like some pet dog, at least until the drinks began to flow. Between them they had some of the crudest verses to the Elven Maiden drinking song she had ever heard. They had been reasonable thieves, she supposed, for former freelancers, but their going would not be missed much. They seemed to have spent more time talking and drinking than doing anything else.

She took her gaze away from the three figures and looked around for the others they were to meet. After what seemed to be an eternity, several times involving the ducking out of sight from the approach of patrolling guards, the others met them. Words and payment were exchanged and Tom moved quickly away, soon rising above street level to the Hawks' Highway of the rooftops. She let him go and dropped down silently after the escapees and their new assistants. They moved quickly down an alley and were disappearing from sight as she slowly looked round the corner.

They were headed down into the sewers. Evidently those two did not have their papers in order, though why they had not just gone and paid for some from Blacknose Bill she did not know. Probably too cheap, she supposed. She moved down the alley and pulled aside the drain cover, looking back as she did. She saw nothing but that sense of someone following her was still strong. She dropped down into the sewer and listened carefully. She could just about hear voices up to the left. She quickly followed after them, trying not to get too close to the light she could see up ahead. Evidently these Circle of Light members were not expecting company. Either that or they were amateurs. Only once was she almost caught and that was due to the jitters of *Sivran*. The light had continued ahead but they had stopped by a sewer junction and she almost walked straight into them. It had led to a tense few minutes before one of them, the big one she thought, spoke out.

"Come on, let's go, there's no one there!"

"I'm telling you, someone's following us," said a second voice.

"You're wrong!"

"When am I ever wrong?" asked the second voice.

"Well, there was that time in…" began the first voice, fading away as they made their way back down towards the retreating light.

She had paused for a few moments then followed, fearing that she had lost them. Fortunately they did not seem to be in much of a rush and she had soon caught them up again.

It was at that point that the light went out and she heard them moving back out of the sewers. She gave it a few minutes then climbed up after them. By that point the group had parted and she was surprised to find that they were outside the city. She followed the four out into the woods which, for a city dweller like herself, was rather difficult and only made easier when one of the dear, sweet souls switched their lantern back on for her. Unfortunately, that was the last thing she had that she could be thankful about for her foot must have caught in a snare and she suddenly found herself hanging upside down. She reached up to the dagger at her waist, intending to cut herself free.

"I wouldn't do that if I were you. Drop yer weapons t' the floor and happens we'll not shoot yer, an' may even let yer down," said a voice from the direction she had just come. The feeling of being watched left her somewhat and she then knew the source of the voice.

He is good! She thought and swore.

IX

Naithan stood on deck of *The Osprey* looking out to sea about ready to tear his hair out. Matthew had been gone barely two days and already the call seemed to be pulling. Evidently over such great distances it would be worse, but the constant aching in his arm merely added to his growing irritation with this whole voyage. On their return to Caldor, Captain Sirius would soon find himself in the Chambers for Redirection, if not worse. The man was insufferable and seemed to think he ruled the world. Yet he could not do a thing about it at the moment for they were not far from the Solman capital of Zaron and his plans could not be altered at the moment. He would simply replace the man if his crew were not so restless. It seemed they somehow venerated the man and the fact that Naithan was king seemed to have no effect upon them. In fact, they seemed to positively hate him and since Matthew's departure he had taken to walking round ship with two guards.

He sighed and stared back out to sea, only to see what appeared to be winged fish leaping from the water and flying across the water.

"Sir William, have you seen anything like that at all?" he asked the almost perpetually silent knight.

"No, your Majesty, though I believe they're called flying fish, Sire," he replied. "They jump from the water to avoid danger, so the sailors say, Your Majesty."

In some ways Naithan preferred the sailors' attitude to him over the stern, duty driven knights. Thoughts of the fish took him away for a moment as he watched their colourful scales glitter in the sunshine as they flew. He wondered what it was they were leaping from. As he did so he noticed the water begin to bubble as more and more began to leap from the water. Within seconds it was almost impossible to see the sea beneath their swarming bodies. He heard the irreverent curses of several sailors as they saw the phenomenon for themselves. For them it was probably some sign of ill luck.

"Ships ahoy!" called out the look out.

Naithan looked ahead and saw three large ships bearing down on them.

How on earth did they get that close without notice! Wondered Naithan angrily.

The ships were almost on top of them and there had been no warning whatsoever.

"They're flying the death Jack!" called out the lookout.

Naithan's heart almost stopped. The Death Jack was the flag of Black Heart, uncaught pirate of these seas. Then he shook his head with a wry grin. The pirate had picked the wrong fleet to pick upon this time. With nine ships opposing them, the small fleet of the pirates stood no chance, especially with magic wielding battle knights on board. He grinned in grim satisfaction at the prospect.

Suddenly one of the ships of his fleet seemed to explode with a heart wrenching crack and start to sink. The cause of its demise was a thing of nightmares. Its head was some twenty feet in length, attached to a neck of gigantic proportions, all covered in barnacles. Horns of some six or seven feet in length rose up from the back of its head and it had protective plates that covered most of its green, mottled and scaly skin. Its eyes were relatively small in comparison to the rest of its head, yet behind them sat a malevolent expression of such hatred that Naithan's spine positively tingled with fear. Screams and cries of fear emerged from the sailors of his fleet, yet his knights stood firm. Almost as one they cast forth flames from their fingertips, striking the beast on the side of its head. It roared in pain and turned to the source of its discomfort, jaws gaping wide. A deep growl rumbled out from the depths of its throat and with it came an eruption of white-hot flames that poured down onto the ship. It caught fire instantly and many of the people on deck leapt into the sea's waters screaming in flame.

From another ship volleys of arrows were fired, a few of which even managed to pierce its thick hide. The minor victory was short-lived however as the creature turned its attention upon that ship. It seemed to almost leap from the water as a massive body some seventy feet in length emerged from the sea, glittering in the sun as it went. The creature's entire body then came crashing down upon the poor ship, rending it in two and reducing the fleet down to seven. The three lead ships were then engaged by the three pirate ships as all came crashing together in unison. Grappling hooks were thrown across and balistae fired from both sides at close range. For some reason, the knights' magical abilities seemed to provide little advantage for them as they fought, many of their spells falling short of the enemy ships and occasionally even just disappearing into thin air.

The sound of splintering wood once again filled the air, informing Naithan that another ship had fallen prey to the sea creature. Now nothing lay between it and *The Osprey*. It turned its attention towards Naithan's ship and his knights prepared for battle. One smart thinking warrior fired lightening at the creature which caused it to thrash about in pain. Unfortunately its massive size combined with its movements to send waves of tremendous sizes out at the ships. *The Osprey* rocked violently and threw many of its occupants to the deck. Naithan was washed away from his knightly guard to the other side of the deck. As he pulled himself to his feet, sea water pouring from his clothes and hair, he found himself surrounded by the ship's company.

"Tis your fault that this do be 'appening to us it be," cried one.

"That be Giarna herself t' wreak vengeance on ye," said another, a malignant gleam in his eyes.

"Tis true. We shall never be saved till he who spurned her has been sacrificed to her domain!" said another with a desperate glare.

"I'm your king," cried Naithan drawing the sword he had taken to wearing at his side. "You cannot sacrifice me to this creature."

"Yer the one who upset her. Yer put yerself in her disfavour. Tis your fault and you should pay the punishment!"

The sailors leaped on him almost as one and Naithan lashed out with his sword. What then began was a hopeless, desperate struggle between them. Naithan cut down sailors left, right and centre, yet still they came. Sea spray shot across them and black smoke bellowed out from the burning ship, obscuring the view. At some point Naithan lost his sword and his footing, yet did not give up the struggle. Biting, kicking and screaming, his eyes streaming tears from sea water and smoke, he fought with tooth and nail to remain on deck. Yet even the arrival of three of his personal guards could not help him.

He felt himself suddenly fly through the air and smash against some wooden panelling. His head began to spin and he found he was surrounded by water. He kicked and struggled to get to the surface, his lungs burning for air as he went. As he emerged from the water and his vision cleared he beheld a sight of awesome, terrifying magnitudes. The creature, jaws wide open, came crashing down upon him and around him.

Suddenly all was dark…

X

Oliver looked over the streets as night began to fall, satisfied with the silence that also began to drop. Crime had all but disappeared in the city now, all thanks to his initiative. Those foolish, greedy thieves thinking that he could be bribed had also helped it. It seemed that those he now had deep in the palace dungeons had been largely responsible for the majority of city crime. Without them the remainder had lost their heads, so to speak, and seemed to be running round and round in circles. He still had not found the one who had broken into his house, despite the guards had been investigating for almost a month now. He had tried to force the confessions from the thieves but it seemed none of them knew who the most recent burglar had been, though it was possible that they were holding back. Until they told him everything, though, they would not be leaving the dungeons below the palace. He had stumbled upon quite by happenstance when he had followed a poor deaf, mute idiot that he had noticed wandering through the servant corridors, and viewed it as part of Toric's plan. Clearly Oliver was meant to use these dungeons.

When he had finished extracting information, of course, they would be severely Redirected until they became the model citizens of the new city. The king would barely recognise it when he returned from Sol. His position of City Protector would be secure.

He would not finish there however. He had noticed in his travels that the people were not as devote followers as he and the king were, and this was another problem he intended to tackle. Worship on the Holy Day was to be compulsory and any not found in their local temple would be taken in for Redirection. Oliver could not understand why the king had not pushed the matter in such ways before, but felt that now was the time to do it. They would also have to crack down upon the heads of the heathens and pagans that plagued this city. Their subversive movements would have to be strictly monitored and controlled to ensure that no young Caldorians were corrupted by their lies.

He could not seal them off completely, for the city needed their trade. Therefore he decided to limit their movements to the docks and marketplace. That should keep them in their place. He smiled contentedly as he wrote down the orders required to enforce these actions. The king would be so pleased on his return.

XI

Meredith shifted uneasily in the wooden cage she had been uncomfortably imprisoned within for the past day and a half. Throughout her stay, the man who had captured her had questioned her exhaustively as to her motives for following the Circle members as she had. She had finally been allowed to rest and eat, though she had spent much of her time planning her escape from them, as it was apparent that they were not going to be of any use to her. Her secret heel contained several emergency lock picks and the lock seemed to be a simple one from what she could see. If she could distract the guard long enough she might even be able to break free, but the trouble was that they all seemed to watch her every movement like a hawk, rotating every half an hour or so to prevent any from getting tired or bored. It was one of the few parts of this organisation, along with her captor, that seemed to have any semblance of professionalism about it.

"Leave us," said her captor to the guard as he entered.

Meredith looked at him with suspicion. This was the first time he had sent the guard away on entering.

"Meredith of the Guild of Hawks," he said carefully.

He was a tall man and seemed well built for his age, which must have been somewhere around five to ten years older than herself. He had dark hair, unusual for a Caldorian, and deep green eyes that positively sparkled with intelligence. He had a short cut beard on his face that was flecked with grey and gave him an air of distinction. He wore brown leather clothing and moved with the grace of an animal, and a deadly one at that. It was very obvious that this was a man to be wary of.

"Yes, that's what I told you," she replied firmly.

"The accent's not Caldorian though," he said musing to himself. "Sounds more Kolthon in origin, perhaps even the Gal'yak province."

That surprised her. Most Caldorians were not that well-travelled and most would not have guessed her accent to be of Kolthon origin, let alone get her province.

"Yes," she replied guardedly. "I had a few troubles there so came here to ply my trade. The punishment here is a lot more lenient than in Kolth."

"That's a matter of opinion," replied the man softly.

Meredith knew what he meant. There was no death penalty here, but the Redirection Chambers could make you wish for death.

"What are you going to do with me?" she asked.

"Do with yer?" he asked. "Why let yer go of course, so long as yer guarantee not t' reveal our secret."

"You have my word on that," she replied calmly.

"I'll take that as enough," replied the man slowly. "Yer companions are at present trapped in the dungeons hidden deep with the bowels of the palace, through which yer would have to pass to get there. There's supposed to be another exit, though finding it would be a mammoth task."

"Thank you," she replied, surprised by this sudden outpour of information.

"Don't thank me yet. The palace will not be easy to get inside. Since Councillor Oliver took control, the guards there have been quadrupled. He is absolutely paranoid about thieves breaking in and is spending large amounts of time exhorting the guards to find the last thief that broke into his house. He has even put up a small reward for any information leading to his or *her* capture."

The look he gave was such that it told her that he knew who the *her* was.

"Thank you again."

"You'd need the Shadow's own skill to get in there."

That made her pause for a moment. The Shadow, famed knight killer of Theldar; such a person would jump at the opportunity to harm the king's plans. The gossip of the city had said that he had been captured, though some instinct told her that was not the case. Anyway, it gave her a direction to look in, for the man was correct. Even she was not good enough to risk an attempt on the palace.

"May I go now?" she asked, itching to get started.

"Certainly, but may I ask one more question?"

"Other than that one? Of course," she replied.

The man smiled yet otherwise did not acknowledge her barbed comment.

"What will you and your companions do if you release them?"

"How do you mean?"

"Well, with the restrictions as they are, your business will be a little limited, won't it?"

"Yes, I hadn't really thought about it. I suppose that we shall just lie low until the king returns then resume business as usual," she replied.

"But what if the king is pleased with the results of the Councillor's experiment and rescinds your agreement?"

"Well," she replied, thinking through the problem.

It was entirely possible that the king could see it as having worked. The Hawkmaster had never actually confirmed the agreement on King Naithan's succession to the throne, and this king could well deny its validity. That would cause a lot of problems.

"You admit, it is possible," said the man as if reading her thoughts. "He is also introducing new reforms that are beginning to upset the citizens based on compulsory temple worship and the like. King Naithan may not be the best king we've had, but he's better than that Councillor, unless he takes up the ideas being introduced here as his own…"

"What are you suggesting?" she asked, beginning to guess where this was leading.

"All I'm suggesting is the people let the king know how much they disapprove. That would be especially true if they took to running the city themselves until his return…"

"That would seem to be a good solution," she replied slowly, "though I couldn't speak for the Dark Circle."

"Dark Circle?" asked the man with an amused glint in his eyes.

"It's a name that the Guild Council took for themselves, sort of parodying your organisation."

The man chuckled softly and she allowed herself a smile.

"Of course, I leave it to your discretion, but if they do agree, then let me know and we'll try and work through details of such a solution."

"How will I find you?" she asked quickly.

"Just pass a message on to your friend Tom Jones and he'll see it's delivered."

"And who shall I address the message to?" she asked as the man began to unlock her cage.

"Tyrone Pathfinder," replied the man, "Leader of the Circle of Light."

XII

Marie looked down on Galen with misery. Despite all her ministrations, his fever had not broken and he had been gradually slipping away from her. She was sure that it had to do with that wretched device he clung to so dearly. It was killing him and there was nothing she could do about it. His arms and legs were pitifully thin and she had barely been able to pass food into his mouth during the few periods when the waking nightmares seemed to cease. The fortunate thing was that the weakness in his arms and legs had prevented him from damaging himself too much more. However, his strength seemed to increase tenfold during the worst periods of the fever and she had been forced to strap him down on the bed on more than one occasion.

She had also been forced to move on by several innkeepers who had heard his screams and felt that he could pass on whatever disease he had. She was now in the worst part of town where screams in the night were more common place and it was only her link with the ring that had saved her from some of the more brutal attacks that occurred on women here, despite the curfew.

She was at her wit's end. She wanted desperately to help him recover, yet could do nothing. When she had tried to remove the device and destroy it he had almost lost control completely and had even managed to pull one of his straps away. It had been a pointless attempt anyway, the fragile looking lens in the centre resisting all attempts to shatter it. She had given it back to him and for almost an hour it had been calm. She had thought that he might be about to recover, but it seemed that it had merely been the prelude to the worst attack she had witnessed. His fever seemed to rise to boiling point and his pale face had flushed red. It had to be the last such attack, for no one could survive such a fever. Even now she could see him slipping away into death.

She screamed and wept and felt on the verge of collapse, nervous exhaustion almost taking her into hysteria. Then a feeling of calmness flowed over her, as often did when the ring spoke to her.

"Why sobbeth thee over one so debased as he?" it asked.

"Because it wasn't solely his fault. He wouldn't be like this if it weren't for me. It was I who spoke to the blacksmith about Galen's mother. She didn't approve of me and her hold over him was almost complete. She wouldn't have let us married, so I tried to have her removed to the Redirection Chambers so that I could get him to marry me whilst she was away. I didn't know that Adam would start a witching, or that they would burn her. I started this madness, and I wanted to do what I could to make amends!"

"To leave him to sleepeth in death would be such a kindness," replied the ring.

"You don't understand," she sobbed. "My actions have condemned him to eternity in Thenril's Pit! If I could take that place then I would. But it doesn't work that way!"

"What would his continued life bring to change such?"

"If I could get his forgiveness and help him heal some of the harm that he has done then we could both be saved. Do you see?"

"I see not as thou doest, but thy despair doth wrench me to my core. When first you bested me then did but asketh for mine aid, thou didst complete one part of mine prophecy of making. I now believe that I hath the choice to completeth the second part. I do this for thee, Mistress Marie. I may be able to aid in his recovery, though it would destroy me as I am forever."

"You can help him?"

"Yes, and I will. You must placeth me upon his finger and I shalt do the rest. Though from then I shall be no more yours but his to serve and never again may we speak, for my presence upon him shall sustaineth his life and if removed shall he die."

Marie looked at the ring confused. Could she truly ask this of the ring?

"Please, do it now for he fadeth fast and if he is gone too far from this realm then I

shalt not be able to help."

She removed the ring from her finger and slowly placed it upon Galen's finger.

"Goodbye, and thank you," she said softly.

"Goodbye Marie, and thank thee, for soon I shall be free…" replied the ring fading softly from her mind.

As she watched the ring glowed softly upon his finger and immediately Galen ceased to move. She could see that he still breathed and felt his head. The fever had broken.

XIII

Demons dragged him through the seven levels of hell, each inflicting more pain than the first. He had gained his just desserts for all the evil he had done, yet that provided him with little comfort against the perpetual pain he was forced to suffer, and would suffer for eternity. The thought was enough to make him mad but the sanctity of madness was never an option in this desolate, darkened place of evil. He screamed again for what was one of an infinite number he would make, yet that no longer brought any comfort. He had wept and begged for mercy, his tears burning to vapour even as they left his eyes, yet forgiveness was also not an option of this Damned Land. The demons, creatures like those he had witnessed in life in the Shadow world, tore at him with their teeth and claws, eating him as they did. His body convulsed in pain and screams could once again be heard.

Suddenly everything went calm and silent. A glowing form appeared before him and all the pain left his body.

"I can save thee from this peril though hast entered, though ye must give thyself completely unto me. There is one who wouldst that thee earn thy redemption ere you finally perish and I shalt give thee life enough to do so, it thee doest agree," said the form, alighting on the ground before him.

Tears of joy surged through his eyes. A chance of redemption, an offer so rarely given to one such as he. He sobbed his acceptance gratefully.

"I'll do anything, anything!" he cried.

"Then give thyself up to me," said the figure softly.

He closed his eyes and opened his heart. He felt the being's touch on his skin and then an overwhelming sense of calm as energy flooded through him. The peace was momentary however, for with the energy came images, thousands of images…

…He saw a being of light and energy swirling before him. He saw it change into the shape of a great fanged beast then leap at him. His own form changed as they clashed and fought. He lost…

…He was in a crystal case, trapped and alone; so very alone. He

fought to destroy it but failed and he heard a voice.
"You will serve me forever…"

…Images of people flooded before him. All of who had fought him. All of who had lost to him. Women, children, elves, goblins, all had failed before him…

…The final of these images was of a woman who seemed somehow familiar to him. They had fought and he had lost. At last he was free and the being of light screamed in frustration and anger. He was free…

XIV

Marie woke from her dreamless sleep feeling a little empty. In the short time she had worn the ring she had grown accustomed to its near constant presence in her mind and now it was gone she felt somehow alone. She looked up at the bed containing Galen and found he was not there. Suddenly awake she looked round and saw a form sat in the corner of the room. Looking closely she could see it was Galen, though he was not as she would have expected him to be. His body was no longer broken and thin. His hair was fully restored and the gauntness of his face had gone. He looked as if the illness had never touched him, or at least that he had been fully healed, though he seemed strange somehow, darker in some way. She looked into his eyes carefully and for a moment they seemed completely dark and infinitely deep. Suddenly they were blue and very tired.

"I don't suppose you would get me some food?" he asked softly. "I feel like I've not eaten in a long time, and I need the energy to complete my task."

"What's that?" she asked, going to the cupboard where she kept some food supplies.

"Redemption, Marie. Redemption."

CHAPTER TEN: Preparations and Prisons

I

The sun rose slowly in the western sky, its red dawn light gradually spreading across the ruined city of Grelchi. It mingled with the fog that lay low in its streets giving the air a surreal and hazy feel to it. Every now and then it reflected off the dazzling armour of the knights who were moving slowly through the swamp-ridden streets. Occasionally the ring of metal would echo out from the more deserted areas as goblins ambushed the knights who sought them. It was a battle that had been going on for weeks now and there was little hope of it ending any time soon. The goblins knew these streets far better than their opponents and were much more experienced at this style of warfare.

What neither side knew was that this mass movement of the knights to clear the streets was merely a ruse to cover and protect the activities closer to the heart of the city. These were being co-ordinated by Matthew in an attempt to find the ancient entrance to the resting-place of the second part of the sceptre he sought. The search was not going well and Matthew was beginning to get impatient. Time was running out for him, the blood-link already calling him to return to Naithan. He just had to find it before he returned. He was sure that he would need it before their visit to Sol had ended and this would be his only opportunity to search for it before the return home.

The first part of the search had been simple, the goblin scroll in his possession had all but stated that it had been stored beneath the palace and even without that information it would have been obvious. The ancient palace was the most complete of all the buildings in the city and it positively hummed with magic, which made it dangerous to use anything other than old fashioned, non-magical methods to search for it. He had no desire to set off some ancient trap by blundering around with spells. Yet the palace was massive, bigger than any he had ever seen and a tribute to the ancient goblin architects, as well as confirmation of their former glory hinted at in some of the older books he owned. Unfortunately it meant it was too large for one man to search alone in a week and he had been forced to allow some of the more experienced and powerful knights of the army to know some of the information so as they could help him look.

He had not told them the truth, of course, mentioning something about the possibility of ancient treasures here that could help in the financing of the war. The problem was that the men, being the muscle-headed knights that they were, felt cheated of their first taste of real combat in the entire conflict. That meant they were not searching as thoroughly as they could because they were too busy moaning about their lot.

Matthew sighed. He was beginning to believe the goblin scroll. It was an ancient piece of work and one of the few in existence. Part of the goblin philosophy was that words, when written down, became eternally trapped. To write something down was not to allow for change and evolution, as was often the case in the oral tradition of the people that often changed and altered its stories to suit the modern situation. It was something else that the Caldorian priests of Toric had taken with them from these people. The Kolthons and Solmen both had a Book of the Gods for their respective religions, the Kolthon being considerably larger having absorbed all of the various religions of the peoples in its Empire. Yet in Caldor, the Word of Toric was a living being that gradually changed from generation to generation. Though the essential foundations of its beliefs never changed, the method of teaching and fable like tales changed as Caldor did, keeping it in contexts of the contemporary worshippers.

However, despite this belied, the goblins had written this work, a piece that was the pride of his library collection, and he had managed to finally decipher it, something his predecessors had been trying for generations. One of the most prominent statements it had made was that the *Headpiece of Prophecy doth lie where none can reach it.* He was beginning to believe it as well. The entrance to this place seemed to be nowhere, despite all their thorough checking.

He sighed again and rubbed his eyes. He had been up all night looking and his head was beginning to feel a little light. He decided it was time for a break and returned to the main chamber. He closed his eyes and allowed himself to view the illusion he had cast over the central star symbol that could prove so disruptive to the priests. It was still there, he noted with relief. His original illusion had rapidly deteriorated after barely a day, probably due to the strong magical radiance around it, and he had been forced to design a rather complex illusion of a damaged, overgrown wall around it. He was glad to see that it was holding, for the moment.

He turned away from it with its oddities wandering around his mind. It seemed strange that what was, essentially, a non-magical image for a human wizard to concentrate upon should be so well protected. Goblins would never have been able to use it and only he would have known the reason for its existence. It was possible that it had been somehow enhanced to improve travel, but why he had no idea. Teleportation using such an image was relatively safe and comfortable. All it did was highlight the spot to any wizard around. It's Kilsbur Effect, its spellprint, was rather obvious among all the priestly marks and would make it stand out to any wizard, though priests would probably not know its significance. His dual ability with magicks allowed him to see such effects of both types of magic, rather than resort to the guesswork that wizards used to guess priests magic and vice versa for the priests. It was certainly an enigma all right.

He bent to drink from the small water fountain that still worked in the corner of the hall. The priestly magic of these creatures had once been very powerful, probably equalling some of the more powerful Caldorian priests…

Suddenly the solution to both his problems struck him and he paused. If priestly magic had been used to seal the sceptre in, the chances were that one day another would unseal it and take the artefact. As far as he could recall, the goblins had suffered greatly under the Elven occupation of their lands and part of that was due to the sceptre. They would have wanted to bury it where none could find it. As they had no reason to foresee their own fall, they would have assumed that such a threat would have to come from their goblin kind, even if they were only looking and had no malevolent intentions.

To prevent that they must have gotten a human or elf to seal the entrance for them with sorcery! He laughed giddily. The scroll was correct. Sealed in such a way, no one could enter, but they had been arrogant enough to assume that they were the only ones who would look for it. They had not counted on a human wizard searching for it! The writing it down on paper had probably even been a piece of well-crafted design to fool their people. Goblins felt that writing prevented change and they had written of the permanent incarceration of the headpiece. No goblin would have tried to find something that was written down as *unfindable.* The gullibility of these creatures had to have been their downfall!

He walked back to his illusion, allowing himself to look at what truly lay beneath it. It took a lot of searching with his eyes through the strange, complex pattern that rippled out from the star. It also made them ache as he searched and his head felt even lighter. When he finally found it he almost broke into hysterical laughter. It seemed so obvious now that he looked. He reached into a pouch and took out some sand. As it slipped gently through his fingers he worked through a spell in his mind. Having formed it perfectly, he spoke the words and threw the sand over the star. As it flew it began to glitter then glow. When it reached the centre, it suddenly dropped to the floor and began to spread out in all directions. It moved round adhering itself to the magical resonance it had found. When it had finished, it outlined a glowing object in the shape of a trapdoor in the floor. He smiled. A simple invisibility shield concealed it!

The smile dropped from his face. The glowing energy that had been sand had not stopped moving, as it should have done. It had begun to run back to the centre leaving streaks of light across it in an almost marble-like effect. It then began spinning round and round, creating a spiralling vortex of light on the floor. Matthew looked round frantically and noticed that the energy of his magic was reacting to the complex patterns of magical energy around it, even though it was priestly magic. With horror he realised that in his haste he had set off some kind of complex, deadly trap. He summoned all the energy from within he could muster and began to create a protective shield around him. Yet as he released his energy, it drained away from him towards the vortex. It fed on the sorcererous energy and suddenly began to grow. As he saw that happen, he felt himself being dragged towards the spiralling vortex.

He changed tack and summoned in all the energy around him and began to pray. He launched the energy at the vortex, hoping to break it apart. Once again it absorbed the magic and grew again, now covering half the floor of the hall. Panic gripped him as he now found himself on the edge of the vortex. Nothing he could do could defeat it. He felt himself slip towards it. It had been made wizard and priest proof. He was going to die and Naithan with him. He almost screamed in anguish. He was now approaching the centre and his body felt as if it were being ripped apart in all directions at once. He looked down at the glowing blue energy and could almost see teeth and eyes at the centre.

Eyes, he thought, feeling suddenly calm. *They seem so familiar…*

Then the likeness vanished and he saw something that gave his frightened mind hope. They were not teeth but cracks. The energy before him was a combination of priestly and wizardly magic so intertwined that they could have almost been cast by one man, but that was impossible, for Matthew was the only man in recorded history to have this talent. The cracks revealed this to be the truth. They were tiny inconstancies that had occurred when the warding spell had been cast. The two had been close when casting, possibly even mind-linked, but they had not been one person. That gave him his hope, for the cracks could be forced open, though only through a perfect blend of the two magicks, something only he could do. This trap had been designed as invincible and he was the only one able to wield the two in flawless combination. Yet time was not one his side. He could already feel his physical form begin to unwind as it entered the vortex, though the pain seemed somehow muted.

Ignoring everything, he drew on all the energy of both forms of magic he could gather and began creating a spell like no other ever created in history. Melding the two energies as one was perhaps the most complex process he had ever done, yet when he had finished he found that he had never felt so alive. It struck him that this was pure magic that he was dealing with, and revelled in the moment. Yet he still had a task before him. He channelled the energy in its pure form into the cracks he had seen in the vortex, though only via a tiny trickle. He pushed it through the gaps and allowed it to worm its way through all such inconstancies throughout the warding spell. Panic began to grip once more for he could feel it beginning to unravel the intricacies of his mind and he knew that he had to act; now.

He changed the trickle of energy to a sudden outpour, flooding the cracks of the spell until they could hold together no more. The seams of the spell split wide apart, and the energy began to spin off erratically. Matthew noted with shock that they were now completely unstable and was barely able to throw up a protective shield before the explosion of pure energy erupted throughout the hall. Even so, he found himself flying through the air at a rapid speed. Breath and consciousness left him as he forcefully struck the back wall and slid to the floor.

II

Meredith was about ready to concede defeat. It seemed her instincts were wrong and the Shadow had indeed been captured. It had taken a lot of searching, but she had managed to find some who had seen him, though their descriptions had varied greatly from evil demon with horns to the father of a woman's child. Many reports she had discounted, as the money she offered around to jog memories seemed to inspire some creative responses. However, there had been a group of people that had mentioned the strange witch burning incident that had occurred here some weeks ago, another of the odd traditions of this *peace-loving* people. They had reported that one of her dark demons had risen up from the shadows of the flames, untied her and then leapt through the fire at them. Most had fled, though one or two had seen his face before they had done so. The description, minus the horns of course, had matched that of a streetwalker she had spoken to a few days before. The whore had been one of the original people to actually see this *Shadow*, though most had discounted it as drunken ramblings.

One of the witnesses from the burning claimed she had even seen him confront the guards and lose, though the witch had used her sorcery by then to vanish into thin air. That had given her hope. The Shadow may well have been captured, but it seemed whatever device he had used to Shadow Travel, something she had read about once, had gone with the woman. From there however, she had seemed to reach a dead end. The description of the woman could have matched any of a hundred Caldorian women and often varied in the details that could have narrowed it down. The closest she had come to finding her had been when she found a landlady of a nearby inn had said that she had thrown out such a woman about three days before the witch burning.

She sighed and rubbed her tired eyes. She had been working almost non-stop on this search knowing that the longer it took the more likely her fellow hawks would be placed in for Redirection. The fact that it had not been done immediately had been the source of some confusion and relief for her, but it looked like that particular respite was going to go to waste. She took a large mouthful of the frothy ale before her and determined to get herself very drunk. It looked like she was going to have to move on again and she just as she had been getting used to this city. Tiredness began to drag her eyelids together.

"'Scuse me dear," said a woman's voice behind her and making her jump.

"Yes?" she asked, a hand instinctively going to the dagger at her side.

"You the one that's looking fer a woman an' her fella?" asked a rather plump, if rather dirty woman stood there.

"I might be," she replied slowly. "Why?"

"Happens I just might know where they is," she replied.

Meredith was instantly awake. It could be another dead end, but any chance was better than none at all.

"Where?" She asked.

"Now I'll not says a word till I've seen the colour of yer money," replied the woman.

Meredith took out three golden mareks and placed them on the table. It was more money than the woman could expect to earn in years of work. Her eyes bulged at the sight and Meredith realised that there was something not quite right about the woman.

"Two for the information and the last for your silence," she said simply.

The woman's hand shot out quickly to grab the money but Meredith was faster and clamped down on the coins.

"You've seen their colour, now tell me what I want to know," she said slowly.

For added emphasis, and by means of a threat, Meredith partially unsheathed her dagger and allowed its blade to glitter in the light of the lamps. The woman caught the message and gulped nervously.

"Well, I was walking the streets over in Fish-Side and I heard these 'orrible screams. Well, Fish-Side is known fer its terrible screams, but yer see, the thing is, well…sometimes there's good pickings on such people as what was screaming, so I went fer a looksee. Well, I saw this woman and a chap like what you described in a small room. Well, 'e didn't look all that well then all of a sudden like, he got well. Well I says to myself that 'taint natural, 'taint. I went to speak to the knights but they ignored me so I says t' Thenril with 'em. Then I heard yer was lookin' fer 'im so I says to myself…"

Meredith slammed her dagger into the table.

"The name woman," she said softly. "Give me the name of the street or inn she is staying in."

The woman gulped nervously and her eyes began to dart around. Incidents such as this were common, however, and all there were pointedly ignoring the exchange.

"Puddle Street, *The Cat's Gut* inn," she all but squeaked.

"Thank you," said Meredith, pulling the dagger from the table and getting to her feet. "Take the money and bother me no more."

She walked quickly out of the pub and into the streets. The sun was beginning to set over the city and she knew she had to be quick. This accursed curfew was truly beginning to get tiresome. She all but ran through the streets towards Fish-Side, the more unruly section of the city. Despite her profession, Meredith always felt uneasy in this particular area of the city and therefore quickened her pace as she went.

It took almost an hour to get there and by then darkness was already falling around her. As she reached the inn the curfew bells sounded out across the city. The street around her was full of people quickly hurrying into the various buildings, so she took her cue from them and entered the inn. It was a dive, even when compared to some of the flea pits that existed around here and the man behind the bar was the most dishevelled, drunken wretch of a slob she had ever had the grace of Sivran to see.

"One room fer one night," she said in her best Fish-Side drawl.

"One geldon," said the man with a burp.

She could not believe her ears. One geldon for one night! She supposed that was one way to profit from the curfew. She was basically trapped in the inn now and forced to pay whatever price the innkeeper wanted. She bit her lip angrily and paid the man his coin. He had the temerity to actually weigh it and ensure it was genuine. At any other time she would have struck out at him with her tongue. She swallowed down the words however, and even had the grace to smile when he grunted and pointed upstairs. Evidently this place was too cheap even to run to proper door locks. She started up the stairs and saw a clean faced and blond haired girl who could have matched the description perfectly. She barely acknowledged her presence and proceeded to her room. She wondered how best to approach the couple and speak with them. She entered the cesspit that was her room and slid the bolt across. As she did so she felt the touch of cold, sharp steel push against her throat.

"Now tell me, dear," said a soft, male voice in her ear. "Why have you been looking for the one who calls himself the Shadow, and I want the truth mind you. I wouldn't want to have to spoil that pretty little neck of yours by splitting it open now, would I?"

III

Light that was the first thing that Naithan could remember after the beast's mouth had clamped down around him. At first he had thought he had reached the Celestial Palace of Toric on high. But instead of winged heralds to greet him it was a bunch of unshaven, unwashed, swarthy faces looking down upon him. His second thought had been that somehow he had failed and that he was down in the Pit of the Damned.

Though he had been incorrect in his assumption, what he was now suffering was a close parallel to what Thenril's realm must truly be like. He was on board the ship of a pirate known only as Blackheart who had, it seemed, been the source of the attack on his fleet. He had no idea how many ships were left but their total destruction seemed not to have been the sea marauder's main intention. That had been the capture of Naithan. It appeared that Blackheart wished to ransom Naithan back to his own kingdom.

Until then, however, Naithan was a prisoner and therefore treated as one. He was kept in chains in appalling conditions, left for hours alone in the hot depths of the hold. He was only allowed water and food three times a day and only on those occasions were his hands allowed to drop from above his head where they were usually kept chained. Naithan had no idea where they were or how he was going to get out of this situation. He only hoped that Matthew was all right and that he would be able to find him before the blood-link killed them both. Sometimes it seemed that the link was more of a curse than anything else, though they had been fortunate this time. All those on his ship had been killed, at least according to Blackheart and had Matthew been there then who knows what might have happened.

Of course it was highly probable that they would never have been sneaked up on in the first place. If that Captain Sirius had only listened to his commands and obeyed he would not have been too busy to notice the arrival of the two ships. At least they had suffered their just desserts. There was no path from the deep water to the Celestial Palace, as the old saying went.

Naithan wiped his head upon his sleeve. It was very hot in this hold, very hot indeed.

"He was talking to hisself again," said the voice of his demonic guard who generally sat just out of sight. "Something about water an' palaces."

"Let me look," came the reply.

It sounded like the captain Blackheart, or was it Sirius? He could not really recall. Everything seemed so faded and unreal at the moment. Was this the way that the blood-link killed? He had been told it was very painful and the screams of his mother's personal sorcerer after her death had seemed to confirm this. Yet if it was, why was it working already? Had they truly been apart that long? Time seemed to have lost all meaning down in this dark pit. He looked up and saw a strange face he had not seen before peering down at him. Behind him was the captain.

"Yes," said the man looking closely at him. "He's definitely feverish all right."

"Well I could 'a told yer that meself!" replied the captain rolling his eyes. "What I wants t' know is, is it catching, an' will it kill 'im? I don't want t' have gone through all this only t' find there'll be no payoff!"

The man closest to him put his hand on Naithan's forehead and closed his eyes, muttering some prayer or another.

"It's not catching, and it shouldn't be fatal," said the man, "though I can't see its source. It's unlike anything I've ever seen. With Giarna's help I can stave off the worst of the fever and allow him to sleep through most of it."

Giarna! The word went through Naithan with a cold horror. This was a heathen priest. A pagan, willing to practice his dark rites on Naithan. He pulled away from the man's torrid, fetid touch. How dare he attempt to corrupt him so! The man looked surprised at the movement and moved to touch him again. Naithan pulled himself out of the way.

"Stay away from me," he all but screamed. "Keep your filthy claws off of me."

The man simply ignored him and moved to touch him again. Chained and helpless as he was Naithan used the only weapon available to him. He bit the pagan's hand. What then followed was, to Naithan, a medley of images and confusion as the Thenril spawned demons around him struggled to pin him down. Then, when held firmly down under four men, his arms screaming in pain as they were pulled tightly against the manacles, the man grabbed hold of him and a slow, evil darkness slipped over him and he knew no more.

IV

Meredith could not believe it. Caught again! She was truly beginning to slip, though this time she could forgive herself for her captor had cheated. Evidently he could spring straight from the shadows and the power seemed to have an unsettling effect on his appearance. When looked at directly, this Shadow seemed nothing but an ordinary man, yet when glimpsed from the corner of her eye, his pale body seemed almost insubstantial, as if not totally there. It would not have mattered too much if he had remained seated or stood still somewhere where she could keep focused on him, but he constantly paced about the room as they talked.

That they were talking was surprising to Meredith. It seemed that her enquiries about him had aroused his interest and he had sent this girl to set him up. The small blond woman looked nothing like the large, filthy one she had spoken to, but the clothes and padding were still hanging from the back of the desk chair. For falling for that ancient trick she certainly could not forgive herself.

"So what exactly, is in this for me?" he asked, turning a suspicious gaze upon her.

That made Meredith think. There were very few people who were not susceptible to financial rewards but she got the impression that this was one of them. Given the ease with which he had captured her and the nature of his strange *powers* it was highly likely that the promise of vast riches would be rather useless. If he desired such things then he could surely get them for himself with less than half the risk.

"It would be a way of getting back at the king and his knights," she said slowly.

The man's hatred of knights was legendary and some of the things he was supposed to have done to them made her shudder.

"I no longer do revenge," he said quietly, looking towards the woman sat quietly in the corner.

"Then I don't know," she replied simply. There was nothing she could think of to offer him that he could not get himself. "All I can do is ask for your assistance. The man and his hatred of thieves rivals your…"

She paused, not knowing whether or not to push this man too far. He finished her sentence for her.

"My hatred of knights. Please, go on."

"And all I wish to do is get them out from that prison under the palace before he does something quite horrible to them. I've seen some of the results of the work he does on such people."

The image of Jack's bloodied head, floating in the sewer appeared in her mind. It had been a shock to find out that the man responsible for killing Jack, the man she had robbed, was the same man who now ran the city.

"I've probably done worse, what does this all matter to me?" he asked, sounding incredibly bitter.

"Galen, don't," said the woman quickly. "Remember the agreement. This could be the start of it. Saving a few people from the likes of men such as you once were."

It was the first time the woman had spoken and Meredith had no idea just what she was talking about. Galen, if that was his name, seemed to understand however, for he visibly winced as she spoke.

"All right, I'll do it," he said sourly.

"Fantastic!" she replied. "I'll get the plans necessary to show you were to go…"

"Not necessary," interrupted Galen. "I know the prison well enough. Wait here. I'll be back with your *friends* in an hour or so."

Meredith could not believe the arrogance of the man. It was not even possible to reach the palace in an hour. He stepped into the shadows and vanished, reminding her that he was not about to use the usual methods to release the Dark Circle. She settled herself down and looked around uncomfortably. It was then she was reminded of the woman's presence.

"I don't believe I got your name when I arrived," she said.

"Marie," replied the woman as she set about tidying the room.

Meredith got the impression that the girl obviously did not want to talk and realised that this could be one of the longest hours of her life.

V

Matthew coughed as he came round to consciousness and found he could taste blood in his mouth. He got to his feet and rubbed his head groggily. The world span momentarily and he was forced to support himself against the wall. He looked over at the pattern and realised in horror, that his illusion had been destroyed by whatever magic had fought with him. He realised just how powerful the trap had to have been because destroying magic without fulfilling its prophecy was probably the most difficult thing in magic to do. Even the simplest of prophecies took so much power to destroy them outright that most spell casters would never be able to wield safely.

Now was not the time to wonder, however, for not only was the illusion gone, but the door had been revealed to all. Matthew could not afford to allow others to meddle in this matter. He staggered over to the still glowing trapdoor and examined it closely. There was no handle, or any physical method of opening it, which meant it had to be magical. He cautiously probed round the magical auras with his magic, testing and checking for any other traps. His caution was rewarded with results. He found a trap, almost as cunning as the first, requiring both forms of magic at once to circumnavigate it.

He pulled the two energies into his grasp once more, his senses and emotions suddenly awash with life. He carefully channelled through the cracks in the trap to study the release spell bound beneath it. After some time examining it he found he had discovered the key and that was the pattern on the floor. Unlike the patterns in the Caldorian cities, this had not been built manually into the floor, but magically etched there by some long forgotten wizard and priest working in tandem. The ten outer points evidently represented the ten aspects of sorcery, as dictated in the Kolthon tomes of writing and the twelve central points seemed to indicate the twelve High Gods of the Kolthon religion. In Kolth, priests were considered paramount among the people, and therefore that pattern had to be manipulated first.

He released a little of his combined magicks and folded each of the stars upon themselves, so that they pointed inwards and their golden colours seemed to merged as one. The process left him with a twelve-sided golden polygon within a ten-pointed star and as he watched the shape began to slowly spin round in a circle. He ignored the unsettling motion and then concentrated on the outer, ten-pointed star. He began the process again and folded each of them in on themselves. Their edges did not meet, as had those of the inner star, yet their outer edges touched to form another polygon around the first. It began to revolve in the opposite direction and every so often one of the inward points of the outer polygon would touch a corner of the smaller, twelve-edged one inside. As they did, a burst of colour erupted in a small fountain that showered towards the exact centre of the pattern. Matthew noted with wonder that each colour was different and seemed to depend upon which point had touched which corner, red from one, green from another.

Soon there were myriad of colours in the centre, swirling within the square of the trapdoor he had already revealed. The colours began to mix and mingle, forming new and vibrant colours that mixed with others to create yet more unusual and often beautiful colours. Gradually the number of colours began to lessen as each mixed and merged with the other. As they did so, they appeared to become brighter and brighter, bringing tears to his eyes. Soon there were but three colours left that all converged at once. Suddenly a flash of brilliant, white gold light erupted up into the sky then disappeared.

It took some time for Matthew's sight to return and adjust to the now dark and gloomy looking surroundings. As they did so, he noticed that the pattern had completely vanished and that in its place was a gaping hole in the floor. He released most of the energy, keeping some as an emergency measure then looked down through the square hole in the floor. His heart pumped rapidly with excitement. There were stairs within leading down into the darkness.

It was then that he also heard voices approaching from outside the hall. The knights had to have either heard the explosion or seen the light and come to investigate. He had to prevent them from entering with him. No one must know of the sceptre. He quickly barred all the doorways with joint magic, using wards similar, though not as lethal as, that he had faced only moments ago. He then drew on a little more magic and created a small glowing ball of light to light the darkness in the stairwell.

He stepped down cautiously onto what appeared to be granite steps beneath him. He could see that they seemed almost new and could have almost never been used. The first step took his weight and appeared perfectly stable. The second was the same and he soon found himself working his way down the dim, chilly stairs. He rubbed his arms as the chill reached them and he briefly regretted not returning to better provision himself for this trip. The swamps of Grelchin were usually humid and it was essential to wear as little clothing as possible. He had no idea how the knights managed to leap around here in their armour and such. However, the humidity seemed unable to reach this cold, stone passage and he found himself feeling decidedly chilly.

Suddenly he found himself plummeting downwards into darkness as his foot touched what had to be illusionary steps. With barely a thought he unleashed a spell to slow his descent and summoned the ball of light to him. As it lit the area around him he saw that he was slowly falling towards a series of sharp, rusty, metal spikes. He had fallen for an ancient trap that appeared so often nowadays in the adventure fiction that Kolthons seemed so fond of reading. Cursing himself for his own foolishness he waited till his feet just touched the tip of them before casting a second spell to raise him out of the pit.

He alighted on the first solid step after the illusionary step and gave his heart a chance to slow down once more. For the first time he began to regret his decision to take this journey alone. However, it was too late now. He had to strike while the iron was hot, as his father had been so fond of saying. He sent the ball a little way ahead of him, took a deep breath and then continued down into the darkness.

VI

Galen entered the dark realm and looked about in wonder. There had been no nausea, no pain and no fear. This realm seemed somehow familiar to him now, and even the strange creatures around him seemed somehow less threatening. He had learned a lot since his recovery, and one of them was the extent of the ring's power.

As he moved towards the palace and its prison, he found himself thinking back on his incarceration. He had been so grateful when Marie had removed him from that hell-spawned pit where he had been forced to undergo such nightmarish dreams. It had been more than he deserved, he believed, but he had still felt relief. The dreams still came, though only at night now when his mind was more open to receive the small brass item's images. He knew that he could shield himself then as well, but felt that this was part of the suffering he would have to endure as part of his redemption. As was this rescue mission, though how rescuing a bunch of thieving crooks and returning them to the world above would help him redeem himself he had no idea.

He ignored his misgivings and continued on his way through the dark streets of this shadowy image of Theldar towards the dungeon. It was a simple matter getting there, yet the danger would come when he emerged in the prison, for he had no idea where any guards were. There were sure to be more guards there now, with so many prisoners now trapped in the small cells.

Suddenly his vision seemed to blur slightly and he saw a shadowy image of a man sat in the corner of the corridor he had been about to enter, for he had no intention of suddenly appearing amongst a bunch of desperate, angry and rather jumpy thieves. Instinctively he knew that it had to be the position of a guard in the real world. He looked around and saw another shadowy figure marching towards him. He felt a slight shudder as the image moved through him and for a moment he had a burst of thoughts that were not his own. They were also not the most pleasant of thoughts either.

Taking note of that odd phenomenon for future reference, he moved carefully to the other end of the corridor. He looked round carefully and saw no image other than the passage, then slipped through the shadow. He almost gagged as he emerged, for the smell in this place was fetid and rotted. Apparently they were being subjected to the same treatment as he had experienced on his visit here. He moved quietly over to the nearest cell.

"Hssst," he whispered to try and get the occupants' attention. "Who wants out of here?"

"We all do, of course," came the eventual, muttered reply.

"Good," replied Galen. "Well, tell the others in your cell that I'll be inside soon and it'll not be by the usual methods so don't go jumping me when I appear."

"Who are you?" asked the voice.

"The Shadow," he replied with a slight mocking bow. "So you know what I can do."

The man looked suitably impressed. Of course, no one but the Shadow could have gotten this far without raising the alarm.

"I'll just speak to your companions in the other cells and then I'll appear," he said quickly.

He moved stealthily from cell to cell, repeating the message to members of each cell. There appeared to be some twenty members of this Dark Circle, all of whom had been crammed into four cells designed to take only one man. As he turned to return to the first cell he all but walked into a guard patrolling the corridor. His heart leaped to his throat and he stood there frozen in panic. The guard just walked straight past him however and continued his patrol. Galen's eyes followed the guard in amazement and he went to wipe his brow with his arm. It was then that he realized that it was almost translucent, with only a dark, shadowy haze to indicate where it was. Suddenly it was solid once more and he stared at the ring in amazement. It evidently had more powers than he had ever realized.

He slipped into the shadow world and moved to the first cell. He decided to emerge from under the only bed within the cell, though at least they had such luxury. It would be safer than appearing in the midst of them, for if one moved at the last second he would appear inside the person. He had only done that once before and the resulting sight had not been pleasant to look at. It was one of a thousand memories he no longer wanted.

He emerged and crawled out to the people inside. Even despite his warning some jumped and went to grab for knives they no longer possessed. He stood in their midst and looked at them.

"The Circle member Hawk Meredith sends her greetings and prepares for your return," he said quietly, reciting the words the woman had given him to prove his allegiance. "Now, where we are about to go is not a very pleasant place and I will even have to leave you there for a moment when I collect your companions. You will have to join hands around me as I take us and when there you must not let go until I say, all right?"

They all nodded in agreement and linked hands. He wondered why not one of them had thought to question him in any way, but pushed the thoughts away. What he was about to do he had not done in years and was very difficult to achieve. In order to protect these men in the Shadow Realm, he had to detach them somewhat from being completely within that realm, leaving them effectively trapped be tween the two worlds. He needed to do this so that he could free them all at once, going from cell to cell and using the Shadow Realm to free them. He could have done it bit by bit, by taking each group out of the prison individually but that would have given the guards chance to notice that something was amiss and, besides, he had said he would do it in an hour.

To achieve their protection he would literally transport part of their physical body two would actually exist in the same place to the Shadow Realm, leaving the rest in the real world. It would mean that whilst they would mainly exist in the other land, they would still be partially present here in the real world. It would hopefully mean that they would be visible and protected in both worlds at the same time as they waited for him to free everyone. Guards glancing in from the real world would still see them in the prison whilst in the Shadow Realm, the part of the thieves that the shadowy forms their would crave most of all, and detect instantly on their arrival, would remain here in the real world. Without this and the scent it created, the creatures would just ignore the thieves and leave them to themselves.

However, the whole process was extremely complex and difficult and required complete concentration. He cleared his mind and visualised his intentions, letting them flow through the ring towards the people. Everything went dark for a moment and suddenly they were no longer quite in the real world.

He left them there, noticing that many of them were sweating with fear already and deemed it wise to hurry. In his experience, if he left it too long then one would crack and break the circle, bringing them fully into the Shadow Realm and leaving all of them open to the merciless attacks of the creatures. Galen paused a moment. These memories were not his own, as he had never attempted to do this before. He sifted through his memories and found that it seemed full of fragments of other lives.

The sound of a guard moving nearby brought him back to the current situation and he shrugged off the eerie feeling all those additional memories gave him. He proceeded to shift all four groups of five men to the dual existence and looked them over. Most were covered in welts, bruises, cuts and scars and most seemed to have suffered a great deal at the hands of the guards. Knowing that most would need treatment for their wounds and soon, he went to the first group.

"You two," he said, pointing to the two most mature and, hopefully, least panicky of the thieves. "Break the circle and link with me. No one else move."

He went to the two and almost had to prize their hands apart to join the circle. The break brought them all fully into this Shadow Realm and the link with him would protect them all. He imagined the cell door to be open then gently led the terrified men and women through it. He then proceeded to each of the cells and got them to join the circle he was already a part of. It was rather crowded in the corridor by the time he had gotten them all to join together, and the circle was more of an elongated ellipse, but it was sufficient to protect them all.

"Now," he said slowly. "I will release you two and I want you to link up together. Then all of you move with me. As long as I am in the centre of you all, you will all be safe. Break the circle and then you will all be at risk."

He did as he said and entered the centre of the circle. He expanded the ring's aura of protection to its limit and then began the slow journey to the outside world and freedom.

VII

Oliver sat in his office looking at the report on his desk with outrage. Not only had that maniacal, knight killing Shadow gotten loose from the palace dungeon but now that wretched thieves' council had also managed to work their way to freedom somehow. He now had some idea of the problems that the king faced and he ruled an entire nation of people such as these. He glowered at the report once more then tore it to shreds and threw it away.

It looked like he had been a little too lenient with these people. He had read books on the other nations and found that many offered the death penalty for such crimes. Though against his general beliefs, Oliver believed that there were some criminals beyond all redemption or treatment. Men and women such as those had abused Toric's gift of life to them, and therefore they should have such a gift forcibly removed. Yet that would not be enough to deter criminals. The people of Caldor had to see what earthly punishment they would suffer if they broke the laws. The knights would also have to be tougher on curfew breakers and pagans. They would be given the choice. Convert or die. Oliver smiled, his anger slipping away. He could see it now. A city of peace and tranquillity where all feared the hand of the law and so avoided it. It would be perfect for when the king returned.

He shook himself from his reverie. If the city was to be ready for the king's return then he had to start work. He set out the proclamations of the death sentence in writing for the street heralds to call out to the citizens and placed the names of those to whom it would be attached. The court judges might object, but he was ruler of this city for now and they would heed to his demands or face dismissal. All thieves would face the axe, without fail. They were Thenril's earthly demons. He called his page in.

"Yes, milord," said the boy with a low bow.

"Take this to the city scribes. I want it proclaimed on every street corner and in every tavern, inn and pub," he said imperiously.

"Yes, milord," replied the boy with another low bow.

The boy had learned his lessons in court etiquette well and the people of Theldar needed such lessons themselves, for children rarely heeded anything other than violence. He smiled. The city would be perfect for the king's return, just perfect.

VIII

Matthew watched incredulously at the large stone ball as it rolled back to its original position. He was living in a Kolthon adventure tale. He had been shot at by poison darts; attacked by bladed pendulums; survived rock falls; been swarmed by illusionary spiders, forced to walk over a chasm on an invisible bridge and finally outran a large, rolling stone ball. His spell energy was almost wasted by these events and he was not far from collapsing with exhaustion.

Of course, many of the traps could have been avoided without using magic, but it had become an instinctive, second nature to him now to defend with spells. He realised that this was probably the intention behind the traps and hoped that there were not too many more challenges ahead of him. He made his way through the cobweb filled and dusty passage. His glowing ball of light was beginning to fade, its time based prophecy rapidly approaching its completion. Matthew had not thought it would take so long to search this underground maze and was once more regretting his haste in entering alone. The corridor reached a dead end and he almost cried out in despair. In addition to all the traps there had been quite a few dead ends and this was the last possible passage to search. Could it all have been an elaborate, yet deadly diversion?

Something caught his eye. It was a carving in the wall at the end of the corridor, barely visible in the dim light. He cleared off the mosses that clung to it and almost gaped in shock. Beneath it was the carved image of a human, and not just any human. It was the exact image of Sir Caldor, first knight and ruler of the kingdom that now bore his name. It was almost identical to the statue that could be found Theldar's central square.

On the left hand side of the wall was the image of a goblin, stood in almost an identical pose to Sir Caldor. Both held identical swords unsheathed and held pointing towards the centre of the top edge of the wall, much like knights when standing honour guard in what was known as the arch of swords. Into the blades of the swords were etched words in ancient goblin script. All he could pick out from them were the words tomb, Caldor and Malch Gru'an-Ar. He moved to the centre of the wall and saw that there was a thin crack that ran down the entire length of the wall. It had to be the entrance. Yet he could not see how to open the door, if that was what it was. He ran his finger down the crack and as he did the mouths on the statues began to move and speak, one in Old Caldorian and the other in goblin speak. Matthew dredged up all his knowledge of ancient languages and attempted to translate the words.

"Enter thee the tomb of they who once did fight in brotherhood. If thee seek to honour they then welcome are thou ist. If thee seek to do they harm, then ware the doom that awaits thee."

As the mouths closed the wall split in two and swung inwards. Inside was a small chamber with a vaulted ceiling, and small statues looking down on him. In the centre were two biers, upon one of which were lying the skeletal remains of what seemed to be a goblin. In its hands was a sword that once probably rested upon the creature's chest. He walked closer and examined the sword. He was amazed to see that it was an exact replica of Tristan's sword, Caliburn. The hilt was only different in one respect. It had the head of a human, that of Caldor upon it. What was now perceived as a trophy design on the King's Knight's sword was probably the graven image of this goblin here and not a threat or reminder of the goblin menace and cruelty at all. Matthew wondered how much of Caldor's history had been perverted like this and why. He reached down to touch the sword to see if it too was magical and suddenly it moved.

Taken aback Matthew jerked away, drawing what little energy he had left to himself. Before him stood a ghostly image of a goblin, the one who the carving had evidently been based upon.

"Thou hast disturbed this place of rest. Now thou must die," said the voices of the statues behind him.

The goblin before him spun the sword round in a complex pattern he had once seen Tristan use in practice. It was one of the most complex forms in swordplay and Tristan, the best swords master in Caldor, would look clumsy compared to this display. Matthew realised that he stood little chance. It was then that he saw the amulet hanging round the ghost's neck. It had to be the headpiece of the sceptre. It matched the description perfectly. He had made it and with this realisation his resolve stiffened and he pulled on all the energy he could muster. He had to defeat this creature and take the headpiece. Even with only two pieces of the sceptre he would be able to produce some of the most powerful prophecies in Loden.

The goblin sprang at him with its sword rising in an arc towards his head. His old training barely saved him, especially as the slash was quickly followed by a downward slice designed to catch those quick enough to move out of the way. He threw himself forward and past the creature, rolling across the floor before staggering to his feet. The creature was already upon him before he had time to think and slashed at him again. Without hesitation he cast a spell and the sword hit an invisible barrier he had placed in front of himself. The creature's sword glowed softly and it struck the barrier. The barrier shimmered once but held.

Unfortunately, Matthew knew that it could not hold out for very long, having only been created to give him a moment to think. He knew that most spells would not work on the phantom before him except those involving the aspect of spirit. Unfortunately that was an aspect neither he nor his predecessors had ever studied much. There was only one possibility and that was known as a spirit blade. He had not wielded a sword for quite some time, however and knew he would not stand up to a hand to hand combat with this creature.

The barrier crackled as the creature struck again and Matthew knew that one more hit was all it would take. A thought suddenly came from somewhere in his vast store of knowledge and experience and he knew how he could even the odds a little. He quickly cast the spirit blade and armour that created a translucent sword and armour around him. The blade seemed to contain a flickering blue flame within it and the armour seemed to have a soft blue mist swirling through it. He then unleashed a second spell and jumped into the air as the barrier came crashing down under the goblin's ferocious attack. The creature looked momentarily confused at the empty spot where Matthew had stood. This was his opportunity. He flew down from the ceiling swiftly and silently, bringing the spirit sword to slash across the creature's back before returning quickly up to the ceiling, out of the creature's reach. It shuddered as if in pain and looked round. Matthew noticed with horror that the creature seemed no more injured than before.

The ghostly goblin then showed extraordinary intelligence for a creature of its type and looked up at Matthew. It then did something completely unexpected. It took its sword and threw it with unerring accuracy and speed straight at Matthew. Mustering all the skill and speed he could, he managed to knock it away with the blade of his own sword. He noticed that it bit deep into the edge of the sword and that it left a deep crack in the blade. When he looked back to the creature he noticed it was more transparent than before. Evidently the creature's power was somehow related to the sword and the sword's weakness was the spirit blade.

Matthew breathed a momentary sigh of relief. The creature was not indestructible and he had been fortunate enough to discover its weakness. He waited on high for the creature to throw the sword at him again, yet it seemed to have learned its lesson. After collecting its sword it had remained almost stationary, just watching Matthew for the next move. Matthew groaned as he felt himself sag in the air slightly. The spell was running close to its prophecy and he would soon be back on the ground. There was nothing for it. He would have to risk another attack, though this time the creature would be prepared.

He turned and dived at the creature, swinging the spirit blade around wildly in the hope that it would somehow strike the creature's weapon. The goblin entered into a complex defensive spin and Matthew knew he had no chance of breaking through the pattern, but he was now going too fast to pull away. He closed his eyes and screamed angrily as he neared the spinning sword. He felt the goblin's sword strike to his left, right, back and head almost all at one instant. Sparks flew in all directions and Matthew crashed to the floor. The spirit blade faded from his hand and the armour around him dispersed into the air. Matthew closed his eyes and waited for the final killing blow.

He opened them again when none came and looked around cautiously.

He found no sign of the creature. He got to his feet and discovered that he was completely unharmed. The spirit armour had done its job and protected him. But why had the creature disappeared? He looked around and saw the sword on the floor, broken into four pieces. Suddenly the truth dawned on him. The armour had been of spirit, and it had evidently been that which had damaged the blade when it had struck him. He almost laughed hysterically. He had burned out the last of his energy attempting to evade the blade and all he had needed to do was let it hit him!

He sagged to the floor in an exhausted heap. His mission would soon be over and he would be able to heed the call of the blood-link and return to Naithan. The thought gave him a final burst of energy he needed. The headpiece of prophecy was his for the taking. He crawled over to the broken shards of the sword and found, to his horror, that the headpiece was gone. He got up and looked to the bier, breathing a sigh of relief as he did. The headpiece lay within the goblin's skeleton where it had once lain on its chest. Fighting back the euphoria of victory that threatened to overwhelm him, he reached in and placed his hand around the ornate claw that marked the top of the Sceptre and that had once held an emerald rose in its grasp. The metal was cool to the touch and the carving upon it of intricate detail. He closed his eyes to savour the moment and gently began to lift it into the air.

Suddenly there was pain. He opened his eyes in shock and looked to his hand. He saw, to his horror, that it was encased rose coloured crystal that seemed to be growing from the bier. He tried to move his hand but found it had become attached to the goblin's resting-place. Panic seized him and he reached out to the magical energies at his command. They were not there. He had expended almost more than he could handle without rest during this journey and no longer had the strength to even reach out to it.

The final and most devious trap in this entire underground complex had caught him. He could almost believe that the entire place had been designed for this moment. Any wizard would have done as he had and only they would have been able to get this far. He doubted that any wizard would have had enough magic left to defeat the final trap.

He cursed himself for being a fool and tried to think of a way out. He knew that it was hopeless though. The crystal was growing up his arm at an alarming pace and he knew that it would probably encase him within an hour. He had no hope of rescue for the shield he had erected in the courtyard's doors would last for over a day, by which time he would then be totally encased in crystal. He would die and the king would not be far behind him.

He cursed the day that the wretched blood-link had been passed to him on Naithan's coronation. The previous Lord Priest had told him of the difficulties the parasite would cause, though it would be worse for the king if he did not realise that the link had been broken. He knew the history of this curse. In the past, kings' and queens' advisors had often sought to harm their rulers in order to get their own way. The link had been used to ensure that it would never do it again. The link was not magical, as such. It was in fact a parasite that existed in its millions within his and Naithan's blood. Yet each of the individual parasites were somehow connected to a creature of higher consciousness. The unfortunate thing was that the male and female of each species could not co-inhabit the same body, for they would tear it apart competing for whatever nutrients they required. Yet neither could exist without the other, so they had to exist in two bodies and keep them close enough together to ensure the telepathic connection that they maintained between them could remain strong and keep them alive.

They had their benefits of course. When passed from one host to the next they took much of the host's knowledge with them and passed on to their new hosts. It was because of this that Matthew was as powerful as he was, for he had the power and experience of countless sorcerers within him. Unfortunately that would not help him in his present situation. He screamed in frustration and rage as the crystal wrapped itself around his elbow and moved towards his shoulder. He was going to die, killing Naithan in the process and there was absolutely nothing he could do about it.

IX

A ringing in Tristan's head disturbed his thoughts and he felt Caliburn vibrating in its scabbard. They were approaching the Great Eastern Highway that ran towards Belthanor and the atmosphere had been growing increasingly thicker with each passing hour. Matthius was forced to lead Belthar around at all times, the big man looking terribly thin, pale and exceptionally blind. Without a guide the big man stumbled, tripped and fell over every obstacle he encountered. Yet still the two refused to say why this was so and why Belthar needed time alone. It seemed that the more ill Belthar became, the more obstinate he became. Matthius had looked on the verge of breaking the silence on several occasions but each time Belthar had cut him off. What made matters worse was the fact that the whole group was certain that they were being watched. It was a feeling that increased tenfold with every step they took towards the Highway. Yet the ringing in his head had momentarily disturbed him.

What was that? He asked Caliburn.

"Another part of my prophecy of making being fulfilled," replied the sword softly.

The sword had been slowly introducing the various ideas and concepts of magic to Tristan over the past few days and Tristan felt he understood this particular part well enough.

You mean the magic that keeps you alive? he asked fearfully.

He had to admit he would miss the sword's presence if it were to suddenly disappear.

"In a way, yes," replied the sword. *"My sister sword Thalus was killed by power that both protected and harmed. It's the second condition of my prophecy completed."*

What's the next one? Asked Tristan.

"I am forbidden to tell you," replied Caliburn. *"It must run its natural course and to tell you would alter the events that followed as you either tried to prevent it or accelerate it."*

I would not, replied Tristan indignantly.

"It matters neither way. I am simply forbidden to reveal such information. I'm sorry. You'd best be on alert. I'm sure we're being watched as well."

Caliburn's statement made Tristan uneasy once more and took his mind off the sword's prophecy. He looked around and felt a shudder run down his spine. He was positive they were being watched, yet he could see no one. He looked round at the trees that surrounded the small trail they were travelling along. There was an unnerving silence in the air. Even animals were making no noise. That could only mean that there were humans around, yet still he could see no one.

"We're here," whispered Matthius, pointing to the paved road ahead.

Tristan motioned for them to stay where they were and crept slowly forward. He looked up and down the road and could not see a single soul. That too unnerved him. It all stank of a trap. Unfortunately they needed to cross this road to continue their northern trek towards Kolth. Matthius had been equally reticent about using his magic to get them across the barrier and he could not blame the boy. Trust was not a bond that any of them truly shared and his and Groltch's treatment of Belthar was less than exemplary. Yet they still travelled with him, for reasons he could not fathom. They would have to go across individually and pray to Toric for their safe passage. It was some fifty yards of uncovered ground to cross and he did not like it one bit. Yet there was no other choice. He returned to the others.

"We will go across one by one and hope for the best," he whispered to them.

"No!" said all three almost as one.

He looked at them in astonishment.

"We need to go across individually so that the others can help out if one encounters difficulties," he said in his best command voice.

For the first time in his life it failed to work.

"I not wish to let them go alone. Who knows what they do out of reach," said Groltch, eyeing the other two suspiciously. "And who go first.

I sure that we all spend many days to come fighting about it. Groltch think it best we all go and hope Toric watch us."

Matthius eyed Tristan angrily.

"You don't expect me to allow Belthar to stumble across that road unaided do you?" he asked angrily. "Torslud. I'm his friend and wouldn't dare subject him to that humiliation. He's sick and needs help."

"I can do well enough on my own. Thank you very much," grumbled Belthar angrily.

He evidently resented having to be treated as an invalid and had been growing steadily testier as time had passed.

"Fine!" he said, throwing his hands to the heavens. "We will go as one then. I just hope Toric truly is smiling on us today."

They grouped closely around Galahad and went to the edge of the trees, peering out over the road. There was still not a sign of life, though little traffic was to be expected this late in the evening. They nervously began to edge their way onto the road. When nothing happened, they grew a little bolder and began to stride across the road. Suddenly Tristan felt as if he had walked straight into a wall, even though there was nothing to see in the middle of the road. Knights appeared out of nowhere and they found themselves completely surrounded. He could see Groltch dart back towards the trees they had just left but he seemed to strike something solid too and knights were also riding up out of the trees. One thought came to his mind.

Magic!

Matthius seemed in the midst of casting a spell and Groltch was clutching his staff with a dangerous glint in his eyes.

"Take no chances with them!" commanded the Blue Knight leading the forces. As one the knights drew their swords and slashed them in Tristan's direction. It felt like a thousand hammers suddenly struck his head and the consciousness was knocked away in a wave of pain.

X

Meredith could not believe her ears. The two circles, Light and Dark were actually planning a revolt. Admittedly the resolve of the Hawks had been stiffened by their desire for revenge against their torturer and the recent proclamations of the introduction of the death penalty for criminals.

That had the whole city writhing in anger and the knights and city guard had been forced to quell disturbances on more than one occasion already. Many had not seemed too eager to harm their own people though; so many disturbances and protests had gone by unmolested. Yet they were actually sat here planning a revolt, something she would never have believed she would involve herself in. Kolthon politics had been enough to put her off the life completely. Even more surprising was the fact that she had been elected Hawkmaster of the Dark Circle, for the old Hawkmaster had disappeared around the time that the king had left for Sol. It explained why these fools had gone along with the ridiculous plans to steal from the city treasury.

She looked over at the leader of the Circle of Light, Tyrone Pathfinder, the man who had so successfully captured her. They had negotiated the initial agreement that lay the foundations of their relationship. They had agreed upon who would be responsible for what activities. The Circle of Light would go among the people and stir them up to a fever pitch of outrage. They would also contact certain knights that Tyrone had assured them could be relied upon to aid them in the actions. Many of these would assist the Hawks in their task, which would be to place themselves in the various strategic positions, ready to take them over when the revolt broke out. The Shadow had agreed to aid them get to the more sensitive and guarded positions that Tyrone did not have friendly contacts with.

The thieves would also be given the Lord Protector, Oliver Talbot, to *do with as they pleased.* The malicious glint she had seen in the Dark Circle members' eyes had made her forget that they were peace loving Caldorians who abhorred violence. She had seen the wounds that the Shadow had treated after they had returned to his room and she could not entirely fault them for their desire for revenge.

Then had come the difficult part. What sort of government they would set up after they had taken over? It was agreed that it would be a temporary one that would be relinquished on the return of the king. However, the Circle of Light had hinted that the king might not necessarily be the same one who had ruled previously, though she had been unable to get the exact details out of Tyrone. It was even possible that he did not know the exact details himself.

They had agreed that the two councils would work together to rule, but the head of that Council had been a subject of hot debate. Both circles wanted one of their own to lead the unified council, and they had almost come to blows over the question. The answer had come completely from the blue from Marie who, for the most part, seemed to have been overwhelmed to silence by the number of people shouting around her. She had suggested the Shadow, Galen Faithe, as his true name was. Of course, his dark past would not be revealed to the general public and only the Circle members would know the truth. He would be completely answerable to the joint Circles and his lack of allegiance to either side made both think that he would be easy to mould to their way of thinking. Meredith had observed Galen closely during the planning and felt that it was a rather rash decision on the part of the two Circles and Tyrone appeared to agree with her. Galen was a lot more dangerous than anyone was giving credit for, but they had both been over-ruled by their Circles. Now all that remained was planning the coup, which was beginning to bore her rigid. She had truly not wanted anything to do with this, but she seemed to have no choice.

"Shall we leave these children to their games of revolution?" asked Tyrone with a sharp smile. "I could do wi' a drink after all that talking. I'm sure they'll let us know what we've to do when we get back."

She looked at the man carefully. He was of middling age, though he had lost none of his powerful physique and he had certainly been skilful enough to catch her.

"Of course," she replied, feeling a little curious at the invitation. "I would be very interested to know just how you kept up with me all the way through Theldar like that. I'm not usually that easy to follow."

"What, and give away me secrets?" asked the man with a youthful, almost impish grin. "I couldn't do that. It would rob me of my mystique!"

"I'm sure I could never do that," she replied, slipping quietly away from the huddled, whispering revolutionaries. "Do you think they'll notice we've gone?"

"Well they will if yer don't stop making all that noise as you leave. I distinctly heard that cushion hit the floor when yer stood."

"Well I'm certain I heard your clothes rustling as you moved. Don't you know silk is much better at moving quietly than all that smelly leather you're wearing?"

"Silk? Who wants t'run around looking all fancy like? And have yer ever tried making silks disappear int'the undergrowth. I'm tellin' yer, it's almost impossible t'get such clothes that 'aint all gaudy like. I bet yer two drinks I could move more quietly in this than yer could ever hope ta in those fancy clothes"

That began a long evening's conversation and drinking match in the inn's bar that found them staggering rather foolishly up to their respective rooms into which Meredith collapsed in a hazy, drunken stupor that had her wishing the room would stop spinning round so inconsiderately.

XI

Hannah cursed her luck. All had gone according to her initial plans. She was ideally suited, in her new position as chief guard, to be present at the locking up of the prisoners after their capture. But it seemed that the governor was determined that none should escape him and had restructured the whole garrison to ensure that the guarding of the cells was to be tripled until the arrival of the knights who had been pursuing them throughout the countryside.

That had also included all servants' corridors through which she had intended to lead them. Releasing them would be easy, for she had access to the keys. Getting them out would be another matter entirely, especially as she had to get them to trust her somehow as well. They had been pushed around and toyed with enough to mistrust the intentions of anyone they encountered.

She was also limited in her time to only a few days, as the prisoner escort would be arriving within that time and then her opportunity would be lost. That would have to wait till the morning though, for they were still all unconscious after being struck by some spell of one sort or another. The knights had tried to pretend it was due to bludgeoning them, but she knew otherwise. It seemed that King Naithan feared the possibility of foreign spies even in this bastion of security.

She nodded to one of the guards and returned to *her* room and looked at the guard whose position she had taken. The woman seemed incredibly thin and drawn. It would not be long now before the poison finally took her to death, giving Hannah yet another reason to act fast. She hated being rushed, but it all added to the challenge and as she retired to bed a thousand and one plans began to form in her mind. It was quite some time before her mind settled enough to allow sleep to intrude upon her thoughts.

XII

Karene sat glaring into the campfire that was being lit. It seemed she would never catch up with that blasted King's Knight. It had been the fault of that officious little man in Grathnac, Justace Strongman, or whatever his name was. He had managed to delay her by five whole days. All she had done was enquired whether people matching the description of Tristan and his companions had been seen passing through the city and if so, which direction they had taken. He had then produced form upon form to fill out, each listing thousands of questions he had insisted needed answering.

She had managed to discover, by her own enquiries, that something had happened at the palace, though she had found it almost impossible to discover an account of the exact events. In the end it had come from Justace himself, who had informed her that he himself had been personally responsible for their capture, but that they had escaped soon after. He had feigned the need to cover his master's embarrassment at the act and asked her to fill out some forms of secrecy that said Lord Anton Gethrel had not been involved in the incident. She could understand the Lord's need to cover up the facts of Tristan's escape, for it would lead to a loss of his standing amongst his fellow shire leaders. She could not understand why she had to fill out so many forms in order to give her word that his secret would be kept. What had frustrated her further was the fact that once she had signed and filled out all the forms, the officious little man then proceeded to burned them to prevent them incriminating Lord Gethrel.

She had set out at full speed, using all the powers at her disposal to try and follow them, managing to finally pick up their trail some two days ago. They could not be more than a few days away at least. Victory was close enough for her to almost touch, yet they had several horses almost go lame today, forcing them to set up camp early and the delay was chaffing her. She had not wanted to waste vital spell energy on healing them. They would probably need it all when they caught up with them.

"Sar Skellan," said a voice in her head, making her jump. *"Knight Commander of the Claws of Belthanor speaking. I have your quarry in my prison. Proceed to Belthanor at once to receive him and escort him back to Theldar."*

Yes Sir, she replied as the voice faded from her mind.

Fury now erupted in her. She was being reduced to a mere escort. The glory of capturing him had been denied to her, again. She stormed over to the fire and kicked it over.

"Mount up," she commanded. "Those with injured horses should heal them or get those who can to do so. We ride at once to Belthanor."

The knights of her command moved as one, all packing and mounting with speed and precision. Within half an hour they were up and riding out of the clearing, Karene's hopes dashed to pieces. At least she would get there as soon as possible indicating that she was not far off catching him. Shaking her head bitterly, she led her knights into the night towards the ignominious duty of prison guard.

XIII

Anton smiled as he decoded the report that had just been delivered to him. It was late and he had been about to retire to bed when the special message from his Theldarian contact had reached him. He looked again at the words, magically fused into the paper.

City brewing with trouble. Governor has followed in the footsteps of Black Henry. Revolution planned even as I write. Situation ideal for your offer of protection.

Brief and to the point. The foolish governor, one of the many Theldarians the Redirecters had worked upon, was doing better than could be expected. Only a fool would introduce the folly of public executions, and Oliver was the ideal candidate. The Circle of Light just to lead a revolt, as in ancient times, and they would unwittingly lay the ground for his triumphant entrance to the city as harbinger of peace. With the Hanton families behind him and both the king and his brother out of the kingdom, a take-over would be simple.

He rubbed his hands together in glee. Years of planning and laying the groundwork would finally bear fruit. He opened a bottle of vintage port and supped it in celebration before retiring to bed. All that now remained was for his agent to retrieve Tristan so that he could marry him to his daughter and everything would be complete. Naithan would not have a legitimate leg to stand upon. He slept and dreamed of crowns and thrones.

XIV

Tristan came round, his head throbbing in pain. His arms and legs were chained together. He was lying in a dark, reasonably chilly room. As his eyes slowly adjusted to the darkness he noticed other forms in the cell with him, for it had to be a prison. He saw that he lay there with his three companions, all of whom were chained up in a similar fashion to himself. Two of them were groaning and slowly raising themselves up off the floor. The third, the largest of the three, lay still and his breath came in shallow gasps. One of the other forms, probably Matthius, pulled himself towards the large man, who had to be Belthar. The boy examined him carefully and groaned in dismay.

"What is it?" asked Tristan. "No more secrets. What is wrong with Belthar?"

Matthius seemed to hesitate, a battle probably raging within him.

"He's dying," said Matthius, choking on tears.

"We see that," said the other form, the thick accent revealing it to be Groltch. "But why he die?"

"Because he hasn't returned to his own form in too long," came the odd reply from the wizard.

"What do you mean, *his own form*?" asked Tristan suspiciously.

"Druids worship and protect nature, yes?" asked Matthius miserably.

"Yes, that is well known," replied Tristan quickly.

"Well, humans and goblins are not the only ones who do so, and they are not the only ones who wish to protect it either. Animals revere Gathra, just as much, if not more so than humans. They often take a lifelong, secret vow, to protect and help nature."

"How does this affect Belthar?" asked Tristan, feeling confused.

"Humans are the biggest threat to nature, as their body allows them to manipulate and destroy much more than the average animal. To combat such actions, the animals must be able to communicate with humans and have the ability to undo what the humans do. To do that they take on human form, though not completely. They give up their sight when human, to prevent them being tempted by the world they would see. Few animals see as much colour, or experience as many visual sensations as humans do and I'm told that it can be very tempting to try and remain human, which usually leads to madness for them.

"One of the other limitations, however, is that they must not remain too long in human form. They have to return to their natural state at certain times of the year, or after a certain length of time. Belthar hasn't changed back to his natural shape in too long and with the first moon going new tonight and the second in a few days' time, his power is so low that he will die unless he can change form. I fear he may even have to go to a sacred grove to do it as well because he is too weak to do it unaided."

"So Belthar is not human?" asked Tristan in shock.

"Of course not," snapped Matthius. "Haven't you heard what I've been saying?"

"What he really then?" asked Groltch.

"He's a bear," said Matthius, a sob emerging from his throat, "and he's my friend."

A gentle mew from Matthius' black cat brought the boy's hand down upon its head and his sobbing lessened. Yet Tristan barely noticed, his thoughts swirling round at once.

"Why he not tell us sooner? We let him change," said Groltch, sounding almost as stunned as Tristan felt.

"It's part of their oath of secrecy. I only knew because I stumbled into one of their sacred rituals when a spell of mine went wrong. No non druidic humans are supposed to know, lest they try to harm them, or use them for profit in some way."

Tristan let the subject drop and stared into the darkness. It was one mystery solved, though there were still plenty of others, such as the presence of Fluff, Matthius' cat in this cell. Surely they would not have put it there with them. It always seemed to be around when the boy needed it, but never in other circumstances. Belthar's true form did not explain why they still travelled with him. Matthius' evident power was another. He was sure one so young should not be able to do half the things he did and there were times when the boy seemed far older than he looked. All these questions and each with no answer; Tristan could feel his headache getting worse and he sighed, settling down to sleep. When sleep did finally take him, it was filled with dreams of bears and men.

XV

The Spymaster looked at the report with incredulous horror. That stupid man could not seriously be introducing the death sentence to the city. That was likely to incite the citizens to riot and revolt, and there was no guarantee that the knights would put down the unrest. The Spymaster put her hand to her head in frustration. She had been getting very close to the source of the corruption in the Redirection Chambers. Now she was going to have to drop it and return to Theldar to sort his mess out once and for all. She could leave an agent to continue her work but that would be too great a risk to take. She had protection against the machinations of the

Redirecters should she get caught. Her agents did not have that luxury, though, and she did not want her quarry to realise they were being stalked.

She tore the paper apart in frustration, going to her bundle of clothing in which her many disguises were kept. For speedy travel, she decided that the costume of a Royal Herald would bring her the least interruption. She could have used her Shadow Crown of course, had she thought to bring it, but knew it was still safely stored within her keep in Teldin, another place she would have to stop before heading towards Theldar. However, thinking about it was not doing it, as her mother had said on occasions, so she hastily donned the disguise. Within a few minutes she was mounted up and tearing off towards Teldin, though she thought she would first pay a visit on the errant knight Tristan, in Belthanor, his capture being the only good news in the report. She had a lot of work to do.

XVI

Oliver looked out from the balcony of his palace apartments over the silent city of Theldar. It was a glorious sight to behold, a hundred flickering lights, united in silence. This would be the city he would hand over to the king on his return. The many knights he had deployed in anticipation of such a response had squashed the unrest of the day. It would take a while for the Theldarians to become adjusted to the new system of justice, but they would soon realise that it would have little effect on the majority of their lives, so long as they obeyed the law. Only those with too much to lose in the new system, in other words the guilty, would shout too loudly against his decree, and he would have them watched like hawks for any misdemeanour.

He sucked in a deep breath of the silent, glorious night and drank in the sight of the peaceful, slumbering city. Everything was starting to run so smoothly now. The first executions would happen at midday tomorrow and after the people realised the truth of his proclamation, they would embrace it with open arms. He could see it now, all playing out in his mind as he turned back to his chambers. Tomorrow would be the start of a wonderful new era in Caldorian history. Justice was coming to the people.

CHAPTER ELEVEN: Violence and Violets

I

The sun rose slowing over the Western Ocean. As it did it lit the white streets of the ancient city of Theldar. Yet there was not the usual bustle to be found as people went to work. Almost nowhere had opened up as its residents moved in stunned amazement to the central square. The rumour was that executions were to be held at midday and, though none could scarce believe it, they had gone to see the truth with their own eyes. In the centre on a raised platform were the beheading blocks. There were ten in all, lined in a neat, straight row with the statue of Sir Caldor looking down on them. Nothing about them seemed sinister, yet all that looked had no doubt as to their purpose.

People wept and others wailed. In some realms, bloodletting such as this was to be cheered and watch in festival. For the people of Theldar it was a dark nightmare to be either endured, or stopped at all costs. Those who favoured the latter were already moving their way through the streets, mingling unseen with those here to endure the city's shame. In the palace, city council buildings and various sights of strategic importance, men and women were gathering, all awaiting the midday bells. On the rooftops, archers set themselves quietly up and many knights exchanged their ornamental blades for those of a more lethal quality.

When all had reached their places, time seemed to stand still. Though hours yet stood before the noon sun shone down upon this abomination, most stood ready before the sun had even completed its rise from the sea. Throughout the morning, barely anything stirred in the city, all stood in fearful watchfulness. Not even the wind dared stir up more than small dust devils through the streets filled with Theldarians. Time dragged on slowly and it seemed days had passed before the sun reached its ascension to stand high over the city and look down in silent judgement.

The bells across the city rang out the twelfth hour toll and slowly the crowds parted. Into their midst were taken the ten to be executed today. As the condemned men and women looked to the people of the crowd, most of them looked away or hung their heads in shame. Those who did meet their eyes had the look of grim determination on their faces, or shamed anger. The procession made its way slowly into the centre of the square and a wave of anger and disgust followed it. As one the people of Theldar were stirring with rage, as they once had in the reign of the Black King. As the procession reached the execution blocks and mounted the steps, the people of Theldar began to move restlessly about, their voices slowly rising in protest.

When the prisoners were stood behind their blocks, the murmur of anger became a low rumble. As each one was forced to kneel with quick, hard kick to the back of their knees, the rumble had become a growl and by the time the executioners were poised ready, it had grown to a positive roar of rage.

Just as each masked executioner raised their swords to sever the prisoners' heads, they all fell to the floor, almost as one. Each had some ten or fifteen arrows protruding from their bodies. The act silenced the crowds instantly, as everyone waited for some form of reprisal from the knights who encircled the execution platform. When none came the crowd cheered and massed towards the prisoners, working to free them from their bonds. At that act, the city of Theldar erupted into a flurry of motion and activity. Riots broke out as knights tried to subdue the ecstatic people and within minutes the city was in the grip of a revolution.

II

Gareth was near frantic now. He knew something of the link between Matthew and his brother and knew that if anything had happened to the wizard then his brother's life could well be in danger. Unfortunately, it seemed that there was no way to help Matthew if he was in trouble, which was quite likely considering the amount of time he had been gone. The shields he had erected over the doorways to the great hall were proving very strong and even the most powerful of his men were having difficulty tearing them down. One had even tried destroying the wall around it, but they were proving almost as indestructible as Matthew's spell. In anger he unleashed one of his more powerful spells at the doorway. It shimmered under the impact but still held strong. Peggy, his horse that was stood at his side, whinnied softly.

"It's all right," he said soothingly. "I'm not angry at you. I just need to get in there to help a pack mate."

The horse snorted and shook its head at him.

"What do you mean, use the sky?" he asked, looking at Peggy quickly.

Peggy neighed slightly and pawed the ground. Suddenly it was all clear to him. He had been such a fool. He had spent so much time in this war thinking of ground tactics, he had forgotten about those of the air.

"Summon the air riders," he commanded a squire. "Inform Sar Mystra that all are to be mounted and ready for flight."

The squire bowed and ran to perform his duty whilst Gareth ordered another to saddle Peggy for flight. The large hall had no roof and even Matthew was not powerful enough to cover the entire two hundred square foot of air in the time he had had to cast the spell. Cursing himself for his own stupidity and incompetence, he mounted up and patted his horse on the neck.

A few moments later, the First Company of the Golden Eagle Regiment rode round the corner, wings already showing. Gareth cast the spell and felt Peggy shudder beneath him as the wings sprouted from her side.

"Sar Mystra, follow me over the walls to the great hall. The Lord Priest may be in danger on the other side so land your troops in battle readiness."

"Yes Sir," she replied with a bow of the head.

"Ride out!" he called, wheeling Peggy round and encouraging her into the sky. He patted her neck gently as she left the ground to soothe her. She was not all that comfortable with heights, but was probably the bravest horse he had ever ridden. Gareth fired several balls of magical smoke over the protected area. It hit the magical shield and some started to sink to the ground where the magical barrier ended. It was large enough for them to fly through and so they were all soon on the other side of the wall. As they landed all knights dismounted and formed a perimeter of steel around the horses.

"The objective is that hole, men," said Gareth quickly, pointing at the trapdoor. "We need speed and caution. Sar Mystra, divide your troops into teams of three. Ensure that each contains at least one specialist and warn caution. We have no idea of the terrain or possible traps so ensure that the first groups issue reconnaissance information about the ground and area they encounter."

"Yes Sir," said Sar Mystra with a bow of the head.

Gareth watched as she swiftly divided the men up and sent them towards the hole. The First Company was among the most elite troops they had here in Grelchin and Gareth felt a little pride watching them get to work with skill and precision. The first group surrounded the hole whilst the next made their way inside using spells to enhance their sight in the darkness. Almost at once there was a scream and the Specialist, the name given to the most proficient of magic wielders, reacted at once. Even from a distance Gareth could see that it was a levitation spell of some kind and the word came back that steps three to eight were all illusionary. By that point, though, the lead knights were already hitting another trap. According to the report, poison darts had ricocheted off the lead knight's armour, though had done little else.

The first casualty occurred after that when a bladed pendulum had swung out and sliced a knight in two. Things progressed at a slightly slower pace after that, as knights took more care to test the ground ahead of them. The entrance was clear now for Gareth, so he entered, then walked gingerly down the magical constructs designed to cover the hole hidden by the illusionary steps. As the darkness enveloped him he used a spell to enhance his vision. Everything seemed to turn grey, though he could now see almost as clearly as he could in daylight. It was also enhanced to allow him to see magical auras, or spellprints, more clearly as he did not have Matthew's natural skill in such matters.

He could see recently cast barrier spells over the dart firing holes and the bladed pendulums lay scattered across the corridor floor, destroyed by fire bars, spells that created fire hot enough to melt firestones. Their use had been a little excessive here, but they had killed a knight so Gareth could understand and forgive their usage. The rest of the journey continued thus, irritating Gareth in the fact that he was useless and forced to follow on behind whilst his men took the risks. Unfortunately, that was one of the roles of a good commander and especially him as the Knight Marshal in charge of the armies. He should not have even been here, though he reconciled his conscience with the fact that one of his duties was, as personal protector to the throne, and rescuing Matthew would constitute rescuing the king.

He passed cautiously over a bridge that his magical sight told him was there but that all other senses screamed was not. He was not afraid of heights usually, but walking on what seemed to be air over a seemingly bottomless chasm was enough to make even him feel a little queasy. It was on reaching the other side that word came back that Matthew had been discovered. The description of his incarceration in crystal made Gareth's blood run cold. Were they too late? He ignored all protocol and safety procedures and charged down the corridor to the chamber in which he was said to be encased.

He burst through the large door, startling the two men and went to Sar Mystra who had reached the chamber already.

"What's your assessment?" he asked, examining the crystallised statue of Matthew in the centre of the tomb.

Matthew seemed to be holding an amulet in his hand, and looked as if he were screaming silently in pain. The sorcerer looked extremely pale and there was no sign of life from within, though it had some form of vulgar beauty about the way the crystal had formed around him.

"It appears that the Lord Priest still lives, though we have found no way to damage the crystal. It seems impervious to any form of physical harm and magical attacks upon its surface merely reflect off. We lost two knights learning that lesson," said Sar Mystra with a resigned sigh.

"Have you tried sound?" asked Gareth.

"Sound, Sir?" asked the Blue Knight.

Gareth's mind raced. He had remembered the state visit of the Imperial Theatrical and Musical Society to their palace when he had been a child. One of the singers had managed to shatter a crystal glass with her voice alone. His mother had not been too impressed with the demonstration as crystal glassware was very expensive, but the image had stuck in his mind ever since. He had even done some experiments with his own magic to test whether he could develop a weapon with it, though he had met with little success. It might work here though, especially as he was not aiming the magic directly at the crystal.

"Sound shields up!" he commanded quickly.

One of the lessons he had learned in his experiments was that sound could often incapacitate soldiers and so had developed defences against such spells. He saw magical auras spring up around him as he erected his own barrier then began casting the spell. He knew that crystal generally needed a high note, but could not risk harming anyone, Matthew especially, by starting too high, so began on a soft, gentle note. He then slowly increased its pitch until he could feel it in his head, even through his sound shield.

He intensified the note a little more and felt his ears begin to ring. He knew that he would not be able to go much higher and remain safely protected. Fortunately he seemed to have struck the correct pitch for the crystal around Matthew had begun to visibly vibrate. He tweaked the pitch just a little higher and the crystal began to grow cracks. It shimmered and shivered, seeming to almost glow as it did and millions of cracks began forming across its surface. As they did so a loud ringing emitted from the crystal, strong enough to penetrate the sound shields around his ears. He felt them pop painfully and almost lost his concentration. The prophecy for this spell had been to continue until he ceased to actively control it with his mind.

Suddenly the crystal shattered, sending millions of tiny, razor sharp shards flying out towards the surrounding knights with lightning speed. Gareth was barely able to erect a magical shield before the shards washed over him and, from the muffled screams he heard, he knew that several others had not been quick enough to do so. As the crystal dust and shards settled to the floor, Gareth noticed with horror that Matthew was lying prone upon the floor, the amulet still gripped tightly in his hand. Fortunately, for him, the shards had flown outwards and not inwards, though the wizard did not look at all healthy. Ignoring the screams of pain of some of the knights who had been hit by the exploding crystal, he went to Matthew's side. He was relieved to see that he was still breathing, though it was very shallow.

"Sar Mystra," he said, hoping she had been one of the quicker thinking knights.

"Yes, Sir," she replied, sounding shaken but unharmed.

"Detail four men to take him upstairs and get some priests to attend to any injuries. Then prepare him for transport. I leave for Belthanor on departing this stinking hole."

"Yes, Sir," replied the Blue Knight.

When the knights had taken away the unconscious wizard, Gareth turned his attention to the other knights. Seven had failed to erect adequate barriers and only two of them were still living. The sight made his stomach turn. The crystal had torn straight through the knights, even puncturing their strongest plate mail coverings. The two who were still alive could not last much longer, their bodies being the bloody pulp that they were. He nodded to two knights and indicating the screaming victims. Without a word the two knights drew their swords and killed them, dropping to their knees in prayer as they finished. Gareth turned away from them, enraged at their death. That wizard and his reckless behaviour had needlessly cost him the lives of several of his best knights. Sar Mystra disturbed his thoughts.

"Sir," she said quietly. "We found this on the floor amongst the crystal."

She handed him a sword with a broken blade. His eyes widened in shock at the sight of it. It was Caliburn, the King's Knight's sword. On closer inspection he realised that it was not quite the same as Caldor's ancient weapon. Upon its hilt was moulded the face Sir Caldor, rather than the image of a goblin that could be found upon Caliburn. Taking all the pieces in his hands, he held them close for a moment, wondering what its significance was. He was a soldier, though, and allowed himself only a little time to ask questions. He then took the scabbard that lay on the bier, slid the broken sword inside then took it outside and up to daylight. He had his brother's life to save and that took precedence over everything.

III

Oliver could not believe his eyes. The city was awash with chaos as peasants ran amok through Theldar. What had happened to the knights? Why were they not enforcing order? And why were the people rioting over a bunch of thieves? Could they not see that they were evil and that the world would be a better place without them?

All these questions flooded through his mind as he watched the chaos and havoc swirl through the very streets he had thought to make so orderly and peaceful. As he watched, he noticed that many of the crowds had begun moving slowly in the direction of the palace. Fear and panic suddenly clawed at the pit of his stomach and he felt himself go pale and cold. For a moment the world span before his eyes, then he regained his senses and took a hold of himself. He marched to the door and opened it.

"Guards, organise a sally forth onto the streets and bring order to them," he commanded haughtily.

The knights looked at him with a mixture of disgust and horror showing in their faces.

"Fight our own people?" asked one, sounding horrified. "I think not."

"But they are rioting and destroying the city," said Oliver, almost shrieking as he spoke.

One of the guards pushed past him and went to the balcony.

"They don't appear to be destroying anything," said the knight, forgetting to say *sir*.

Oliver went over to join the guard and looked down. His assessment seemed to be correct. What had seemed to be reckless rioting had turned into something of a peaceful, if noisy, march. Though the march seemed calm enough now, he knew it would only take a little encouragement to change the situation.

"Fall out the garrison!" he commanded the guard. "The palace is in danger!"

"I don't think he ought t' do that," said a voice behind him. "His best bet would be to arrest you and escort you to the dungeon."

Oliver span round and saw two heavily cloaked figures stood behind his desk. One looked remarkably familiar to him. There was something about the way he moved.

"You see," said the voice of the other figure. "This is a revolution, and I'm afraid you've just been deposed."

The man pulled back his hood to reveal dark hair flecked with grey and a bearded face with sparkling blue eyes.

"And you two intend to rule in my place do you?" he said, more bravely than he felt.

He was still able to use the sword at his side and the knight behind him would help even up the odds. All was not yet lost.

"No," said a voice behind him. "I do."

He spun around again and saw the knight removing his helmet. A cold shiver went down his spine. It was the man who had first escaped the prison dungeon. A man who had single-handedly made the city cower with fear at night.

"You th…th…the Shad…d…dow," he stuttered in panic.

"I'm glad you recognise me," said the man with a smirk, "because you'll know what I'll do to you if you don't co-operate, and I promise you, it will be far more imaginative than any of those perverted games you've ever come up with."

Oliver all but yelped at the thought.

"Take him away," said a feminine voice behind him.

He spun around once more, now knowing how those children's spinning tops must feel like. The other figure had de-robed to reveal a rather attractive, if hard looking, woman. She had long auburn hair, something of a rarity in the southern kingdoms. He had only seen it once and that had been hanging down the back of the thief who had escaped his trap. Suddenly he realised where he had seen her before. She had been the one to steal from him. Rage consumed him and he drew his sword, heedless of the risk. Suddenly the Shadow was before him, appearing out of nowhere and draining Oliver's rage away with a single look.

"I told you," said the man with an evil smile. "Be nice or I'll have to be nasty to you."

Oliver gulped down the last of his anger and gave the man his sword. As he did so, two rough looking men came and grabbed his wrists. He recognised both as two of the thieves who had come to him hoping to gain a deal and had ended up in the prison. They had also escaped and the look they gave him let him know that they had not forgotten the *games* he had involved them in. He knew the gleam that was there too, for he had seen it in his own eyes on many occasions. These men wanted revenge. They led him out of his office and he felt his legs begin to give way. Much as he had enjoyed watching the games, he had never believed he would become the victim of one. Suddenly the shock of it all overcame him and he collapsed to the floor.

IV

Naithan woke up with a tremendous headache feeling incredibly sick, though better than he had for ages. As his eyes went into focus he noticed a face looking at him.

"Yeah," it said with a grin. "He be all right. The fever musta broke last night. This fella's a strange chap, but a strong 'un an' all."

"Clean him up then," said a figure stood above the first.

Naithan took time to actually look at the man. He was a tall, muscular man with a dusky tanned skin and short-cropped black hair. His face had a scar down one side, running from underneath a patch that covered his eye, to his jaw. His bare chest also showed scars from numerous fights and his single blue eye had a look of harshness about it that Naithan had never seen before. The man turned away and climbed up to what had to be the deck.

"You be sittin' still, now, while I gets you good and clean," said the rather wizened looking man. A strange look suddenly came across his face. "You've passed your first test, the test of sickness. Like Caldor, there'll be others, but you can pass them. Keep faith and all Loden will bask in the light of Toric."

"What did you say?" asked Naithan, fearing that the fever had returned.

"Only that's yer was in a fever an' that yer not lookin' yer prettiest. But don't yer worry yerself about that. I'll fix yer up good an' proper. Yer've gotta look yer best when they presents the ransom demand," replied the old man, his face returning to normal.

Naithan looked at him suspiciously, but nothing else changed as the man fussed around him. In some respects the old man reminded him of Luca, in his mannerisms and constant prattle. It actually made him relax and he only flinched slightly when the man bared the blade of the razor and put it to his throat. After the man had finished, Naithan actually felt reasonably clean and fresh, though his head still throbbed a little.

"Right then sir," said the old man. "Let's get yer up deck an' get yer lookin' pretty fer yer viewin'."

He was led up the small ladder and found his eyes weeping tears of pain as he entered into the bright sunlit day. He was taken to the one eyed man who he assumed had to be the captain. Next to him stood what seemed to be a wizard, judging from the robes he was wearing.

"Ah, good, you're here," said the one eyed man with a vicious grin. He pointed to the robed man. "You, connect us up."

The wizard flinched and began to cast a spell on a mirror they had on deck. Naithan was impressed and found himself wondering how this wizard, evidently powerful if he could control that sea creature, had been cowed by a mere pirate.

"I know how fast you can do this, boy, so don't try and waste time," said the captain with a growl. "Yer know what happened last time, don't yer?"

Naithan thought he saw the wizard rub his arm slightly as he sped through the casting of the spell.

Is it possible that they're blood-linked? he wondered silently.

That could not be the answer, though, for in his case it did not allowed either one to force the other to do something they did not wish to as seemed to be the case with these two. He decided it would be worth further examination, though closed off such thoughts for the moment. The wizard had finished his spell and there was now an image on it. It was of a woman, his sister in fact.

"There yer go, me darlin'," said the captain, suddenly gaining a thick accent. "He's all safe an' sound, but that won't last if yer don't pay up. Stuff like this'll kill 'im!"

He motioned to the old man who had cleaned Naithan up earlier. He took out a vicious looking hook and walked over to him with a vicious grin on his face. Naithan tried to back away but found his way blocked by other sailors on the ship. The old man took a big swing and Naithan felt pain erupt in his stomach and stars appeared before his eyes. The man twisted the hook before wrenching it out, leaving him the lie on the floor. Naithan groaned in pain and pushed his hands to his stomach to stem the flow of blood.

"Heal 'im!" said the Captain with a mocking bow.

The same old man returned to Naithan and he found himself cowering away from the malicious creature.

"Don't yer worry now. I'm jus' here t' make yer pretty like so's yer don't go spillin' yer guts all over the deck. The Captain don't be liking that."

The old man placed his hands on Naithan's head and he heard himself whimper in fear. He mumbled something and breathed over Naithan's face. The smell of fetid, rotten fish filled Naithan's nostrils and he felt ill, though as he breathed in he felt the flesh of his stomach slowly begin to knit together. The feeling was quite nauseating and unsettling, but it was painless and actually eased the pain in his stomach.

"You have one week to leave the money on Devil's Isle or we leave the corpse, okay?" asked the Captain.

His sister looked visibly pale and seemed to nod her assent as the image faded from the mirror.

"Take 'im back below," said the Captain, dismissively.

Naithan felt himself being grabbed roughly by many hands then dragged across the deck. Suddenly he was falling and he felt himself slam against the floor.

"I'd better be chainin' yer back up again. Can't have yer runnin' 'bout the ship like some sorta ship rat now, can we?" asked the old man, scuttling down the ladder.

Naithan looked closely at the old man and realised with a start that he could not see a trace of sanity in the old man's eyes. He remembered an old quote of his mother's. *Toric often puts words in the mouth of madmen, for they have no mind to lose when his presence touches theirs.* He smiled as the old man chained him back up again to the wall. Toric had spoken to him. This was to be another trial, like Caldor had been forced to endure all those years ago. He would pass this one. He had truly been chosen. He allowed himself to become lost in the world of his imagination, taking him far away from this hellhole of a ship.

V

"Well, what are we goin' t' do with him then?" asked Jarek.

Meredith was beginning to grow tired of this debate. The Dark Circle wanted to punish Oliver as he had punished them and the Circle of Light had wanted him redirected. It was the first of what would probably be many such disputes between the two Councils and this one seemed about ready to tear the fragile alliance apart. She had used all her scant knowledge of the Great Game so frequently practised in the Kolthon Empire just to keep them from going their own separate ways.

It had been easy enough to convince the citizens to leave them in power as a proxy government until the king had returned, though once again she had caught hints from Tyrone that the king may not be the one they all expected. She liked the man and did not expect to know everything about him. There were things about her she kept from him, yet all the hints he kept dropping did excite her curiosity.

"I have an idea," said Galen, startling the arguing sides.

"What?" asked Jarek.

"We'll hold a trial, publicly. All his crimes will be put up before the people to hear and we'll let them decide what is to be done with him," he said, simply.

"That's absurd," said Judith, of the Circle of Light. "Peasants won't know what to do with him."

"Then we'll let them decide upon the options. We'll give them a list of the punishments and let them decide. Everyone shall have a vote. Whatever the answer, we'll abide by it. That way people out there," he said, gesturing to the window facing onto the city, "don't feel that we're as bad as he was. If we just make him disappear, either to a dungeon for torture or the Chambers for something similar, then they may feel that they've been cheated, or worse, that we executed him."

They all looked at him with suspicion.

"Remember, we only rule here because of the goodwill of those out there and the knights in here. The knights have already shown us that they most likely won't fight the people and that leaves us pretty much unprotected, for the moment. We need to gain their trust if we're to survive here."

"He's correct," said Tyrone quickly and Meredith threw in her assent.

She looked at the two councils trying to propose an argument against it. However, what Galen had said was true. They were here by the grace of those citizens out there and only there as caretakers at that. He had them both. He would merit careful observation, for he was evidently a very astute man. Especially that comment about the knights. It was known that he was in the midst of negotiations with their leader at present, one Sar

Petra, the results of which none of them could predict. It was certainly going to make for an interesting few weeks, especially as she was not entirely sure how the other shire rulers would take to this rebellion.

VI

"Welcome, my dear friends, welcome," said Anton, ushering his companions into his private audience chamber, or study, as he liked to call it. "I hope you both had pleasant journeys here. What with autumn drawing on now, it's getting a bit nippy nowadays."

"Cut the chit chat," said Lewis Hanton, Count of Kempshire, throwing off his wet travelling cloak and taking a seat.

He was a lean man with dark brown hair, thin face and sharp blue eyes. His hair was cropped short after the new Kolthon fashion and his clothes were neat and very utilitarian. He was a complete contrast to his brother, Darren Hanton, Count of Harkshire, who was big set with long, sandy blond hair and deep brown eyes. He wore much more fashionable, brighter clothing and moved with a more relaxed rhythm than his higher-strung brother. Even sitting the contrast was obvious. Darren was sat comfortably in the chair, almost slouching across the cushions, with a lazy air about him and Lewis was sat with his back to the fire and with the chair turned around so that its back would protect his chest if attacked.

Looking at them now it was plain to see why court gossip had it that they did not share the same father. Anton had known their parents, however, and could see that Lewis took after his mother, the Kolthon Senator's daughter and that Darren was the spitting image of his father. One thing they both shared, though, was a keen intellect combined with a good measure of ambition. It was for that reason that they were here today.

"Well, don't keep me in suspense, I have to get back to Kelvaria as soon as possible," said Lewis, drumming his fingers along the back of the chair.

"Oh dear, not having any serious trouble I hope?" asked Anton, motioning to his new personal servant to pour them all some port.

He had taken Hannah's advice and once again she had been proven correct. His old servant had been a spy, so Anton had sent him to the country estate to look after his daughter. He was sure she would love that.

"I wouldn't be here if it was serious trouble, now would I?" asked Lewis with biting sarcasm, another trait inherited from his mother. "It's just some deranged stable boy who swears he saw a unicorn and that it spoke to him. Ever since then it's said that miracles have been happening wherever he happens to be. It seems some poor saps now believe that he's the high priest of the great unicorn and have been following him round listening to every word he says as if it's Toric's own truth. Well, you know how these fads can catch on if you're not careful, so I intend to nip it in the bud before it goes beyond a joke."

"Very wise too," replied Anton, making a mental note of the situation.

It was always wise to have emergency plans and you never knew when such information would come in useful.

"Well, what's up then?" asked Darren, taking a long swig of port.

He was possibly the more dangerous of the two, for he always concealed his intelligence behind a wall of silence. It always seemed that he was overwhelmed by his brother's presence but Anton suspected that it was actually Darren who was the more dominant of the two. He nodded to his servant to leave the port and leave them in peace.

"Good news is what's up," replied Anton with a smile. "It seems that our years of careful planning are finally beginning to bear fruit."

"Really?" asked Lewis. "What news, pray tell, do you have that we do not?"

"I have recently heard from some of my discrete sources, that there has been a little rebellion in Theldar. Apparently, the governor left in charge during the king's absence seemed to think it a good idea to introduce capital punishment, with public executions."

"So that's what you wanted with the Redirecters," said Darren quietly, almost as if to himself.

Anton was barely able to hide his surprise. The man knew a lot more than he was letting on.

"Yes," replied Anton. "We sort of, doctored his treatment, shall we say, in the hopes that such a situation would arrive. It usually is in times such as these."

It had also been a lucky decision, for Naithan had not acted as other monarchs before him in most matters, and his erratic and often well made decisions had been one of the reasons he had been unable to move until now.

"Well, what is Helena doing about it at present?" asked Darren.

"Nothing, unfortunately," replied his brother, taking both Anton and Darren by surprise.

"How do you know?" they asked, almost in unison.

"Well, it seems that a certain pirate, Black Heart I believe, somehow managed to get his hands on the voyage plans of the king. I believe he has a pet sea creature that was quite capable of dealing with a few ships. Anyway, it seems that our poor king has been captured and is presently being held for ransom. Helena will be quite occupied for a while, especially with her other brother mired in the swamps of Grelchin."

Anton could scarcely believe his ears. Though Lewis was not admitting he had done it, it was certainly daring enough a plan. One that could most definitely work to their advantage. Even if Gareth did return with his forces, he was too much of a lap dog to try and take power for himself. There was something about the concept of honour that seemed to go to knights' heads and often seemed to somehow remove all deviousness from them. His only thought would be of restoring the throne to his brother, not of taking it for himself. Anton was glad that chivalric ideals had never taken hold of him. Looking at the other two it was obvious that the opportunity available to them was ideal.

"What about Tristan?" asked Darren. "You promised that he'd be with us. From what I hear, he wasn't too keen on staying here with you."

"Tristan's being dealt with even as we speak," replied Anton with a smug smile on his face. He had received a message from Hannah only today that all was proceeding well. "I have my special agent working on it right now."

He enjoyed watching Darren wince at the mention of Hannah. He had once questioned her special talents and had been on the end of them when she took affront to his lack of confidence in her abilities. It had cost him dearly to regain his family jewels stolen from his treasured *impregnable* vault.

"How long until we move then?" asked Darren.

"I'll need about a week to recall the rest of my knights in Grelchin, and I think I can muster another couple of battalions from the doctored troops still here in Caldor," replied Anton.

"It'll take me about that myself," said Darren quickly. "I've already had a few clearing land in the new territories, so it'll not take that long to recall them all."

Anton looked at Darren with suspicion. It seemed he had decided to claim land even before it had been apportioned out. They obviously had more ambition than even he had credited them with. It could be that he would have to deal with them sooner than he had previously planned.

"Very well then, we move next Thensday, agreed?" asked Anton.

"Agreed," said the other two in unison.

"Will you be staying for a light supper before you leave?"

"No, we've both got things to do, I'm afraid. This was merely a passing visit on our way to pay respect to our parents' grave. We are grateful that you allowed them to be buried here when our family fortunes were not as they are now."

"You're welcome," he said, acknowledging their thanks.

When their parents had died before either of their children had been able to inherit, the Lansdowns of Harkshire had taken their county of Kempshire and paupered the boys. It was a credit to them both that they had been able to gain not only their ancestral lands back, but to also destroy the Lansdowns and take their lands in the process. All had been done with little help from Anton, though he had sheltered them until they had been old enough to fight back. Their lack of a need for a mentor was one of the reasons why they would eventually have to be disposed of, for they were natural born conspirators and, unlike most, very successful ones.

"Well good night to you both. Safe journeys and Torsluck till next we meet."

"Good night," replied both with a bow.

"We know our way to the tomb," said Darren, "so we would not impose on you the burden of showing us out."

"Why thank you good sirs, and good night," he replied.

They bowed as they left and closed the door behind them, leaving Anton alone in the room. He sat long into the night staring into the fire, eyes glazing as he thought of the crown finally going where it belonged, upon his head.

VII

"Damn!" swore Hannah, rushing through the corridors. "Blast and Hellfire!"

She ignored the looks she got from the servants at her use of language. Her plans, so neatly prepared and laid had come crumbling down around her ears. She had been all set to free them tonight, even to the point of drugging the guards' drinks so as to move out unopposed. Then the blasted message had come through. Prince Gareth, Lord of bloody Belthanor had decided that he was to make an unexpected visit. The whole fort had gone up in a swirl of turmoil and strife. Ordinarily she would have loved such a diversion, but this time she had chosen the guise of a woman essential to the preparations of such a visit. It had tested her skills to the limit and she felt that more than one person suspected something about her behaviour. She had managed to shrug it off as the stress of organising everything, but knew that their suspicions would not go away. She would have to wait until tomorrow evening now, for she would be busy from dawn tomorrow.

She swore again. She could not risk playing sick, for priests around here took any opportunity to examine patients and one would have likely turned up to her room that day. She could not think of anytime more suspicious than night in which to skulk around with four escaped prisoners. Yet it had to be tomorrow evening, for Prince Gareth would have returned by the morning. She scowled at the run of Thenril's luck she was suffering from at the moment.

She reached the door to her, sorry, Cassandra's room, unlocked it and stormed inside, doing all she could to refrain from slamming the door in frustration. Cassandra did not slam doors. She locked it behind her and saw to the fire and lanterns. It took a while and she longed to be back where she had servants to do such things for her. She took a deep breath and sat down in front of the fire.

It took a while to calm down and it was then that she noticed the noise. It sounded like the buzzing of flies. She groaned, got to her feet and walked to the bed. She checked the forehead of the real Cassandra and rolled her eyes in disgust. The woman had to have died during the day and was already beginning to rot. That was one problem with the poison she used, it seemed to accelerate the decaying process after it finally killed its victim. By tomorrow evening the smell would detectable outside, even with the door closed. She had no choice at all now. It would have to be tomorrow night or never, and never was not an option. She dropped to the floor and rolled under the bed. Hopefully the smell would not sink and she would be able to get a decent night's sleep. She closed her eyes and issued a prayer to Toric asking that all would go well tomorrow, before drifting off to a troubled sleep.

VIII

Galen sat high up on the judges' platform and the world span before his eyes. He was still having the bad dreams, though it was not lack of sleep that was troubling him. Ever since his revival he had not quite felt exactly healthy. He had suffered from severe stomach cramps and dizzy spells from that moment and one had just struck.

He closed his eyes and took a deep breath. Feeling a little better, he opened them once more and for a moment everything seemed dark and somewhat unfocused. It was not long before his sight had returned to normal and he was able to concentrate on the proceedings. Fortunately, it was not important for him to be aware of everything that was going on around him. This was not a trial, more a sentencing, and this time the people of Theldar would decide Councillor Oliver Talbot's fate, not him. All he had to do was announce the final result and oversee the administration. Unfortunately it was taking more time than was expected, for they had turned out in their thousands to place a vote and it was taking some time to count them.

They had been forced to draft in some one hundred volunteers and hope that they were honest enough to make the count truthfully. It had taken the best part of a day already and did not look like finishing soon, despite the hopeful pronouncements of the collectors that they were *almost there.* They had been almost there since noon.

Galen sighed. It seemed there was a lot to this ruling business. He did not know why he was bothering, but he knew this was a chance to give something to the people of Theldar to make up for some of the pain he had caused them, though he was not sure exactly what yet. Another wave of dizziness struck him and he closed his eyes. He had better think fast, because he was not sure exactly what time he had left on Loden. Whatever Marie had done to bring him back did not seem as though it would last all that long.

"The count's done sir," said Jarek, running up to the bench.

"At last," muttered Galen quietly.

He opened the folded piece of paper and read the results. He smiled at the results, for it was the sentence he had come up with and voted for himself. Oliver was to be Redirected then exiled from the city for eternity. He stood up and announced the verdict at the top of his voice, to which he got a roar of approval. Some ninety percent of the voters had been in favour of the sentence. Only ten had gone for the death penalty, all of whom Galen could probably name.

The room span around violently and he found himself on the verge of collapsing. He dropped to the main floor, his task done, and all but ran to the back door. As he reached it he felt a hand clasp his arm. He turned and saw Marie.

"What's wrong?" she asked worriedly.

"Nothing, I'm just a little dizzy, that's all," he replied tersely.

"Do you need some help?"

"No, just leave me to myself," he snapped, almost snarling.

He regretted it the instant he saw the hurt in her eyes but she span away from him and disappeared into the crowds. He turned back to the door and passed through it, his stomach beginning to cramp and churn. He staggered through the corridor to the door at the end. He turned the handle and found it locked. Snarling angrily, he passed under the door before he even realised what he had done. He sat in the large chair that stood before the fireplace that seemed to dominate this room. For some reason, the pain was always less here and he felt his stomach ease.

He found his eyes going to the dancing shadows created by the flickering flame. As he watched, the reality of his situation dawned on him. Whatever Marie had done to him to bring him back was only temporary and did not sit well with his physical form. He was slowly dying and time was running low. He thought again of the hurt in Marie's eyes and decided it was for the best. He could not afford to get close to anyone, for he had nothing to offer. It was whilst pondering this that he realised he still loved her. He had spared her at the village out of a final act of love, and he was doing the same again, though this time he hoped it would be to ensure she would feel no pain over him or his actions ever again. He would have to be cruel for a while just in case, by any whim of Toric, she still had any such feelings for him, but it would be better in the long run.

He turned his thoughts away gazed at the beautiful shadows created by the flames, losing himself to their hypnotic waltz across the walls and floors.

IX

Hannah had not felt this tired in years. She had been on her feet almost all day using every ounce of skill and quick thinking she had organising the knights and lower reaches of the castle for the arrival of Prince Gareth. Now she had to ignore her aching limbs and arrange the escape of four prisoners, one of whom was in no fit state to travel. The big man looked on the verge of death and it was obvious that only a visit to a sacred grove would heal him. Shifting him down to the lower levels unnoticed would be almost impossible, yet she knew they would not leave without him. What was it about knights and their honour? She sighed and made her way to the armoury where their weapons had been stored. She collected them all together, only to find that the King's Knight's sword was not where she left it. She searched round frantically and found nothing.

"Damn and Hellfire!" she swore, grabbing the first sword to hand.

She would have to be quick. The sleeping drug that she had mixed into the guards' drinks would not last all that long and she did not want some enterprising young officer to find his soldiers asleep on duty and raise the alarm. It took her some ten minutes to reach the cell, for she could not appear hurried, lest it raise suspicions. The walk seemed to last an eternity and she was relieved to see the guards all still fast asleep at their posts. The poor knights would receive quite a dressing down come the morning.

She went to the cell and peered in. There was no torch inside so she could see little through the viewing grid.

"Hsst! Is anyone awake?"

"Yes," came the familiar voice of the King's Knight.

It seemed that he had sat awake in vigil over the big druid since their arrival. From what she could gather from the conversations she had overheard them having, he seemed to believe himself somehow responsible for the druid's condition.

"I've come to help," she whispered quickly.

"It's too late for that," replied the knight despondently.

"Snap out of it," she hissed angrily. "If it's your friend you are worried about, then don't. I believe there's one of his kind's holy places about an hour's trek north of here. If we can get him there then we might save him."

That was the one thing with knights and their chivalric code, at least with those who genuinely followed it. An appeal to their honour and sense of duty was enough to persuade them to do practically anything.

"Truly?" asked the knight suspiciously.

Evidently he was not as naive as many of his type.

"Yes," she replied, recalling the one time she had been there.

It had been one of the few places she had ever felt truly content, though she had always known that it was just a side effect of its holy nature.

"I will go with you then. If you lie…"

That truly shocked Hannah. Evidently he had become slightly embittered by his recent experiences. She shook off the thoughts and unlocked the door.

"You," he said suspiciously.

"It's only a disguise," she replied quickly. "Screw your eyes up tightly. You'll see it blur and then will be able to make out the body beneath the disguise."

He did as instructed and screwed his face up in disgust as she allowed her disguise to blur somewhat, revealing a little of the form she usually used.

"Magic," he said, almost spitting the word from his mouth. "Very well, can you release us then?"

She placed the keys in the manacles that chained his arms and legs and he stretched out.

"Give me the keys," he said abruptly. "I'll wake the others and release them. It'll be better that way. You watch for the guards."

She nodded her assent and gave him the keys, then went to stand by the guard sleeping on the stool as if talking to him about some matter or another. She heard muttered whispers echo out from the cell then the sound of movement. Looking around quickly, she returned to the doorway.

"I have your weapons, if you'd like to take them before we leave," she whispered hurriedly.

"Good," replied the knight.

He came out and took them off her.

"I'm afraid they've stored your sword away somewhere safe, so I brought this one instead," she said, passing him the one she had grabbed.

He looked at it and seemed to frown. His eyes went vacant for a moment before he looked back at her and returned the sword.

"This will not be necessary," he said quietly, sounding almost a little despondent.

A look of resignation crossed his face, followed quickly by one of disgust. He muttered a few words and the air shimmered around him and the sword and its scabbard appeared at his side, firmly attached to his belt. Her eyes widened and she sneered as she thought of his disgust at her use of magic. His hand went to his side and he almost looked disappointed to find the sword there.

"Come on," she hissed, desperate to be away. She just wanted to deliver them to Anton and be done with them and this entire accursed mission. "We need to get out of here tonight. Prince Gareth arrives tomorrow and with him all chance of your escape."

She only hoped that the financial reward would be worth all of this hassle. It was certainly the most problematic quest she had undertaken. She threw her hands up in exasperation as they struggled to get the big man to his feet. He struggled a little and a hand caught on the leather necklace that hung round the knight's neck. She heard it snap and the ring of metal on stone rang out in the near silence of the corridor. The stupid knight actually went to pick up the item and left the goblin and the boy to pick the druid up alone.

"I'll get it," she snapped, vowing to up and leave them to it if one more thing went wrong.

She knelt down near where she had heard the item dropped and saw the glint of metal. She picked up the item and found it was a ring. She took a long look at the item the knight valued so much and suddenly went deathly cold. It was made of polished gold around which was wrapped a thin band of silver. She knew what this ring signified. It was a ring of the High Circle of Light, one worn by one at the very top of the organisation of which she was only a junior member. Either he was a member of the High Council, which was highly doubtful, or he was under the protection of one who was.

Her world was suddenly turned upside down. How could she betray either one of her trusts? She had vowed never to take a quest, in which the needs of the two organisations clashed, for she had feared such a dilemma. She returned the ring to the knight, her thoughts swirling around in turmoil. Tristan evidently did not want to be with Anton, so what was her correct course of action? She wanted to scream in frustration.

"Come on," said the knight. "Let us get moving."

She turned and began to lead them down the corridor, even forgetting to close the cell door to delay discovery. Only one thing was on her mind. Which party would she choose loyalty to?

X

Matthius Faldare struggled under the weight of his giant friend. Concern for the big man's health was pre-eminent on his mind. He was not, and never had been, a strong person and supporting the huge frame was proving to be a struggle, despite the diminished size of his friend. He had never seen him in such a state before. He had seen him weak before. It was on one such occasion that he had followed Belthar to his sacred grove and witnessed the truth of his friend's species. Yet this time was different. His face was drawn tight and his hair falling out in massive, bloody clumps. He truly feared that Belthar would not make it this time. He stumbled and almost fell to the floor. It was the goblin, Groltch who caught him.

"You leave Belthar to me," said the goblin in that thick accent of his.

"You follow with woman and help keep men away."

Matt had no idea what he could do to help. Half the time he never seemed able to control his spells, coming up with many weird and some not so wonderful results. Other times they seemed to be erratic, either being more powerful than he intended, or in no way powerful enough. His mentor had died some two years ago having imparted barely a single iota of his knowledge, and he had been muddling on his own since that point. It had been during that time he had met Belthar and joined up with the Circle of Light, largely in the hopes that one day he would meet a runaway wizard who would teach him all he needed to know. In that time, the closest he had come was this wretched knight who refused to admit he used magic and seemed less schooled in it than he was.

He shook his head and looked back at Belthar. He wished he had never met that knight and his wretched goblin friend. It was entirely their fault that Belthar was in his present danger and if the druid died, he would never forgive them. Tears welled up in his eyes and he blinked them away. This was not the time to cry. They had to get out of here and over to that grove the woman had said existed in the woods north of the city. He prayed to Toric that they get there safely then returned his thoughts to the present situation.

"Hsst!" whispered the woman. "Someone's coming. Stay still."

Time seemed to slow down as they waited, with only the approaching footsteps marking its passage. He petted Fluff on the head, who had managed to curl up inside the large pouch in his robe. It brought him at little peace of mind, as the action often did in times of stress. The footsteps drew closer and Matt felt himself begin to go light-headed. He released the breath he had been holding, feeling the blood rushing back to his head.

As it did so, the owner of the footsteps emerged from the side passage ahead. It was a robed boy about his own age and as he stepped into the corridor they were hid in, he turned his head and looked directly at Matt. Their eyes locked together and he gasped in shock. They were violet, like his own. The man seemed as shocked as he and as they locked gazes time seemed to halt. He felt a thousand images seem to pass between them, none of which he could see clearly. Yet one theme ran through them all. Hatred. Pure, unadulterated hatred and it made him shudder as it passed between them. He felt like he had known this boy forever. Correction, he felt he had hated that boy forever. The boy was the first to break the still silence and react. His hands moved to his pouches and began to mouth through the words of a spell. Matt recognised it instantly and groped for the components of the counter spell.

He was too slow and with the sudden realisation that he was to die he saw the lightening leap from the man's fingertips.

XI

Hannah had watched the exchange between the two boys with horrified fascination. They were almost completely different in every physical way describable, saving their eyes. However, when they looked at each other they seemed to be almost identical in some way that was almost impossible to explain. Time seemed to slow down as the stared at each other and she was horrified to see the hatred that seemed to erupt between them. It was blind, unreasoning hatred, the like of which she had never seen nor ever wished to see again.

She gasped in shock as the lightening began to arc from the other man's fingers and a thousand thoughts flashed through her mind. She thought of her father, disappointed that she had not delivered Tristan to him. She thought of the Circle and their disappointment at her failure to deliver Tristan to freedom. She thought of her father's grief at her death, and of the shock when her true identity was revealed to him. She thought of the boy. It was obvious that he was going to fail to defend against the attack and that he was also the only one who could defend them against their opponent. But most of all she thought of the fact that her failure would be total. She would not even get a half victory, and that thought riled her most of all. She had never failed and she could not do anything to prevent from failing this task. But she did have a choice. She could fail completely, or partially. She chose to fail partially.

With a speed that she would have never credited herself with, she leapt across the corridor in front of the boy and into the lightning's path. She was surprised to feel it hit her, amazed at the velocity of her leap. Her body convulsed as the lightening crackled through her, her muscles twitching and jerking as it did. Burning pain seared through her and she felt herself clinging to the edge of consciousness. She struck the wall on the other side and collapsed to the floor, her body twitching and convulsing as smoke rose up from it. She looked up and saw that it had worked. The boy wizard was still touched, unharmed. She took pleasure in the fact that her failure would only be partial…

XII

Rage borne of hatred seeming to span aeons flooded through Matt, bringing his power alive to his touch. The lightening had passed through the woman, but she had slowed it enough to give him a chance to defend himself. Now, he counter attacked. Bars of white-hot flame flew from his fingertips at the hated form before him. The boy dived to the floor and the flames seared through the stone wall at the end of the corridor. The boy retaliated with the same spell and Matt contemptuously deflected it away with counter spell. The violet eyed man leapt to his feet and disappeared down the corridor as Matt unleashed rocks of ice at him. He ran to follow him, bouncing lightening off the walls down the corridor as he entered. He vaguely heard the cries of his companions behind him but he paid them no heed. All that mattered to him was the violet-eyed man.

He turned into the corridor just in time to see the boy turn up a spiral staircase. He ran after him and suddenly the floor around him exploded in red light. Looking down he saw a complex pattern of light pulsating around him, sending red beams up and around him. They began to wrap around him and he realised that he had been caught in a ward of binding. Coursing with anger he sent a complex counter spell spiralling in blue light around him. It sliced through the red light and exploded through the walls. Now positively glowing with energy he tore up the stairwell, using his magic to cut through all the traps his quarry had left behind.

At the top he reached a door that had been magically bound shut. He unleashed his energy onto it, causing it to erupt outwards in a million splinters. He stepped out and onto the roof of what was the central tower of Belthanor. As he emerged the stone of the turret he had emerged from suddenly exploded, showering him with stones and rock. He unleashed the white fire out in all directions, turning the stone to molten rock that slid harmlessly round the shield he had erected and began melting through the roof.

As he stepped through it he saw the man with the violet eyes. Here was a time of reckoning.

XIII

Tristan watched the conflict between Matthius and the violet-eyed man with stunned amazement. He called out to his companion as he ran after their attacker but the boy paid him scant attention and disappeared round a bend in the corridor. He looked to the fallen woman and was amazed to see her body changing. He looked to Groltch.

"I manage Belthar, but not long," he said, understanding his silent plea. "Go see woman."

He gently allowed the rest of the weight of Belthar to rest on the ranthe and dropped to the woman's side. He was stunned to see that he knew her. It was Anton's daughter Miranda, a face he could see even through the blackened visage. He cradled her in his arms and she coughed, flecks of blood splattering his clothing.

"My insides are like jelly," she muttered, "but I didn't completely fail."

"You did not fail at all," replied Tristan softly, not completely sure what she was talking about, but trying desperately to reassure her.

"I didn't?" she asked, her features lighting up briefly. "Oh good.

Didn't want to fail. Mustn't fail…"

He cradled her close.

"Wait," she coughed, her breath coming in short gasps. "Take scarf, for goblin. If…the wizard doesn't get back…use to hide him. He just wears, and rest is eas…"

Her words were cut off by a sudden fit of hacking coughing. As suddenly as they had come, they ceased and her head lolled to one side. He closed her eyes and offered a quick prayer to Toric to receive her soul before gently laying her on the ground. He was amazed to see that the scarf around her neck was untouched by the lightning strike, despite its fragile and delicate silk material. Remembering her last words he gently unwound it and put it in his belt pouch.

"Help," grunted Groltch, sagging towards the floor.

Tristan returned to his companions and took some of the weight off Groltch. Even in his wasted condition Belthar was a heavy man, or bear.

"Let's go," he muttered. "We've got to get to the stables and find Galahad. Can't carry him all the way."

"Groltch agree, but where out?"

"Do not worry," replied Tristan. "I know the way."

Having trained here for some eight years Tristan knew his way quite well around the central tower and was able to steer them through the less busy corridors. The hardest part turned out to be getting the big man safely down the narrow, spiralling staircases. They were designed to make it difficult for attacking warriors to fight as they climbed, but it also meant it was difficult to carry big men down them. They managed, however, and were soon staggering out of the building and into the courtyard. As they emerged a loud explosion erupted from on high and spots of liquid fire fell to the earth around him. The sound soon attracted onlookers and the courtyard rapidly filled up with people. This served Tristan well for it meant that all eyes were looking up and he was able to lose them in the crowd. Groltch was able to conceal himself against Belthar's large form and no one seemed to notice the ran-the as they staggered into the stables.

They moved into the darkened stables and gently lay Belthar in some hay. Tristan whistled softly and a familiar whinny came from the third stall on the left. He went to free the horse then thought of the ran-the, who was crouching down in the darkness to prevent anyone looking in from seeing him. He went over to Groltch and handed him the scarf.

"What this?" asked Groltch, taking it and examining it closely.

"It is a magic scarf," he replied.

"How it work?" asked Groltch.

"I am not entirely sure," replied Tristan.

"Don't worry, I'll explain it to him," said Caliburn softly.

How do you know? Asked Tristan suspiciously.

"I touched her mind before she died. It was the last thing she was thinking of as it went dark. I thought it best to do it as she was fading fast," replied the sword hesitantly.

Thank you, replied Tristan. "I'll see to Galahad."

He left Groltch to his instruction and opened Galahad's stall. He whinnied with pleasure and rubbed his nose gently against Tristan's arm.

"Good boy," he said softly. "Belthar's hurt and I need you to help us carry him."

Galahad seemed to understand perfectly and stood patiently waiting to be saddled. Tristan chose a broader saddle, usually used for carrying armoured knights and strapped it on. He slipped on the bit and bridle before leading the horse to where Belthar lay. For an instant Tristan thought the druid was dead, but noticed his chest rise gently with relief. He turned and felt himself start as he saw a young boy stood in the stalls next to Belthar.

"Groltch your squire," said a familiar voice from the child's lips.

Tristan had to admit that the scarf worked very well.

"Now for the difficult bit," he said, looking at the prone form of Belthar.

"Use magic," said Caliburn softly. *"You could even soften the ride for him with it and make the journey a little less hazardous for him."*

How? Asked Tristan in resignation.

It was the only way they could safely do this.

"Listen carefully, and I'll guide you," replied the sword slowly.

The sword guided him through the basic principles and he slowly cast a spell to lighten Belthar and enable them to get him atop Galahad. Once that was achieved he then used another to cushion him against falling off or any harsh knocks.

"See," said Caliburn. *"That wasn't so hard now, was it?"*

Don't push your luck, thought Tristan angrily, feeling tainted inside.

"Let's go," said Groltch quietly.

Tristan nodded in agreement and led them back out into the courtyard. It was still filled with people and the battle still raged on top of the central tower so it was relatively easy to move through to the main gate unmolested. He was astounded to find that the great gate stood open and unmanned. In all the time he had lived here he had never once seen such a sight. He looked back at where Matthius now fought. He felt a little guilty at leaving the boy, but Belthar would die if they delayed. He slid his hand into his pouch and found the slightly scratched coin Matthius had given them all those weeks ago. If Matthius needed to he could get to them. He only hoped that the boy would remember and return, for he had seemed completely obsessed by attacking the other boy. He shook his head sadly. He could not worry about everything. He turned and headed out into the city, fleeing to freedom once more.

XIV

Sir Markus Luther, Green Knight and night guard duty-man could not believe his eyes. He had only been recently knighted before being posted here and had found his duties rather boring. He had spent more of his time polishing armour and guarding the gate than fighting evil creatures, as he had always believed the knighthood was all about. He was sick to his back teeth with constant drilling and parading and had been feeling low.

That had been until this week. First was yesterday's news that Prince Gareth, Knight Commander himself was returning, hopefully for more troops, and now this. He had heard an explosion from within the walls of the fortress and had emerged to see it raining fire. He had then heard lightning and thunder crash and had looked up to see two glowing figures fighting across the roof of the central tower. It seemed a titanic struggle with energies far greater than those he could ever muster being unleashed back and forth between the glowing combatants. Sheets of flame and ice struck out at each other and wind and stone crashed together. The very ground shook with one attack and parts of masonry had begun dislodging from the weaker sections of the fortress.

Suddenly a pillar of flame struck out from the heavens at one of the figures, knocking it momentarily off balance. Like any true warrior, the other combatant attacked while the other was in a weakened position. A swirling wind span out from the figure's outstretched arms and struck the other full on. It knocked it off the top of the tower and the figure plummeted towards the earth, disappearing out of sight behind the Tower. Without a thought he raced towards the area, diving through the awestruck crowd that had gathered to watch the battle. He had to find out who it was.

XV

Groltch helped Tris weave the horse through the rapidly filling streets of Belthanor. The sounds of Matt's battle could be heard even at this distance and was attracting the attention of all the citizens, all who seemed to be in fearful awe of the magical energy being unleashed. Every so often, the dark, almost moon-less sky would suddenly erupt in light and colour, fade away almost as quickly. Groltch wondered at the powers being unleashed up there and found himself asking how one so young could be so strong. There was definitely something the boy was not telling them.

He looked back and saw a column of flame strike down from the skies. It was followed by an unnerving silence, which seemed to indicate them battle's end. He wondered who had emerged victorious and found himself unsure which one he would have preferred to win.

He told himself off for his uncharitable thoughts and concentrated on the journey out. He realised with a start that they were already out of the city and not far away from the trees. He looked back in confusion.

"Belthanor was designed as a fortress city. It cannot get too large else the walls become almost impossible to man. It has only once ever been breached, and the weaknesses that were exploited to do it were removed almost immediately after the city was regained."

Groltch looked back in amazement. Now that he looked he could see that it would probably make a formidable place to defend from. Human architects, it seemed, did not always follow the slap dash construction he had frequently seen in Caldor so far. He took one last look then entered the trees once more.

XVI

Sir Markus moved cautiously to the motionless body on the floor. He knew that whoever it was, it was a person of some power and to be dealt with cautiously. He heard a snarl to his left and, drawing his sword slowly, turned to look. Stood there on a pile of fallen masonry, was the largest black beast he had ever seen. Its fur was short and sleek, though bristling in anger and its eyes almost glowed yellow. Razor sharp teeth shined at him from its snarling mouth. With a roar it leapt at him, knocking him to the floor and pinning him down. It put its mouth close to his face and he could smell its fetid, almost sulphurous breath. It opened its mouth and roared. Markus lost control of his bodily functions as fear gripped him in its cold fingers. Then the creature leapt away and was gone. He lay there, still as a rock for some time and only stood when someone looked over at him. By that time both man and creature were gone.

XVII

Matt came round with his head throbbing and his back aching. He appeared to have somehow made it outside, though he had no idea how. He vaguely recalled a face and violet eyes, but after that, there was nothing. He looked around and saw a large group of people all stood around looking up. He looked up and could see nothing. He wondered where the others had gotten themselves to. He decided to risk a spell and formed an image of a scratched coin in his head, around which he put the familiar image of Belthar. A soft mew at his foot and a slight tug of his robe made Matt subconsciously pick Fluff up and put him in a pouch. Having completed the image and petted the kitten, he cast the spell, finding himself suddenly in an explosion of fern leaves in front of a very startled looking Groltch.

CHAPTER TWELVE: Rest and Rescue

I

"How are we going to find it?" asked Matthius, looking around the trees angrily. "Without that woman we'll never find the grove."

Tristan found himself agreeing with the boy. There had been a grove of some sort near his home in Havelock, but he had never actually been there and seen it. He had no idea how they were supposed to find it.

"Ask Galahad to lead you," said Caliburn, breaking his thoughts.

How will he know where to go? Asked Tristan, feeling confused.

"Galahad is closer to his animal nature than you humans and ran-tha," replied the sword. *"He doesn't have any awkward permanent conscious thought present barring him from his instincts. He can lead with you there by instinct alone."*

Humans are not animals, retorted Tristan angrily.

The Word of Toric said that man was greater than the common beast and everyone knew that humans were special. He thought about that for a moment then looked to Belthar. There was proof that this was not necessarily so. He suddenly found that he was not surprised that they concealed the truth of their form under a veil of mystery. Priests of Toric would come down strongly against such pagan claims and work to force them out of Caldor.

He sighed and felt sorrow at what his people had become. Yet he knew that if he could learn, then so could others. He decided to try something. He closed his eyes and let go of conscious thought. It was difficult, trying to clear all words from his mind, but he slowly achieved it. His breathing slowed and altered as his mind worked into the subconscious. He allowed his awareness to sink into his base, instinctive needs, food, rest and safety. As he did, the world around him seemed to sing out to him and he felt a strong need pulling to the left. A pack mate was hurt and needed safety. The pulling cried out to his mind that safety was nearby and instinctively he began walking towards it.

"What on Loden are doing?" asked a voice, bringing his consciousness back to a more active level.

"The grove is this way," said Tristan simply, looking hard to find the words.

Both Groltch and Matthius looked at him with perplexed expressions on their faces.

"How you know?" asked Groltch.

"Instinct," replied Tristan firmly.

"Great," said Matthius, throwing his hands up in the air in disgust. "We're trusting my friend's life to your *instinct.* Fantastic."

"What made you fight that wizard?" asked Tristan simply. "You used magic the like of which I have never seen."

"I've told you already," replied Matthius. "I don't remember what happened, just seeing him in the corridor, then coming round outside the keep. Something in me seemed to react to him and just somehow knew how to react."

"Instinct," said Tristan. "You allowed instinct to guide you and it saved you. That is what I am doing now."

"Great! Fantastic! Wonderful!" replied Matthius sarcastically. "My *instinct* damn near got me kill…"

The boy's voice broke off as they broke into a clearing amidst the trees and a strong sense of peace and tranquillity washed over them all. In the centre of the clearing was a pool of water that seemed impossibly round for a natural occurrence. Around it were stood stones of granite and lime forming a circle. Light seemed to rise out of the pool and all around animals of all shapes and sizes were facing towards the pool.

The perfectly calm waters suddenly bubbled and churned before rising up into two twisting spirals of clear water that seemed to dance around each other. As they watched, the spirals began to shift and change, gradually forming two humanoid figures. They glowed in blue light and the two figures took on solid form.

A breath of astonishment escaped from his lips. They appeared human like, though no human he had ever seen had possessed such beauty. A man and woman with delicately formed features stood atop the water and looked around them. Their skin was perfectly smooth and held a slightly bluish tinge and their long hair seemed to swirl about their heads as if still in flowing water. They wore no clothing, yet Tristan felt nothing but awe for them. They stepped from the pool and moved along the animals, touching their heads as they passed. Some turned and left quietly afterwards, and others seemed to shift in form, becoming human like in appearance. Others simply lay down and died, their bodies sinking silently into the ground. The two creatures walked gracefully towards them, their bodies seeming to sway as waterweed in a gentle stream.

The male creature reached them first, looking deep into the ranthe's eyes. Groltch's eyes widened and he smiled, sinking to the floor asleep. The woman moved to Tristan, her green-blue eyes holding his momentarily. They seemed to hold a measure of sadness in them and she turned away towards Belthar. By now Matthius had sunk into sleep and Tristan wondered why he still stood awake.

The two creatures raised Belthar off of Galahad and the female touched the horse's nose. He seemed to bow his head, before lowering himself to the floor in sleep, his saddle and bridle seeming to just fall away. Yet Tristan's eyes did not leave the unconscious druid's form as the two creatures took him to the centre of the pool, their feet seeming to rest upon the water's surface. They held him aloft and light seemed to swirl around them. As he watched, the big man's body slowly shifted and turned. The clothing fell away and the huge, muscular torso could now be seen, writhing and twisting in a fascinating, if somewhat disconcerting way. Fur erupted along his flesh and his face elongated into a snout. From his hands sprang long claws and the thumbs shifted away as his paws were formed.

The two creatures open their mouths and music seemed to flow from their lips. It spoke to Tristan of trees, water and life. It seemed to surround him consume him and grow within him. He held up his head and laughed with joy, then looked back to the bear that was Belthar. He noticed that the two creatures seemed to speak to him. The bear seemed to nod its head in agreement and slowly all three began to sink into the water. The waters bubbled as they began to wash over their heads and the light of the pool began to fade. As it did, so too did the music around him. As it disappeared, he heard two voices speak to him in unison, one male and one female.

"For all there are choices. You were allowed to see this to see the choice of one you know. In your future, two paths will open up before you. One will be of ease and comfort, yet could ultimately end worse for all. The second will be towards much pain and suffering, yet could ultimately lead to the good of all. Neither is certain to ultimate victory or defeat, though both have more likely outcomes. You shall see the choices this night and when the time comes you may be ready to make your decision. Think hard on the visions you will see tonight and prepare if you can. Sleep well and stay strong, oh Knight of Two Days."

With that Tristan felt his eyes slowly begin to close and a dream filled sleep wrapped around him…

II

Gareth tore through the night sky on Peggy with Matthew magically secured behind him. He had travelled as fast as his horse could manage with his magical aid to keep her strength up and had almost reached Belthanor in record time. Yet he knew that even that might not be enough.

He had spoken to the Field Priest Commander that had tended to the High Priest and the woman had said that the damage to him was neither spiritual nor physical, but magical. The crystal that had trapped him had sapped away almost all of his innate magical energies and without an infusion of such energy Matthew would just waste away. Unfortunately, that energy had to be given before the last spark of magic left his body, else he was lost. His body could survive for a while after, but no amount of magic would then be able to save him. Some of his most powerful knights had tried to infuse him with energy, yet their complex energy transferral spells could not give him the power to sustain him long enough that he could begin regenerating his own. Gareth knew of only one person on the whole of Loden who could possibly do that and he was presently staying in Belthanor. Matthew had told him of his student's amazing ability to transfer vast amounts of raw magical energy from himself to other people. Gareth just hoped it was enough to save Matthew's life.

The towers of his fortress appeared on the horizon and he spurred Peggy on all that harder. She snorted her compliance and increased the beat of her wings fourfold. As he approached he noticed that something was amiss. Parts of his central tower seemed to have been blown away and there were several fires.

He shut his mind to the problem. This task was all he needed to worry about at the moment. Several of the knights riding in advance began their spiralling descent into the courtyard to prepare for his arrival and he saw them all dismount almost before their mounts had set foot on the earth. As Peggy began her own spiral downwards, there were already several men stood in the courtyard bearing a stretcher to take the injured Priest.

Gareth dismounted the moment Peggy's hooves brushed the cobbled floor and helped two men off-load the unconscious Matthew onto the stretcher.

"My private chambers, now," he commanded, leading the way.

The crowds parted before him, most looking stunned to see him. He also noted that two of the knights on night watch were not at their posts and realised that discipline had deteriorated since his departure. That would soon change. Evidently Lady Julia's talents for administration did not extend to the keep knights.

He swept the thoughts away as he raced through the corridors to his private chambers and was relieved to see the strange eyed boy stood there waiting for them. He had to admit to himself that it was probably the first time he had been happy at the sight of this strange youth.

"Have you been briefed of the situation?" he asked the boy as Matthew was brought in and laid upon the bed.

The boy nodded and Gareth noticed that he seemed very tired. He hoped that he was not too exhausted to help Matthew. The boy waved the others away and knelt at Matthew's side, placing his hand on the Priest's forehead and closing his eyes as he did. After a few minutes he looked back at Gareth.

"He's very far gone," said Jalim, "but it is possible to save him, though I'll need to bond with him until he is able to produce his own energy. It is dangerous, yet he needs it to survive."

"Whatever," he replied quickly, silently chaffing over any delay.

"As you wish," said the boy, turning back to Matthew.

It was as the boy did so that Gareth saw a strange look in the boy's eyes. They had seemed a lot older than the face they inhabited, and he also recalled that the boy's voice, so seldom heard, had sounded even stranger than usual.

He brushed aside his worries. Jalim provided him with the only hope that he could save his friend and thereby save his brother as well. He stood and anxiously watched as the boy entered a trance and muttered a few words. He then knelt there in silence for what seemed like hours but was probably only a few minutes. Nothing appeared to be happening, at least according to his eyes. Yet his sixth sense told him otherwise and he could feel the hairs on his body stand on end as what had to be vast amounts of energy poured from Jalim to Matthew. For the first time he realised the full extent of the vast power the two men before him possessed. His own meagre talent was like a small drop of water compared to the ocean that was theirs. He found himself feeling glad that they were on his side.

"It's done," said Jalim, rising unsteadily to his feet.

"Will he survive?" asked Gareth looking at the deathly still form on the bed.

"His body will, though his mind faces a fight to survive against madness," replied Jalim in that odd voice once more. "In that, no one can help him save himself."

Gareth ignored the voice and nodded his thanks. The boy shook his head slightly and his eyes briefly glazed over. He then yawned and stretched his arms, his eyes blinking as if to ward away sleep.

"Prince Gareth, what are you doing here?" asked Jalim starting as if seeing him for the first time.

"You just linked with Matthew to save his life," replied Gareth slowly, suddenly worried by the boy's odd behaviour.

The violet-eyed boy looked at the still wizard and his features creased momentarily.

"Oh yes," said Jalim, almost to himself. "Sorry. Linking in such a way can often disorientate you for a while afterwards."

"That's all right," replied Gareth, still feeling a little unsettled. "Go and rest up. We shall speak further on the morrow."

"Thank you, my lord."

With that the boy bowed and left Gareth alone with Matthew. He went over to the bedside and looked down on the still form and saw that he seemed to be asleep. The eyelids suddenly flickered open and he saw that the eyes were twitching around violently. However peaceful the sleep may look, one glimpse at those eyes told Gareth that the battle within the wizard was far from peaceful. Despite all this, the amulet Matthew had been seeking was still clasped firmly in his hand. Gareth hoped that it was worth the effort and risk that it had posed.

"We need to talk," said a voice behind him.

He spun around and drew his sword, summoning a spell to mind as he did.

"Now calm down," said a familiar figure in the shadows.

Gareth smiled. Naithan's *Spymaster* had come to pay him a visit. The smile dropped quickly at the sight of her serious expression.

"Will he survive?" asked the Spymaster.

"I think we'll know better in the morning, but I believe his chances are good," he replied, with more conviction than he felt.

He knew how much the Spymaster would fret if she thought the king's life was in danger. But then, Helena had always been like that over their baby brother. He shook his head and smiled briefly at the thought of Naithan's face if he ever found out who his Spymaster actually was. No, he knew how Naithan would react. He would ban her from the role and try to replace her with some man or another. In some things their brother was a little archaic in his views, but he was still king. If he commanded Helena to stop, then she would without question. Therefore it was better for them all if he remained blissfully ignorant. But such things should not concern him at present.

"What is the problem?" he asked.

"Unfortunately," began Helena, "even if he does survive, we're not out of the fire yet."

She loved to use their mother's expressions. Sometimes he felt that she believed herself to be mother over her two baby brothers.

"In what way?" asked Gareth, the hairs on the back of his neck prickling with a dark premonition.

"The most important thing is that Naithan has been captured by Black Heart and he's demanding a ten thousand marek ransom to be delivered to Devil's Island before next Torsday, else they'll kill him."

"You'll not pay him?" interrupted Gareth in shock and anger. "I'll take the fleet out and hunt him down. He can't stop an entire armada."

"How long will it take to muster that, brother dearest?" asked Helena softly. "He'll be dead by then, and even if you do track him down I believe he has some control over a sea dragon, and even an armada may not stand up to its attacks."

"Sea dragons are the stuff of myth!" snorted Gareth, silently conceding her point on the ships.

To get the ten ships prepared for Naithan's visit to Sol had required months of preparation. For an armada, that could extend to over a year. Letting the matter drop he turned his thoughts to more practical ideas.

"It managed to destroy over half the ships when it attacked," replied Helena. "Not bad for a story book creature, wouldn't you say?"

Gareth merely shrugged. His sister rarely stated things unless she had facts to back it up.

"The surviving ships are following at a discrete distance, concealing their presence in the usual way. I was hoping the Matthew would be well enough to save him. As it is, they need to be reunited soon or else their link will kill them."

"I'll be ready by morning," said a weak voice behind them.

Helena moved back into the shadows to conceal her features. Gareth, and their late mother, had been the only ones to know of Helena's special role.

Relief flooded Gareth as he turned back to Matthew. There lay a very strong man, though incredibly tired. Needing to talk more he muttered a quick spell and Matthew drifted back to sleep.

"We're getting sloppy," said his sister, relief evident in her voice.

"Tough circumstances," replied Gareth simply.

"Well, at least we can use Matthew, that's one thing," said his sister, half to herself. "Now, there's another reason why you cannot go gallivanting off after our brother."

"What's that?" asked Gareth warily.

"Recall those troops you don't need in Grelchin. There's a revolt in Theldar that you need to put down."

"A revolt?" asked Gareth incredulously. "How in Toric's name did that happen?"

"It seems our city *protector* had a tampered Redirection a few years back. He appears to have felt he could introduce the public death sentence. Well you know how those ideas often end up."

"Yes," replied Gareth angrily. "I'll leave in the morning with the city garrison. We have to get there before some council member feels the need to get himself crowned on the stone of Mara'dor."

Mara'dor was the mythical city of Toric, words that seemed to ring loud bells in some forgotten quarter of his mind, and the stone was supposed to have been the first stone placed in creating the temple there. Kings and queens had been crowned on it for generations and any would be king had to be crowned there. Legend said that it would weep blood if any other than the true ruler of Caldor were to sit upon it.

"I think one is already well down that particular track," replied Helena.

"What do you mean?"

"I'm certain that the corrupt Redirecters were working for one of the Royal Council members and with the crown particularly in mind. Do you know that they've been sowing seeds of treachery among the knights? Not blatantly, only giving them the feeling that someone other than Naithan was the one true ruler; a feeling that there was something not quite right about him."

"You mean someone's planned the whole thing?" he asked incredulously.

"Maybe not every aspect, but it certainly looks the part of some plot or another. I'll have to search further before I can make any solid conclusions, but that is the way it looks at the moment."

The frowning, thoughtful look on her face made him realise that he had the best tasks of the family. He could not stand all that cloak and dagger stuff. He would prefer a good, well-fought battle to a sneaking in the dark anytime of the year.

"I have to go now. There's work to be done. Send Matthew to Helena when he awakens and she'll brief him from there," said his sister, keeping up the fiction they had created years ago.

"Will you get there on time?" asked Gareth.

"Of course" she replied with a smile. "You know that you're not the only gifted one in the family. I'm there already! Take care and get Theldar back for us."

He stood and watched his sister slowly fade to nothing. How many times had he been fooled by her illusions? He had lost count and never really cared. She was as good as there with him when she did those things.

He shook his head with a smile. Though more powerful in many ways than their brother, what with their *special* talents, it was Naithan's very lack of those powers that made him king. Though he did not know it himself yet, the most important rule of succession was that no king could be magically talented. No one knew why this rule existed, but it was the most strictly enforced rule in the land, which was why Naithan, youngest of their mother's children, had been chosen as king. Some said that it went back to the ancient days when the fear of magic was so strong that the people simply refused to accept a sorcerer for a king. Gareth believed it had more to do with the blood-link that was passed on from generation to generation, though what the exact problem was he dared not guess.

Whatever the reason for its existence, it was still the most fundamental law of kingship and several of the greatest houses had been brought down by their inability to sire non-magical children. The Tara'nons had almost suffered that fate themselves. Their father, Richard had died mere months before the birth of Naithan.

He looked back to Matthew, turning his thoughts away from unpleasant memories and, on seeing him still slumbering peacefully, turned and left the room, posting two guards outside the door to ensure that he suffered no interruptions. He then went to his war office and began to look over the tactical maps of Theldar. Hopefully there would not be much of a fight, but if they did opt for armed resistance, the taking of the city could be the most difficult battle of his life to date.

He called for some of his tactical officers and the rest of the night was then whiled away discussing the various plans that could be used. It was almost dawn by the time they retired for sleep and he crashed to his bed in an exhausted slumber. He could not be wakened until late the next day. When he finally did wake up, he found that Matthew had already departed, though that barely bothered him. He had his plans for the recapture in place, thought it would take time to muster the troops required. In the meantime, he had a fortress to repair. It was going to be a long few weeks.

III

Matthew arrived at the patterned platform of Teldin shortly after midday. The link with Jalim was still in effect and he was surprised by exactly how much energy the young wizard could muster. It was almost equal to his own in some ways and with the two combined he doubted that any unlinked wizard could challenge him. He wondered just how long Jalim would be able to maintain the connection, and over how great a distance. With Naithan imprisoned he could have need for it soon. At the thought of Naithan his arm throbbed painfully and he felt his chest constrict. He needed to get back to the king before the blood-link killed them both.

"My Lord, the Lady Helena will see you in her chambers at once," said a page, bowing low before him.

Momentarily startled he merely nodded his assent and followed the girl through the palace corridors. Within minutes he had entered the private audience chamber of Princess Helena and had seated himself before her. She was a small woman whose presence could often fade into the background and be overlooked, yet Matthew knew that this could change in an instance. At full flow a giant would seem small compared to her. Being the oldest of the three siblings, she had often bullied the younger brothers into doing what she wanted and it was a talent she still possessed to this day.

"I assume you know the basic situation?" she asked, getting briskly to the heart of the matter.

"I know that Naithan is presently being held captive by Black Heart and that the pirate has some type of control over a sea creature. I also know that over half the fleet was sunk in the pirate's attack and that the rest were badly damaged. Other than that, I'm in the dark," he replied.

"Well, my brother's *friend*," said Helena with the sneer she always used when talking about Naithan's Spymaster, "reliably informs me that the four surviving ships are not that badly damaged. They used illusionary magic to make it seem that they were close to sinking and let Black Heart think he had escaped. They are presently following him under magical disguise, though not too closely for fear that Black Heart's wizard will detect them. Two more ships are also on their way there. One was part of the original fleet, though was damaged in a storm and had to put into harbour here for urgent repairs. She left a few days ago with my Royal Galleon. Naithan will need that ship to impress the Light of Heaven, and he'll need to do that if he truly wishes to convert him to Toric and convince him that he is a suitable suitor for his daughter.

"Unfortunately, that does not help us at the present moment. Our pursuing ships can't get too close for fear of attracting the wizard's attention, and therefore the sea creature in its wake. The remaining knights on board are not powerful enough to free him themselves and so it's all down to you. That's if you're ready and able to, of course."

For the first time Matthew regretted the fact that the more powerful knights had been left here in Caldor. Naithan had been adamant that the ancient secret that the Caldorian knights used sorcerous magic be kept, and that had meant taking those of a lesser power with them, for the more powerful knights exuded an aura of power that would have been unmistakable in any close examination. He was lucky in that his own aura could be explained as godly magic.

"Even minor magic would work if enough was used though," protested Matthew quickly. "Why didn't they use it in the first attack?"

"Why do you think?" asked Helena softly. "My brother's command that no one was to sacrifice to Giarna put our knights in a difficult fight on two fronts. That creature appears to match the description of Giarna's form exactly. Sailors are a superstitious lot, and who wouldn't be living on something as fickle as the sea. They believed that they had angered the ancient goddess and the knights had to put down a mutiny whilst protecting their ships at the same time. It was all they could do to survive!"

Matthew had to agree with her on that point. Naithan could be a little blinkered when looking at other religions. It was easy to see why the Solmen, a race of seafarers, would worship creatures such as that, beasts that could tear away their only protection in seconds. He wondered if control of a creature such as that would ever be of use to them. He would have to seek out the control device once he had freed Naithan. At that thought his arm throbbed painfully, his chest constricted and his vision swam. Time was running out for them. Helena seemed to notice his reaction.

"Is everything all right?" she asked. She was probably one of the few people who knew of their link.

"Fine," he replied, blinking the dizziness away. "But it won't be for long. I'm afraid I'll have to leave you now. Forgive my haste but the link is nearing its limits and time is short."

"Go! Quickly," she replied with a nod.

Matthew pulled the energy from within and formed it around himself, curving beams of light around him, rendering himself virtually invisible, though any knowing what to look for would spot him immediately. He then released more of the sweet energy, ripping open a gateway before him. It was a slower method of travel than simple teleportation but ensured that he would appear were he wanted and would allow him to see what the situation was before he arrived. He brought the image of Naithan to his mind and an image appeared in the gateway before him. He could see his friend chained to the wall and another man leaning over him. Naithan looked extremely ill and for a moment Matthew thought he was dying. It seemed his friend was suffering more from the link than he was at present. The man seemed to be talking to Naithan so he waited until he had finished and left the cell before stepping through the gateway.

IV

"Yes, all signs of fever have completely gone," said the ship's wizard, looking at Naithan carefully. "I cannot see why you should still be so weak. It's like something is slowly killing you from within."

Naithan knew what it was, though he was not about to give his secret away to the gentle man before him, even though it was a secret they held in common. The past couple of days had been full of new experiences for him. The old man who had almost gutted him on deck had not been around since that day and his only human contact had been with the wizard Uther.

Their initial contact had been brief but as Naithan's condition had begun to deteriorate they had spent more and more time together, Naithan slowly gaining the man's trust. He had learned that the man was indeed blood-linked to the pirate, though it had been an unintentional bond. Black Heart had killed the wizard's former blood-linked partner and the link had transferred to the killer, something Naithan had never heard of before. His link had been transferred to him on his mother's deathbed, following a tradition that went back centuries. It seemed that the creatures involved did not always require human help to transfer, and also that one was always more dominant than the other.

It was in this way that Black Heart was able to control Uther, though it seemed the poor wizard suffered terribly whenever it was used. The man also hated the pirate with a vengeance, for his former partner had also been his wife of some ten years. Unfortunately the link prevented him from gaining revenge.

"That's all I can do for you at present. I'll have to go now, unless he senses I'm doing more than just healing you," said the wizard softly.

That too had been a shock for Naithan. He had always believed that Matthew was the only dual magic user, though this man could do both. It was the only way the artefact controlling the sea creature could be used, something else he had learned from the wizard. He was a learned man, much like Matthew, and had found his months on board this ship had been allowing his intellect to stagnate. Though no genius, Naithan had found his education and learning had allowed him to get Uther to open up and reveal things that would have normally remained hidden in any other situation.

"Thank you Uther," he replied with a sigh.

"Besides, I believe your rescuer is due to arrive," said the wizard quickly. Naithan tried to ask what the man meant, but was interrupted. "I only ask that he kill me first, and that he use flame. They can't escape the flames, and I do not wish to be the one to die from the link. It is supposed to be the most painful thing to experience and I believe he deserves that more than me. Let that be my revenge."

Naithan watched in silence as the man left, wondering at the fire that had briefly flashed in the man's eyes. The air shimmered slightly before him and suddenly the ache in his arm vanished.

"It's about time you showed up," he said quietly to the air before him. His friend was obviously magically hidden and whilst the thought of such magic scared him, he knew it was a vital defence.

"I'm going to free you and take you away," said a voice by his ear, making him jump. Matthew could move very quietly at times, even without his magic.

"No," replied Naithan quickly. Though he had only known Uther a few days, he felt closer to him than anyone he had met in years. "We're not letting them get away with this."

"I thought you might say that!" said Matthew, sounding exasperated. "It's much simpler if we just leave them to it. The conversion of Sol must be our main objective."

"I will not leave murderers such as him on my seas," hissed Naithan, angrily. "We will destroy him and put the fear of Toric into any who think of following in his footsteps."

"As you wish, my lord," said Matthew softly.

His friend often capitulated to his commands and Naithan found himself wondering, for the first time if it was not solely due to his superior rank. Could his blood-link also be used as Black Heart used his? It was a question he would have to ponder on later. For now, however, there was the problem of capturing and destroying the pirate's fleet.

"What is the present situation with my ships?" he asked and Matthew gave a detailed reply. From that plans were formulated and discussed in hurried whispers until a suitable one was found. Matthew then vanished to inform the other ships in their fleet and Naithan was forced to wait in the dark with silent anticipation for his final moment of freedom. Uther would get his revenge.

V

Siege. The very word sent a shudder down Galen's spine, yet that was what they were facing. It was an inevitable outcome to his actions in taking over the city. He had hoped that the moment would not be so soon, yet the Circle of Light's informers had told them that Prince Gareth was already back from Grelchin and mobilising troops. They could be marching even now as the two Circles met to discuss their actions.

"What do you say?" asked Jarek, looking to him.

"My views are very clear and simple. We are to fight for the freedom of this city. Tyrants have ruled long enough. I say that we should govern ourselves and not by some man who can rule solely because his parents did before him. The only way to maintain that is to fight. If that means a siege, then let it be so."

Most in the circle did not share his mistrust of kings, and the Circle of Light had openly discussed who to replace Naithan with on the throne. The members of the Dark Circle were more open to his views, however. They seemed to be enjoying their new found power, though they would not like his ideas if they were successful in outlasting the siege. Most would probably find themselves voted swiftly out of office for more *respectable* candidates.

"Then we of the Dark follow your lead in this, Lord Protector," said Meredith with a bow. She appeared to have become the spokesman of the Guild of Hawks in the absence of their old leader.

"We of the Light also concur with the Lord Protector's wishes," said Tyrone, bowing as he spoke.

He wished that they would not use such a title, one he had never sought, yet it was a continuation of the old, of sorts, that allowed the public in general to accept the changes as legal. One had even suggested that he be made king, an idea he had swiftly quashed. He had no intention of ruling to his death as king.

The compliance of the Circle of Light's members made him suspicious. He was sure that they had some secret agenda that they were following, though he had been unable as yet to ferret it out. However their agreement left only one vote to be cast and that was the most important of them all. That was from the Circle of Steel, as they fashioned themselves. The knights and guards of the city had almost unanimously voted to remain with the citizens and help maintain order. Why they had all given up their oath to the king so quickly he did not know, yet another mystery that needed solving at some point. He rubbed his eyes and yawned. So many things to do and so little time. He felt himself fade away briefly and saw the glazed looks of those around him as they pointedly ignored it. It was one of his new gifts that many chose to ignore.

The knights had joined them after much negotiation and become part of what was becoming known as the Triad of Theldar, though they seemed uncomfortably close to the Circle of Light in views in his opinion. They too had voted for the election of another king, though they had been undecided upon whom the honour should be bestowed. In that, however, their vote was of little consequence, being the newest of the three groups. In matters of defence, however, they were the most vital of all. Without their aid, Theldar would most probably fall at the first sight of troops approaching the city. With their aid, they would stand a chance.

He looked to Sar Petra, speaker for the Circle of Steel, awaiting her vote. She was a master of ceremony and very shrewd in the game of politics. With this vote her newly formed party was gaining more power and control. She paused long enough for those around her to fully realise their dependence on her vote before casting it.

"The Circle of Steel votes with the Lord Protector. We shall defend the city with our lives. To this we swear on the Light of Toric."

Her reply stunned those around her. Such an oath was not sworn easily or lightly. In one move she had placed herself firmly on the side of the city with more conviction than anyone else in the room had mustered previously. She bowed a perfect bow, fully an inch lower than Tyrone's bow, indicating her subservience to Galen's wishes was greater than his. It placed the knights firmly in his camp and had radically altered the balance of power within the Triad. She was a very wily diplomat indeed.

"Then it is decided," said Galen slowly. "We fight on till death. Prepare the defences, you are dismissed."

The councillors stood and left as one, leaving him alone with Marie.

"That includes you," he said, coldly looking through her.

She bowed stiffly, cold anger and pain in her eyes. She left without a word and he moved to the balcony that looked out over the city. Night had already fallen and the thin light of the waxing moons' did little to illuminate the sleeping city. Memories surged through him, memories that were not his own and he found himself wondering, not for the first time, what he had become. He was neither the Galen of before, nor the Shadow, but something else entirely. Galen had not been a politician. The subtle underplays he had seen today the Galen of old would have missed. He had gained more than life and power with the ring. He had gained knowledge too, some of it ancient.

A flash of foreboding overcame him and he had a sudden vision of a city in flames appear before him. That was something of the old Galen coming through. He had sometimes seen things that had once happened, or were yet to come. He found himself wondering which that vision had been. It was with a chilling certainty that he realised that it was an image of what was yet to come.

VI

Tristan woke with the dawn and rose to his feet. Hunger gnawed at him and he was surprised to see food awaiting him and the others already eating. He sat down and joined them, a sense of peace filling him. His sleep had been filled with visions and he knew the time would come when he would have to decide what to do. One way led to peace, the other to strife, yet one could be the salvation of many. He had a lot to think on and barely noticed the others around him.

He looked around at the glade in which he had seen such wonders the previous night. It now seemed devoid of life, though he could feel it all around him. The pool no longer seemed perfectly circular, though it was not far from it and much of the sense of magic seemed muted, almost dull. He sighed, knowing he would never find such a place again and finished the fruits before him. It was Matthius who was the first to disturb the silence.

"Where's Belthar?" he asked, looking around.

It was with those words that Tristan noticed the druid's absence, something he would have considered impossible considering the man's size.

"Look to the pool," said Caliburn in a voice that seemed almost audible.

They all looked round to see the calm waters begin to bubble and churn. The waters parted and with a roar a giant black bear reared up, water streaming from its shaggy fur. The morning light sparkled and span through the falling drops creating a halo of light around the massive creature. It roared once more and lifted its large paws to the air. As it did so, the light shimmered and the fur began to recede from its body. It shrunk in size and fingers seemed almost to grow from the outstretched claws. Its muzzle shrank back into itself and the eyes began to fill with a milky white fluid. Its hind legs convulsed and the knee joint inverted upon itself. Within moments the familiar form of Belthar was climbing from the pool.

Tristan sat in awe at the sight of such magic and found he had to remind himself to breathe. He then flushed briefly as he noted that the man was naked, though it seemed he had no genitals as such to cover. He turned away and allowed the druid to put on the clothes that were lying by the pool.

"So yer guys know about me now then?" he asked, sounding a little tired and melancholy.

"Yes, and we will keep your secret," replied Tristan softly. "We are sorry for putting you through all this."

"There was nothin' to be done about it, I'm afraid," replied Belthar. "'Twas my own fault, not yours. But, what's done is done, as your kind are fond of sayin'."

"It as you say, all done," said Groltch, looking round slowly. "What we do now?"

Tristan had no idea. He knew where he would have to be, but had no idea how to get there or when it was due to happen.

"There's a place near here where we can rest up and get foodstuff," said Belthar slowly. "But it's a secret place and I hope you'll keep it, especially you."

The druid looked directly at Tristan with those blind eyes. He wondered what secret would be so shocking to him that he would have to be singled out.

"It's a village nearby called Dilatch," he continued and Tristan saw Groltch start at the name.

He looked at the ran-the closely but he merely returned a blank look of innocence.

"Dilatch it is then," said Matthius, looking dubiously towards Belthar.

Tristan felt a prickle of anger at being kept out of whatever secret the three of them seemed to be sharing. Even Caliburn was being suspiciously quiet, as if it too was in on their plot. Pushing the anger away he went over to Galahad who was grazing contentedly upon the grass. The horse looked up and whinnied a small greeting. He patted the horse's nose and took out a brush to groom him. He busied himself with the task whilst the others packed away their belongings and Matthius sought out his kitten, which seemed to have decided to play a quick game of hide go seek with the young wizard. He finally caught it and carefully placed it in his pouch, its loud purr audible even from Tristan's position at the edge of the clearing.

"Let's go then," said Belthar briskly, leading the way from the trees.

Tristan led Galahad out of the clearing and felt the urge to take one final look back at the clearing. As he did he thought he caught a glimpse of the female spirit he had seen that night, watching him with those large oval eyes. He blinked and the image was gone, yet the sorrowful expression he saw on her face was to haunt his dreams for many nights to come.

VII

Karene woke up with a start. She had been dreaming and her dreams had been interrupted by a premonition. That was all she could call it, for she had found herself dreaming of a castle and the name Teldin had whispered in her mind. She knew without doubt what it meant. She had to get to Teldin. Tristan had to have somehow escaped from Belthanor and Teldin would be his destination. She roused the knights with her and ordered them to mount up, ignoring their complaints. She was going to waste no time in riding there. She would even ignore getting more supplies at the fortress, even though it was less than a day away. The chance of victory was still hers. She led the knights out of the clearing they had camped within with the dawn sun and rode hard to the main highway. She was so intent on leaving quickly that she did not notice a beautiful humanoid figure with sad oval eyes watching her departure.

VIII

Rufus Manne, otherwise known as Black Heart, Terror of the High Seas, looked out at the dawn as it rose up from the western horizon over the Endless Sea. It was always his favourite time of the day, as it reminded him of the day he had wrested control of his first ship in a mutiny, some ten years ago. He had never felt so alive and it was the same whenever he won a victory at sea, though the beast he now controlled had lessened that thrill somewhat.

He closed his eyes and breathed in the salty air, revelling in the wind as it rushed through his hair. Never could you be more free than here on the sea, and he sometimes wished he never had to dock to dry land, but few ever felt this strongly about the ocean and would need time a shore to revel in drink and women.

His thoughts were disturbed by a commotion on the lower decks. He turned to see a strange robed man on board his ship. It had to be a wizard, for no one else could get aboard his ship without notice. He summoned his own wizard on deck.

"Kill him!" he commanded the man when he emerged from below, his instincts telling him a trap was being sprung.

The strange figure stretched his arms outwards and light sprayed out in all directions. Ships suddenly appeared amidst his own and his fears were realised as knights suddenly appeared on his decks. He cursed angrily. He thought Caldorians had no use for magic. He shouted out to his men to fight and then drew his sword, knowing that they could not rely on their sea beast this time. He could already see that his wizard was in the middle of a terrible battle with the enemy sorcerer. The ship rocked suddenly as fire exploded from the two wizards. His senses came to life and he was reminded of that first day once more.

The mutiny had begun and people were fighting everywhere. Without thought he cut down one of the officers who had appeared before him, the man screaming as he tried to replace his intestines. Yet he paid it no thought, he was going to be the one to run this ship. No more would he be forced to demean himself to the harsh officers, or that filthy wretch of a captain. Even as he thought of him, the man appeared on the deck below him and he knew what he had to do. Another officer leapt at him and they traded blows. Yet Rufus did not keep his eyes off the captain on deck. He would revenge himself on that man. He cut down the officer, receiving a nick in return.

The ship reeled suddenly, throwing those less balanced than he off their feet. He saw his opening and leapt onto the lower deck, crashing into another officer as he did. He got swiftly to his feet and engaged another man before him, momentarily losing sight of the captain, the man who had taken his eye. Snarling in rage at the man before him he savagely sliced the man up, ignoring the slight cuts and nicks he gained in the process. He wanted the captain and nothing less.

A fellow mutineer cut down an officer beside him and he saw his chance. The captain was fighting another but the mutineer backed down at the sight of Rufus leaping to attack. The captain spun around and faced him, a cold look of contempt on his face. He gave a contemptuous salute and Rufus snarled, slashing his sword out in attack. The ship rocked again and flames danced past him. He dived to one side to avoid the now falling mast and rolled to his feet. The captain was upon him instantly and their swords clashed together violently, jarring his hand slightly.

Rufus found himself losing ground rapidly and looked for some way to reverse the trend. To his left he saw a piece of sailcloth in flames blowing in the wind. He grabbed at it with his free hand and threw it at the captain, causing his attack to falter. Now was the time of Rufus' attack. He advanced, anger fuelling his strength, his blade flashing out left and right, forcing the captain backwards. The ship shuddered violently and the captain lost his footing. Rufus saw his chance and sprung out for the kill.

The sword sliced through flesh and the captain suddenly vanished, the illusion fading before his eyes. Pain flashed across the back of his legs and they gave way as the severed hamstrings snapped backwards. He collapsed to the floor and saw the king, the man he had held prisoner, stood before him. He realised the trap that had been sprung as he looked around. Most of his men were dead, some probably from his own blade. He looked up angrily at his former prisoner.

"Kill me now then," he snarled, gritting his teeth in pain.

"Oh no," said Naithan, kicking Rufus' sword across the deck. "That's far too light a fate for you. Look on your fate and know true pain."

Rufus looked in the direction of the king's icy cold, fanatical stare. He was just in time to see his wizard erupt in a ball of incinerating flame. A high pitch scream seemed to slice his head in two and his world exploded in pain.

IX

Naithan watched as the man's eyes bulged out in pain as Uther died. He saw blood leak from the man's ears and eyes and the pirate known as Black Heart screamed in pain. His body writhed and twitched as it almost tore itself apart as the creature within him fought its way to freedom. The look of pain on the man's face was horrifying, yet it was his just desserts. As the light of life left the man's eyes, he felt the creature within him stir as if in fear. He looked to Matthew and indicated the pirate's body. Matthew seemed to struggle for a while to find the magic and he felt his own stomach churn as the parasite within him began entering a terrified frenzy. He looked to the pirate and saw the blood red haze tearing its way out of every orifice and wound.

He looked back to Matthew worriedly, not knowing how this parasite would react with his own. Suddenly resolve filled the eyes of his sorcerer and the pirate's body exploded in flame. The creature within him settled immediately, though he still felt a little queasy at the sensation of such an unusually active movement in the parasite within him.

"We've got to get off of here," said Matthew as he rushed towards him.

Naithan could hear the ship splintering and cracking about him.

"We have to get the circlet!" he replied quickly.

He needed control of that sea creature.

"We don't have time!" cried out Matthew, side stepping a burning log of wood as he did.

"We have to get it!" he commanded.

"All right," said Matthew. "It's this way!"

He followed his friend who had spent the day after they had been reunited following Uther around learning everything he could about the man. His was a small cabin, yet he was evidently privileged, for few had a room to themselves on a ship this size. He waited as Matthew dug through the man's drawers and chest, using his magic to force the locks. Sea water washed against Naithan's feet and he realised just how far the ship had already sunk.

"Quickly!" he cried.

"It's not where he left it!" shouted back Matthew. "He must have hidden it. We'll have to leave it!"

"No!" he cried, angrily. "We have to have it."

He waded into the cabin to help his friend, for the water was now almost up to his waist. He began to frantically dig through the various components Uther possessed in a vain search for something he had never seen.

"We've got to get out before we drown in here!" screamed Matthew fearfully. He had never been all that good a swimmer.

"We stay until it's found and that's an order," said Naithan, the tone of his command cutting out like ice.

"Very well then, but you'll have to let me do something then," said Matthew angrily.

That meant magic, something Naithan abhorred, but he knew he needed that circlet.

"Very well," he growled. "Do it!"

The man began casting his spell as the water reached his shoulders and Naithan instantly began to regret his decision. He was just about to break the man from his spell when he was grabbed by Matthew and forcibly pushed under the water. Frightened and angered he gasped one final breath of air and held his breath. He struggled to free himself from his *friend's* grasp and rise for air. It was a struggle and by the time he had broken free the water had filled the small cabin. Panic filled him as his breath began to give out. Matthew was drowning him. How could he? His head began to spin and his lungs began burning for air.

Naithan felt fists ram into his stomach and his breath was forcibly expelled from his lungs. He instinctively breathed in and water filled his lungs. He coughed and spluttered slightly, yet suddenly found his head was beginning to clear up. Confused he looked round and saw Matthew swimming before him, breathing in water. Naithan took a second breath, ignoring the urge to choke. His head cleared further and his eyes opened in amazement. Matthew turned his head and pointed to the back of his neck. Running down its entire length was a set of gills, like those fish possessed. He slowly reached behind his neck and found the same to be the case with his neck. As he breathed in, water surged into his lungs, yet much passed out through the gills on his neck. Horrified at the abomination he had become he would have screamed if he could, but that was not possible.

Matthew turned and continued his search of the water filled room and Naithan pushed aside the thoughts of the gills and joined him, vowing to speak to the wizard at some point about this moment. The search took some time and he could feel the pressure of the water around him begin to mount up as the ship continued to sink. He also noted the growing coldness of the water and could see the encroaching darkness. It was Matthew who eventually found the circlet, a small golden crown with a central silver disk upon which the image of a dragon was etched in gold.

They turned as one and swam through the door to the ocean beyond and began to make their way to the surface. A shadow passed across them and a chilling certainty filled Naithan. The creature was out here, somewhere above them. He looked to Matthew and saw from his eyes that he had realised the same fact. He knew the reason for the look of panic in them too. Matthew always liked to study devices before putting them to use, never leaving such things to chance. Now he would have to act first and hope he could work the device. Naithan prayed silently to Toric as Matthew placed the circlet upon his head and concentrated. The shadow passed over them once more and Naithan fought to keep his panic down. Matthew smiled and Naithan breathed a sigh of relief.

The relief was short lived, however. The shadow covered them once more and he saw the creature was now swimming down towards them. Icy fear, colder than the water around them shot through Naithan as the beast drew closer and closer. He had to struggle to stop himself from thrashing around in a frenzied panic. His prayers went out once more to Toric and he closed his eyes, hoping for the best, yet fearing the worst. He felt the creature's massive form brush past him and the moment of truth arrived.

X

"Well, is there any sign of them?" asked Admiral Dysan fearfully.

The knights in the long boats below shook their heads in reply, sending a shiver of fear down his spine. How was he going to explain the failure of their rescue attempt of the king to Princess Helena? He had seen the ship go down after a fearful battle and had retrieved all the knights who had survived the conflict. Several even claimed to have seen the king enter a cabin as the ship went down, increasing his fears as to the wellbeing of the king. The ship had now been under some thirty minutes. All was lost.

He signalled the winch operators to bring up the long boats and re-secure them to the deck. As they did so the watchman called out in alarm. He looked out across the sea and saw the waters bubbling and churning violently.

"Battle positions!" he commanded quickly.

He had not been involved in the first conflict, yet he had heard the stories of Giarna's beast and feared the worst. They were confirmed as a huge head emerged from the water, jaws gaping wide.

"Archers, loos…hold," he called, his voice catching at the sight before him.

Atop the great beast were sat two familiar figures, the King and the Lord Priest, both clearly still alive. Relief and awe filled him as he saw the sunlight glitter through the water dripping from the beast's gaping maw. He watched silently as it glided towards his ship and gently, almost reverently, lowered its head to the main deck, allowing its passengers to board.

"Well don't stand there gawking," said the king briskly, walking past him as if nothing extraordinary had happened. "Let's get underway. We need to be in Sol as soon as possible."

"Yes, Sir," said Admiral Dysan, watching as the creature sank beneath the water's surface.

"And show me and the Lord Priest our quarters. It feels like I've worn these clothes for days, and I'm sure the sea water will ruin them," continued the king, walking towards the stern of the ship.

"Yes, Sir," he replied, slowly recovering from his shock.

He turned and ordered the cabin boy to tend to the King's needs whilst he began ordering his sailors to set sail. Within minutes they were underway, yet he could not help looking back over their wake and wondering if that great beast was still nearby…

XI

Anton looked at the two reports on his desk with mixed feelings of anger and pain. Prince Gareth had somehow gotten word of the revolt and was already marching his troops to attack the city. Belthanor was several days closer than Grathnac to Theldar, which meant Anton would arrive too late, though he had made plans for such a possibility.

What troubled him more was the report on Tristan's escape. A woman had been killed in the incident and had confirmed his worst fears. His daughter Miranda was not out at their country estate, he had ridden out immediately on reading the report and had found that his *daughter* was in fact one of the ladies-in-waiting. His daughter, always a wilful child had gone and gotten herself killed, allowing Tristan to escape. He hoped that they would return here, but that was a slim hope at best. That part of his plan had failed, and he was going to need another wife if he was to produce an heir.

"The troops are ready," said a voice from the doorway, disturbing his thoughts.

"Thank you," he replied. "I'll be there anon."

The woman bowed and left him alone once more. He took one last look around the study. If he had his way, it would be the last time that he would see this rat infested dump. He vowed that as King he would never visit this wretched city again. He left the room and closed the door behind him before making his way down the stairs beyond. A few minutes later he was riding out of the palace gates to blazing fanfares that would hopefully be the last he heard in this stinking city.

XII

Galen looked out over the crowds of people spread out before him, all of whom were cheering loudly. Years of experience he had never had, had helped him speak to so many people. He could recall countless speeches in countless languages over countless generations, none of which the man known as Galen had ever performed. He had instinctively known how to move the crowd, to wrap them up in his words and feel his passion. He had begun with an appraisal of the situation and the introduction of martial law to the city. Yet he had followed them with promises of greater freedom once the dark times were over, and they had cheered him. He had spoken for almost an hour, sometimes coaxing, sometimes cajoling, yet always affecting the crowd before him.

Humans never change, came the unbidden thought in his mind. It was his own thought, yet not, like many things about him since his brush with death.

He raised his arms high and led a final cheer before leaving them to their own preparations. He saw a few leaving quickly, men and women who would probably have left the city before the day was over. The rest would stay and fight, for good or for ill, as was often the case after his speeches.

He shook the thoughts from his head angrily. They were not his thoughts. He felt unclean at his actions, using his powers to make people fight what would be a hopeless fight. He saw that with each passing day, the old Galen within him crying out with visions of death and destruction. Yet the new Galen sneered and ignored the old, pushing him away and striving to become whole. He would rule these people, as none of his kind had done successfully before.

His kind. What did he mean by that? He was not human; the ring had changed that, but were there others out there like him? He did not know. He walked through the various fawning courtiers, all of whom had decided to stay in the hopes of gaining a better position with their new ruler. Some had even hinted at his possible claim to the throne, given his last name. An old herald had been brought forward who had managed to trace his ancestry back to the ancient Royal House of Faithe, one of the first ruling families of Caldor. It was a tenuous link that required a leap of imagination, though he had not dismissed it immediately, as he had once done before. The new Galen had paused to think on it a moment before rejecting it. That scared him more than anything else.

Not for the first time, he cursed the ring on his finger. Yet he could not rid himself of it, for it was keeping him alive. He caught his reflection in a nearby mirror and shuddered at his partially translucent form. The ring was only keeping him alive for a short time and he found himself wondering what purpose it had him in mind for.

He pushed the thoughts away and went and sat down in his darkened room. He found light very irritating these days.

"He must be dead or a long way from the city," said a voice behind him, making him start.

"You're sure?" he asked Meredith cautiously.

He had sent her on a mission to search out her former guild master to determine the reason for his absence. He needed a strong leadership and did not want an unknown element appearing from nowhere and disturbing the balance of the Triad.

"Yes," she replied softly. "All trace of him vanished when the King left for Sol. There were rumours that he was a courtier in the palace, hence giving us our royal protection. If they were true, then it is possible he is presently in Sol, if not, then he must be dead, for he would never vanish so suddenly otherwise."

"Very well, so that settles the matter now then?" he asked quietly.

"Yes," she replied almost sadly. "I have been elected the new Hawkmaster and shall take the permanent position on the Triad."

"Good," he replied, smiling to himself in the darkness. "You may go."

He waited until he felt her presence leave before chuckling openly. She made the perfect sword to Tyrone's shield. He had seen the two drawing closer together day by day and knew that as long as that remained so; their respective loyalties to their Circles would be compromised, making a permanent alliance difficult to come by. That only left the Circle of Steel, and that was the group he distrusted most of all. With the other Circles entangled as they were, he could leave them for a while and concentrate on the knights and their motives. He chuckled once more then lit the fire and watched the shadows dance.

XIII

Luca moved his chair closer to the fireplace and closed his eyes, drinking in the sounds around him. It was not often that he got to visit his daughter and his grandchildren at home. His duties to Naithan usually prevented him, even those that the king was not truly aware of. Yet this trip to Sol had given him such an opportunity and he intended to use it well.

He opened his eyes, drinking in the smells of even-sup. His daughter could cook as well as his late wife and the smells reminded him of those wonderful times. He took a deep breath of air and gloried in the world around him one last time. As he breathed out, he saw his wife waiting at the doorway and he smiled. He got to his feet and the world faded away in the light of his wife's smile.

XIV

The sun was setting as they approached the clearing in the woods. Groltch smelled the air as the scent of vis'nar was carried to him on a gentle breeze. Visions of home and hearth flooded through him and for a moment he was almost overcome with emotion. There was no mistaking the smell of baking vis'nar, a spicy bread that his people favoured. There were ran-tha nearby, here in Caldor. His knees went weak and for a moment he feared he would not be able to walk the final steps. A homesickness the like of which he had never felt washed over him at the thought of seeing his own kind once more. He had fancied them all dead. His travels through his kingdom here to Caldor had been one long sojourn of death and destruction. He had not seen one trace of his people in that journey, a fact that had made him more determined to kill the king and stop the slaughter.

A surge of energy filled him and he pushed his way to the front of the group, making certain that he was the first to emerge from the trees. His heart soared as he saw the village before him. It was filled with life and laughter, ran-tha younglings racing round the small green and many ran-tho, women of his kind, preparing the communal even-fest meal.

As he approached, he saw several turn and look their way. One clapped her hands and one of the children raced into the heart of the village. Within moments ran-tha of all ages were rushing out to watch them approach. One, obviously the Greater Elder judging by his clothes, moved to the fore and approached him, eyes glancing to his companions in a silent question. He motioned to Tristan and the others to stand still as he approached. As he neared them he noticed that this was not a typical ran-tha village. Many had tribal tattoos, something he had never had chance to earn, and there were markings of many different clans of many different provinces. These were obviously refugees, though why they were hidden here, in Caldor of all places, he could not fathom. Yet as he approached, he saw that they were stood in the traditional greeting Triad of Greater Elder, Master Tenget, and High Mis-lah, the tribal priest.

"Welcome, lost one, to this place of peace," said the Greater Elder in ran-tha in perfect Caldorian. He pressed four fingers together and bowed slightly in the ritual greeting used in such situations. "Enter now and know our hospitality."

"Enter, lost one," began the Master Tenget, duplicating the ritual bow of the Greater Elder, "and know that your shadow is mine to protect whilst in the shade of our walls."

"Enter, lost one, and may the light of Toric illuminate you whilst you reside in this place of peace," finished the Lord Mis-lah, repeating the greeting bow.

Groltch returned the bow, holding it for three beats of his heart, one for each of the village elders.

"I, Groltch, son of Mar-loutch, thank the Triad for its gracious hospitality and gladly accept it with joyful soul," he said, straightening up as he did. "My shadow is yours to protect till I depart."

"The Triad welcomes too, those of the Light who follow in your wake," said the three elders in unison, startling Groltch as they did.

This was not part of the traditional ran-tha greeting. He had not known how he was to get these strangers invited into the village boundaries, as most humans had been banned since the time of the great flood.

"Welcome, Wizard of the Arts, whose knowledge spans the ages," said the Greater Elder, turning to Matthius and speaking fluently in Caldorian. "Enter now and know our hospitality."

Groltch could do nothing but stare at this turn of events. The Triad were treating the three behind him as Triad members themselves. Stranger too was the fact that Matthius returned the bow, albeit a little clumsily.

"Welcome, Master of the Sword, protector of shadow," said the Master Tenget. "May we not find cause to join battle during your stay."

Tristan returned the bow gracefully.

"Welcome, Druid of Gartha, priest of the godless ones," finished the High Mis-lah. "Lord Toric bows to one more ancient than he."

Belthar returned the bow and all three humans voiced the ritual reply as one.

"Don't worry," said Cal's voice in his mind. *"I thought it would keep things running smoothly if they knew how to respond correctly."*

Did you reveal what they were to the Triad? he asked suspiciously.

"To that I must confess ignorance," said the sword, soundly genuinely confused.

"Now that the formalities are over, I bid thee enter our humble village and sup with us," said the Greater Elder, using an old form of Caldorian. "I hath taken residence with my joined one… my wife, so that thou hast a roof to protect thee and thy companions from the elements."

Groltch found himself unable to speak from shock. Rarely would a ran-the give up his freedom and independence in such a way for a stranger.

"I see thou art startled by the many ways in which things be different here," said the Greater Elder softly, looking at Groltch as he spoke. "This war that doth destroy us be'ath a war of change. If we darest not change, then we shall all die. But that is for later talk. Thou and thy companions must needs be hungry after thy visit to the sacred place. Tis said you spent two days in sleep there."

That too surprised Groltch. None had spoken of their experience in the druid's grove. He had been touched by dreams and visions he prayed were not to come true. Yet at the mention of the grove, one vision suddenly flared back into his mind and he felt a shiver of fear run down his spine.

"The guardians of the grove instructed us to thy approach and did bidst that we welcome all as we have thus," continued the Elder, seemingly oblivious to Groltch's sudden discomfort.

He allowed himself to be led through the village, drinking in the sights and sounds around him. Other than the occasional peculiarity, such as the differing tattoos, it was just like many a ran-tha village, including his own, and everything part of him cried out for home. He was taken to the central hut of the village and shown inside by the Greater Elder.

"Here are your quarters, at least for the night. Stay and freshen up if you wish. A steam room is just beyond if you have need of it," said the old ran-the to Groltch before turning to the humans behind him. "I'm afraid space is limited in our village, as more and more refugees arrive here each week than can be housed. You will have to share this accommodation with each other this night."

"Thank you for your concern," replied Tristan with a slight bow. "It will be more than adequate for our needs. Toric shine on your generosity."

Groltch flinched, waiting for an outburst of shock and rage from the aged ran-the, but none came. He merely nodded in thanks, understanding showing in his eyes. Evidently the ran-tha of the Western Realms had not lost all contact with humans and knew of their shared religion. Groltch found himself wondering how two races who shared the same god had ever managed to drift so far apart from each other.

"One will come for you when the even-sup has been prepared for you," said the Elder, bowing as he left them.

The first thing Groltch did was strip off his clothing and all but run into the sweat room, a much more wholesome method of cleaning than this human idea of immersing yourself in water. He sat in the steam, scraping off the grime for what seemed like a heavenly eternity, before leaving and dressing himself in proper, ran-tha clothing that had been brought in for him whilst he had been steaming. He looked round for the others and saw only Tristan, who was sat at the small window looking out on the village green.

"Everything all right Tris?" he asked quietly.

"Everything seems so ordinary," said Tristan, largely to himself. "The children, the playing, the life. Why do the taleweavers always portray it so differently?"

Groltch had no answer and decided to leave the human in peace. The knight had seen his world overturned and everything he believed in destroyed in a way not so dissimilar to his own experience. Groltch also knew that Tris needed his own space to solve the dilemmas that such a trauma had produced.

He left the building and almost immediately walked into the Master Tenget. She stopped and stared at him with piercing eyes.

"You're the one then," she said, sadness filling her voice. "Being so far away I had hoped that I was wrong, but you are the only one."

"What do you mean?" he asked, feeling more than a little disturbed by her strange words.

"Reach out with your thoughts to your amulet. Feel for others of our kind out there in the wilderness," she replied.

Groltch had forgotten about the methram about his neck, given to him by his own Tenget before he died. He had barely finished his training and had needed to fully reach his adulthood before he should have truly possessed it, yet time had been short. He was now old enough to bear it, though he had none of the tattoos he should have gained during his rite of passage. It had been his lack of tattoos that had caused the Triad to address him as the lost one, one without a clan.

It was because of all this that he had little idea what she meant him to do. He did not wish to appear unworthy for the amulet, though none could forcibly remove it from him, even on death. He emptied his mind of though, finding the centre of being that all warriors needed to attain if they were to become masters. He then formulated an image of the amulet around his neck in his mind. It took little effort, and he focused his whole being around the device. After what seemed hours he felt his awareness spreading beyond his normal level. He found he could feel the presence of the Master Tenget before him, burning like a star in the darkness of the hidden world around him.

"You have found me, but search for others out there," said the Tenget softly.

He spread his awareness out further, searching for other lights in the night. His mind soared across the land, searching high and low. He travelled across plains, forests, swamps and lakes, stretching to the edge of his now vast awareness looking for other tengeti. Yet none could be seen and all was silent and dark. He returned to his own body with a heavy heart.

When his eyes opened he saw a painful flash of disappointment cross her face.

"My awareness never could reach that far, and I had hoped I was wrong. We are the last two tengeti of our race. The humans have almost succeeded in their quest, for we were among the best of our kind."

Groltch went cold. The only two tengeti left in the realm. That meant the humans had killed thousands and thousands of ran-tha in their cold-blooded war. Rage washed over him and he almost cried out in despair. Yet his control was there, as it always was and he pushed the pain away. He could not help his people in a cold mission of revenge. His failed attempt on the human king's life had shown him that. The only way he could divert the war was to somehow precipitate a new threat from other human kingdoms. That meant going to either Sol or Kolth. It meant remaining among humans and leaving this small haven behind. Yet he knew that he had to do it. The spirits of the glade had almost told him as much. They had spoken in his dreams. The salvation of his kin was in the darkness of the north, whatever that meant. He closed his eyes and renewed his blood vow.

As he opened them he noticed the Master Tenget looking at him with a strange light in her eyes. He opened his mouth to make an excuse to leave her company. She took his arm gently, halting the words before they were uttered.

"I see great things of you, Groltch, son of Mar-Loutch," she said softly, the look of the Sight passing briefly across her eyes. "Fear not. You are worthy of the title Tenget, for few could do what you have done thus far, or will do in times to come. Live on and fight, lost one, and bring us our salvation."

She turned away suddenly and ran quickly down a small alley. Groltch resisted the urge to follow, knowing he would probably find no trace of her passage. He turned and paced through the village, losing himself to thought on her words. It seemed only a moment before he was summoned for even-sup, yet he felt that he had aged years in that time. He began the meal and lost himself to the night's revels.

XV

Galen raced through the streets of Theldar in the Shadow Realm towards the eastern wall. A guard had reported that he had seen torch light approaching in great numbers and he was now on his way to confirm it. He emerged into the dark night of the real world just in front of a guard who started at his sudden appearance.

"Where are they?" he asked.

"Where do you think?" came a voice behind him.

He whirled round to see Sar Petra stood there, looking out over the wilderness beyond the walls. The knights had spent the night evacuating and evicting all whom lived outside the outer walls and then burnt it all, leaving the approaching army no cover close to the walls. He looked to the leader of the Circle of Steel.

"I got word shortly after you, my lord, and thought it best that I take a look myself," she replied to his unasked question.

He knew it to be a lie, for her quarters were close to his own and none could move as fast as he when travelling in the Shadow Realm. She had to have been informed first showing that the loyalty of the knights was connected to her.

"You will also need a guard, you realise. You would be the likely target of assassination now," she continued, ignoring his silent gaze.

He knew her ploy here. She wished to become more powerful

through close association with him. If she could gain his trust then it was possible he would be more amenable to her requests.

"Thank you for your concern," he said quietly. "I'll take your suggestion under consideration. Yet there is another more pressing matter to discuss."

He looked out over the wall for the first time and saw the approaching lights. They were evidently making no secret of their approach, probably hoping that their mere presence might induce surrender.

"How will the knights take to fighting their own kind?" he asked softly, so that the patrolling guard would not hear him.

"Well, for they follow us," she said, equally as quiet. "There have been a number of us that for some time had begun to question our training and teachings. Those of us in the higher ranks of the order ensured that those of a like mind were kept close in the event of an emergency such as this. Of course, many would reject you if they knew of your past."

Galen went quiet and felt a chill run down his spine. She knew his true nature. How she had found out he did not wish to know, but it was a complication he had hoped to avoid.

"How many know?" he asked softly.

"A few," she said with an edge of steel in her voice. "Enough to spread the word should I die in odd circumstances."

"Those days are over for me."

"Not entirely," she replied, glancing out over at the advancing torches. "You'll kill a few more before your life is out, I guarantee it."

He nodded and looked back out on the night.

"What will it cost me for your silence?" he asked, knowing that knowledge always had its price.

"Only that you take in a personal guard, for your own protection," she replied. "I've heard your plans and believe in them. I do not intend to lose you to some stray arrow or to an overzealous assassin."

Galen looked at her suspiciously. There had to be more than that, though he could not fathom at present what that may be.

"Very well," he replied with resignation. "How many would you *recommend*?"

"Not many," she replied. "Ten should suffice."

"Very well. Send them to my quarters at dawn. I think I'll need some sleep before then. I'll have to be fresh for this siege."

"As you wish," she replied with a bow. "I'll oversee these preparations and make sure no one starts getting jittery."

He nodded his ascent and made his way down the stairs. He could travel in the Shadow Realm, but always found it harder to keep himself together both emotionally and physically after such sojourns. Even now he was feeling weak and lightheaded. The world faded briefly around him and his stomach clenched tightly together in pain.

He stood still for a moment and collected himself together. He could feel the other self, the darker, more ancient self, pushing at him in his weakness, trying to take over completely, yet the old Galen was stronger, though not by much. He found himself wondering how long it would be before his old self lost. He pushed the thoughts from his mind and returned to the palace. He arrived to find his guard there waiting for him. She had evidently been confident of his answer. He nodded to them briefly then retired to bed, knowing that the morrow would be a long day.

XVI

Groltch staggered back to the hut he was staying with, supported between Belthar and Tristan. He had gotten himself well and truly drunk this night and felt all the better for it, though he knew he would regret it in the morning. The Greater Elder had taken the opportunity of the occasion to invite him to stay and Groltch had been highly tempted to agree and remain here. Yet he had seen the Master Tenget's eyes following him, though they had not spoken again, and he had refused. It had been then that he had begun consuming copious amounts of alcoholic beverages, knowing that this would be his first and last even-sup for a long time. Now he was being helped home by his best friends in the whole of Loden, as he had repeatedly told them all.

"Even you, Matt," he had said. "I knowsh you ushe magic an' everyfing but…you is still Groltch's friend."

The boy had seemed a little embarrassed by the show of emotion, though he too was a little worse for the alcohol. He recalled having sung a duet with the boy, though Matt had had to teach him the words. It had been a somewhat bawdy song about an elven maiden, or something. He could not really recall it now, though he was sure others would probably remind him in the morning. As he recalled, some ran-tho had blushed quite visibly at a few of the lyrics.

"Here's yer bed," said Belthar, helping him down to the floor. "Do yer need a bucket, or something?"

Groltch had been sick twice on the way here, but felt he would not need to do it again. His head had already cleared up somewhat and he was feeling much less queasy.

"Groltch fine," he said, lying down on the floor. The world began to spin so he closed his eyes and found that only made things worse. "You go back to sup. Not finished there yet. Groltch be out soon. Just needsh a resht."

"I think we're all done now. We've got an early start in the mornin', if yer recall," replied Belthar.

"An early morning?" asked Groltch, shuddering at the thought of such a thing.

He was going to feel very rough in the morning. The big man reached down and touched his forehead, which seemed to be spinning in all directions. The big man uttered a few soft words and the world righted itself. His head cleared and tiredness swept over him. Within moments his snores were reverberating around the hut.

XVII

Field Knight, Sar Alice of the Arrows of Northshire, moved slowly through the night camp, inspecting it in minute detail, or at least seeming to do it. They were now back on home territory and should be safe from attack, though she had only ever experienced one in her involvement in the Eastern war, as it was now being called. The goblins had put up little resistance in her battles, though she had heard reports of bloodier conflicts occurring deeper within the goblin lands. Yet that was of no consequence now. Her orders were simple, if a little unusual. She was to march immediately with her troops to the capital, Theldar, and aid in a siege. It had to be an exercise, though why it was necessary so soon after their conflict in Grelchin she had no idea. Her thoughts were disturbed by the sudden appearance of an advance scout. Old habits were difficult to lose, even in home territory.

"What's your report?" she asked of the Green Knight.

She knew that it would be the same as the other five she had already received, but the forms had to be observed.

"You'll not believe it, Sar," replied the soldier, sounding a little out of breath. "There's an enemy encampment not some five miles from here."

She looked at the man in surprise. An enemy encampment this far behind enemy lines had to be impossible. She reached out and used her talents to ensure that he spoke the truth. The result was equally surprising. There were indeed goblins in Caldor. Cold rage consumed her at the thought.

"How many?" she asked quickly.

"Only four hundred or so."

Four hundred, she was a Cyan Knight, leader of five hundred and that was more than enough to take the goblins. She had been involved in conflicts where their numbers had more than doubled her own.

"Very well," she replied. "Give your report to the Blue Knights and inform them that we break camp immediately. Then get some food."

"Yes Sar," replied the Green Knight with a swift bow.

She watched as he rushed off to the Blue Knights' tents, fuming silently at the thought of goblins polluting these precious lands with their devil worshipping ways.

"Come the dawn and they will pay for their insolence with their lives," she muttered quietly to herself.

She turned and returned to her command tent, instructing her squires to make ready her departure. Before the midnight hour had passed the five hundred troops were on route to the goblin encampment. By dawn, they were ready to attack.

CHAPTER THIRTEEN: Swords and Shields

I

Tristan was woken by a gentle shove from Belthar. He had not slept all that well during the night, partly due to Groltch's loud snoring and partly due to the confusion thrown up by what he had seen of the ran-tha village. Even knowing Groltch, he had not been prepared for what he had seen. Groltch was not some rare, noble exception to the general rule that his people were evil, much as Tristan had secretly hoped. He saw in these people the same values he had seen in his own village, and other human villages he had visited since. They had even had their own version of a taleweaver at the feast last night, telling tales in High Caldorian in honour of their human guests.

That had been the biggest shock of all. He had grown used to Groltch's broken accent and odd phrases of Caldorian, believing to the end that it was a sign of the ran-tha's lesser intelligence. Yet many in the village spoke his language fluently, something he doubted few humans could manage if the situation had been reversed. Everything he knew and believed was false, and he had had to face that fact last night. Their High Priest had spoken to him and they had touched upon religion. He had been able to see common elements in both their theologies, though they had both altered in the years of their political enmity. It had helped him come to terms with his feelings, however, for many ran-tha harboured similar feelings about humans, placing them as the worshipers of Thenril and that had allowed Tristan to feel that he was not alone in his former intolerance.

It had also helped to know that this village had been founded by Caldorians to aid the ran-tha fleeing the knights. It meant that there was hope for them all for greater understanding, if people could be shown this side of the story.

"Aren't you ready yet?" asked Matthius, disturbing his thoughts.

"Sorry," replied Tristan. "I am afraid I am still a little tired. How are you Groltch?"

"Tired and head hurts, but not as bad as I should be…after all that drink," came the whispered reply.

Evidently Belthar's magic last night had only lessened the effect of the drink, rather than removed it completely.

"You can thank Belthar for that," said Tristan, rapidly pulling on his clothing.

"'Twas nothing," said the druid with a shrug. "We needed to be goin' early and I didn't want you too hungover to move."

"Groltch thank you anyways," said the ran-tha, still keeping his voice low.

"We'd best be going now, before the village wakes up," said Matthius, also sounding a little worse for wear. "I've heard that ran-tha farewell ceremonies can go on quite some time."

Tristan had heard that too last night and could still remember the advice of the one they called the Greater Elder last night to leave before dawn. In ran-tha society that was often considered polite as it meant that the villagers would not have to throw a sumptuous farewell banquet. Only close friends would stay long enough to merit such attention, though their etiquette said that any departure should be met with a feast. Though they were not the evil creatures he had imagined them to be, they were still a strange lot, all things considered. He made his way outside and found Galahad had been saddled and provisioned already, probably on the instructions of the village elders.

He took a deep breath of the morning air and looked out at the false dawn. There was a crispness and cold bite about the air that reminded Tristan that autumn was drawing on. He wondered just how much time had passed from his flight from Theldar. It seemed an age ago since he had been King's Knight, though it was probably only a couple of months in actual time.

Belthar emerged from the hut, drawing in deep breaths of air as he did so. Matthius and Groltch, who were both looking a little off colour, quickly followed him.

"Shall we depart then?" asked Tristan.

"Certainly," said Belthar with a mock bow. "I wouldn't want to outstay my welcome."

The other two merely nodded their assent. Tristan turned Galahad about and led the way out of the village, pausing only once to glance back at the village. From his vantage point and in this light, it could have been any number of villages in Caldor. He sighed and continued out, wondering just where his life was going to lead him next.

II

Naithan looked at the golden spires and minarets of Zaron as the light of the dawn sun struck them, making them seem to almost glow. The domes and spires towered above the rest of the city that, though nothing compared to the dazzling white palace of Theldar, was impressive nonetheless. The streets were nothing like the sweeping avenues of his own marble city, seeming to crowd in upon each other. Buildings appeared to have been constructed in very much a haphazard manner that spoke of little planning. There was also too much colour and decadent display of wealth in what appeared to be the rich quarter of the city. Despite this there was a spirit and energy about the city, or at least so it appeared from on board his sister's flagship the *Golden Swan.*

The Prophet of Light, Sulan XXV, had been instructed of their arrival and of the pirate problems the day before, news to which the Royal Vizier, Zakar, had been suspiciously unsurprised about. They had agreed that the meeting should be at dawn, which suited Naithan's plans perfectly. He intended this to be the dawning of a new age in Solman history, and he wished the history books to record this symbolic event with relish.

As they neared the docks he saw the royal party gathered to greet him. There were around one hundred men and women gathered in their most colourful and expensive clothes, along with three elfants, upon one of which was probably seated the Prophet. Surrounding them were some two hundred black clad warriors, all members no doubt of the Shar-meer, the Solman elite royal guard.

Naithan waited in silence as the other ships of his fleet docked and off loaded their passengers and Naithan was proud to see the knights move out and line up in perfect formation. It had been worth the awkward difficulty of transporting their horses by ship just for that moment alone. It was only a shame that his most honoured knight, the King's Knight, was not there to finish the effect. Yet the man was still in Caldor and Naithan held on to the hope that he could take the man and bring him back into the light. He shook away the thoughts and looked to his friend.

"Will they be able to detect you from here?" he asked quietly.

"Not yet," replied Matthew. "Do you want me to start the spell now?"

"Yes," said Naithan, gritting his teeth.

Matthew muttered some arcane phrases and a breeze picked up around him.

"It's done," said Matthew softly. "They will now see you as a towering man of almost godly bearing. It's an old trick that others have used before, but it's the done thing. You're the most powerful man in your kingdom and you want to make it look like you're out to imprint that firmly on their minds."

"Thank you," replied Naithan dryly. "I'll take you're lessons on the Royal Game to heart."

Naithan knew why he had requested this trick. He wanted those ashore to think of him as a man inflated by his own importance, someone too arrogant to see through their machinations. He sighed wearily. The Royal Game, enjoyable as it could be, would be one of the first things to go when he finally converted all men to the rule of Toric. If god himself did not sanction disobedience and dissent, then Naithan certainly would not. He adjusted his robes nervously and turned his thoughts to other things. He was carrying as little magical protection as he could safely do to reinforce his anti-magic stance and his thoughts were not secure from the probing spells of the Prophet's wizards. He opened his mind outwards, neatly folding the parts he wished concealed under other thoughts of a similar, yet less dangerous nature. It was an old trick taught to him by his mother when he was younger and one that Naithan treasured dearly. *A man's thoughts were his own save unto Toric* she had frequently said to him when teaching him.

"Ready to go?" asked Matthew softly.

Naithan concealed his startled jump and merely nodded calmly, as if his pause had been wholly intentional. He had not even noticed the ship reach the pier. He mounted his horse and rode it out onto the deck, his appearance being announced by a loud fanfare of bugles and longhorns. He rode the horse to the gangplank and urged it cautiously onto the precarious walkway. He knew that magic was being used to ensure that the horse had a stable footing and that it could even see the wide pathway before him but Naithan still had to gulp down a shudder of fear. An invisible bridge of air constructed of magic was not the best thing to reassure him of an uneventful ride.

The horse lifted its head high and all but pranced across the thin wooden plank, making him twice as nervous as before. They had both trained at this but that was not all that reassuring. He kept his head high though and rode with the dignity befitting his status. As he reached the other side a long, royal blue carpet was rolled out before him by four servants, leading to the central elfant. He allowed himself to appear a little impressed and self-satisfied at their gesture as he rode his stallion onto it, before nodding to his knights as they knelt their horses as one before him.

The Solmen were not to be outdone on this point and all bowed as well, allowing their heads to fall a fraction below the height of his knights. What impressed him more, however, was the fact that all three elfants knelt with them, an impressive feat for creatures that size. They all raised their long grey noses and trumpeted together in a sound not too dissimilar to that of the buglers and it took all his strength to retain his composure in the presence of such creatures.

"Welcome to ye, Lord of Caldor," said a voice, booming out across the crowds. "I bid you greetings and happiness in all things."

"I thank ye most kindly," replied Naithan in his best Solmanese, the language of Sol. He dismounted and knelt down in a full bow, ignoring the startled gasps from his men. If it startled them, it would hopefully do the same to Sulan. "I humbly request permission to stay in your great city. I recognise your Lordship in this great land and do agree to obey you whilst within these borders."

Naithan risked a quick glance up from his prostrate position and saw, with relief, a host of satisfied smiles on the faces of Sulan's Viziers. Evidently he had bowed enough in accordance with their traditions, though the bow had been of the Caldorian type.

"Thank you for your kind words," said the voice, now much closer to him than before. "I bow to you and your glory."

Sulan proceeded to bow in accordance with Solman tradition, which was to go down on both knees and bow the face down until it almost touched the grounds. From the shocked gasps of the Solmen around him Naithan guessed that the bow was not a common one for the Prophet of Light to use. They stayed in their respective bows for what seemed like an eternity before they both rose to their feet as one.

"Your actions and hospitality do me honour, First Prophet," said Naithan quietly. "May my visit bring many blessings down upon your household."

The Prophet nodded in thanks then swept his arms towards the great elfant behind him.

"I have taken liberty to prepare you transport to my palace, if you would be gracious enough to accept it," said the man with a playful glint in his eye.

Naithan suddenly went cold. The man before him was evidently an expert in the Game of the Council. Sulan must have seen through his act of indifference to the great beasts and was now using his fear of them against him. Yet Naithan could not refuse an offer set in such away, especially as the elfant was one of the sacred animals of this realm and to ride one was to be blessed.

"Oh course I shall accept such a kind and generous offer," he replied with a slight bow of the head, trying to conceal a flash of panic. "And as we journey, perhaps we could begin our discussions on matters of state, such as the punishment of the pirates who waylaid me on my journey."

Sulan seemed momentarily taken aback, though only an experienced player of the Game would have noticed it. That gave Naithan a moment of hope and with that came the courage to approach the elfant kneeling before him. Sulan was good at the game, but not the best. Naithan knew he had a challenge on his hands, even with Matthew's aid, yet it would not be an impossible one. He stepped carefully onto the creature's outstretched leg and slowly pulled himself up into the small carriage upon its back. The Prophet leapt up quickly after him, showing an ease and grace that revealed his years of riding such beasts.

Naithan swallowed hard as the creature rose up to its feet and pointedly avoided looking down. As the beast began to move away towards the shining golden palace ahead, Naithan forgot his fears as he began to talk to Sulan. Though they only touched upon niceties initially, with Sulan pointing out the glories of his city, the Game had already begun and Naithan intended to win.

III

As the sun began its ascent over the marble city of Theldar, Gareth watched his troops as they began to surround his brother's dazzling city. His first hope of a quick and peaceful end to the revolt had been dashed upon his arrival. The gates had all been closed and men had armed the walls of the city, their weapons drawn in preparation. He had sent a squire to announce his arrival and had received jeers and taunts in return. Several had even dared loose arrows at the poor boy, even though he had ridden under the white flag of truce. He had not given up all hope though, for it was possible that the citizens would retreat once they realised that he would use armed force against them. It was for that reason that he was sending several units to the various gates, for he was going to try and force entry as quickly as possible whilst shedding the least amount of blood.

A squire came rushing towards him and stood before him in a full salute, breaking his train of thought. He nodded to the girl and indicated that she should speak.

"The troops are all in position, Sir and are ready to attack," she said breathlessly.

"Excellent," he replied quietly. "Inform the heralds to sound the attack."

"Yes, Sir," she replied.

She gave a quick salute before dashing off to relay his orders. He stood calmly and quietly, watching the heralds as they raised their trumpets to sound the attack. He hoped fervently that they would not break under the strain and that all went well. Almost all the knights he had here were not battle tested, as those who were had not yet returned from Grelchin.

The trumpets sounded and the knights moved as one towards the gate, letting out a great battle cry as they did. Almost at once, arrows began raining down into the troops and the deadly shower felled many of the attackers. He cursed angrily at the arrogance of those who had fallen.

None had truly believed that Caldorians would shoot arrows at them and had not raised their shields high to protect themselves from such an attack. Those who had survived the initial volley were now, rather belatedly, pushing their shields high, their lesson in war learned at a heavy cost.

The defenders immediately dealt another lesson out as the attackers looked to the skies for arrows. They had approached grouped together in order to attack the gates, not noticing that they had been left open to reveal the portcullis. As they looked up and raised their shields from their bodies, arrows flew out of the holes and cut into the unsuspecting attackers. More troops were cut down and Gareth decided that enough was enough. He had sent the force out merely as a test of the defenders' resolve and had been shown that it was one of steel. He motioned for a squire to approach. The same girl he had spoken to earlier approached.

"Sound a retreat," he said wearily, "then inform the commanders I would like to see them when the camp has been fully set up."

"Yes, Sir," she replied with a salute, swiftly running off to carry out her instructions.

He began to turn wearily to his tent as the retreat was sounded, but was brought about by the sounds of trumpets from the city itself. He looked back and saw with horror that the portcullis was rising swiftly and that there were mounted knights riding out at them. He called for the head runner.

"Quickly," he said, trying to hold down his horror. "Instruct the commanders to organise a defence. Get archers out there. Cover their retreat and have pike-men set up lines of defence. Go!"

The young man turned swiftly, calling to his runners to pass on the messages quickly. Gareth cursed himself angrily. The sloppy defences and responses of the goblins had made him complacent and he had not even bothered to set up the most rudimentary necessities of an attack. He was now about to pay for such laxity. He rushed to his own troops and called for them to mount up as the thundering sound of the city's horses grew louder. He could hear the screams of the dying men and did not need to look to see whose men were dying.

"Let's go," he said angrily to the nearest of his commanders.

"But Sir, you can't lead men…"

Gareth cut him off with a move of his hand.

"I can and I will," he growled, driving his spurs into Peggy's flanks.

He rode out towards the city and led his knights directly at those who were now in his camp causing so much chaos and destruction. As he drew nearer the knights of the camp saw him and soon their discipline began to override their confusion. Yet just as that began to occur, the signal for retreat was sounded and the Theldarian knights broke off their attack, retreating in an orderly fashion that made Gareth's face flush in shame and anger. He bellowed out the command to charge and raced after the retreating riders. At his back he could hear others calling to him but their voices became insignificant as rage consumed him.

He smiled triumphantly as he neared the back of the last of the Theldarians, a smile that soon dropped from his face as arrows began falling around him. He wheeled Peggy frantically round towards his own camp, feeling a stab of fear as an arrow glanced off his armour. That should not have happened as he had a protective shield spell around him. Cursing more than ever he started his return gallop, only to feel a searing pain rip through his shoulder. His head screamed in pain and the world spun around him. The last sensation he felt as darkness swept over him was of the taste of mud and blood in his mouth.

IV

Galen watched the battle with adrenaline surging through his body. He could not believe that the plan had worked so successfully, though part of him seemed to feel no surprise at all. More astounding than that, however, was the fact that he had even enticed their commander out onto the field. The man was truly a fool. He commanded the soldiers of the battlements to loose their arrows at the knights charging towards the city. He saw the panicked looks on their faces as they wheeled their horses around in an attempt to escape. But nothing could stop him now. The commander of the besieging troops was in range and Galen intended to make use of it. Arrows rained down on them and he realised, with horror, that none seemed to be touching him. Many even ricocheted off in different directions as if striking an invisible shield.

Magic. The word sliced coldly through him, bringing a horror he could barely contain. If they had magic, they could not be beaten. Yet he could win here and now, came a thought from deep inside of him. He was not subject to the usual laws, by his very nature. His arrows would pass through the shield. He grabbed a bow and some arrows off a nearby munitions boy who was running passed. He notched an arrow, aimed and released, completely oblivious to the fact that he had never used such a weapon before and that he should not have been so adept at it. The arrow flew true, slicing through the invisible shield. Yet its presence knocked the arrow off course and it merely glanced off the knight's shoulder. He notched another arrow and released, taking into account the angle of deflection, and this one struck flesh. A flash of triumph danced across his face as the knight fell from his galloping horse. It soon turned to anger though as another knight turned back and bent over the fallen form. By his shouts it was obvious that the commander was still alive. Soon others were running towards the fallen man.

"Release your arrows at them," he commanded and another volley of arrows flew from the walls.

They all burst into flame, however, and disappeared into dust. He commanded another volley to be fired and that suffered the same fate. He knew then that he had lost his moment and his slim chance of victory was over. He commanded them to cease and walked away slowly to his chambers. He sat down in the darkness of his windowless room and glared angrily into the still glowing embers of his fire, losing himself to dark thoughts. He had never even thought that he could come up against such magic. He stood no chance against such opposition. He heard the cheers of the city erupt at their victory and shuddered at the thoughts of their jeers when he announced their surrender. He would not lead people into such a hopeless fight.

A knock on the door made him start and he sat in silence, hoping they would go away. The knock came again, this time with more force. When he answered with silence once more the person behind the door spoke.

"I know you are in there," came the familiar voice of Sar Petra, "and I know why you are skulking there as well. You fear the magic."

Galen looked swiftly to the door, suspicion sweeping over him.

"What would you know of magic?" he asked slowly.

"Only that knights use it, and not just those outside these walls," came a voice to his right.

A ball of soft yellow light appeared before him, lighting up the room in an almost natural light and he saw that she was stood at the opposite end of the room from the door. He sneered at the ball of light before him.

"What good are parlour tricks such as this against magic that burns up arrows?" he asked bitterly.

"What seems like a simple parlour trick to some can be a deadly weapon in the hands of another," she said cryptically.

The glowing ball suddenly shot towards the hearth and exploded in a ball of flame. The darker, magically tainted half of himself recoiled in horror at the nearness of such a destructive force, yet before the ball had left he had felt not a single twinge of danger. The ring's powers seemed able to detect threats to its safety yet had been fooled by her trick. She was evidently quite powerful.

"I see you understand the significance of what I just did," she said with an amused gleam in her eye. "Knights rarely go far in the Order if they are not blessed with such power, and many of my order are here and loyal to you, my liege."

He looked at her carefully as his brain fully digested the news it had received. With the power she was offering they might well stand a better chance than he had ever hoped of succeeding. Yet he could never allay the suspicions that constantly stalked the dark recesses of his mind.

"What would you ask in return for the use of such gifts?" he asked.

"Only that the Light speak first and the Steel speak last in all matters of debate and vote," she replied softly.

Galen was surprised at the seeming lack of importance of such a request. It took a moment to fully understand the intention. The Circle of Steel seemed somehow constantly opposed to the Circle of Light and the ability to speak last in a debate would be of great advantage to them. They would have time to consider counter arguments to those presented by the Light and their words would be the last heard on voters' minds, adding more weight to their worth. Sar Petra was a very clever woman indeed, yet he needed her magic to win this conflict.

"Agreed," he said, closing his eyes briefly in resignation. "Now go and make the arrangements necessary to protect us from their magic."

"As you command, my liege," she said, giving a slightly mocking bow. "Though I would warn you, beware the eyes of the Light, for I am sure I see a plot against you within them."

Galen nodded his head in understanding. He already had similar suspicions of his own. He had sent Marie to spy on them and report any plots they may have directly to him. He would have used Meredith and her hawks, but she seemed to be getting too close to Tyrone, and both seemed hostile to the power of the Circle of Steel. Marie was the only one he could trust and by sending her away from him, he was also saving her from further pain and suffering. He felt himself fade away once more and turned his thoughts away from the precious woman.

He cursed himself and solidity returned to his form. He was above such emotions as love, and yet, somehow he was not. He stood and began pacing the room in frustration, his thoughts turning to Marie once more. He had sent her away to save her from more pain, yet he had sent her into a situation that could lead to more physical harm.

Sickened at himself and his manipulations he turned towards the door and opened it wide, allowing the light of the day to flood in. It washed away his thoughts as he heard the cheers of the crowds and the thoughts of Marie dwindled under the thrill of the public exultation he would feel once more. He was a battle leader once more and the humans would worship him for it.

V

Groltch walked quietly through the woods, content that at least some of his people were safe. It had been a glorious time and he had thought briefly of remaining there with them, yet their confinement would have been too much for him. He knew that they were still only living there by human consent and that if the human knights were to discover their location, they would be killed without a thought. He had to seek out help for his people, for their stories led him to believe that there were not many of his kind left. He was still left with that haunting feel of emptiness the amulet had left him when he had sought out other Tengeti. For so many to be dead did not bode well for others of his kind. Kolth was his only hope, though he had no idea how he was going to set about gaining their support. He just had to hope that he could find some way once he reached there.

Screams from behind him destroyed his reverie and he spun around, fear mounting inside him. The trees behind them blocked his view yet he was sure he knew what was happening. More screams erupted into the air and he clearly heard the sounds of battle. Anger filled him and reason left him. He sprinted back down the path towards the village, ignoring the cries of his companions. He emerged onto the ridge above the valley it was set in and looked down on a scene of carnage and bloodshed. Knights were riding through the tracks, cutting down ran-tha on all sides, yet many were fighting desperately to stay alive. Magical fire exploded onto those groups where resistance was greatest and especially upon one figure, who seemed as yet untouched by such magicks. The Master Tenget stood in the midst of the swarming knights, her sash-wa blades spinning in a dazzling dance of death. None could get near her and live, but she was old, even among the Elders, and she was weakening quickly.

Without a thought he ran down the ridge into the fray, his long staff bringing down a knight from its horse. As it lay there on the ground, momentarily stunned, Groltch saw an opening in its metal shell around its neck. He brought the staff down hard and crushed its windpipe, leaving it gasping for air on the ground. He took up its sword and discarded his staff, forgetting his vow to Tristan. Knights were killing his people and no vow would have made him hold back from fighting them.

He lashed out at the next knight to approach him, flicking its sword from its hand into his own. Now armed with two swords, he cut the knight down as it looked at him in surprise. Groltch paid that little attention however, and focused on the whirling melee of Master Tenget. The swords twirled in his hands as he attacked the next knight his skill far out matching that of the human before him.

Yet it was still an annoyance, just one more delay that prevented him from reaching his goal. Another knight attacked, swirling its blade in an impressive offensive pattern. Groltch found himself momentarily on the defensive and rapidly lost one of his swords. Thinking swiftly, he grabbed for Belthar's dagger at his side. He then spun out of the knight's reach, forcing him to move in to attack. Groltch blocked the knight's sword blade with his own and locked it momentarily with the hilt. He used that moment to bring the dagger round in one swift move. Its thin, pointed blade slid through the protective chain and into the human's kidneys. The knight doubled over in pain as Groltch twisted the blade, then the human collapsed to the floor as his sword came down on the its exposed neck.

Groltch moved away and attacked another knight, bringing it down with a ruthless efficiency that he would not have credited himself with, and with that knight's fall he found himself facing the Master Tenget.

"Well met," she said breathlessly, appearing glad for the respite. She saw the concern in his eyes and smiled. "I'm not as young as I was."

"Is there anything I can do to help?" he asked, spinning to block another knight's blade as he did.

"There's always the meld of course," she replied, placing her back to his.

Groltch winced as her elbow jarred into his back. Their styles were not compatible, though ran-tha sword styles rarely were. They were just too independently minded to co-operate in such a way, though that was what the meld had been designed for. It was the sole purpose of the amulets that hung around their necks. It allowed them to meld their thoughts and actions together so that they fought as one. In years gone by there had been armies of such warriors, all fighting in unified groups, defeating all who came against them. That had been before the Breaking of course, the cataclysm that had turned their lands to the swamps they were now.

Another elbow jabbing him in the back reminded him of where he was and what he was doing. He brought his sword round and another knight fell to his blade. A meld had its problems of course, and was quite a risk to take as it could often lead to the deaths of both parties if the meld was not completed successfully. He felt her sag against his back and knew there was no choice. A meld was the only option. He stepped forward and cut down yet another knight to give him a moment's breath.

"Let's us bond as one," he intoned, dredging up the memories of the ritual from his early lessons.

"My mind to your mind, your mind to mine," she said, fiercely cutting down the knight in front of her and turning to face him.

"My heart to your heart, your heart to mine," he replied, grasping hold of the amulet. It began to grow warm in his palm.

"As one we stand, as one we fall," she replied, finishing the brief mantra.

They placed their amulets together and they flared up with light. A part of Groltch's mind noted that the knights around them fell back at this, yet it was soon swept away under the power of the meld. He felt energy course through him and a multitude of visions flashed through his mind. Experiences and thoughts of the Master Tenget swamped his mind, from her birth to the present moment. In the split of a moment he knew more about her than any being alive save herself. The feeling was exhilarating, though only lasted a moment for at that point all individual thought stopped. They were now one and they fought as one.

Their blades flashed out in dazzling patterns that combined their two styles in perfect formation. As they moved through the knights their weapons slashed out relentlessly, hacking down knights in all directions. Suddenly magic lashed down at them, striking at their bond and they screamed as one, both doubling over in pain. A knight took advantage of this, bringing its sword down upon them. They screamed in pain and knew death was upon them. Yet it did not come, either in magical or physical form. They looked up and saw that all was confusion. Flames erupted everywhere around them, burning up knights as it did. A vast creature tore at others, ripping them to pieces with its claws and teeth and in another part of the village, Death rode in on a white stallion.

They turned their thoughts away from these strange visions and pushed away their pain. With a cry of battle lust they leapt once more into the fray and more knights fell to their blades. The battle raged on around them and everything seemed to blur as one. Pain and anger flooded through their brain as blades came down upon them. They retaliated in kind, ripping open great wounds and driving in killing blows. The din of battle rang in their ears and then suddenly it all became too much for them. The world turned black and their fight was over.

VI

Tristan heard the cries and screams and looked back towards the village. He was in time to see the small form of Groltch disappearing down the path. He called out to stop him yet the ran-the seemed oblivious to his cries.

"Wouldn't you be, if Caldorians were being attacked?" asked Caliburn in his mind.

Tristan ignored the sword and turned Galahad around to bring him back to the ridge that overlooked the village. Belthar and Matthius followed him, both seeming a little stunned at the noise. It was a feeling soon shared by Tristan as he looked out over the bloody melee in the village below. Knights were rampaging between the houses, cutting down ran-tha as they went. Tristan went cold with fear and anguish. If they knew whom it was they were killing, the knights would stop, of that he was sure. Yet he had no idea how he could stop them; let them see what he had seen.

"*Wake up and see what's plain before you,*" said Caliburn's voice angrily in his mind. *"They are killing innocent creatures and there is no way they will stop. You have to do something!"*

"We have to do something," said Matthius, echoing the sword's words.

"Groltch seems to be doing well enough," he said, somewhat more coldly than he had meant.

It was true though. The ran-the had gotten hold of a sword from somewhere and seemed to be carving his way through the knights towards the old Weapons Mistress they had met last night.

"Yes, but there's so many of them. We have to help," continued Matthius.

The boy seemed unable to take his eyes off the battle below. They saw a sudden flash of light strike out against the Weapons Mistress then fade away.

"In Cal's name, they've got magic!" said Matthius in horror. "Torslud. They don't stand a chance."

"She survived it, did she not?" he asked looking round at the boy.

"How can yer be so bloody cold?" asked Belthar with a dangerous rumble in his voice. "After all these people did fer us? Yer willin' t'just stand here and watch 'em die? Well I won't do it."

As the last words left Belthar's mouth they became a vicious snarl and suddenly his face began to contort as a large, tooth filled muzzle emerge and the eyes lost their milky white colouring. His huge frame twisted and turned until it had completely transformed into something different. Yet it was not the form of a bear, as Tristan had expected. The creature before him seemed like some kind of hybrid between man and bear. Its shape was vaguely humanoid, yet much larger than any human Tristan had ever met. Its body was covered with fur and muscle and its human like hands ended in claws. Most frightening of all, however, was the visage of the creature. It had lost all semblance to that of a human, snarling like a rabid creature, except in its eyes. They were no longer the milky white of Belthar, or the deep brown of a bear, but tawny yellow eyes that seemed part human, part beast. Behind them lay a cold, intelligent, yet terrifying rage that seemed to cut straight through Tristan.

The creature that was Belthar turned and raised its muzzle to the air in an angry roar, before racing down the hill. As Tristan watched the beast go in stunned amazement he noted that Groltch had met up with the Weapons Mistress and they now appeared to be fighting as if possessed by demons. He could barely recognise Groltch's weapon style as they fought and found himself almost hypnotised by their dazzling movements.

"How can you think about things like that when people are dying?" asked Caliburn in horror.

"They are not people, they're goblins," replied Tristan, forgetting to keep it to his mind in his anger.

The sword's presence faded from his mind and he instantly regretted his remark. He saw that Matthius was looking at him in disgust.

"You think you're so pure and righteous," he said softly, anger lacing his voice with steel. "Yet you stand here and allow these people to die because they are not human! You disgust me!"

"Well I do not see you down there fighting," retorted Tristan venomously.

A flash of light disturbed them and they saw Groltch and the Weapons' Mistress double over. Matthius muttered some words and swung both his arms round in a wide arc, sending a beam of fire into several knights.

"That is because I don't need to be in the middle of the battle to fight it," said Matthius, turning his back on Tristan as he spoke.

Tristan walked away and felt Caliburn fall from his side. He glanced down at the sanctimonious blade in disgust. No one here could possibly understand what he was going through. The knights down there stood for all that he had once believed in and he could not bring himself to accept that everything was false. He had to have faith in the knights, all of whom had been fooled like him.

He looked back at the battle and gazed at the horrors of war, something he had never been close to before. He found himself able to pick out the tiniest details, even from a distance. He could see a knight fall to the savage attacks of Belthar, his body literally being ripped apart. He could see Groltch and the female goblin cutting down humans with ruthless efficiency. Elsewhere there were knights collapsing to the floor in flames, struck down by Matthius' magic.

Yet it was only in these small pockets of resistance that any knights were being harmed. In most other areas of the village it was the goblins…the ran-tha…who were being killed. Some held weapons in their hands, yet others did not, and some were cut down even as they fled. Suddenly one scene caught his eye and he found himself looking down on a ran-the mother with child. She was on her knees and holding her arm up as if that would stave off the sword of a knight stood towering above her. He could not see her face but she was obviously pleading with him for mercy. The knight's mouth moved in reply and Tristan saw the words he spoke as clearly as if he had heard them. *No mercy.*

No mercy. The words rang in his mind accompanied by a cold shiver down his spine. Mercy was the first and greatest of all virtues a knight could aspire too. All knights were told that in training and all believed in it, the only code known to have come from Sir Caldor himself. At least that was what he had thought before. Evidently that too was a lie. At that realisation, the last flame of his ideals spluttered and died and a part of Tristan died with it. He walked over to the sword still lying in the grass and knelt down to retrieve it. He felt some resistance as he pick it up and also felt it tremor slightly. He drew it from its scabbard and walked slowly to Galahad, cold rage slowly consuming him. He mounted up and raised Caliburn up to the heavens.

"Today I die," he said softly to himself.

Galahad reared up onto his hind legs and Tristan galloped into the battle, his sword lashing out with deadly accuracy as he did. Within moments the icy battle rage had taken him and battle was all he knew.

VII

Matthius was more than a little stunned by the apparition that tore past him and thundered down towards the village. The brief glimpse of the knight he had caught had shown him that something had changed in him. There had been a look behind Tristan's eyes that had sent a shiver of fear down his spine. Yet he could not let it distract him. The knights in the field had been surprised by his sudden attack and he believed he had disabled the most powerful of the knights, yet it seemed that all of them had some passing familiarity with the arcane arts. Some had even begun returning his attacks, though they had generally been inept attempts that had posed no real threat.

A knight reared out of the bushes with a yell, startling Matthius and breaking his train of thought. Panic gripped his mind and he stumbled backwards, his arms flailing about as if acting alone from his body. The knight before him grinned viciously and raised his sword up to bring down the killing blow. Spells tumbled like water through his thoughts and he found he could catch none to defend himself. His thoughts whirled in furious circles, panic pushing them faster and faster.

Suddenly a snarling black shape leapt from the bushes and bore the knight down to the ground. The sudden disappearance of the threat focused his mind and a spell flashed up before him. Without a thought he unleashed it at the fallen attacker and flames consumed him. Matthius was immediately sickened by the dying man's screams and he averted his eyes from the sight of burning flesh melting from bone. A shudder went through him as the smell reached his nostrils and then, all at once, it was gone. He looked back and saw blackened remains smouldering on the floor before him, though only of his human attacker. Of the black creature that had saved him, there was no sign.

His confusion was soon forgotten, however, as he felt the tingle of power run through him. Somehow he felt more alive than he had a mere few moments ago and he could not understand why. Normally, the magical energies would have left him feeling tired and drained, yet now he felt more vibrant than he had before the battle had even begun. The energy filled him and thrilled him to the point of insensibility.

He turned back to the battle and unleashed more spells at the knights. Several fell down dead, yet Matthius barely noticed. The ecstasy of using the magic was upon him and all other considerations had faded to insignificance. Energy flowed through him, lashing out at knights in all directions. Some threw up magical shields to protect themselves and he found himself laughing in manic delight at their pathetic attempts. He was alive with magic and none could stop him. More and more energy filled him and with each wave of magic came a greater awareness of life. Already he could hear sounds of life from miles around, and he also found that he could see minute details on the people involved in the battles below.

A small voice in his head called for caution and cried out that something was wrong. One of his age and experience should not be able to wield so much power. It also warned him of the consequences of using too much magic, yet Matthius ignored it. Around him he was aware of voices calling to him, yet he heeded nothing. No one here could stop him from wielding his magic. He was invincible. Energy coursed through his veins and he cried out in ecstasy.

Suddenly the flow stopped and disappeared. He groped desperately for the energy but found himself shielded from it but some outside force. He tried to lash out at it to break himself free, yet he was too weak to break through. The real world then broke through to his senses and his body began quivering with exhaustion. He saw that Tristan was stood before him, concern creasing his face.

"I am sorry," he said quietly. "I had to do it, or else you would have burnt yourself out."

Confusion muddled through Matthius' mind. Tristan could not have shielded him. He could not even stand other people using of magic, so there was no way on Loden he would stoop to using it himself. The confusion cleared suddenly as an explosion of pain ran throughout his now burning muscles. Yet the moment of clarity was only brief for immediately afterwards came the darkness of unconsciousness…

VIII

Tristan looked at the carnage and destruction left after the battle. Bodies littered the battlefield and, most disturbingly, the majority of them were knights. Somehow, against the odds, the ran-tha had succeeded in pushing back the knights. In fact, if Caliburn was to be trusted, those who had managed to withdraw from the conflict had done so in a rather disorderly manner, scattering out in all directions, meaning the victory was truly theirs. It was only a small victory, however, as they all knew that the knights would be back, and probably in greater numbers than before. It was for that reason that the ran-tha had begun preparations to leave almost immediately on the finish of the battle. They were very organised, dividing tasks up equally to ensure that everything was seen to, including the bodies that received proper funerary rites, even the bodies of the knights.

He looked away, the sight of so many dead threatening to overwhelm him. He especially wished to avoid the bodies of those men and women he personally had killed. The images of their faces were all too vivid within his mind. He had not known any of those he had killed, the Caldorian army had grown too large for such intimacy, and for that Tristan thanked Toric for his small mercies. Even so, their presence haunted him and he had to struggle to push them to the back of his mind. He walked over to Matthius's unconscious form and watched Belthar as he tended to the boy.

"He'll be fine," muttered the big man without turning round. "I don't know what yer did to 'im but it doesn't look permanent."

"Good," replied Tristan, turning away again.

That was another problem he did not wish to face. He had used magic in this battle, its power being one of the few reasons he still lived now. He hated himself for it, and for the fact that he burned with the desire to do it again. Half of what he had done had been under the guidance of Caliburn and he could probably not recreate the effects even if he tried. That shield he had thrown around Matthius was one such example. It had been very painful to do it and for a moment he was able to feel just how much magical energy the boy had been channelling. It had been amazing. Had Tristan tried to hold even a tenth of the power it would have torn him asunder. He was certain that the shield had only worked because the boy had not been expecting it.

He turned his thoughts away again, trying to avoid any such feelings. He decided to seek out Groltch whom he had last seen nursing the Weapons Master. He wandered through the streets, pointedly ignoring the bodies being carted away by the ran-tha, and made his way to where he had last seen Groltch. It was only a few minutes before he found them, and from the look of things, they had not moved. They appeared to be talking to each other in that strangely lyrical language of theirs.

He moved closer, not wishing to intrude yet desiring Groltch's company. As he moved, he gained a clearer view of the Weapons' Mistress's wounds. She had a deep wound in the stomach, one that would eventually prove fatal, though the passage to death would be long and painful. It was a wound that even the most skilled of priests would have had difficulty healing. He saw a dagger in Groltch's hand and tears in the ran-the's eyes, and a cold shudder went down his spine. Killing the Weapons' Mistress was the best option, but he was not so certain that he could do it if he were in Groltch's position.

He moved to leave, determined not to see the act, yet the Weapons' Mistress saw him and beckoned him closer. He knelt beside her and took hold of her outstretched hand. She grasped his hand briefly, before reaching to her neck. She removed something from her neck and placed it in his palm.

"You fought well today," she said softly in Caldorian. "You are a true master, wear this and remember, always, what happened today. Whatever else happens in your life, see this and remember. Let it be your strength."

Blood began to spurt from the wound in her neck that Groltch had just formed with the dagger. She looked to the ran-the and smiled.

"Mish'nar, Groltch, Tenget di Mathen'ra fel," she said, the light of life fading from her eyes.

"Stel'nar masnit di Toric, Mar-tenget Maslatch di Glatch-nar," replied Groltch, gently closing her lifeless eyes. "Match-nar di'na vel dis."

With these words Groltch placed the dagger in his own palm and drew it sharply across it, drawing blood as he did. The ran-the looked to Tristan, tears and anger in his eyes.

"I swear here to bring down king and bring misery to all who hurt my people," he said, hatred flowing from his voice. "That which she gave you will show you why."

He looked down at the item she had given him and saw that it was an amulet like the one around Groltch's neck. He placed it round his neck and for an instant flashes of another life tore through his mind. He staggered as if struck by an unseen force and for a few moments was unable to think. When his thoughts cleared, there came a burst of knowledge, years of practise in weapons, some of which he had never seen before, let alone used. Yet he knew if he had been given any one of them at that moment he would have been able to wield it as if he had used it all his life.

"An Amulet of Life," murmured Caliburn with an almost reverent whisper. *"You must be the first human to wear one since the time of Caldor."*

The Amulet of Life? Asked Tristan.

"A powerful item that allows to ran-tha to merge their lives and experiences in such a way that they can fight in perfect unison. It was once the only way that ran-tha could fight as units rather than individuals," replied Caliburn, not really clarifying the situation for Tristan.

"We must leave," said Groltch, breaking Tristan's thoughts. "Best if we go now. Sooner I go, sooner I can return."

Tristan nodded in agreement and moved away to where he had left Galahad tethered. As he did he noticed that he felt the presence of Groltch move away and the amulet grew a little colder. He touched it and for a brief second an emptiness filled him, one that he knew should not have existed. For that brief moment he was truly aware of how many ran-tha had been killed by his people. Anger and rage filled him, washing away the feelings of sorrow he had felt for the knights only minutes ago. He touched the hilt of the sword at his side softly.

As soon as we are gone from here I want you to teach me everything there is about magic, he said coldly.

The sword seemed to almost quiver at his side.

"As you wish," replied the sword meekly.

They saw to Galahad and they were soon joined by the others, Matthius now conscious and seemingly ignorant of the events of the battle, including his own part in it. It took them but a few minutes to prepare to leave and before the sun had hit its midday peak they were once more on the move, headed north towards the Kolthon Empire.

IX

Tyrone looked out over the battlements at the troops beyond. It had been almost a week now since their arrival and initial, only attack. It seemed as though they were content to wait for the moment. It was quite probable that they were presently waiting the full recovery of their commander. His sources had informed him that the arrow wound he had received had festered somehow, almost killing Prince Gareth, and without him, the army seemed at a loss as to what to do. Yet it was not those troops he was looking for. He still had the other report provided by his sources in his hand. The true heir to the throne, the Earl of Seronshire, the previous queen's elder brother was on his way to the city. For some reason, the past few generations of kings and queens had not succeeded by the traditional law of first born rule and that was no doubt the reason for the growing corruption among them. It had been under Queen Anne that many of the new laws had been enforced, including the one that had taken his son from him.

The blast of several bugles broke him from his reverie and he looked out across the walls. In the distance he could see movements of horses and soldiers emerging from the northern, eastern and southern forests. The armies of Lord Anton and his allies had arrived, exactly as expected. Now all he had to do was convince Galen to allow them in. There would be no more bloodshed. No Caldorian would be forced to fight his kith and kin. He turned and left the battlements, meeting up with Meredith as he did.

"They're here then?" she asked softly. He looked at her in alarm. He had not told her of the plans of the Circle of Light. "You didn't think your plots would go unnoticed, did you?"

"Have we been that obvious?" he asked quietly.

"Only to those who know where to look. I think it best that you revise your plan though," she replied.

"What do you mean?" he asked quickly.

"Galen will never agree to the coronation of a new king, and the circle of steel will be against you as well. They all see benefits to a continuing freedom. You've heard some of Galen's speeches. He is becoming enamoured with the ideals of leadership and justice."

"And the Dark Circle?" he asked slowly.

"I speak for them and I cannot guarantee that they will support you. I believe we are evenly divided and mine would be the casting vote," she replied.

"Then the matter would be decided. You will vote with me."

"It is not that simple," she replied wearily. "It has become common knowledge that I share your bed as well as your views. It would be seen as favouritism on my part and I would find the vote would turn against me."

"Then you'll vote against me?" asked Tyrone, barely keeping the hurt from his voice.

"I don't want to have to vote on this matter at all," she replied quickly, placing her hand on his arm, "and if we play it correctly, I won't have to."

"You have a plan?"

"Of course I do. It's quite simple really. With a simple move we can neutralise Galen and alienate him from the Circle of Steel."

"You mean that we should reveal his past, as the Shadow?" he asked, his mind running over the possibilities.

"Yes, and not just to the Triad, but to the populous in general," she replied. "We will use his own weapons against him. He has often talked of the need for popular support. If we remove that from him he will be nothing. He will not be able to stop us from opening the gates and allowing the new king entry."

"When would you suggest you do it?" he asked.

"As soon as possible. If we don't we'll lose the initiative and could find ourselves caught short."

"You know, it's times like this when I realise just why I like you," said Tyrone with a playful smile.

"You mean to say it's not due solely to my ravishing good looks," she replied, a smile playing across her face.

"Well," began Tyrone, losing himself for the moment in the banter, "there is always…"

They continued in this fashion as they worked their way through the streets, heading towards the small headquarters of the Circle of Light. Unbeknownst to either of them, a small, almost shadowy figure that had been following turned abruptly away, heading towards the palace, in search of Galen Faithe.

X

Gareth felt a wave of dizziness and nausea sweep over him as he rose unsteadily to his feet.

"Sir," said the chief healer at his side, "I really must protest. You are not yet strong enough to leave your bed. The sickness you suffered took a lot of energy from you. It will be at least another week until I would be prepared to declare you fit for duty."

"Well I'm Prince of the Realm and not subject to your reports," replied Gareth angrily. "I have idled enough time outside these walls and intend to be back on the offensive immediately. I can't well direct the battle from within this wretched tent now, can I?"

The priest looked a little startled, and maybe even a little afraid, yet he stood his ground before the entrance.

"There are others that can see to the battle, if you wish to attack the city. Why only this morning Lord Anton and..." the priest trailed off quickly as he realised what he had said. Evidently they had not believed him well enough to meet with his uncle.

"That settles it then," he said, glowering angrily at the man. "My uncle would see it as a great insult to him that I had not greeted him as soon as I was able and I am able now. Squires, dress me."

The tone of voice he used brooked no refusal and suddenly the tent was a flurry of action. Squires raced to prepare him for his meeting and Gareth found himself fighting to control his vision. He reached out to the magic briefly and cast a small spell to settle his stomach, though the effort of casting it almost saw him collapsing completely and his vision blurred violently. When he was able to see clearly once more he found that the squires had ceased in their work.

"Did you not hear me when I said quickly?" he asked, all but growling in anger.

The squires went white and doubled their pace. Within moments he was fully dressed and ready to meet with his uncle. He took up his staff of office, primarily to remind his uncle of his position, but also because he knew that he would have need of its support, and swept out of the tent. At least that was the intention. He found that such movements made his dizziness worse, and so he dropped to a slow dignified march towards the blue and yellow tent of Lord Anton.

He brushed aside the guards at the entrance and walked in unannounced. His uncle looked up, seeming momentarily surprised at Gareth's arrival but it was swiftly replaced by that ingratiating smile of his that always set Gareth on edge. He had never had much time for his uncle who seemed to have spent most of his life in a useless search of hedonistic pleasure. Yet he was here and with him were two other Shire Lords, the Hanton brothers Darren and Lewis. It appeared, from the relative bustle from the three new camps around him that all three had arrived almost exactly together, as if it had been planned that way.

He pushed the suspicious thoughts away. His uncle was many things, a drunkard, a lecher and a violent man, yet he was no traitor.

"Greetings, uncle," he said with a short bow.

"Greetings to you, eldest nephew," replied Anton with a bow of his own. "We were not expecting you up and about so soon. We had heard your health was not as it should be and deemed it necessary to begin tactical discussions in your absence. Had I known you were healthy enough to join us I would have waited, though I feel it vital that we begin the recovery of the king's city immediately."

"I take no offence at your actions," replied Gareth formerly. "Your concern for my brother's city echoes my own and it gladdens me to see it. What conclusions have you reached?"

"Well the first is to wait a while, to allow our troops to make camp properly and to allow the people in Theldar to see the full might of the troops arrayed against them," began Anton slowly. "If we are lucky then we will only have the casualties of your initial assault upon our consciences."

Gareth had expected the barb and there it was. He and his uncle, though always politely formal to each other, had never been very close. In fact, there existed more antipathy between them than either would care to admit and Anton could not have avoided mentioning Gareth's reckless charge. Yet now was not the time for petty rivalry and so he ignored it, vowing to ignore any other such comments thrown at him as well.

"And if our numbers are not enough to scare them into a peaceful submission?" he asked.

"Then we will have to fight them of course, and crush them that they may never rise again. No one should be allowed to rebel against the authority of the king."

Gareth was surprised by the anger in his uncle's voice and eyes as he spoke those words. He stifled it, however and turned his matters to those of the siege. His uncle and the Hanton brothers proved to be able strategists and he found himself talking with them well through the day. He became so engrossed that he almost forgot his recent weakness until his legs threatened to give way beneath him. He begged leave to retire and staggered back to his tent shivering as the afternoon heat began to fade. Autumn was fast approaching and he needed to be inside that city soon. He did not much fancy a winter siege.

He retired to his quarters and lay there a while, thoughts and plans of the up and coming battles playing through his mind. The illness won out however and he soon found himself drifting off to sleep. His dreams were filled with death and destruction, war and glory.

XI

Galen sat in his study listening to the outlines of Sar Petra's plans for the defence of the city. They were sound plans and quite original thinking, for a knight. Most revolved around magical barriers and weapons, as she seemed to be under the impression that those outside would be more reluctant to use spells against the city for fear of turning the citizens against them. Galen had pointed out that their own use of magic could be viewed that way as well and she had shown him how it was possible to conceal their spells, and confine them to largely knight defended areas. There were flaws of course, but there always were. He had some plans of his own, but was loathed to share them, as it would mean revealing more about himself than he felt he could.

Their meeting was interrupted by a knock on the door.

"Come in," he commanded, and the door opened allowing Marie to enter. "Have you found something?"

"Yes," she said looking pointedly at Sar Petra.

The knight raised one eyebrow questioningly and made to leave but Galen waved her back down. He had to trust someone on the Council with his secrets and at the moment the only ones who seemed to be on his side were the knights. He almost laughed at the irony of it.

"What you have to say, you can say before the both of us," he replied.

Marie shot Sar Petra a withering look of jealousy that made Galen start in surprise. He pushed the worrying conclusion he reached away for the moment.

"I followed them, as you asked, and found that they intend to replace you with a king, the Lord Anton, one of those who arrived with the troops this morning," she began. Galen nodded. He had expected as much, yet knew there was more to come. "They plan to expose certain facts about you to the public in the hope that it will lead to your downfall."

Once again she looked pointedly at the knight sat with him, though Galen had not needed it to inform him just which facts they intended to reveal about him. He looked to Sar Petra with concern. He knew that she knew the truth about his past, but was not sure whether her seeming indifference to his crimes would last if revealed to the whole city. Would they stand by him in such a situation? The knight answered his question even before he asked it.

"It's all right," said the knight softly. "I was one of those who aided in your capture, Galen, and you had even killed some friends of mine, yet I still stand with you."

However, there was a vicious gleam in her eyes and Galen shuddered with fear. He had been too ill to truly recall the faces of those who had captured him, yet as she spoke the words, the memory of her face flashed before him. She had said then something about a dead lover, and Galen wondered if she spoke truly, or whether she now intended to take revenge…

XII

Sar Karene Skellan rode up to the sentries stood on guard at the gates to the city of Teldin. She passed him her papers and waited patiently whilst the guard and his captain struggled through the written words. She was surprised that they could read them at all, as many city guards could not read or write that well. Then again, the Princess Helena was noted for her love of learning. It had been she that had first worked hard upon improving the city library, making it the wonder that it was today. It was said that she even allowed peasants to enter it, if they could read of course. Why anyone would bother with such things she could not imagine, but then nobility were renowned for their strange ways.

The guards moved back towards her and saluted in the manner befitting her station.

"We have sent a messenger to prepare your quarters, Sar, and I will lead you and your troops to the garrison where you may rest up. We will send men tomorrow to aid you in your search for this errant knight," he said, saluting once more.

Karene smiled to herself. At last, she was somewhere that she could organise a proper strategy for Tristan's capture. She only hoped that her guess would prove correct.

"Thank you, Sir," she replied. "Lead on."

She was led through the cobbled streets past the various half-timbered buildings that gave it a look reminiscent of Kelvaria, though the streets were a little cleaner. Within a few minutes she and her troops were garrisoned and she retired to her new quarters. She spent a little time finalising the details of her plan before blowing out the flame of her lantern and retiring to bed. It could not be too long before Tristan would arrive and this time she would not lose him.

XIII

Matthew bent closer to the two pieces of brass like metal that formed parts of the device known as the Sceptre of Prophecy. He had been studying their intricacies as much as was politely allowable on this journey and believed he had found a way of utilising their combined powers without the need for the connecting piece. With just these two pieces he felt it highly probable that his Prophecies would now be more powerful than he could manage alone, though not by much. He found himself frequently wondering just how powerful the prophecies would be when the sceptre was complete.

He pushed the distracting thought away. He had to focus on the present. These pieces had to be the key to their plans. They had already begun their attempt to open Sulan to the Light of Toric, though their initial attempts had been ineffective so far. Sulan XXV was a very intelligent and perceptive man who would not be swayed by mere argument and rhetoric alone. Magic was required, yet the Prophet's Viziers kept such a close watch on him that any such intrusion would be immediately noticed and destroyed. This meant that Matthew would have to do something deemed impossible by all modern scholars and wizards. He was going to have to cast one magic, whilst concealing it with another, masking spell. It was believed impossible, yet he knew it was not, at least for him. The problem was that the masking magic would have to be of his weaker, priestly powers and the amount of energy required was directly proportional to the amount of energy used in the spell he intended to mask. A spell that was strong enough to alter someone's belief would mean a masking spell beyond the power he could handle alone. It was in this that these two pieces of the sceptre would help him, for they could provide him with the power he needed, though only just. He just had to be certain, and that was difficult without actually casting the spell and finding out.

He sighed and rubbed his temples as his head began throbbing once more. He really had to get more sleep, yet with the many functions he had to attend each day, the night was the only time he usually had to work, and he had strong suspicions that this was the intention of the Solmen. This was the first time since they had arrived that he had had a moment to himself. Yet this time was to be fleeting, as they were due to attend a banquet tonight in honour of Serinda, the Prophet's daughter and Naithan's intended bride, if all went well. He shook his head, angry at the way his thoughts had begun drifting again, yet he did not have time to think on it too long as he was disturbed by a palace servant.

"The banquet is prepared for you, Great Lord," said the man in Caldorian with a bow. "Your king requests that you attend him."

The servant bowed again then walked away backwards about twelve paces. He then turned and left as Matthew sighed. He had been to more banquets this visit than he cared to recall and was sure he was beginning to gain pounds in weight. He quickly checked himself in the mirror and cursed as he recalled the pieces of the sceptre still lying on the table. He wondered if the servant had seen it, certain the man had been a spy. He closed the box he stored them in and muttered the words of protection to activate the invisible protective runes on its surface. They glowed briefly and he stored the box away in his trunk. He then turned and left, preparing to meet his future queen.

XIV

Galen marched quickly to the public podium, still shocked at the turn of events. Sar Petra had not wanted revenge, and had truly forgiven him his crimes, something the cynic inside him still could not believe. Yet more importantly, she had given him a plan to counter those of the Circle of Light. It was a plan that could lead to disaster, yet it was his only hope. He had convened a public meeting and was now racing to the square to give what would have to be the speech of his life. Sar Petra and Marie were presently headed off in different directions, hopefully fulfilling other parts of the plan. He hoped that it would all occur in time, for he knew that even now the rumourmongers of the Circle of Light were spreading round whispers about his past, that would soon become full-fledged rumours, much of which untrue and more ghastly than the truth.

He reached the podium and found his head suddenly spin at the sight of the crowds before him. Never before had he seen so many on the streets and he knew that if the plan failed he would not survive the ensuing events. At that moment he felt an overwhelming desire to run. He felt his form momentarily fade away and he almost gave in to the temptation. Yet he did not run. He had not felt the joy of power like this in centuries and he did not intend to give it up now. He shook his head, trying to clear them. He had not lived centuries. He was barely a quarter of one century in age, let alone being of more than one. He looked out to the chattering people and raised his arms. After a few minutes he was received by a general silence.

“People of Theldar,” he began, his voice booming out across the square.

That gave him some comfort as it meant that Sar Petra had returned. He only hoped she had been successful. He pushed the worries away and concentrated on the speech.

“People of Theldar, I have betrayed you.” He waited for the shocked murmurs to die down. “I have concealed things from you, things of my past that once harmed many of you. At this moment, some among you will have heard the rumours about me presently flying around the streets, alehouses and marketplaces. Many concern my past and former crimes. Some are of the vilest of natures and unfortunately, many are true.”

The murmurs of shock rippled around the square and he let them, before continuing his confession. He revealed everything, from start to end, laying himself bare before the crowd, sparing no quarter, telling no lies. It pained him to speak and on occasions it was almost all he could do to remain upright. At some point Marie came and stood beside him, supporting him and giving him much needed comfort. As he drew near to the end of his speech, he felt drained of all emotion and energy, yet he was not finished.

"Since I have come to rule you here, I have tried to be fair and to correct some of the wrongs I have committed. I offer no excuse to my actions and stand here at your mercy. I give myself unto your judgement and submit myself to your will. I have but one final act to make before I do so. Here in Theldar a travesty has occurred that none but a few know of. That is the execution of prisoners. It was a foul deed sanctioned by the king that I chanced upon in my travels. Upon becoming your protector, I was reviled by the men's actions and forced them into prisons for their crimes. Yet what they did was on the orders of a king who could have them killed for refusing. What I did was far worse, and for a far lesser, more petty reason than theirs. I command that they be forgiven and released. I ask you honour this as my final act as Protector, and now leave myself to your judgement."

He fell to his knees and gasped for breath, doing everything he could to stop himself from fading to safety. He was now in the hands of the people. He heard someone mount the podium and he prayed to Toric that it was who he hoped.

"You, Shadow, killed my husband, by your foul deeds," said the voice of Sar Petra, "yet in you I see the hope of Theldar. It was Toric's First Commandment to the great Prophet Ramathus that the highest, most noble virtue of all should be mercy and forgiveness. It is this way that we Caldorians have striven to live for centuries and one that I do not wish to revoke now. I forgive you and pray that you continue leading us. You have shown great strength in revealing all to us and I pray that you help us fight to remain free of tyrants who execute men."

She bowed down to him and kissed his head gently before moving away. Then another knight approached, another who had known one of his victims, and he forgave Galen his crimes. One by one, all those related to his crimes came forward and forgave him. Then came the former executioners, all coming forth to ask forgiveness for their crimes and to thank him for his mercy. The whole ceremony took close to an hour before it was complete. When it was he stood and looked to the crowds. They stood in silence watching in what could only be described as reverent awe. Sar Petra moved to the front of the podium.

"I, Sar Petra, Leader of the Circle of Steel, come forth and forgive you, Galen Faithe, once known as the Shadow. I call for you to remain our protector in all things and lead us to freedom as Sir Caldor once did."

Meredith then stepped forward, surprising Galen, for he had not seen her arrive, or Tyrone who he could now see stood behind her.

"I, Meredith, Leader of the Dark Circle, come forth and forgive you, Galen Faithe, once known as the Shadow. I call for you to remain our protector in all things and lead us to freedom as Sir Caldor once did."

All eyes then turned to Tyrone. He looked like a trapped man and for a moment Galen felt pity for him. One glance at the crowd was enough to know that somehow he had won them over. Tyrone could not make his plan work and would have to either accept the loss or risk becoming known as a man bereft of compassion and mercy. He stepped forward to the edge of the podium and looked out across the crowd. There was but a moment's hesitation before he too repeated Sar Petra's words and when he finished, a cheer erupted from the crowd. Galen felt tears well up inside him as the knowledge that he had succeeded and only a small part of him laughed at the gullibility and foolishness of the human being.

XV

Matthew hurried back to his room as fast as a man could who had been forced to dine on eleven courses of sumptuous, rich food. He had left the banquet as soon as etiquette had allowed him for he had felt the runes go off on his box. He knew the servant had been a spy, he had just known it. Now he stood the risk of losing all. The wards had fired, but that did not mean that the pieces of the sceptre were safe, especially as he now knew where the third piece was kept. The daughter of the Prophet had worn a thin, intricately laced crown of gold and silver, studded with many diamonds and sapphires, yet the centrepiece had been a simple brass rod, one of the two middle sections of the Sceptre of Prophecy.

Yet as he had noticed the piece, he saw that the Royal Vizier, Zakar, had noted his interest. The man had retired early, complaining of a sickness of the stomach and shortly after Matthew had felt the wards being triggered. It had to be Zakar who had set them off and Matthew knew the Royal Vizier was among the more powerful wizards of this realm.

He hurried through the silk canopied corridors, desperate to get to his room in time. He rushed into his room, mentally preparing any spells he might require if he were going to have to fight for the box. He saw the Vizier stood over the blackened body of what could have once been a human, though the flesh had all but melted away, leaving identification all but impossible. That made Matthew suspicious, as the wards he had set did not have the power to do that much damage. The Vizier turned as Matthew entered and sighed. Matthew noticed that his box was in the Solman's hands.

"I'm sorry your Excellency had to see this," he said with a small bow. "I was in my chamber when I felt a surge of magic from your chambers. Of course I made my way here with the fastest of haste to find this thief burning upon your floor. He had this box in his hands yet I was not in time to save him, nor find anything out about him. I am truly sorry that you had to see such things here in our lands."

The dusky skinned man handed Matthew the box. He looked at it carefully and noted that it did not appear to have been opened, though he could not risk checking the contents in front of Zakar.

"Thank you," said Matthew guardedly. "Pay it no mind. It is not possible to be completely safe against those who would steal from you."

"It is as you say but I can but apologise most profusely that your possessions were not safe in here in the heart of our realm," replied the Vizier with another bow. "If you a fear for your possessions, we can offer you the protection of our royal vault."

There it was. Matthew looked for anything suspicious in the man's expression that would leave any clue, yet he was too good a player of the Royal Game. He looked nothing other than the model concerned Vizier offering the protection of the royal vault. Matthew had the suspicion that his possessions would be in even more risk if they were left there. Yet he could not show his suspicions, else he and Naithan would have lost footing in the Great Game.

"I thank you for your humble concern about my meagre possessions," he replied, echoing the man's bow. "There is little of worth here that I possess save this box, which I fear has more worth than its contents. Yet I will convey your offer to my king, for there are items in his possession worth far in excess of all mine combined. I am sure he would feel more secure if he knew that such things were safely kept within your most secure rooms. Now, if I may be excused, I feasted rather heavily upon the fine delicacies served at the banquet tonight and am in need of a rest that I may digest it better."

"Of course," replied the Vizier, with a quick bow, his eyes flicking for just a second to Naithan's quarters.

Matthew smiled to see his ploy so obviously fallen for by the Vizier. By Toric the man was good at the Game, trying to lull Matthew into the belief that his comments on the king's wealth had successfully misdirected him to the king's chambers. Matthew resisted the urge to rub his throbbing temples. Playing the Game on this intense level was enough to drive a man insane.

Matthew bowed as the Vizier left and watched as the man walked deliberately in the opposite direction to Naithan's room. Matthew knew there would be another way to it from that direction and that the Vizier would be sure that Matthew would see someone headed in that direction at a later time. The man must have eaten, slept and dreamt the Royal Game since his childhood, and he was a merely a Solmen. It was said you had never seen a good player of the Game until you met a Kolthon noble who could convey a thousand messages with just the blink of an eye.

He shook his head and entered his room, the headache seeming to lessen a little as he entered the relative privacy of his chambers. Of course there were at least ten spy holes in various parts of the room and it had taken Matthew an hour of casual wandering to locate them all and find the few positions he could sit in safe in the knowledge that he could not be observed. He could not sit in them very often otherwise the spies would become suspicious and begin trying other methods to discover what he was about. It may have been that he had sat there too often already, the thief's attempt on his box being the ultimate result of those actions. For that reason he purposely did not check the contents of his box, but merely reset and slightly altered the protective runes on its surface. He placed it in his trunk and then retired to the silken sheets of the bed, a luxury he would have to import to his chambers in Caldor. He had never felt anything so smooth against his skin, not even garments made with magic.

He did not intend to fall asleep at that moment, but found the tiredness of the past week's activities suddenly catch up on him and his eyes began to close with heaviness. As the eyelids cut off the images of his room, he saw a suspicious character creep past his doorway in the direction of Naithan's room. Evidently tomorrow Naithan would learn that a thief had tried his rooms too…

XVI

"Why did you do it?" asked Tyrone angrily.

"I had to," replied Meredith. "You saw how the crowd were reacting to him. He gave them what they wanted to see. He and that wretched knight outmanoeuvred us. To stand against him would have been to stand alone against a mob. I did what I had to do to survive."

"And to Thenril with the consequences for others as well, I suppose," replied Tyrone with a glare.

Galen smiled to himself at the exchange. He had followed them the moment they had left the podium and in their anger with each other they were not acting as cautiously as usual. That, along with his gift to fade out of sight, made shadowing them all the more easy.

"It means we'll have to resort to the other plan now though," said Tyrone bitterly.

"You did not honestly think Galen would live through this, did you?" she asked softly. "If he had not have done what he did, our actions would have caused his death, and even if he had survived that, Anton would have had to make an example of him, even if it was just to the other Lords. He was dead the moment he was selected as Lord Protector."

Galen's eyes narrowed angrily at the woman's statements, though she was only echoing the thoughts of the other voice that sometimes spoke in his head.

"I know," replied Tyrone softly. "I just wish it didn't have to happen that way. It's not my way."

"I know," she replied with a smile. "Unfortunately, it's the way of politics."

"Knowing that doesn't make it any easier though, and after his display today it will be a lot harder to kill him without martyring him."

"Why not use his martyrdom to our advantage then?" she asked quickly.

Galen could tell she had once lived in the Kolthon Empire. Her grasp of the Game almost equalled his and her mind was quick to seek advantage in disadvantage. He shook his head as if to shake the thoughts away. He had never been to Kolth, let alone played this Game.

"How do you mean?" Tyrone asked, looking around cautiously.

Galen allowed himself to fade into shadow a little more, accepting the lessened clarity of sounds and images that accompanied it. Now that they were back to serious plots, their careful, suspicious natures were in play once more.

"Well, have Anton meet him as planned, and have the guards kill Galen. Then allow Anton to place the blame on others," said Meredith quietly, her words almost inaudible to Galen in his present state. "Surely he has those he wishes to dispose of. He could capture Galen's *killers* and lead them into the city, putting the blame for Galen's death on them. He can then ride on the martyrdom of Galen. The people of the city will follow him to avenge his death, and he will be able to crush Prince Gareth's army…"

The words faded as they entered the building that housed the Circle of Light. There was some type of magic surrounding them that he could not pierce, that being the main reason he had originally sent Marie to spy on them. At least he knew some of the details and could prepare for it, though the instinct born of that other voice told him that he would need to follow Tyrone a little further, even if he could not hear his words.

He stepped through the barrier, shuddering at the tingling pain it sent down his spine as he did. He would know all there was about this plot and he would be prepared, regardless of the cost to him. He walked through the corridors until he found them and saw them looking over a map of the city with words and diagrams all over them. Though in code, it was simply done and he had no problems reading their ciphers. Within a few minutes he had learned all he felt he needed and left to make preparations of his own…

XVII

Anton sat alone in his command tent looking at the ciphered note he had just received. The plan provided did not look like one of Tyrone's making, yet it was sound enough. They were to meet and Gareth's knights, secretly placed there earlier, would spring out and kill the man. Anton would then have those men captured with his own knights and force them to *confess* that Gareth had planned it thus from the beginning, gaining him the support of the city.

In the fight that killed Galen, he would also have one of the Hanton brothers killed, drawing the other closer to him with the thirst to avenge his brother's death with Gareth's head. Anton smiled with pleasure. Everything was starting to go his way and soon he would be king. He retired to bed, yet found his mind too active for sleep and his thoughts swirled in a maelstrom of glory and glee. The image of him on the throne with the crown of Tir'nin on his head surfaced again and again and continued even in his dreams when they washed over him with the darkness of sleep. With them came the words he had longed to hear for many years.

Long live King Anton, Light and Hope of Caldor.

CHAPTER FOURTEEN: Schemes and Studies

I

Anton waited anxiously for news on Gareth's health. He had been surprised by his nephew's sudden appearance yesterday at their meeting, especially as the priests attending to his wounds had said that Gareth was unlikely to be mobile for several more days at least. That had suited Anton's plans perfectly and he had thanked Toric for his kindness on learning of his nephew's condition. Unfortunately Gareth was evidently a strong man and it had only been towards the end of their deliberately long meeting that the strain had begun to show upon Gareth's face. Anton hoped that he had tired the man enough to allow him the chance to enact the first phase of his plan. Someone tapped upon the tent flap, breaking Anton's thoughts.

"Enter," he commanded, trying to sit as if completely at ease.

The Lord Priest Yain entered and bowed before him.

"You sent for me, my lord?" he asked as he bowed.

Anton allowed the insult to slip, though he would not forget it. Yain would pay for it when he was king. No one should speak before him, unless they were bidden to do so. Even the most stupid of his servants had learned that lesson quickly enough.

"Yes," he replied languidly. "I was just wondering as to the health of Prince Gareth. Our meeting yesterday was overly long and, despite my protestations to the contrary, he plainly refused to retire until it was completely finished."

That had been the easy part. Gareth was very much like his mother in that he refused to give in weakness and could be stubborn about continuing with his tasks as if nothing were wrong, even to the point where he was risking his own health. A few well-placed phrases about how ill he looked and how he should retire to bed had pushed the man to stay and talk even after there was nothing left to discuss.

"When he left he seemed a trifle unwell and I hoped he would not be too sick to reach his tent, though my servants who followed him informed me that he made it that far, at least."

"Yes," replied Yain. "He was more than a little exhausted when he returned last night and has many days to rest before he can be said to be truly fit for duty. Unfortunately, he is not a man to take advice concerning his health, as your lord has no doubt seen for yourself."

Anton almost shouted at the man in rage. How dare he voice opinions about one of the royal blood in such a way? He would truly come to know the meaning of suffering when Anton was king. However, he controlled his rage tightly, not daring to let loose his anger at this crucial moment in time.

"Yes, I have," he replied with a nod. "I hope he will be allowed to awaken in his own time this morning. We have no need for haste today."

"It was our intention to allow him such," replied Yain with a nod.

Anton breathed deeply, concentrating on his exercises to retain emotional control. How dare they take such a decision without consultation with a member of the Royal Family? His sister and nephew had allowed the sanctity and position of the monarch to slip during their rule, yet another reason for him to take what was rightfully his.

"Good," he replied, centring his emotions in a state of balance. The Karsisian mystic had taught him well. "I'm glad to see my nephew in the care of such capable hands as yours. You may go."

"By your leave, my Lord," replied Yain with a bow.

The man turned swiftly and left the tent, leaving Anton alone once more. That gave him the moment's calm he needed to prepare himself for what he was about to do. When he felt ready, he rose slowly to his feet and passed through the tent opening, emerging into the morning sun. It was not much past dawn, despite the lateness of the hour, for the long nights of winter were rapidly approaching, and the horizon appeared to be filled with clouds, many of them dark and threatening. The first autumn storm was most definitely on its way, if not today then certainly tomorrow and this fact strengthened his resolve. He was not a man used to braving the elements and he thoroughly intended to be installed in the luxury of the palace when the rains finally struck.

He looked around and saw that his honour guards were already awaiting him and that both Darren and Lewis Hanton were stood with their entourages. All bowed with a salute as he surveyed them and he nodded briefly to his Magenta Knight, Archknight Sir Alex Mel'ar. The knight raised his sword in salute and command as the honour guard moved to surround Anton.

The banner man then came forward and hoisted the red and white flag of peace so that it flew beneath the blue and yellow colours of Anton's House. Under that flag he should be safe, though he knew that Sir Alex had probably also cast protective spells over him in case the Theldarians chose to disregard the flag. It was not necessary, of course, for Anton was adept in some forms of magic and could probably create far more superior shields than his Archknight, though that was a talent he kept to himself these days. It would be unseemly to have a king of Caldor use magic in his own defence when he had loyal followers to do it for him.

"Let's go," Anton commanded, and his troops moved out in perfect formation.

He was pleased to see that neither the knights of Darren or Lewis matched his for their precision marching.

It took almost an hour to reach the outer walls of Theldar thanks to the slow pace of the ceremonial march and it gave time for the walls to become crowded with spectators. Anton smiled to himself, satisfied that all was working well so far. He needed as many people to hear his speech as possible and there was less of a chance that fighting would commence if non-military personnel were at risk of being harmed. The fact that none of them had loosed arrows at them as yet was a good sign. Evidently he had supporters within the city troops thanks to his allies in the Redirection Chambers.

He commanded his troops to halt some thirty paces from the wall and he signalled the buglers to begin. The fanfare they produced was certainly fit for a king and was enough to silence the spectators on the city's walls. A herald stepped forward and Anton felt only slightly annoyed as nerves struck the young woman and she stumbled whilst approaching the walls.

"People of Theldar," she began, her hands shaking as she held out the scroll before her. Evidently she had risked a quick glance at the scroll's contents before leaving, giving her some right to be nervous. "Before you stands Lord Anton Gethrel, Earl of Seronshire, and his companions and allies, Count Darren Hanton, Lord of Harkshire, and Earl Lewis Hanton, Lord of Kempshire. With them come three vast armies, greater than any number you can muster here against them, despite the protection of these walls. With them arrayed against you, you would stand no chance of victory, yet that need not be the case. For at present they surround the troops commanded by Prince Gareth, Duke of Kelranshire and if they were to ally with you, they could be easily crushed. It is for this reason that the great Lord Gethrel comes seeking a parlay with the Lord Protector of your city."

By the end of the speech, the herald had blanched considerably and the tremble in her hands had become a violent shake. Anton looked at the reaction of the crowds stood upon the wall and smiled. There was still suspicion in the faces he could see, but many held expressions of surprise and hope. At that moment the crowds parted and a dark figure appeared at the edge of the wall. A shudder went down Anton's spine as he looked at the figure and he had the strange sensation that he thought he could almost see through the man, if indeed it was a man. He got the distinct impression that what he could see was not entirely human.

He pushed down the desire to order the man shot by his archers and as he did he realised that it was unlikely that arrows could kill such a fiend. He found himself regretting his decision to meet with this man face to face. The man raised his arm high in the air, a blade glistening in the morning sun. Whatever he was, he was a master of ceremony and symbolism. Even from here Anton could see adoring, awe inspired gazes from those people closest to him. This Lord Protector was a dangerous man indeed.

"I am Galen Faithe, Lord Protector of Theldar," said the figure, his soft voice carrying further than was natural. Anton had the unnerving feeling that the man was stood directly before him, rather than thirty paces away. "It is my duty to see these people safe and you are indeed correct to point out the odds. Yet this would not be the first time that the few have survived the attacks of the many. One has to think of the victories of Sir Caldor the Great and his One Hundred at the Siege of Rathamoor."

Anton knew the legend of the siege. It was said that one hundred knights had defeated some ten thousand legionaries of Kolth defending the keep in the mountain pass of Rathamoor, though any learned man would know that history tended to exaggerate such figures. Unfortunately, this Galen Faithe was not appealing to learned people, but to the mythical ideals of the commoners around him and Anton could see that the man's ploy was working. Already there were many faces hardening in resolve against him. This was a man Anton could learn from, if it was not for the fact that he had to die.

"Yet even the Hundred needed aid when battling the combined might of Kolth and Sol on the plains of Tir'nin," replied Anton loudly.

Tir'nin, the site of Caldor's greatest victory and the moment he had crowned the first monarch of Caldor, Queen Angeline. An image of the beautiful crown flashed before his eyes, yet he pushed it down. He had to remain focused.

"True enough and it is for that reason alone that I will consider your request. You will receive your reply at dusk. Look to the skies of Theldar at this time. If you see the doves of peace sail through them, then we shall parlay on the morrow. If you see the black crows of war darken them then be prepared to meet our army at dawn."

Anton listened and watched, impressed by the looks given to this unsettling man by those around him. He had no doubt that at that moment those nearest him would have leapt into the flames of Haden if he commanded them to. Anton wished he too could inspire such devotion. There had to be some trick to it. It truly was a pity that the man would die with the dawn, regardless of the answer given tonight.

"It will be as you command," he replied, biting back the bile in his throat as he bowed slightly to this peasant.

Galen bowed in return and turned, seeming to vanish into nothingness as he did. As he faded whispered words filled his ears.

"You have but five minutes to remove yourself from these walls before the command to release arrows will be given to my archers. Please note that those with *special* skills have been commanded to aim for you and your defences will not be enough to still all of them. If my archers are forced to attack, the crows of war shall fill the sky and blood will stain the field," said the soft, sibilant voice, sending chills and shudders down Anton's spine.

He commanded his troops to begin a forced march in retreat, suddenly aware of just how many archers were lining the walls before him. He praised the intelligence of Galen's actions, even as he cursed them. This quick retreat would raise Galen's standing in the eyes of the spectators on the walls. The might of three armies forced to make a shambolic and disordered retreat, for none had been prepared for the sudden order, and there was nothing he could do about the humiliation it brought. At least not today, anyway.

II

Galen looked round at the Triad leaders sat before him. Tyrone and Meredith seemed a little more on edge than usual, as well they should be, and Sar Petra sat in complete silence, as she had a wont to do in these situations.

"Well," he asked slowly, "what do you advise?"

He scanned them all and noted that all seemed a little hesitant to answer him, though Sar Petra's silence was understandable. She took her right to speak last with great seriousness, often not saying a word until the others had had their say. Yet none seemed able to bear silence for any length of time and eventually Tyrone broke it first. He spoke with slow and measured words, as if he were being very careful exactly how he phrased what he thought.

"The Lord Gethrel did have a point about the odds levelled against us," he said softly. "If all were to lay siege against us at once we would have little chance of success."

"So you would bow before his threat and subject us to his rule?" asked Meredith angrily, though Galen could hear the faintest traces of falseness in her attitude.

These two made an ideal couple and he had no doubt that between them they would argue out all the possibilities as if in some genuine debate. Not many days ago he may have fallen for such a ploy, but not now. He knew parts of their plot and also knew which direction they were moving towards. He allowed them to approach agreement on setting up a meeting with this Lord Gethrel, under strict guidelines of course, before he turned towards Sar Petra.

"And what do you think?" he asked softly, enjoying the look of surprise on all three faces. He had to give credit to Sar Petra for her fast recovery though. "You are, after all, our military arm, and best suited to comment upon the options before us."

She bowed slowly and looked around carefully at each of them, her cool demeanour disguising her rapidly moving thoughts. Galen found that if he allowed himself to fade into shadow a little he could almost see them, spinning round her head. He wondered if he would ever be able to read them clearly, but had to bring himself back fully into the real world as she appeared to reach a conclusion.

"What both say has merits. It is true that without aid we are likely to fail and that if we allow them to take a hand we are likely to find ourselves under a new king. The Circles of Light and Dark point out these views very clearly and both are also correct when ascertaining that speculation gets us nowhere," she began and Galen smiled. She had seen their plan immediately.

"I will also say that we must meet with him at dawn, but not for the reasons pointed out by my two associates. What they have failed to recognise is the fact that Anton made it clear to all those on the walls that there was an alternative option and if we are not seen to explore it, then we will lose some of the public support we have gained thus far. Therefore, I suggest that you meet with him, alone in a room, just you and him. If he has something like a satisfactory agreement towards aiding our predicament, then we reply in kind. If he gives the wrong answer, then I suggest we clearly show him our resolve to fight on regardless of the odds."

Galen looked at her closely and saw something else in her eyes, a meaning he could not quite fathom. He decided he would need to speak with her later on the subject.

"Very well," he said slowly. "I see that for the first time we are all in complete agreement on the issue. Lord of Light, Lady of Night, go search out sufficient numbers of peace doves to signal our message. We will send the terms of the meeting after their flight, so have the scribes prepared to write them out once we have decided upon them. Lady of Might, I need to discuss certain security arrangements for his visit here. We would not want anything untoward happening to the Lord Anton upon his visit here, now would we?"

He pretended not to notice the startled glances of Tyrone and Meredith, or the mischievous gleam that suddenly appeared in Sar Petra's eyes.

"As you wish, Lord Protector," they all replied in unison.

Tyrone and Meredith bowed slightly and left. He allowed them some time to be about their business before turning to speak to the now silent, demure knight.

"You know they mean to kill me in this meeting, don't you?" he asked slowly.

"Of course," she replied. "It is what I would do if I were them."

"But you are not them."

"Exactly, and I will be there to defend you when the time comes," she replied.

"Why, may I ask?" he said softly. "I killed your husband and you forgave me. I massacred knights, many of whom were your friends, and you forgave me. I even prepare now to kill still more knights and use your knights as my weapon, yet you follow me. Why with all this do you stay loyal to me?"

"Simple," she replied quietly. "I have no need for kings and would-be kings. They are nothing but betrayers of trust."

"Why do you say that?"

"I was not only a knight, but a Shadow Runner, a member of a ring of spies in the employ of the king's Spymaster. I was sent to discover who had been tampering with the Redirection Chambers in order to loosen the bonds of loyalty to the king. To do so I was subjected to weeks of their Treatment until I felt my own loyalty waver. I began to yearn for a true king, one who should have inherited the throne by ancient rites of succession. A king such as Lord Anton, who was passed over twenty years ago in favour of his younger sister, Queen Anne. To make matters worse, they had stripped him of his House, naming him Head of House Gethrel, a lesser house with no real claim to the throne."

"What has this to do with your loyalty to me?" he asked slowly. "Surely you should still be loyal to this Lord Gethrel then."

"The weeks of Treatment made me wise to their ways, and that made me strong. I was able to resist their charms and even remember some of the horrors they placed upon me to enforce my loyalty. When I left I vowed to give my loyalty to one whom asked for it and never for one whom commanded it. You have never done that, so I give my loyalty to you, someone who stands for more than a petty rising against a petty overlord; a man with dreams so large that they may never be fulfilled."

He looked at her with undisguised amazement. What dreams did she talk of? He had no such grand dreams, just the desire to make the life of the people in the city a little more free and just. Memories rushed through him of other such men over many ages and realised that in times when justice and freedom were scarce, to seek to restore them could inspire awe. Was that not the whole point of the legend of Sir Caldor, his struggle to free the humans from the yoke of goblin tyranny?

He shut the thoughts away and looked back to the knight before him. She had restored the cool demeanour she had momentarily dropped and looking at her now he could not picture her as being capable of the emotional outpour he had just witnessed.

"We have work to do, if you are to survive this meeting tomorrow," she said quietly.

"I know of their plans, and even the place they intend to set the trap," he replied acting as if nothing had just passed between them.

"Good, then we shall let them lay their trap and then surprise them with one of our own."

He nodded in agreement then looked to her for a while in silence. He did not know if he should do what he was about to do, but loyalty such as hers was not all that common and essential to him if he were to have people he could trust around him. People like Marie. He had already given her the gift, though she did not know it. He had done it before sending her away to spy on Tyrone's activities, hoping that it would give her some protection from the dangers. He had done it secretly because he did not want her to see his care for her that underlay the gift, or to draw her any closer than was necessary. He was dying. His end was near and he did not wish to bring any more pain into her life than he already had.

"Are there many among your troops who could offer me such loyalty as you spoke of?" he asked cautiously.

"Why?" she asked, her eyes narrowing with suspicion.

"I ask because I would like those who are to be the ones who aid me spring our trap," he replied.

"That would be a wise precaution," she admitted, suspicion still hovering in her expression.

"But it would also be to my detriment if such loyal followers were to be lost at such a crucial stage in my plans," he continued.

"I don't see where your logic is taking us," she answered.

"Simply to the fact that I have the power to save them, to give them a gift that will protect them in times to come, even in battle. With it, they would become an elite force, loyal to me, but also loyal to my ideals. Speak to those who would follow me faithfully and offer this gift. If they accept it, bring them to me tonight after the release of the doves and I shall bestow it upon them as well, that is if you wish to accept this gift from me."

"What would the gift be?" she asked slowly, and he told her. Her eyes widened. "You can do that?"

"Only to a few, maybe fifty, so ensure that those you ask would be best suited to the task. That is, if you wish to accept it from me."

He could have done a lot more than that, but not without risk to himself, and fifty would be more than adequate for the task.

"I would be honoured if you were to make me the first of such an elite group," she replied with a gentle bow.

Galen could not help wondering if the bonds of loyalty placed upon her in the Chambers could still be affecting her now, with only the master's name being changed. He moved his mind off such thoughts, for even if he were correct, it was of no consequence as it suited his purpose and she would never be any the wiser to the fact. Galen shuddered angrily, hating the thought even as it had sprung from the dark recess of his mind and he almost refused to bestow the gift upon her. Yet this was too important to do any differently, so he placed his hand upon her shoulders.

"You say that you were once known as a Shadow Runner," he began, summoning the energy from within. "Well now you will join a new group whose title shall bear more truth than that. No blade not forged of shadow and light shall touch you, and shadows will light your paths." *As long as I do live,* he added mentally, not wishing to unleash this power unlimited into the realm. "I name thee Sar Petra, first of the Shadow Knights, warrior elite of Theldar."

His body shuddered as the energy left him and his head swam in dizzy circles for a moment. When he looked down he saw Sar Petra's form shimmer slightly and for a moment she was almost translucent, before her body solidified once more.

"Rise and be reborn," he intoned, momentarily closing his eyes.

She stood and he saw a stunned look of amazement upon her face. Marie's reaction had been similar, though she had not known the source of the sensation he had passed on. He found himself wondering just what they felt during the process, for it brought only pain to him, though not immediately. After bestowing it upon the knights tonight, he did not expect to sleep at all that night. But it was a necessary sacrifice. He closed his eyes quickly and gathered his thoughts together. There was still much to do and he could not afford to lose his focus.

"As you wish, Lord Protector, High Shadow Knight," said Sar Petra, as if she were obeying some order he had uttered. "I shall round up the most loyal knights at once and then return to aid you plan your strike."

He looked her and realised that she had just answered one of his thoughts. His eyes widened in shock, before he allowed himself to drift partially into shadow. The thoughts he had believed he could see earlier were now most definitely circling around her head, as clear as the morning sky on a cloudless day.

He allowed himself to return to the solid realm. He hoped that she could not read his thoughts as clearly as he could read hers, and a voice deep within his mind told him that she would not even be able to see their outline. He ignored it, despite the relief it brought, and nodded his assent for her departure. She left without a word and left him wondering if what he was doing was a wise thing. The voice in his head told him that it was, yet he had learned long ago not to trust it. As that thought sprung from his mind he believed he heard the other voice laugh, then suddenly it spoke, its words as clear as his own thoughts.

Thou art truly an able pupil, and thou hath heeded my first lesson well. Trust no one.

It broke out into laughter once more and Galen pushed it away, a shiver of fear running down his spine. He turned back to gaze into the blazing fire whose heat he could barely feel. The laughter faded softly, yet he found no comfort in this fact. Was he going mad? Was this the final curse brought on by the gift of that he had received, to enter Thenril's Realms a gibbering madman?

He received no answers to the questions and he found his thoughts drifting on to the meeting tomorrow. Then came the pain and he gasped in shock. He bore it as best he could, taking little comfort in the fact that this would be but a shadow compared to that which he would feel come nightfall. He avoided calling out, knowing that it would soon be over then, as suddenly as it had come, the pain vanished, and he was left in peace to plan once more.

III

Gareth was awoken by the voice of his second in command, the Grey Knight Sir Valence Shieldbearer.

"I don't care if Toric himself had come down and commanded that Lord Gareth sleep without disturbance," he all but shouted. "The commander needs to be informed of these events."

"But sir," came the voice of that odious Priest Yain, sounding shocked by Sir Valence's appalling use of blasphemous language. The man had been the son of a pig herder, though birth rank had little to do with the knightly orders nowadays. It did lead to some interesting encounters between commoners and noblemen, though. There were some things that Treatment could not simply erase completely from a person. "I must protest most strenuously that his Lordship is sick and in need of rest."

Gareth heard the sound of swords being drawn and he quickly rose up from his cot. Though now a priest, Yain had, like all magic wielders, once been trained in the knighthood. If he was not careful the bloodshed outside could be terrible, not something he needed at this moment in time. He wondered what had so agitated Sir Valence to make him forget himself so and threaten a Lord Priest of Toric.

"Father Yain, please allow Grey Knight Valence to enter my tent," he commanded in his most authoritative voice.

He saw the silhouetted outline of the priest jolt in surprise and hurriedly move away from the entrance. Within moments Sir Valence had pushed aside the tent flap and entered. He was a tall man and his frame was lean and muscular, despite his age. His hair was thick, wavy and light brown, though it was heavily streaked with grey, as was his bushy moustache. He wore the ceremonial surcoat of his office over a more serviceable and less extravagant suit of armour. If Gareth did not know better, he would say that the man was dressed for battle, though that could not be so for he had yet to order the attack. A cold shiver ran through his body as yet another terrifying premonition overcame him. He looked into Valence's deep set, icy blue eyes for confirmation and was not pleased to find it.

"What has happened?" he asked quickly.

"Forgive the intrusion, Sir," replied Sir Valence briskly, "but I felt that the news I bear was of too grave a matter to leave until the afternoon."

"Do not concern yourself and present the report."

"Yes Sir. There is treachery afoot. Lord Gethrel has offered to ally himself with the Theldarians and it appears that the Lords of House Hanton are with him. It leaves us surrounded on four fronts and in an almost hopeless position."

Gareth felt sick to the depths of his stomach. How the Grey Knight could stand there and deliver such news in so neutral a tone of voice was beyond him.

"Have the Theldarians…" How he hated that term. "…accepted his offer?"

"They will answer by bird this evening, though that will only tell us if they agree to meet to discuss the alliance. I fear we will not know the outcome until we are set upon by the armies around us," replied the knight.

"So you think they will accept his offer?"

"They are rightfully suspicious of his motives, but I cannot see them refusing. It is the only chance they have for success," replied Sir Valence gravely.

Gareth rubbed his eyes as his vision blurred momentarily. How had this happened? What was he to do? The thoughts swirled around in his head, making his nausea all the stronger. The tent flap parted, disturbing his thoughts.

"A messenger to see you, My Lord," said one of his squires. Evidently Yain had gotten tired of door duty.

"From whom?"

"He wears the livery of House Gethrel and wears the cloth of peace on his arm," replied the girl quickly.

"Send him in," he replied wearily.

A boy of no more than thirteen years of age entered, wearing the blue and yellow colours of House Gethrel and the white armband with the red cross that was the ancient symbol of peace.

"What is your message boy?" he asked, more gruffly than he intended.

The sandy haired boy quickly handed over the piece of parchment and withdrew whilst Gareth broke the seal and read it. Gareth recognised the spidery handwriting of his uncle. It read:

To my eldest nephew,
By now you will have learned of my supposed treachery and will be most angered by it. I ask that you only give me time, for things are not what they seem. I believe that the one who leads these "Theldarians" is the one once known as the Shadow, and that he has somehow bewitched the city. I believe that his death will end the charm and prevent the need for further bloodshed. To this end I intend to meet with him and, with the aid of some loyal followers within the city, end his reign and restore the city to your capable hands.

I'm sorry if this all seems sudden, but I have been led to believe that those of the city are preparing another sally forth soon and felt that haste was of vital necessity. I hope you can forgive me the small duplicity and find it in your heart to give me the chance to prove my loyalty to your brother, my nephew and our king, Naithan Tara'non. I also ask that you tell no one of my plan until it is complete, for I fear our security is compromised and that spies are abound in our camp.
Yours Loyally,
Anton Gethrel.
Long Live the King.

Gareth read the letter again and started as the words began to fade from view. He had forgotten that his uncle shared his talent for magic, though he did only use it on rare occasions, so it was not surprising he would forget.

"What do we do, Sir?" Asked Sir Valence, appearing to show no interest in the note Gareth held.

He did his best not to jump in surprise, for he had forgotten that the Grey Knight still stood there. He looked to Sir Valence, his thoughts still sorting through the words of his uncle's message.

"We wait," he replied wearily.

At that Valence's stoic demeanour was briefly overtaken by a look of surprise, if a mere widening of the eyes could be called that. On Valence, such an expression spoke volumes.

"You may leave, but prepare the troops. It may be that come the morrow we will have a fight on our hands," he commanded.

Sir Valence bowed and left the tent, leaving him alone with his thoughts. He tried to puzzle through the words of the note, searching for possible hidden messages. Not for the first time he found himself longing for the council of his sister, in her guise as Spymaster, yet she was apparently busy elsewhere at present. The last communication he had received had been the news that Naithan was safely arrived in Zaron, and that had been some days ago.

His brow furrowed as a headache began to throb in his temples. He rubbed them absently with his fingers, scowling. He had never been one for the Royal Game and he was beginning to feel that Anton shared Naithan and Helena's talent for it. Just thinking of a few possible hidden meanings within those few lines was enough to drive one insane. But he would play his uncle's game, for now, whatever it was. He just hoped that whatever the man had planned did not backfire on him, unless of course it aided Gareth's cause.

He was distracted from his thoughts by the entrance of Yain to his tent. The man spoke to him yet all he could hear was a faint buzzing. It was then he realised that he was feeling very light headed. Cursing the illness that had made him so weak, he allowed himself to be led to bed and unconsciousness claimed him.

IV

Matthew closed the book slowly. He had been allowed into the Great library of today Zaron for the first time on this visit and had been making the most of the opportunity. He had requested this privilege on their arrival but it had taken until today to gain the permission he had needed. Even so, he was sure he had been followed in and that he was, even now, under close scrutiny by the various library guards. That had made him cautious and he had collected together a large number of texts to peruse, burying the one he truly sort in their midst. Its title was simply known as *The Dark and the Light* and was the only known history of the Second Elf War that had continued on into the period of reconstruction that had followed it. Matthew hoped that it would contain additional information on the workings of the Sceptre, though he knew it was probably just a vain hope.

To disguise his intentions he had taken other books for perusal in the Reading Room, including the massive *History of Loden*, written by the greatest historian of all time, Marconious the Blind of Kolth. Admittedly he had lived many generations ago and the history reached nowhere near even his own time, his blindness hindering him in his final years and the Yellow Plague taking his life at the pitifully young age of forty one.

Matthew screwed his eyes closed and rubbed them with his hands, the flickering candlelight starting to strain his eyes. Blindness was the curse of all great scholars, for it was known that sunlight and magical light could damage the paper and parchment, so most were read in windowless rooms such as this with only candle light to see by. It was a curse he hoped he would never suffer, though at this moment in it would have been a blessing, as it would have forced him to cease his work.

Yet he could not rest. This was because in order to disguise his intent, he had to read through most of the books within their chronological framework and, unfortunately, in the vast span of Loden's history, the Second Elf War was considered something of a recent event. It had taken him most of the day skimming rapidly through the books allowing his strong memory to pick up enough information to answer the Vizier's inevitable questions at supper, to finally reach the book he actually wanted to read.

It was bound in soft leather purportedly created from the skin of the legendary Krakars, dangerous reptiles that were said to have swum the Great River of ages past. The leather did have an unusual feel to it, though it was not dissimilar to the snake skin bound books he had in his possession in Caldor. He pushed away the enquiring thoughts and concentrated on skimming through this book as quickly as was possible without making any spies suspicious whilst retaining the relevant information.

Fortunately it was a slim book, though many of the pages seemed to have been damaged by some great fire. There were even signs that it had been damaged by water as well and Matthew found it surprising that they kept the book at all. In fact, he was sure that it would have been destroyed if it were not the only known copy in Loden. He looked back briefly at the cover and wondered why it had survived all these incidents seemingly undamaged.

He allowed that thought only a moment of his time though, and raced through the book to the part he had been searching for. When he reached it he almost screamed in frustration, for these pages too had been burned and water damaged so that any writings were beyond recognition. Of all the things he had been prepared for, this had been the one he had dreaded the most. All his searching and subterfuge, his headache and throbbing eyes had been for nothing. He had wasted a day that he could have spent in his chambers examining the Sceptre for a way to combine and utilise its powers, only to find a blackened, crumbling page that did not contain even one legible word.

His vision blurred, the throbbing in his eyes grew in intensity and it was all he could do to prevent himself throwing the book away. He took several deep breaths and allowed himself a chance to calm down a little. He had known from the start that he had stood only a slim chance of gaining anything useful from the book, and had to reconcile himself to the fact that he had been correct in his assumption, yet there had always been hope…

He pushed the thought away, knowing that it would only cause him to lose control once more. He pushed his thoughts out to the calm still of the mountaintop where he and his father had once climbed to many, many years ago. It had been there that he had truly felt at peace and found the memory a soothing one, despite the melancholy that accompanied it, as he was reminded of his deceased father. The calmness came quickly and he found himself wondering if this was somehow due to his father's spirit watching over him.

He smiled at the fanciful whim and then looked back at the book. The calmness within him was consumed by shock at what he saw there. For an instant what was left of a page shimmered and seemed to reform itself, though only as a shadowy, translucent image. Words flared suddenly across the new page in letters of flame that burned brightly for a few seconds before fading to nothing. The illusionary page shimmered once more then winked out of sight, as if it had never existed.

Matthew sat there a moment, stunned by what he had seen. The book had told him everything he needed to know, or at least confirmed his own suspicions. The brief flare seemed to have burned the words into his mind. He looked round warily, partly wondering if anyone had seen the incident, whilst also searching for any trace of the magical page's origin. Looking around he could see little in the way of spellprints, though that could mean nothing. He himself had used mirrors and other such devices to cast spells from a safe distance.

He looked back at the page and saw a slight shimmer around the air where it had been. It was a spellprint and seemed to indicate that the magic had come from him, though he had not felt anything. He was not certain, but found himself believing that he had somehow triggered a spell, maybe even a Prophecy, when opening the book. It had been used to disguise an un-charred page, making it look like its damaged companions, and had waited to this moment to reveal its contents one last time. Matthew smiled. Evidently Toric was smiling down upon him.

Movement from a reader in another area of the room made him start as he realised he had spent too long on this page. He stretched out his arms and yawned, hoping his pause would be taken as one due to tiredness, before continuing with his reading. It was not an easy task, for his mind now swam with plans and ideas that distracted him and eroded his ability to focus on the words upon the page. To cover for that he allowed himself to yawn frequently, and seem to almost doze off on occasions. After what he considered was a considerable length of time he shook his head violently, as if trying to shake away his drowsiness. He then rose to his feet and went towards one of the many, ever hovering librarians.

"I'm afraid that tiredness is getting the best of me," he whispered in

Solmanese. "Would it be possible to take those last few books with me to my chambers, that I may read them when I have had the chance to rest?"

The look of shock that crossed the librarian's face was enough to make Matthew smile. He suppressed the urge and concentrated on looking tired.

"I'm afraid that would be unacceptable, sir," the short man replied with a worried frown. "Even the Prophet himself may not take a tome from the sanctuary of Sashad, Keeper of Knowledge."

"Of course," replied Matthew, trying to appear remorseful. "In my tiredness I forgot myself. I am sorry to have insulted you."

"That is already forgotten," replied the man with a bow. "You are not of our lands and it is not for me to expect you to know all of our customs as well as we do ourselves. We can aid you in a small way though."

"Truly? In what way?"

"We are able to put aside books you have yet to read in a small sanctuary so that you may return to them when you need to," replied the librarian.

"You can?" asked Matthew, as if in delight. "That would be most useful to me if you could do so. I am trying to prepare a small treatise on history and books such as those would prove most useful to my studies."

"These are histories?" asked the librarian, looking closely at the books. "Ah yes. That too is my passion. I have even written a small tome on the subject myself, if you would be interested in reading it."

The man sounded almost shy about the subject, yet his eyes shone with enthusiasm.

"I would be delighted to," replied Matthew with a smile. "If you would place it atop those you leave for me in the sanctuary, then I shall read it upon my return,"

"Very good, sir," said the Solman with a bow. "I will place them in my private sanctuary. All you need do on your return is ask for Farhid and I shall attend to you."

"Thank you," replied Matthew genuinely touched. "I shall do so, though needs must I now retire. I thank you once more for your assistance."

He gave a small bow from the waist, in the Solman fashion, then turned and left, returning his thoughts to the words still burning in his mind. Already a plan was forming in his mind and he needed to speak with Naithan immediately.

V

Zakar Melzanor, Grand Vizier to the Prophet of Light, sat alone in his offices, trying to puzzle out the actions of their Caldorian guests. They were a strange group that had proved themselves to be almost unreadable. Their actions and moves in the Great Game made no sense and often seemed contrary to each other, though not in the planned way he would have expected had they been out to deceive him.

It was almost as if they could not play the Game at all, yet at times he could see understanding in their eyes as to the meaning of their actions. Caldorians had never been renowned players, yet their actions seemed almost as complex and expertly played as some of the greater Clans of the Council of Kolth, and that made them dangerous.

He looked at the character profiles again, trying to form a mental picture of them in his mind. The king seemed to be a religious fanatic who enjoyed nothing more than a debate on theological ideas and differences, though that seemed to be in an attempt to persuade the Prophet to allow him the honour of marrying the Princess Serinda by stressing the similarities in their religions. Yet even though the Prophet had done the unprecedented thing of allowing Naithan to see her before the day of the wedding rites, Naithan had not yet offered the bridal payment yet. He seemed content to prattle on about the glories of Toric, never realising that his chance of marriage was slipping away from him with every word. Yet the Prophet seemed to enjoy the debates with the king, even though he was a far superior debater and theologist than the Caldorian, and did not seem to take offence at the king's actions.

Zakar could not fathom the behaviour, though he was sure that it was somehow related to the behaviour of the Lord High Priest, Matthew. He seemed to be the better of the two at playing the Game, for he had found every spy hole within his room as if by chance and continually picked one of the three blind spots to sit in when about one of his hidden tasks. Zakar was sure it had something to do with the two pieces of magical brass rods he kept in that small box, one that could, by rights, only be used by wizards. Yet the man was a priest, for he himself had felt the man's healing powers used upon himself when he had visited Caldor with Ambassador Mahjats some two months ago.

That was another mystery, for all historical records stated that the Lord Priest of Caldor was in fact a wizard kept to guard the king against the foul magicks of their enemies. Matthew appeared to be the first true priest to hold the title, yet he also seemed able to use sorcery. No one could ever use both magicks, it was a known impossibility, like that of turning truly invisible with magic, yet, as the ancient phrase went, if one had eliminated the possible, the impossible, however improbable, was the answer. If the man had somehow managed to work a way around the barrier between the two magicks, then he was the most intelligent, and potentially powerful, man Zakar had ever met, and that scared Zakar more than anything he had ever known. Against a man of such intelligence, even his own towering intellect would be dwarfed and useless. He would make an interesting opponent in a game of Shak'ar. If the man was as intelligent as Zakar believed, he would most probably have learned ways to win, even if playing black.

A knock sounded gently at his door and he set his thoughts aside.

"Enter," he commanded and Farhid, one of his assistants at the Temple of Sashad entered the room. "Well, what did he do?"

"Histories," replied the man as he began a full bow. "I have taken them to my sanctuary and looked through them, though I have been unable to see anything of value there. He even picked one that was so burned that it was almost illegible in parts."

"Thank you," replied Zakar, his mind racing. "You have done well for one of your station. However, you did more to presume upon that which you were not asked to presume upon. After you have taken me to the sanctuary, report to your confessor and have him order you flogged three times."

"Yes sir, forgive me sir," said the man with a dutiful bow.

"I did," Zakar replied. "If I had not then I would have suggested one hundred lashings. Lead on."

The little man bowed once more then led him out into the canopied corridor. He paid it no mind, for he was one of the few officials who had little use for such silken luxuries. The billowing silk would constantly shift in airy rooms and corridors, acting as a distraction to the mind. His quarters, save the audience chamber, were all bare of such things.

They passed out of the palace and into the streets, Zakar pulling the tail of his silken head scarf, his hadar, across his face to hide his features. It would not do for one of his station to be seen walking through the streets, but there were times when a litter was too conspicuous a method of transport.

He walked through the bustling streets, keeping his eyes to the floor as any dutiful servant would, and even stopped on occasions to glance over wares in various stores, where messages from other assistants were waiting for collection. Usually he had others perform such menial tasks, though he liked to do it himself on occasions, for there were times when things needed his personal touch to ensure all still ran smoothly.

Even despite the stops, the journey to the gilded entrance of the temple did not take long and he soon found himself in the sanctuary of Farhid.

"Go now and find your confessor," he commanded. "Do not return to these chambers before dusk. To do so would forfeit your life."

"As you command," replied Farhid, bowing as he did.

Zakar watched him leave then turned his attention to the books piled before him. They were in two piles and he assumed the lesser of the two was the pile read by the Lord Priest, a view he was soon abused of when he saw the blackened pages of a book amidst the greater pile. If the Lord Priest had truly read them all in the limited time the man had been given then evensup would be interesting tonight.

That was of no consequence at the moment, however, and he reached out to take the book. It did not appear damaged from the outside, one of the unusual properties of Krakar skin, but the pages inside were just as Farhid had described, all save one. One of the pages was warm, as if the flame had only recently taken it. He smiled and placed the book inside his robes. He prayed briefly to Sashad to forgive him the crime he was about to commit and vowed to be lashed a hundred times in penance. Even the Grand Vizier was not immune from the death penalty and taking a book from Temple grounds was crime enough for such punishment. Yet there were tests he needed to perform on the book before then, and they could only be done in his laboratory. He would learn the plans of the Caldorians and if they meant harm to the Prophet, then he would stop them.

VI

Matthew was woken by Naithan's voice as he entered his bed chambers. It took a few moments to shake the sleep from his brain and focus upon his friend's words.

"…So what did you want?" finished the king, leaving Matthew momentarily confused.

"…I…needed to speak with you about the Prophet," he said, throwing up a quick spell to ward their conversation against eavesdroppers. "In particular, we need to discuss his conversion. How went your discussion?"

"Not well," replied Naithan, his face suddenly seeming drawn and haggard. "He talks me round in circles and none of my arguments touch him. How can such an intelligent man err so gravely?"

"Thenril gives his followers, witting or unwitting, words of guile and deceit to confuse and test the true follower," replied Matthew, quoting one of the many mantras taught by Toric. "You've told me that one often enough, have you not?"

He felt a stab of fear slice through him as he saw the uncertainty in Naithan's eyes. It was a look he had never expected to see from his friend when discussing such matters.

"I know, but somehow, here in this land of heathens, I feel alone, as if Toric is not here with me," replied Naithan.

"Impossible!" replied Matthew in shock. He was not the most devoted follower, yet even he did not question Toric's omnipresence. "He's everywhere. You know that!"

"Do I?" asked Naithan, turning upon Matthew, anger flaring up in his eyes. "I speak with the prophet and his words confuse me, as you say. They make me question things and that scares me." Matthew did not know how to reply. "I have left my kingdom and since then nothing but ill fortune has beset me. I have been captured by pirates, lost Theldar to rebels, failed in both my objectives here in Sol, and the dreams have ceased as well."

"The dreams?" asked Matthew in surprise. Naithan had not spoken of this before.

"Yes," replied Naithan sadly. "Since the first day I arrived here I have felt the dreams approach me, yet they cannot reach me. It is as if they are barred, sealed away from me by a greater power, yet there is no greater power than Toric. I have slept the dreamless sleep of death here, every night a reminder of what is to come."

"Only if you fail," replied Matthew slowly. Working around his friend's religious ideas was going to be difficult. "Perhaps this is what it means. Always you say Toric is testing your resolve by giving you dream after dream of pain and torture, to make harder and more worthy for the task ahead, is that not so?"

"Yes, that is what I have always believed," replied Naithan slowly.

"Then consider this another test," replied Matthew. "He is forcing you to examine your own faith to see if it is strong enough to survive the trials ahead of you. If you look into your soul deeply, you will find the resolve you need. Your questioning can only make you stronger in the end."

He could see a little change in Naithan's expression and Matthew knew that his words were having some effect. Unfortunately he knew it was not going to be enough. He would now have to enact his plan alone, for he was going to have to boost his friend's faith whilst converting the Prophet.

He sighed and looked at the king. He had never realised those dreams that tortured him so were so important to him. They had spent so many years trying to remove them, or block them and Matthew would have thought Naithan should feel better for the rest he was now getting. Yet it seemed the dreams were part of the strength in his belief. He had had them since the day of his coronation and obviously viewed them as a sign, either from Toric or Thenril, though Matthew would never believe the second possibility. He found it hard to believe that Toric would be so cruel a god as to inflict such pain, yet even if it were Thenril creating the dreams, it showed Naithan that he was doing what was needed.

"Will you be all right?" he asked his now silent friend.

"Yes. I will need to retire to my chambers and pray for guidance though. I shall not attend evensup tonight. Can you inform them that I am ill and have taken to bed early? There are things I must do."

Matthew nodded and Naithan got up and left the chamber. He watched him go, worry racing through his mind. He hoped Naithan was not cracking under the pressure.

He rubbed the sleep from his eyes and set back to the work he had been doing before sleep had taken him. He yawned and wondered if he should request any of the coffee he had tasted here. It was stronger than the Kolthon brew he was used to drinking and was supposed to act as a stimulant to the senses. It was also able to ward off sleep, assistance he knew he would need in the long night ahead of him, for tomorrow he had a miracle to create.

VII

Groltch did his best to control his anger. The human knight could be so stubborn sometimes. They had reached the edges of Teldin over an hour ago yet they had still not decided on who should enter the city. They had decided that unanimously that they dared not risk another trap waiting for them and that it would be safer if only two of them were to enter and see about booking passage out of Caldor. It was highly likely that the northern borders would be patrolled and was too great a risk to chance, so sailing from the kingdom still seemed the best option.

Groltch was still not sure he'd be prepared to trust his life to one of those flimsy wooden vessels, but had been out voted. That was not the source of the present argument though. That was due to the debate over who would enter the city to book their passage. Tristan had immediately volunteered and had set the argument rolling, largely between Tristan and everyone else. Everyone knew that, noble as his ideals were, they were not conducive to entering a city covertly. The man had argued that he had changed and that he would be able to do it, which was blatantly untrue. Oh, he had changed since their fight at the village but he was certainly not the best candidate. However, Tristan remained obstinate and the shouting continued.

"Fine," said Tristan sourly, breaking Groltch from his thoughts. "Matthius and Groltch can enter the city. Just be warned, I will not be entering the city to rescue you when it all goes wrong."

Groltch looked at the human quickly. There had been an edge to his words that had sent a cold shiver down his spine. The human seemed positive that things were destined to go wrong, and the knight's sleep had been restless, as if he were dreaming of unpleasant things. Of course, they had all slept restlessly since that day, except Belthar of course, who would probably sleep through an earthquake, and he had merely put it down to dreams of the fight. Could he have had a portentous dream? Groltch smiled at himself. He was becoming as bad as a youngling for such fanciful imaginings.

"Well Groltch, are you ready?" asked Matt, looking at him.

Groltch turned his thoughts away from Tristan, who was now sat a little way away and staring out into space.

"Yes. Groltch ready," he replied, still feeling a little distracted by his friend's behaviour.

"Then hadn't you better transform yourself then?" asked Matt, whose body was already shimmering as it transformed.

Groltch touched the scarf around his neck and closed his eyes. It was difficult to get the details exactly correct and he had spent many days practising with it since he had gained it. He should hopefully look like one of the Solmen, as they were called in Caldorian, one of the humans from Sol. He had never seen one and it had taken a long time for him to build up an adequate picture in his mind so that he could change form. His vision blurred and pain stabbed through him, telling him the process was underway. When it died out he looked to Matt who nodded approvingly. He then mounted Galahad, who had been transformed into a large black stallion and Matt took his place as a servant leading the horse. As they moved off towards the city he thought over the story they had prepared. He was to be a travelling tourist from Sol with a Caldorian guide to show him the sights of the kingdom. He had thought it a rather strange custom, this visiting a place just to see it. Ran-tha rarely ever felt the need to leave the environs of their village, but the others had assured him that it was quite common among humans.

Thinking of that conversation reminded him of Tris, for it had been then that he had first begun to notice the changes in the human knight. He was normally a quiet man, yet he had become more and more withdrawn since the battle and Groltch had often seen him gazing out into nothingness, a look of despair and concentration playing across his face. There were also several occasions when he swore he had seen strange occurrences happen shortly afterwards, as if Tristan had been using magic, a thought that almost made him snort with laughter. He had also been willing to let Matt cast a disguising spell on him as well though, so Tris was evidently warming to the idea of magic.

The sound of people distracted him and he turned his thoughts to the present situation. As he looked around he saw that there were a large number of humans labouring around this area, moving large slabs of cut stone towards the edge of the city. As he looked around, he saw that they were in the process of creating a large wall that would end up surrounding the whole city. He thought it odd that such a development was coming so late, then realised that in the distance was another such wall. Between them were many houses and shops, though most of those around him looked quite ramshackle and worn down.

As they moved through the central street he saw that the quality gradually improved and even saw some buildings undergoing complete reconstruction. All these new buildings looked of similar design to those in Kelvaria, with their half wood and half-stone pattern. Evidently this was a successful and thriving city, though why so many humans could wish to live so close to so many others was beyond him. He had heard the stories of the great ran-tha cities of the Golden Age, but doubted there was much truth behind them.

The voices of human younglings disrupted his thoughts once more and he watched them scamper around the streets hollering and shouting at each other in whatever game they were playing. At least those younglings had a little more freedom than others he had seen. Most of those he had seen working the fields could not have been much past eight cycles in age and certainly not old enough yet to be of useful employment. Yet again the differing habits of the humans caused a stab of homesickness in his heart. He ignored it though, trying to act like an interested tourist, looking at everything with a wild-eyed wonder, taking in all the sights they could. As they approached the gate in the completed wall, the guards glanced at them before waving them through. As they had planned, Groltch raised his palm up and commanded Matt to halt. He then beckoned the wizard to him and spoke softly to him in his native language.

"This is stupid. This won't fool them. Why are we doing it at all?"

Matt smiled and nodded his head, as if he understood every word Groltch had uttered. He then turned to the first guard.

"Excuse me sir," said Matt politely. "My master asks me to ask you the location of the finest alehouse in the city. He has the desire to sample some Grathnacian drinks, and wishes only the best."

"Not from these parts, is he?" asked the guard suspiciously.

"No, from Sol," he replied loudly. Groltch smiled and nodded his head, as if he were reacting to mention of his homeland. Matt then softened his tone to an almost conspiratorial whisper. "His gold is good though and he is very free with it. I'll see that you're well rewarded, if you would tell us of the best inn."

A glint of avarice appeared in the man's eyes and Groltch had to stop himself smiling. The plan could work after all.

"I tell you what," said the guard, smiling at Groltch as he did. "I'm just finishing my shift now, so I can give you a personal escort there. You know there are a number of footpads and such around. An obviously foreign gentleman would be considered easy pickings to such criminals."

Groltch concealed his horror at the plan, still trying to smile and look around vacantly, as if he could not understand a whit of Caldorian.

"That would be most kind, sir," replied Matthew, tension edging his voice. "I'll make sure the Solman rewards you generously for your kind sacrifice."

Groltch's eyes widened at that and he glared at the wizard as he returned to the horse.

"Well that seem to work all right," said Matt in thickly accented ran-tha. Groltch smiled and looked to the guard. "You never knew speak your tongue Matt could. We best follow guard, for that would be perfect cover for us. Any human who does question us shall receive reply better than we two alone could give."

Groltch smiled at the guard again and bowed in thanks, as if he had just been told of the man's offer. It was all a show though, for inside his stomach was churning. He hoped the boy was correct in his hypothesis. Groltch was a ran-the keen on organisation and he hated it when plans went awry, as they had a wont to do when he was with these humans. He was suddenly reminded of Tris's certainty that things would go wrong and the shudder of fear ran through him again. The methram around his neck, often able to sense danger nearby went cold for a moment and Groltch found himself praying to Toric that the knight was wrong.

"What be wrong with you?" asked Matt, pointing to several buildings as if giving a small tour. "You do look like death herself."

"Nothing," replied Groltch, looking around trying to appear enthralled by it all. "I'll be fine."

"Here we are," said the guard, indicating an inn called the *Golden Goblet*.

Groltch smiled and allowed Matt to help him down from Galahad. He then handed the guard a handful of golden mareks, making both the guard and Matt look down in shock.

"I thank you for your help, good sir," Groltch said slowly, as if struggling to find the words.

The guard bowed, still looking stunned, and then left them alone.

"Do you realise how much you gave him?" hissed Matt angrily.

"Enough to make what you whispered seem enough," replied Groltch.

"You heard that?" asked Matt, his eyes widening in surprise. "I added that on the spur of the moment. I'm sorry."

"Don't be," replied Groltch. "If our pursuers ask the guards about who came into here today, he will remember only a rich fool and his servant. Not poor…fleers…"

"Runaways." interjected the sword quickly. Groltch had gotten rather used to having it ride around in his mind with him, helping him with his Caldorian, though he still had difficulties on occasions.

"…runaways…"

"Thank you," said Matt, sounding relieved. "Shall we stable the horse then?"

"Yak," replied Groltch in his own tongue once more. "Could you also hire us a room? It would make us look a little less suspicious."

Matt seemed to comprehend and took the money Groltch gave him. The ran-the looked through the door and saw Matt talking to a bald headed human stood behind the door. Groltch tried not to stare, but it was difficult. He had not realised that humans had Mes-trecha as well, though Matt seemed to treat the human as if it were like any other. This was going to be a very expensive inn indeed. The Mes-treche clapped his hands together twice and a human youngling came running out to him. The child took Galahad's reins and led the horse to the stables.

"You won't believe how much he charged us for one night's rent," muttered the wizard as they walked away.

Groltch felt sure he would but even he blanched at the price Matt told him. Even the High Mes-treche of his village had not charged such fees for his services. But this was a city, and quite a large one at that. It took them almost an hour to reach the docks and when they did, Groltch's eyes widened in shock at the size of them. He had never seen the docks of Theldar, only those of Kelvaria, and Teldin's docks more than dwarfed them.

Finding a ship that would take them away from Caldor would be much easier than they had originally thought, though getting to them could be a problem. They were bustling with activity as the dockers loaded the many crates onto the many ships docked there. Fishermen were there too, many seeming to prepare their boats for sailing, others sat on the dockside mending their nets. In other areas, drunken humans swayed out of the various taverns and bars, several of them all but colliding into Groltch as they went.

Everywhere smelled of salt and humans and Groltch suddenly felt himself being briefly overwhelmed by it all. He was not one for crowds and he had not realised that there would be so many people here. He turned to Matt to ask if they could rest a moment and found, to his horror that the boy had disappeared among the many bodies pressing around him. He fought to keep down the panic and tried to push his way through the humans to find Matt, yet there was no trace. His head swam and his vision blurred. His breathing became ragged and his mind screamed at him to flee.

The rational side of him suddenly took hold and he forced himself to breath calmly and slowly, beginning his exercises to calm his mind. He was not given time to complete them, however, as the crowds parted around him and he found himself facing a contingent of some twenty knights all marching towards him. He pushed himself at the crowds that only minutes ago he had been desperate to leave. Unfortunately they were too tightly packed together and so he just stood there, holding his breath as the knights marched passed him. He waited for the moment that they would turn and confront him, but they merely ignored him and marched on past. He released his breath and turned back to try and find Matt once more, colliding into someone as he did so.

"Watch where you're going," said a vaguely familiar voice.

He looked up and saw the female knight that had almost caught them in Kelvaria, the one Tristan had called Sar Karene. A look of recognition crossed her face and she examined him closely.

"It is you," she hissed, confusion flaring up in her eyes. "My spell should show your true form but can only give me a sense of…"

Groltch turned to leave and as he did he felt his muscles suddenly freeze up. The methram round his neck went icy cold and fear cut through him like a knife. She had caught him with magic.

"You're not going anywhere," she said walking round him slowly, a triumphant grin on her face. "So tell me. Where is he?" Be warned, any answer that does not satisfy me will be met with intense pain to which you will be unable to scream at. Do you understand?"

"Yes," he replied, determined to withstand whatever torture she was preparing to devise.

He did not need to, for at that moment the docks suddenly exploded with flame and a familiar presence entered his mind.

"Fear not," said Cal. *"The cavalry has arrived!"*

With those words came mobility and he turned to run. He immediately collided with a dock worker that seemed to have the same idea and they both fell to the floor. He pulled himself to his feet and saw that chaos now ruled the docks. Everything seemed to be on fire, including some of the humans working on the dockside and even buildings near him. A human ran past, screaming as the flames enveloped them and as he moved out of the way, he felt invisible tendrils of magic try to wrap round him. Panic began to grip him, but they vanished suddenly, as if they had never been.

He did not have time to puzzle it out though for he found himself crashing to the ground and as he twisted to land safely he saw what had caused his fall. It was the knight Karene, and she had thrown her full weight against him. He began to struggle to try and free himself but found she had expertly pinned him down. She moved her face close to his and smiled.

"You are going to stay with me now, and I shall use you to bait a trap for Tristan, as he seems to have some strange fascination with you," she said, shifting her weight to keep him pinned as he struggled to free himself. "You don't realise…"

She was cut off by a high pitched scream and both looked for its source. Not too far away several burning crates had collapsed, trapping a human youngling with long blond hair. It was alive and unburned at the moment, yet that would not last long, for the flames were rapidly approaching the child. Karene looked at him, indecision showing in her face, though it was not there for long. She bent closer to him once more.

"It seems I will have to let you go," she said with regret, "but I, unlike you, am not a child killer. Just tell Tristan this when you reach him. No matter how far he runs, no matter where he goes, I shall follow him, and I shall find him. Even if he runs to the depths of the Dark Realms and back, and he and all those who aid him shall regret it when I catch him."

With that she leapt to her feet and dashed to the youngling. He let her insult slip by, knowing that this could be his only chance of escape. He rolled to his feet and took a moment to watch the knight rescue the child. He then began pushing his way through the panicking mob. Initially it was difficult to make his way through the crowd, but suddenly those around him started yelping and moving out of his way, as if they were being hit by some invisible shock.

"Run towards the inn," called Caliburn. *"Help is coming!"*

He made his way out of the docks and soon found the crowds thinning, and with it his own sense of panic. He looked back warily, suddenly getting the strange sensation he was being watched. A momentary flash of panic filled him as he realised that he had allowed the disguise to drop in his flight. Cursing himself he scanned the streets, but could see no one looking at him. He was distracted by the sound of hooves clattering on the cobbled street. He looked down a side street and saw Tristan galloping towards him on Galahad, whose illusion had also faded. The knight slowed the horse a little, before wheeling round towards the eastern gate.

"Here we go again," said Cal wearily in his head.

Groltch found himself agreeing with the sword and he wondered if he would ever leave a human city without the need for haste.

Thank you for the fire, he thought to the sword. *It was a little excessive though. You injured innocent humans.*

"The fire was not our doing," replied the sword. *"We arrived as it exploded."*

Groltch felt relief at that. He would have found him hating them if they had risked that youngling's life and killed others like it just to save him. It did leave him the question of where the flames had come from. It was then that he remembered the wizard that had aided Sar Karene in Kelvaria, and the other one Matt had fought in Belthanor. Had the young sorcerer encountered one of them? He suddenly found himself very worried about Matt's safety as they raced out of the gates past the startled guards.

VIII

Karene cursed her luck as she carried the girl to safety. She had just had that wretched creature in her hands and had held the key to capturing Tristan, only to lose it again. Now she was back to her original position.

"Sar Karene," came the voice of Sir Jax in her head.

Yes Jax, she replied, a little too brusquely. *What is it?*

"I have spotted the errant knight and am in pursuit. He is headed out of the city. Request permission to follow."

Request granted, but follow them only, and report to me their position regularly, she replied, suddenly hopeful once again. *And Jax?*

"Yes Sar?"

No heroics, she warned. *You can't take them on your own, no matter how good you think you are."*

"As you command, Sar," he replied, his voice fading from her mind.

"Are you all right?" she asked aloud, her attention turning to the girl.

She replied by mutely nodding her head. Fear had obviously put her in shock. Karene embraced the girl and gently stroked her hair.

"It's all right now," she said softly. "You're safe here."

The girl began to sob and Karene closed her eyes in sadness. Whoever had started that fire would have a lot to answer for, though that would have to be a matter for the city guards. She had other duties to attend to, once the fire was under control and the people safe. Her thoughts began to spin off as she allowed her mouth to speak soothing nothings to the girl. Tristan was almost her prisoner.

IX

Matt turned round and found that Groltch had been lost in the crowds. He scanned the many faces of the people around him, but found it was all to no avail. The unfamiliar form Groltch had taken was too dissimilar for him to find in the midst of all these strangers. It was made worse by the fact that there were many Solmen on the docks, Teldin being one of the central trading ports of Caldor, and found that they all seemed alike, their dark, dusky skin confusing to his eyes. He spied one that seemed similar to Groltch but he merely glared at Matt as he tried to approach him.

After that he gave up searching. They had agreed to meet up at the inn if they became separated, so he paid it no mind. He reached down to his large pouch and absently scratched between the ears of his kitten, causing a loud purr to emanate from him. He looked down feeling mildly confused. He was certain that he had left Fluff behind with Belthar for safe keeping though the kitten did have, like most of his feline brethren, a strong will of his own. This was not the first time he had turned up where Matt had not been expecting him. He stroked him a couple of times before continuing his search through the bustling docks.

He soon found himself gawking at the many sights around him.

Selene was miles from the coast and he had never seen the docks in Kelvaria, yet the sheer variety of activity was astounding. All around him people from many nations hurried from pillar to post about their business. He saw dockers hauling crates on and off ships, what had to be fishermen mending nets and foreign sailors clambering about the rigging of the many magnificent ships. Most fabulous of all was an elegant tall ship that seemed to have been built to mirror the shape of a bird, down to a long arching neck at the prow. Its sails were folded at the moment, yet strangest of all was the fact that there was no rigging. All the tales he had ever heard of ships had talked of the need for rigging, yet this apparently needed none.

"Ah, I see you are admiring our ship," said a voice softly.

Matt started and he looked round, finding himself staring into the oval eyes of what had to be an elf. His jaw dropped in disbelief. The elves of Veltharia were known for their secrecy and reclusive ways, yet here was one stood before him, its ship dock mere feet away. He took a long look at this being around which hung so much myth and legend. It was tall and slender, measuring almost seven feet in height, and its limbs seemed almost out of proportion to its form. The fingers were long and so thin that they looked as if they would break under the slightest pressure. Its clothing was of an elegant cut, the shirt and breeches being made of the finest green silks and they seemed to move as if alive as the wind ruffled them gently. On its right shoulder was the clasp of its cloak, designed to form a butterfly with dazzling jewels being used to colour its wings. More amazing than this was the cloak it held that seemed to be almost insubstantial and so fine that it appeared almost invisible to the eye. More surprising than this was the fact that none of the clothing seemed to have any stitching and there was no evidence of seams covering anywhere that would need stitching.

Strangest of all were the elf's facial features. Its eyes were slanted towards its long, thin nose, and their irises were a soft lilac in colour. The face was longer than seemed natural and this was accentuated by its high cheekbones and finely chiselled chin. The skin was of a light grey hue and its ears had long lobes and slanted up into slight points. Its long hair was silver and gold, which was braided with green and blue ribbon and wrapped once round its long neck before trailing down its back. It was the most amazing thing Matt had ever seen. It was beautiful, if in an alien way, and he found that he had lost his voice in wonder.

"The ship's rigging is made of the same material as the cloak you see me wearing," continued the elf, ignoring Matt's silent gaze. "It is so fine that from a distance it is invisible, though it is stronger than the toughest steel. Would you like to come on board for a closer look?"

Matt wondered what had made this beautiful creature start talking to him, a mere human, and the offer to board the ship made his eyes open wide in amazement. He had the chance to go on such a wondrous ship with such beautiful creatures. He nodded his head and began moving towards the slender, graceful gangplank. Suddenly there was a hissing and growling from Fluff that made him pause a moment. He reached down to soothe the animal. Fluff screeched and spat as his paw came out, claws extended, and scratched his hand viciously. The pain cut through the euphoria he had been feeling and his head suddenly felt a lot clearer.

He looked to the elf and found that whilst still beautiful, it had lost the awe-inspiring aura he had felt. Its lilac eyes widened in shock as Matt turned to move away and it swept its arm out towards him. Invisible threads of magic leapt out to catch him and Matt threw up a shield, cutting them off immediately, shocking the elf once more. He tried to keep down his own shock, for he had just used magic without the usual forms, and what was more, it had worked. How he did not know.

"You are the *Mattenrar*," said the elf, its eyes narrowing to slits, giving the creature an almost feral look. "Get him! But don't kill him."

Several armed humans leapt at him from the crowd, though no one else around seemed to be paying them any attention. Looking round he saw that none of the people on the dock seemed to see what was happening to him. He stumbled back, knowing that somehow they had cut him off from aid, leaving him alone. He looked back and saw that he was edging towards the sea, causing a stab of fear to slice through his heart. He was not much of a swimmer and rarely swam beyond his depth, finding that his chest seemed to tighten and his breathing became ragged when his feet could not touch the ground. The water behind him was of a deep port for ships, their depths unimaginable to Matt.

He had to act. He summoned his magic and concentrated, bars of flame leaping from his fingertips at the men. Two were instantly melted in flames and the other three collapsed to the floor, screaming as they burned to death. Energy flooded through every pore of his body and he felt more alive and powerful than he could ever dream of.

He turned to the elf in time to see it launch another magical attack at him. He used his power to swat the attack away and sent the flames at the elf. Its cloak wrapped itself around it as the flames struck and it stepped through them completely unscathed. Matt gaped in shock and barely noticed another man leap at him. As he did he spun and flicked a bar of flames at him, causing him to crash to the floor, screaming in agony. Matt knew he was too late, though, for the distraction would have been enough to allow the elf to prepare another attack and Matt doubted that his own magic would harm it.

He heard a loud snarl from the elf's direction and turned in time to see a large black beast pounce upon the elf. The elf screamed and began grappling with it, though was barely able to fend off the creature's claws that were currently tearing through its clothes. He watched the scene for only a second before turning to flee, drawing more magic to himself as he did. Two more men ran to attack him only to be consumed in Matt's flame bars. Energy flooded through him and as it did came a terrifying revelation. Each death brought about by his magic seemed to give him more power. If he were to kill just a few more people the he could well end up being powerful enough to deal with the elf. He drew the energy towards him, preparing to destroy the humans now running around the docks in panic, his conflict at last reaching their notice.

He smiled at the thought of the power it would bring him and unleashed a torrent of flame. As he did a small voice screamed within his mind and the horror of what he was unleashing struck him with the force of a charging horse. He screamed as he did, knowing it was too late to recall the flames, yet somehow he managed to alter the spell as it left him, sending it up into the skies around. He forced out all the energy he had, feeling sickened at its source and the flames exploded outwards, setting light to the buildings, ships and crates around him. Fortunately not one touched a single human, a small mercy for Matt.

Suddenly the energy vanished and the flames stopped issuing from his fingertips. Matt slumped to the ground, tears of shame and fear flooding from his eyes. If he had unleashed that flame on people he would have killed almost all of them. Was this how magic was? Fear and misery twisted his stomach. Now, more than ever, he missed his master's gentle teachings and he knew just how little he knew of magic.

Instinct made Matt turn around and he saw the elf staggering towards him, blood flowing from many large wounds on its body. Matt was surprised that the creature was still standing with that many injuries, let alone walk with them. Matt got to his feet, turning away from the elf and merging into the crowd. He allowed himself to get lost in the screaming crowds of fleeing humans and ran from the docks into a maze of alleyways and streets.

He ran until his lungs burned with each breath and his legs felt as if they were turning to jelly. He looked back and saw no sign of pursuit, so allowed himself a chance to rest. It was then that he realised he was truly lost. He tried to keep the panic down but failed, knowing that if he were in the wrong part of the city any number of crimes could be committed against him and he would have no defence. He had almost completely burned out his magical energies with the flame and doubted if he could even muster up enough energy to conjure up a candle flame.

He hung his head wearily, wondering where he should go. At that moment, the large black animal that had attacked the elf on the dock appeared from the alley to his left. It padded slowly towards him and a cold wave of fear swept over him. It had several wounds to its legs and torso, but still looked strong enough to finish off one weak human, such as himself. He closed his eyes, waiting for its pounce. It did not come and Matt almost jumped from his skin when he felt it nuzzle its head against him. He opened his eyes and looked warily at the beast. It looked like a large black cat of some description, with yellow eyes seaming to gleam in the light of the now setting sun. It wandered a little way down the street then looked back at him.

"You want me to follow you?" he asked if, feeling a little foolish and nervous.

It seemed to nod its head then edged its way further down the alley. As it did Matt heard footsteps behind him and turned to see the elf staggering across towards him, many of its wounds already seeming to be partially healed. Matt looked back to the large cat in the alley and, after a quick prayer to Toric, followed it down the alley. He heard the elf break into a run and the beast snarled, leaping suddenly into a shadow. Matt followed its example and found the world suddenly swirl around him. Colours merged and span as one and he found himself feeling sick at the sight of it all.

Suddenly all was gone and he found himself on a path in a dark forest. The road seemed ancient and was made of some black substance that crumbled at his touch. Next to him stood the large cat, waiting for him. It twitched its tail then began padding quietly down the road. He followed it, aware of many eyes looking down upon him.

Movement flashed in the bushes around him and his eyes darted after them. The creature before him roared loudly and all sound stopped, the feeling of being watched vanishing with the noise. After that he found no fear of this place and had the strange sensation that somehow he was at home. It was queer, but the trees, as strange as they were, seemed similar to those of Caldor, though much larger and more ancient than any he had ever seen before. Even so, he had the strangest feeling he had been here before, a long time ago. The feeling sent a shudder down his spine and nervousness gripped him once more.

Suddenly the cat stopped and motioned to the shadow of a particularly large tree before them. He looked at the cat questioningly, noticing that many of its wounds were beginning to heal already.

"Does this get me back?" he asked, feeling foolish once again at talking to an animal. He thought suddenly of Belthar in his natural form and suddenly it did not seem so strange.

The creature nodded and Matt moved closer. He gingerly reached out to scratch it between the ears and it began purring loudly.

"Thank you," he said with a smile then stepped into the shadow.

The world swam before him and he appeared in a familiar stretch of road. Just as the world began to steady itself, it swirled suddenly again, the soil rising up to meet him.

X

Belthar paced angrily around the clearing, muttering and cursing to himself. That knight was a bloody stupid human being. The moment Groltch and Matt had left the knight had gone after them. Belthar had tried to stop the man but something in the tone of his voice had stopped him in his tracks.

"If I do not go now, Groltch will be captured and all will be lost," he had said, and Belthar's instincts had told him Tris was correct.

The man had been touched by the water spirits in the sacred grove on High Festival and had obviously shown him visions of the future, as they had Belthar when they had restored him in the pool. If Tris's had been anything like his own then there was a dark future ahead for them. He had let the knight go and prayed to the Spirits that he was successful.

He had listened to the knight go before turning back into the clearing and discovering that Matt's wretched cat had disappeared on him. He had spent over an hour searching for him, using scent and his powers to seek out its mind, yet all had drawn a blank. The creature was evidently out of range and, therefore, too distant to search for. Matt was going to be livid when he returned.

A noise to his left made Belthar turn away from his thoughts. Matt's scent seemed to spring out from nowhere and he heard the boy collapse on the floor. It was immediately followed by the sound of Tris's horse bursting through the bushes from the other side of the clearing. He could smell the scents of both Tris and Groltch and with them came traces of fear and adrenaline. From the sounds of things, it had not gone well.

"Are we leaving?" he asked quickly.

"As soon as you are ready," replied Tris.

Belthar picked up Matt gently and heard the soft mew of his kitten. He turned to face Tris whilst opening himself up to the lifelines of the forest that would allow him to navigate them safely.

"I'm ready," he said gruffly, channelling some energy into Matt to restore some vitality to him.

"Let's go then," said Tris, riding Galahad out into the bushes. "Can you hide our trails?"

"I'm already doing it," he replied, sending out his requests to the animals around them.

Already he could feel their presence as they began restoring the soil and covering the land. In a few minutes it would seem as if they had never been there. That left only their scent trails, but that would be covered by the larger, shyer animals after they had left. He then masked their personal scents, as he had done on many occasions before, and followed Tris out of the clearing. As he did he found himself wondering what the former knight would do if he ever found out how often he and Matt had cast magic upon him.

XI

Galen watched Tyrone as he sat alone in his room praying to Toric. He had thought to leave the man alone to his prayers, but felt to do so was to risk losing the man. Tyrone was probably the best hunter Galen had ever met and his skills were incredible. He knew that he was being stalked somehow, despite all the powers Galen was using to cloak himself in shadows. This could well be the last in a long line of ruses used by the man to shake his pursuer.

The man finished his plea for forgiveness for the evil deed he was about to do and looked around the room. The man seemed to focus directly on Galen and he felt a shudder run down his spine. The man's instincts seemed infallible. Tyrone's eyes took on a look of resignation, as if he knew what were in store for him, before it changed to one of resolve. Galen heard the man mutter something.

"If I'm going t'die, let it be following my ideals."

Galen looked at the man with new found respect. He knew that the plan would fail, yet was still going to follow it. That was a rare courage for a human. He shook off the thought. He was human, or at least he had been once.

Tyrone moved off out of the room and he followed. The man removed a grate to the sewer system and dropped through it, closing it behind him. Galen allowed himself to seep through the grill, the sensation of his senses becoming fluid still making him feel distinctly uncomfortable. It was one of the powers he did not enjoy using too often.

The man was already some way down the tunnel by the time Galen had reformed himself enough to follow and he had to rush to catch him up. Tyrone went through what seemed like miles of tunnel before he clambered up into sunlight. Galen followed and found himself somewhere in the trees outside Theldar surrounded by some twenty knights.

For a moment he had the worrying thought that the plans had been changed and that this was now the site of the ambush, yet found this not to be the case. Tyrone was merely stood in the centre outlining his plan to these warriors. Satisfied that all was going well, Galen seeped back into the sewer and returned to the city, making a note of the tunnel's whereabouts. That was one weak link he could not afford to leave open after the morrow. He slipped back in through the gates of the palace and past the Shadow Knights guarding his chambers. They still had a lot to learn. As he re-formed once more he found Marie was sat in his chambers, watching him.

"Did all go well?" she asked.

"Well enough, though I still do not know what role the hawks will play. Did you follow her?"

"Yes," she replied. "What did you do to me?"

"What?" asked Galen, looking at her swiftly.

"I followed her and suddenly she looked round at me," replied Marie softly. "But she didn't see me. She looked right through me as if I wasn't there, just like they do around you sometimes. Have you turned me into one of *them*?"

"I needed to protect you," he said quietly.

"Protect me?" She asked, turning on him with anger blazing in her eyes. "If you didn't send me away then you wouldn't need to taint me to do it. You could do it yourself."

"Is that what you think it is? A taint on my soul?" asked Galen angrily.

"No," replied Marie. "But those Shadow Knights are your weapons, you told me that yourself. Tools to help you protect a dream. Does this make me one too? Is that all I am to you? A weapon?"

"No," replied Galen softly.

She had tears in her eyes and Galen felt pain.

"I send you away to keep you from me," replied Galen. "The king's torturing dreams plague me constantly and I feel myself slipping away more and more with each day that passes. I'm not going to live on this realm much longer, and wished to spare you the pain of losing me again."

"So instead you pain me every day with your cold remarks and snide comments?" she asked softly.

"No," he replied, taking her in his arms, feeling the heat of her body against his. She shuddered at the cold she felt from his frame, but wrapped her arms around him. "I love you, and would never wish to hurt you."

The realisation made him start and the cold, sinister part of his mind recoiled as if struck. His body seemed more solid than it had in days and for the first time in weeks he felt warm.

"I love you too," she replied, drawing him into a passionate kiss.

As she did the amulet that brought his nightly torture, now kept hanging from a chain around his neck, fell to the ground, shattering as it did. It was not the last garment to hit the floor that afternoon and Galen lost himself to a passion he had thought long dead…

XII

Marie left Galen as he slept his first night of peaceful sleep since the village. She looked down upon him, her heart soaring. The old Galen had returned to her that night and she had allowed herself to believe that they were back in Ashby. As she looked at him now, she saw his form shimmer slightly and was reminded that such thoughts were just illusions. They were both different now, and the love they felt was different, yet somehow stronger.

She turned and slipped from the room, heading back in the direction of Meredith's chambers. She knew that there was still some unfinished business to attend to there. She knocked on the door and entered immediately, finding Meredith sat at her oak desk.

"What do you want?" she asked, looking a little disgruntled.

Galen knows your plans," she replied simply, watching the surly expression disappear at once. "He has planned to repel it and arrest those involved."

"Why do you tell me this?" asked Meredith slowly.

"Because I know that you are not stupid and that in your own way you love Tyrone," replied Marie. "If you want to keep hold of your position and help save Tyrone's life, you will help us."

"And if I don't?" asked Meredith slowly.

"Then you'll die," replied Marie quietly.

"It is not wise to threaten me in my own quarters," said Meredith, calmly revealing knives up her sleeves.

"If you can cut through air with those then go ahead," replied Marie, allowing herself to change slightly and moving her arm through the chair.

When she had removed it there was a large white patch where her arm had been. She changed back and tapped the white area with her now solid hand. It crumbled to dust.

"What do you suggest?" asked Meredith, seeming to be unmoved by the scene.

"Galen will have people such as myself, Shadow Knights awaiting your assassins in the room…" began Marie.

"And you wish my Hawks to deal with Lord Anton's knights that will be there to capture those assassins?" filled in Meredith, a slight shake in her voice. Her eyes were locked on the white dust on the floor that was now eating through the rug there with an audible hiss.

"Yes," lied Marie, covering her shock. They had not known that part of the plan. Evidently Anton was planning on capturing the knights who killed Galen for some purpose or another. She had hoped to get someone other than the Shadow Knights to protect Galen, but now the original plan had to stay, with Meredith's addition that her Hawks take out Anton's knights.

"If I do it will Tyrone live?" Asked Meredith.

"Yes," replied Marie, "and you will keep your council position. I cannot guarantee Tyrone's position though."

"What guarantee do I have that you will do this?" asked Meredith.

"The same guarantee I will have from you that you will not betray me and have the Hawks aid in the assassination attempt," replied Marie. "My word."

They looked at each other for a few minutes before Meredith spoke.

"Done. Shall we discuss how it is to be done now?"

"It is as good a time as any," replied Marie. Though we shall have to be there for the release of the doves."

"That doesn't give us long then."

"Let's get to it then."

They made their plans as quickly as possible then hurried to get to the ceremony, Marie praying to Toric that she had done the correct thing.

XIII

The sun set slowly in the eastern sky and all across the city eyes looked to the heavens, waiting and watching for the reply that all knew was coming. The black crows would mean that by dawn they would be outside the city gates, fighting the armies camped there. The white doves would mean that they had chance for a peaceful solution. Storm clouds loomed over the sea and all hoped that they were not omens of doom.

The last few red rays of the sun's light slowly began to fade and suddenly the sky was awash with doves of purest white. Yet as they flew more than one person observed that the red light of the sun reflected off their white feathers giving them all a red tint and many people thought that the sky seemed awash with blood.

CHAPTER FIFTEEN: Augury and Ambush

I

The sun rose over the castle and he knew that the moment of truth had arrived. On this day he would have a choice, pain or life, with neither outcome liable to succeed, though the path of pain would better serve it. Outside the walls the knights were waiting. He donned the armour borrowed from the Countess and mounted Galahad, riding the horse out into the stormy morning. As he emerged the knights watched him, including her, and he raised his sword up in challenge. The moment of choice was about to arrive…

II

Tristan woke in a cold sweat, the false dawn just beginning to fade. The dream was the same every time until the moment of his choice then a multitude of possibilities would then spin out their stories in his dream. Each ending was different, though usually the path of pain led more often to the path of truth. This was not always so, for there were times when he failed to bear the strain and his actions led to greater suffering to others, just as occasionally the path of joy would lead to a greater goodness for all. He had hoped that the dream given to him that strange night in the druids' grove had been false, but the events of the previous day had proved that hope spurious. He had tried to prevent it, but everything had happened as predicted.

He could have left them to be captured in the city, but knew that he would be unable to do so. They were his friends, Groltch especially, and as he had tracked them towards the city he had realised that he had never had friends before and that made his choice harder in the end. The path of pain generally led to a separation between him and his friends, yet the path of joy could often lead to greater danger to them, even though he was there to aid them. His head hurt trying to sort through it all. A soft spattering of rain began as the edge of the storm moved over them. He knew that his time of choice was fast approaching, possibly even days away.

"You're awake early," said the sword in his mind, sounding a little distant, *"and you're doing well to keep me out. I almost didn't get in."*

That's because I need time to think, replied Tristan quietly. *Time on my own, with my own thoughts.*

"So you still think to go ahead with this insane plan of yours then?" asked Caliburn angrily.

Yes, and when the time comes you will aid me, sword, replied Tristan. *I am your master after all.*

"Yes Sir," replied Caliburn without a trace of sarcasm and sounding even a little saddened.

Tristan had discovered only the night before that the sword's enchantment had been designed to ensure it obeyed its true owner, regardless of whatever the command was. Of course, the fail-safe had been that its true owner must be true of heart, so that the sword's powers could not be used for evil, but for Tristan it meant that when he issued a command, the sword obeyed. That had explained why the sword had not even told Groltch of his plan and also why it would not try and stop it when the time came.

You saw what happened yesterday, said Tristan softly, ashamed to have upset the sword. Caliburn too was a friend, and probably the closest of them all. *It all went just as they showed me, down to every detail, and you said yourself that they were like most animals in that a lie was an unknown concept in their mind.*

"But I also said that they could only show you the truth as they saw it," replied the sword. *"Which would be with different perceptions to yours. Things may not be as they appeared."*

There will be no argument, Cali...Cal, thought Tristan firmly. *It must be as I plan, for otherwise the moment of truth will be harder for me to face. I may have to sacrifice more than either of us can imagine in gaining us the chance we need. You've seen the futures. You've been there with me. Most are not good and if it gives us a chance to change that then I will do it.*

"I know you will, but I will miss you," replied the sword sadly.

And I'll miss you, all of you, even the wizard, replied Tristan with a half-smile.

"You're not that bad a sorcerer yourself, for a beginner," said Caliburn with a soft buzzing laugh.

I had a good teacher, replied Tristan and he felt the sword's flush of pride. *But you know what Karene said to Groltch. If I remain then she will pursue us until time itself ends. The dreams merely confirm that. It will be better this way, for all of us. I just hope I can make the correct choice when the time comes.*

"You will," replied Caliburn gently. *"You are strong, probably the strongest I*

have served in many centuries, including Sir Caldor. His remained blind to certain truths, even until the end."

I thought you were created for him though?

"In this incarnation yes, but the source of what I am has existed far longer than you can ever imagine," said the sword sounding almost weary, *"and have served many masters."*

But not many more, replied Tristan.

"Not in this incarnation, no," replied the sword. *"Not many more at all."*

Tristan lay in silence and the heavens unleashed their watery fury. He rose to his feet and wandered outside the shield Matthius had created to protect them from the elements. He seemed to have fully recovered, though he had seemed loathed to use his magic, and had looked as if he had bitten a sour lemon as he had cast the spell. Yet that was a mystery not to be solved by him. The boy had spoken to Belthar and, despite the companions growing friendship, he knew that he would never be truly close to either of them.

He raised his head to the heavens and allowed the rain to pour down his face. The water was cold yet invigorating and he suddenly felt more alive than he had in years. He was reminded of the time when he had sneaked out the house out into the rain of a thunderstorm and had stood there, much like this, for hours. His father had eventually discovered him and dragged him back to bed. Tristan had shortly come down with the flu and his mother had had to nurse him back to health, but it had all been worth it.

Tristan's thoughts paused a moment as he thought of his mother. He realised that it was probably the first time since he had been knighted that he had thought of her. Even at his knighting ceremony the thought that it was sad his mother was not there to see him had been but a distant one. Yet now her memory was strong in his mind, her blond hair, her gentle grey eyes, and her musical voice. Tears mingled with the rain on his face and he mourned her death once more. She had died of the green plague only months after his night visit to the rain. He had felt it had been entirely his fault at the time, for bringing the sickness into the house, not realizing that it was different to what he had been ill with, though its symptoms were similar.

Lightning flashed in the sky and Tristan's tears ceased. He finally felt truly at peacc.

"Well done, said Caliburn softly. *"You're finally free of the Treatment's effects. As they train you, they wish to inspire loyalty, so to do so they suppress the memories of the people you love most in life, transferring that love into the image of the king. To be truly free you have to bring back those memories. Now you are ready."*

"Not yet," replied Tristan not realizing he had spoken out loud. "There are things we've yet to do and others yet to meet."

As the words came out of his mouth he felt a shiver go through him. It had been said that his mother had possessed some small gift for the Sight, and that on occasions prophecies would come unbidden. The words he had spoken were not based upon the dreams, but even as he spoke he could see the image of a madman and a woman carrying a bow, and another fleeting image of a hawk. Was it possible that he possessed the talent as well and had that it too had been suppressed?

"Yes," said the sword softly, confirming his fears. *"Now you're truly free."*

III

Anton disliked the rain, especially today. The day of his first day as king should have been one of sunshine and warmth with the Winged Heralds of Toric playing the sweetest music of triumph as he walked and the golden light of the Celestial Realm lighting his way. It should not be one in which he had to tramp through the wet mud like some peasant and enter the city with flat wet hair and dripping garments. It would demean him in the eyes of the Theldarians and he was sure that it was for this reason that the terms had stated he should do it. They had arrived with the rain last night, shortly before the midnight hour and much later than he had intended to retire to bed. Another trick of this Galen, he was certain. The message runner had arrived, delivered the terms in a perfunctory manner that had insulted Anton almost to insensibility. When he was king, no one would speak to him in such a curt manner. No one.

No one will ever see me wet and bedraggled either, came his thoughts, bringing back to the present situation.

He had just reached the edge of the city archers' range and now the second term would be adhered to. He nodded to his honour guard and they all dropped back fifty paces. They were allowed to enter the city with him but had to remain too far away to aid him. Galen had agreed to meet with him alone, though in return for such faith Anton had to walk the streets of Theldar alone, to all intent and purposes. It was yet another attempt to humiliate him before the *Theldarians* by this Lord Protector. The man would die, and by his own hand. He patted the dagger on his belt. It was enchanted in such a way that it could never be found by any who searched him. He just hoped that Galen did not have a similar such weapon.

"Who goes there?" Came a voice at the gate and Anton swallowed back the bile he felt at the woman's arrogance.

"I, Anton, humbly seek entrance to the mighty city of Theldar," he replied as humbly as he could, another term of the treaty.

This Galen seemed well versed in the Great Game, especially in the areas of humiliating opponents, but he would not take the bait. He would remain icily cold, even at the point when he killed his opponent. It was one of the few lessons of his father he could recall. He had been one of the greatest swordsmen that ever lived and he had always claimed that this was because he never lost control of his emotions in a fight. Anton was never very good with the sword but had been one of the few that had ever beaten him in a duel. He had spent months studying his father until he had learned what could irk him. He had then baited his father, goaded him and taunted him and the man had exploded into a flurry of attacks that would have killed Anton had they struck. But he had dropped to his knees, rolled to one side and brought his sword up under his father's guard and struck the blade home. A perfect, controlled and accurate hit. The courtiers watching had stood in stunned amazement at the move which had been clean and legal and meant instant victory for him.

The look on his father's face had been one to savour however, as the shock of finally losing hit him hard, allowing Anton some small revenge for all the humiliations his father had ever inflicted upon him. He later hated himself for destroying his father's self-image though. The man had never lifted a sword again and could never look at Anton in the eyes again. The powerful man had slowly wasted away on the throne, losing his vigour and ability to rule well. Many courtiers and even Council members had seriously considered forcing his abdication and had been preparing to enact it when his father's heart had finally given out. Anton had vowed never to be as weak as that and had kept himself cold.

"You may enter," said the guard opening the gate.

Her pause in considering his request had been two heartbeats off insulting. Yet he remained in control and stood there silently, waiting for the portcullis, then the gate, to open enough to allow him entrance. He walked into the streets, keeping fierce control of his emotions. He had not been here in person since the day of his sister's coronation. Then he had stood in the great temple watching the crown being placed upon her head and had vowed never to step foot in the city again until the day when it was he sat in that throne. It had been on that day that he had been cast out from House Tara'non to be placed as the Head of House Gethrel, one of the furthest power bases from the queen. Evidently they had feared them, so he had given them no cause to and bided his time. It had needed patience to wait the twenty-five years since that day to prepare the ground and now all that stood between him and his goal was this upstart of a peasant now ruling this city, the city that held *his* crown in *his* vaults.

As he walked through the city it seemed very different from his last visit, with many buildings now seemingly built of marble, though he knew that they were largely facades and that the older, half-timbered buildings still lay beneath them. It made for an impressive sight as he entered, however, and knew that had been why the streets closest the gates had been transformed first. This was an awe-inspiring first image of the centre of Caldorian power, yet the room to which he was headed was certainly not. He knew that it was a small, poky tavern basement in an area of the Southern Quarter not yet covered with marble. It was an inauspicious place, unsuitable for its grand purpose, yet it would have to do. He would walk away from it a king in all but name.

It was not a long distance to the small two-storey building, but it felt like it took an age to get there. Its tall thin windows were stained with smoke and the white paint of the upper storey was flaking away. It was tiled, as in the Kolthon fashion, and seemed to lean slightly to the right, the upper storey overhanging part of the alley beside it. Outside it were several errant knights standing with their swords drawn.

He approached them slowly, aware that his own troops were still some distance behind him and showed his open palms in the ancient sign of peaceful intent. As he drew near he noted that discipline had obviously slackened since the revolt of the city, for their salute to him was sloppy and out of time. It was just what he expected of them. Without nobles to guide them they were nothing more than peasants in armour, though they could still gut him with deadly efficiency if he did not watch his step. He walked up to the Blue Knight stood to attention at the door.

"I am Lord Anton of the House Gethrel," he said formally. "I am here to meet with Lord Galen of the House Faithe, Lord Protector of Theldar."

"I know," replied the knight with an insolent tone. "If yer Lordship wouldn't mind, we've orders to search yer fer weapons."

"You have my word as a noble that I bear none," replied Anton heatedly.

"A Lord's word 'aint worth spit in this city, sir. So if yer don't mind, we'll search yer now. Don't yer worry. Them knights of yers will have the same chance t'frisk the Lord Protector when he arrives. Yer can stand an' watch if yer don't believe it."

Anton sighed and closed his eyes, allowing the humiliation of letting commoners touch his person wash over him. He smiled within when their hands slipped unknowingly over the magically hidden dagger then entered the building, refusing to show his lack of trust for Galen.

Besides, he needed to be within the small cellar room first to make certain that Lewis Hanton and the knights loyal to Gareth were there and ready to spring the trap at his signal. Behind them were hidden some additional knights loyal to Anton and together with Darren and the knights that had accompanied him into the city they would kill most of Gareth's knights, leaving only one to use when framing Gareth for the murder of the Lord Protector.

It was fortuitous that his honour guard were not immediately on hand to enter the room, as Anton intended for Lewis to be dead before they entered. The Hanton brothers were too dangerous to allow both of them to live. They shared a bond of loyalty that could eventually see them turn on him, and together they could probably achieve it. It was too great a danger to ignore, though the risks of his plan had almost made him change it.

He had ordered a knight loyal to him amongst those waiting with Lewis and Gareth's troops to kill him as the fighting erupted, claiming that the man had rushed Galen and been struck down. She would be the one to survive the attack and would be there to confess to the truth of the events that were about to happen; truths that he had drummed into her before the mission. If it failed, or others were allowed to live, then it could all crumble down around him, yet it was a risk worth taking. He prayed to Toric that his knights, some of the best of his army, would do their tasks well.

"Welcome, milord," said a dirty, fat, and balding peasant who appeared to be the proprietor of these premises with a bow. "The chamber below is set."

The malicious glint in his grey eyes and the slight smile on the man's face signalled the true meaning. The knights were all in place and waiting. The man opened a small doorway beyond which a thin, steep stairwell descended into the ground, light by several gas lanterns set into the walls. He found himself mildly surprised to see them there, for they were a relatively new invention from the Kolthon Empire. Even his castle had yet to install the expensive items.

He masked his surprise though, and climbed down the steps through the dank corridor. They soon led to a door that stood open and he cautiously entered, half-expecting Galen to spring a trap of his own. He found the small square room empty, save for two elegantly carved wooden chairs with velvet cushions stood facing each other in the centre. Between them was a table upon which glasses and a bottle of wine stood open. The room itself seemed to have no other exits, though he knew that there were at least four hidden doors with knights behind them, waiting to spring out at the correct moment.

He moved over to the chairs and looked at them closely, still fearing some trap. They were high backed chairs and atop the back were carved dolphins leaping over the ancient symbol of peace, a circle divided in two by a swirling line, one side blackened and the other painted white. He recognised them as chairs from the palace, but swallowed his anger. He was close to his victory. He reached over and smelled the wine on the table, wrinkling his nose in disgust. It was some cheap Kolthon wine, and not even a vintage one at that.

He took a seat and looked once more around the room. Shadows flickered around it, created by the four lanterns set into the wall, and seemed almost menacing. Some even seemed to take on human form briefly, yet he forced himself not to think about it. They were merely shadows, their dancing forms playing upon his fears, and in this place he could not yield to such passing fancies. To do so would mean death. Yet still, he could not help thinking that there was something odd about them.

"Good morning, Lord Anton," said a soft voice, making him start.

Galen Faithe stood at the entrance regarding him, and Anton felt a slight chill run down his spine. From here the flickering light made this man seem like a creation of shadow and nothing more. He forced down the fear. This was a man, no matter what his powers, and if he thought Anton defenceless to his magicks then he would be sorely mistaken.

"Good morning Lord Galen," he replied bowing his head gently. "I hope you do not mind that I seated myself."

"Not at all. That is why the chairs were brought here."

The man sat and Anton got his first chance to see the man up close and found the awe lessening. He was a thin young man, though his haggard appearance made him seem much older. His dark hair was streaked with grey and his clothes could not disguise his thin, bony form. Only when he looked at the eyes did the creeping fear return to Anton's stomach, for they were dark, the light of the room making them seem almost black, yet behind them burned a fire the like of which he had never seen. As he looked into their dark depths he fancied he could see images of his own death playing amid them. He blinked away the images and smiled at the man, feigning all the confidence he could muster.

"Would you like something to drink?" asked Galen, gesturing to the bottle on the tale.

"No, I think it best we dispense with all the formalities," replied Anton quickly. "We both know the danger of the armies outside and the longer I am away the more time Lord Gareth has time to react to my actions. Haste is of the essence."

"Of course. What do you offer?" asked Galen, taking the seat opposite him.

"I offer only this. I will aid you fight the armies outside these walls and bring about their defeat. I will then take the kingship of Caldor." Galen's eyes narrowed dangerously at this and Anton quickly continued. "I offer you the independence of Theldar and the lands that surround her to the range of thirty miles. In return, I expect your aid in combating the troops and that you present me with the crown of Tir'nin."

"What is there to prevent you from betraying me?" asked the man suspiciously.

"I will offer you my only child, my daughter Miranda, as hostage," replied Anton, hoping that Galen did not hear the catch in his voice as he spoke of his daughter. He prayed that news of her death had not reached

Theldar yet. "If you wish, I will even offer you her hand in marriage to cement the peace between us."

"That'll not be necessary," replied Galen quickly. "You speak plainly, for a noble."

"I am a plain man, despite my status. Do we have an agreement?"

"Let me think on it," replied Galen, rising to his feet.

The dark man began to pace slowly and deliberately around the room, seeming to be deep in thought. Anton felt his palms sweat, despite the coldness of the room and he found his eyes warily following the man around the room. The shadows flickered menacingly once more and many even seemed to part before Galen. Anton looked suspiciously around the room, trying to see any traces of magic. He could just make out the slight shimmering and smiled to himself. The man was trying to frighten him with illusions. He would not succumb to such simple tricks. Even so, he could not shake the feeling that there was something more to them than mere illusion.

"Agreed," said Galen, standing before him, spitting on his hand and holding it out to Anton.

Anton suppressed a shudder at the crude tradesman of agreeing to a bargain. He removed his gloves and spat on his hands, feeling somehow soiled as the spittle slid down his hand. He grasped the hand of Galen with his right hand as his left hand rapidly drew the dagger at his belt. Now was the moment to strike. The blade arched up towards the surprised man's neck at an incredible speed and sliced through it. Straight through it, as if it was not there. He looked at the man in horror, realising that he no longer felt Galen's hand in his grasp. He appeared almost translucent and seemed to be made solely of shadow. The man laughed a soft, yet terrible laugh.

"You thought you could kill me with that?" asked the man with contempt, his dark eyes now seeming bottomless.

"No," croaked Anton, struggling to maintain his fear.

His dagger had passed straight through him as if he were air. The man was a demon! Yet it would not stop him claiming his rightful place upon the throne. Anger filled him and he cried out, leaping backwards out of Galen's reach. Doors opened around him and the knights, led by Lewis Hanton, leapt out to attack the man. He sensed them summoning forth their magic and smiled. Galen was soon to be dead. One of his knights slashed out with his sword that was glowing in a soft magical light. It caught Galen on the arm and Anton smiled as the man cursed in pain and blood began to flow. He was mortal then, and that meant he would die.

He looked round and saw Lewis approaching him with another knight at his back. Now was time for the greatest gamble. He nodded to the knight and she responded in kind, bringing a long dagger out in a vicious arc. It swept out and slid across the man's throat. Confusion followed by anger flashed into the man's eyes as he collapsed to the floor desperately clutching his neck and trying to utter the words of a prayer. Anton smiled. The man's spells would aid him to no avail, for all those of healing powerful enough to save him required words. He looked back to the battle and noted angrily that two of the knights had been cut down and that Galen was still alive. He growled angrily, he needed one of these fools to kill Galen. Was he going to have to do this himself?

He made to move then noticed the shadows flickering angrily around his men. They shimmered momentarily then as if from nowhere twelve knights in almost translucent black armour appeared around his men. He shouted a warning, but it was too late, for many died before they even knew of the danger. Anton's momentary panic abated when heard noises from the both the main entrance and those of the hidden doorways. His reserves were on their way. He knelt before the dead body of Lewis Hanton, feigning rage and grief at the man's death, praying that Darren would see this as he entered.

It was then that he realised that the sounds he heard from without were from the clash of metal on metal. He looked to the one of the secret doors and saw several of his warriors battling their way backwards into the room. He looked at the main entrance and saw that barely half their number had made it through and there was no sign of Darren. He dropped the body and looked back to the attack on Galen. Only one of Gareth's knights still stood and none of Galen's troops seemed harmed in anyway. Anton also noted that Galen was still alive and and gasped with horror when he realised the fiend was making his way towards him.

"Retreat!" he cried out. "Cover my retreat!"

The female knight who had assassinated Lewis looked to him and nodded, turning to face Galen.

"This way, my lord!" called a from behind him. Anton turned and headed towards the voice. Stood by one of the previously hidden exits was one of his knights.

"This way is clear!" called the knight.

Anton ran towards the exit then stopped short suddenly; before him stood one of the dark knights.

"You're going nowhere," he said with a grim smile.

"Don't be so sure," replied Anton, unleashing a spell.

The man's eyes widened as the horrors he thought he saw approached him. He would be crippled by fear in moments and his heart would probably give way with shock. Such was the power of spells of the mind. Anton stepped past him and entered the passage beyond.

"The way is clear, Lord," said his knight. "We were set upon by assailants in thieves garb, but were able to take them down."

"Good work," replied Anton as he rushed past. "Hold the door as long as you can!"

"Yes Lord!"

As Anton entered the corridor he heard a terrifying scream and knew the man upon whom he had cast an illusion had died. Anton closed the door quickly and cast a spell of sealing upon it, the effort bringing him short of breath. He had no great Talent and even these few spells were tiring him. He forced it away, knowing that his pursuers would soon find a way round the barrier and would soon be chasing him. He muttered a brief spell and a ball of light appeared in his hand. The light revealed the bodies strewn across the corridor. His men had won, but at what cost. He cursed silently. He had been assured that the Dark Circle were on his side! He picked his way through the bodies trying not to slip in the pools of blood on the floor. As he moved he thought he heard sounds behind him. They must have already gotten through his wards. Panic-stricken he released his light spell and began to run and disappearing into the darkness.

IV

Galen looked around at the carnage angrily. Four of his Shadow Knights had died in this fight. Had they known to enchant their blades, or had it been just luck? Galen was not sure but one thing was certain, the enemy knights had been harder to kill than he had expected. He cursed again as pain flared in his shoulder. He would have to be more cautious in future.

He looked to the *knights* who had searched Anton on his arrival. One approached him and removed her helm.

"Well Meredith, what happened?" he asked the thief quietly.

"Some resisted, even after we had taken their Lord captive and he had ordered them to drop their weapons. It seems that Treatment works better on some than others," she replied quietly. "I lost several hawks because of that. As for the tunnel fights, I've yet to hear the total cost."

"We all lost people today," he replied gently.

"Yet I'm about to lose another more dear to me," she said, turning her eyes away bitterly.

Galen ignored her sadness and changed the subject.

"What of Anton?"

"He is fleeing through the sewers," she replied, still keeping her eyes averted. "My scouts report that other knights have begun massing at the entrance to the secret passage. As was planned, they await his decree if your death to enter secretly and help him subdue the city."

"Do you think they will try to enter still?"

"As I told you this morning, if Anton manages to escape then he will be angry and will send them in to attack us. It will be a setback to his plans, but he seems to be a man with many plans and I doubt he was not prepared for this possible outcome. That is if he escapes of course…"

"Oh, he will escape all right," he replied darkly. "Let him send his men in. The rest of the Shadow Knights are in place and will seal their doom."

He saw Meredith shudder and smiled. Anton would pay for killing his men.

V

Anton staggered through the sewers, his breath ragged and his heart thumping heavily in his chest. He was not a young man and not fit enough to keep up this sort of pace for long. Yet he had to, for he could still hear the sounds of his pursuers around him. He had narrowly avoided capture so far and had almost stumbled straight into the arms of three patrols. Fortunately, they were as sloppy as those who had guarded the tavern were and he had evaded them.

He saw thin beams of light appear ahead of him and he smiled. He was almost safe, yet he had one thing to do before he left. He had planned for this eventuality and knew he would need to allay the suspicions of Gareth. He had not believed that he would need such a plan, but he was a cautious man and glad of it at this moment.

He would exit, covered in blood and report the failure of his plan, yet he would bring the city to Gareth with the troops he had arranged to wait outside. Though initially he had planned to use them to help maintain order as he took over, and to reinforce the walls, now they would act as an invasion force that would enter the city and open it up for their armies. Anton would emerge as the liberator and his standing on the Council would be elevated. He would then have to wait again, for another chance to grab the throne. He smiled. He had waited this long for the crown; he could wait a while longer.

However, he needed to be convincing in his tale of the events concerning the trap's failure. They had arrived and he had been attacked before the talks had barely even begun. The knights had leapt out and fought valiantly to protect him, but found themselves ambushed by warriors of Galen. Lewis Hanton had been killed there, battling to save his life and Darren was missing, presumed dead, having fought outside, desperate to enter. Anton had barely escaped with his life and had battled his way through the sewers to freedom.

He looked down at himself with a wry smile. He had been completely untouched by the day's violence, something he had not counted on when preparing the tale. Yet he had to be injured, to add strength to his tale. He took out his dagger and sliced off part of the leather strips that held it to his waist. He put them in his mouth and clamped his teeth down hard upon them. He then raised his dagger and brought it down across his arm in a vicious slash. Pain seared through him and tears streamed from his eyes, a small grunt passing from his clenched jaw. He smeared the blood now flowing across his clothing, before opening another wound upon the arm. He wanted to scream, yet knew to do so would prematurely alert the knights outside, as well as the enemy pursuers, so clamped down with all his might upon the leather.

Two wounds were not enough though, and he brought the dagger in a short thrusting motion along the side of his stomach, the searing agony almost knocking him unconscious, yet he endured it and slashed himself again and again, until wounds, light and heavy, criss-crossed his body. By the time he finished his last cut, his body had numbed to the pain and he knew shock was not far away. He also knew that death now hovered near him as well, for he was losing a lot of blood. He looked to his first cuts and nodded with a hazy satisfaction that they had begun clotting, giving the appearance of slightly older wounds.

He got to his feet, though he could not remember sitting down, and staggered to the light. It seemed far more distant than before and a stab of fear cut through him as realised he might die before he reached it. The pain began to returning and Anton felt his vision swim. He wanted to lie down, to sleep, knowing the pain would go away. He shook his head, determined to keep walking, yet the light seemed no nearer. He staggered and fell to one knee. He should not have made so many cuts. Why had he done it?

He tried to drag himself to his feet but found his head swimming to violently. Death was coming to him. He cried out. He did not want to die, yet already he could feel its icy touch. He called to Toric to let him live, to let him continue, and Toric replied. An angel appeared before him with dark wings and flowing hair. In her eyes he saw beauty and pain, and he felt himself lifted into the air.

"I was commanded to let you live, so I'll not have you dying on me," he heard her mutter as he floated through the air.

Light appeared above him and for a moment his vision swam with blackness. He felt himself sink to the floor, before he was suddenly hoisted high into the air and into the light. A face appeared before him.

"How is he?" asked a voice.

"Bad," came the reply of another. "But I can stabilise him for the journey to the camp."

"Good," came the first reply once more. "Take whoever you need and get him there as swiftly as possible."

"What do you intend to do?"

"Exactly as ordered. These butchers have betrayed us and now we go to enter and open it for our troops."

"Toric go with you," came the second voice again.

The face loomed over him again.

"Torslud!" he cursed. "How are you still conscious? By the light you're strong. But you need to heal and you can only do that asleep."

A hand waved over his eyes and blackness followed it.

VI

Sar Petra watched as the enemy knight lifted Lord Anton from the passage to the air above before returning to her post. She allowed herself to shift, so that her body no longer existed fully in the realm of life. She shuddered as she did, but knew it would be vital if the enemy attacked. Galen's plan had sounded insane and she was not sure that when the time came she could go through with it. There was no guarantee that they would be protected by his gift when they sprang the trap and she feared that he might even be sacrificing her and her knights to remove her opposition. She pushed the thoughts away and looked to the others around her.

He was not about to sacrifice them, intentionally at least. She had seen that much in her vision, one of the many she had been struck with after she had thrown off the effects of the Treatment. She believed that she had been subjected to so much Magic of Prophecy in the Redirection Chambers that after her mind had been freed she had been able to see them in what seemed to be visions of the future. That was how her rational mind saw it at least, but her irrational mind had cried out that she had been granted the mythical Gift of Sight, but that was nonsense. The future was not set. Yet she had seen it when she had met Galen for the first time. In his hands lay the key to Caldor's future. She had seen it clearly, and somehow she was inter-linked with it. It had been such a link that had made her reveal her motives to him that day, and another such one that had made her take his gift. It was as if she were being twisted by some powerful force to fit a pattern already there and though she did not like it, there was no way to battle against it.

"They're coming," said the advance scout in Shadow Talk, the words forming in her mind as if they were her own.

Make ready, she commanded, setting her mind at rest and bringing the calm she would need to cast magic. *Unleash the spells on my command only.*

She felt a wave of acknowledgement and felt the nervousness of the knights around her. She was not surprised. If the Gift did not protect them, then almost none of them would survive to tell Galen. Yet it soon settled into resolve and she felt a strange sense of peace; a feeling of complete trust. She could feel the gentle brush of Galen across her mind and knew the source of the calm.

The sound of movement allowed her thoughts to focus and she visualised the spell she was about to cast. She felt the others do the same and soon all had the same image in their minds. It was incredible. They were preparing to unleash a spell as one, a spell more powerful than any of them could cast alone. It had been deemed impossible to achieve such a thing by all the great authorities on magic, yet here they were, doing just that.

"How far, do you think?" whispered a voice down the passage.

"Forty feet, maybe more. Any sign of guards?" replied another.

"None," came the reply. "Send the all clear."

Petra could narrowly make out the shape of the man creeping towards her and narrowly felt a stab of sorrow for him. But this was war, and she had chosen her side, as he had his, though it may not have originally been his will. She pushed such thoughts away. They would only lead her to doom. She breathed in a long, slow breath and counted to twenty before releasing it again. As she did, she heard the sound of the rest of the enemies approaching. It would not be long now. Soon the lead knights had reached her and were walking past her, yet she had to let them move on.

She had placed herself in the centre of the group, putting her full faith in Galen's Gift, which meant waiting for the signal from those furthest from the passage's entrance. The wait seemed to last an eternity and she felt the threads of fear wind through the Shadow Knights again. She prayed briefly to Toric and found others doing the same. As she completed it the signal came. She released the energy of the spell and felt the spells of the others channel through her and enter her own. Power filled her and for a moment she felt a flush of unbelievable joy, a surging sensation that left all her senses tingling. She drew her sword and thrust it at the ceiling, the other knights following her lead. It passed through the stone as if it were air yet where it penetrated black cracks appeared and began to spread like rapidly growing vines across the ceiling. The cracks grew and multiplied and soon they began to join with those of the other Shadow Knights' swords, forming small chasms as they did.

Dust and pebbles began crumbling down to the floor and the whole ceiling creaked ominously. The enemy knights, who now surrounded her as they made their way towards Theldar, looked around in concern and saw the cracks. She heard curses and cries and many began to try and back out of the tunnel, but it was too late. The ceiling gave way and tons of earth and rubble came crashing down around them. Petra shuddered at the heart wrenching screams of agony as the stone collapsed, then all was black and still.

VII

Joseph pulled himself out of the rubble of the cave in and groaned in pain.

He looked back and his heart cried out at the sight behind him. His lantern lay on the floor, its flame still flickering. Its light revealed a gruesome scene. Rocks and earth littered the passage, blocking it completely, interspersed with the blood and bodies of those who had perished in its fall. He had been lucky. He had been walking at the rear of the column, and had been able to leap to safety on seeing the cracks above him. They had seemed to just stop in a line, just a foot ahead of him, and he had correctly surmised that magic was afoot here.

The walls and ceiling had been too strong for them to collapse so suddenly. He looked back and was visited by a living nightmare. Black creatures, humanoid in form flickered and shimmered, emerging from within the rubble, walking through it as if it were not there. One approached him and knelt before him. Its eyes flickered in demon light and its voice hissed menacingly.

"Return to those of your camp. Tell them what happened here and let them know us. We are the Shadow Knights. We are death to all who oppose us."

Its hand reached down and touched his, tracing an intricate pattern of a skull upon it, leaving his hand cold. Blue light glowed and the image scored itself onto his hand. He lost his resolve and screamed, getting to his feet and fleeing. The creature did not pursue him and it was many hours before he eventually made it to his camp. There the Prince himself questioned him, but his answers brought only fear and rumour. Within one day the rumours of these demon killers had spread throughout the ranks of the waiting knights and when the order to attack the walls came the following day, many found themselves staring up at them, wondering if they were to be the beasts' next victim…

VIII

"Why have you not yet asked me for the hand of my daughter in marriage?" asked Sulan XXV, his question coming from out of the air.

"I was unsure of your customs in this field," replied Tristan with a start. "It is known that no child of a Prophet has ever been married to one outside the blood of Sol."

"That is untrue, for there were three wars averted by alliances of marriage, two to the Prelates of the Western Provinces of Kolth, Garlus and Mertikus, shortly after our rebellion against the overlordship of the Empire. The third was with one of your own ancestors, Edward Tara'non, Fifth Earl of Daranshire during the Second Elf War when only the western provinces of our two realms still fought for freedom."

Naithan could recall that part of family history from younger days, though there had never been any mention of a Solman princess being wed to Edward, though Krystal had been a rather unusual name for a Caldorian woman. He pushed the thoughts aside. He could afford no lapses of concentration when talking to this intelligent man.

"That was something unknown to me," he admitted, hating to show ignorance in any subject, particularly that of his own ancestry.

"It was to me until a few days ago," replied Sulan with a smile. "I discovered it by chance when reading an ancient text on the wars. I believe your Lord Priest has similar interests in such an era."

"He has been known to study history," replied Naithan warily.

"It is a wise man who seeks to learn from the mistakes of the past," said Sulan with a nod.

"He has often said much the same."

Sulan smiled and Naithan fought back the desire to like him. He was a pagan and therefore an enemy, until he could be converted of course, but that seemed highly unlikely. The man seemed untouched by any theological argument and, more annoyingly could often argue Naithan's points better than he himself could. Naithan had to admit that the man was a more skilled player in the Game than he would ever be.

"But back to my original question," said Sulan, his dark eyes flicking quizzically to Naithan. "Do you intend to ask for my daughter's hand?"

"That I do," replied Naithan. "Yet, tell me. Why do you offer her so readily? The three examples you gave of marriage outside these borders all occurred in times of need for your realm. Are you in need?"

"I will be honest with you, Naithan, King of Caldor. My position here is not strong and I am forced to travel constantly among the Princes, staying with them and controlling them by displaying the force of arms I can still muster. The Empire knows this and seems intent on stirring dissension in my people to divide us so that it may re-conquer us."

"You're sure of this?" asked Naithan quickly.

"Of course," replied Sulan. "They always look for the opportunity to retake these lands. They have never accepted our freedom, despite the generations during which we have enjoyed it. Yet it is more than that. I know that sometime soon war will unleash itself upon Loden. A Great War that will make yours with Grel-Chin seem but a swell in a teacup. In such a war we would be weak alone, and I intend Sol to be strong. Therefore she needs allies. I could never convince the Princes to ally with Kolth for the animosity is too strong, but there is no history of such hatred between our lands. We are both small and alone would face complete destruction. The Empire will be less inclined to attack us if we were allied by something such as the marriage of my daughter to you. It might even prevent a large war from even starting. You have heard of the horrors inflicted in the last such war, and this would be far greater than that, I fear. I wish Sol to survive and she stands her best chance with you."

Naithan could not fault the logic of the man's reasoning.

"There is also the fact that I feel you may need our help soon as well," continued Sulan, looking out of the corner of his eyes to Naithan.

"What do you mean?"

"Despite your attempts to hide it, we know of the rebellion of your city, our Seers have watched it closely. Your brother's siege cannot break it alone, for if it does, you will no longer have a throne. One of your family seeks your crown and should you not be in the palace when it falls, he shall win it."

Naithan felt the room go very cold and he was reminded of his dreams, now so distant. One such dream had spoken whispers of the treachery Sulan spoke of and he knew the man's words to be true.

"I see that you know it to be true," said the Prophet softly. "With my aid, my ships can have you back to your city in time to prevent this."

Naithan pushed down the anger he felt inside. Always the man twisted his thoughts, seeming to always gain the upper hand in their conversations. Never once had he felt that he had been the victor in these conversations and now, even though he had gained one of the things he had come to this accursed realm for, once more it would be on terms beneficial to Sol. He looked to the Prophet and as he did so, the man handed him the small crown his daughter had worn the one time Naithan had seen her, at the banquet.

"I give you this crown as proof of my word. My daughter and her crown shall not be reunited until she has been united with you in marriage," said the Prophet solemnly.

He looked at the crown and saw that its centrepiece consisted of an ornately carved brass tube surrounded by jewel encrusted gold and silver leaf motifs. Yet the tube was all that mattered, for it was part of the Sceptre of Prophecy they sought and now they owned it. That was the second of the three objectives they had had on arriving here. That left only the third, the conversion of the Prophet.

IX

It was all Matthew could do to keep himself from screaming with glee as Naithan took hold of the crown. However, he had to maintain his silence or else all would be lost. He had no idea what Naithan would do if he became alerted to Matthew's presence in his mind, yet it had been the only way to get close enough to Sulan to cast the necessary spell. He had created a link with Naithan's mind with priestly magic and allowed himself to become almost one with him, as he had when rescuing him from the Shadow's poison. Yet he had shielded himself from becoming completely immersed with his sorcery, allowing his and Naithan's conscious thoughts to remain apart, allowing them to both operate independently. He had then sat in his room with the two pieces of the sceptre in his hand, their power linked by a combination of magicks, ready for the correct moment. It had not arrived yet, for Naithan had yet to begin talking of Toric and seemed entranced by the crown in his hands.

Matthew smiled and released a small spell of searching through Naithan's hands to the crown. He felt the tingle of power and felt the energy of the piece in the crown reach out to him, as if seeking the other two pieces already within his hands. He smiled, knowing that his plan would work. Through Naithan he could work the magic needed to convert the Prophet to the Light of Toric, the king's body acting as a conduit to his power.

It was the only way he could get close enough to the Prophet when he was not surrounded by his magic-wielding Viziers. It seemed that the Grand Vizier had known about the fact that Caldorian monarchs were not allowed to possess magic, and it had therefore been deemed safe for the Prophet to walk alone with the King.

Matthew had now solved that problem with his ability to use both magicks to merge his thoughts and powers with Naithan. Even so, it should have been almost impossible to attune himself well enough into Naithan's mind and body so that he could use him to cast his spells. His only theory was that somehow the blood-link between them allowed it to happen, though he was not sure how. It was definitely worth researching at some other point.

"We still haven't discussed fully the problem of our religions though," said Naithan, his words sounding like the shadow of an echo in Matthew's ears.

He allowed Naithan's vision to supersede his once more. They were stood on the Prophet's private balcony that looked over the Three Tiered Gardens for which Zaron was most famous. Even with the hazy, second hand images he received from Naithan their beauty was astounding. Yet Matthew had no time to admire it for the time for his magic was fast approaching and there was one more thing he had yet to try, now that they had the third piece of the Sceptre. He gently coaxed Naithan's subconscious mind to look down at the piece, then shift Naithan's grip so that the piece of the sceptre pushed into the palm of his hand. That done, Matthew then drew thin strands of his magicks together, linking them in a tight weave, before passing them through the pieces in his own hands and into the piece in Naithan's hand, linking them with a triangle of magic. He was amazed to feel the pull of an invisible vortex that seemed to emanate within the triangle of magic. His magic prepared, he then returned to the conversation.

"But such a thing would lead to chaos in my kingdom," replied Sulan to whatever question Naithan had answered, *"even if I were inclined to convert to*

your teachings. Unlike you, though I am the First Prophet, there are another fifteen who can overrule me in matters of religion, if they banded together."

"All the more reason to convert to Toric, for he would allow no such dissension. His teachings are of strength and goodness. Is it not true that you revere even those of malicious leanings?"

Matthew shuddered. Naithan must have been getting truly desperate to speak out so openly about his desire to see the Prophet converted.

"That is true, but then our gods preach harmony and balance, that to exist there must be both good and evil," replied Sulan slowly, sounding a little angry.

"Yet you say that a Great War is coming and that you need to be strong. If you follow your philosophy then you will remain weak and divided," replied Naithan quickly.

Matthew had to act before his friend ruined matters. Already Sulan's eyes where narrowing angrily, something Matthew had never thought he would see in the mild, reserved man. He drew forth the spell from within and coaxed Naithan to gently brush the Prophet with the hand holding the crown. As the sceptre touched the Prophet, Matthew was ready. He knew that the Prophet had been surrounded by protective spells and also that he did not have the time to sneak round them all, therefore he decided to simply smash through them with all his energy. It was an attack that would hold many risks and would need more power than he could muster alone, so he channelled his through the vortex swirling between the linked pieces of the sceptre. His jaw dropped at the power that erupted from it towards the prophet, it was over ten times that which he had pushed through it.

He felt the wards around the Prophet spring to his defence and arch out towards his attack, yet they withered under the searing power that raged through them. They struck Sulan with such force that Matthew saw the man drop to his knees, tears falling from his eyes, yet that could not distract him. He had to retain control of the spell throughout its duration, for this illusion had to be perfect…

X

Sulan XXV, First Prophet of the Fifteen Gods of Sulad'aur, fell to his knees as power the like of which he had never felt engulfed him and surrounded him. His anger at the Caldorian king faded to nothing and joy filled him, bringing tears to his eyes. He looked out at the gardens beyond the balcony.

Suddenly they seemed to be in flames and the palace crashed around down around him. Soldiers swarmed around them, dressed in the armour of the elite Death Warriors of Kolth, killing and destroying everything in their path. Everywhere there were children dying under the swords of the attackers, women screaming as they were brutally raped and houses burning. His joy turned to fear and horror at the sights that he saw. What was happening here? Why was it happening? How could he stop it?

With that thought came a sudden lull in the images and as he watched, the flames seemed to move closer to him.

I CAN HELP YOU PREVENT THIS, said a commanding, yet gentle voice around him.

It seemed to come from the flames, yet also from the earth, yet also from the air. It was everywhere yet nowhere. He could even feel it speak from within himself. He was aware of a great and powerful presence surrounding him.

"Who are you? What are you?" asked Sulan in awe.

I AM ALL . I AM EVERYTHING. I AM TORIC, came the voice.

"Why do you speak to me? Why now?" he asked.

BECAUSE I HAVE WATCHED YOU AND DEEM YOU WORTHY.

"Worthy of what?"

BECOMING MY HIGH PRIEST IN THIS REALM.

"But I worship the gods of my kingdom," he replied angrily.

THEY ARE NOT TRUE GODS. I AM THE ONLY ONE. THEY ARE BUT DECEPTIONS OF THE ONE-EYED WOLF, THENRIL, DEMON OF DARKNESS.

"And you are but a vision in my mind," replied Sulan swiftly.

I AM SO MUCH MORE, replied the voice. *FEEL MY POWER AND LEARN.*

Blue light swirled outwards from the flames around him and cocooned him, lifting him up on wings of air. Energy flooded his every sense filling him with a sense of ecstasy he had never felt before and he found tears of the purest joy flooding from his eyes, each drop transforming into diamonds as they fell. Around him, winged beings of fabulous beauty surrounded him and music of pure and melodious sound filled the air around him. He found himself short of breath as it was stolen by the most spectacular vision of all, a golden palace just as he had always pictured the Sulad'aur.

NO, THIS IS NOT THE CELESTIAL PALACE OF YOUR GODS. THIS IS MY HOME, OF WHICH THE PALACE OF YOUR GODS IS BUT A POOR IMITATION. LET ME SHOW YOU.

The energy coursed through him and his vision swam for a second before clearing once more. Stood before him was the golden palace once more, its minarets and spires reaching to infinity. Yet something did not seem the same as before, as if something was amiss.

YOU FEEL IT, DO YOU NOT. THINGS ARE NOT AS THEY APPEAR.

A tall man in yellow and red monks' robes walked from the temple, his face radiant and peaceful. It could only be Hala'dar, god of peace, harmony and inner balance. The man smiled, his smile lighting the corners of Sulan's mind. He felt peace and calm wash over him and felt the need to live and study as the teachings of the god had ordained.

SEE HIM NOW AS I DO, whispered the voice. *SEE WHERE HIS TEACHINGS WILL LEAD YOU.*

The body of Hala'dar shifted and shimmered, becoming the hunched form of a great black beast, a one eyed wolf that seemed to smile at him. He then saw himself sitting in the cross-legged position of meditation, his mind, body and spirit in perfect peace and harmony. He was as he should be. Yet all around him the kingdom of Sol was crumbling down, the armies of Kolth cutting a path of destruction through the heavy forests, rolling hills, and many cities. Yet all his people did was sit, sat in perfect harmony as their bodies were slain.

Another god before him, his rotting body, riddled with cancerous sores naming him Zipharon, god of disease and decay, appeared before him. Again Toric allowed Sulan to see how worship of this god would worsen his kingdoms problems in the great war to come, and he was not the last to appear in such away. Giarna, goddess of the sea, nature and life appeared and visions followed. Ash'mar, goddess of death and the after-world was next, followed by Bel'ami, god of the seasons, harvests and fertility. On and on they came, Luranthio, the moon god, chasing the sun goddess Solnar and Hethica, goddess of famine and barrenness following Drel'nadar, goddess of love and passion. Nihilan, god of chaos and destruction raged past afterwards, swiftly followed by Seshad, god of knowledge and wisdom. The twins, Shapul god of mischief and ill luck and Lupash, goddess of fortune and good deeds came next and the god of war and rage, Gam'eht, followed in their steps. Even the great Al, blind mediator of the gods, lord of justice, appeared, his links to the one eyed wolf revealed. All of the Fifteen were revealed and their truths laid bare before him. Then he saw the palace for what it was, a poor copy of the first, its gilded paint flaking, its plaster cracked. Sulan wanted to scream. It was not so. It could not be so.

Peace filled him suddenly and Toric's presence could be felt once more.

BE AT EASE. YOU ARE MORTAL AND ALL MORTALS ARE FLAWED. THENRIL IS THE BEGETTER OF ALL LIES, FATHER OF ALL THAT IS EVIL; MOTHER TO ALL MISCHIEF; STEALER OF SHADOWS. HIS POWER IS GREAT AND IT WILL BE THAT WHICH WILL BRING THE VISION I SHOWED YOU TO PASS.

Sulan found himself suddenly back in his city. The flames of the burning houses were still burning and people around him were still dying. Looking at all the attackers he found that when he looked at their shadows he could see them shift unnaturally and for brief moments he could see the dark shadow of a wolf.

"Is it too late?" he asked the voice of Toric.

IT IS NEVER TOO LATE. THIS IS BUT A POSSIBLE FUTURE, AND WITH MY AID IT WILL NEVER HAPPEN.

Another image flash before him and he saw his Shar-meer marching triumphantly through the streets of Kolth, their shadows blazing with light.

"So you command me to follow you and then you will save me," he said suspiciously.

"I command none who do not follow me," said a voice, softer than before. The flames of the city seemed to have taken on an almost human form. "I am no commander of obedience. I set just rules for my worshipers to follow and offer rewards to those who do so. Those who do not, sell themselves to Thenril, from whom I may never retrieve them, such is the Great Pact of Creation, as spoken of by my priests."

The flames had now taken on the shape of an old man in white flowing robes. It looked much like the images taleweavers created when speaking of the Caldorian god.

"Yes, I take on a form now that you will recognise, to make you feel at ease," replied the god, as if reading his thoughts. "And yes, the images I have shown you may not happen, even if you remain in ignorance. I show you only the most probable outcome of such actions and even if they do come to pass, your people will survive. Much reduced in power and quality of life, but you will endure, as you have before."

Sulan felt his mind cloud with confusion. He felt as if he had been turned around many times and found himself feeling slightly sick.

"You are an intelligent man and I do not expect you to change your worship immediately, yet at this time you have the greatest chance to learn much of me from my most holy of followers. Go and think on it."

"How do I know that you are not just some illusion, conjured by magic just to change my views? How do I know that you truly exist?" asked Sulan hurriedly, noting that the body of the old man was turning back into flame. The man smiled softly.

YOU DON'T. LIKE ALL MY FOLLOWERS, YOU WILL JUST HAVE TO HAVE FAITH, THOUGH I CAN GIVE YOU ONE MIRACLE. IN ALL YOU KNOW OF MAGIC, CAN ILLUSIONS CREATE DIAMONDS FROM TEARS?

The form faded and with it the images. He found himself back on his palace balcony, Naithan knelt worriedly beside him.

"Are you well?" he was asking. "Should I send for a physician?"

"No," replied Sulan softly. "I am fine, though I feel a little unwell. I feel I may have to cut our meeting short today."

He saw worry lines etched into Naithan's features and he found himself gazing deeply into them, searching for any trace of guile or deceit, but he could find none. He was a good judge of character and he knew that whatever had just happened had not been done by Naithan. The fear and concern in his eyes could not be faked.

"Are you sure?" asked the blond man.

"Yes, I am sure. Please forgive my impoliteness."

"There has been no insult here," said Naithan, getting to his feet. "I would hope we can meet again when you are in better spirits."

"Of course," replied Sulan quickly. "I find myself intrigued by your talks on theology. I would like to learn more about your god."

He saw the look of pleasant surprise on the man's face confirming that he could have had no part in the illusion. That did not rule out the possibility that his advisor, this Lord Priest Matthew, had acted alone however. He would have to speak with Zakar soon, though first he needed to get to a temple and pray for guidance. He waited for Naithan to leave and before rising and as he did he heard a soft tinkling as something fell from his silk robes. He bent down to retrieve it and found two diamonds lying on the floor. He placed them in the palm of his hand and looked at them. The light of the sun sparkled through them and he noticed that they had been cut perfectly into the shape of tears…

XI

Zakar was worried. He had been moving along the hidden corridor that ran adjacent to the one in which the Prophet and the King had been walking and had seen his ruler collapse to his knees in a most unusual way, as if he were gripped by some unseen vision. The Vizier had been immediately suspicious and had sent out spells to see if magic were being employed. He had found no trace whatsoever and that had shocked him. In fact, the whole area around the King and Prophet seemed to contain no magic whatsoever, even though there were charms and wards around Sulan to protect him. They, at least, should have been visible. Yet there was nothing, as if they had been blasted away, but only powerful magic could do that and he had sensed nothing.

He felt the hair on the nape of his neck rise up and a cold sensation of foreboding swept over him. Something was wrong. His senses seemed certain that magic was being used, but his rational mind told him that there was none, unless the wizard had found some way to mask his spells. The rational part of his mind screamed that it was impossible, yet he knew he had ruled out the possible. He spared it no more thought, trusting to instinct. He flicked the sandals from his feet and began to run towards the chambers of the Lord Priest. His spies had informed him that the man had merely been reading one of his books but something told him they had been mistaken.

"Guards, follow me," he commanded as he ran past two sat talking on cushions.

He heard them fall in step behind him and soon they were joined by two others. Zakar prepared some spells and prayed they would be enough to hold the powerful man. As he neared Matthew's chambers, his instincts warned him that strong magic was being used and he soon began to see traces of it around him. He found himself balking at the prospect of facing this man. The shimmer of the magic was so strong that the corridor seemed to swim before them and even the guards behind him seemed able to see it. He found himself regretting his rash actions, yet knew that they were essential. He prayed to the gods that Matthew would not be expecting him so soon and that his defences would be down long enough for him to attack him effectively. He motioned the guards to slow the pace and crept near the door. The magical aura here was so strong that Zakar felt he was going to be sick.

Suddenly it ceased, indicating that whatever spell it was had ended. Now was his moment and he did not hesitate to act. He forced open the door and slammed a shielding spell onto the startled wizard, for wizard he had to be. Zakar smiled. The man was defenceless.

"Guards, seize this man," he commanded, and four men rushed in.

XII

Matthew staggered under the impact of the shield that slammed down around him, cutting him from his magic. Cursing, he spun round and saw four armed guards running towards him. He was trapped in this wretched room with no power.

With some power.

The thought came unbidden to his mind and he found that he could still feel the link with Jalim, faint though it was. The boy never ceased to amaze Matthew. Somehow he had maintained a link over such a long period of time without a break. The boy even seemed all the more powerful because of it, something logic and knowledge of spellcraft told him was impossible.

He ducked under the leaping grapple of one of the men and dived to the floor, the pieces of the sceptre falling from his hands. Looking around he saw that the guards had discarded their swords so as to take him more safely. He smiled grimly. They were about to learn a costly lesson. He sprang for the nearest sword, noting the positions of the guards around the rooms. Two seemed to have taken up positions at odd points along the walls and Matthew decided that they must be guarding secret passages, though he had never discovered any himself. The other two were already advancing on him.

His hand touched the hilt of the sword and he grabbed at it, rolling to his feet and turning to face the nearest guards as he did. They seemed a little taken aback at the move and their approach slowed a little. The sword seemed a little unwieldy, most of its weight seeming to be towards the tip of the blade, but he could use it. He smiled at the guards. All wizards of Caldor, high or low, had been trained by the knighthood and he was no exception. The training took over and his stance steadied. The guards noted this and hesitated a moment before attacking. It was all that Matthew needed. He sprang at them, lashing out with the flat edge of the sword. His aim was true and the blade cracked hard against one man's skull, its heavy tip felling the man at a stroke. He then turned and smashed the sword's hilt into the face of the other man and he felt his nose smash. Blood began seeping out and the man staggered, though remained standing.

Now was the time for a little magic. He channelled a small spell, hoping that the spellprint left by his present spell would mask it. Matthew flailed at the man with a wild left punch that grazed his chin. However the man twisted as if struck with great force before slumping unconscious to the ground. That only left the two still stood at the edges of the room. He gave one no chance to move, throwing his sword at him with all the force he could muster. It spun awkwardly through the air and Matthew fired a quick spell at it. The hilt struck the man and he slumped to the ground knocked unconscious by the invisible, electric shock his spell had delivered through the sword. He turned to the last guard who now had a sword in his hand.

"Give in now and I won't kill yer," said the man with a vicious smile. Matthew could see that this was probably the most dangerous of his opponents, as he wore the robes of the Shar-meer, elite warriors of Sol.

"Drop your sword and I won't kill you," he countered, his words carrying more courage than he felt.

The man shook his head and smiled, before running into attack him with his sword raised high. Matthew felt a momentary flash of relief. The guard was more foolish than dangerous, though that could still end in his death at the end of a sword. He steeled himself before stepping inside the man's guard, wrapping the man's sword arm with his own. Without thought he spun with the man, using his momentum against him and rolled him into the air over his hip. As the man came crashing down to the floor, Matthew slid his hands towards the hilt of the man's sword, using his weight to break the guard's grip. He grabbed the sword and it spun easily through his hands and soon it was pushing against the man's throat.

"Yield," he said softly.

"Never," gasped the winded man. "Death first."

"As you wish," he replied drawing the sword across the man's neck.

He turned to Zakar, who still stood in the doorway.

"You Caldorians are of a hardier stock than I had thought," said the man with a smile.

"He would have killed himself any way. Is that not the way of your Shar-meer?"

"It is true," said the man. "He was defeated and had to accept your mercy. In this kingdom that means slavery and most warriors could not live the life of slave."

"And you?"

"I'm far more practical," he replied and unleashed a spell.

Matthew saw blue tendrils of smoke wrap around him and knew now was the time to draw the energy from Jalim. Power surged through him and he struck out at the shield around him, shattering it and causing Zakar to double over in pain. Matthew, now in contact with the remains of his power, attacked Zakar's spell and trapped the Vizier in his own magic.

"I believe that now makes you my slave," he said slowly.

The man stared at him defiantly for a moment then dropped in shame as fear passed through his eyes.

"Yes, Master."

"Then listen, slave," said Matthew moving to pick up the pieces of the sceptre. "Slavery does not exist in my lands and may it never be so. I will release you and even help you."

"How?" asked Zakar slowly.

"I believe your Prophet may be on the road to converting to the religion of my kingdom. If he does, then your position here could be greatly enhanced if you were to become the Lord Priest of these lands."

The man seemed interested, though he would, for Matthew now had both pieces of the sceptre in his hands and was using a spell to play on the man's lust for power to bring him to their cause. In under ten minutes he was in complete agreement, a willing accomplice in their plans and the guards were back at their posts, all knowledge of their fight erased. Of the dead man, no more was ever seen. Zakar seemed to be skilled in the art of disposing of corpses. By the time Naithan had arrived at his chambers it was as if nothing had happened.

He seemed a little shocked at the turn of events and with the third piece of the sceptre in his hands. Matthew took it from the king and placed the whole crown in the magically warded box with the other two pieces. He then sat and listened to Naithan's version of the events, feigning shock and surprise at the correct moments, as well as including his congratulations.

"I think things are going well," said Matthew, echoing Naithan's thoughts. "I will contact Gareth tomorrow to learn how the siege goes and if how far they are from success."

"Can we trust him though?" asked Naithan, the gleam in his eyes making Matthew nervous.

"Of course we can. He would have done something before now if he had been the one plotting against you."

"Yes, you're correct, though I don't like this place. It makes me edgy."

"We'll soon be gone from here," said Matthew, trying to be reassuring. "I also think I may have worked out a plan to help us speed along the conversion of the Prophet."

"Really?" asked Naithan quickly. "How?"

"It would involve magic," he warned.

"No matter. I need to return to my lands before I lose them. Anything we can do to speed that moment will be considered."

That statement alone put the fear of Toric in him. For Naithan to readily agree to the use of magic was a strong indication of how bad things were getting. He outlined his plan and Naithan agreed, once again all too readily. They then left for the next banquet in their honour. When they arrived they learned that the Prophet was not to be dining with them this night. Apparently he was still feeling unwell. The meal passed in polite conversation with the viziers and princes, before they both retired to bed. Tomorrow was to be a big day and even Matthew was asleep before the midnight hour was struck.

XIII

Sulan sat alone in the temple of Al, praying for guidance. The vision of Toric had disturbed him and he sought answers from his gods. For the first time in his life they felt distant and though he sat in meditative prayer all night, not one answer came. As the sun's light began to brighten the morning he gave up and retired to his quarters. These questions he was going to have to answer alone…

CHAPTER SIXTEEN: Monsters and Mayhem

I

A cold breeze cut through the dark morning air and Karene found herself shivering a little. She drew her cloak around herself and removed a pair of fur lined gloves from her saddlebags. They were one of the few luxuries she allowed herself, the ermine fur being a delight to her calloused hands. She looked round to the knights under her command, now somewhat more numerous than before, and gazed down at the cyan plumes at her side with pride. For her efforts in yesterday's fire she had been given a field promotion and was to be trained up after her quest to capture Tristan had been completed. That was if it was completed, of course.

She scowled at herself angrily. She was close to him now and Jax was keeping her constantly informed of their progress. It seemed they had veered off into the woods once more and were determined to make it out through the old Grelchin border. They stood little chance of that and she would be upon them long before they even had the chance to discover that Caldorian Knights now patrolled it. She looked to her troops. They were ready to move out. She absently fingered the new badge of rank that now clasped her cloak around her. She would not be satisfied to remain a Field Knight. No cyan feathers could satisfy her. She would be the first female knight to take on the mantle of the white feathers, the King's Knight. She brushed the thoughts aside and looked to the new Blue Knight of the company.

"Order the march," she commanded.

Sir Aaron saluted and followed her orders with commendable speed. She looked back to the streets of Teldin, the grey light of pre-dawn giving it an almost menacing look. A cold shudder ran down her back and she found herself questioning the chances of success in her quest. She scolded herself silently once more, trying to put it down to the eerie look of the city. Yet even as they rode out passed the gates she still could not shake of the feeling that something was destined to go terribly wrong…

II

The Earl of Harkshire, Lord Darren of the House Hanton winced as light penetrated the darkness of his small cell and stung his sleep filled eyes. Evidently the torture he had been steeling himself would soon begin. He could not understand why they had not done so already, in an attempt to get him to tell them the plans for the attack of the city.

"You'll not get anything from me," he growled defiantly.

"I'm not expecting to," said the voice he had come to associate with this man once called the Shadow.

"So it's just for your own amusement then?" he asked bitterly.

"Of course," replied Galen with what sounded like a soft chuckle. "There's no tactical advantage to doing it." Darren tried not to wince at the thought of the terrors he could already imagine were to come. "I mean, releasing you only gives them another man to fight us with, and one such as you, a leader, can bring them morale."

"What are you saying?" asked Darren suspiciously. He was not sure exactly where the conversation was going, or what the man was implying.

"I'm going to release you," came the stunning reply.

"I'll not take mercy from the hands of my brother's killer."

He forced down the stab of pain that the statement caused. He could not show weakness in front of this man.

"I did not kill your brother," replied the man softly, "and neither did any of those in my command."

"Liar!"

"Why would I lie to you about this?" asked the man softly. "Do you think I wanted him dead?"

Darren did not answer.

"What good would that do me?" asked Galen softly. "I don't want this war, I just want to let these people rule themselves free of the lies perpetrated by those of your kind. I don't want to see them die under the swords of those who might even be relatives. If Prince Gareth leaves, he will have my assurance that we will do nothing to threaten Caldor. We don't want to fight you."

"You know what the answer to that will be, don't you?" The man nodded gently, the lamp in his hands revealing a pained expression on his face. "Why does a cold killer such as yourself care for these people?"

"Because they gave me a second chance, a chance to redeem myself, and I intend to try to make good on that chance," replied Galen.

"There can be no redemption for murderers such as you," he spat, angry at the man's hypocrisy.

"I'm aware of that," replied the pale faced man with a wince. "But I do what I can."

Darren found himself shocked by the honesty he felt in Galen's words. A question formed in his mind and he ventured to ask it, angrily fearing that he already knew the answer.

"If you claim that neither you nor your spawn killed my kin, then who do you claim did?"

"Anton of course," replied Galen.

A part of his mind had whispered such suspicions already, here in the dark. He could still remember the horror that surged through him as he saw his brother in Anton's arms through the door. It had been the shock of seeing it that had led to his capture. As he had been taken prisoner, the suspicion had voiced itself, yet he had brushed it aside, as he did again now.

He shook his head angrily. Anton could not have done it. He had been like a father to them both.

"You don't think he could have let two dangerous allies close to his bosom?" asked Galen softly. "A madness is running through his family. A sickness perhaps. They trust no one and use everyone. With each generation it is growing stronger, and I fear that in Naithan it will become all consuming, as it has become already to your ally."

Something again rang true about Galen's words, but he was a cautious man by nature. He looked to Galen as the man began to remove his chains.

"Either you're a brave man, or you have great faith in my words," he said slowly, "to free me from my bonds alone."

"You couldn't kill me if you tried," replied the man wearily, not bothering to look away from his task. "Not even if I desired death and embraced your sword within my ribs myself. Let's get you to freedom. Your brother's body has been released to your armies for burial. If you examine the body, you'll find the cut mark across his neck that killed him could have only come from behind."

With those words he rose and was led into the drizzling haze of the dawning sun.

III

Gareth surveyed the knights as they prepared for the next attack of the siege. This would be the first real challenge to his troops. Until now, none had believed they would truly be attacking the city and would not do so until they had to kill their first Theldarian. Only then would Gareth know if his troops had the will and morale to push ahead and take the city.

He pushed away any negative thoughts. His troops would fight and would fight well, that was all there was to it. The city had to be retaken from these criminals. He motioned to the runners to pass on the command to attack, though that was only a formality for the benefit of any foreign observers hoping to learn something of their tactics. He was already telepathically linked with the three Grey Knights under his command and they in turn were linked to the Magenta Knights under their command and so on, meaning that all those in command would be able learn whatever they needed to know to fight well. The theory was that they would be able to move as one, reacting together with a fluidity that could meet successfully with any battlefield shift of fortune, though it had never been tested in actual combat. There had been plenty of mock training battles, but never any actual combats, even in Grelchin, for there had been little need for it. Here, though, they were facing knights trained in his own tactics and that made them very different prospect.

"*Red cross showing*" came a voice in his mind, rising above the gentle murmurs that were the other Grey Knights' thoughts.

"*Surrender?*" he asked Sar Sophia.

"*I don't think so,*" came the reply.

"*Watch and wait,*" he commanded them all at once, receiving their obedience at once.

Of course, he would still have to wait for a runner to reach him with the news before he could act on it but it was good to see the procedure working as planned. The girl arrived just as another report from Sar Sophia rose into his thoughts.

"Sir, they've raised the red cross, Sir" said the girl crisply.

"*It's a prisoner release,*" said Sar Sophia quickly. "*They're returning Lord Hanton, Lord Darren, to us sir.*"

"Sar Sophia wishes to know how to proceed, sir."

"Wait and watch," he replied and the girl saluted, turned and ran to her task.

"*Wait until I speak with him before acting,*" he commanded the Grey Knights. "*I need to know if he has any intelligence on them.*"

They all knew the intelligence he spoke of. They had all heard the report of the young knight who had escaped the sewer cave-in that had wiped out almost an entire corpus of knights. He had been scared half to death and kept talking of black demons, shadow knights that could survive being buried alive by rock without a scratch. It had been a worrying report, particularly when a Battle Priest had searched the man's mind to discern the truth and had collapsed in a fit of fear. Even now the man would not leave his tent, and that made Gareth worry. It was that threat he feared more than that of his troops not fighting. Five hundred knights had been killed by shadowy knights who seemed able to tear stone down around them and walk away unscathed. Whatever dark pact this Galen had made was terrible indeed and he intended to ensure that Theldar was cleansed of it. Nothing should be allowed to despoil the holy city.

A pale, yet apparently unharmed Darren walked up to his command arena, disturbing his thoughts.

"What news?" he asked.

"None," replied the man wearily. "Only a message."

"A message? What is it?"

"I was told to tell you this. *Leave now and peace will be restored. We will challenge none. Attack us now and feel our wrath.*"

"What did he mean by *feel our wrath*?" asked Gareth.

"I don't know," replied Darren shaking his head. "I believe it has to do with some weapon they used yesterday. What that was I do not know."

"Shadow Knights?"

Darren looked at him blankly. Gareth pushed his mind away from such a topic, swallowing down his fear.

"What of the people of Theldar. With what spell does he have them ensorcelled?"

He saw the man's head whip up and his eyes scan him close, an edge of fear tingeing his eyes.

"None that I could see, but then I don't have the Talent, so would not be the best judge of things. They seem to be genuinely supporting him, but why I know not."

Gareth looked at him closely. He would have to be carefully observed for a while, to ensure that no spell had been used on him, though that was a matter for later. Now was the time for the attack. He sent out the command telepathically, dismissing the lord as he did so, then signalled for the buglers to sound the attack. Pushing away the image of the white streets of Theldar stained permanently red with blood he began the co-ordination of the first battle for Theldar's freedom.

IV

Tyrone shivered in the morning chill, his bones aching and his eyes heavy from a night of misery spent in the stocks. He had suffered jeers, spits and worse from the people around him, and he stank of the horse dung that had been picked from the streets and smeared into his clothes and face. He had vomited at that and the contents of his stomach still lay in a congealed pool at his feet. Only one person had shown him any kindness, Meredith, though how she had the gall to say she still cared for him after her betrayal he did not know.

Now he was to suffer the final humiliation. He was to be judged that morning before any that was interested to see it and people had been gathering since before the dawn cockerel had even crowed. He was to suffer some dramatic scene like that, which had robbed him of success in his first plan. He knew that somehow Galen would twist this to his advantage and somehow walk out of it more popular than ever. He forced down the bitterness.

"Are you ready?" asked a familiar voice behind him.

"I told you yesterday. I have no wish to speak with you after all you've done," he replied angrily.

"If I had not, he would have killed you," she said angrily. "I did it to save your life."

"I'd rather die than face whatever he has planned for me."

He felt her hand brush past his shoulder.

"Please, don't ever say that," she said softly, yet he refused to soften his heart.

"If you're not here to free me then go."

That had been another galling point of the events. None of the Circle of Light had come to free him and some had even been there to spit at him.

"Fine," came Meredith's reply. "I'll leave you to your misery."

He heard her footsteps fade away from him and felt a stab of pain in his heart, yet he refused to call out after her. It was she who had betrayed him. He settled himself down and prepared to await the predictable penny show he was about to become. He did not have to wait long.

Barely an hour had gone before fanfares blared out, announcing the official arrival of the Triad members to Justice Square, as it was rapidly becoming known as. A cheer erupted from the gathered crowd and he saw that the square was now packed with people. He doubted that there had ever been as large a crowd in the history of this city's brief independence. Evidently the events of yesterday had boosted support for the Triad immensely, particularly Galen. Tyrone found himself doubting whether the man could now ever be removed from office without causing a full-scale riot or other such civil disturbance. He closed his eyes bitterly, knowing that it was partly his fault and feelings of regret flooded through him.

"People of Theldar," came the voice of Galen from behind him, his soft voice somehow seeming to reach every part of the square. "Here before you is a man who betrayed us and tried to have me killed."

The crowd began to jeer and taunt him, and he found himself glaring at them angrily.

"No," said Galen softly, silencing them all at once. "Don't jeer him. He did what he thought was the correct thing to do, the right thing to do, and no man deserves punishment for doing what he thought was right. But his plans involved death, and more importantly, murder, my murder. As such, I claim the right to punish him myself, if that be my wish."

Tyrone could see the crowds gazing up at the man behind him, some with an intense look of adoration that was frightening.

"But punishment is not my wish," he continued. "I have committed many crimes in my life, and have been forgiven for them, so why should I not forgive a man for doing what he felt was right?"

Tyrone could see that he had the crowd under his spell, though why that was he did not know. Galen's speeches were not all that good, if looked at on paper, yet somehow, when Galen spoke them, people listened. Tyrone realised that in some way, this was probably one of the most powerful men he had ever met.

"The answer is of course, that there is no reason. I will forgive him, and all those who worked with him. He is even free to retain his seat on the Triad council."

Tyrone started with shock and saw many in the audience do the same.

"You wonder why?" asked Galen rhetorically. "I'll tell you. He loves this city and the people within it and will do all that he feels is right for it. Yet in doing what he was doing, he misguidedly threatened the city. Therefore, to ensure he does not do so again, he must make an oath, if he wishes to remain within the city limits. He will swear an oath, not to me, but to the city and its people. He must swear to protect the city, independent of any other causes. What say you to my offer?"

The crowd remained silent as Galen moved into his line of sight and Tyrone felt the eyes all fall upon him. He realised that Galen had outmanoeuvred him once again. If he refused the man's offer, he would be sent into exile, forever abandoning his cause. Yet if he swore the oath, he would be betraying much of what he believed in, though would remain in a position of power, if the Circle of Light permitted it. He could well find himself returning to power only to lose it to another. Of course, if he did stay, he would still be near to Meredith. He closed his eyes, the pain of indecision filling him. What could he do?

"You have two choices, my friend," said Galen softly. "One is to go and forever leave, the other is to remain with me and help us build up a better place for all."

Tyrone knew that he could do something if he remained, yet to yield to the man's offer would be an act of weakness. He heard footsteps to his right and caught the faint trace of Meredith's perfume on the air. He closed his eyes, hoping to drown everything out, yet knew he could not. He could not be parted from her, despite her betrayal, and he could not leave the Theldarians to the whims of this man.

"I…accept your offer and agree to swear loyalty to the city," he said softly, though his words seemed to ring out across the square.

"I'm glad you did," replied Galen quietly. "This city will have need of you."

Tyrone looked to the man as he spoke, wondering at the brief moment of truthfulness in his tone. Yet the calm, composed player of the crowds

Tyrone had come to know rapidly replaced it. He waited quietly as Galen raised the keys above his head and released him from the stocks. Tyrone felt his body begin to give way but he steeled himself for the event, determined to show no more weakness. He knelt before Galen and swore his oath, choking on the words as he did.

"I see you, Lord of Light," said Galen quietly, "Keeper of the Sacred Scrolls. Rise and face your city anew."

As he spoke he pressed a tightly rolled scroll into his hands. He looked at it and felt his jaw drop. It was the only written page containing the words of Toric, and only given to a new High Priest. He looked to Galen once more, who had now turned back to the stunned crowd.

"From now on, the Lord of Light shall be protector of the spiritual wellbeing of all Theldarians." Tyrone could see more than one priest now glaring angrily at them. "Now, as has ever been, we shall worship Toric, but no more will we restrict teachings to those solely of our god. Now all have the right to worship whom they wish and where they wish, save upon the grounds of other holy temples. We shall be free."

There was a great roar of applause from the crowd and Tyrone had time to absorb the news. Religious practises of other kingdoms had only ever been permitted in the dockside area before now.

"Come, friend," said Galen, stretching out his hand towards him as he spoke. "Take my hand that we may seal our agreement."

Tyrone clasped Galen's hand, still shocked from his announcement and was not prepared for the sudden jolt of energy that passed through him. He looked at Galen , suspicions stirring up his fear.

"What was that?" he asked, his dry throat feeling very rough and painful.

"Just a little guarantee to ensure your continuing loyalty," he replied with a pleasant smile that almost verged on maniacal.

Tyrone's heart sank. He had been truly tricked. For a moment he had believed the man and now he was trapped, his fate now tightly bound to that gaunt, pale man.

"Go now," he said softly to Tyrone. "Rest up and clean up. There are many things to do today and I need all the *loyal* hands I can get."

Tyrone gave a brief salute before preparing to return to his quarters. As he left the square he noticed that a group of priests seemed to have found Galen's pretty speech not to their taste and would doubtless be preparing to plot something. Sometimes such people were so stupid. They had conspiracy printed all over their cautious actions and most, even those untrained in the art of body reading, could see it.

He decided to begin his work now and decided that his bath could wait. He slipped out behind the priests and followed them, preparing a report in his head even now. He would find a way out of Galen's grasp, though he would now have to wait a while. As he continued his way through the streets he heard a distant rumble and terrible cry of voices. It seemed that the siege of Theldar had truly begun…

V

Zakar rushed through the silk canopied corridors, cursing the gods as he did. How could he have been so stupid? His treachery was going to lead to the ruin of his kingdom. Civil war would soon be erupting throughout the provinces and all due to these damnable Caldorians. He entered the sorcerer's room without knocking and sat before him in the only part of the room where he could talk unheard by the many spies in the outer walls.

"You seem a little upset," said Matthew, barely taking his eyes off the three pieces of metal tubing before him.

Zakar recognised one as the centrepiece of the princess's crown. He ignored the slur that their vandalism of the sacred heirloom invoked.

"You see well," replied Zakar sourly. "Your plans have succeeded and my realm is undone. The Prophet of Light, the gods watch his spirit, has converted to your religion."

"That is good, then, isn't?" asked Matthew, still seeming to be thoroughly absorbed in his study of the tubes.

"No, it is not," replied Zakar acerbically. "He realises that to remain ruler of this realm would be to incite rebellion, so he will stand down as its ruler, leaving the question of succession to the Great Council. I have been undone and the kingdom will sunder, for it was so before my lord's accession to the throne. All will be turmoil once more and we shall be left to the savage mercy of the Imperial Lion!"

"Why has Sulan decided to stand down, exactly?"

A thousand curses upon the man. How dare he take such news as if it were no consequence!

"He knows that a ruler of one faith cannot lead people of another, so he stands down for one of the *old faith*," said Zakar sourly.

"He doesn't think to convert his people to the true faith?"

At last, there was the hint of worry in the cursed man's voice.

"Of course not. He would create an outcry and be deposed himself if he were to announce his conversion and enforce theirs. He may have had a vision, but those in the city have not and would surely revolt at his atrocity. A Prince cannot rule Sol if his Palatial City is not his own."

"What if the people were shown the truth of their ruler's conversion, and the power of Toric?"

"It would have to be a mighty vision indeed for such a change in the whole city's perceptions."

"Then if it is what is needed, then I am sure that Toric shall oblige," replied the infuriating man, returning his gaze to the pieces of brass before him.

"What do you mean? Do you have some plan?"

"Be at peace," said Matthew, using Zakar's native tongue. "All is now in the hands of Toric. If you are true to us then all will be well. You are dismissed."

The wizard turned back to his work, ignoring Zakar once more and he found himself forcing down a growl of rage. How dare this man dismiss him as a servant, yet he could play their game, just a little longer. He had no faith in these outlanders but had little choice but to follow them for now.

He nodded his head in a cursory bow and left the room. He set his mind to looking for an opportunity from the chaos that was to erupt. He could see none for now, but there were always moments of choice available if one looked in the correct direction. All he had to do was discern which direction to look in.

VI

Galen moved about the battlements, inspecting his troops. They had held well against the first two onslaughts, even those who were not used to combat, though some sections had been hard pressed and had almost allowed breaches in their defences. It was not good enough. This was the first day of actual fighting and he could not afford the loss of morale that would follow any serious breach in the walls. They had to win this day with fewer losses than they were already taking. That meant he had to unleash his knights' magic soon, much though he hated the idea. Sar Petra had argued against it, yet it was the only way. He needed to lessen the morale of the besiegers as soon as possible and so he had to show them that he commanded the magic of his forces. Unfortunately, as Sar Petra had pointed out, that would force them to retaliate in kind, but it was necessary. He could not send his Shadow Knights into the combat, as Sar Petra had advised, for he had another purpose for them and needed them rested.

A roar erupted from beyond the walls as the third attack charged towards the city and Galen relayed messages to the knights to unleash their magic if breaches looked imminent. He hated ceding this so early in the conflict but the day had to be won well. He moved back from the walls and across to the observation post as his archers let forth their first volley of arrows. The screams of men began to reach into the air and he closed the sounds off from his ears. It was not a pretty war, but he had seen far worse. He shook his head angrily. He had never seen wars before, this was his first, yet still he could recall the stench of blood and the screams of men, from countless other wars, some remembered thing from whatever kept him alive.

He knew that they were not his memories, yet could not separate them from the present conflict. Fire suddenly ripped out with a loud explosion and he jumped, fearing himself in the muddy trenches once again, then realised with a start that it was magic that had created the flames this time. He pulled his thoughts back to *this* conflict and saw yet more explosions erupt along the walls as more of the city knights unleashed their magic. He waited for the fires of retaliation, yet none came. In fact, the attackers sounded the retreat and began to flee back to their camps. Explosions and lightning rained down upon them as they did, the city knights gaining more confidence as they used it.

Yet still no magic was returned. He quickly gave the command to cease the magical attacks, fearing that they would use all their strength in one go. He did not wish to remain defenceless against their counter magic. Yet still it did not come. He waited long through the day and saw nothing. He sent out shadow knights to spy for him and anxiously awaited their results. It was Sar Petra who came to report the news.

"Well, why do they not attack now?" he asked impatiently.

"They are unsure how to react Sir," she said softly. "They still think of the battles to come and do not wish to reveal the level of magic they possess to foreign spies."

"Then the gamble worked then?" he asked with a smile.

"This time, yes, but I doubt it will for much longer. They will not tolerate the losses they received today. I fear that their ultimate decision in the council they hold will be to retaliate with magic."

"Then they still meet to discuss this, even now?" he asked incredulously.

"They have probably contacted the king to request permission to use magic, for Gareth will not move without his brother's consent," the knight replied.

"Then we can expect no further attacks today?"

"Probably not," replied Petra.

"Good, then instruct the knights to create a fog. We strike at them now," he commanded.

"But that would be revealing ourselves too soon," she replied, unable to keep the shock from her voice.

"I believe that this fight has to be won quickly," replied Galen quickly. "If not, then I fear we will lose."

She looked at him quickly, evidently trying to read his expression, yet he kept his face impassive. She could not know of the vision he was presently caught in. He could see the city in flames and the king marching through the streets with painted warriors. In Naithan's hand was a severed head and Galen did not have to look at it to know whose head it was. He watched Petra leave as the vision ended with him staring into his own vacant eyes. He had to win this fight, yet part of him knew it was lost already. Yet he could not back down. He looked back out over the walls and saw the fog rising from the earth already. Soon the world would be lost in haze and shadow and his special knights would do their work…

VII

Gareth waited impatiently for Matthew's reply to his request. They had to be able to fight magic with magic, yet Matthew seemed to be taking an eternity with his reply. Apparently they were at a crucial stage in their plans with the Prophet of Sol and he would be unable to contact him for some time. He could do nothing without the use of the more powerful magicks they had at his disposal.

"Excuse me sir," came a voice from his guard. "I think you should see this."

Gareth glared at the man for his temerity to speak to him without permission but went to look at what the guard spoke of. He peered out from the tent and found that a dense fog was rising from the ground, carried out from the earth's moisture by the familiar shimmer of magic.

Knights, he thought out to those still linked with him. *Beware an attack!*

Already he knew it was too late, from screams were erupting from all directions. More worrying still was that none of the command knights linked with him and worse still, when he reached out his thoughts to them he found that they were not there. He summoned forth magical armour to protect him.

A scream gurgled from his right and saw his guard drop to the floor, blood spurting from his throat. Of the attacker there was no sign. He felt a blade slide across the back of his invisible armour and turned to face his astonished attacker. He saw that it was a young man, dressed in dark armour and armed with a short sword. Gareth drew his own weapon and prepared to meet his attacker. The man lunged at him in a clumsy attack and he parried it away with ease, or at least he should have done. Instead he found that the dark knight's sword cut straight through his own and glanced off his armour of magic once more. Gareth strove to counter attack quickly, forcing down a sudden surge of panic and found to his horror that the blade of his sword shattered into a thousand shards. He backed into his tent, panic surging through him as the man smiled coldly at him. Gareth knew that his magic shield would not hold off his attacker for long, being only a temporary measure designed as a last defence for him. Already he could feel its energy fading around him.

He looked to his attacker quickly, and noted that for a moment the man seemed almost insubstantial, before becoming solid again. Panic tightened its grip upon him at the confirmation that this was no ordinary knight before him. His eyes flicked around the room quickly, looking for something to fight with. He was forced to duck back from another lunge from the attacker and twisted away from the blade. As he did so he collided with a chest and found himself tumbling to the floor, knocking over one of the small tables as he did.

The knight raised his sword and sprang as Gareth scrabbled desperately for a weapon. His hands closed around a sword hilt and he threw it at the leaping knight. As he did so, he rolled to his left in a desperate bid to escape and saw the knight fall to the ground, blood spilling from his chest. He looked to the attacker in surprise and saw that the hilt was that of the broken goblin sword he had found in Grelchi. For a moment he thought he saw a translucent blade protruding from the man's back, before the hilt clattered to the floor. He picked up the fallen hilt and looked at it in stunned amazement, before turning his thoughts to more pressing matters.

He scrambled to his feet and ran from the tent, listening for sounds of combat. He heard only silence, though he thought he could see the red haze of fire in the distance. Panic surged through him momentarily before he realised he could not even hear his own breathing. He reached out with his magic and dispelled the silence that had been created, feeling relieved to hear the shouts of men and women. Yet there was still no sound of combat and as he reached out with his magic he found that none around him appeared to be fighting and the shouts came from those fighting fires in the supply wagons.

Can anyone hear me? He thought out with as much force as he could muster, hoping to make contact with his commanding knights.

He received word only from those of the cyan plumes and below. It seemed the attack had been aimed at the high ranking officers, reducing his ability to command efficiently. He cursed them and began to collect telepathic reports from those knights skilled enough to provide them. The news was not good from any of them, most talking of black demons springing from nowhere to kill and burn all they touched. Gareth knew that if left unchecked, this fear would spread through the camp like a plague and eat away at the knights' morale. It had to be stopped, and the only way to do that was to show them that their attackers had been human. He went back into the tent to see to the body, only to find that it had vanished, leaving nothing but blackened earth behind it.

VIII

The streets of Zaron began to fill up as all its citizens came out to hear the proclamation of their prince and Prophet Sulan XXV, or so it seemed to

Naithan, sat on the raised dais at the top of the palace steps. It had been well situated, for from here he could see all the way down to the harbour and it was probable that he, or at least the dais he presently stood upon, would be visible from down there. There could not be a more auspicious view from which the proclamation of the prophet's conversion could be seen from, yet something filled Naithan with nervousness. It was not the crowds, for he had addressed numbers such as this before, and today it would not be his words to which it the people would be listening, nor Matthew's plan to begin the conversion of the city, it was something in the manner of the others upon the stage, including Sulan himself. All the princes of the various regions were in attendance, ostensibly to be there as witnesses to the betrothal rites he and Sulan's daughter were to undergo. What they did not realise, of course, was that they would be here to witness the beginning of a new order for Sol. The touch of Toric was now reaching into this kingdom, offering to bring the purity of light and truth to its people.

He smiled contentedly to himself. His victory here was almost enough to remove the sour taste of Theldar's rebellion from his mouth. He offered a quick prayer of thanks and felt the nervousness slip away somewhat. Toric was with him once more. All would be well. His night's sleep had even seen the return of his dreams, a sure sign that Toric was pleased. Yet despite it all, he could not shake the feeling that something was going to go wrong. He looked to Matthew only to see that intense stare of concentration he had when thinking through difficult problems, or when working magic, though why he needed to do so was beyond Naithan. Everything was going to plan, as far as he knew, anyway. He found himself wondering if his advisor was keeping something from him.

His thoughts were distracted by the arrival of Sulan and his daughter the princess Serinda to the dais. He stood and bowed with the other princes, keeping up the pretence of servility for just a little longer than the rest, shaming them as he did so. He had to prove himself more a servant to Sol than they were, else the people would have suspicions about his role in Sulan's conversion. Sulan waved his hand and all the princes stood behind him sat as he made his way to the front of the platform. The man looked to his High Vizier, Zakar, briefly and upon seeing a slight nod from the small man, turned to face his people.

"People of Zaron," he said, raising his arms out towards them as his voice boomed across the city. "I have summoned you today to announce news of the most joyous nature. My daughter, the princess Serinda, is to be wed."

A great cheer arose from the citizens before him and Naithan felt himself moved, despite himself. The reaction of his citizens would be more one of apathy than anything.

"The great king of the mighty Caldor has appeared here to offer his suit and I have accepted, though I will be heavy in my heart that this will mean she will have to leave this fair city. Yet through this marriage there shall be strength and the oppressors of Kolth will find us with powerful allies if they dare ever to take our lands once more!"

At this there was yet another cheer, though this was a much fiercer, more bestial cry, as if the mention of Kolth brought out the crowd's most base, primeval feelings of rage and triumph. It made Naithan shudder and he suddenly found himself glad that he had made the Solmen his allies and not his enemies.

"Yet I have more news, not of so happy a tune for you my people."

Naithan's ears pricked in alert at this. He started, almost rising from his seat to ask him what he meant. A hand clasped around his arm and he felt Matthew gently press him down, reminding him of his place. He looked to his friend wondering if this was what he was worrying about but got no reaction. Matthew's brow was still furrowed in concentration. Naithan looked back to Sulan.

"In the many days I have been with the king of this great nation Caldor, I have been shown that the gods of the heavens are not my gods any more, and that their great one god, Toric, is god of my heart. As such, I am no longer worthy of leading you my people, along the seven paths of truth anymore. I therefore must stand down as your leader, and in turn, as prophet of our nation."

This news was greeted with a deathly, stunned silence from both the crowds below and the princes with Naithan on the platform. He felt a cold sense of dread shudder through his spine. His plans had come to nought. His alliance was now a worthless millstone around his neck and he was now obliged to help a heathen kingdom in matters of international importance. He moved to stand once more but felt Matthew's grip upon his arm tighten ever so slightly. He looked to his friend once more but saw only that infuriating blank stare of concentration. Naithan repressed a shudder of anger that suddenly coursed through him. His friend had known this was going to happen and had not warned him. How dare he!

"Have faith in Toric and pay attention to what now goes on!" said Matthew in a soft whisper. Naithan turned his attention back to the Sulan and saw chaos erupting around him. Already four princes had leapt to their feet to issue their claims as the next Prophet of Light, their allies and companions moving to join him. Others had leapt up to Sulan to protest, undoubtedly his allies in the Grand Council, all calling for him to renounce his new faith and take back the Throne of Light and some were moving towards Naithan, drawing their swords as they did. Matthew's grip on his arm released and he immediately stood to face his potential attackers.

"You have caused this!" hissed one, his dark eyes glittering menacingly. "You and your god will now bring us to ruin!"

"He is not my god," growled Naithan angrily, drawing his own sword as he did. "He is the god of us all, whether you believe it or not!"

"Toric has no claim over us!" snarled another. "Ours are the gods of the seven heavens. They are everything. They are all!"

"Compared to the power of Toric, they are nothing. They are merely shadows, created by the king of shadows, the one eyed wolf Thenril!" replied Naithan, bringing his sword up to block one of their initial attacks.

"Stop this!" thundered the voice of Sulan over the chaos. "He is a guest in my house and I will not have any bloodshed over my decision. I claim the rite of abdication, to choose my successor. I will then enter exile from these lands and trouble them no more. There will be no chaos!"

"You would leave us in a position such as this, allied with a man who calls us devil worshipers? Nay, by your abdication and his marriage to your daughter you make him a prince among us! Able to sit at our Council's and listen to our business. By what right to you think to do this. You are becoming as bad as he is, thinking to command us as a king would, and not as a prophet!"

"I claim it by the Rite of…"

He was not allowed to finish for an earth-shattering roar from the city interrupted his words. All on the platform turned round and saw a monstrous form rise from the waters of the docks, smashing up Naithan's ship as it did. Naithan knew he recognised it, and looked to Matthew, who shook his head ever so slightly, meaning for him to look back to the chaos below. Naithan did as his friend asked, angry by this turn of events and wondering exactly what the wizard had in mind. It seemed the wizard had seen fit to alter their plan somewhat. The creature roared once more and flames erupted from its mouth, engulfing one of the warehouses. This added to the growing chaos of the streets as people began desperately trying to run away, or fell to their knees in supplication to the personification of the greatest goddess in their pantheon, Giarna, goddess of the sea.

The people in the streets were not the only ones to have dropped to their knees, for most of the princes and warriors on the platform and done so as well, all with their heads bowed and all muttering prayers of supplication. It was not long before he and Sulan were the only two left standing. Even Serinda had dropped to her knees, Naithan noticed, suppressing the anger and disgust he felt at the sight.

The creature roared again and he could hear the sound of more buildings erupting in flame. The people kneeling on the platform all flinched visibly, before one got to his feet. It had been one of those who had moved to attack him before.

"Where is your god now?" he asked with a sneer. "You have brought the wrath of Giarna down upon us all!"

"I AM HERE," came a voice from his mouth.

Naithan's eyes widened in surprise, as did those of the men around him. Naithan wondered what was happening and gasped as energy the like of which he had never felt flooded through him. His senses seemed to leap with life and all around him was light and colourful. Everything suddenly seemed more real, more solid, and more beautiful. He felt like he could do anything if he just put his mind to it. The power was intoxicating.

"Think not of the power," said a voice softly in his mind. Naithan found it to be familiar in some way, though he was not sure exactly why. What he did know was that power radiated behind those words. *"We seek only to enlighten these heathens to the Faith."*

"I WILL REVEAL THE TRUTH TO YOU ABOUT YOUR GODS THROUGH THIS MY GREATEST SERVANT!" came the voice from his mouth.

"Go to the docks!" commanded Toric within his mind, for it could only be he that spoke.

Naithan turned and walked to the edge of the platform. He had thought to use the stairs, but they led back into the palace and he needed to show Toric's power with as little delay as possible. He closed his eyes and put his faith in Toric, stepping off the thirty-foot high platform.

IX

Matthew struggled to retain a look of composed serenity as Naithan stepped off the platform. The blood-link had warned him of his friend's plans, but only just in time. He reached out with the power he was channelling through Naithan and formed a bridge of light beneath the king's feet, allowing him to gracefully descend towards the docks. He felt sweat and tears run down his face, yet restrained himself from wiping them away, for they were not his tears. Matthew had done something that could lead to both their deaths if it were not done correctly. He had reached through the blood-link between them and allowed their thoughts to touch in such a way that Matthew could use his power through Naithan directly, using only his energy and his thought patterns. It was dangerous because Naithan's body and mind were not accustomed to the powers and drains that this magic would cause and if it entered a state of shock, it could well kill Naithan and Matthew with it. Yet it was necessary to do this. Matthew had to be seen as having had nothing to do with this event. Already he had felt the probing magicks of several of the princes' viziers, all of which seemed to have expressed surprise at Matthew's lack of involvement.

When Naithan returned he too would be subject to such probes, but by then it would be too late to find anything. Naithan had as much talent with magic as a dog had with a sword and they would surmise that it truly had been a miracle, and that Toric truly had spoken. Matthew's patchy memories from earlier High Priests given when he had taken the burden of the blood link told him that it had been done before and that in ancient times it had been done on regular occasions. This was the first time it had been attempted in recent generations though, and the first time ever that it had been done without the monarch's knowledge or consent.

That was possibly the most dangerous part of all, for if Naithan tried to take over the link then there was no telling what could happen. He could draw enough to kill them both, and even Jalim whose faint link Matthew could still feel now. If he was not careful, Naithan could probably draw enough magic to destroy half the city, for Matthew was also linked to the three pieces of the sceptre he had attached around his wrists. It was a very large gamble, yet it was one that had to be taken. If all went well then Sulan would not have to resign the Throne of Light and Sol would begin its conversion to the true faith.

He pushed these thoughts aside and looked back to the scene below. Naithan was now nearing the docks and the sea creature that was ravaging them. Matthew turned his thoughts back to retaining control of the beast, the only magic he could use safely, for somehow the circlet of control seemed to radiate no magic even when in use. It was probably due to the use of his two magicks, but that was not important. He turned his gaze to the scene below.

X

Naithan looked up at the beast before him and knew fear once more. Despite the energy surging through him, he could still feel his most primal instincts calling for him to flee, to survive. Yet he stood his ground. The power of Toric was now radiating around him and he knew that nothing could harm him now. The creature roared in rage and flames leapt from its mouth towards him. He held back a scream and trusted to the power of Toric.

The world became a mass of red, orange, blue and yellow as the flames washed over him, yet no heat came from them, at least that he could feel. Behind him another warehouse exploded in flame and some of the cobbled stones around him began to melt in the heat, yet Naithan did not feel even the slightest change in the temperature. He smiled and looked at the beast that seemed to look down upon him in confusion. It roared another bellow of rage and its huge maw came down around him, sending another shudder of fear down his spine. He could smell its fetid breath as the darkness of its mouth closed around him and its teeth brushed round his clothes. Naithan stood his ground, determined that he should move no inch and found that beast was unable to touch him in anyway. The power of Toric was too much for the beast.

Naithan smiled, before praying out to Toric to aid him in his moment of triumph. He raised his arms in the air, his hands briefly brushing its slimy tongue, then threw out the power of Toric. Light leapt from his arms into the creature's throat and it screamed in pain. It reared its head into the sky and recoiled from Naithan, Toric's power still pouring from his palms.

"I AM THE WILL OF TORIC," came the voice from his mouth once more. "BOW BEFORE MY SERVANT AND SHOW ALL WHO IS THE TRUE GOD. THE ONE GOD!"

The creature screamed once more and looked as if it were going to return to the sea, before it lowered its head to the ground at Naithan's feet. He could not help but notice a look of pure anguish in the creature's eyes as he did so, yet he ignored it and stepped up onto its head, turning back towards the city. It raised its head back into the air until he could see almost every part of the city in one glance and looked to the people who were now looking up at him with an awe that startled him.

"PEOPLE OF SOL. I AM TORIC, THE ONE GOD, AND YOUR PROPHET HAS CHOSEN WELL. HE IS DESTINED TO RULE YOU TO GREATNESS IN MY NAME. ACCEPT HIM AND YOUR NEW FAITH, FOR NONE IS AS POWERFUL AS I AM, NOT EVEN THE GREATEST ON THE FIFTEEN CELESTIAL GUARDIANS, AS I HAVE PROVEN. BUT KNOW THIS ALSO. I AM NOT A GOD OF DESTRUCTION, BUT OF CREATION, AND TO PROVE MY WORD I RESTORE ALL THAT YOUR FALSE IDOL DESTROYED."

Naithan felt his arms stretch out involuntarily towards the burning buildings and light leapt from them. The fires were quenched almost instantly and the buildings reformed, yet Naithan did not feel it would be enough. He stretched out with the energy and channelled it with his own idea. Somewhere, some part of him seemed to scream out in fear but he did not heed it. He was following the will of Toric. The buildings exploded in a dazzling, golden light that made his eyes water and his head swim.

The beast lowered him to the floor and as it did the power and strength left him. He slumped to the ground, the dark fingers of unconsciousness stretching out to claim him, yet he had to see if Toric's will had worked. He looked up and saw exactly what he had hoped to see. Every part of every building that the flames had touched had been rebuilt, entirely with gold. Then came the darkness…

XI

Jalim Freewielder, apprentice to the High Priest of Caldor, Matthew Kelreon, sat in a laboratory within the central keep of Belthanor, fortress city of Caldor, muttering angrily at the menial spells he was being forced to work through with the other apprentices, or squires, in the room with him. He was far in advance in his studies when compared to these fools, but it was strictly regulated by age here and he was still only a youth of sixteen, meaning he was only allowed to study magic of the third order, as they put it. They set so many rules and regulations about their magic that none could see the beautiful simplicity of it all. Even the greatest wizard he had ever known, Matthew, seemed to find difficulty with his concepts of magic. They seemed to wrestle with it, bind it in words and strictures, rather than allowing it free to do what it could.

"Master Jalim, if you would please concentrate on the task at hand," came the firm voice of Sar Karinda at the head of the class.

Jalim sighed and looked back to the work, trying to ignore the sudden surge of energy as it left him. Matthew was evidently drawing off him once more, so it was good, in a way, that he was only working simple magicks at present. Whilst the aftermath of giving others energy often left him feeling more powerful than before, the act itself was very draining and left little room for him to perform his own magic.

A small mew from the floor disrupted his thoughts. His cat Misty was there.

"Go back to the room," he hissed to the snowy white cat. "You'll get me into trouble again!"

Misty had done that on more than one occasion already, and Sar Karinda, with her infamous allergy to cats, had seen that he had faced the cane on several occasions for allowing him in here. However, no amount of shouting, cajoling, and bribing could keep Misty from him sometimes. The cat had very much a will of his own and went where he pleased. He mewed again and paced worriedly around the stool legs. Jalim felt a stab of worry. Misty had an uncanny sense for detecting danger sometimes. It had saved them both from several dangerous incidents when he had still been a boy running with the street gangs of Kelvaria.

Misty mewed again, following it with a hiss. Jalim looked round anxiously wondering what was disturbing his cat. His vision swam and suddenly he knew exactly what it was. He could feel the energy leaving his body turn from a trickle to a rush, then from a rush to a torrent. Whatever Matthew was doing was likely to kill both of them if he continued. Jalim could give a lot of energy, but he had limits and they were rapidly approaching. He tried to control it, slow it down somehow, and when that failed, to shut it off completely, yet all were useless. He was going to die and there was nothing he could do about it. His vision was suddenly filled with white and he felt Misty's claws dig into his face. He screamed and tried to throw the cat off, losing his balance as he did so. He felt the world spin around him and everything exploded in pain as his head hit the floor.

The last thing he could recall was a sense of relief as the unconsciousness severed the connection.

XII

Tyrone watched silently as the priests plotted together about bringing the end of the Shadow's *reign of terror*, as they called it. He knew that their plans were nothing but air though. The chance to oust the man had gone. All his dreams were gone as well. His honour; his sacrifices; all his hopes; all had gone the way of dust. He got up and walked out of their chamber in disgust, partly at them, partly at himself, for he knew he had given his word, sworn fealty to that man, in a way, and that he would report them. What had he become? A petty snitch for a petty man, that was what. Yet he would not leave, and knew that he could not, even if he wanted to.

He walked out on the streets shadowed by the darkening skies and witnessed the celebrations of the citizens of Theldar as they rejoiced in the success of the first day of combat. It would not last, he knew. These were people unused to war, or the fact that they were destined to lose. They could last for a while, perhaps even for a long period of time, but they could not hope to win, isolated as they were. Eventually they would starve, and he knew he would still be here, clinging on to his hopes to the end. He just hoped that Tristan was doing better in his new life.

At least then it won't have all been for nothing, he thought sadly, walking back to the palace, and the monster he had helped create.

XIII

Groltch watched Tris with concern. The human had not been himself since the fight at the village. He had always been the quieter of the two humans he travelled with, well three if you wished to include Belthar and he certainly looked human, yet these past couple of days he had been unusually quiet. He only spoke when answering questions and the answers he gave were always short and succinct, leaving no option for conversation. He had even taken to keeping watch alone, something the others did not seem to mind, for both seemed to sense the difference in him and felt uneasy about it.

The truth was that it made Groltch uneasy, but he refused to allow the human to force him away. Groltch considered the man a friend, and, for his people at least, that meant not abandoning him to the melancholy that seemed to be tearing Tris away from them. He moved to sit closer to him as Tris prepared to take watch. The other two were already well on the way to sleep and Groltch judged this to be the best time to speak with the knight. Tristan still seemed unable to trust the others and was even more taciturn than usual, if such a thing were possible. When they were in earshot and he often refused to answer them at all if it could be ignored politely enough.

"What wrong with you?" he asked, deciding that the direct route would probably be the best approach.

"Nothing," replied Tristan shortly. The knight looked round apologetically and for an instant, Groltch saw a flash of the old Tristan. "I am sorry. I did not mean to snap at you like that. It is just that I have had a lot on my mind since the fight."

"I know, but it over now," replied Groltch softly. "It time to move on."

"I just cannot do that at present," replied Tristan quickly. "I killed people on that day, people whose names I could have known. Have you ever done that before?"

Groltch shook his head. He could not say he had even killed a single member of his race before, let alone one he knew.

"Then you cannot understand. I always thought I would be able to shut it out, but I cannot. It will stay with me until my death."

The finality of the statement made Groltch worried and he looked closely at the human, who seemed to have returned to vacantly gazing into the fire. He would be no good on watch in that state. Not knowing what else to do or say he drew he sword.

"You sleep, or rest," said Groltch softly. "I watch first. Not disturb you though, I know you need to think. Watch would only distract you."

Tristan turned to look at him accusingly, before his face sank into a weary smile.

"Thank you. You are a true friend and I will value that forever."

Again the knight used words that unnerved Groltch. It was like the human was expecting to go away shortly. Tristan held out his hand in the Caldorian symbol of friendship and Groltch took it.

"We friends," he said with a smile.

"Until death," replied Tristan softly.

With that he turned away and wrapped himself within his bedroll. Groltch moved closer to the fire as a breeze whistled through their camp. Autumn was fast approaching and Groltch found himself thinking of his village at harvest time. The memories brought tears to his eyes and he blinked them away, looking back to Tristan.

"I don't know what it is to kill my own kind," he whispered to himself in his own tongue. "But I know what it is to see them all slaughtered."

Tristan stirred and Groltch saw that he was asleep already. That was one thing about Tristan, his warrior training prevented him from not taking advantage of an opportunity to sleep.

Suddenly the knight moaned and began muttering to himself. Groltch moved closer, wondering if anything the man said would reveal something he would not say consciously. Yet it all sounded like nonsense and there was only one phrase he could make out, repeated over and over again, something about the night of two days or some other such nonsense. As far as Groltch was concerned, all nights had two periods of day, that of the morning and evening.

Suddenly he found himself feeling guilty at eavesdropping over his friend's dreams, and returned to his position on watch, looking up at the stars, tracing out the constellations of the Golden Sword and looking for Mesunrus, the flying unicorn, western herald of the autumn. It was not visible yet, at least as far as he could see through these trees, but it would not be long, and then the harvests would begin. He lost himself to memories once more and soon drifted off to sleep, despite his efforts to stay awake. He need not have worried though, for out in the woods stalked a guardian, one who had watched over them every night since his master had joined them, and would do so as long as he remained with them…

CHAPTER SEVENTEEN: Siege and Sacrifice

I

"How is the king?" asked Zakar as Matthew left Naithan's chambers.

"He's doing fine for the moment," he replied wearily. "That willow leaf resin seems to have restored his spirits somewhat, though he's still a little weak."

"Does he have any memory of the events of the ceremony?"

"None at all," lied Matthew. Naithan had some idea what had happened though not that he had come close to destroying them both and Jalim with it. Matthew was not sure how the boy have been able to close the conduits of power between them all but he was glad that he had, for it had saved them all. "He seems able to recall things such as the ceremony proper, but the rest seems locked out to him. It must be the way of Toric, for to recall such contact with so great a mind would no doubt drive a man to insanity."

Zakar gave him the look of suspicion that he always used when Matthew spoke of the incident. There had been extensive investigations by all the viziers and princes in the days since Naithan's battle with Giarna, and all had ended with the same result. There was no hint of any magical ability in the king whatsoever and he had possessed no items of magic to trick them. None had felt Matthew's use of magic, for it had not emanated from him and none could prove it to be a fake.

It was the golden buildings that had proved the miracle though. For generations alchemists, particularly in Kolth, had been looking for the stone of power that could be used to transform base metals into precious metals, and had never come close. Even the Kolthons had deemed it impossible, yet Naithan had done it, and not even with metals. He had physically altered substances of completely different natures and transformed them into solid gold. How it had happened, Matthew did not know, nor did he wish to learn. The effort had drained three people, used up the energy of one of the most powerful items in Loden, and almost destroyed the entire city. It was not worth contemplating. That they had survived and nothing had been destroyed was a miracle in itself.

"You know, there are those who now claim that the golden buildings have the power to cure. Already people have begun crowding around them in great numbers," said Zakar slowly. "I had always thought that I would never truly believe in anything, but your king may have changed that, if we are proved victorious in our next battle."

The next battle, he thought slowly. *Theldar. Yes, if we lose there, we will lose the allies here, and the throne.*

It was the only thing now standing in their way. It was a battle they could not afford to lose.

"We will be victorious," he replied with more confidence than he felt.

He had communicated with Gareth every day since the siege had begun and there seemed to be no change in the situation. Gareth's troops were continually thrown back by forces becoming rapidly proficient in siege defence and were attacked every night by the Shadow Knights against whom there seemed little defence. Gareth continually requested that he be allowed to use his magic but Matthew had continuously refused, knowing that if they did, they could use Caldorians fear of magic to their benefit, allowing them to execute those leaders of the rebellion under the charge of witchcraft. It was one of the few crimes they could probably use the death penalty publicly on, though it would have to be done with the citizens' support. They could not risk another rebellion.

"When will the ships and your forces be ready?" he asked Zakar.

"They are ready with a word from your king to sail with the dawn tide, if he so desires," replied Zakar with a bow.

"So soon?" he asked, astonished at the speed in which they had organised it all. It had taken months to prepare for the Caldorian mission here.

"Of course, they will do anything for the High Lord," replied Zakar with a smile.

The High Lord, a name once given to the goddess Giarna, now transferred to her conqueror, Naithan. Matthew had not thought to ask him yet how he felt about the god-like status the Solmen seemed to be giving him. He doubted that the king would be able to take the news well in his present, weakened state.

"And how long would you estimate it will take us to reach Theldar?" he asked.

"A month if unaided, just over a week if we are allowed to use our wind wizards," replied Zakar, again with a bow.

"That quickly?" he asked, again surprised.

"There are very strong deep under currents that run down the coast. Our ships are aware of their presence and able to drop under sails beneath the keel to capture them and move us all the more rapidly south. If the winds favour us as well then we are able to make our ships glide like swans through the water."

"Thank you," replied Matthew, glad that they would be able to resolve the problem quickly.

"We do require a favour in return, however," said Zakar slowly, as if unsure how to proceed.

"Anything," replied Matthew more quickly than he had intended.

"There are some…princes who will be accompanying you and the ships to aid in the siege of Theldar. His exulted one wishes that you see that they see their fair share of heavy action in the battle," said the small man, handing him a parchment with several names scrawled clumsy in the Caldorian letter forms. The Solmen still relied on the more archaic glyph and symbol language that gave their writing an almost alien, magical look to it. Matthew found that he recognised most of the names there.

"These are all those who stood against him at the ceremony…" he said slowly, not liking the vicious glint in the Grand Vizier's eyes. "You mean that you want us to arrange for them to be where the fighting is most dangerous…"

"Yes," replied Zakar quickly. "Here in Sol the Great Game is played for higher stakes than it is in your realm. These are all princes who openly questioned the Prophet's rule, and as such have insulted him. He does them honour by allowing them to die in battle and they are aware of it. If he were to leave them unpunished then there would be people left to plot his demise. It cannot be allowed, but these men too have enemies, all of whom will ally to Sulan if given the chance, and the power…"

Matthew felt his mouth go dry. The politics here made the games of the Royal Council seem tame in comparison.

"It will be done as you have requested," replied Matthew formally sealing the agreement.

"The Prophet will thank you eternally for your assistance," replied Zakar with a bow.

"If I may now have your leave to depart…"

"Yes, you may go," replied Matthew wearily, turning towards his own chamber as he did.

He did not need to hear the gentle pad of the man's sandals to know he had left. There was something about his presence that was beginning to truly unsettle Matthew. Much as something about the odious little man Malcolm had often done in Theldar. He entered his chamber and began preparing some willow leaf resin for himself to drink. He needed it to give him the energy he required to retain the pretence that he had done nothing strenuous these last few days.

As he prepared the bitter drink, he found himself wondering just how Malcolm was coping with his new "border" lifestyle. He found himself smiling, despite himself. The weasel-like little man would absolutely hate it all.

"Matthew," came Gareth's voice in his mind. *"We need to talk."*

Matthew sighed as he turned his thoughts to Naithan's brother. He could almost guess what they would need to talk about, and knew that it would not be a short conversation.

The willow leaf resin had gone cold and solidified by the time they had finished. By then Matthew also knew that they would have to leave on the morning tide, regardless of Naithan's health. The situation there was becoming critical and they needed a swift victory. He got to his feet and went to inform Naithan of the problems, leaving the tar like resin untouched upon the table.

II

"Do you require my assistance today, ma'am," Malcolm asked the Lady Michelle an'Tharon with a bow.

"Not today, thank you," she replied, seemingly distracted with tending to her plants. "You are so efficient that there is nothing left to do. You may have the day to yourself."

She turned back to her plants and began muttering to them softly, leaving Malcolm with no work to do, once again. He had no idea why he had been sent to this hellhole of a place. She had given him the day off, the third in as many days, but the village was almost two hours ride away and it was very much a border village with none of the luxuries and civilities you would expect in the city. He turned to return to the study to reorganise the household finances again, though that only consisted of meaningless paperwork.

"Oh, Malcolm?" she asked suddenly.

He turned round swiftly, hoping she had finally thought of some work in that flighty brain of hers.

"Yes ma'am?"

"Is there any word from Erin?"

Malcolm scowled angrily.

"No ma'am, she's no doubt still out hunting, I dare say."

"Thank you Malcolm, I do worry so. Could you ask her to see me when she returns? I think it's time she learned the responsibilities of ladyship. Don't you?"

"Yes, ma'am," he replied, barely concealing his snarl.

There was absolutely no possibility of any treachery in this household. The mother was too flighty and her daughter Erin was too headstrong and childish to entertain such thoughts. The only possible news he could report was that they often fought over every subject available and these usually ended in Erin storming out into the forests with her falcon and disappearing for several days in a sulk. These were hardly events worth his attention, yet they were all he had.

He was sure this had been the idea of Naithan's ridiculous brother Gareth. The oafish man had always resented his obviously superior intelligence and had arranged for him to be moved so that he would suffer. But the man would be eating his words now, sat outside that city in a siege that by all accounts was not going well for him. It was a small comfort, but one he clung to in this damp, draughty castle here. When the king returned Malcolm was sure he would be returned to his rightful place in the palace. He returned to his office, opened the accounts file and sat there transferring the funds from one section of the household to another. It was not even like he could actually even arrange for some of the money to disappear for the chief steward kept an eagle eye on the purse strings. He sighed and went back to his pointless paperwork.

III

"Damn," cursed Gareth angrily as he broke off contact with Matthew. *How goes the battle?*

"The same as before," came the reply. That meant that what the defenders lacked in numbers they were certainly making up for in magic. He felt his hands were being tied in this conflict and his troops were suffering because of it. *"Have we permission to retaliate?"*

No, keep it the same as before, he replied, which meant that they could use magic if they used it discretely. Gareth could give them that much. *Begin the retreat.*

Again they were retreating, leaving the defenders feeling that they had won another victory and his own troops' fury at their inability to respond in kind. Even from here Gareth could see the flashes of the defenders' magic. The morale of his troops was rapidly on the decline, especially as they could not get a decent night's sleep, as the darkness was the time of the so-called *Shadow Knights*. Warriors from the city who stole into their camp night after night, killing where and when they pleased, striking horror into the hearts of his knights and leaving nowhere safe.

He himself had been attacked three times already, and he knew that other commanders suffered similar fates. They had all began to rotate their sleeping quarters now, save Anton who was still too ill to be moved, though he seemed safe from their attacks, something that Gareth found a little suspicious. Admittedly, the man was no threat to the city in his present condition. He slammed his fist down upon the table in his command tent angrily.

"Temper, temper," came a female voice from behind him.

He spun round and saw his auburn haired sister Helena stood in the doorway. He smiled and they moved to embrace each other.

"What kept you so long?" he asked as they hugged each other.

"A little problem at home," she replied. "It seems that friends of the Errant Knight managed to enter my city and destroy half the dockside warehouses."

"Torslud!" Is everything all right?"

"Yes, that wolfhound knight of yours, Sar Karene was there and she organised a very quick rescue operation. I gave her a field promotion for the effort. She saved my treasury almost two thousand mareks by her quick thinking."

"I'll see it's honoured when she returns. Is she any closer to finding him?"

"I think she is close now. I believe she had a knight trailing him when she left. I don't think it'll be long now before she catches up with him."

"Well, that's some potential good news then."

"And the return of our brother isn't another then?" she asked, arching one eyebrow mischievously.

"How did you know? I only found today…" he asked, stunned at the extent of her knowledge. She was certainly the best suited of all of them for her task. He decided it was best to let it go unanswered. "Of course it is, but that leaves me with at least a week during which to lose more troops to this cursed siege."

"Is it truly going that badly?" she asked softly.

"Don't you know already?" he asked caustically.

"The reports I get are hardly believable," she said slowly. "Demons leaping from the night, tearing away the souls of those they touch. The light and power of Toric showering down from the marble city to save its righteous people. They're all rumours that I've heard over the past few days and I've had no reports from my own sources, or your messengers. What am I supposed to do with such news?"

"You mean none have reached you?" he asked in shock. He had wondered why there had been no reply from her until now.

"None, though I did find a few well-rotted corpses. I think you'll have to order them to move with more care from now on. Just because they're in their own kingdom, it does not mean they are safe."

"That's true, we may have been a little complacent."

"Only a little?" she asked sarcastically. Gareth chose to ignore it. "So what can you tell me then?"

He relayed all the information about the attacks, including the attacks on him by the Shadow Knights, including the only way he had discovered of killing him, with the damaged sword from Grelchi. She picked up the broken blade that he now kept close by him at all times looked at it closely.

"It's certainly magical, and all the pieces are as well," she said thoughtfully. "It could be possible to re-forge it, if the right smith were found."

"Do you know of such a man?" he asked quickly.

"Yes, but *she* lives many miles away. I fear you would not get it back in time to be of any use."

"Could any smith forge it?"

"Well, probably, though it might lose some of its potency," she replied. She had always been the more adept student in sorcery. "It would just depend on what its prophecy of creation was. It certainly couldn't harm to try."

"I'll have it done immediately."

Helena smiled quickly.

"No one could ever accuse you of standing still on such problems. Make sure the smith is aware of exactly what it is you have given him. One who is skilled in magic would not go amiss either."

"I've already thought of that," he replied quickly. "Haarken is in the camp and he used to handle Caliburn on frequent occasions."

"Good," she replied absently. She turned her head back to him suddenly. "I thought he was dead?"

"It was considered best if it was thought that way. He's working on a special project for Naithan," replied Gareth, somewhat smug that his deception had fooled his sister's extensive network.

"Never mind," she said, shaking her head in bemusement. "The important thing there is these knights, and for that I will have to investigate the situation for myself."

"Are you sure that's wise?" he asked in concern.

"Of course it is, and this is something I wouldn't risk anyone else upon. Besides, I have my own way of dealing with them if needs be."

Gareth did not like the inference in his sister's tone of voice and decided to change the subject.

"I assume you brought your troops with you as well."

"As many as can be spare…"

A sudden roar of battle from outside the tent broke her off.

"They sally forth sir," came the voices of his commanders all at once.

"Be warned! The Shadow Knights ride with them…" came one voice, cutting off with a scream as the speaker died. Gareth spun round, clasping the broken blade in his hand as he did, and saw one of the dark knights before him. He raised his guard and prepared to attack, but was surprised when

the attacker just keeled over dead with a gaping wound in his back.

"I have my ways brother," whispered Helena's voice in his ear.

He searched round for her but could see nothing. Shrugging of the confusion he raced into the battle outside, closing his thoughts off as two more of his commanders died. Once more his upper levels of command were being destroyed by the Theldarians. Roaring out an angry challenge he leapt into the battle in an attempt to rally his troops.

IV

Galen watched the attack from the battlements with a smile. He had seen the arrival of more troops to besiege the city and had decided to take the initiative to prevent the Theldarians from getting disheartened. He had also decided to send forth his Shadow Knights as well, in an attempt to damage their hierarchy once more. He hoped that this time they would take the leader down for he had now killed three of his Shadow Knights, each one slicing through him like a hot knife. He had not realised that their deaths would cause such pain though part of him recognised it, as though he had suffered it before.

Suddenly it happened again, this one worse than before. The pain actually felt physical to him too, as what felt like a sword sliced through his back. It was all he could do to keep from screaming out in pain and he put his hands down onto the wall and leaned forward, taking deep breaths as he did so.

"Are you all right?" asked Marie, who had been stood next to him. She slipped her arm round him, her hand brushing past the spot where he felt the pain. He winced and forced himself to take a deep breath.

"Fine," he replied through gritted teeth.

"No you're not!" she replied, her voice rising in shock. "You're bleeding!"

He reached his own hand to his back and found that she was correct.

"Shadow magic!" rasped a voice in his head, fear lancing through the words.

Galen felt his body shudder and knew a moment of true panic and his body faded momentarily, Marie's hand almost slipping through his form.

"I need to rest," he said quietly, turning to Sar Petra. "Sound the retreat when you see fit."

"Yes sir," she replied crisply. "I'll see that it is done."

He nodded his thanks and allowed Marie to help him down the steps as his body returned fully to its corporeal form. As they moved he felt something he had never felt before, the presence of someone he did not know moving around in the Shadow Realm. He looked round, allowing his vision to shift spectrums so that he could see into the plane without actually entering it but could see nothing. The presence was still there however. Whoever it was, they were good at moving out of sight from the eyes, but inexperienced when moving around in the Shadow Realm. Every step they took seemed to resound like a thunderclap through the streets. Even his own knights were not that heavy footed. It had to be an interloper, somehow protected as the ring had once protected him. He sent out a warning to his knights to listen out for them, for even they would be able to hear the person.

"Do you want them killed?" asked Sar Petra in his mind.

No, just observed if possible. It is one who can kill you as if you were like any other being. I've lost too many of you to risk it at present.

"As you command," came the reply.

"Come on," said Marie, "and don't worry about it. I can protect you to some extent. Better than those *Shadow Knights* of yours, anyhow."

She could never quite keep the contempt from her voice when she spoke of his personal guards, but he could not blame her for that. They all felt similar envy towards her; the bonds of loyalty created by the shadow magic ensured that, though he sometimes felt that with Marie there was something more to it than that.

He paid it no mind and relaxed as he felt Marie's presence quest out into the Shadow Realm. She was definitely the best of all his followers at it, her probes being like faint whispers in the breeze compared to the elfant stomps of the intruder. It probably had something to do with her contact with the ring, though he could not be sure. Some humans had a natural affinity to the so-called Shadow Magic. He pushed the thoughts away. He was as much human as she was.

"Yes you are," said a voice softly in his mind. *"And that is what will kill you."*

V

Groltch was beginning to tire of it all; the constant journeying; Tristan's growing silence; and the continuous banter of the wizard and the druid. It was all too much. They had decided to head towards Grelchin and leave through its, hopefully, less protected borders into Kolth, but had decided to take the most concealed, awkward, and uncomfortable path Thenril could have ever devised, at least that was how it felt to Groltch.

They seemed to go through every dense bush, bramble and thicket they could find. They frequently crossed over streams and fords, masking their trails and scents as far as was possible and Belthar had even once suggested they go up into the trees until Groltch had reminded them that Tristan's horse was hardly fit to involve itself in such an action. Belthar had admitted the truth of it, though not without some quiet grumbling to Matt.

The factioning that had been occurring over the course of their journey seemed to have grown worse and there were times when no one spoke of an evening, not even Matt and Belthar. Matt was another who seemed to be somewhat preoccupied, though Belthar was somewhat more adept at bringing the boy out of it than Groltch was with Tristan.

To make matters worse, Groltch was positive that they were being followed. He mentioned it shortly after they had fled Teldin, and had caused them all to search the area thoroughly, only to find nothing. Belthar had complained about it being an intense waste of time. Ever since, however, they had followed this awkward, slow and tedious path through the woods. Evidently Belthar could feel the presence of unseen eyes around them, even if he would not admit to it. Just thinking about it gave Groltch shivers of worry down his spine and gave him goose bumps.

He looked around the forest once more, unease tickling the pit of his stomach. His eyes twitched this way and that, his senses telling him something was wrong. He noticed Belthar's ears twitching and he even saw Tristan's hand move towards Caliburn's hilt. Suddenly there was a loud scream above them and as Groltch looked up he could not believe his eyes. Screaming ran-tha were leaping from the trees to attack them…

VI

Erin an'Tharon, daughter of Lady Michelle an'Tharon, Countess of Northshire, wandered through the woods near her home, watching for her hunting bird to return. It was a pastime she had enjoyed since her father had first shown her the wonders of hawking when she was still very young. Her mother had disapproved, of course, she always seemed to disapprove of anything Erin enjoyed doing. Archery, for example, another skill taught to her by her father and a sport for which she had some small talent. Yet the day her mother had found out about her father's secret lessons she had all but screamed the house down, shouting at her father. He had taken it as always, sitting at his desk, stoically ignoring her protests, as immovable as the rock in the fiercest storm. He would weather her protestations and her shouting and eventually she would relent, allowing Erin to do what she wanted, so long as she kept up her studies in becoming a true lady.

Her mother seemed obsessed with tales of the ancient times, when women were ladies and men were gentlemen, times when each sex had clearly defined roles in life, and she had tried to instil the values into her daughter, to no avail. She had sat and attended her lessons, of course, and could probably recite the seven virtues of womanhood, walk as if she had a book upon her head and perform several of the other "dog-like" tasks she had been expected to learn as a good and dutiful lady. However, she had never really taken the values to heart. The lessons had come thick and fast, especially after her father's death in a hunting accident, something her mother could never forget. She had also prevented her from joining the knighthood, especially after she had run away from home at the age of nine to go and join them. Her mother had enlisted the aid of the entire garrison in the search, and Erin had been forced back in all but chains. It had not been the last time she had ran from home, and each time generally occurred after any fight she had with her mother.

The last argument had been an old one about Marak, their falconer. After her father's death and in a desperate attempt to escape the continuous boredom of etiquette lessons she had found refuge in the falconry. There she had met Marak, a twenty something peasant, as her mother had described him, and in him Erin had found a father figure. He enjoyed falconry and was very adept with a bow, and so had begun to continue the lessons where her father had left off. Her mother had gone livid when she found out, screaming about how unbecoming it was for a young lady to associate with a man of lower station and had tried to ban her from seeing him, leading to her second attempt at running away.

Surprisingly it had been Marak that had found her and brought her back, raising his standing somewhat in her mother's eyes, but not by much. He had patiently endured her screams, much as her father had, and then quietly pointed out that the things that Erin enjoyed could be quite dangerous for the untrained. He then went on to state that, as she was going to do them anyway, that it was better to do it under the eye of those trained in the arts.

Her mother had backed down and relented, possibly seeing something of her husband in Marak's eyes, and they had been allowed to "associate". However, as time had gone by her mother had grown more and more concerned about their ever nearing relationship that she had tried to ban her from seeing him again, insisting that now was the time to begin the search for a proper husband for her.

Erin did not yet feel ready to marry or even to court properly yet and this had driven her mother into one of her many, irrational rages. Erin had left and not returned for several days now. She knew she would not go far, and so did her mother, so both left it alone. Erin also knew that eventually she would accede to her mother's wishes, at least visibly, and begin to seek a suitable husband.

She sighed angrily and looked back to the skies, looking for the falcon, or more properly, tiercel, for it was a male peregrine, another thing her mother disliked. According to the ancient handbooks, those of royal blood should use falcons, the female of the species, yet Erin preferred her "nobleman's" tiercel as it was the best hunting bird they possessed.

Its piercing cry broke her thoughts and she looked back to the sky, her cares slipping away as she watched his graceful spiralling descent to the ground. In his talons was a fresh kill that he deposited on the ground for her to inspect. She smiled and nodded to him, signalling to let him know he could eat. He bent his neck and began to tear strips from his kill, looking around between mouthfuls. Suddenly he let out a cry and flew up to her shoulder. It seemed to look pointedly towards a particular area of bush. This pricked her curiosity and she moved closer to see what was there that could possibly have startled her tiercel in such a way. As she crept silently forward she slipped the bow from her back and nocked an arrow. She was surprised to see a man crouched within the bushes and found herself take a step back. She knocked against some foliage and the sound startled him. He looked round and gazed directly at her, his blue eyes seeming to cut straight through her. He was a well-built man, around six-foot in height and well-armed. She could see at least three weapons, a sword and two daggers, from here and knew instinctively that he would have more.

"You see me? At least you're not with them," he muttered angrily to himself. "Though I've no doubt given myself away. That goblin doesn't miss a trick."

He started as he realised that he was talking aloud and focused his attention back on Erin.

"Well you've just cost me time," he muttered angrily. "I'd teach you a lesson if I had the time and you weren't of royal blood. Tell any that you saw me and that won't save you, so remain quiet if you wish to live."

She mutely nodded her head and he turned away, moving back into the trees, vanishing from sight as he did. She stood there frozen for a while and only relaxed when her tiercel leapt from her shoulder to return to his food. She found herself wondering just who the man was, and how he had known anything about her. She looked down and saw that she still wore the velvet blue cape her mother had given her some years before. Blue was the Royal colour and could only be worn by those of royal blood. Well that explained how he knew her, for only the most desperate peasant would risk Redirection to wear such a cloak. As to whom he was, she guessed she would never know other than that he was a violent man well trained in the ways of stealth.

As to what he was doing, she should be able to learn that if she tried, though the use of the word goblin had unnerved her a little. Goblins lived far to the east and would never be here, especially as the war had driven them deep into their homeland. Her curiosity piqued, she moved cautiously over to the spot where the man had been crouched and bent down to look around at the ground, all the time fearing that he would return. She looked back to Soarer and saw him quite happily tearing away at the food, so assumed the man had truly gone, then looked back to the ground.

It took her a while to find what he had been looking for and had involved all of her skill at tracking to find it though. In the ground before them, somehow seeming to pass through seemingly un-passable terrain were a series of tracks, so well concealed that they seemed almost invisible. They seemed to be of four humans and one horse though it was difficult to tell. It was only the regularity in the formation of the marks that had alerted her to the fact that they were more than just natural marks, and it was only the horse tracks that had alerted her to the fainter human tracks in the first place. Whoever had done this was an expert, one she would not mind meeting.

She began to edge her way down the trail carefully, following the awkward tracks as best she could, forgetting completely about the possible danger she could face at the end. At present there was only the adventure of this strange encounter, something to break up the otherwise boring monotony of endless days sewing, avoiding her mother and hunting in the trees. She did not mind the hunting, but always dreamed of more, though had never quite taken the step towards complete freedom. Even though she was almost nineteen years of age now, she had still never been further than the county bounds without her mother at her side, and excitement rarely came to her. She was determined to make the most of the opportunity.

A scream suddenly cut through the air ahead of her, making her jump as it did. She got to her feet and listened out carefully for any further noise and was rewarded with the clash of metal on metal and the sound of curses and screams. She hurried towards the sound, nocking an arrow once more into her bow.

It did not take long to find the source of the conflict and soon found herself looking across a clearing filled with chaos. Creatures that could only be goblins were leaping onto four humans from the trees with wicked curved knives in their hands. They began to set upon the humans savagely and the humans fought back with equal savageness. All except one, who seemed to be merely fending off her attackers with a staff. Erin aimed towards the creature before her, intending to kill it and help the poor girl out, but was suddenly greeted with a sight that both confused and frightened her. The woman's form suddenly shimmered and changed, becoming like that of the creature before it.

Confused she lowered her bow and watched the fight. It was unlike any of the stories she had ever read or heard. There were no honourable challenges, blood seemed to fly everywhere and the screams of the dying were horrific, almost human like, which made it all the more worse to see. She suddenly found herself doubting her resolve to kill the goblin that stood before the thing that had been a woman. She had killed before, on many a hunt, but never anything that even remotely resembled a human. She wanted to turn away, to not see any more, but found herself strangely drawn to the conflict before her.

VII

Groltch fought back the tears as he fended off the ran-the's attack, praying to Toric that he would listen to him.

"I'm one of you," he cried. "Listen! We are friends. We can help you!"

His attacker did not listen though and continued his violent attack, a dangerous gleam in his eye. He reversed his attack suddenly, dropping below Groltch's weapon and giving him a nasty wound along his arm. He sobbed in misery and pain as the realisation that words would not stop his opponent. He change the spin of his staff from a defensive one to an offensive one, beginning his attack with a well-executed disarming manoeuvre in a final attempt to stop the ran-the. The curved blade flipped through the air, but the attacker simply ignored the loss of his weapon and leapt at Groltch, forcing him down onto the ground. He released the breath from his lungs to prevent himself from being winded and drove his foot into his opponent's stomach. He then used the momentum of the fall to roll the attacker forward, then over his head into the ground. Groltch winced as he heard the sickening sound of his opponent's neck breaking.

He rolled to his feet and found himself with a moment to spare, so looked at the battle raging around him. Belthar was in full battle frenzy, roaring and swinging that great staff around like a man possessed and Tristan was once again the cold, ruthless killing machine that he had been in the village, facing down three opponents with ease.

That left only Matthew, who seemed to be stumbling over the words of a spell, as well as the ground, whilst two more ran-tha approached him. Suddenly the boy fell to the floor and the larger, male ran-the sprang to attack. What happened next Groltch was never quite able to recall but as the ran-the leapt, a patch darkness seemed to detach itself from the surrounding scrub and sprang at the ran-the, pitching him into the bushes next to him with a terrifying roar. The ensuing scream was short lived and there was the sickening sound of tearing flesh.

The ran-thi, the female, leapt in to attack the human boy, who seemed to have knocked himself out when his head struck the floor. Groltch allowed his body to react without thought. In one motion his hand went to the dagger at his belt, drew it, and threw it, his aim at its lethal best despite the tears in his eyes. The blade sank deep into her throat and blood fountained out, spraying Matt with blood as her twitching, dying body, landed on his unconscious form.

Groltch closed his eyes and prayed for forgiveness at his sin. It was then that he noticed the silence in the clearing. The battle was over and there were now ten dead ran-tha around the clearing. Tristan shook himself, as if coming out of a daze and his faced creased with anguish. He turned to Groltch and for a moment they shared a look of pain, for they had both recognised one of the dead ran-tha. She had been one of the girls who had served them in the village, not more than two weeks ago. Groltch could not remember her name and that galled him more than her death at his hands.

He looked to the others and saw them all moving towards him, seeking to comfort him. He shook his head and for once they all listened, leaving him alone in the clearing. He looked down and prayed to Toric, begging that he receive their shadows to the celestial palace then closed his eyes to the world.

"Traitor!"

The words, spoken in ran-tha, cut through him like a knife. He spun round to see another of his kind racing towards him, holding a long scythe over his head. Groltch was unarmed and in no mood to kill again. Let this be his punishment. He heard his companions return to the clearing and cry out in warning, but he just stood there. He had killed his own kind, and the punishment was death. He felt at peace and looked into the eyes of his attacker, only to see them glaze over in lifelessness, the feathered haft of an arrow protruding from his chest. The ran-the collapsed to the floor, the scythe falling with him.

Confused Groltch looked round and saw what seemed to be a human female, holding a bow in her hand. She had auburn hair, a colour he had never seen on a human before, and wore a blue cloak wrapped around brown hunting leathers. Her skin was pale and her blue eyes seemed to glitter in the light. For a moment she seemed akin to one of Toric's heavenly messengers, her blue cloak acting as her wings, then the illusion shattered and he saw only a frightened, probably quite young, human female, her knuckles white as she gripped her bow tightly with a shaking hand.

VIII

Helena knew she was being followed. She had never once seen her pursuers, yet she knew they were there, and had been for some time. She knew that almost no one could usually track her when she wore the crown. She knew its shadow magic somehow concealed her, and with her other talents, made her the ideal spy, as had been her mother's intention. Yet here, in this realm, with these Shadow Knights in pursuit, the crown seemed only to act as a lure, as a flame was to a moth. Unfortunately if they found her it would mean a lot more trouble for her brother. She could probably take some with her, but that would not solve Gareth's problems.

She had to find a way to neutralise their threat as quickly as possible, and she could only do that if she remained free. It meant she had to make a decision and quickly. When reviewing her options, there was no real choice.

She removed the crown. She felt a moment's confusion among her pursuers and knew that she had to use it. She began to race through the streets of the empty, black Theldar of this dark realm. Around her she could already hear the sounds of the creatures that inhabited these streets. She could almost hear them sniffing the air, suddenly aware of the scent of her unprotected life now crying out temptingly to them all. She went to turn down an alleyway and suddenly realised that the creatures were there already.

She turned back and leapt for a wall, scrabbling up it, hoping that it would somehow stall the creatures, and began to continue back towards the palace. She had to reach the private room, one specially designed to mask the crown's power, created by an ancient Lord Priest so that he could practice magic unseen from foreign eyes. She could only hope it would mask her use of the crown from her pursuers, or else she was truly in trouble. Almost like she was now, as the wall was rapidly coming to an end and in the street beyond were more of the creatures, waiting for her.

Cursing her luck she slowed down and looked around her. There was a building to her left, a small one-storey affair, and her only hope. She jumped at it, stretching out her arms as she did so. Her hands found purchase in the thatched roofing and she was able to pull herself onto the roof. She looked around and saw the palace only a few streets away. She could make it!

She ran along the roof then slid down the side closest to the palace, hoping the short fall would not injure her. As her feet touched solid ground she rolled her body, allowing it to fall completely to the floor, before rolling back onto her feet into a loping run. Her muscles were beginning to strain and her lungs started to burn, yet she could not stop, the adrenaline coursing through her body. This was spurred on by the sounds of the creatures behind her as they gradually drew closer and closer. They seemed to show no sign of tiring and Helena knew she would have little chance of out-running them.

She turned a corner into the street that led to the palace gate and found herself stumbling to a halt. Stood on guard, in mockery of the real world, were two Shadow Knights. At that moment she knew she was doomed. Destined to fail. She almost collapsed with the realisation. She had to take the protection of the crown, and doing so now would alert the guards to her position. It would not take much for them to find her after that. She choked back a sob as she removed the crown from her belt and raised it to her head. The creatures were now almost close enough to touch her, and she dared not risk that.

She paused a moment before placing it upon her head, her sharp eyes catching sight of something. The creatures had stopped moving towards her, and some had even moved back, just at the sight of the crown. She did not need it touching flesh to protect her, though she would need to be wearing it when she wanted to leave. Hope flared once inside her and she began to move carefully back away from the guards. Fortunately, they had not seemed to see her, their forms being slightly translucent. It was possible that their eyes saw only the real world, or that they saw both and that she was disguised by the confusing images. Whatever the reason, they had not approached her, nor did they seem able to sense her presence. She had time.

She moved away towards the servants' gates, hoping that they would not think to guard them as well. As she moved, the creatures moved with her, always staying around her, but never going too close to her, or the crown at least. She had never felt so unnerved before, their forms pushing as close as they dared. It was enough to make her mind spin close towards panic, but she had to retain control. She had to concentrate her breathing, take one step at a time and keep focused.

"Each step I take gets me one step closer," she muttered to herself, over and over again, using it as a mantra to retain some semblance of self-control.

Time seemed to stretch out into infinity for her, but eventually she found herself at the gate and saw, with relief, that it was unguarded. She willed the gate to be open and stepped through, the creatures still following, though no longer surrounding her. They seemed to recoil at the entrance to the palace, and hesitated before following, giving Helena a little welcome relief. The oppression of their presence was not so bad when it came at her from only one direction.

"Well, well," said a female voice behind her. "Look who it is! The Princess Helena has come to visit the Protector."

Helena turned round to see a Shadow Knight stood before her. She searched her memory for the face was familiar and soon placed a name to it.

"Sar Petra, I see," replied Helena, taking a little pleasure in the look of shock that registered on the knight's face.

"I see your reputation for flightiness is ill deserved," said the knight, recovering her composure.

"And I see your reputation as a traitor is well deserved," countered Helena quickly.

"I see you are of quick wit as well, it seems," replied Sar Petra with a sneer. "Well let's just see how well your wit serves you against those creatures then shall we?"

As she spoke, her sword flashed out, striking the crown from Helena's hand. A shriek arose from the creatures and Helena felt a moment of abject terror. Then the knight's hand clamped around her wrist and the creatures wailed once more.

"All I have to do is release you and they will come down and devour you," said Petra with a snarl. "So you'd better be on your best behaviour."

Helena felt hysteria build and for no reason she could recall she brought the palm of her hand up to slap the woman's face, for how dare one of her station even think to lay hands on her. It was a childish act from a thought more in keeping with those of her mother. It also had dire consequences. The knight scowled in rage, releasing her grip and smacking Helena across the face with the back of her hand.

Helena's world seemed to explode in pain and she felt herself reeling to the floor. Around her she heard the roars of the creatures and she closed her eyes, prepared to meet her fate, the hysteria fading to resignation. It was only when she heard the screams that she realised it was not her that they were attacking, but Sar Petra. Helena moved to open her eyes then thought better of it, the screams were horrifying enough. She did not wish to see what had to be done to a human to make them produce such inhuman sounds.

Instead she waited for the screams to cease, and tried to edge towards where she had seen the crown fall. She was almost there when she heard a moan before her face. She risked opening her eyes and saw one of the creatures leaning over her. In its hands was the crown. She recoiled in terror, before realising that this was the only creature around. She looked at it closely and almost thought she could see human eyes in what should have been its face. It stretched the crown out towards her and she saw that smoke was rising from where the crown touched its blurred flesh. She nervously took it from its "hands" and was surprised to see it drop into what appeared to be a full knightly bow. Even more surprising was the fact that it altered its moans, as if trying to speak, and she heard it utter what she thought was her name. It then roared as if in pain and fled from the corridor, leaving her alone. Of Sar Petra, there was no sign. Not even any blood.

Helena pushed the thoughts away, locking them safely within the depths of her mind and continued down the corridor. It did not take her long to find the room and she swiftly put the crown back on, feeling a little relieved to have made it. She stepped back into the warmth of her world and revelled for a moment in the array of colours that assaulted her senses. It took only a few moments more to realize she could hear voices from the door outside.

She opened her mind to the magic of spells, knowing the room would shield her activities from any knights nearby. She took out the components needed and formed the spell needed in her mind. She threw the glittering glass dust at the wall where it seemed to attach itself and shimmer slightly. Slowly the wall became translucent and on the other side she could see the very man she had come to spy upon, the Lord Protector himself, Galen Faithe.

She quickly cast another spell to enhance the strength of her ears and settled down to watch the proceedings. It seemed that what they were discussing would be of great use to Gareth indeed, though when she returned it would be via normal methods. She had no desire to return to the shadow realm again. Even now, locked away as it was deep within her mind she could still hear the scream of the knight, and see the pleading look of anguish in the eyes of the creatures. They would haunt her dreams for a long time to come…

IX

Tristan felt his jaw go slack at the sight of the young woman with the bow and his vision swam momentarily.

"You're sure the plan will work?" Erin, leaning across the table.

"Of course," replied Tristan quickly. "I've used it before. There'll be no problems at all. Just concentrate on getting them out of the keep."

It was the girl of the vision. The time was fast approaching for him to make the choice and he was unsure as to what his answer would be. He felt himself go weak at the knees.

"Easy girl," came the gruff voice of Belthar. "He's a friend. There's no need to point that thing at him."

"I just killed it, like that," said the woman, sounding a little dazed.

Tristan suddenly felt like an oaf. He moved over to her and gently took the bow from her hands. He then cautiously put his arm around her and led her out of the clearing.

"I think it best we go and make camp whilst Groltch deals with the funerary rites for the bodies," he said, leading them towards a likely spot, whistling to Galahad to follow. He heard Belthar and Matthius follow behind and it was not long before they had found a suitable spot. He sat the girl down and looked closely at her. She seemed a little shocked, though life did seem to be reappearing in her eyes.

"You'll be all right here," he said trying to be reassuring.

"Is it always like that, to kill?" she asked softly.

"It's never easy, lass, never," said Belthar as he sat Matthius down, who was still a little dazed from his fall.

"Where's Fluff?" asked Matthius looking round.

He was answered by a soft mew as the small cat walked out from the trees. Tristan was still amazed the Matthius had yet to truly lose the animal.

"Oh my," said the woman, getting to her feet. "Soarer!"

Tristan looked at her in confusion, wondering if she was still in shock. He was shocked to see her put her fingers in her mouth, then whistle loudly in a most unladylike manner. He was even more amazed to see a falcon come spiralling down from the skies to rest upon her shoulder.

"You know, you should not do that," he ventured to say. "They should be allowed to stand only upon your hand, for they have a tendency to peck at eyes…"

"I know what I'm doing," replied the auburn haired woman shortly. "If you would just leave me for a moment so that I may tend to him in peace."

Tristan bowed his assent and moved away. He walked over to Matthius and Belthar.

"Is he all right?" he asked Belthar, who was tending to a bump on the back of the boy's head.

"Aye, he'll be fine, don't worry," replied the big man softly. "I'm more worried about your…our friend out there. I think he needs someone right now, and I don't think Matt or I will do."

"I know," replied Tristan sadly. "I shall attend him anon."

"Still able to pull out the old formal lingo I see."

"Needs must," Tristan whispered in reply. "Our guest wears the Royal Blue. We had better be upon our best behaviour this night if she stays."

"Royal Blue?" asked the big man in wonder. "I had thought I could smell wartwoad, but that is only found many miles north of here. I'll watch my mouth."

Tristan smiled and turned away, only to feel Belthar's hand turn him back.

"I know we've not gotten on all that well of late," said the big man gruffly. "But we are friends and do feel for him. Could you pass on our regrets till we see him personally."

"Certainly," replied Tristan with a sad smile.

He went out to the clearing where they had fought and found Groltch stacking the bodies together, including one that seemed to have been mauled by some savage beast. They spoke no words, for none were needed. They had both done this before and so set about the unpleasant task with grim determination lining their faces. It took most of the afternoon to stack the bodies and set the fire, and they both stood and watched until the flames had died down. By the time they returned in the direction of the campsite night was already well under way.

X

Anton coughed, waking himself from his slumber. His whole body seemed to burn with pain and it took him a while to orientate himself. He could remember wounding himself, and had vague recollections of fever dreams, but little else.

"You're lucky," said a familiar voice somewhere near his feet. "The fever broke today and you're likely to recover."

Anton managed a weak smile and moved to sit up, but found the action too painful.

"Water?" he asked his voice grating as it did.

"Certainly my liege," said the voice.

Now was it Darren or Lewis? Their voices sounded so familiar without the face to remind him. Suddenly a memory flashed up before him. The dead Lewis in his arms, or was it Darren. He could not recall now.

"Yes, you know who it is, don't you?" The voice was soft and insinuating. Its tone sent shivers done his spine. "And I know exactly what you did. I would have never believed that man, had you not spoken in about it in a fever dream."

"That's what it was, just a dream," stuttered Anton quickly.

"No, your fear now only confirms it, but don't worry, I'll not kill you for it. There are plenty of other ways to gain revenge upon those who betray you, and I intend to use them. Here's your water."

Anton felt it pour across his face as the dark form loomed above him and he gulped down what he could, his dry throat allowing for nothing else.

"You'll come to regret not killing me as well," said the voice.

Then the figure was gone, the candle lighting his tent blown out, and he found himself alone in the darkness. Very alone.

XI

Jax made his way carefully back down the tracks, praying that the disturbance with the girl had not ruined his hopes of tracking. He had already reported in to Sar Karene and she had told him that the girl was most likely Erin an'Tharon, only daughter of the Lady of Northshire, though it mattered little to him. Had he had the time, he would have killed her and left no trace, as he had done on many occasions before. He was one of the true Black Knights, royal assassins to the king, though he had not been ordered to do so for some time. He was here purely to watch over Sar Karene and ensure that the White Knight, Tristan was not killed in the capture attempt. Karene's desire for the White Plume was well known enough to make her a risk, but she was also the best tracker near enough to give chase, next to himself, yet he had been ordered to watch only, and protect Tristan if the need arose.

"I told you," said a voice behind him. "There was fighting here."

"Well that's obvious," said another. "What with all the flattened ground, blood and broken weapons. I'd say this was the scene of a fight."

"Yeah. All right. Shut up," came the first voice again.

"Hmm, goblins," said the second voice. Jax crept closer to try and see who the speakers were. They did not sound like any of those he had been following previously. He had to make sure they did not pose a threat. "We always miss out, don't we? I remember that time with the dwarf, what was his name again?"

"Jack," said the other voice absently. Jax's eyes widened in surprise for a second before his ears registered the actual name spoken. "I also recall that time when you were left hanging from a tree branch…"

"Yeah, all right," said the second voice sourly.

Jax could now see two silhouettes moving round a clearing that, as they had correctly surmised, had seen a battle recently. One was a tall, hulking figure of a man, the other smaller and lither. He could see the hilts and pommels of two great swords protruding above the back of the tall man and the smaller held a longbow in his hands.

"Someone burned the bodies," said the taller figure, looking at a charred heap in one corner of the clearing.

"Who would do that?" asked the second figure, moving over to inspect it. "I mean…they're only goblins…"

"And you're only a human!" said the first voice. "You forget that in this land goblin is just a derogatory human term…"

"Shh," said the second voice. "Someone's watching us…and when did you start using such long words?"

The figure seemed to ignore the small man's last comment and drew his large swords. Jax cursed. It could be that he was going to have to kill these two fools. He examined them quickly as they both scanned the trees. The taller looked the most dangerous opponent, though he would be slower than the shorter.

"You can come out from there," said the smaller figure, pointing his bow unerringly at Jax.

He muttered another curse, knowing that he could do nothing from this range and that he would have to emerge and get closer. He stepped out from the bushes. He could not believe it. First a mere snip of a girl and now this bearded fool with a bow. He must be slipping.

"Now there's no need for that fellas. I've got no cash and am not worth the trouble," he said, marking out his paces as he walked.

"We're not going to rob you, we just hoped…thought you might be out to rob us, that's all. We've not been attacked by bandits for so long we're beginning to lose our touch," said the taller man, stepping forward.

There was something about the larger man's grin that unnerved him, though not as much as the numerous scars he could see criss-crossing the man's arms.

Ten paces, almost in range…

"As you can see fellas, I'm not armed for such a venture," he replied, smoothly reaching down to the daggers on his back.

Fifteen paces…perfect…

"Knife!" shouted the smaller man.

Suddenly everything seemed to happen at once. Jax drew his daggers as he felt an arrow strike his shoulders. He released the daggers, one at each. The one aimed at the smaller man struck the air where he had been stood, the man having dropped to the ground, and the second aimed at the taller man glanced off one of the large swords. They were now spinning at what seemed to be impossible speeds and Jax knew that his death was imminent.

The last thing he heard were the words.

"I told you he was a bandit. Why else would he have been tracking those people like that!"

He collapsed to the floor and death claimed him…

XII

Erin looked quietly into the fire, listening to the sound of the goblin sharpening his knife by the fire. It had been an interesting night to finish off an interesting day. She had gained her first taste of adventuring and other than the killing part of it, which she had hated and could still not think of without tears brimming to her eyes, it had been what she had expected. They had sat round the fire, exchanging stories, telling jokes, well the large man, Belthar, had done most of that, and eating what they had caught.

It was the kind of life she could grow accustomed to, she was sure, though she was not sure how they would react to her tagging along with them, not that they would have much choice in the matter. Yet despite all the jollity of the evening, other than the understandable sorrow of the goblin, there seemed to be a lot of tension and secrets between them, though she guessed that was always the way between such adventurers. She had her own secrets as well, and she had no doubt that she would discover theirs, in time.

A moan from the boy, Matt, made her jump and she looked round the camp. The violet eyed boy seemed in the midst of a nightmare and she longed to wake him, but feared it would not have the desired effect. She left it and decided to try and get to sleep. Tomorrow was now open to new adventures for her and she wanted to be awake enough to enjoy them…

XIII

He stood in the midst of the city, his power unstoppable. None could harm him. None could touch him. He was a god. He sent his energy arching across the street, killing everyone it touched. With each death he became more powerful, and stood one step closer on the road to godhood. Powerful wizards came and stood against him, yet they too fell to his power and he laughed, for he knew none could stop him.

His heart went cold. There was one who could stop him, the man with violet eyes. Matt knew that, and as the realisation came the man appeared before him.

"I am here to stop you," said the man quietly.

"And I am here to kill you," replied Matt coldly.

"Let the contest begin then," said the man.

Matt nodded and unleashed the full fury of his fire magic at his opponent. The man threw up a shield, deflecting the energy back at Matt, and he barely turned it away in time. The contest then began in full earnest. It raged on for hours, neither one giving in, both struggling with all the power they had, which had become considerable on both sides.

So powerful that the battle raged on into days, then weeks, then years, then generations, then millennia and off into eternity, or so it seemed. Always they fought, often with different names, yet the prize was always the same. In the end one always triumphed supreme to claim the prize. This time it was Matt's turn to lose. The energy of his opponent consumed him and oblivion took him…

XIV

Matt awoke with sweat pouring from his brow, the dream disturbing him as it always did. He could not understand it, did not know why he had them, or what they meant. They were always the same format though the battles were always different as well as the outcome.

"I need help," he whispered to himself. "I have no idea what is happening to me."

"Yer need to go t'Kolth my friend," said Belthar beside him. "Go to the Great Academy and they'll teach yer what yer need t'know."

"Will you come with me?" he asked softly.

"If I can I will," replied the big man, his voice seeming to drift away a little.

Matt did not find that reassuring in the slightest, but he let the odd comment and laid his head back on the ground.

"When I go to Kolth I will enter the Academy, and I shall be the greatest wizard there is!"

"Of course yer will boy. Of course yer will…"

CHAPTER EIGHTEEN: Duty and Destiny

I

"How much longer will it take?" Naithan asked the captain as he looked out over the bow of the ship, marvelling at how fast these sleek boats seemed to cut through the blue waters of the sea.

"At the rate we are travelling, only two more days," replied the captain in awe. "I've never known the journey to go so fast. These ships are amazing, and the winds we are getting are like none I have ever seen before. Toric must be guiding our hand on this voyage."

Naithan smiled contentedly. All was going better than they had hoped. They had only been journeying for a few days, three at most, and they were almost home already. Even though he knew that the former Wind Priests, newly converted to Toric, were controlling the winds, it was still a miracle, for their magic had obviously been enhanced by their conversion to the true faith. Matthew had hesitantly suggested they use them, lest they not reach Theldar in time and he had agreed.

However, he was still a little distrustful of the speed at which the Solmanese had converted to the faith, but Matthew had convinced him that it was due to the miraculous nature of the defeat of the great sea goddess Giarna in Zaron. That incident was still a little hazy in his mind, though he could remember certain parts clearly. He knew Matthew had been in control of the beast and had already reprimanded him over some of its actions. Naithan could still see the image of its great maw clamping down around him vividly in his mind, especially when he closed his eyes, and even now it made him shiver. The effect was muted of course, by the feeling of Toric's touch upon his soul, and in some ways he wished he could remember more than just the joy at god's touch.

It was not to be, however, and he knew Matthew was probably

correct when he had said that Naithan's mind would probably go insane if he recalled any more. It was enough to know that Toric stood with him in his fight and all the fear and doubt he had felt in the Solmanese city had left him. Even the loss of Theldar only troubled him slightly, for he knew that they would return victorious and that the city would fall quickly upon his return. Everything was going according to plan, though Gareth's lack of success to date was frustrating to say the least. Admittedly, after Sulan's warning, he did not want Gareth to succeed before he arrived, yet it would have been a nice endorsement of his armies had they conquered it immediately. Unfortunately that was not the way of siege warfare. Naithan also took it as a sign that he was meant to return and claim the city as a reaffirmation of his god given rights.

He looked up at the sun above and saw that it was approaching its zenith. It was almost time for him and Matthew to communicate with Gareth once more. He turned to walk away and the world spun briefly before his eyes. He put his hand upon the rail to support himself and cursed his weakness. It had been the same since that day in Sol, and Matthew had told him that on occasions it had even led to him passing out and fitting upon the floor. Fortunately his friend had been the only one to see them so far. The sorcerer was presently working on the healing magic required to solve his problem, though he had been unsuccessful as yet.

When the dizziness had passed, he inhaled deeply before making his way down to the main deck, past the ropes that held the "under sail". That had been quite a marvel to see and his own captains had been making notes on the technique. They were apparently used to catch the deep under currents of the sea, or something, and meant that the ship could often move at fast rates, even when there was no wind. They had been rather excited about the prospect and had spent most of the first day pestering him to allow the release of funding for investigation into the design. It had positively worn him out and he had given them a grudging agreement that he would send a writ to the Chief Exchequer when they returned, if they had any funds left in the Royal Treasury when they returned. He had no doubt that the rebels had probably stolen everything they had before he arrived.

He knocked on the door to Matthew's cabin and entered, pushing all thoughts of his beleaguered city out of his mind.

"How are you?" asked Matthew, coming over to see him as he entered.

"I had another dizzy spell a moment ago," he replied wearily, "but it wasn't as bad as previous ones."

"Good," said Matthew, examining him with a practised eye. "It might mean that the effects were only temporary. We can't take it for granted though. You'll have to keep me informed and I'll keep working on the cure if I can."

"You do realise that I'm not here to have you check out my health, don't you?" asked Naithan sourly. He hated it when Matthew went all fussy over him like this. "We need to contact Gareth and inform him of our arrival time. I'm sure he could use the aid."

It galled Naithan that his high commander of the army could not defeat the rabble of a rebellion, but they were fighting without their entire arsenal. It was absolutely imperative that the other kingdoms, even those of their new allies, Sol, did not suspect the full extent of the magical powers at the command of his troops. They would learn, in due course, but for now he needed all the advantage he could get.

"Certainly," replied Matthew briskly, fidgeting slightly with the circlet on his head.

Naithan swallowed down his suspicions. Since the incident on the docks Matthew had insisted on wearing the circlet at all times. He apparently did it to ensure that the great beast it controlled never strayed too far from their ship as, at least according to Matthew, if left to its own devices it could stray quite a distance away. If it did that, it could then take a while to respond to the circlet's call. However, the thought of the sea creature swimming below their ships sent a cold shiver through him and brought back visions of the two times it had trapped him in its maw. Unfortunately it was a vital part of their plans to reclaim Theldar, so Naithan could not really demand it be sent away.

Matthew began preparations for the spell, disturbing Naithan's train of thought. He settled himself down for the unnerving experience of talking to his brother through Matthew.

II

Galen sat back wearily in his chair, aware that another of his Shadow Knights had perished under the cursed sword of Gareth. The pain was not as bad as usual, or it could just be that he had grown accustomed to it. After the death of Sar Petra, which had been more painful than he could have ever imagined, other deaths seemed somewhat muted and dull by comparison.

He closed his eyes, pushing back the sadness he felt at her death. She had been a close advisor with a sound grasp of tactics and many people had felt her death. More had died upon the walls than usual since that day and they had not repeated any of their initial victories either. This was all despite the lull that had occurred in the fighting over the past few days. It was almost as if their opponents were awaiting something, for the attacks had been more a show of force than any real attempt to try and break through.

"Of course it is," said the voice in his head. Galen had come to realise

that it was something other than his own subconscious, unless he was going mad, and he severely doubted it. Whatever it was, it possessed many memories, much of which seemed to leak into his own thoughts. There were times when he could not tell were the voice ended and he began, though not at present. *"They await the arrival of King Naithan of course."*

"He's returning?"

"Of course he is," said the voice, sounding almost irritated. *"You didn't think you could take over his city and not expect him to return to reclaim it, did you?"*

"Of course not," he replied sourly. "I may be only human, but I'm not stupid."

"Well, return he does and with him comes a large fleet. He will attack through the harbour whilst his brother attacks the walls. You will be surrounded and defeated."

"Is there anything I can do?" he asked, rubbing his now aching temples with his hand.

The thought of everything collapsing around him and all the dreams he had dying was not a pleasant one.

"Only hold off the inevitable," replied the voice softly. *"Scuttle ships in the harbour to slow their access, use our powers in a more general fashion on a wider number of knights, trusting that their loyalty to the fight will be enough. In the end it will come to no avail."* Galen winced at that statement. *"And of course, there is always surrender."*

"Never," replied Galen angrily. "I will not allow this city to go down without putting up a fight."

"What of the people you care so much for?" asked the voice slowly. *"Would you throw their lives away needlessly?"*

"Since when did you care about that?" he asked bitterly.

"I have always cared," replied the voice sadly. *"That was why they trapped me in that ring, as punishment for aiding your people."*

"What?" he asked, surprised despite himself.

"It matters little," said the voice. *"Whatever happens, you will die, even if you flee. My aid slowly eats at your form, killing you from within. Had you not been dying when I aided you then it might not have been so, but all I do is slow the process down. One day soon, you will die, unless you truly give yourself up to shadow. Then you can escape. Only then…"*

"What do you mean?"

"Galen?" asked Marie's voice behind him. "Are you all right?"

"Yes," he replied wearily. "I'm just tired, that's all."

"I thought I heard you talking to someone."

"Yes, a Shadow Knight contacted me," he lied. "Apparently there are ships sailing towards the city, a fleet of them. They can't be more than a few days away, if that. We will be enclosed between two armies, trapped and doomed."

"Is there no way that we can win?" she asked worriedly. She rounded the chair and sat before him.

"None that I can see," he replied, looking past her at the fire beyond. "Though we could always surrender…"

"Never!" she replied fiercely, making him smile. He believed that this would be the attitude of most Theldarians, at least he hoped so. The voice had been correct though. He would have to speak with the people and present them with a choice. He would see to it later.

"Come to the Shadow, escape with me…" came the voice again.

"So we stand," he said, mostly to himself.

"Of course," replied Marie quietly.

"We were never married you know," he said, surprised at the words that came from his mouth, voicing one of his many regrets.

"I know, but it never mattered," replied Marie, holding his hand gently.

"It does," he replied, with more conviction in his voice than he had intended. "We shall do so today, before the sun has set." She looked up at him, her eyes wide. "That is…if you wish to…"

His voice faltered to a halt, and he found himself suddenly a little unsure.

"Of course I do," she replied softly, moving to hold him close. "But that is still a little while off yet, and I can't wait till then to visit the marriage bed."

He looked at her and saw the mischievous gleam in her eyes.

"But there is so much to do…" he protested, yet allowing her to draw him to his feet.

"All that can wait a while, can it not?" she whispered softly in his ear.

"Only a while though," he conceded.

"Then we'll have to be quick then, won't we?"

He allowed himself to be led through to his bedchamber. He allowed the worries of the moment to drift away as the scents and sights of Marie filled his thoughts and he lost himself to the moment. Yet through it all came the voice.

"Become one with shadow, escape with me…"

III

Krista Goldheart, once priestess of Solnar, goddess the sun and purity, now priestess of Toric, the one god, sat before the altar in meditation. At least that is what it would look like to any that entered her chamber in search of her. It would guarantee her privacy, for none would dare interrupt her in such a pose, regardless of which faith she was. It gave her time to fully comprehend the changes of the past week, for more than religion had changed.

The politics of Sol were now in turmoil. Six of the principle enemies of Sulan XXV were now on their way to the southern kingdom of Caldor, destined to die with honour, something that had led to a greater respect for Sulan. He could have simply hanged them as traitors, dooming their spirits to wander the seven roads for eternity.

She took a deep breath and tried to adjust her thinking. The seven roads were no longer there, only the golden straight path to the Celestial Palace and the black and crooked road to the Shadow Realm of Thenril. She would have to get used to thinking in those terms if she were to make the most of her new position. She had always been a practical person and from an early age she had seen religion as her mode of getting to the upper echelons of power. The rigid caste system of her land did not reach into the religious orders, where any of talent and ability could rise to power. The present Prophet, Sulan XXV, had his roots in a third tier family, all of whom had risen to first tier on his ascension to the golden throne. Whilst she did not expect to follow exactly in his footsteps, she already had access to more power than most other fifth tier members, with the new religious position in Sol, she could see options for further rises.

This was due, in part, to her heritage, once a hindrance to her. Her grandmother had married a man from the kingdom of Caldor, a minor noble from a dying house that no longer existed, against the wishes of her family. She had been thrown out of the family and driven from the first to the eighth tier, yet remained devoutly attached to him until her death. Her grandmother's contact with him had opened her eyes to the teachings of other religions, ideas that had passed on down to her father, Melkor Goldheart, who had in turn passed them onto her. When alive he had been very astute and had managed to raise the family's position to the fifth tier by arranging his and his two sisters to be married to prominent families. He had also tried the same for Krista, but she had refused. To be married off to some fourth tier noble was not her plan for life, for it meant a life of servile existence where there was no freedom.

She could recall sitting on her grandfather's knee as a girl, listening to his tales of women knights, and queens ruling the kingdom, and had dreamed of something like that for herself. Yet in these lands, women could not hope for the freedom to do as they wished. There were some Solmanese women who gained immense power and privileges, such as the concubines to Sulan and the various princes, or priestesses. In general, however, they were confined to the role of wives and householders, something she abhorred more than the thought of servility, the lowest tier in the order of things. So she had entered the priesthood and that of Solnar specifically as it was a celibate order, and her father had cast her off, abandoning her to her fate. She did not even know if he still lived, though she acted as if he were dead, for it was easier to bear the sadness that way.

Being cast off had also aided her cause, although only slightly. The High Priestess of the time had been so wary of accepting one with "tainted" blood and faith lines that she had almost been refused entry into the temple. Her father's actions had separated her from those lines, in a sense cleansing her of the taint, and she had wondered more than once if that had been her father's intent all along, though she knew she would never learn the truth.

It had gained her admittance into the order, though not full acceptance. The taint of her heritage had dogged her steps over the eight years she had been a priestess and even now there were those who would look away when she passed. Now, though, her heritage had earned her a special place in the new order emerging from the Prophet's conversion, and the startling defeat of Giarna by Toric. Her own conversion to the new faith had not been looked upon with as much suspicion as those of the other priests and priestesses of the various orders. Many had viewed her as a partial, if not a complete, worshiper of Toric for many years and were not surprised by her sudden change of heart. There were even some that viewed her as a herald of the new era, a prophet of sorts born precisely for this day.

Krista viewed all their ideas and beliefs with a cynicism that would have made her grandfather proud. She had never truly believed in any of the religions and her atheism had been proved by the fact that her prayers were still answered and seemed as powerful as any cast by true believers. Seeing Giarna rise up from the waters had startled her for a while, but the carefully orchestrated fight between the beast and the Caldorian king had restored her confidence. She had no idea how they had achieved it, for she had been one of those to probe King Naithan for magical talent and he had none whatsoever save a tiny residue of something unusual that only she had been aware of. She believed it probably had something to do with the circlet she had seen his priest Matthew hide away after the miracle of Giarna's defeat. It seemed to absorb magic, yet radiated none, from what she had seen of it.

Whatever the truth of the matter, though, it meant good news for her. Her knowledge of the Word of Toric, basic as it was, had proved to be a stepping stone into the high circles of power, for she had been expected to help in the teaching of the new ways to the various princes. It was a position envied by her fellow priests and she knew that she had gained more enemies by doing so, but she was now in contact with some of the most powerful men of Sol.

At the present moment she was in the House of Alash'an-min, the second most powerful clan of the kingdom. Its Clan Chief, Minrash, was the greatest enemy of Sulan XXV. Minrash had lost the election to the Golden Throne to Sulan, yet he was also a very intelligent man. In the moments after the announcement of Sulan's abdication he had been the first to leap up and protest, no doubt fearing some ruse or another. It had saved his life and drawn him closer to the Prophet's circle, making him more dangerous still. He was one of the few princes to remain here in Sol with the Prophet whilst others aided their new ally. The man had protested that it was safer for the Prophet to retain a faithful powerful ally in the troubling times of change that were to come. The man had even insisted that Sulan send a priest learned in the ways of Toric to his household to teach him the new ways.

Krista knew the truth, though, for she had overheard the man yesterday talking magically to some of his allies. She had used her own magic to spy upon his vizier's spell and learned some very interesting facts. She could still visualise their discussion now, in her trance-like state of meditation.

"You're sure that you will reach them that soon?" asked Minrash in surprise. "Truly, this Toric must sail with them."

The sarcasm in his voice was unmistakable to Krista. She stretched out the magical flows, attaching one to that of Vizier Sha-lim's spell of communication, puncturing a minute hole in its thread, allowing her to siphon off some of the information. She had suddenly found herself smelling the freshness of the salty sea air and knew immediately that he spoke with one on their way to Theldar. Minrash spoke again.

"Are you certain your men will be in place?"

"Yes, Excellency," replied the man on the ship. "Fully three quarters of Sulan's allies will perish in the fight, confirming the treachery of the Caldorians."

"Good," replied Minrash, sounding genuinely pleased. "With his allies dead and his alliance with Caldor weakened thus it will be easy to engineer his downfall."

Krista had broken off her spell and retired to her quarters to think. She spent the whole day in in meditation, thinking through the best course of action. She had two options before her, and they were not simple ones. She could leave Minrash to his plans, and prepare to make the best she could of the new situation, something she could do forewarned as she was. The second was potentially more dangerous, yet the rewards were of higher value too. She could inform Sulan and act as a spy, dishonourable as it was, helping him to neutralise the threat. If Minrash succeeded, she would most certainly die hanging from the nearest tree. If Sulan won, she would be in a position of trust with the Prophet himself, and have access to more power than she could ever imagine, especially as he was renowned for his fairness. He was the first Prophet in years to have sent a female ambassador to a foreign realm, relying upon her skill to negotiate without thought to her sex. It was true that he probably used them as any other tool, but then that was the way of rulers.

Minrash, on the other hand, was a traditionalist through and through. He had even attempted to curb entry in to the priesthood to those of improper caste, and was an unlikely source of power to her.

It meant that there was no real choice in the end. She could stay and wait until Minrash had succeeded, having gained more enemies along the way, and hope she could avoid the sweeping repercussions of the reaction to Sulan's conversion; or she could risk everything and hope she could help Sulan XXV to victory. She finished her meditation with a quick prayer to Toric then departed in the direction of her sleeping cell. She would devise a way of communicating with Sulan privately and hope for the best. She looked up to the heavens.

"If you truly are up there, please shine your blessings down upon us," she murmured briefly. They were going to need all the help they could get.

IV

Gareth was not a happy man, despite the dead Shadow Knight now being removed from his tent. The blade that had killed him had shattered again, precisely along the tears of the original breakage and would have to go back for its third re-forging. At least the bodies had ceased disappearing. The lack of corpses had started rumours that the Shadow Knights never actually died and had nearly destroyed morale in the troops. Why they had stopped disappearing he did not know and Helena had not been seen since she had gone to the city to learn what she could about these Shadow Knights, so he could not rely on her to find out.

He sighed; he seemed to be getting nowhere fast. Naithan had instructed him to lessen the offensive in preparation for his arrival and the morale of his troops had hit an all-time low. The previous night he had gone out in disguise, in the manner of all legendary war leaders, to hear for himself the campfire talk. What he had heard had not pleased him. They all spoke of the Shadow Knights with awe and fear, despite the confirmed deaths of nearly ten of them now and all talked of the bad omens. These ranged from peasant superstitions he had thought crushed from them in Redirection, to rumours too close to truth for comfort.

The king's capture by pirates was mentioned, and many claimed that the king had died. There were others saying that Caldor had deserted them when the King's Knight had fled Theldar, and that they were doomed to fail until he returned. Tristan's flight was one they had hoped well covered over, but there were people in this camp who had heard of the knight causing chaos in the city streets of Theldar, all those months ago. Many called him Caldor, but others still named him as Tristan, though in their eyes it was one and the same thing. There had not been a King's Knight in four generations that had inspired the awe that Tristan had. He was held by many as the perfect knight, his record of seventy successful jousts, which was, unusually for rumour, not far from the truth, was held by many as proof of his perfection.

Most disturbing of all was the fact that not one of them truly believed they could take the city, and it was galling for Gareth to hear it told, for he knew that knights without victory in their hearts would never win. It was a problem that would have to be dealt with swiftly.

His thoughts were suddenly disturbed by a great cry from outside his tent, and he rose to see what the noise was all about. He opened the tent flap to the most amazing sight. Riding into the camp, pennant flying, white plume sparkling in the sun, came the King's Knight in all his glory. The change in his soldiers was immediately noticeable. The man dismounted and strode purposefully towards the tent in his full glittering armour and Gareth found his mouth gaping open in surprise. The man knelt before him, raising his visor as he did.

"I hath returned from the quest thou hadst required of me, and offer thee my services in the forthcoming battle," he said, performing a full knightly salute as he did.

Something prickled at the back of Gareth's mind and he knew that something was amiss.

"Enter, great knight, and find shelter in my tent," he said, unsuccessfully trying to imitate the formal manner of address used by the knight.

The man bowed once more then followed him into the tent.

"Well, tell me," he said, turning to the knight. "Just how did you get the armour out of Theldar in one piece, and how have you managed to fit it on?"

"Trade secrets, dearest brother," said his sister in that infuriatingly smug tone she often adopted. "I felt the troops needed a morale boost, and thought this was the best way to provide it."

Gareth smiled slightly and took a seat as she began to struggle to remove the complex, ceremonial armour. Her face, which had not dropped the illusionary mask of Tristan's visage, scowled as she struggled with the many clasps and buckles.

"Well, are you just going to sit there and smile at me or will you decide to help me?" she muttered angrily.

"You wish me to squire for you dear sister. I'm long past knighthood for such a menial task. Do you wish me to summon a squire for you?" he asked, enjoying the brief moment's levity.

"Only if you want them spreading rumours of the stretched lady in the King's Knight's armour and destroying what little morale I given them," she replied sourly.

He got to his feet and helped her remove the armour as her face returned to the familiar shaped that he recalled. It took some time to help her out, his days as a squire truly forgotten and at the end they both felt weary. He looked at his sister and noticed what she had meant by her term *the stretched lady*. In order to fit into the armour she had used a spell to stretch her form somewhat, the same spell she was now using to return to her usual dimensions. Fortunately her tight black clothing had stretched with her.

"So what do you have to report?" he asked, sitting himself back down.

"I've figured out how to remove the power of the Shadow Knights," she said, casually pouring herself some wine from his table. "We just kill their leader, this Galen, and their power fails. It was simple really."

She sounded a little annoyed with herself. Helena had always hated it when she missed what should have been obvious.

"And you can arrange for that can you?"

"Not at the moment," she replied. "He's got himself too well protected. But in the midst of the all-out attack two days hence it should be an easy matter reaching him. Killing him will probably take all the skill I have though."

Like Naithan and Matthew and him, Helena had studied in Belthanor, training in the knightly ways. It was obligatory for most sons and daughters of noble houses. It was generally considered an honour, though some sometimes chose not to send their children there, and if they were not magically gifted, they were generally allowed. The last to have done so was the Countess of Northshire some years ago.

"Why not leave it to someone else?" he asked, knowing exactly how she would respond.

"No one else will be able to get close enough I'm afraid. So you'll have to find some other fool to wear the armour during the attack."

"What?"

"Well, if you want them to fight at their best they'll have to have him fighting with them."

It was true enough. He hated his sister's intelligence at times. He could work his way round the tactics of a battlefield, but had little time for anything else. Even his magical skills came to him with difficulty at times. He ceded the comment to her.

"Do you have any other news?" he asked quietly.

"Only a warning, really," she replied quickly. "Keep your troops out of the fighting as much as possible, and give me at least until dawn before making your attack on Theldar."

"Why?" he asked, cold shivers running down his spine as he spoke.

"Well firstly, it'll give me time to free the priests that are going to secure the gates for you from the inside, and secondly, I believe he is planning to create a vast number of these *Shadow Knights* tonight at his wedding. They'll be waiting on the walls for your attacks, and will decimate your troops when they fight. If I'm in time, they will have lost their powers before the attack."

"Advice noted," he replied. "We'll devote tomorrow to the completion of the siege engines."

"Good, then I'll leave you to it. I've preparations of my own to tend to."

With that she got up and, unusually for her, walked out from the tent through the front flap. Admittedly she went using an illusion of Tristan with the supposed mission of paying his respects to the princess, but it was unusual nonetheless. He was sure she would send a suitable replacement for the fake Tristan in due course, so decided to try and sort some of the administrative headaches caused by the last round of Shadow Knight attacks. He had not yet gotten round to creating some field promotions yet so sat down and began to read through the officer recommendations. Try as he might though, he could not get the terrifying image of hundreds of shadow knights on the walls, raining death upon his troops out of his mind.

Yet it also set him to wondering. If they had that particular magic, Caldorian knights would be truly invincible. For a moment he regretted the need to kill Galen, but he knew it had to be so. They had to take the city before any plans for the Kolthon Empire could be laid, and the only way to do that was to kill him. He sighed and returned to his work. If only the man had surrendered when he had the chance.

V

Tristan was starting to lose patience with Erin. She was certainly not acting her eighteen years at all, or maybe she was, he could barely recall his eighteenth year, even though it was only five years previous, or was it six? The blasted treatment had a lot to answer for. Even so, she should not be here, though he knew they would not be rid of her. She was the girl of the vision and would be there to the end. He could not explain this to the others though, for they would have probably ignored him.

They had all decided that she could not come with them but, as she was of the Blue Blood, she had decided that she would stay. Nothing they had said had persuaded her to leave and most of it had made her want to stay more than before so they had decided to try and bore her away. They had reduced their already ridiculously slow pace to one that even a snail could have bested; they continuously doubled back upon themselves, tracing out old tracks for much longer than was strictly necessary; and had taken almost four days to cover four miles. Yet nothing they did could dampen her enthusiasm, her experience with killing the ran-the seemingly forgotten.

They had finally given up and decided to allow her along, as if they had any choice in the matter. They had started the day at a full walking pace. Unfortunately she had taken their former caution to be standard, and had already begun to imitate them extensively. It meant that despite trying to move at a faster pace, they could not, for she was constantly stopping them with suspicious finds. Each time she was positive that she had found something important and each time they had wasted time following it up, only to find nothing. It had taken them the whole morning to convince her that they finally felt safe enough to travel without as much caution. It truly was like having a young child with them and he could not help but smile at Caliburn's cruel suggestion that perhaps she had been dropped upon her head as a baby.

"This is strange," she said, for the hundredth time today. "I've never seen this path here before."

"And I expect you know every path and trail in these woods," replied Belthar sourly.

Tristan was not the only one losing patience with the girl.

"No!" she replied defensively. She pointed to another trail pointing north. "But I know that particular trail. It leads up to my home. I use it all the time and I've never seen this one leading off from it. It's too large and well-worn to be a new trail. It's got to be something important!"

"Are yer sure girl?" asked the big man.

"Positive," she replied. "I climbed that tree there hundreds of times when I was younger. I even carved my initials on it as well. You can take a look for yourself, if you want."

Belthar merely raised his eyebrow to the barbed comment and shrugged his shoulders.

"I guess we'd best check it out then," he grunted. "Matt, can yer detect anything?"

Matthius shot him an angry look. He was still not happy that the man had divulged the truth of his calling to the girl. He muttered a few words and shot his hand out in the direction of the path. Tristan saw the magic ripple the air before them and realised with shock that he could see a faint glow.

"Powerful wizards can often see the hidden effects of other's magic, especially when thrown about as sloppily as that," said the sword, answering his unasked question.

It made a change. Caliburn had been unusually quiet since Tristan had divulged his dream and plans. The sword had tried to persuade him off that course of action and Tristan had refused to back down, swearing the sword to silence, a vow that it had kept almost literally.

Thank you, he replied. *Does that mean there is magic there?*

"Well, there's certainly a magical residue there," said Matthius, answering the question for Caliburn.

"We had better be careful then," replied Tristan, drawing his sword and readying his mind for the few spells he thought he had now mastered. He still hated the thought of using magic, but knew, with disgust at his lack of willpower, that he would use it if needed, regardless of how he felt about it afterwards.

They all cautiously edged down the trail, weapons drawn. Tristan saw Erin's face draw tight and he realised that her endless chatter and activity was designed to keep her mind from the killing she had done. Now, with possible danger ahead, she was being reminded of it constantly. He tried to catch her attention, to try and ease her fear a little, but she just stared resolutely ahead, bow drawn in readiness. He turned his attention back to the trail and prayed to Toric that she would not snap under the strain.

The trail opened out suddenly into a small clearing within which was a ramshackle wooden hut. The clearing seemed to be lit by unusually bright sunlight, as if summer had returned, though the day had been overcast just a few moments ago. He felt the hairs on the back of his neck prickle and he knew that something was not right here, other than the sunshine. The whole clearing simply pulsed with magical energy.

"It's just an old hut," said Erin, relief showing in her voice.

She stepped out into the clearing as they all cried out in warning and looked around smiling. Nothing had happened. Tristan breathed a sigh of relief and heard the others do likewise. They entered the clearing after her, though still with a little more caution. By the time they had all stepped in, she was at the door and knocking on it.

"Is anyone in?" she called out. "Hello? It seems empty enough."

"You have to be more cautious yer know girl…" began Belthar, but his words were lost on her as she opened the door and went inside.

"Poo! It smells a bit in here" came Erin's muffled voice from within.

"Come out of there," said Tristan angrily. "It is very rude to enter other people's property you know!"

"You sound just like my mother," she retorted. "Besides, this is on my land and I have right of entry to any home in our demesne."

He was now close enough to see inside the building and could see her looking at several scraps of parchment.

"What have you got there?" he asked.

"Now who's being rude?" She replied. "It's just a bunch of riddles, that's all. I mean who's ever heard of a *bird without wings* or the *master of the dark past, lord of the light future*, and what does it mean by *on the night of two days*?"

"The night of two days?" he asked moving closer towards her. The creatures of the grove had said those words when they gave him his vision. He suddenly found this place very cold, despite the warm rays of sunshine pouring through the gap in the leafy canopy. He drew close to the hut and was about to enter when a scream from behind him caused him to pause. He turned round and saw the filthiest person, if they could be called such a thing, he had ever had the misfortune to meet.

"My place, this," he said in a gravelly voice. "You not allowed here. Only for the special one and me is this. Me and the special one."

"We are sorry to have intruded. We will leave you in peace now," replied Tristan, moving away from the hut, but keeping himself between it and the creature. He hoped Erin would take the hint and leave as quickly as possible. The creature, however, seemed to take no notice of him whatsoever. It just kept babbling on to himself.

"Special one. The master said I hads to wait for the special one. *The one of pure heart.* Then he says I can rest. Only then mind you. A long time t'wait for the special one. A long time."

"What is it?" asked Erin behind him, evidently leaving the hut as she spoke.

Suddenly the creature's eyes seemed to clear and they focused on the girl behind him. It screamed again and rushed directly at her. Its sudden movement startled Tristan and it was able to get passed him in a couple of bounds. He spun round with his sword as Erin shrieked and he saw the creature pounce upon her. Tristan wasted no time, leaping to attack and bringing Caliburn slicing across the creature's back, causing it to howl in pain. Erin lashed out with her feet, forcing the creature off of her. As she did so, a blur of feathers and claws descended upon the creature as Soarer flew to the defence of his mistress. Belthar and Matthius also rushed in to aid but by then the creature was dead.

"Are you all right?" asked Tristan, turning back to Erin.

"Yes I'm…"

"Tristan!" called out Matthius.

He spun round in time to see the creature leaping back to its feet, its fatal wounds vanished.

"Pure of heart, pure of heart, I've seen the pure of heart," it chanted before racing off into the trees.

Tristan spared no time in thought and leaped into pursuit. He thought he heard the others follow but could not be sure, and did not truly care. He needed to know how someone could survive such wounds unharmed. He tore through the trees at break neck pace, desperately trying to keep up with his quarry but found that the creature was much faster than he could ever hope to be.

He stopped and dropped down to look for tracks. There was nothing. Cursing he looked round, listening for sounds of its flight. He caught the sound of distant plants being pushed aside and he made his way towards it. He approached cautiously until he heard Matthius's familiar cursing. He stood and approached.

"Did you find anything?" he asked, making the boy jump in shock.

"No, the Greenman's long gone," he replied.

"The Greenman?" asked Tristan.

"Have you never heard that term before?" asked the boy in surprise. "It was a common myth. He is supposed to be immortal and always talk in riddles. To see him is to see the future and past all at once, whatever that means. It's an ancient legend, stemming from the time of the Second Elf War. He was supposed to be the most loyal servant of the dark elf Kaneril who stayed loyal, even when the elf was killed, or captured, whichever you believe. But his master's death left him mad, along with the immortality that had been bestowed upon him that he may serve in perpetuity."

Tristan looked at the boy in alarm. His eyes had glazed over and he did not seem all that aware of the words coming from his mouth. His eyes then rolled and he blinked, looking at Tristan as if he had just seen him.

"How did you know all that?" he asked.

"All what?" asked the boy in confusion.

"All that information about the Greenman."

"Oh, I probably studied it somewhere," he replied vaguely. "Should we keep looking or head back to the others do you think?"

"I think it best we head back," replied Tristan slowly, his eyes searching Matthius' face for any sign of deception.

Matthius nodded his assent and turned back. It took several minutes walking before they finally entered the clearing, though it was not exactly the same as when they had left it. The sunlight had vanished, as had most of the clearing. Only a small area, where the hut had stood, was clear of any bushes or plants.

"What happened?" asked Tristan quickly.

"It just disappeared," said Erin in a small voice. "Just like that."

Her face was pale and even stroking the bird upon her shoulder seemed to bring her little comfort.

"It's all right girl, no harm came t'yer," said Belthar gruffly.

"Could you take me home please?" she asked suddenly, her eyes revealing both her youth and her fear. "I would go alone, but I'm scared it might come back."

Belthar looked at her in alarm, and Groltch seemed a little upset, as it would take them further out of their way. Tristan's training and sense of honour was too strong, though. He also knew deep within his heart that the moment of choice would occur there, in her home.

"Don't worry, we will see you home safe," he said, his heart sinking slowly. There was no escaping it now.

VI

Hunger. It had known hunger in its long life, but never as bad as this, and in the corner, chained in magic, was its only hope of sating its hunger. All it had to do was touch the creature and its sweet life energy would drain and it would be full. But this was the last of its food. After this, there could be no more until it was free, and that could be a while yet.

It moved over to the mouth of the cave across which the magical barrier shimmered threateningly at its approach. To touch it was to know oblivion. When they had first been placed here many generations ago they had tested it. It had been how the first couple had died. Another had gone mad after several generations of confinement, but not the creature once known as Kaneril. Not the creature once feared across the face of Loden. It had survived, living off the energy of those trapped with it, using what little magic it could send past the barrier to influence the events of the world outside. It was the magic of dreams and shadows, yet it was enough.

Kaneril had been there when the magical shield's prophecy had been created and impossible as it had sounded when cast, Kaneril had managed through the long years to finally gather together the pieces needed to fulfil it and release the shield, releasing the creature when it did. Kaneril had even begun preparing the world for its triumphal return, and this time it would rule all. Yet first it needed to survive. Its magical energy was beginning to ebb, its dream magic suffering the most. Even the puny dream shield over Zaron had been enough to prevent it, draining Kaneril's energy needlessly.

The creature beside him whimpered, knowing that it would not survive as Kaneril had promised. The humans would not reach here in time. Kaneril allowed its thoughts to roam over the land to Caldor, where it found those it needed, making their dreary way to the female's castle. The image dimmed a little as its powers ebbed once more. A few years previous it would have been able to hear their words, but not now, not without the death of the creature behind it.

It was one of Kaneril's own kind, though a pathetically weak one. It had been the strongest of the others, but none had matched Kaneril for power. The Master of Shadows had, but Kaneril had trapped it in the ring, siphoning off its power when needed. Until that human female had freed it. Kaneril hoped that in doing so she had assigned it to oblivion. That had been the only failed part of Kaneril's plan so far, and now there was a city in revolt, chaos, the bane of Kaneril's long life.

"Master," came an ancient, yet familiar voice in his mind. *"I have seen the one of pure heart. Come at once..."*

The voice faded and Kaneril felt the draw of the ancient spell. It had been for this reason that it had saved the last one un-consumed. It reached out and touched the cowering creature, feeling its energy seep through it. The call of the spell grew stronger and Kaneril intensified the drain, drawing as much energy at once as was safe. Suddenly the creature before it vanished and the spell triggered, just in time. Kaneril felt its form shift, allowing it to appear partially before his ancient servant. It was a sign of the shield's weakening strength that Kaneril was able to do such a spell, allowing it to almost physically touch the outside world.

"The one of pure heart was here master," said his servant, grovelling before him.

"You gave him the bracelet?" asked Kaneril quickly.

"Yes Master, though there were others with her, so I had to do it quickly, without notice."

"No matter," replied Kaneril with a smile. "Now he has it, he won't be able to let it go. Even the sword will not be able to stop its powers."

"Can I rest now master?" begged the creature pitifully.

"Yes, you can," replied Kaneril softly.

This human had existed for generations past his own lifetime, waiting for the day the knight, this Tristan, armed with only the knowledge of the shield's prophecy in his mind. It could not have been easy for this short-lived creature to bear, and it had remained faithful to the end. Kaneril placed its hand upon the servant's head and he sighed.

"She was very beautiful," he said as his life left him. "Just as I had dreamed she would be…"

Kaneril's eyes turned towards the human, concern flaring up.

"You said she?" he asked the now cooling corpse. "She? You did not give it to the knight? You fool! The plans are ruined! You fool!"

Rage consumed Kaneril the like of which it had not felt for generations. This bumbling human had ruined its plans. Centuries of planning all come to nought! Despair filled it as it felt the pull of its prison, calling it back. In an act of spite Kaneril destroyed the fool creature's body with flame, a pointless action that wasted energy. But that did not matter now. Kaneril knew it would die in this stinking cave, as its captors had always planned.

It returned to its prison, rage giving way to despair. Then came a flicker of hope, a human trait it had picked up in its many years of contact with them. Perhaps the fool had been wrong. The geas Kaneril had placed upon the fool human was too powerful to allow for mistakes. He had to have been wrong. Kaneril, still strong from the feed, stretched out its senses, seeking the knight, deciding that it should just wait and see before giving up all hope of escape…

VII

Tyrone watched the wedding with a feeling of contempt and disgust. It was a grandiose affair that made a mockery of the situation they were in and yet the Theldarians were lapping it up like puppies with milk. Could they not see that they were doomed? Galen had all but said so in his speech after the ceremony, yet they had all cheered wildly and agreed to fight on, like mamrats to the cliff.

They had then decided to finish the foolery by agreeing to join the ranks of the Shadow Knights now, to aid the campaign. The thought made him shudder; hundreds of these men fighting, immune to many forms of attack, slaughtering the attacking knights. There was even to be a sea-borne division to attack the fleet sailing at great haste towards them, purportedly carrying King Naithan with it. Despite all this they were going to fail, and yet none save Galen and himself seemed able to see it. Why else would he have had his marriage now in war than if there were no chance it could occur in more peaceable times?

He looked away at the queues lining up to enrol in the elite force and decided to retire to his quarters.

"Where are you going?" asked Meredith, who had been sat at his side for the ceremony.

"T'bed," he replied bitterly. "I've no stomach t'watch fools march blithely t'their deaths."

"Then you won't be joining them then?"

"Why would I even want ter?" he asked with a snort.

"To gain revenge, why else," she replied.

He turned and looked into her deep brown eyes and saw an angry fire burning there.

"Revenge of that sort is not my way. Besides, I gave my word t'serve the good of the city. I don't think I could go against that, even if I tried. The bond that the vow created is like none I've ever felt."

"Is allowing thousands of men to perish defending a city that cannot possibly hold for the sake of that murderous madman's dream what you would consider good for this place then?"

"No, but what can I do?" He looked at her for a while. "Yer're planning something, aren't yer?"

She glared at him defiantly.

"That would depend."

"On what?" he asked slowly.

"On whether you will help me or not," she replied quickly. "It involves no deaths, not even of that man, and could even save lives."

Tyrone was interested despite himself.

"I'd have no problem listening t'hypothetical plans," he said slowly.

"It involves those priests you arranged to have imprisoned."

Tyrone winced at that thought. He had reported to Galen all he had heard and Galen had imprisoned the men, just as he had feared. He had not even thought to hide their plans from Galen, though he was never sure if it had been due to his vow or simply due to plain cowardice on his part. They now spent their days in the dank prison cells beneath the palace.

"Well, what of 'em?" he asked gruffly. He did not like being reminded of the episode.

"Just this," she began. "It would be possible, hypothetically speaking, to release the aforementioned men of god and lead them out to freedom. From there they could be left to their own devices, where they could possibly make their ways to the various gates, securing them for the more peaceful entry of the opposing armies."

"And how would that benefit the city?" he asked with a sneer.

"You would be restoring its spiritual diversity, and by allowing the armies in you would prevent them having to fight their way in, inflicting the necessary casualties that such a violent approach would entail."

By Toric, she's gotta wickedly devious mind thought Tyrone, though he merely asked "Why could you not do it, or some of your Dark Circle?"

"We have…other tasks to attend to," she replied cryptically. Her eyes forbade him to enquire further.

He thought about the idea for a moment. It would be a ridiculous gesture that would not save many lives, but it could save some. It would also allow him to make up for the wrong he had committed. Those men had not had the strength to carry out their plots. They might not even have the courage to liberate the gates. But it would make him feel a little better about himself when he sat alone in the darkness.

"I think it time we joined this great army," he said quietly, praying that he was doing the right thing. So often before he had thought that what he was doing was right, so often it had turned out wrong.

They made their way to the back of the queue and waited in silence with the rest of the fools. Tyrone closed off the excited chatter of those around him and concentrated on the procedure he was about to undergo. Meredith merely clasped his hand and stared ahead, seemingly calm and serene. When she had made up her mind to do something she then went ahead without doubts a trick he wished he could master. As it was, all he could do was wait and worry.

It seemed to take an eternity for them to finally reach the steps of the great plaza that led to the courthouse and an eternity longer to make it to the final step. As he moved forward he found his mouth opening in shock. Galen seemed but a reflection of a man, worn to beyond exhaustion by the task he was doing. At his side was Marie, her support invaluable in keeping him upright.

"What are you doing here?" asked the man in a thin, but suspicious voice.

Tyrone looked into Galen's eyes and saw that despite the worn body, his eyes were awake and alert. He kneeled before the man, suddenly worried that his own face would betray him.

"I do this for the good of the city," he replied, more calmly than he felt. "Just as I vowed to you."

"Look at me," commanded the man quietly.

Tyrone looked up and found himself caught in the man's piercing stare. He felt trapped there and panic welled up inside, yet the man merely nodded and placed his hand upon Tyrone's head. He felt a jolt of energy pass through him and the world went black for a few seconds. When his vision returned he found that everything seemed a lot greyer than before, made worse by the dark clouds overhead.

"It is done, you may go," said Galen wearily. "And Tyrone…"

He looked at the man and words formed in his mind.

"Save as many as you can."

His eyes opened in surprise and he found himself begin to shake. Meredith came to his side and supported him slightly.

"Come on now," she whispered. "You did well, but don't give the plan away now."

Tyrone looked back at Galen but he was busy with the next enlistment. As they walked from the plaza, he wondered just how much the man truly knew of their plans. Whatever it was did not matter though, for he had not stopped them when he could.

As they walked over to their chambers, the first drops of rain began to fall and by midnight, a full storm was in progress, yet out in the plaza, people were still lined up to take the Shadow Knight blessing…

VIII

Naithan sat in the cabin, looking across at Matthew, now speaking with Gareth's voice. It was one of the most unnerving things he had ever encountered and even though they had done this every day since leaving Sol, he was still not used to it, nor would he ever be. Even his eyes had changed to match the deep blue of Gareth's eyes. Fortunately this was to be the last of such communications for a while, for they would be at Theldar in the early hours of the morning, despite the rain now crashing down outside.

"So all will be ready at dawn then?" he asked.

"Yes, sir," replied Gareth formally, as he did in such conferences. "Our troops will attack at dawn. If the emissary has done his work then all should go well for us."

The Emissary; the code word for his Spymaster in open communications such as this. Naithan had been impressed by the work he had done this time.

"Then we shall attack harbour-side at dawn with you then, and I shall meet you in the palace."

The palace, being one of the central points of the city, was the ideal meeting point for the two forces.

"Do you still insist on moving at the fore front of your forces, Naithan?" asked Gareth, losing his formality in concern for his welfare.

"Of course," replied Naithan, "and nothing you say will stop that."

"Well, you know my stance on the matter," replied his brother softly.

"Yes, it is noted," he replied a little more coldly than he had intended. "You are dismissed."

"Yes sir. Toric guide you."

"And you."

Matthew's eyes went vacant for a moment before they returned to their usual grey colour.

"Thank you," he said to his friend, rising and leaving before he too lectured him on the need for safety, as he inevitably would.

This was his city he was returning to claim and he had no intention of being seen as a man to cower behind his soldiers in such a battle. The greatest kings of old had ridden to combat with their troops and Naithan could see no difference in this. If he was to crush this rebellion, he was going to have to be seen being a strong king that no one would even dare think of rebelling against again.

He moved out to the prow of the boat, ignoring the rain lashing down at him and looked for any sign of his kingdom rushing past them. He could see nothing though, and returned to his own cabin.

This is a fine way to welcome the returning king, he thought darkly.

IX

Groltch did not like the way this journey was going. He had not been best pleased to learn that the human female they now travelled with was of the same blood as the man he had tried to kill, for in ran-tha custom, she was as guilty as him for the crimes committed against his realm despite her youth. This had been complicated by the fact they were now taking her to her home, where they had been promised safe haven for the night. This made things doubly confusing, for custom also dictated that it was impolite to kill any who offered the Shen-la, or shelter of home, even if they were blood sworn enemies.

Groltch was aware that to humans this would seem strange, yet could not help feeling like he was betraying his own kind by doing this. He had vowed to kill the House of King Naithan, and that would include her, and those of her house. The only way to get round this would be to call a Shak, a truce, but there was no independent master to formalise it. He had no idea how to deal with this problem and needed to talk to someone.

He moved across to Tris, who had reached a level of silence that was scary. Most of the time it was as if he wandered around in another realm, seeing and hearing nothing of this one. He was like some sort of automation of ancient tales, such as the Garlum, the strange statue of flesh that moved as if alive, yet was not. But he needed advice.

"Tristan," he said softly to the knight.

He looked down at Groltch.

"Where's Galahad?" he asked.

"The girl tends to him," replied Groltch.

They had decided it was unwise to allow him to keep tending the horse whilst in such a distracted way and Erin had leapt at the chance to do it.

"Good, because I'll be needing him soon," replied the knight, his attention drifting away.

"I need to talk with you," continued Groltch slowly. "It about the girl."

"What about her?" asked Tristan, his attention rapidly fading.

"I have blood debt with her family, yet cannot kill her, for she has offered shelter of home and it bad to do this."

"Kill her?" Tristan asked, his attention instantly focusing back onto Groltch. "You can't do that."

"Groltch know this, but not sure what to do. Ran-tha custom very strict on this. Can only not kill if a truce pact formed by a master."

"No, you can't kill her," said Tristan, not seeming to her him. "A Master? Does this not make me a Master?"

He pulled out the methram they both shared, the only two left on living creatures.

"Yes, but you not know…"

"Groltch, son of Mar-loutch, I Tristan, son of Tyrone, Swordmaster to the Pathfinder Clan, bid thee kneel," said Tristan in fluent ran-tha.

Groltch's eyes widened in shock, but he did as bidden.

"I bid thee to hold Shak towards Erin, daughter of Michelle, Huntsmistress of Clan an'Tharon, and her mother, Michelle, daughter of Michael, head of the Clan an'Tharon, until such time that I bid thee not too."

"I, Groltch, son of Mar-loutch, hear and obey thee, Tristan, son of Tyrone, Swordmaster to the Pathfinder Clan. Shak will be held until such time as you release me, though only to those who offer Shen-la this day."

"It is agreed. Break this bond and face the wrath of Toric."

"Break this bond and I shall bare my throat to the fangs of Thenril."

They both bowed in the ran-tha fashion and turned back up the trail. Groltch looked at Tristan in curiosity.

"How you know what to do?" he asked.

"The medallion does more than pass on weapons expertise, but also other things that, though new to me, are so common to you that you would not notice it. We're here."

Groltch looked out from the break in the trees and across almost half a mile of fields stood an ancient castle, set upon a hill, with stone walls around it and a deep looking moat surrounding it.

"Castle Carrador," said Matt, his eyes glazing over. "Site of Caldor's greatest victory against the Kolthon army. The original keep here was built as a boundary marker, until the river Fye widened and altered course in the great catastrophe."

Groltch shuddered as Matt spoke. Something told him that this was the site of momentous events. He prayed to Toric in the hope that at last, their stay in at least one Caldorian residence would be free of incident. Somehow, though, he knew that they had been cursed with the luck of Thenril on this.

"Come on," cried Erin loudly. "If we hurry, we'll make it before nightfall."

Groltch sighed and followed the others now well on their way to the fort.

X

Tristan wandered through the castle halls, looking at the various tapestries, displays of arms and paintings on the walls as if in a dream. It was all too familiar to him. He had seen them all in his dreams night after night since their visit to the Druid's grove. Even the scents were familiar, as was Groltch's ever-hovering presence behind him.

"Impressive, don't you think?" he asked, pointing to an elaborately decorated sword.

Groltch moved to examine it, drawing the blade and studying it closely, just as he had in countless dreams before.

"No, the blade flawed," replied the ran-the, Tristan mouthing each word as he said it. "Will break when you most need it, I assure you."

Tristan smiled and winked at the section of wall where he knew Malcolm would be hidden, noting down all the details of his visit. In his dream this action had made the man jump up and run for shelter. He smiled at the thought then turned down a corridor that led to the servants' stairs. Just as in the dreams he had seen enough to convince him that this was the place.

The evening's meal had been what had initially confirmed his suspicions, as it had rekindled the memories of the dreams to the vividness they now were. He bade Groltch good night as he mounted the stairs, noting the sword's position for future reference. Not that it mattered, for the only future Tristan saw at present was the morrow, the day of his decision. He retired to bed and a dreamless sleep, awakening only once in the night to prepare for the next day. It was almost time…

XI

"Mother! Would you just be quiet!" snapped Erin angrily. "How was I to know who he was?"

"You weren't. Though you would have known had you paid attention to your lessons," replied her mother in her usual waspish tone. "Now you have us harbouring an Errant Knight! We'll have to report them."

"No!" cried Erin angrily. "I promised them a place of safety for one night. I gave them my word!"

"Your word means nothing to criminals."

"Yet my life does? They saved me mother. They had no need to, but they did. They looked after me and provided me safe passage home, though it took them away from their original course, all for no reward. Do those sound like the actions of criminals?"

"No, but they are the actions of responsible adults, something yet to see in you," her mother replied angrily. "If you had not run off they would not have had to rescue you, now, would they?"

"There's no talking to you mother, you're so stuck in your ways it's untrue!"

She got to her feet and stormed out of the dining hall, thankful that the others had retired already. She stormed through the corridors, barely avoiding that weasel Malcolm, and sprang up the stairs two by two, entering her room and slamming the door. She knew the act to be childish, particularly as her mother would not hear it all the way down in the dining hall, but it made her feel better. She got onto the bed and began to sob angrily. How dare her mother take away what she had promised?

"Erin," said a soft voice at her window. She looked across and saw Marak sat on the lip, regarding her in that stern, but gentle way of his. "I've spoken to your mother. She has relented a little. She said to tell you that if they were gone at dawn and out by the hidden routes then she would claim it all to have been a dream, albeit a strange one."

Thank you," she said softly.

"I did nothing I haven't done before, but you'd best rest now."

She smiled and cleared her eyes.

"Yes sir," she said with a mock salute. She then paused to look at him as he prepared to descend the way he had come. "Do you ever worry that someone will see you?"

"No, I've done it often enough to know the best way to escape notice. Besides, it's not something people would expect to see."

"That's true," she replied with a smile. "Well goodnight then!"

"Goodnight," he replied, slipping from the window and out of sight.

She refused the impulse to run and watch, as she had done numerous times before, knowing that tonight, as on all nights, she would doubtless see nothing. She turned and prepared herself for bed before preparing her equipment for the next day. The confrontation today had proved that she and her mother could not live peaceably under the same roof. Despite the fear she felt at the prospect, she decided that tomorrow she would leave for good and travel with these four *outlaws* to wherever they were headed. Tomorrow would be the beginning of a new life.

XII

Malcolm raced back to his room. He had gotten over his initial panic at the thought that Tristan had discovered his hiding place. The wink just had to have been a twitch or something. Now he simply could not believe his luck. Tristan had delivered himself straight into his arms. He mounted the stairs to his draughty room and continued on up to where he maintained his messenger pigeons. He rolled up the coded note and attached it to the leg of his fastest flyer. He would have to think of ways of detaining them here of course, though the guard here would not be much use, being the aged militia not needed for the siege at Theldar, but there were ways. Tomorrow would mark the end of his days in this miserable hole. He could hardly wait. He released the pigeon then retired to bed, his head buzzing with plans for his triumphant return to Theldar.

XIII

Karene glared into the campfire angrily. There had been no word from Jax since he had bumped into Lady Erin in the trees, and that did not bode well. Tristan could be long gone by now, and with him her chance of promotion. She cursed her confounded luck and spat into the fire.

"Movement in the brush," came a sentry's warning. Within seconds everyone in the camp had drawn their swords and stood ready for combat.

"False alarm," came another cry, "it's only Jax."

Karene started in surprise. She had ordered him to follow them and if he was here then it could only mean that Tristan was close by.

"Bring him forwards at once," she commanded and the men rushed to aid him. She found herself blanching at the number of wounds crossing his body. It was a miracle that he had survived at all. He staggered over towards Karene, collapsing into her lap.

"Tristan, Castle Carrador," he croaked as the life faded from his eyes.

Karene closed his eyes, breathing deeply to cover her excitement. They could be at Carrador by dawn if they left at once.

"Our quarry is at Carrador, we must ride at once," she commanded, getting to her feet.

"What of the body?" asked Sir Simon.

"We need to ride at once, but you and two men may stay and prepare the funerary rites."

"Yes Sar," he replied with a salute and a slightly crestfallen look. He would not be there in time to witness her triumph.

She barely noticed, for she was already breaking camp in preparation to ride to the castle. Within minutes her knights were charging out down the road at full gallop, a rate they would not keep for long, but it felt good to actually be doing something. Come the dawn and they would have the King's Knight in chains…

XIV

Sir Simon, Green Knight of Teldin, watched as his companions as they raced off to capture the King's Knight. It was the last clear memory either he or any of his fellow knights were to have of the evening. The rest of the night would appear as a dream to them that none could truly recall. All had agreed that a mist had risen up around them as they began their grim work, and all could remember the light. None were exactly sure what happened next, though Simon was adamant that he saw the glowing figure of a man like creature rise from the corpse and then lift it in its arms. Another could recall a pool nearby that the creature and the corpse both sank beneath, and the third swore on the truth of Toric that he had seen a more feminine blue creature in the pool. All remembered that the pool vanished once their heads sank below the surface.

Only Simon could recall the final strange occurrence of the night, though his companions both swore that it did not happen at all. Simon was positive that he saw two figures emerge from the bushes from which Jax had emerged. One had been tall and covered in scars, the other short, bearded with long black hair, braided into a tail with raven feathers.

"So that's how they do it here," the tall one had said.

"I told you that body got up and walked away," said the other.

"It's a little old fashioned though," said the tall one, "all that, *man struggles to his companions and dies giving the important message*."

"That's destiny for you, I guess," replied the other.

"I suppose so, though it never happened to us."

"Yes it did," replied the shorter of the two. "Remember that time when…"

The voices faded away as the two walked off into the mist and Simon could recall no more until dawn when he had awoken refreshed, ready for the new day.

CHAPTER NINETEEN: Death and Destruction

I

Dawn.

Tristan looked out on the pre-dawn light through the window in the chamber he had been given as residence for the night, feeling at peace for the first time in many months. All the problems, debates and confusion were gone from his mind. His course was set. He knew that the moment of decision was upon him, and knew he would do what was necessary. It would not be an easy course, but then he had always been taught that it was wrong to back down just because the task would be difficult.

A glint of metal caught his eye and he knew that they were there, just as the dreams had foretold. It was not going to be a long wait. He smiled happily, knowing that all was ready. The door opened behind him.

"Good morning Groltch," said Tristan without turning, knowing how that would startle his friend.

He turned round to face the ran-the and realised that he truly was his friend and for a moment Tristan found himself regretting his decision. Groltch would do what was necessary to save his people and Tristan knew he would do what he could to aid in that.

"There are knights outside castle," said the ran-the softly.

"I know," replied Tristan, gesturing to the window. "I can see them from here."

"They demand you be sent out to them," said Groltch.

"I thought they might. Will the lady of the castle release me to them?"

"She not yet risen, but they not open gate to them, even though castle surrounded. The woman, Erin, have told the guards to keep closed. Groltch…I think she have a plan to escape here."

"She probably does," he replied, his thoughts returning to his dreams. Of course she would have a plan, and he would aid them in it. "I will join you in the hall anon."

"You all right?"

"I am fine, Groltch," he replied with a smile, "as will you be. We'll get out of this, rest assured."

"I know that," replied the ran-the with a smile. "We always get out. We always run."

Not this time, he thought, but merely smiled at his friend's words.

Groltch turned and left the room, leaving Tristan to his solitude once more. He looked back down at the knights gathered by the drawbridge over the moat and took a deep breath, a sudden tremble of nerves striking him. He would have to remain focused if he were to succeed today. He then turned back to the chest by the luxurious four poster bed he had spent the night in. He had to smile at the strangeness of it all. Only twice in his life had he ever been able to sleep in a room alone and each time he had been a virtual prisoner at the time, once to the schemes of Anton and now to destiny.

"You are sure there is no way I can persuade you from this course?" asked Caliburn, gently entering in upon his thoughts.

None at all, he replied.

"Then all I can do is wish you Toric's blessing then," said the sword quietly.

Thank you, he replied, removing the few possessions he had from the chest and packing them up neatly. He then turned and left the room.

He made his way down towards the hall where they would all be sat planning their escape. As he passed by the spy-holes that he knew that Malcolm would be hidden behind, he sent out a quick spell, putting him into a deep sleep. His dreams had told him that this would keep him out of mischief for at least two hours. He entered into the hall. The others were all dressed and ready and Tristan was not surprised to see that Erin seemed packed and ready to leave with them. He could also hear that they were arguing about it as he entered.

"Look gal," said Belthar, his voice rumbling ominously. "Kolth is a very dangerous place fer the likes of you and yer only likely t'get yerself killed if yer come with us."

"You have no command over where I can and cannot go and I have decided to go with you," she replied petulantly. "Besides, who else here can speak their language, eh? The goblin here can't even speak Caldorian properly, let alone Kolthon."

Groltch winced visibly at her words and Tristan could see the dangerous glint of anger in the ran-the's eyes. The situation could rapidly dissolve if the subject were not changed swiftly.

"All this is just academic debate if we get cannot find a way to get out of here past those guards," he said, startling Matthius and Erin as he did.

Tristan was used to the almost magical hearing of Groltch and Belthar.

"'Tis true enough," replied Belthar grudgingly.

"It's simple enough," replied Erin smugly. "I know numerous ways out of this place, all of which could lead us passed the knights, and none of which I'll show you unless I can come with you."

"You will actually find that they are all presently guarded by knights," said Tristan, smiling at her startled reaction.

"How do you know?" she asked suspiciously.

"In the Royal Chancery and Ordinance Offices in Theldar there are numerous detailed plans of every castle and keep in Caldor, and many of those from Kolth and Sol. There are also copies of these in Belthanor, all of which are required study materials of every knight," lied Tristan, refusing to reveal the source of his information. "I can remember studying these plans, with all its secret exits, and surmised that others would also be able to recall the details, so took a brief look. They are all guarded."

"Oh," replied Erin, looking much deflated. "Then we're stuck. Unless we could use magic…"

Matthius shook his head mutely. "The only spells I could use to transport us away are dangerous unless I know every aspect of our destination, or if someone I knew very well was stood in a clear space." He looked meaningfully at Tristan with these words. "To use them without this could be fatal to us all."

"Why not just make us invisible?" asked Erin, leaning towards him.

"Despite what you may think, magic cannot do everything and unfortunately, making someone or something invisible is an impossibility," he replied wearily. Tristan could already see the boy's dread of what would happen to him after his capture crossing his face. "I can make things seem different from what they actually are, but not make it seem like it isn't there at all."

"Oh," she replied, looking deflated once more.

"There is one way, of course," said Tristan, quietly interjecting.

Suddenly four pairs of eyes were looking directly at him.

"What?" they asked, almost as one.

"I could demand the Right of the Challenge," he said simply.

The Right of Challenge was an ancient practice among the knighthood for protesting one's innocent. Anyone who had gone errant and fled the knighthood, or any accused of a crime or falsehood, had the right to challenge the best knight in the field of combat. In the case of the errant knight, it would often be required that he or she fight a succession of at least half those from the party sent to retrieve him. If the errant knight were successful they would be able to return to the knighthood in honour, with a trip to the Chambers their only punishment. If they failed, they would find themselves demoted to the rank of squire and forced to endure many doses of Treatment before they could return to the knighthood, and they rarely ever regained the rank they had formerly held. In Tristan's case, he doubted that he would retain the white plume, even if he won the Challenge.

"There are too many of them for you to fight and win," protested Erin. "Even if your reputation for jousting is deserved."

"I probably could, though it would take some time, but that is not my intention," replied Tristan. There was no way he would return willingly to the knighthood. "All I will do is issue the Challenge and, by the rules of the engagement, I must see all the knights I may face. That will clear the way for you to leave through the exit. Even if they do not recall all of the knights, it will leave fewer for you to face when you leave."

"You mean kill them?" asked Erin with shock. "Is that why they hunt you? For killing knights?"

"No," replied Tristan. "They seek me only because I fled from their ranks and aided Groltch in his flight from the city. But the important fact is that they seek *me*, and so they will recall all the knights when they see me ride onto the drawbridge, especially if the portcullis is lowered behind me. This will leave you clear to escape. I assume that you can ride horses from the northern tunnel, so that is what you will do, whilst I sit and wait in prayer before my first challenge. That will give you at least ten minutes to escape. Then I will raise my sword to signify the start of the Challenge, but also my intention to flee. Have your men raise the portcullis and I shall use Caliburn's power to create a flash of light bright enough to startle them and give me time to flee after you. We can then drop the portcullis after me and I will follow you with all speed to the border. Once across we shall be safe, for the knights will have to gain permission from the king to leave the kingdom, which he should be loathed to do."

He looked round the table and saw all four working through the plan in their minds and he knew he would have to act fast if he were to prevent them from seeing the flaws in his design.

"You're sure the plan will work?" asked Erin, leaning across the table.

"Of course," replied Tristan quickly. "I've used it before. There'll be no problems at all. Just concentrate on getting them out of the keep." All was going just as he had dreamed. "Come, there is little time to waste, if we are to be away swiftly. If I may borrow a suit of mail from the armoury, or even plate, if there be any to fit me, so that I will at least look the part. Also I would like to take a sword for my companion here, for I fear the staff is not his best weapon."

Erin nodded in agreement.

"Shall I send for a squire to attend to you?" she asked softly.

Tristan breathed a sigh of relief that she had accepted the plan easily.

Knowing from the dream that she would had not been assurance enough for him and he was still waiting for something to occur differently, fearing that it could all be a trick, but all was going exactly as he had seen. Matt and Belthar were already beginning to move into action and he could see Groltch's fear of riding a horse solo rising in his eyes.

"No, that will not be necessary for Groltch has enough knowledge to aid me and I think it best that we involve as few others as possible in this. If you could send forth a herald though and announce that I request the Peace of Parley, it would make my task a lot easier."

"Certainly," replied Erin, moving towards the door. "You know where the armoury is I suppose."

"Of course," he replied. "Unless the room's function has been altered in the past fifty years?"

"No," she replied, "probably not in a hundred."

"Thank you," he replied, motioning for Groltch to follow him.

"How you know I can put armour on?" asked the ran-the when they were finally alone.

"I told you before. This amulet allows me to recall things about your culture, one of which is that to become a tenget you have to have learned how to dress a warrior in any armour," he lied. It seemed that he was getting quite good at the skill once so alien to him. "I would not expect anything different from you."

"Oh," replied Groltch, and they walked on towards the armoury. "You're plan…"

"I know, there are flaws, but it is all we have. The issue of the Challenge should hopefully surprise them, allowing it to succeed."

He could see that Groltch did not fully believe him but was glad that the ran-the ceased questioning him.

They walked into the armoury and Tristan made his way to the almost bare sword racks. He pulled out several in a row, making test swings with each as he did. On the fifth sword he turned to Groltch and offered him it.

"Try this one," he said, trying to sound deep in careful thought.

Groltch went through a series of warm up exercises with the sword, expertly finishing it off with a flourish. Tristan had been correct in his assumption. The ran-the was a good swordsman. Not the best of course, and he would probably never be a master of the blade, as Tristan was, but he would do better with it than with the staff and dagger he had been using previously. Groltch handed the blade back to him.

"Well weighted," he replied. "Almost perfect for me. You good judge."

"I was the King's Knight," he replied with a shrug that he hoped looked suitably casual. "I would have not been fit for the position if I could not judge such things."

Groltch looked at him with a penetrative stare but said nothing.

"Would you allow me to do something?" Tristan asked hesitantly.

"What?"

"Would you allow me to knight you?" He saw the ran-the's eyes open wide in shock and rushed out the explanation he had prepared. "It is just that in my culture no one not of the knightly orders would be allowed to wield a sword of such a length. It is considered an honour, even if there are many now who defile the plume now. And I would like to honour you as your kind did when they gave me this medallion."

That at last seemed to decide Groltch and he dropped to one knee in the perfect knightly bow, surprising Tristan despite the dream's forewarning. He turned the flat of the blade towards Groltch and lightly tapped him twice on both shoulders.

"I knight thee in the name of Toric and for the honour of Caldor," said Tristan formally. I dub thee knight of the Green Order. Arise Sir Groltch, son of Mar-loutch."

Groltch rose to his feet and Tristan turned the sword's hilt towards him. The ran-the accepted it and brought the hilt to his lips. In Tristan's ears he heard a slight ringing and knew that another of Caliburn's Prophecies of making had been fulfilled, leading the sword one step closer to destruction.

"When Tu'ran-tha and human stand one as tengeti and knights..." came Caliburn's voice with the ringing, confirming his suspicions.

"Let's get to the armour and see if we can find anything that fits," said Tristan, pushing his thoughts back to the task at hand.

"Yes," replied Groltch, his voice thick with emotion.

It did not take them long to find a suitable set of armour, Tristan having known where to look already. Groltch made an able squire, his nimble fingers attaching and strapping the armour securely in place. They worked in swift silence and were soon making their way back to the main hall, Tristan trying to re-accustom himself to the feel of wearing armour as they walked. It felt as if an eternity had passed since he had removed his armour alone in the woods outside Theldar. They found the others ready to depart and Tristan bade them well before moving to leave the keep. He could see doubts and questions in the eyes of the others, so kept moving to prevent them from attempting to alter the plan.

"Toric's speed and blessings to you all," he said as he left and he and the ran-the left the keep to the front courtyard.

He barely heard their farewells, his thoughts focusing inwards as he prepared himself for the struggle ahead and moved to where Galahad awaited him. He was being held by the silent falcon-master Marak they had met on the previous day, who bowed and moved to the gate house on Tristan's arrival. That gave the knight some relief for he had found that there was something unsettling in the man's deep-set eyes, something that Belthar had noted too, and had found his silent presence that night unbearable, even for the few minutes they had been in contact. Yet he had been in the dream too, so nothing was amiss. He turned to mount Galahad and noted Groltch still stood there.

"Why do you wait?" he asked quietly.

"To say goodbye, and to thank you, my friend," replied the ran-the in his own tongue. "Good luck in your quest."

"And you in yours," he replied, feeling a little unsettled. This had not been part of the dream, though the dream had never really shown much of him leaving the keep but had jumped from the keep to his wait upon the drawbridge. He looked into his friend's eyes and saw that the ran-the knew something of his intentions. A moment's fear crossed over him, before he realised that Groltch was not here to stop him, only bid him farewell.

They bowed to each other formally then turned away, Tristan leaping up onto the horse's back. Tristan looked down and Groltch passed him up a lance with which to ride out with. At its tip fluttered the white pennant of his rank. He turned to thank Groltch, but the ran-the was gone, the tradition of his people being that they should not look back upon each other lest Thenril's luck curse them. As he turned back towards the now rising portcullis and rode out beneath it, the heavens opened up and the rain came pouring down. Tristan ignored it all and he focused his attention forwards, ready to face his moment of choice.

II

As the dawn sun began to emerge from the Great Western Ocean, the city of Theldar began its final preparations for the conflict that was about to erupt around it. Surrounding her upon the land stretched vast numbers of knights, foot soldiers and priests, all awaiting the command to attack. Dotted in amongst them were the powerful war wizards of Sol, newly arrived from the vast fleet presently blocking the entrance to the harbour, known as the Jaws of Death to those of the city. These ships too were prepared, their oars out in readiness, their decks lined with soldiers from both Sol and Caldor and a giant, dark form could be seen swimming beneath them.

Before these ships and lying just beneath the waves were the sunken ships hastily scuttled in a vain attempt to close the harbour off from the encroaching ships, the masts of some still visible above the swirling seas. On the other side of these defences lay harboured seemingly abandoned ships swaying in the tide, though hidden within them were the dark knights of shadow, stood only partially in this realm, yet ready to defend the bay with their lives.

In the city itself, bathed in the red morning light, stood other such knights, intermingled with the ordinary soldiers and warriors, all prepared to fight with the same determination as those on the ships. The sun's rays reflected off the white city walls and all knew that its colour was not merely warning of the weather to come, but also of the blood that the rain would wash away.

The silence of the day was broken by a cheer from the forces outside the city walls and as the defenders looked on, a magnificent sight emerge from the ranks of the besieging army. Astride a magnificent white horse rode forth a knight in glittering armour, his white plume unmistakable to any that saw it. The White Knight had come to lead the attack upon the walls, with the mighty sword of Caldor, Caliburn, at his command, and the will of Toric riding with him. As he drew his mighty sword and raised it high into the air a glow enveloped him as he drew upon the will of Toric, and for the first time that day the defenders knew true fear. Even the Shadow Knights felt the icy claws of panic and terror clutching at their hearts, for whilst the White Knight was only one man, he had never been defeated in war or combat. When one saw him charge onto the battlefield against you, it was to see your own defeat riding inevitably towards you.

The knight called out a prayer to Toric and his mighty steed rose up high onto its hind legs, its front legs pawing the air angrily. As its mighty hooves crashed back to the earth, a mighty ripple flowed across the ground towards the eastern wall. As it struck, the wall groaned and cracked and parts of it crumbled to the ground, its protective spells ineffective against the might of Toric. The defenders found themselves thrown to the floor and at that moment a mighty roar erupted from the attacking troops as they charged across the open ground, bringing their siege engines with them.

Out in the bay the dark form beneath the sea waves sped unerringly towards the sunken ships, a great wave accompanying it. Masts shuddered and disappeared beneath the surface as the great beast tore the ships apart into driftwood. It did not halt there, however, but continued on towards the seemingly abandoned ships, smashing through their hulls as if they were not even there. The knights inside struggled in vain to flee the vicious attacks, yet failed, for those who did not drown were swallowed by its great maw, never to see light again, gaining the dubious honour of being the first casualties of the battle. Behind the creature sailed the fleet of ships, the great swan prow of the central ship marking itself as the king's ship and it was as they entered through the Jaws of Death the battle for the walls began in earnest.

Naithan II, King of Caldor, First Lord of Theldar and Light of Toric had returned to retake his city, and with him came the chaos and fury of battle.

III

A time of beginnings;

Karene was not sure exactly what was going on and that annoyed her. She had ridden up half expecting to find Tristan imprisoned and ready for transport back to Theldar when she had arrived this morning, yet had found it not to be so. It seemed that they were presently harbouring him, claiming not to have known who he was. Worse still, when she had informed them of the truth and of her quest, the servant she had spoken to, a tall man with grey, unsettling eyes, had informed them that she must wait outside until he had contacted the mistress of the castle.

It had been then that she had ordered her troops to surround the castle, knowing full well that most had some type of bolt hole for emergencies, and determined to ensure that this time Tristan would not escape. She had only just finished overseeing this when the man had returned, informing her that Tristan had asked for the Peace of Parlay, effectively acting as if he were still a knight. Unfortunately, until he was stripped of that title by the king, he could still claim rights as a full knight, and the king had never once done so, as far as she knew, so she had to abide by the laws. That meant waiting until he deemed himself ready to come out and talk with her. Of course, she could not spring a trap upon him when he did because the rules of honour said that it was not allowed and, if she were to successfully challenge for the White Plume, then she could allow no such smears of dishonour to stain her claim. So she would have to wait and see what he had planned, and pray he still abided by the codes and laws he was claiming rights under.

"What do you think he plans, Sar?" asked Sir Aaron, her Blue Knight.

"I have no idea," she said, concealing a yawn. The ride that night had been tiring for them all. "Just ensure that the knights are alert and ready for any trickery."

"Do you think the White Knight would do that?" he asked, his tired eyes widening with shock.

Karene looked at him quickly and saw a sense of awe in his eyes. Despite everything, all his treachery, all his falseness, Tristan still held the respect of knights akin to that of a legend. It was incredible, and dangerous. She would have to remain doubly wary upon their journey back to Theldar.

"Sar, they open the portcullis," reported a green knight, bringing her attention back to the castle.

She watched in amazement as a fully armed and armoured knight rode out on the back of Tristan's horse. She wondered what ploy this was, then realised with shock that it was actually Tristan in the armour. The hairs on the back of her neck prickled as though she had a premonition of what was coming. It took but a glance at the white pennant flying from his lance to confirm her suspicions. He was going to demand the Rite of Challenge, and there was nothing she could do about it. Already the knights around her were shifting awkwardly, the more intelligent of them realising that they were going to have to joust him this day. She cursed her impatience, and the fact that this would come upon such a hard night of riding. None of her troops would be completely on form today, the tiredness weakening their reactions.

Tristan, on the other hand, looked truly refreshed and awake. She had been on the end of his lance that day when he had defeated all his doubters in one day and, despite his faults, there was no one here that could best him, even on a good day. It was even possible that he could win the Challenge and ride back vindicated of all crimes, making her long hunt a worthless quest with little glory.

"I would speak with you, Sar Karene," said Tristan in a loud, formal voice.

She urged Saracen towards the knight slowly, swallowing back the bitter taste in her mouth. He seemed so calm and serene that she knew he was in full control of this situation. He knew exactly what he was doing and that made her face scowl in an anger she could not disguise. He seemed not to notice, however, galling her even more. As her horse made his way slowly onto the drawbridge, Tristan dismounted his horse and went down into a full bow.

"I assume you mean to take the Rite of Challenge?" she asked, barely keeping the bitterness from her mouth.

"It is my right and duty, Sar" he replied calmly, not looking up at her once. His grasp of honour had not abandoned him here, his actions and movements faultless. "I would see my opponents, if I may. All of my opponents."

She bowed, knowing that she could do little else, especially as the majority of the knights here under her command were watching. She could not be seen to dishonour him in any way, though there were a couple of knights she could still leave on patrol who would not complain of the duty.

She wheeled Saracen to face the knights awaiting the outcome of their words.

"The Knight Errant claims his Rite of Challenge. I shall summon those of us not here to witness the Challenge then he shall be given his time to make peace with Toric, which I suggest you all do yourselves. It shall be done here, under the sky before the eyes of Toric, so that all will know the outcome to be just."

The silence of her knights showed that they all realised the severity of the situation, and the strength and skill of their opponent. More than one had dropped their head in prayer already.

She rode up to join them and sent the orders for her knights to return, which took more than a few minutes to achieve. When they had arrived, she was pleased to see that not all had returned, a few having correctly interpreted her instructions. She looked back at Tristan and smiled to herself.

"You'll not have the day all to yourself," she muttered with satisfaction. If her quest was to be made meaningless then so would his. She would have his companions, if she could not have him.

IV

Galen watched as the battle unfolded in the streets below the palace, unsure exactly what to do. They had attacked sooner than he had expected and he knew that they must have realised he had ways of eavesdropping upon their battle meetings, and planned around it. That meant that the first magical shock wave from the King's Knight had gone un-countered, severely damaging the strength of the outer walls. At the same time, he had felt the deaths of his Shadow Knights on the ships in the harbour and knew that the bay was open to attack. Those he had stationed in the light keeps on the Jaws of Death had also met with a quick end, though one had managed to get through a report that two of the enemy fleet were now in flames. However, that was merely a scratch on the dragon's leg, as the expression went. What made matters worse had been that he had still been in the palace when it occurred, not with the troops where they could see he had not abandoned them. He stopped his thoughts and resumed his walk.

"Are you all right?" asked Marie.

She had stayed close to him ever since their marriage and even now, as they made their way to the battle, she would not leave. He had asked her and pleaded with her to let him go alone, but she had refused. He could see that by her eyes she had decided to die with him this day, and that made him bitter. He had promised himself he would never hurt her again, but he had, so much so that she would not live with it.

"Nothing," he replied softly. "I'm just feeling the city's pain, that's all."

"You shouldn't have done it, you know," she said again. "It drained you too much. Last night you were constantly fading in and out, as if all control had left you. You almost killed yourself!"

"Better that they fight as protected as I can make them, than die without," he said simply, as he had every time she had raised this question.

The hairs on his neck suddenly prickled and the voice in his mind whispered a warning. He stopped suddenly and looked around.

"What is it?" asked Marie worriedly.

"Someone's here," he said looking in every shadow he could see.

The raining, now coming down quite heavily, was doing its best to obscure everything.

"Who?"

"The one I felt before, the one who could enter the Shadow Realm," he replied.

"Truly?"

"Yes, and I think I know what they intend to do," he replied. "I must find them."

"I'll go with you," said Marie quickly.

"No," he snapped back quickly. "You're needed on the battlements. My presence there must be felt, even if I am not there. You will have to be that presence. I'll find you once I've killed this intruder."

"You're sure?" she asked.

"Yes, now go!"

She turned to hurry away then turned back to him, her eyes brimming with tears.

"I love you Galen," she said, her voice thick with emotion.

"I love you too," he replied, pulling her close for a final embrace.

She hugged him back fiercely, then pulled herself away and rushed down the street. They both knew that they would never see each other again in this life, yet he could not dwell upon it. He entered the Shadow Realm and then reached out with all his senses, searching for the tell-tale signs and traces of intrusion upon what he had come to view as his realm. It did not take long, his opponent's trail standing out like a blazing torch in the sky. He made his way swiftly through the streets, constantly searching out his prey, allowing his senses to extend out through the shadow realm, heightening them above the level of even the most proficient hunting hound. After some ten minutes of tracking, he slowed his pace, his instincts telling him something was wrong.

"Run, run away," came the voice again. *"It's you're only way."*

Never! He thought back angrily, though the rising hairs on his neck told him he was not alone.

"You never fool with the man of a Kolthon woman," said a familiar voice. "Have you never heard that before?"

He turned round and saw Meredith stood there, partially in shadow, her use of the shadow powers being what had warned him of her presence. Around her were stood others from the Dark Circle, all of whom had accepted his gift the night before.

"He was going to betray me," said Galen, slowly reaching for his sword.

"Kill her, kill her now," screamed the voice in his head angrily.

"So was I, so why should you worry about it? I did what was

necessary to survive. As did you," she began, "and I know that you *forgave* him his crimes. However, you used me against him, turning him away from him. You allowed him to be humiliated and degraded in front of the entire city and used his own love of the city against him. For that I seek vengeance. I'll see you hang."

Her words confused him, for she had been one of the reasons that Tyrone had survived, though he did not have time to think on it for as she spoke a dagger flashed from her hands at him. It passed straight through him and her eyes widened in shock.

"You thought that because you were of part shadow you could harm me, did you?" he asked with a mocking smile.

He moved closer to her and grabbed her wrist, draining the shadow power from her. She screamed in pain and her eyes rolled as she slipped into unconsciousness. Her power removed, she faded back into the real world. He turned to face the other members of the so-called Dark Circle that had ambushed him.

"Anyone one else like to try that?" he asked with a sneer. As one his assailants winked out of existence.

"Yes, I would," came a voice from his right, and with it came the boom of someone unskilled entering the shadow realm.

He spun to face his opponent, whose form was almost completely cloaked in shadow even though it stood in the middle of the street.

"Flee," screamed the voice in his mind. *"This one can harm you!"*

Fear crept down his spine but he drew his sword and dropped into a defensive stance. It took but one look at his opponent's stance to realise he was out matched. For the first time in his brief rule of Theldar he regretted not keeping a personal guard at his side at all times.

"If you give in, I'll let you live," said the shadowy form, softly.

"Never!" he cried angrily, leaping to attack.

"That's a shame," said the other figure, parrying his thrust with ease.

Galen pressed his attack, fighting with the ferocity of a cornered beast and actually forced his opponent to give ground. Unfortunately that did not mean he once broke through his opponent's defensive sword patterns. Galen snarled angrily, his world now revolving about the here and now. This fight was all that mattered. His opponent changed his defensive spin to one of attack and Galen's energies were transferred to putting up any defence he could. Somehow he managed to fend off all the blows and even managed to turn once more to the attack.

Suddenly an image formed in his mind and he knew the opening in his opponent's attack, the flaw that would bring him victory. He continued his savage attack, forcing them to give ground once more and waited until the hole in his attacker's defences appeared. As it did he lashed out like a viper, his blade slicing straight through the gap and into his stomach. Yet the blade moved through it is if it were air. Galen pulled his sword back in shock and he heard his opponent laugh.

"To kill one so completely enwrapped Shadow you need a weapon of magic," said the figure, his voice taking on a distinctly feminine cast.

"Tis true, tis true!" gasped the voice. *"Escape, flee…"*

"Fortunately, I'm so blessed with such a blade," continued the figure, her gleaming blade lashing out suddenly.

Galen lifted his blade up in defence and felt it shatter under the blade of the now glowing sword. A chip fell from his attacker's sword, but the rest remained intact as it sliced through his neck. For a brief moment he had the strange sensation of falling as the world spun around him.

"Flee!" came the voice in his mind and with it darkness…

V

A time of endings.

Groltch watched with sadness as Tris rode out of the keep. He had felt his friend's unhappiness and knew that what he was doing was to aid them in their escape. He hoped he would have the chance to repay the favour, though doubted it. Tris had certainly never expected to see him again, his eyes had revealed that all too clearly.

He waited until the portcullis was lowered behind the knight then turned back to the central tower of the castle. He found himself almost bumping straight into the strange human male, Marak. There was something about the man that was somewhat unsettling, though Groltch had decided not to raise his doubts to the others. They would have merely thought him worrying over nothing.

"Let us go," said the man in fluent ran-tha.

Groltch's eyes widened in shock. He pulled out his medallion and checked his reflection in its polished back, yet found his disguise still functioning. They had all thought it best they keep up his disguise here, and he had thought that only Erin had known. Evidently she was a little too free with her tongue. In ancient times she would have been punished for such, though today such punishment was merely used as a threat to frighten naughty younglings.

"As you wish," he replied quickly.

"I'm to show you to the tunnel, and I speak your tongue for there are some here who would report our words. This way we are safe," replied the man in what had to have been the longest number of words Groltch had ever heard the man string together.

"Good," he replied. "Is it far?"

"No," replied the tall man, disappearing suddenly behind a tapestry hanging from the wall.

Groltch followed and found a dark doorway beyond. He could not hear the quiet man's footsteps so followed behind quickly, almost running straight into him once more. He cursed and paused for a moment to let his eyes adjust to the dark. He was startled to find that they did not adjust, and the corridor remained inky black.

"This tunnel is spelled so that only those who have travelled them can navigate them safely. Place you hand on my back and stay with me if you wish to survive the trip."

Groltch shuddered and stayed close to Marak as they continued to move through the passage. It seemed to run between two walls and continued on for around twenty paces.

"Stairs," warned Marak quietly.

Groltch felt the floor drop away beneath his foot. He lowered it slowly and found a step that marked the top of a spiralling stairwell. He made his way gingerly down it and, after what seemed like an eternity, finally reached the bottom. They proceeded to walk for what seemed like an age, and every so often Marak took a left or a right without warning. From the slight change in air pressure he felt as they moved, Groltch guessed that they were currently navigating a maze of passages under the keep.

Eventually the stone floor gradually gave way to earth and the darkness was suddenly broken by light from the ceiling. Groltch had never been so happy to see such a sight in his life. He looked back down the corridor what little he could see of it confirmed his suspicions. It appeared to have numerous passages leading off from it.

"It looks like it was safe to leave," said the man ahead of him, disturbing his thoughts. "Good. You can track?"

"Yes," said Groltch quickly.

"They will have headed north down an old game trail just by the exit. Go and meet up with them. They have your horse there. I'll return to signal Tristan to flee, and Toric's speed to you all."

"Thank you," said Groltch quickly, but Marak was already walking back down the tunnel.

As the human entered the ensorcelled part of the corridor he seemed to suddenly vanish. Groltch shuddered and turned back to the light. He made his way slowly towards the it and found it was a small hole in the ceiling that was barely large enough for him to squeeze through. He wondered how they had ever managed to get the horses through it, then realised that the tunnel ended in thick scrub that could probably be shifted to allow access to larger animals. It was a very dangerous hole to have for a fortress and Groltch found himself wondering just how long this would remain undetected in a war.

"I told you I saw people riding this way," said a voice beyond the brush. "These tracks are less than an hour old!"

"Let's trace them then," said another as a horse whinnied.

Groltch steadied his breathing before he pulled himself silently up out through the hole, praying that all the humans were down the bank by the tunnel's main entrance. He blinked away the water from the rain that had now turned into somewhat of a downpour, and crawled on his stomach towards where he had heard the voices. He found himself looking down a rocky escarpment that seemed to drop straight down into a bush. The two knights he had heard where stood looking intently and the bush in front of the tunnel entrance.

"They seem to come from this rock face," said the first one.

He was taller than the second and had a long growth of red hair under his nose that Tristan had once told him was called a moustache. One had dismounted from his horse to read the tracks while the other remained on horseback.

"Don't worry where they came from yet, just where they're going," said the mounted knight. "If we can catch those he travelled with then we are likely to get promotions."

The other nodded his assent and moved to mount his horse. Groltch knew that he had to act fast. He drew the sword from his side and judged the distance between him and the mounted knight. He then took a deep breath and rose silently to his feet. They did not see him and so he sprang at the knight on the horse with his sword raised high. It was a desperate gamble, he knew, but it was all he had. He grunted in pain as he crashed against the human's metal armour but was surprised to feel the weight shift beneath him and found himself falling off the horse with the knight.

They crashed heavily to the muddy ground and he felt the body beneath him go limp, though he allowed no time to consider it. He rolled to his feet, sword at the ready and found the other knight moving to attack him. The human came at him with a classic opening attack that Groltch parried with ease, bringing his sword around swiftly under the swing for a counter attack. Both he and the knight were surprised at the speed his strike went and his blade sliced through the armour on the man's chest.

Unfortunately the knight recovered from his shock before Groltch and brought round a swift double-sided attack, forcing Groltch to put up a desperate series of parries. The speed of his blade saved him and he was able to draw back a little to assess the situation. The man before him was a good and canny fighter and not one to take lightly, but he seemed to attack without thought of defence, and defend without thought of attack, only taking opportunities as they arose. This could help Groltch plan his attack. A good feint could draw his opponent into making an ill-considered attack.

A groan from behind him informed him that the other knight had merely been winded and would soon be back on his feet. He had to move fast. He unleashed a blistering series of attacks, startling his opponent and forcing him to give ground a little. Then Groltch acted as if he had grown over confident, over reaching himself in his final two spinning attacks. The knight took the bait and stepped in to take advantage of the hole Groltch had left. He reversed his final attack quickly into a strong parry, forcing the knight's sword low as he did, leaving his entire torso open to attack. Groltch wasted no time and brought his sword up against the knight's neck. Sparks flew as his sword cut through the chain mail protection and blood began spurting from the wound. He cried out in pain, dropping his sword as his hands went to his throat.

Knowing the human was now no threat he spun and leapt at the other knight, who was now pulling himself to his feet. There was no contest in this fight, Groltch's quick reactions soon bringing about the knight's death. He then took time to look around, but could see no one else, so cleaned the blood of the now dull, but well-balanced blade and returned it to its scabbard. He looked down and ensured the magical scarf he wore concealed the blood he had shed then made his way along the tracks towards the others. As he did he reached out to Tris with the medallion and knew that the combat was almost upon him, for the fire of fear and tension were there, though riding over all such emotions was a serene calm that startled him. The few other times Groltch had reached out with the medallion's powers he had received only feelings of confusion and turmoil.

He offered a prayer to Toric to watch over his friend and added another for himself asking that their paths could cross again sometime. He then turned his thoughts to the future. His time fleeing through Caldor was over and when next he walked these lands it would be with an army rushing forth to aid his people against this kingdom's armies.

VI

Gareth watched the battle sat astride Peggy, angry that his forces were still having such difficulties. He had gone against his sister's plan to wait until she contacted him, knowing that Naithan would attack with his ships at once and that he would doubtless lead the attack into the city. He had argued against it, but his brother had been adamant. He had to be seen fighting with his troops, as had the kings of ancient times, putting himself in risk as he did. Gareth was determined to reach at least as far as the palace before Naithan, so that at least that was free for the king to walk through safely. Yet the attack had not gone well, after the initial show of attack by the King's Knight.

That attack had caught the defenders unprepared but all of the other spells the Solmen war wizards had used were countered to some extent by the defenders. This meant that they had to rely upon the more awkward and less effective siege engines. Unfortunately the walls now seemed lined with black knights, all of who seemed indestructible and who had cut down his knights like corn in the autumn. He had then been forced to concede his troops the use of magic, for there was no other way to harm them. Helena had left this morning with the magical sword with the aim of ridding them of this problem and if she failed it seemed that there would no way to breach the walls as long as the Shadow Knights defended them.

"Sir, the gate, it has opened," came a report from one of his front commanders.

A trap? He asked in reply.

"No, tis held by priests, Sir," came the reply.

As he finished his report commanders fighting near the other gates reported similar incidents occurring at the other gates.

Use them then, he ordered.

Now was time for him to act. He commanded his relief troops to charge in to attack. He decided that he would join the attack, the need to do something taking over his need to command. Some part of him knew that it was foolish, but his troops had to see him in the battle, just as they had to see Naithan fight. He was the commander of the armies and he had to prove that he could and would fight. He dismounted Peggy and joined his troops, knowing that the city streets were not the best place for cavalry attacks.

His forces surged forward and he made his way towards the east gate. As he arrived he found that many had already moved into the city beyond and others had begun attempting to secure the walls. Most were dying at the hands of the shadow warriors. He nodded his thanks to the robed priests still stood guard in the doorway and charged through, coming face to face with his first dark knight of the day. He brought his sword round and brought it through in a swift attack. The man before him was unskilled in warfare and it was only his partial transparency that saved him from the killing blow. Even so he shuddered as if in pain and stepped back.

Suddenly a great scream erupted from the man before him and countless others around the city, the sound briefly drowning out those of combat. It was one of incredible pain, as if a great beast had been mortally wounded, and immediately after that the man before him sagged slightly, his body becoming fully solid. Gareth smiled and brought his sword round swiftly, ending the man's life in one blow. Helena had done her work well. He now knew the battle could be won and pressed on into the city.

The fighting extended only part of the way into the city's streets, the defenders not having time to work their way back to the second defensive walls and Gareth knew the end would now be swift, for the Theldarians were effectively surrounded, or would be soon. However, that did not mean there would not be others in the palace. He drew off several companies from the fighting and commanded them to follow him. It was a strange experience running through the city that had once been his home constantly looking round for any that might harm him and he knew that Theldar would never be the same again. He pushed away the sadness he felt at that and focused on his task.

They raced through the streets facing little resistance until they reached the palace where a small group of Theldarians had gathered together in a last ditch attempt to defend themselves. The fighting here was brief, quick and vicious and he lost too many of his men securing the palace and all its grounds, losses he knew he would come to regret. The number of casualties in this campaign were far in advance of those suffered in the Goblin War and it would take some time to recover the numbers required to attack Kolth, but that was a matter for later. He made his way through the corridors with his guards, but found the inner sanctums here abandoned, though sounds of combat behind him told him that this was not so throughout the palace. A shadowy form broke away from the wall and he and his knights turned as one to face the threat.

"Relax," said a familiar, indistinguishable voice. "I merely bring a gift for you to deliver to the king who fast approaches the palace."

"What?" he asked, keeping the recognition from his voice. Some of the knights with him were of Helena's forces, though none seemed to recognise her. She was truly adept at her profession.

She handed him a sack and Naithan's crown.

"One is for the head of our king, the other is the head of the would-be king," she said quickly.

He took them from her and turned back down the corridor. He knew by now that it was pointless to offer thanks for she would have vanished before the words had left his mouth. He marched down towards the throne room, knowing that it would be the first place his brother would head for on reaching the palace. He smiled grimly. Despite all the initial problems, the day was going well, and it was still not long past dawn.

VII

The birth of a new day;

Erin waited impatiently for Groltch and Tristan to arrive, trying to shelter from the pouring rain. She had decided it best to leave for the tunnel at once, so as to move as soon as the knights had been recalled and get their horses out into the open. That had been the most difficult part of the plan, for that had involved opening the large exit to leave by, and that was not easily opened. It had taken their combined strength and Matt's magic to force the boulder covering the exit aside and none had been able to roll it back, despite their efforts.

It had been Belthar who had thought of the best way to conceal it and he had used his druid's magic to cover the gap with thick scrub and brush. She had stood gaping in amazement as the plants had suddenly sprung up from the ground and meshed themselves across the dark opening in the escarpment. Belthar had explained that all areas of ground had seed just waiting for the opportunity to grow and he had just provided them with such a moment.

"What's keeping Groltch?" asked Matt irritably for what had to be the fifth time.

"Be quiet, will yer," grunted Belthar in annoyance. "He had t'make his farewells, you know that."

"Why?" asked Erin. "Tristan will be back soon."

"That's true lass," said the big man softly, "but all plans are but a house of cards yer know, it takes but a single breath to destroy it. For Groltch's kind, leaving without bidding farewell is to bring bad luck down on both parties involved."

"Oh, I see," she replied, not really understanding.

It seemed there was a lot in this world she did not know or understand, but she would in time. She felt free for the first time in her life, all burdens and responsibilities lifted from her shoulders. She was going to finally experience life as she never had before and the thought excited her, though it frightened her a little too.

She placed her hands in her pouches and was surprised to find a metal bracelet in one. She removed it and looked at it closely. It was a beautiful thing made of gold and silver weaved to make a complex, enthralling pattern that caught the light and made it sparkle. Etched along its many ribbons of metal were ancient looking, illegible runes that seemed to almost pulse with light as she looked at them. She gazed at it admiringly, wondering where it could have possibly come from. She knew that she certainly did not own an item such as this and she had never seen it among her mother's collection of jewellery. Even if she had, she would have never placed it in a pocket of her travel clothing, for it was too precious a thing for that. She was reminded of Marak's visit the previous night and suddenly she knew the only possible source for the bracelet. His kind probably used letters different from hers and he would certainly wish to give her a gift to remember him by. She smiled at his gesture and slipped it on round her wrist. The fit was perfect and it suddenly felt as if it were meant to be.

"There you are," came Matt's voice, disturbing her thoughts. "What kept you?"

"Some knights didn't go fight Tris," replied Groltch quickly. "Others probably around. We must move now."

"But what about Tristan?" asked Erin in alarm.

"He not coming. He know that if he stay with us, they follow us forever. It best he stay, lead them away. We not see him again," replied the goblin, its voice sounding thick with emotion.

"Come on then, let's go," said Belthar, turning to mount the horse, seeming a little unsure of himself. Matt seemed uncomfortable mounting his horse too.

"You mean, that's it? We'll just leave him?" asked Erin, outrage sounding in her voice.

"Of course, if yer want his sacrifice t'be in vain," replied Belthar irritably.

"Sacrifice? You mean he'll die?"

"No, tis unlikely lass," replied Belthar with more softness. "They've had the chance to do that before. They'll not kill 'im, but it will be as good as though. He'll lose his freedom. That's his sacrifice."

"Oh," said Erin, a little mollified by the thought.

Still, nothing was quite going as planned. The rain was coming down heavily and she was already soaked through. The knights had not all gone to watch the Challenge and some had waited to catch them, against all precepts of honour. Tristan would not be joining them, allowing them to capture him so that they could go free, though that was more in keeping with noble precepts. In fact, she reasoned, it was even possible he could win the Challenge and return with only a visit to the chambers as his punishment. He was, of course, known for being unbeaten in combat.

No, things were not as bad as all that, and she was now on a true adventure, seeing the world for the first time. She began her ride down the trail with a light heart. Her new life was beginning.

VIII

As their ship approached the dock Matthew prepared himself for the battle, the sword at his side feeling strange and uncomfortable after so many years without the need to wear one. Yet today it could stand as the only thing that kept them alive. Naithan's mad decision to stand in the thick of the battle could spell the end for them both. It only took one of them to die for the other to follow on rapidly so they could not separate for they needed to watch over each other.

This was especially true with these Shadow Knights running around. The king's Spymaster seemed confident that he could neutralise the threat, but Matthew was not leaving anything to chance. Magic would be the only way to stop them and he would have to use it sparingly. For the first time in many weeks he was entering a dangerous situation without

Jalim's link. He had contacted Belthanor the previous day, to learn that the boy was recovering from some violent unknown seizure. Matthew could have told them the cause, but knew that all Jalim needed was rest, and did not wish to reveal the truth about his apprentice's powers to anyone. That meant he was left with his own not inconsiderable powers to defend them with.

Priestly magic was best used for such creatures as these knights, for their power lay in the spirit, and fortunately, the many times he had found use for such magic since the goblin's assassination attempt had meant he had grown quite considerably in its power. He hoped he had grown enough though…

"Are you ready?" asked Naithan, disturbing his thoughts.

"Of course," he replied with a smile, covering the sudden fearful trembling that had begun in his stomach.

He had never been in a battle such as this before and was not sure how he would react. He wished he could be as calm as Naithan seemed to be, but such strength just would not come to him. He reached for the calm he would need to cast magic and prepared himself for the first spell. He unleashed it as they began scrambling from the deck of the ship and then the fury of battle washed over him.

Afterwards he was never able to fully recall the events of the day with any real clarity, unlike many others he spoke with afterwards. He could recall the smells and constant noise, the clash of steel and the feel of flesh and blood as his sword sliced through his enemies. He could recall unleashing spell after spell, often mingling it with his swordplay in a way that later left the surviving wizardly viziers in awe of him. He could remember the Shadow Knights as well, with their unsettling gazes and their vicious attacks, and the relief he felt when at last they all became mortal once more.

He had no recollection of reaching the palace, or the rain that had poured from the skies, only of awakening on his bed, his valet Eward waiting on him with food and water. Only then had he realised that for the first time the two magicks had blended so perfectly that they had worked almost as one. For a brief while he lay there, remembering the pleasure it had given him and he knew that he had used magic almost as the elves themselves used it. He was truly going to be the Merlin. All that he needed was the remaining two pieces of the Sceptre of Prophecy.

IX

The death of a dark night.

Tristan remained in silent prayer on the drawbridge, ignoring the rainwater trickling down his face and steeling himself for the events ahead. He hoped that Groltch survived the attack of the knights, one part of the dream that had never been clear, leaving him with only the vague impression that the sword would tip the balance, which way he did not know, but he wished Toric's speed in his journey. Yet here and now, Tristan could not worry about such things. He needed to be focused, prepared and ready to fight well. This would be his greatest challenge so far, and he would need every resource at his disposal. He had seen that the other knights were tired and that would work in his favour though it would not be long before he too began to tire whilst those awaiting the next bout would be slowly recovering their strength.

His mental count reminded him that his time for prayer was fast departing so concluded his meditation and brought his sword to his lips. He kissed its blade, dedicating the fight to Toric and rose slowly to his feet, taking one last look at his blade. Caliburn had never looked so magnificent, its blade shining with an almost magical glow that seemed to push aside the rain's attack, leaving it clean and ready. He mounted his horse, leaving his lance on the drawbridge, its pennant hanging limply over the moat. He had never intended to use it, for today he would only need his sword. As he settled himself in his saddle and the first of his challengers rode out to the tourney ground to face him, the portcullis behind him began to rise slowly. That was his sign, he knew. The others had reached safety and he was signalled to follow them. He had made his decision though. He raised his sword high into the air and coaxed Galahad into rearing onto his hind legs.

Let them see the White Knight in full glory, he thought sadly, then unleashed the spell.

X

Naithan could not understand why his friend remained so calm with the battle looming before them as their ship moved to dock in Theldar. Neither of them had ever seen true combat, especially not of this kind, yet Matthew stood next to him, serenely surveying the scene, as if it were just another ordinary day. Naithan had to admire him his courage, for he was now already beginning to regret his decision to lead the troops into Theldar. Yet he could not back down now, for he had made such an issue over it in their final meeting. Both Matthew and Gareth had tried to change his mind, Gareth in particular and Naithan had found himself stubbornly digging his heels in on the subject. This had been fuelled by a slight, nagging suspicion that, despite how often he dismissed it as a ridiculous idea, kept returning to his mind to haunt him. Gareth had consistently insisted that he be the first to the palace, ostensibly to ensure there were no assassins lurking nearby.

However Naithan's thoughts kept constantly straying towards the fact that the palace was where the crown and throne were and that meant that was where the sovereignty of the kingdom was. It was a stupid, almost paranoid thought, but whispered words in the back of his mind kept reminding him of the fact that someone had been tampering with the knights' Treatment. This someone had been eroding their loyalty to the point that his King's Knight had fled his presence and others now fought his troops in defence of this pathetic rebellion. This kind of tampering could only have originated from a Council member, and who was best placed to do this than his brother.

Even if, as was most likely, Gareth had no part in it, and entertained no thoughts for the throne, it did not rule out the possibility that Thenril whispered in his ears. It would be a great temptation to some and not all were blessed with his own strength to resist it, unless these worrying thoughts themselves were being placed by the One Eyed Wolf to sow dissent between him and his brother...

He pushed the thoughts away angrily. Following such lines of thought would only feed the feelings of worry, leading into a downward spiral of paranoia, something Naithan could not afford to do, especially today. Of course if Gareth had truly wanted to take the throne he would have done so earlier, or been the first to agree to Naithan's plan to lead the sea-borne troops into combat, hoping that he would die in the fight...

"Stop it," he muttered to himself as the ship began to moor along one of the few piers not destroyed by the retreating Theldarians. He thought he saw Matthew start at his words and feared he had been overheard, so spoke quickly to cover himself. "Are you ready?"

"Yes, just about," replied the wizard, his cool demeanour slipping slightly as he spoke. At least he felt nervous too.

"Attack!" he commanded those nearest, despite the fact that most had already begun fighting.

This was due to the fact that those on the docks had begun attacking and those of his warriors closest to the gangplank were rapidly engaged in a vicious melee, thus beginning his first battle rather ingloriously. He was not able to lead the troops from the ship and found himself constantly surrounded by his knights, even when he finally made it to the shore. The few that ever broke through the barrier would then explode in flame, or collapse with Matthew's blade in them and for fully half the conflict Naithan's blade did not shed a single drop of blood. In a way he felt glad, for the noise, confusion and smell of blood seemed to muddle his senses, making the whole thing seem somewhat distant, a feeling reinforced by the ringing of blood in his ears.

When one Theldarian did finally reach close enough to fight him he found himself so confused that his first combat was almost his last. It was made worse by the fact that the rain had made the footing slippery and he had stumbled twice trying to evade the man's blows. Yet on the second slip he was prepared for the knight's attempt to use it to his advantage and lashed out viciously as he stepped in close. Naithan felt a rush of energy flow through him as his opponent fell to the ground, the adrenaline of blood lust filling him and others who managed to stray within his reach found him a much more responsive and dangerous opponent.

However, despite the clarity of thought that came with the energy, his later recollections of the events became hazier from this point onwards. He could not recall how many he was forced to slay in order to reach his palace, or when it was exactly that Matthew strayed from his side, and could only remember entering the palace as if viewing the incident from another man's memory.

Once in the palace, though, his thoughts clarified once more and he was filled with an urgency to reach his throne room. He knew that Gareth's troops had already entered and that his brother would not be far behind them and he felt an irrational need to get to his throne first. He sent out knights to check and clear the corridors they passed through, leaving only a few to guard him. As he did he realised that Matthew was no longer there and that made him only more worried, though his rational mind screamed at him he had nothing to fear. The journey to the great chamber seemed to take an eternity and with every step his worry increased, and he found himself searching the shadows for hidden assassins. Even when he entered the empty room and made for the throne he did not feel safe.

Suddenly the great entrance doors swung open and Naithan saw his brother marching towards him. In one hand he held a sack, in the other, he held the crown of Caldor. Fear stabbed Naithan momentarily until Gareth dropped dutifully to one knee before him, offering the crown up before him.

"I return you your crown and city, my lord," he said quickly, "though I wish it were in a better state than you find it."

Naithan was not sure if his brother meant the city or the crown, for both seemed a little more worn and dirty since he had last seen them.

"I thank you brother," he replied, taking the crown and placing it upon his head. He moved over to the throne and took his seat. "What other gift do you bring me?"

"The head of a traitor," said Gareth, reaching into the sack.

He pulled out a human head from the sack, holding it by its hair. Naithan was pleased to see the vacant stare of the man once known as Galen Faithe. He smiled. The Shadow was no more, banished back to the nether regions of the dark realm.

XI

With the sun comes the hope for a fresh start;

Karene watched Tristan going through the rituals of prayer with gritted teeth. She knew he would have it timed to the very second, never once breaching the etiquette of the Challenge, forcing her to abide by the rules as strictly as him. She also knew that he only did it to gain more time for that goblin to escape, as if its life was of worth. It was disgusting and pitiful to see and she just hoped her guards would capture the foul creature, making all his preparations and stalling as worthless as he was making her quest for him. Even a defeated knight in the Challenge had to be treated with respect due one brave enough to face his pursuers in such a way, meaning the journey back would be tiresome and her quest almost fruitless.

If Tristan did decide to return voluntarily, she doubted they would strip the white plume from him either. They would cover over the story, making it out to be some great quest or service he had been giving to the king. They would not want to go through a public stripping of the *repentant* knight, especially with the King's city in revolt. It made her sick to think about it. She could only hope that a person who had run away once would do so again, and then the white plumes would be hers. She would see her ambition realised, though Tristan's present actions meant it would probably take longer than she hoped.

At long last he mounted his horse and turned to face them. He raised his sword high into the air and as he did the portcullis behind him began to rise up. Suddenly his plan became clear. He was going to flee, again. There was truly no honour in the man. He was going to flee whilst in the midst of the Challenge, the most cowardly thing a knight could do.

"Treachery," she cried out. "Ward your eyes from light then prepare to follow. He seeks to flee with his companions."

There were murmurs of protests from some of the knights there, but there were those who had been with her from the start and all recognised the tactic he was about to employ. She hastily raised a spell to defend her eyes and the barrier flew up just in time. Judging from the screams sounding around her, not all her company had been quite so quick to react. At least it proved her point, for to use magic in the Challenge, even that of a magic sword, was considered in breach of the rite and cheating. She had him where she wanted him. The white plumes would truly be hers.

The light faded and she was pleased to see her knights racing towards the castle entrance. What shocked her, though, was the fact that Tristan was not fleeing them, but charging headlong towards them…

XII

A deathly silence dropped over the great city of Caldor. The battle was over, the Theldarians having given in almost as soon as they had been surrounded. The king's armies had won, though the cost had been high. The streets were filled with the blood of the dead, now being washed away by the tears of the heavens, as if they too wept for the death of the city. Its fabulous walls had been destroyed and breached in four sections, some of the damage stretching some two hundred feet in length.

In the streets themselves, the defenders were being herded together by the victorious knights, all facing Treatment at the very least, others expecting that they would be made an example of and prepared for death. Already word had reached them that the Lord Protector, Galen Faithe, was dead and that his head now adorned the palace walls. Many of the prisoners doubted that they would escape a similar fate, but most did not care, for hope was dead.

Yet in small areas of the city resistance continued and some of the newly captured prisoners were released by small warrior bands, disappearing into the complex sewer system beneath the streets. Some of those who witnessed the events claimed that some Shadow Knights survived with their powers intact and that they had been led by the Shadow himself. Others discredited that claim, however, claiming that the troops had been led by a woman, the Lady of Shadow, but whatever the truth was did not matter. Their presence brought hope to the vanquished citizens, particularly those who had believed most fervently in the changes they had wrought.

Naithan II of the House Tara'non had reclaimed his city, but he had not reclaimed its heart and already, hidden in the shadows of the morning rain, plots were being laid against him.

XIII

Fear of a bitter demise

Tristan raced towards the oncoming knights, crying out the ancient Tu'ran-tha battle cry as he did, his glittering sword outstretched before him. The knights seemed startled by his actions and he used it to his best advantage, taking down three knights almost at once, one screaming as his armour dragged him to the bottom of the moat.

He paid it no heed though, spurring on towards the next group of knights that were before him. He knew he had the advantage, for they had been prepared for single, one on one combat, whereas he had planned to fight like this already. He used Galahad's speed and strength to confuse and disorient his attackers, forcing more than one to almost blunder into one another in their attempts to get near him. It would not last long, of course, for their training would soon kick in and they would begin attacking together as a unit, but he made the most of the chaos he had created though, killing three more knights before they finally broke off and reformed.

"We must capture him alive!" Came the commanding voice of Karene, but Tristan knew that many were no longer listening, the blood lust now ringing in their ears.

Yet some evidently did listen for he suddenly felt a surge of power from them and spells lashed out at him. He raised the sword in his hand and energy lashed out at the binding spells, carrying with them lethal stings for their casters. He heard their screams and felt little joy in the fact that only two had managed to shield themselves. One had been Sar Karene.

He wheeled to face those using more mundane methods of attack and fought them once more. This time they were prepared and his strikes were fended off by the tightly formed units, so Tristan lashed out with magic instead. Lightening crackled from his sword and struck their horses, causing them to buck and convulse. It would not kill them, but only a few of the best riders were able to retain control of their mounts.

Pain seared across his left arm and he felt his shield splinter. He spun round to face another knight and slashed out with his sword. It struck the heavy metal chest plate and sparks flew. He felt the sword shudder slightly in his hand and shards fell from its blade.

"See, even the sword's blessing is deserting you," said the knight with a vicious smile.

"Not before I finish with you though," replied Tristan with a snarl. All was going as he had foreseen.

He reversed his swing and found a less protected area. The man screamed and fell to the floor, but not before he had grabbed Tristan and brought him to the ground with him. Tristan sent out a quick mental command to Galahad with magic and the horse reared up, bringing his hooves down upon the knight's head. Tristan scrambled to his feet, wiping the mud from his helm, and moved to his horse. They regarded each other for a moment.

"Go now," he said softly. "Your place is not here. Find the freedom I can never have."

For a moment it seemed as if the horse understood every word, before he snorted angrily and raced away from the fight. As he did so, Tristan sent out a burst of magic, forcing the bridle and saddle to fall away. Tristan did not have time to watch him go for he found the other knights bearing down upon him, their horses now giving them a dangerous advantage. Two moved in close and he sprang to attack, his sword striking home twice, startling his attackers. One fell heavily from his horse, his head smashing into a large stone. The other fell clutching a stomach wound that would take its time killing him.

Tristan then moved back to the moat, keeping the water to his back, negating the advantage of their horses. They intended to take him alive and could not safely knock him into the water with the heavy armour he presently wore. His opponents slowed their pace, discussing their options before dismounting. They fanned out to surround him, holding their weapons in such a way that suggested they would attempt to use the flats of their blades, despite their growing desire to harm him. Karene certainly had a strong command to keep such angry men in check like that.

He waited their attack and when their blades leapt for him, fought like a man possessed. Sparks flew from his blade as he deflected their attacks again and again, often dropping through their defences to inflict wounds upon them. Suddenly he saw a sword arcing towards his head, the flat of its blade looming in his vision.

With a speed he did not think possible Tristan managed to reverse the swing of his blade to deflect the blow. It was barely enough, but as his sword struck that of his opponent, there was a flash of light and the sound of splintering metal. His sword, the mighty Caliburn, shattered into a thousand pieces around him. Slivers of metal lacerated his face and blood began running down his cheeks. Before him the fight ceased as the other knights stood staring at him in shock. All knew of the mighty Caliburn, and that he wielded it and none could believe what they saw. He threw the now useless hilt behind him and their eyes followed it into the water. He used the distraction to draw the dagger that he had taken from the armoury.

"Give up Tristan," came Karene's voice, sounding a little shaken.

"Never," he roared in reply, slicing the dagger across the face of one of his opponents.

The man roared in anger, instinctively lashing out with his sword, slicing Tristan across the neck in his haste. Tristan felt the pain course through him and the world spun as he collapsed to the floor. He closed his eyes and breathed deep, waiting the moment of his choice. Rainwater poured down his face and as the blackness closed in he realised it was not coming. Around him he was aware of the frantic efforts of the knights trying to save him, yet none of it mattered. It all seemed somehow distant and unreal. All that mattered was that the moment of choice was about to arrive.

The world started to fade out completely. He felt his life start to slip away and he realised with a chill that the choice was not coming. The creatures in the grove had lied to him. He tried to cry out in despair, yet could only manage a gurgle. As the darkness closed in around him, the last words he heard where those of Karene, now raised in horror and anger.

"You idiots! You've killed him…"

EPILOGUE: Demons and Devils

Kaneril bitterly withdraw its presence from the human castle, the events there having taken a surprising and horrifying turn. It had not expected the knight's ferocious attack or his subsequent defeat. It could see no reason for it all, but the knight had ensured that Kaneril would die in this light forsaken prison, eternally trapped until it finally faded away. The energy it had consumed from the last of Kaneril's stock would last it a few years, maybe longer, but it would all be to no avail. Hundreds of years of manipulation had been wasted. The despair it felt was draining away any last vestige of rage it had felt. It was resigned to its fate. The mortals had finally won. It had used the sceptre once to create a spell of protection round it so powerful that almost none could harm it. The prophecy had been that only a weapon not forged of humanoid hand could harm it, and they had found a way to do just that. Starvation was their weapon, and they had used it well.

Kaneril allowed itself to drift out to those it felt had betrayed its chance, the ran-the, druid and wizard. They were presently riding out across the border to the human Empire of Kolth, if it could truly be called an empire. The druid and the wizard seemed uncomfortable in their saddles, but the ran-the and the accursed girl seemed fine. For a fickle moment it felt the need to lash out at her, using its powers to make her horse buck and throw her. Suddenly that seemed a good idea. It moved its presence closer, reaching out with its powers to brush the horse's mind. A good scare is what it needed…

Kaneril stopped, a familiar spellprint reaching its senses. It looked closely at the girl. On her wrist was the bracelet his servant had mistakenly given her. It was impossible that she could be wearing it, for part of its prophecy had been that only one of pure heart would be able to wear it, yet she did. Could its servant have been correct?

Kaneril withdrew itself from the scene to think on it. Only the one able to fulfil the prophecy on the shield presently keeping it imprisoned should be able to wear it, so was it possible it had been incorrect? Kaneril had made mistakes before, especially when concerning these unpredictable humans. Could it be that all was not lost?

It smiled to itself as hope rose once more into its thoughts. Such a strangely human emotion, yet Kaneril could see how mortals lived such brief lives with feelings such as this constantly urging that things could still get better. It was strange. All Kaneril's planning had been casually brushed away by the death of one mortal, only to be restored by the mistake of another. Kaneril found itself laughing at the irony of it all.

At this moment it could see why some humans believed devotedly in *fate* and why they would often call it a fickle thing. It slowly returned its form back towards the group, watching them intently, determined not to waste any of its precious energies. Even the king would have to be granted some peaceful nights without dreams from now on. Its saviour was coming and it intended to allow this *fate* no idle chance for irony by allowing Kaneril to perish when so close to freedom; a freedom with which it would punish the mortals for imprisoning it.

For the first time ever in its pitiful existence, mankind would be united under one ruler. They would live prepared, structured lives in which order ruled supreme, their chaotic natures banished once and for all. Of course, first they would have to pay for its imprisonment, and such payment could only be given in pain and blood. All it had to do was wait and revenge would be its reward. The humans would learn the true meaning of suffering…

This tale is to be continued in the second book of *The Annals of Prophecy; The Power of Prophecy.*

About The Author

Mark Kingshott was born in the United Kingdom and spent the early years of his life living in the many places the military sent his father to work. He went to the University of Leicester where he studied History as an undergraduate and spent a year studying in Italy. After he achieved his degree he went on to get a Master's degree in Mediaeval Culture. He then took the next logical step and went on to become a website developer, albeit whilst living in the Tower of London. It was during his time in the Tower (as a resident, not a prisoner) that he completed his first book *The Magic of Prophecy*. He also met and married his wife Dawn, and had his two children, Ashlynne and Ethan Christened there. After a brief spell living in South Africa with his family, Mark now lives in Reading where he is currently balancing time commuting to his day job whilst working on the second book in the series, *The Power of Prophecy*.

www.ingramcontent.com/pod-product-compliance
Lightning Source LLC
Chambersburg PA
CBHW020616310726
48979CB00008B/1505/J